BEACON LIGHTS OF HISTORY.

BEACON LIGHTS OF HISTORY

DR. JOHN LORD

BEACON LIGHTS
OF HISTORY.

By JOHN LORD, LL. D.,

AUTHOR OF "THE OLD ROMAN WORLD," "MODERN EUROPE,"
ETC., ETC.

VOLUME I

PART I.
THE OLD PAGAN CIVILIZATIONS.

PART II.
JEWISH HEROES AND PROPHETS.
(TABLE OF CONTENTS FOR PART II FOLLOWS PAGE 378.)

NEW YORK:
WM. H. WISE & CO.

Copyright, 1883, 1888,
By JOHN LORD.

Copyright, 1921,
By WM. H. WISE & CO.

Entered at Stationers' Hall.

To the Memory of

MARY PORTER LORD,

WHOSE FRIENDSHIP AND APPRECIATION

AS A DEVOTED WIFE

ENCOURAGED ME TO A LONG LIFE

OF HISTORICAL LABORS,

This Work

IS GRATEFULLY AND AFFECTIONATELY DEDICATED

BY THE AUTHOR.

INTRODUCTION

TO FIRST ENGLISH EDITION.

By Sir James H. Yoxall, M.A., M.P.

I AM asked to introduce to the English-reading public on this side the Atlantic a book which millions of American people have reason to hold in affectionate esteem. The request is an honour, for it makes me sponsor to a work already hallowed by success, and of which a student, teacher, writer, or man of affairs can hardly speak too well. Scan it, and you will at once comprehend why American parents who owe to this book much of their own culture are careful to afford their sons and daughters the same opportunity. "'Beacon Lights of History' will help to form you," successful men and women say; "it helped to make me what I am."

That a million of these books have been sold in America "speaks volumes" for the usefulness of them over here. Among a people as practical as ourselves the work succeeded because it is both practical and pleasant. To read the book is to drink at a limpid stream. It teaches the student, it fascinates the leisure of the business man. The fortunate young can learn by it, the adult who never went through a collegiate course finds it to be "just the

INTRODUCTION.

book." It clears the conceptions of the self-educated and systematises their scraps of lore, for into its frame and plan fit the odds and ends of historical and biographical reading which newspapers and magazines supply. But it is also self-contained; in its broad completeness it offers a record of human thought and achievement during six thousand years; it maps the currents which have shaped the course of modern life; it hangs a gallery of pictures up, to show the races, empires, deeds, and ideas of mankind. "I *hate* the 'period' system of teaching history," a student said to me recently. "I know nothing of any 'period' that was not set me." But here in this great book one may study man and historic time as a whole— the chief events and foremost personages in creeds, governments, philosophy, letters, art, education, science, politics, commerce, and war during all periods, and in their chief manifestations. The "Beacon Lights" is a conspectus; it relates and collates.

"Quite what I always wanted," the busy man tells himself, as he takes a volume into his hands beside the evening fire. For the self-taught it is a key-book; it plans and correlates, it expounds the principal references and allusions which other books have mentioned tantalisingly and not explained. It is as the lamp illuminating general reading; it turns vagueness into something like precision, and gradually it leads into the path of regular study; many an American is learned to-day only because he began with this book. The method of the work is a lesson to teachers, and the style an example for us all.

INTRODUCTION.

Though it is history, biography, philosophy, and science "in pemmican," it is literature also; it is anything but tasteless and dry. It can be read in sections and at intervals, or it can form the basis of systematic studiousness. As a book for the fireside shelf, taken down for a chapter at a time, it a little resembles that once-famous book "Half-hours with the Best Authors," but it shows a wider *essor* and scope; another name for it might be "Half-hours with the Best that has been Known, Thought, and Done." It is no scrappy half-hour compilation, however, fugitive in interest, unsustained in conception or execution; the author's eye saw deep as well as far. Dr. Lord was scholar and teacher as well as writer, and he made this book a treasury of philosophic wisdom. Yet its popular title is no misnomer; the village library, the school book-shelf, and the boy's bookcase may house it as fitly as the student's desk.

"Knowledge comes but wisdom lingers." Not information, but the assimilation of information educates; mere instruction cannot make an educated man; there must be mental digestion, there must be selection and rejection in the sustenance of the mind. Now the author of this book was, in the highest and widest sense of a title often misapplied, an educated man; maybe he never expected for his work a recognition so remarkable as it attained, for he always aimed high, and "To give the substance of accepted knowledge concerning the leading events and characters of history" was the aim expressed in his preface. "To present what is true rather than what is new"—he was no clap-trapper, no notoriety-hunter. "Not to be exhaustive, or to give minute criticisms on comparatively unimportant points"—he knew how to select and reject. "Candidly to describe the passions and interests which have agitated nations, the ideas which great men have declared, and the institutions which have grown out of them"—he knew how to correlate and to define. And his book, moreover, has a particular method of appeal; it is history expressed in terms of men. "As the interest in the development of those great ideas and movements which we call Civilisation centres in no slight degree in the men who were identified with them, I have endeavoured to give a faithful picture of their lives in connection with the eras and institutions which they represent, whether they were philosophers, ecclesiastics, or men of action. And that we may not lose sight of the precious boons which illustrious benefactors have been instrumental in bestowing upon mankind, it has been my chief object to present their services, whatever may have been their defects." For "these services certainly constitute the gist of history." That was the mark which Dr. Lord set before him, and the execution became worthy of that aim.

Synoptic and synthetic, selective and collective, this book is made out of that assimilated knowledge which is wisdom, expressed in simple language full of charm. And it pioneers; it is the kind of book which will come to be needed more and more. Every year the scope and minimum amount of necessary study increases; already men

INTRODUCTION.

despair of gaining anything like universal culture, and begin to specialise almost from the first. In every branch of study a conspectus, a book of preliminary knowledge "in pemmican" such as this, will need to be provided, or school-years must inordinately lengthen, and one's bookshelves groan to a staggering extent. Most pemmican books are tabular, dry, and chippy, however this is not. Most pemmican books are the result of spiritless toil by mere book-makers uninspired; Dr. Lord was a scholar and philosopher. To look at his portrait is to perceive a foreign strain in him, probably French, through Canadian or Louisianian ancestors. The French rank highly the skill of the *vulgarisateur,* who simplifies and popularises knowledge; and for that duty the especially French qualities of logical thinking, clarity of language, lucidity in exposition, taste in selection, and a sure wisdom in rejection are required. Dr. Lord wrote from personal research, not at second-hand, as most popularisers do, and he was master of a restrained, delicately picturesque literary style. In tone and taste the book is impeccable; orthodoxy without bigotry is the note of it, and one does not wonder that the praise of clergy as well as of University people in America should have been won.

Dr. Lord has been called the "artist historian," and in his book I find something of the spirit which animates the sculpture by Rodin; obvious is the same emphasis on the great things, and the same omission of such details as ordinary imagination or common experience can add. As you read this book, out of the formless block of the past you see the essentials emerge—the great things, the characteristic and world-influencing things and personages, the things and the men that illustrate and synthetise, the things and men that made each era what it was, the tendencies and currents that have caused the world to be what it is to-day. Here, in print, is something of the art of Rodin and even of Michael Angelo; the "artist historian" gives us the principal features of the past in large, with broad exactitude and suggestive outline. Out of the sheer material block of petrified historical fact he has brought to view the shape of humanity as it was in successive epochs—mankind and the social world as they formed themselves into what they are now; his work can make even the regular student of history conscious of wide connections and large meanings to which specific text-books are often blind. So that this is a book for school and college study also, and not for the leisure of the business man or the man of the world alone. Selection, connection, comparison, and synthesis, that was Dr. Lord's formula. How few other writers have used it so well! I think his method was much the same as that used by all great artists in work of any kind: it was Rembrandt's, it was Shakespeare's, it was Leonardo da Vinci's in science as well as in art; for he sought to detect and reveal the idea and soul of things, no less real, though less apparent, than their exterior and form.

How came he to be able to do this so well? He was not famous, his name has been no European possession. But he had specially qualified himself for his particular

INTRODUCTION.

and consummate work. No great stroke of art ever springs into being; the artist himself has to learn. Dr. Lord lived long and devoted himself to one duty. By forty years of public lecturing to students, and to great audiences of the general public also, he came to know by experiment and observation exactly what the general reader, and often the student, most needs and wishes to have in a book. Then his repeated delivery enabled him to adjust, amend, and polish each lecture ever more and more; continually each was corrected, revised, and improved, until it became as lucid, pointed, compact and concise as might be. While in England he wrote a most successful school-book, "The History of Modern Europe," and later he issued often-reprinted works on the History of the United States, the Old Roman World, Ancient Cities and Empires, and Ancient History for schools and colleges. At the end of forty years of such experience he began to gather his books and lectures together into systematic and final form. Never wearying of the *limæ labor* which is the condition of finish and perfection, he again re-wrote the myriad pages which had scores of times been amended already, and he brought all dates, facts, and attributions into harmony with the most recent evidence. He never ceased to study, he never tired of his work. The revision of the volume "Great Writers" was reserved for his final task, but was interrupted by his death; so that part of the "Great Writers" volume, and the whole of the book on "The New Era" are due to other hands. But they are skilful hands, and nothing in these

INTRODUCTION.

handsome volumes can be considered feeble or out of date.

I have dwelt on the genesis of the book, because that best explains its particular success and appeal. It grew up out of the proved needs of audiences, it was not written *a priori,* or uttered in a breath. The lecturer had tested each step of the author beforehand; what had told in a lecture a hundred times would tell in a book, the author knew. But he did not seek for "telling" things only, he was no charlatan of the footlights; his reading was eclectic as well as wide, and he showed the artist's conscience, which cannot satisfy itself with scamped work. His biographic method, resembling that which John Richard Green adopted later, resulted in history so humanised that ordinary human beings can feed upon it with delight. Emerson said, "There is properly no history, only biography," and Dr. Lord treats the Renaissance, for example, as not so much a mere historical period as the time and stage of Dante, Chaucer, Galileo, Michael Angelo. Reading of men and women, almost with the pleasure of reading fiction you are led along the record of historic truth. Smoothly you sail through historic time and space. From the pagan civilisations you pass to the Hebrew heroes and prophets; from the empires and achievements of classic antiquity you are gradually brought into the Middle Ages, and to the Reformation. "Great Rulers" is one of the volumes—it gathers up the gist of a thousand years. "European Statesmen" and "European Leaders" carry you from the French Revolution to the demand for Irish Home Rule—from Mirabeau

INTRODUCTION.

to Gladstone, with all that those names and the intervening ones imply. "The New Era" paints our immediate past, the Nineteenth Century, in portraits of Spencer, Darwin, Ruskin, Li Hung Chang, Faraday, and Virchow. The special volumes of "Great Women" and "Great Writers" are among the most entrancing of all. Scan the earlier volumes, and then skip to the later, as an experiment—a test; the chapters on Cicero and Roman literature exemplify the just estimates and masterly condensations which make the whole series invaluable, but Medicine and Surgery—Jenner, Hahnemann, Pasteur, Lister, Simpson, and Virchow—in the penultimate volume, are treated almost as ably. These are true "University Extension" books. In the last of them a set of questions on each volume or chapter will afford teachers and systematic students great help.

So that here are six thousand pages of history, biography, art, and letters all in one; pages full of spirit and interest, as well as of philosophy and thought; pages which clothe the dry bones with life, and vitalise the past; pages in which there is a constant elevation and a high appeal. As I know no book of purely English origin which could replace it, I am glad that it is now to be available over here. And I wish I could have written a letter of introduction more worthy of the theme.

J. H. YOXALL.

SPRINGFIELD,
20, KEW GARDENS ROAD,
KEW.
25th May, 1911.

AUTHOR'S PREFACE.

IT has been my object in these Lectures to give the substance of accepted knowledge pertaining to the leading events and characters of history; and in treating such a variety of subjects, extending over a period of more than six thousand years, each of which might fill a volume, I have sought to present what is true rather than what is new.

Although most of these Lectures have been delivered, in some form, during the last forty years, in most of the cities and in many of the literary institutions of this country, I have carefully revised them within the last few years, in order to avail myself of the latest light shed on the topics and times of which they treat.

The revived and wide-spread attention given to the study of the Bible, under the stimulus of recent Oriental travels and investigations, not only as a volume of religious guidance, but as an authentic record of most interesting and important events, has encouraged me to include a series of Lectures on some of the remarkable men identified with Jewish history.

Of course I have not aimed at an exhaustive criticism in these Biblical studies, since the topics cannot be exhausted even by the most learned scholars; but I have sought to interest intelligent Christians by a continuous narrative, interweaving with it the latest accessible knowledge bearing on the main subjects. If I have persisted in adhering to the truths that have been generally accepted for nearly two thousand years, I have not disregarded the light which has been recently shed on important points by the great critics of the progressive schools.

I have not aimed to be exhaustive, or to give minute criticism on comparatively unimportant points; but the passions and interests which have agitated nations, the ideas which great men have declared, and the institutions which have grown out of them, have not, I trust, been uncandidly described, nor deductions from them illogically made.

Inasmuch as the interest in the development of those great ideas and movements which we call Civilization centres in no slight degree in the men who were identified with them, I have endeavored to give a faithful picture of their lives in connection with the eras and institutions which they represent, whether they were philosophers, ecclesiastics, or men of action.

And that we may not lose sight of the precious boons which illustrious benefactors have been instrumental in bestowing upon mankind, it has been my chief object to present their services, whatever may have been their defects; since it is for *services* that most great men are ultimately judged, especially kings and rulers. These services, certainly, constitute the gist of history, and it is these which I have aspired to show.

JOHN LORD.

PART I.

THE OLD PAGAN CIVILIZATIONS.

PART I.

THE OLD PAGAN CIVILIZATIONS

CONTENTS.

ANCIENT RELIGIONS:

EGYPTIAN, ASSYRIAN, BABYLONIAN, AND PERSIAN.

	PAGE
Ancient religions	27
Christianity not progressive	28
Jewish monotheism	29
Religion of Egypt	31
Its great antiquity	31
Its essential features	32
Complexity of Egyptian polytheism	33
Egyptian deities	33
The worship of the sun	34
The priestly caste of Egypt	35
Power of the priests	36
Future rewards and punishments	36
Morals of the Egyptians	37
Functions of the priests	37
Egyptian ritual of worship	38
Transmigration of souls	39
Animal worship	39
Effect of Egyptian polytheism on the Jews	41
Assyrian deities	43

CONTENTS.

	PAGE
Phœnician deities	48
Worship of the sun	49
Oblations and sacrifices	49
Idolatry the sequence of polytheism	52
Religion of the Persians	53
Character of the early Iranians	54
Comparative purity of the Persian religion	56
Zoroaster	56
Magism	58
Zend-Avesta	59
Dualism	62
Authorities	64

RELIGIONS OF INDIA.

BRAHMANISM AND BUDDHISM.

Religions of India	67
Antiquity of Brahmanism	68
Sanskrit literature	69
The Aryan races	70
Original religion of the Aryans	73
Aryan migrations	74
The Vedas	74
Ancient deities of India	75
Laws of Menu	76, 78
Hindu pantheism	77
Corruption of Brahmanism	79, 83
The Brahmanical caste	80
Character of the Brahmans	82
Rise of Buddhism	84
Gautama	85

CONTENTS.

	Page
Experiences of Gautama	86
Travels of Buddha	90
His religious system	91
Spread of his doctrine	91
Buddhism a reaction against Brahmanism	92
Nirvana	93
Gloominess of Buddhism	94
Buddhism as a reform of morals	96
Sayings of Siddârtha	98
His rules	99
Failure of Buddhism in India	102
Authorities	103

RELIGION OF THE GREEKS AND ROMANS.

Classic Mythology.

Religion of the Greeks and Romans	107
Greek myths	108
Greek priests	108
Greek divinities	109
Greek polytheism	110
Greek mythology	111
Adoption of Oriental fables	111
Greek deities the creation of poets	113
Peculiarities of the Greek gods	114
The Olympian deities	115–119
The minor deities	119
The Greeks indifferent to a future state	122
Augustine view of heathen deities	123
Artists vie with poets in conceptions of divine power	124
Temple of Zeus in Olympia	124

CONTENTS.

	PAGE
Greek festivals	126
No sacred books among the Greeks	127
A religion without deities	132
Roman divinities	137
Peculiarities of Roman worship	138
Ritualism and hypocrisy	139
Character of the Roman	140
Authorities	141

CONFUCIUS.

SAGE AND MORALIST.

Early condition of China	146
Youth of Confucius	147
His public life	148
His reforms	150
His fame	151
His wanderings	151
His old age	152
His writings	153
His philosophy	158
His definition of a superior man	159
His ethics	160, 162
His views of government	161
His veneration for antiquity	163
His beautiful character	165
His encouragement of learning	166
His character as statesman	167
His exaltation of filial piety	169
His exaltation of friendship	171
The supremacy of the State	172

	PAGE
Necessity of good men in office	172
Peaceful policy of Confucius	173
Veneration for his writings	174
His posthumous influence	175
Lao-tse	177
Authorities	179

ANCIENT PHILOSOPHY.

SEEKING AFTER TRUTH.

Intellectual superiority of the Greeks	183
Early progress of philosophy	185
The Greek philosophy	185
The Ionian Sophoi	186
Thales and his principles	187
Anaximenes	189
Diogenes of Apollonia	190
Heraclitus of Ephesus	191
Anaxagoras	192
Anaximander	194
Pythagoras and his school	197
Xenophanes	198
Zeno of Elea	201
Empedocles and the Eleatics	201
Loftiness of the Greek philosopher	203
Progress of scepticism	204
The Sophists	205
Socrates	207
His exposure of error	209
Socrates as moralist	210
The method of Socrates	213

	PAGE
His services to philosophy	214
His disciples	215
Plato	216
Ideas of Plato	218
Archer Butler on Plato	221
Aristotle	222
His services	226
The syllogism	227
The Epicureans	229
Sir James Mackintosh on Epicurus	230
The Stoics	231
Zeno	231
Principles of the Stoical philosophy	233
Philosophy among the Romans	237
Cicero	238
Epictetus	240
Authorities	245

SOCRATES.

GREEK PHILOSOPHY.

Mission of Socrates	250
Era of his birth; view of his times	251
His personal appearance and peculiarities	252, 253
His lofty moral character	254
His sarcasm and ridicule of opponents	255
The Sophists	255
Neglect of his family	256
His friendship with distinguished people	257
His philosophic method	258
His questions and definitions	259
His contempt of theories	260

	Page
Imperfection of contemporaneous physical science	260
The Ionian philosophers	261
Socrates bases truth on consciousness	262
Uncertainty of physical inquiries in his day	262
Superiority of moral truth	263
Happiness, Virtue, Knowledge, — the Socratic trinity	264
The "dæmon" of Socrates	265
His idea of God and Immortality	268
Socrates a witness and agent of God	270
Socrates compared with Buddha and Marcus Aurelius	270
His resemblance to Christ in life and teachings	271, 272
Unjust charges of his enemies	273
His unpopularity	274
His trial and defence	275
His audacity	276
His condemnation	277
The dignity of his last hours	278
His easy death	279
Tardy repentance of the Athenians; statue by Lysippus	279
Posthumous influence	280
Authorities	280

PHIDIAS.

Greek Art.

General popular interest in Art	283
Principles on which it is based	284
Phidias taken merely as a text	284
Not much known of his personal history	285
His most famous statues; Minerva and Olympian Jove	285
His peculiar excellences as a sculptor	286
Definitions of the word "Art"	287
Its representation of ideas of beauty and grace	288

CONTENTS.

	PAGE
The glory and dignity of art	289–291
The connection of plastic with literary art	292, 293
Architecture, the first expression of art	294
Peculiarities of Egyptian and Assyrian architecture	294
Ancient temples, tombs, pyramids, and palaces	295
General features of Grecian architecture	296
The Doric, Ionic, and Corinthian orders	297, 298
Simplicity and beauty of their proportions	299
The horizontal lines of Greek and the vertical lines of Gothic architecture	300, 301
Assyrian, Egyptian, and Indian sculpture	302
Superiority of Greek sculpture	302
Ornamentation of temples with statues of gods, heroes, and distinguished men	303
The great sculptors of antiquity	304
Their ideal excellence	305
Antiquity of painting in Babylon and Egypt	306
Its gradual development in Greece	306
Famous Grecian painters	307–309
Decline of art among the Romans	310
Art as seen in literature	311
Literature not permanent without art	312
Artists as a class	313
Art a refining influence rather than a moral power	314, 315
Authorities	316

LITERARY GENIUS.

THE GREEK AND ROMAN CLASSICS.

Richness of Greek classic poetry	321
Homer	322
Greek lyrical poetry	323
Pindar	323

CONTENTS.

	PAGE
Dramatic poetry	324
Æschylus, Sophocles, and Euripides	325–328
Greek comedy: Aristophanes	328
Roman poetry	330
Nævius, Plautus, Terence	331, 334
Roman epic poetry: Virgil	335
Lyrical poetry: Horace, Catullus	336–338
Didactic poetry: Lucretius	338
Elegiac poetry: Ovid, Tibullus	339–341
Satire: Horace, Martial, Juvenal	342, 343
Perfection of Greek prose writers	344
History: Herodotus	345
Thucydides, Xenophon	347–349
Roman historians	349
Julius Cæsar	351
Livy	353
Tacitus	354
Orators	360
Pericles	362
Demosthenes	363
Æschines	365
Cicero	366
Learned men: Varro	371
Seneca	372
Quintilian	373
Lucian	374
Authorities	377

CONTENTS

	Page
Dramatic poetry	321
Æschylus, Sophocles, and Euripides	325-328
Greek comedy: Aristophanes	328
Roman poetry	330
Sævius, Plautus, Terence	331, 334
Roman epic poetry: Virgil	335
Lyrical poetry: Horace, Catullus	336-338
Didactic poetry: Lucretius	335
Elegiac poetry: Ovid, Tibullus	339-341
Satire: Horace, Martial, Juvenal	342, 343
Reflection of Greek prose writers	341
Theory: Herodotus	345
Thucydides, Xenophon	347-349
Roman historians	349
Julius Cæsar	351
Livy	356
Tacitus	357
Quintus	360
Polybius	363
Demosthenes	365
Æschines	366
Cicero	368
Derived men: Varro	371
Seneca	372
Quintilian	373
Pliny	374
Aulus Gellius	375

ANCIENT RELIGIONS:

EGYPTIAN, ASSYRIAN, BABYLONIAN, AND PERSIAN.

BEACON LIGHTS OF HISTORY.

ANCIENT RELIGIONS:

EGYPTIAN, ASSYRIAN, BABYLONIAN, AND PERSIAN.

IT is my object in this book on the old Pagan civilizations to present the salient points only, since an exhaustive work is impossible within the limits of these volumes. The practical end which I have in view is to collate a sufficient number of acknowledged facts from which to draw sound inferences in reference to the progress of the human race, and the comparative welfare of nations in ancient and modern times.

The first inquiry we naturally make is in regard to the various religious systems which were accepted by the ancient nations, since religion, in some form or other, is the most universal of institutions, and has had the earliest and the greatest influence on the condition and life of peoples — that is to say, on their civilizations — in every period of the world. And, necessarily, considering what is the object in religion, when we undertake to examine any particular form of it which has obtained among any people or at any period of time, we must ask, How far did its priests and sages teach exalted ideas of Deity, of the soul, and of immortality? How far did they arrive at lofty and immutable principles of morality? How far did religion, such as was taught, practically affect the lives of those who professed it, and lead them to just and reasonable treatment of one another, or to holy contemplation, or noble deeds, or sublime repose in anticipation of a higher and endless life? And how did the various religions compare with what we believe to be the true religion — Christianity — in its pure and ennobling truths, its inspiring promises, and its quiet influence in changing and developing character?

I assume that there is no such thing as a progressive Christianity, except in so far as mankind grow in the realization of its lofty principles; that there has not been and will not be any improvement on the ethics and spiritual truths revealed by Jesus the Christ, but that they will remain forever the standard of faith and practice. I assume also that Christianity has elements which are not to be found in any other religion, — such as original teachings, divine revelations, and sublime truths. I know it is the fashion with many thinkers to maintain that improvements on the Christian system are both possible and probable, and that there is scarcely a truth which Christ and his apostles declared which cannot be found in some other ancient religion, when divested of the errors there incorporated with it. This notion I repudiate. I believe that systems of religion are perfect or imperfect, true or false, just so far as they agree or disagree with Christianity; and that to the end of time all systems are to be measured by the Christian standard, and not Christianity by any other system.

The oldest religion of which we have clear and authentic account is probably the pure monotheism held by the Jews. Some nations have claimed a higher antiquity for their religion — like the Egyptians and Chinese — than that which the sacred writings of the Hebrews show to have been communicated to Abraham, and to earlier men of God treated of in those Scriptures; but their claims are not entitled to our full credence. We are in doubt about them. The origin of religions is enshrouded in mystical darkness, and is a mere speculation. Authentic history does not go back far enough to settle this point. The primitive religion of mankind I believe to have been revealed to inspired men, who, like Shem, walked with God. Adam, in paradise, knew who God was, for he heard His voice; and so did Enoch and Noah, and, more clearly than all, Abraham. They believed in a personal God, maker of heaven and earth, infinite in power, supreme in goodness, without beginning and without end, who exercises a providential oversight of the world which he made.

It is certainly not unreasonable to claim the greatest purity and loftiness in the monotheistic faith of the Hebrew patriarchs, as handed down to his children by Abraham, over that of all other founders of ancient religious systems, not only since that faith was, as we believe, supernaturally communicated, but since the fruit of that stock, especially in its Christian development, is superior to all others. This sublime monotheism was ever maintained by the Hebrew race, in all their wanderings, misfortunes, and triumphs, except on occasions when they partially adopted the gods of those nations with whom they came in contact, and by whom they were corrupted or enslaved.

But it is not my purpose to discuss the religion of the Jews in this connection, since it is treated in other volumes of this series, and since everybody has access to the Bible, the earlier portions of which give the true account not only of the Hebrews and their special progenitor Abraham, but of the origin of the earth and of mankind; and most intelligent persons are familiar with its details.

I begin my description of ancient religions with those systems with which the Jews were more or less familiar, and by which they were more or less influenced. And whether these religions were, as I think, themselves corrupted forms of the primitive revelation to primitive man, or, as is held by some philosophers of to-day, natural developments out of an original worship of the powers of Nature, of ghosts of ancestral heroes, of tutelar deities of household, family, tribe, nation, and so forth, it will not affect their relation to my plan of considering this background of history in its effects upon modern times, through Judaism and Christianity.

The first which naturally claims our attention is the religion of ancient Egypt. But I can show only the main features and characteristics of this form of paganism, avoiding the complications of their system and their perplexing names as much as possible. I wish to present what is ascertained and intelligible rather than what is ingenious and obscure.

The religion of Egypt is very old, — how old we cannot tell with certainty. We know that it existed before Abraham, and with but few changes, for at least two thousand years. Mariette places the era of the first Egyptian dynasty under Menes at 5004 B. C. It is supposed that the earliest form of the Egyptian religion was monotheistic, such as was known later, however, only to a few of the higher priesthood. What the esoteric wisdom really was we can only conjecture, since there are no sacred books or writings that have come down to us, like the Indian Vedas and the Persian Zend-Avesta. Herodotus affirms that he knew the mysteries, but he did not reveal them.

But monotheism was lost sight of in Egypt at an earlier period than the beginning of authentic history. It is the fate of all institutions to become corrupt, and this is particularly true of religious systems. The reason of this is not difficult to explain. The Bible and human experience fully exhibit the course of this degradation. Hence, before Abraham's visit to Egypt the religion of that land had degenerated into a gross and complicated polytheism, which it was apparently for the interest of the priesthood to perpetuate.

The Egyptian religion was the worship of the powers of Nature, — the sun, the moon, the planets, the air, the storm, light, fire, the clouds, the rivers, the lightning, all of which were supposed to exercise a mysterious influence over human destiny. There was doubtless an indefinite sense of awe in view of the wonders of the material universe, extending to a vague fear of some almighty supremacy over all that could be seen or known. To these powers of Nature the Egyptians gave names, and made them divinities.

The Egyptian polytheism was complex and even contradictory. What it lost in logical sequence it gained in variety. Wilkinson enumerates seventy-three principal divinities, and Birch sixty-three; but there were some hundreds of lesser gods, discharging peculiar functions and presiding over different localities. Every town had its guardian deity, to whom prayers or sacrifices were offered by the priests. The more complicated the religious rites the more firmly cemented was the power of the priestly caste, and the more indispensable were priestly services for the offerings and propitiations.

Of these Egyptian deities there were eight of the first rank; but the list of them differs according to different writers, since in the great cities different deities were worshipped. These were Ammon — the concealed god, — the sovereign over all (corresponding to the Jupiter of the Romans), whose sacred city was Thebes. At a later date this god was identified with Ammon Ra, the physical sun. Ra was the sun-god, especially worshipped at Heliopolis, — the symbol of light and heat. Kneph was the spirit of God moving over the face of the waters, whose principal seat of worship was in Upper Egypt. Phtha was a sort of artisan god, who made the sun, moon, and the earth, "the father of beginnings;" his sign was the scarabæus, or beetle, and his patron city was Memphis. Khem was the generative principle presiding over the vegetable world, — the giver of fertility and lord of the harvest. These deities are supposed to have represented spirit passing into matter and form, — a process of divine incarnation.

But the most popular deity was Osiris. His image is found standing on the oldest monument, a form of Ra, the light of the lower world, and king and judge of Hades. His worship was universal throughout Egypt, but his chief temples were at Abydos and Philæ. He was regarded as mild, beneficent, and good. In opposition to him were Set, malignant and evil, and Bes, the god of death. Isis, the wife and sister of Osiris, was a sort of sun goddess, representing the productive power of Nature. Khons was the moon god. Maut, the consort of Ammon, represented Nature. Sati, the wife of Kneph, bore a resemblance to Juno. Nut was the goddess of the firmament; Ma was the goddess of truth; Horus was the mediator between creation and destruction.

But in spite of the multiplicity of deities, the Egyptian worship centred in some form upon heat or fire, generally the sun, the most powerful and brilliant of the forces of Nature. Among all the ancient pagan nations the sun, the moon, and the planets, under different names, whether impersonated or not, were the principal objects of worship for the people. To these temples were erected, statues raised, and sacrifices made.

No ancient nation was more devout, or more constant to the service of its gods, than were the Egyptians; and hence, being superstitious, they were pre-eminently under the control of priests, as the people were in India. We see, chiefly in India and Egypt, the power of caste, — tyrannical, exclusive, and pretentious, — and powerful in proportion to the belief in a future state. Take away the belief in future existence and future rewards and punishments, and there is not much religion left. There may be philosophy and morality, but not religion, which is based on the fear and love of God, and the destiny of the soul after death. Saint Augustine, in his "City of God," his greatest work, ridicules all gods who are not able to save the soul, and all religions where future existence is not recognized as the most important thing which can occupy the mind of man.

We cannot then utterly despise the religion of Egypt, in spite of the absurdities mingled with it, — the multiplicity of gods and the doctrine of metempsychosis, — since it included a distinct recognition of a future state of rewards and punishments "according to the deeds done in the body." On this belief rested the power of the priests, who were supposed to intercede with the deities, and who alone were appointed to offer to them sacrifices, in order to gain their favor or deprecate their wrath. The idea of death and judgment was ever present to the thoughts of the Egyptians, from the highest to the lowest, and must have modified their conduct, stimulating them to virtue, and restraining them from vice; for virtue and vice are not revelations, — they are instincts implanted in the soul. No ancient teacher enjoined the duties based on an immutable morality with more force than Confucius, Buddha, and Epictetus. Who in any land or age has ignored the duties of filial obedience, respect to rulers, kindness to the miserable, protection to the weak, honesty, benevolence, sincerity, and truthfulness? With the discharge of these duties, written on the heart, have been associated the favor of the gods, and happiness in the future world, whatever errors may have crept into theological dogmas and speculations.

Believing then in a future state, where sin would be punished and virtue rewarded, and believing in it firmly and piously, the ancient Egyptians were a peaceful and comparatively moral people. All writers admit their industry, their simplicity of life, their respect for law, their loyalty to priests and rulers. Hence there was permanence to their institutions, for rapine, violence, and revolution were rare. They were not warlike, although often engaged in war by the command of ambitious kings. Generally the policy of their government was conservative and pacific. Military ambition and thirst for foreign conquest were not the peculiar sins of Egyptian kings; they sought rather to develop national industries and resources. The occupation of the people was in agriculture and the useful arts, which last they carried to considerable perfection, especially in the working of metals, textile fabrics, and ornamental jewelry. Their grand monuments were not triumphal arches, but temples and mausoleums. Even the pyramids may have been built to preserve the bodies of kings until the soul should be acquitted or condemned, and therefore more religious in their uses than as mere emblems of pride and power; and when monuments were erected to perpetuate the fame of princes, their supreme design was to receive the engraven memorials of the virtuous deeds of kings as fathers of the people.

The priests, whose business it was to perform religious rites and ceremonies to the various gods of the Egyptians, were extremely numerous. They held the highest social rank, and were exempt from taxes. They were clothed in white linen, which was kept scrupulously clean. They washed their whole bodies twice a day; they shaved the head, and wore no beard. They practised circumcision, which rite was of extreme antiquity, existing in Egypt two thousand four hundred years before Christ, and at least four hundred years before Abraham, and has been found among primitive peoples all over the world. They did not make a show of sanctity, nor were they ascetic like the Brahmans. They were married, and were allowed to drink wine and to eat meat, but not fish nor beans, which disturbed digestion. The son of a priest was generally a priest also. There were grades of rank among the priesthood; but not more so than in the Roman Catholic Church. The high-priest was a great dignitary, and generally belonged to the royal family. The king himself was a priest.

The Egyptian ritual of worship was the most complicated of all rituals, and their literature and philosophy were only branches of theology. "Religious observances," says Freeman Clarke, "were so numerous and so imperative that the most common labors of daily life could not be performed without a perpetual reference to some priestly regulation." There were more religious festivals than among any other ancient nation. The land was covered with temples; and every temple consecrated to a single divinity, to whom some animal was sacred, supported a large body of priests. The authorities on Egyptian history, especially Wilkinson, speak highly, on the whole, of the morals of the priesthood, and of their arduous and gloomy life of superintending ceremonies, sacrifices, processions, and funerals. Their life was so full of minute duties and restrictions that they rarely appeared in public, and their aspect as well as influence was austere and sacerdotal.

One of the most distinctive features of the Egyptian religion was the idea of the transmigration of souls, — that when men die, their souls reappear on earth in various animals, in expiation of their sins. Osiris was the god before whose tribunal all departed spirits appeared to be judged. If evil preponderated in their lives, their souls passed into a long series of animals until their sins were expiated, when the purified souls, after thousands of years perhaps, passed into their old bodies. Hence it was the great object of the Egyptians to preserve their mortal bodies after death, and thus arose the custom of embalming them. It is difficult to compute the number of mummies that have been found in Egypt. If a man was wealthy, it cost his family as much as one thousand dollars to embalm his body suitably to his rank. The embalmed bodies of kings were preserved in marble sarcophagi, and hidden in gigantic monuments.

The most repulsive thing in the Egyptian religion was animal-worship. To each deity some animal was sacred. Thus Apis, the sacred bull of Memphis, was the representative of Osiris; the cow was sacred to Isis, and to Athor her mother. Sheep were sacred to Kneph, as well as the asp. Hawks were sacred to Ra; lions were emblems of Horus, wolves of Anubis, hippopotami of Set. Each town was jealous of the honor of its special favorites among the gods.

"The worst form of this animal worship," says Rawlinson, "was the belief that a deity absolutely became incarnate in an individual animal, and so remained until the animal's death. Such were the Apis bulls, of which a succession was maintained at Memphis in the temple of Phtha, or, according to others, of Osiris. These beasts, maintained at the cost of the priestly communities in the great temples of their respective cities, were perpetually adored and prayed to by thousands during their lives, and at their deaths were entombed with the utmost care in huge sarcophagi, while all Egypt went into mourning on their decease."

Such was the religion of Egypt as known to the Jews, — a complicated polytheism, embracing the worship of animals as well as the powers of Nature; the belief in the transmigration of souls, and a sacerdotalism which carried ritualistic ceremonies to the greatest extent known to antiquity, combined with the exaltation of the priesthood to such a degree as to make priests the rulers of the land.

To maintain their position of supremacy the priests of Egypt appealed to the fears of the people, thus favoring a degrading superstition. How far they taught that the various objects of worship were symbols merely of a supreme power, which they themselves perhaps accepted in their esoteric schools, we do not know. But the priests believed in a future state of rewards and punishments, and thus recognized the soul to be of more importance than the material body, and made its welfare paramount over all other interests. This recognition doubtless contributed to elevate the morals of the people, and to make them religious, despite their false and degraded views of God, and their disgusting superstitions.

The Jews could not have lived in Egypt four hundred years without being influenced by the popular belief. Hence in the wilderness, and in the days of kingly rule, the tendency to animal worship in the shape of the golden calves, their love of ritualistic observances, and their easy submission to the rule of priests. In one very important thing, however, the Jews escaped a degrading superstition,— that of the transmigration of souls; and it was perhaps the abhorrence by Moses of this belief that made him so remarkably silent as to a future state. It is seemingly ignored in the Old Testament, and hence many have been led to suppose that the Jews did not believe in it. Certainly the most cultivated and aristocratic sect — the Sadducees — repudiated it altogether; while the

Pharisees held to it. They, however, were products of a later age, and had learned many things — good and bad — from surrounding nations or in their captivities, which Moses did not attempt to teach the simple souls that escaped from Egypt.

Of the other religions with which the Jews came in contact, and which more or less were in conflict with their own monotheistic belief, very little is definitely known, since their sacred books, if they had any, have not come down to us. Our knowledge is mostly confined to monuments, on which the names of their deities are inscribed, the animals which they worshipped, symbolic of the powers of Nature, and the kings and priests who officiated in religious ceremonies. From these we learn or infer that among the Assyrians, Babylonians, and Phœnicians religion was polytheistic, but without so complicated or highly organized a system as prevailed in Egypt. Only about twenty deities are alluded to in the monumental records of either nation, and they are supposed to have represented the sun, the moon, the stars, and various other powers, to which were delegated by the unseen and occult supreme deity the oversight of this world. They presided over cities and the elements of Nature, like the rain, the thunder, the winds, the air, the water. Some abode in heaven, some on the earth, and some in the waters under the earth. Of all these graven images existed, carved by men's hands, — some in the form of animals, like the winged bulls of Nineveh. In the very earliest times, before history was written, it is supposed that the religion of all these nations was monotheistic, and that polytheism was a development as men became wicked and sensual. The knowledge of the one God was gradually lost, although an indefinite belief remained that there was a supreme power over all the other gods, at least a deity of higher rank than the gods of the people, who reigned over them as Lord of lords.

This deity in Assyria was Asshur. He is recognized by most authorities as Asshur, a son of Shem and grandson of Noah, who was probably the hero and leader of one of the early migrations, and, as founder of the Assyrian Empire, gave it its name, — his own being magnified and deified by his warlike descendants. Assyria was the oldest of the great empires, occupying Mesopotamia, — the vast plain watered by the Tigris and Euphrates rivers, — with adjacent countries to the north, west, and east. Its seat was in the northern portion of this region, while that of Babylonia or Chaldæa, its rival, was in the southern part; and although after many wars freed from the subjection of Assyria, the institutions of Babylonia, and especially its religion, were very much the same as those of the elder empire. In Babylonia the chief god was called El, or Il. In Babylon, although Bab-el, their tutelary god, was at the head of the pantheon, his form was not represented, nor had he any special temple for his worship. The Assyrian Asshur placed kings upon their thrones, protected their armies, and directed their expeditions. In speaking of him it was "Asshur, my Lord." He was also called "King of kings," reigning supreme over the gods; and sometimes he was called the "Father of the gods." His position in the celestial hierarchy corresponds with the Zeus of the Greeks, and with the Jupiter of the Romans. He was represented as a man with a horned cap, carrying a bow and issuing from a winged circle, which circle was the emblem of ubiquity and eternity. This emblem was also the accompaniment of Assyrian royalty.

These Assyrian and Babylonian deities had a direct influence on the Jews in later centuries, because traders on the Tigris pushed their adventurous expeditions from the head of the Persian Gulf, either around the great peninsula of Arabia, or by land across the deserts, and settled in Canaan, calling themselves Phœnicians; and it was from the descendants of these enterprising but morally debased people that the children of Israel, returning from Egypt, received the most pertinacious influences of idolatrous corruption. In

Phœnicia the chief deity was also called Bel, or Baal, meaning "Lord," the epithet of the one divine being who rules the world, or the Lord of heaven. The deity of the Egyptian pantheon, with whom Baal most nearly corresponds, was Ammon, addressed as the supreme God.

Ranking after El in Babylon, Asshur in Assyria, and Baal in Phœnicia, — all shadows of the same supreme God, — we notice among these Mesopotamians a triad of the great gods, called Anu, Bel, and Hea. Anu, the primordial chaos; Hea, life and intelligence animating matter; and Bel, the organizing and creative spirit, — or, as Rawlinson thinks, "the original gods of the earth, the heavens, and the waters, corresponding in the main with the classical Pluto, Jupiter, and Neptune, who divided between them the dominion over the visible creation." The god Bel, in the pantheon of the Babylonians and Assyrians, is the God of gods, and Father of gods, who made the earth and heaven. His title expresses dominion.

In succession to the gods of this first trio, — Anu, Bel, and Hea, — was another trio, named Siu, Shamas, and Vul, representing the moon, the sun, and the atmosphere. "In Assyria and Babylon the moon-god took precedence of the sun-god, since night was more agreeable to the inhabitants of those hot countries than the day." Hence, Siu was the more popular deity; but Shamas, the sun, as having most direct reference to physical nature, "the lord of fire," "the ruler of the day," was the god of battles, going forth with the armies of the king triumphant over enemies. The worship of this deity was universal, and the kings regarded him as affording them especial help in war. Vul, the third of this trinity, was the god of the atmosphere, the god of tempests, — the god who caused the flood which the Assyrian legends recognize. He corresponds with the Jupiter Tonans of the Romans, — "the prince of the power of the air," destroyer of crops, the scatterer of the harvest, represented with a flaming sword; but as god of the atmosphere, the giver of rain, of abundance, "the lord of fecundity," he was beneficent as well as destructive.

All these gods had wives resembling the goddesses in the Greek mythology, — some beneficent, some cruel; rendering aid to men, or pursuing them with their anger. And here one cannot resist the impression that the earliest forms of the Greek mythology were derived from the Babylonians and Phœnicians, and that the Greek poets, availing themselves of the legends respecting them, created the popular religion of Greece. It is a mooted question whether the Greek civilization is chiefly derived from Egypt, or from Assyria and Phœnicia, — probably more from these old monarchies combined than from the original seat of the

Aryan race east of the Caspian Sea. All these ancient monarchies had run out and were old when the Greeks began their settlements and conquests.

There was still another and inferior class of deities among the Assyrians and Babylonians who were objects of worship, and were supposed to have great influence on human affairs. These deities were the planets under different names. The early study of astronomy among the dwellers on the plains of Babylon and in Mesopotamia gave an astral feature to their religion which was not prominent in Egypt. These astral deities were Nin, or Bar (the Saturn of the Romans); and Merodach (Jupiter), the august god, "the eldest son of Heaven," the Lord of battles. This was the favorite god of Nebuchadnezzar, and epithets of the highest honor were conferred upon him, as "King of heaven and earth," the "Lord of all beings," etc. Nergal (Mars) was a war god, his name signifying "the great Hero," "the King of battles." He goes before kings in their military expeditions, and lends them assistance in the chase. His emblem is the human-headed winged lion seen at the entrance of royal palaces. Ista (Venus) was the goddess of beauty, presiding over the loves of both men and animals, and was worshipped with unchaste rites. Nebo (Mercury) had the charge over learning and culture, — the god of wisdom, who "teaches and instructs."

There were other deities in the Assyrian and Babylonian pantheon whom I need not name, since they played a comparatively unimportant part in human affairs, like the inferior deities of the Romans, presiding over dreams, over feasts, over marriage, and the like.

The Phœnicians, like the Assyrians, had their goddesses. Astoreth, or Astarte, represented the great female productive principle, as Baal did the male. It was originally a name for the energy of God, on a par with Baal. In one of her aspects she represented the moon; but more commonly she was the representative of the female principle in Nature, and was connected more or less with voluptuous rites,— the equivalent of Aphrodite, or Venus. Tanith also was a noted female deity, and was worshipped at Carthage and Cyprus by the Phœnician settlers. The name is associated, according to Gesenius, with the Egyptian goddess Nut, and with the Grecian Artemis the huntress.

An important thing to be observed of these various deities is that they do not uniformly represent the same power. Thus Baal, the Phœnician sun-god, was made by the Greeks and Romans equivalent to Zeus, or Jupiter, the god of thunder and storms. Apollo, the sun-god of the Greeks, was not so powerful as Zeus, the god of the atmosphere; while in Assyria and Phœnicia the sun-god was the greater deity. In Babylonia, Shamas was a sun-god as well as Bel; and Bel again was the god of the heavens, like Zeus.

While Zeus was the supreme deity in the Greek mythology, rather than Apollo the sun, it seems that on the whole the sun was the prominent and the most commonly worshipped deity of all the Oriental nations, as being the most powerful force in Nature. Behind the sun, however, there was supposed to be an indefinite creative power, whose form was not represented, worshipped in no particular temple by the esoteric few who were his votaries, and called the "Father of all the gods," "the Ancient of days," reigning supreme over them all. This indefinite conception of the Jehovah of the Hebrews seems to me the last flickering light of the primitive revelation, shining in the souls of the most enlightened of the Pagan worshippers, including perhaps the greatest of the monarchs, who were priests as well as kings.

The most distinguishing feature in the worship of all the gods of antiquity, whether among Egyptians, or Assyrians, or Babylonians, or Phœnicians, or Greeks, or Romans, is that of oblations and sacrifices. It was even a peculiarity of the old Jewish religion, as well as that of China and India. These oblations and sacrifices were sometimes offered to the deity, whatever his form or name, as an expiation for sin, of which the soul is conscious in all ages and countries; sometimes to obtain divine favor, as in military expeditions, or to secure any object dearest to the heart, such as health, prosperity, or peace; sometimes to propitiate the deity in order to avert the calamities following his supposed wrath or vengeance. The oblations were usually in the form of wine, honey, or the fruits of the earth, which were supposed to be necessary for the nourishment of the gods, especially in Greece. The sacrifices were generally of oxen, sheep, and goats, the most valued and precious of human property in primitive times, for those old heathen never offered to their deities that which cost them nothing, but rather that which was dearest to them. Sometimes, especially in Phœnicia, human beings were offered in sacrifice, the most repulsive peculiarity of polytheism. But the instincts of humanity generally kept men from rites so revolting. Christianity, as one of its distinguishing features, abolished all forms of outward sacrifice, as superstitious and useless. The sacrifices pleasing to God are a broken spirit, as revealed to David and Isaiah amid all the ceremonies and ritualism of Jewish worship, and still more to Paul and Peter when the new dispensation was fully declared. The only sacrifice which Christ enjoined was self-sacrifice, supreme devotion to a spiritual and unseen and supreme God, and to his children: as the Christ took upon himself the form of a man, suffering evil all his days, and finally even an ignominious death, in obedience to his Father's will, that the world might be saved by his own self-sacrifice.

With sacrifices as an essential feature of all the ancient religions, if we except that of Persia in the time of Zoroaster, there was need of an officiating priesthood. The priests in all countries sought to gain power and influence, and made themselves an exclusive caste, more or less powerful as circumstances favored their usurpations. The priestly caste became a terrible power in Egypt and India, where the people, it would seem, were most susceptible to religious impressions, were most docile and most ignorant, and had in constant view the future welfare of their souls. In China, where there was scarcely any religion at all, this priestly power was unknown; and it was especially weak among the Greeks, who had no fear of the future, and who worshipped beauty and grace rather than a spiritual god. Sacerdotalism entered into Christianity when it became corrupted by the lust of dominion and power, and with great force ruled the Christian world in times of ignorance and superstition. It is sad to think that the decline of sacerdotalism is associated with the growth of infidelity and religious indifference, showing how few worship God in spirit and in truth even in Christian countries. Yet even that reaction is humanly natural; and as it so surely follows upon epochs of priestcraft, it may be a part of the divine process of arousing men to the evils of superstition.

Among all nations where polytheism prevailed, idolatry became a natural sequence, — that is, the worship of animals and of graven images, at first as symbols of the deities that were worshipped, generally the sun, moon, and stars, and the elements of Nature, like fire, water, and air. But the symbols of divine power, as degeneracy increased and ignorance set in, were in succession worshipped as deities, as in India and Africa at the present day. This is the lowest form of religion, and the most repulsive and degraded which has prevailed in the world, — showing the enormous difference between the primitive faiths and the worship which succeeded, growing more and more hideous with the progress of ages, until the fulness of time arrived when God sent reformers among the debased people, more or less supernaturally inspired, to declare new truth, and even to revive the knowledge of the old in danger of being utterly lost.

It is a pleasant thing to remember that the religions thus far treated, as known to the Jews, and by which they were more or less contaminated, have all passed away with the fall of empires and the spread of divine truth; and they never again can be revived in the countries where they flourished. Mohammedanism, a monotheistic religion, has taken their place, and driven the ancient idols to the moles and the bats; and where Mohammedanism has failed to extirpate ancient idolatries, Christianity in some form has come in and dethroned them forever.

There was one form of religion with which the Jews came in contact which was comparatively pure; and this was the religion of Persia, the loftiest form of all Pagan beliefs.

The Persians were an important branch of the Iranian family. "The Iranians were the dominant race throughout the entire tract lying between the Suliman mountains and the Pamir steppe on the one hand, and the great Mesopotamian valley on the other." It was a region of great extremes of temperature, — the summers being hot, and the winters piercingly cold. A great part of this region is an arid and frightful desert; but the more favored portions are extremely fertile. In this country the Iranians settled at a very early period, probably 2500 B. C., about the time the Hindus emigrated from Central Asia to the banks of the Indus. Both Iranians and Hindus belonged to the great Aryan or Indo-European race, whose original settlements were on the high table-lands northeast of Samarkand, in the modern Bokhara, watered by the Oxus, or Amon River. From these rugged regions east of the Caspian Sea, where the means of subsistence are difficult to be obtained, the Aryans emigrated to India on the southeast, to Iran on the southwest, to Europe on the west, — all speaking substantially the same language.

Of those who settled in Iran, the Persians were the most prominent, — a brave, hardy, and adventurous people, warlike in their habits, and moral in their conduct. They were a pastoral rather than a nomadic people, and gloried in their horses and cattle. They had great skill as archers and horsemen, and furnished the best cavalry among the ancients. They lived in fixed habitations, and their houses had windows and fireplaces; but they were doomed to a perpetual struggle with a severe and uncertain climate, and a soil which required ceaseless diligence. "The whole plateau of Iran," says Johnson, "was suggestive of the war of elements, — a country of great contrasts of fertility and desolation, — snowy ranges of mountains, salt deserts, and fields of beauty lying in close proximity."

The early Persians are represented as having oval faces, raised features, well-arched eyebrows, and large dark eyes, now soft as the gazelle's, now flashing with quick insight. Such a people were extremely receptive of modes and fashions, — the aptest learners as well as the boldest adventurers; not patient in study nor skilful to invent, but swift to seize and appropriate, terrible breakers-up of old religious spells. They dissolved the old material civilization of Cushite and Turanian origin. What passion for vast conquests! "These rugged tribes, devoted to their chiefs, led by Cyrus from their herds and hunting-grounds to startle the pampered Lydians with their spare diet and clothing of skins; living on what they could get, strangers to wine and wassail, schooled in manly exercises, cleanly even to superstition, loyal to age and filial duties; with a manly pride of personal independence that held a debt the next worst thing to a lie; their fondness for social graces, their feudal dignities, their chiefs giving counsel to the king even while submissive to his person, esteeming prowess before praying; their strong ambition, scorning those who scorned toil." Artaxerxes wore upon his person the worth of twelve thousand talents, yet shared the hardships of his army in the march, carrying quiver and shield, leading the way to the steepest places, and stimulating the hearts of his soldiers by walking twenty-five miles a day.

There was much that is interesting about the ancient Persians. All the old authorities, especially Herodotus, testify to the comparative purity of their lives, to their love of truth, to their heroism in war, to the simplicity of their habits, to their industry and thrift in battling sterility of soil and the elements of Nature, to their love of agricultural pursuits, to kindness towards women and slaves, and above all other things to a strong personality of character which implied a powerful will. The early Persians chose the bravest and most capable of their nobles for kings, and these kings were mild and merciful. Xenophon makes Cyrus the ideal of a king, — the incarnation of sweetness and light, conducting war with a magnanimity unknown to the ancient nations, dismissing prisoners, forgiving foes, freeing slaves, and winning all hearts by a true nobility of nature. He was a reformer of barbarous methods of war, and as pure in morals as he was powerful in war. In short, he had all those qualities which we admire in the chivalric heroes of the Middle Ages.

There was developed among this primitive and virtuous people a religion essentially different from that of Assyria and Egypt, with which is associated the name of Zoroaster, or Zarathushtra. Who this extraordinary personage was, and when he lived, it is not easy to determine. Some suppose that he did not live at all. It is most probable that he lived in Bactria from 1000 to 1500 B. C.; but all about him is involved in hopeless obscurity.

The Zend-Avesta, or the sacred books of the Persians, are mostly hymns, prayers, and invocations addressed to various deities, among whom Ormazd was regarded as supreme. These poems were first made known to European scholars by Anquetil du Perron, an enthusiastic traveller, a little more than one hundred years ago, and before the laws of Menu were translated by Sir William Jones. What we know about the religion of Persia is chiefly derived from the Zend-Avesta. *Zend* is the interpretation of the Avesta. The oldest part of these poems is called the Gâthâs, supposed to have been composed by Zoroaster about the time of Moses.

As all information about Zoroaster personally is unsatisfactory, I proceed to speak of the religion which he is supposed to have given to the Iranians, according to Dr. Martin Haug, the great authority on this subject.

Its peculiar feature was dualism, — two original uncreated principles; one good, the other evil. Both principles were real persons, possessed of will, intelligence, power, consciousness, engaged from all eternity in perpetual contest. The good power was called Ahura-Mazda, and the evil power was called Angro-Mainyus. Ahura-Mazda means the "Much-knowing spirit," or the All-wise, the All-bountiful, who stood at the head of all that is beneficent in the universe, — "the creator of life," who made the celestial bodies and the earth, and from whom came all good to man and everlasting happiness. Angro-Mainyus means the black or dark intelligence, the creator of all that is evil, both moral and physical. He had power to blast the earth with barrenness, to produce earthquakes and storms, to inflict disease and death, destroy flocks and the fruits of the earth, excite wars and tumults; in short, to send every form of evil on mankind. Ahura-Mazda had no control over this Power of evil; all he could do was to baffle him.

These two deities who divided the universe between them had each subordinate spirits or genii, who did their will, and assisted in the government of the universe, — corresponding to our idea of angels and demons.

Neither of these supreme deities was represented by the early Iranians under material forms; but in process of time corruption set in, and Magism, or the worship of the elements of Nature, became general. The elements which were worshipped were fire, air, earth, and water. Personal gods, temples, shrines, and images were rejected. But the most common form of worship was that of fire, in Mithra, the genius of light, early identified with the sun. Hence, practically, the supreme god of the Persians was the same that was worshipped in Assyria and Egypt and India, — the sun, under various names; with this difference, that in Persia there were no temples erected to him, nor were there graven images of him. With the sun was associated a supreme power that presided over the universe, benignant and eternal. Fire itself in its pure universality was more to the Iranians than any form. "From the sun," says the Avesta, "are all things sought that can be desired." To fire, the Persian kings addressed their prayers. Fire, or the sun, was in the early times a symbol of the supreme Power, rather than the Power itself, since the sun was created by Ahura-Mazda (Ormazd). It was to him that Zoroaster addressed his prayers, as recorded in the Gâthâs. "I worship," said he, "the Creator of all things, Ahura-Mazda, full of light. . . . Teach thou me, Ahura-Mazda, out of thyself, from heaven by thy mouth, whereby the world first arose." Again, from the Khorda-Avesta we read: "In the name of God, the giver, forgiver, rich in love, praise be to the name of Ormazd, who always was, always is, and always will be; from whom alone is derived rule." From these and other passages we infer that the religion of the Iranians was monotheistic. And yet the sun also was worshipped under the name of Mithra. Says Zoroaster: "I invoke Mithra, the lofty, the immortal, the pure, the sun, the ruler, the eye of Ormazd." It would seem from this that the sun was identified with the Supreme Being. There was no other power than the sun which was worshipped. There was no multitude of gods, nothing like polytheism, such as existed in Egypt. The Iranians believed in one supreme, eternal God, who created all things, beneficent and all-wise; yet this supreme power was worshipped under the symbol of the sun, although the sun was created by him. This confounding the sun with a supreme and intelligent being makes the Iranian religion indefinite, and hard to be comprehended; but compared with the polytheism of Egypt and Babylon, it is much higher and purer. We see in it no degrading rites, no offensive sacerdotalism, no caste, no worship of animals or images; all is spiritual and elevated, but little inferior to the religion of the Hebrews. In the Zend-Avesta we find no doctrines; but we do find prayers and praises and supplication to a Supreme Being. In the Vedas — the Hindu books — the powers of Nature are gods; in the Avesta they are spirits, or servants of the Supreme.

" The main difference between the Vedic and Avestan religions is that in the latter the Vedic worship of natural powers and phenomena is superseded by a more ethical and personal interest. Ahura-Mazda (Ormazd), the living wisdom, replaces Indra, the lightning-god. In Iran there grew up, what India never saw, a consciousness of world-purpose, ethical and spiritual; a reference of the ideal to the future rather than the present; a promise of progress; and the idea that the law of the universe means the final deliverance of good from evil, and its eternal triumph."[1]

The loftiness which modern scholars like Haug, Lenormant, and Spiegel see in the Zend-Avesta pertains more directly to the earlier portions of these sacred writings, attributable to Zoroaster, called the Gâthâs. But in the course of time the Avesta was subjected to many additions and interpretations, called the Zend, which show degeneracy. A world of myth and legend is crowded into liturgical fragments. The old Bactrian tongue in which the Avesta was composed became practically a dead language. There entered into the Avesta old Chaldæan traditions. It would be strange if the pure faith of Zoroaster should not be corrupted after Persia had conquered Babylon, and even after its alliance with Media, where the Magi had great reputation for knowledge. And yet even with the corrupting influence of the superstitions of Babylon, to say nothing of Media, the Persian conquerors did not wholly forget the God of their fathers in their old Bactrian home. And it is probable that one reason why Cyrus and Darius treated the Jews with so much kindness and generosity was the sympathy they felt for the monotheism of the Jewish religion in contrast with the polytheism and idolatry of the conquered

[1] Samuel Johnson's Religion of Persia.

Babylonians. It is not unreasonable to suppose that both the Persians and Jews worshipped substantially the one God who made the heaven and the earth, notwithstanding the dualism which entered into the Persian religion, and the symbolic worship of fire which is the most powerful agent in Nature; and it is considered by many that from the Persians the Jews received, during their Captivity, their ideas concerning a personal Devil, or Power of Evil, of which no hint appears in the Law or the earlier Prophets. It would certainly seem to be due to that monotheism which modern scholars see behind the dualism of Persia, as an elemental principle of the old religion of Iran, that the Persians were the noblest people of Pagan antiquity, and practised the highest morality known in the ancient world. Virtue and heroism went hand in hand; and both virtue and heroism were the result of their religion. But when the Persians became intoxicated with the wealth and power they acquired on the fall of Babylon, then their degeneracy was rapid, and their faith became obscured. Had it been the will of Providence that the Greeks should have contended with the Persians under the leadership of Cyrus, — the greatest Oriental conqueror known in history, — rather than under Xerxes, then even an Alexander might have been baffled. The great mistake of the Persian monarchs in their degeneracy was in trusting to the magnitude of their armies rather than in their ancient discipline and national heroism. The consequence was a panic, which would not have taken place under Cyrus, whenever they met the Greeks in battle. It was a panic which dispersed the Persian hosts in the fatal battle of Arbela, and made Alexander the master of western Asia. But degenerate as the Persians became, they rallied under succeeding dynasties, and in Artaxerxes II. and Chosroes the Romans found, in their declining glories, their most formidable enemies.

Though the brightness of the old religion of Zoroaster ceased to shine after the Persian conquests, and religious rites fell into the hands of the Magi, yet it is the only Oriental religion which entered into Christianity after its magnificent triumph, unless we trace early monasticism to the priests of India. Christianity had a hard battle with Gnosticism and Manichæism, — both of Persian origin, — and did not come out unscathed. No Grecian system of philosophy, except Platonism, entered into the Christian system so influentially as the disastrous Manichæan heresy, which Augustine combated. The splendid mythology of the Greeks, as well as the degrading polytheism of Egypt, Assyria, and Phœnicia, passed away before the power of the cross; but Persian speculations remained. Even Origen, the greatest scholar of Christian antiquity, was tainted with them. And the mighty myths of the origin of evil, which perplexed Zoroaster, still remain unsolved; but the belief of the final triumph of good over evil is common to both Christians and the disciples of the Bactrian sage.

AUTHORITIES.

Rawlinson's Egypt and Babylon; History of Babylonia, by A. H. Sayce; Smith's Dictionary of the Bible; Rawlinson's Herodotus; George Smith's History of Babylonia; Lenormant's Manuel d'Histoire Ancienne; Layard's Nineveh and Babylon; Journal of Royal Asiatic Society; Heeren's Asiatic Nations; Dr. Pusey's Lectures on Daniel; Birch's Egypt from the Earliest Times; Brugsch's History of Egypt; Records of the Past; Rawlinson's History of Ancient Egypt; Wilkinson's Ancient Egyptians; Sayce's Ancient Empires of the East; Rawlinson's Religions of the Ancient World; James Freeman Clarke's Ten Great Religions; Religion of Ancient Egypt, by P. Le Page Renouf; Moffat's Comparative History of Religions; Bunsen's Egypt's Place in History; Persia, from the Earliest Period, by W. S. W. Vaux; Johnson's Oriental Religions; Haug's Essays; Spiegel's Avesta.

The above are the more prominent authorities; but the number of books on ancient religions is very large.

RELIGIONS OF INDIA.

BRAHMANISM AND BUDDHISM

RELIGIONS OF INDIA.

BRAHMANISM AND BUDDHISM.

THAT form of ancient religion which has of late excited the most interest is Buddhism. An inquiry into its characteristics is especially interesting, since so large a part of the human race — nearly five hundred millions out of the thirteen hundred millions — still profess to embrace the doctrines which were taught by Buddha, although his religion has become so corrupted that his original teachings are nearly lost sight of. The same may be said of the doctrines of Confucius. The religions of ancient Egypt, Assyria, and Greece have utterly passed away, and what we have had to say of these is chiefly a matter of historic interest, as revealing the forms assumed by the human search for a supernatural Ruler when moulded by human ambitions, powers, and indulgence in the "lust of the eye and the pride of life," rather than by aspirations toward the pure and the spiritual.

Buddha was the great reformer of the religious system of the Hindus, although he lived nearly fifteen hundred or two thousand years after the earliest Brahmanical ascendency. But before we can appreciate his work and mission, we must examine the system he attempted to reform, even as it is impossible to present the Protestant Reformation without first considering mediæval Catholicism before the time of Luther. It was the object of Buddha to break the yoke of the Brahmans, and to release his countrymen from the austerities, the sacrifices, and the rigid sacerdotalism which these ancient priests imposed, without essentially subverting ancient religious ideas. He was a moralist and reformer, rather than the founder of a religion.

Brahmanism is one of the oldest religions of the world. It was flourishing in India at a period before history was written. It was coeval with the religion of Egypt in the time of Abraham, and perhaps at a still earlier date. But of its earliest form and extent we know nothing, except from the sacred poems of the Hindus called the Vedas, written in Sanskrit probably fifteen hundred years before Christ, — for even the date of the earliest of the Vedas is unknown. Fifty years ago we could not have understood the ancient religions of India. But Sir William Jones in the latter part of the last century, a man of immense erudition and genius for the acquisition of languages, at that time an English judge in India, prepared the way for the study of Sanskrit, the literary language of ancient India, by the translation and publication of the laws of Menu. He was followed in his labors by the Schlegels of Germany, and by numerous scholars and missionaries. Within fifty years this ancient and beautiful language has been so perseveringly studied that we know something of the people by whom it was once spoken, — even as Egyptologists have revealed something of ancient Egypt by interpreting the hieroglyphics; and Chaldæan investigators have found stores of knowledge in the Babylonian bricks.

The Sanskrit, as now interpreted, reveals to us the meaning of those poems called Vedas, by which we are enabled to understand the early laws and religion of the Hindus. It is poetry, not history, which makes this revelation, for the Hindus have no history farther back than five or six hundred years before Christ. It is from Homer and Hesiod that we get an idea of the gods of Greece, not from Herodotus or Xenophon.

From comparative philology, a new science, of which Prof. Max Müller is one of the greatest expounders, we learn that the roots of various European languages, as well as of the Latin and Greek, are substantially the same as those of the Sanskrit spoken by the Hindus thirty-five hundred years ago, from which it is inferred that the Hindus were a people of like remote origin with the Greeks, the Italic races (Romans, Italians, French), the Slavic races (Russian, Polish, Bohemian), the Teutonic races of England and the Continent, and the Keltic races. These are hence alike called the Indo-European races; and as the same linguistic roots are found in their languages and in the Zend-Avesta, we infer that the ancient Persians, or inhabitants of Iran, belonged to the same great Aryan race.

The original seat of this race, it is supposed, was in the high table-lands of Central Asia, in or near Bactria, east of the Caspian Sea, and north and west of the Himalaya Mountains. This country was so cold and sterile and unpropitious that winter predominated, and it was difficult to support life. But the people, inured to hardship and privation, were bold, hardy, adventurous, and enterprising.

It is a most interesting process, as described by the philologists, which has enabled them, by tracing the history of words through their various modifications in different living languages, to see how the lines of growth converge as they are followed back to the simple Aryan roots. And there, getting at the meanings of the things or thoughts the words originally expressed, we see revealed, in the reconstruction of a language that no longer exists, the material objects and habits of thought and life of a people who passed away before history began, — so imperishable are the unconscious embodiments of mind, even in the airy and unsubstantial forms of unwritten speech! By this process, then, we learn that the Aryans were a nomadic people, and had made some advance in civilization. They lived in houses which were roofed, which had windows and doors. Their common cereal was barley, the grain of cold climates. Their wealth was in cattle, and they had domesticated the cow, the sheep, the goat, the horse, and the dog. They used yokes, axes, and ploughs. They wrought in various metals; they spun and wove, navigated rivers in sailboats, and fought with bows, lances, and swords. They had clear perceptions of the rights of property, which were based on land. Their morals were simple and pure, and they had strong natural affections. Polygamy was unknown among them. They had no established sacerdotal priesthood. They worshipped the powers of Nature, especially fire, the source of light and heat, which they so much needed in their dreary land. Authorities differ as to their primeval religion, some supposing that it was monotheistic, and others polytheistic, and others again pantheistic.

Most of the ancient nations were controlled more or

less by priests, who, as their power increased, instituted a caste to perpetuate their influence. Whether or not we hold the primitive religion of mankind to have been a pure theism, directly revealed by God, — which is my own conviction, — it is equally clear that the form of religion recorded in the earliest written records of poetry or legend was a worship of the sun and moon and planets. I believe this to have been a corruption of original theism; many think it to have been a stage of upward growth in the religious sense of primitive man. In all the ancient nations the sun-god was a prominent deity, as the giver of heat and light, and hence of fertility to the earth. The emblem of the sun was fire, and hence fire was deified, especially among the Hindus, under the name of Agni, — the Latin *ignis*.

Fire, caloric, or heat in some form was, among the ancient nations, supposed to be the *animus mundi*. In Egypt, as we have seen, Osiris, the principal deity, was a form of Ra, the sun-god. In Assyria, Asshur, the substitute for Ra, was the supreme deity. In India we find Mitra, and in Persia Mithra, the sun-god, among the prominent deities, as Helios was among the Greeks, and Phœbus Apollo among the Romans. The sun was not always the supreme divinity, but invariably held one of the highest places in the Pagan pantheon.

BRAHMANISM AND BUDDHISM.

It is probable that the religion of the common progenitors of the Hindus, Persians, Greeks, Romans, Kelts, Teutons, and Slavs, in their hard and sterile home in Central Asia, was a worship of the powers of Nature verging toward pantheism, although the earliest of the Vedas representing the ancient faith seem to recognize a supreme power and intelligence — God — as the common father of the race, to whom prayers and sacrifices were devoutly offered. Freeman Clarke quotes from Müller's "Ancient Sanskrit Literature" one of the hymns in which the unity of God is most distinctly recognized: —

"In the beginning there arose the Source of golden light. He was the only Lord of all that is. He established the earth and sky. Who is the God to whom we shall offer our sacrifices? It is he who giveth life, who giveth strength, who governeth all men; through whom heaven was established, and the earth created."

But if the Supreme God whom we adore was recognized by this ancient people, he was soon lost sight of in the multiplied manifestations of his power, so that Rawlinson thinks [1] that when the Aryan race separated in their various migrations, which resulted in what we call the Indo-European group of races, there was no conception of a single supreme power, from whom man and nature have alike their origin, but Nature-

[1] Religions of the Ancient World, p. 105.

worship, ending in an extensive polytheism, — as among the Assyrians and Egyptians.

As to these Aryan migrations, we do not know when a large body crossed the Himalaya Mountains, and settled on the banks of the Indus, but probably it was at least two thousand years before Christ. Northern India had great attractions to those hardy nomadic people, who found it so difficult to get a living during the long winters of their primeval home. India was a country of fruits and flowers, with an inexhaustible soil, favorable to all kinds of production, where but little manual labor was required, — a country abounding in every kind of animals, and every kind of birds; a land of precious stones and minerals, of hills and valleys, of majestic rivers and mountains, with a beautiful climate and a sunny sky. These Aryan conquerors drove before them the aboriginal inhabitants, who were chiefly Mongolians, or reduced them to a degrading vassalage. The conquering race was white, the conquered was dark, though not black; and this difference of color was one of the original causes of Indian caste.

It was some time after the settlement of the Aryans on the banks of the Indus and the Ganges before the Vedas were composed by the poets, who as usual gave form to religious belief, as they did in Persia and Greece. These poems, or hymns, are pantheistic.

"There is no recognition," says Monier Williams, "of a Supreme God disconnected with the worship of Nature." There was a vague and indefinite worship of the Infinite under various names, such as the sun, the sky, the air, the dawn, the winds, the storms, the waters, the rivers, which alike charmed and terrified, and seemed to be instinct with life and power. God was in all things, and all things in God; but there was no idea of providential agency or of personality.

In the Vedic hymns the number of gods is not numerous, only thirty-three. The chief of these were Varuna, the sky; Mitra, the sun; and Indra, the storm: after these, Agni, fire; and Soma, the moon. The worship of these divinities was originally simple, consisting of prayer, praise, and offerings. There were no temples and no imposing sacerdotalism, although the priests were numerous. "The prayers and praises describe the wisdom, power, and goodness of the deity addressed,"[1] and when the customary offerings had been made, the worshipper prayed for food, life, health, posterity, wealth, protection, happiness, whatever the object was, — generally for outward prosperity rather than for improvement in character, or for forgiveness of sin, peace of mind, or power to resist temptation. The offerings to the gods were propitiatory, in the form of victims, or libations of some juice. Nor did

[1] Rawlinson, p. 121.

these early Hindus take much thought of a future life. There is nothing in the Rig-Veda of a belief in the transmigration of souls,[1] although the Vedic bards seem to have had some hope of immortality. "He who gives alms," says one poet, "goes to the highest place in heaven: he goes to the gods.[2] . . . Where there is eternal light, in the world where the sun is placed, — in that immortal, imperishable world, place me, O Soma! . . . Where there is happiness and delight, where joy and pleasures reside, where the desires of our heart are attained, there make me immortal."

In the oldest Vedic poems there were great simplicity and joyousness, without allusion to those rites, ceremonies, and sacrifices which formed so prominent a part of the religion of India at a later period.

Four hundred years after the Rig-Veda was composed we come to the Brahmanic age, when the laws of Menu were written, when the Aryans were living in the valley of the Ganges, and the caste system had become national. The supreme deity is no longer one of the powers of Nature, like Mitra or Indra, but according to Menu he is Brahm, or Brahma, — "an eternal, unchangeable, absolute being, the soul of all beings, who, having willed to produce various beings

[1] Wilson: Rig-Veda, vol. iii. p. 170.
[2] Müller: Chips from a German Workshop, vol. i. p. 46.

from his own divine substance, created the waters and placed in them a productive seed. The seed became an egg, and in that egg he was born, but sat inactive for a year, when he caused the egg to divide itself; and from its two divisions he framed the heaven above, and the earth beneath. From the supreme soul Brahma drew forth mind, existing substantially, though unperceived by the senses; and before mind, the reasoning power, he produced consciousness, the internal monitor; and before them both he produced the great principle of the soul. . . . The soul is, in its substance, from Brahma himself, and is destined finally to be resolved into him. The soul, then, is simply an emanation from Brahma; but it will not return unto him at death necessarily, but must migrate from body to body, until it is purified by profound abstraction and emancipated from all desires."

This is the substance of the Hindu pantheism as taught by the laws of Menu. It accepts God, but without personality or interference with the world's affairs, — not a God to be loved, scarcely to be feared, but a mere abstraction of the mind.

The theology which is thus taught in the Brahmanical Vedas, it would seem, is the result of lofty questionings and profound meditation on the part of the Indian sages or priests, rather than the creation of poets.

In the laws of Menu, intended to exalt the Brahmanical caste, we read, as translated by Sir William Jones: —

"To a man contaminated by sensuality, neither the Vedas, nor liberality, nor sacrifices, nor strict observances, nor pious austerities, ever procure felicity. . . . Let not a man be proud of his rigorous devotion; let him not, having sacrificed, utter a falsehood; having made a donation, let him never proclaim it. . . . By falsehood the sacrifice becomes vain; by pride the merit of devotion is lost. . . . Single is each man born, single he dies, single he receives the reward of the good, and single the punishment of his evil deeds. . . . By forgiveness of injuries the learned are purified; by liberality, those who have neglected their duty; by pious meditation, those who have secret thoughts; by devout austerity, those who best know the Vedas. . . . Bodies are cleansed by water; the mind is purified by truth; the vital spirit, by theology and devotion; the understanding, by clear knowledge. . . . A faithful wife who wishes to attain in heaven the mansion of her husband, must do nothing unkind to him, be he living or dead; let her not, when her lord is deceased, even pronounce the name of another man; let her continue till death, forgiving all injuries, performing harsh duties, avoiding every sensual pleasure, and cheerfully practising the incomparable rules of virtue. . . . The soul itself is its own witness, the soul itself is its own refuge; offend not thy conscious soul, the supreme internal witness of man. . . . O friend to virtue, the Supreme Spirit, which is the same as thyself, resides in thy bosom perpetually, and is an all-knowing inspector of thy goodness or wickedness."

Such were the truths uttered on the banks of the Ganges one thousand years before Christ. But with these views there is an exaltation of the Brahmanical or sacerdotal life, hard to be distinguished from the recognition of divine qualities. "From his high birth," says Menu, "a Brahman is an object of veneration, even to deities." Hence, great things are expected of him; his food must be roots and fruit, his clothing of bark fibres; he must spend his time in reading the Vedas; he is to practise austerities by exposing himself to heat and cold; he is to beg food but once a day; he must be careful not to destroy the life of the smallest insect; he must not taste intoxicating liquors. A Brahman who has thus mortified his body by these modes is exalted into the divine essence. This was the early creed of the Brahman before corruption set in. And in these things we see a striking resemblance to the doctrines of Buddha. Had there been no corruption of Brahmanism, there would have been no Buddhism; for the principles of Buddhism were those of early Brahmanism.

But Brahmanism became corrupted. Like the Mosaic Law, under the sedulous care of the sacerdotal orders it ripened into a most burdensome ritualism.

The Brahmanical caste became tyrannical, exacting, and oppressive. With the supposed sacredness of his person, and with the laws made in his favor, the Brahman became intolerable to the people, who were ground down by sacrifices, expiatory offerings, and wearisome and minute ceremonies of worship. Caste destroyed all ideas of human brotherhood; it robbed the soul of its affections and its aspirations. Like the Pharisees in the time of Jesus, the Brahmans became oppressors of the people. As in Pagan Egypt and in Christian Mediaeval Europe, the priests exercised tremendous influence; their power in the land was more than Druidical.

But the Brahman, when true to the laws of Menu, led in one sense a lofty life. Nor can we despise a religion which recognized the value and immortality of the soul, a state of future rewards and punishments, though its worship was encumbered by rites, ceremonies, and sacrifices. It was spiritual in its essential peculiarities, having reference to another world rather than to this, which is more than we can say of the religion of the Greeks; it was not worldly in its ends, seeking to save the soul rather than to pamper the body; it had aspirations after a higher life; it was profoundly reverential, recognizing a supreme intelligence and power, indefinitely indeed, but sincerely, — not an incarnated deity like the Zeus of the Greeks, but an infinite Spirit, pervading the universe. The pantheism of the Brahmans was better than the godless materialism of the Chinese. It aspired to rise to a knowledge of God as the supremest wisdom and grandest attainment of mortal man. It made too much of sacrifices; but sacrifices were common to all the ancient religions except the Persian.

> "He who through knowledge or religious acts
> Henceforth attains to immortality,
> Shall first present his body, Death, to thee."

Whether human sacrifices were offered in India when the Vedas were composed we do not know, but it is believed to be probable. The oldest form of sacrifice was the offering of food to the deity. Dr. H. C. Trumbull, in his work on "The Blood Covenant," thinks that the origin of animal sacrifices was like that of circumcision, — a pouring out of blood (the universal, ancient symbol of *life*) as a sign of devotion to the deity; and the substitution of animals was a natural and necessary mode of making this act of consecration a frequent and continuing one. This presents a nobler view of the whole sacrificial system than the common one. Yet doubtless the latter soon prevailed; for following upon the devoted life-offerings to the Divine Friend, came propitiatory rites to appease divine anger or gain divine favor. Then came in the natural human self-seeking of the sacerdotal class, for the multiplication of sacrifices tended to exalt the priesthood, and thus to perpetuate caste.

Again, the Brahmans, if practising austerities to weaken sensual desires, like the monks of Syria and Upper Egypt, were meditative and intellectual; they evolved out of their brains whatever was lofty in their system of religion and philosophy. Constant and profound meditation on the soul, on God, and on immortality was not without its natural results. They explored the world of metaphysical speculation. There is scarcely an hypothesis advanced by philosophers in ancient or modern times, which may not be found in the Brahmanical writings. "We find in the writings of these Hindus materialism, atomism, pantheism, Pyrrhonism, idealism. They anticipated Plato, Kant, and Hegel. They could boast of their Spinozas and their Humes long before Alexander dreamed of crossing the Indus. From them the Pythagoreans borrowed a great part of their mystical philosophy, of their doctrine of transmigration of souls, and the unlawfulness of eating animal food. From them Aristotle learned the syllogism. . . . In India the human mind exhausted itself in attempting to detect the laws which regulate its operation, before the philosophers of Greece were beginning to enter the precincts of metaphysical inquiry." This intellectual subtlety, acumen, and logical power the

Brahmans never lost. To-day the Christian missionary finds them his superiors in the sports of logical tournaments, wherever the Brahman condescends to put forth his powers of reasoning.

Brahmanism carried idealism to the extent of denying any reality to sense or matter, declaring that sense is a delusion. It sought to leave the soul emancipated from desire from a material body, in a state which according to Indian metaphysics is *being*, but not *existence*. Desire, anger, ignorance, evil thoughts are consumed by the fire of knowledge.

But I will not attempt to explain the ideal pantheism which Brahmanical philosophers substituted for the Nature-worship taught in the earlier Vedas. This proved too abstract for the people; and the Brahmans, in the true spirit of modern Jesuitism, wishing to accommodate their religion to the people, — who were in bondage to their tyranny, and who have ever been inclined to sensuous worship, — multiplied their sacrifices and sacerdotal rites, and even permitted a complicated polytheism. Gradually piety was divorced from morality. Siva and Vishnu became worshipped, as well as Brahma and a host of other gods unknown to the earlier Vedas.

In the sixth century before Christ, the corruption of society had become so flagrant under the teachings and government of the Brahmans, that a reform was imperatively needed. "The pride of race had put an impassable barrier between the Aryan-Hindus and the conquered aborigines, while the pride of both had built up an equally impassable barrier between the different classes among the Aryan people themselves." The old childlike joy in life, so manifest in the Vedas, had died away. A funereal gloom hung over the land; and the gloomiest people of all were the Brahmans themselves, devoted to a complicated ritual of ceremonial observances, to needless and cruel sacrifices, and a repulsive theology. The worship of Nature had degenerated into the worship of impure divinities. The priests were inflated with a puerile but sincere belief in their own divinity, and inculcated a sense of duty which was nothing else than a degrading slavery to their own caste.

Under these circumstances Buddhism arose as a protest against Brahmanism. But it was rather an ethical than a religious movement; it was an attempt to remove misery from the world, and to elevate ordinary life by a reform of morals. It was effected by a prince who goes by the name of Buddha, — the "Enlightened," — who was supposed by his later followers to be an incarnation of Deity, miraculously conceived, and sent into the world to save men. He was nearly contemporary with Confucius, although the Buddhistic doctrines were not introduced into China until about two hundred years before the Christian era. He is supposed to have belonged to a warlike tribe called Sâkyas, of great reputed virtue, engaged in agricultural pursuits, who had entered northern India and made a permanent settlement several hundred years before. The name by which the reformer is generally known is Gautama, borrowed by the Sâkyas after their settlement in India from one of the ancient Vedic bard-families. The foundation of our knowledge of Sâkya Buddha is from a Life of him by Asvaghosha, in the first century of our era; and this life is again founded on a legendary history, not framed after any Indian model, but worked out among the nations in the north of India.

The Life of Buddha by Asvaghosha is a poetical romance of nearly ten thousand lines. It relates the miraculous conception of the Indian sage, by the descent of a spirit on his mother, Maya, — a woman of great purity of mind. The child was called Siddârtha, or "the perfection of all things." His father ruled a considerable territory, and was careful to conceal from the boy, as he grew up, all knowledge of the wickedness and misery of the world. He was therefore carefully educated within the walls of the palace, and surrounded with every luxury, but not allowed even to walk or drive in the royal gardens for fear he might see misery and sorrow. A beautiful girl was given to him in marriage, full of dignity and grace, with whom he lived in supreme happiness.

At length, as his mind developed and his curiosity increased to see and know things and people beyond the narrow circle to which he was confined, he obtained permission to see the gardens which surrounded the palace. His father took care to remove everything in his way which could suggest misery and sorrow; but a *deva*, or angel, assumed the form of an aged man, and stood beside his path, apparently struggling for life, weak and oppressed. This was a new sight to the prince, who inquired of his charioteer what kind of a man it was. Forced to reply, the charioteer told him that this infirm old man had once been young, sportive, beautiful, and full of every enjoyment.

On hearing this, the prince sank into profound meditation, and returned to the palace sad and reflective; for he had learned that the common lot of man is sad, — that no matter how beautiful, strong, and sportive a boy is, the time will come, in the course of Nature, when this boy will be wrinkled, infirm, and helpless. He became so miserable and dejected on this discovery that his father, to divert his mind, arranged other excursions for him; but on each occasion a *deva* contrived to appear before him in the form of some disease or misery. At last he saw a dead man carried to his grave, which still more deeply agitated him, for he had not known that this calamity was the common lot of all men. The same painful impression was made on him by the death of animals, and by the hard labors and privations of poor people. The more he saw of life as it was, the more he was overcome by the sight of sorrow and hardship on every side. He became aware that youth, vigor, and strength of life in the end fulfilled the law of ultimate destruction. While meditating on this sad reality beneath a flowering Jambu tree, where he was seated in the profoundest contemplation, a *deva*, transformed into a religious ascetic, came to him and said, "I am a Shâman. Depressed and sad at the thought of age, disease, and death, I have left my home to seek some way of rescue yet everywhere I find these evils, — all things hasten to decay. Therefore I seek that happiness which is only to be found in that which never perishes, that never knew a beginning, that looks with equal mind on enemy and friend, that heeds not wealth nor beauty, — the happiness to be found in solitude, in some dell free from molestation, all thought about the world destroyed."

This embodies the soul of Buddhism, its elemental principle, — to escape from a world of misery and death; to hide oneself in contemplation in some lonely spot, where indifference to passing events is gradually acquired, where life becomes one grand negation, and where the thoughts are fixed on what is eternal and imperishable, instead of on the mortal and transient.

The prince, who was now about thirty years of age, after this interview with the supposed ascetic, firmly resolved himself to become a hermit, and thus attain to a higher life, and rise above the misery which he saw around him on every hand. So he clandestinely and secretly escapes from his guarded palace; lays aside his princely habits and ornaments; dismisses all attendants, and even his horse; seeks the companionship of Brahmans, and learns all their penances and tortures. Finding a patient trial of this of no avail for his purpose, he leaves the Brahmans, and repairs to a quiet spot by the banks of a river, and for six years practises the most severe fasting and profound meditation. This was the form which piety had assumed in India from time immemorial, under the guidance of the Brahmans; for Siddârtha as yet is not the "enlightened,"—he is only an inquirer after that saving knowledge which will open the door of a divine felicity, and raise him above a world of disease and death.

Siddârtha's rigorous austerities, however, do not open this door of saving truth. His body is wasted, and his strength fails; he is near unto death. The conviction fastens on his lofty and inquiring mind that to arrive at the end he seeks he must enter by some other door than that of painful and useless austerities, and hence that the teachings of the Brahmans are fundamentally wrong. He discovers that no amount of austerities will extinguish desire, or produce ecstatic contemplation. In consequence of these reflections a great change comes over him, which is the turning-point of his history. He resolves to quit his self-inflicted torments as of no avail. He meets a shepherd's daughter, who offers him food out of compassion for his emaciated and miserable condition. The rich rice milk, sweet and perfumed, restores his strength. He renounces asceticism, and wanders to a spot more congenial to his changed views and condition.

Siddârtha's full enlightenment, however, has not yet come. Under the shade of the Bôdhi tree he devotes himself again to religious contemplation, and falls into rapt ecstasies. He remains a while in peaceful quiet; the morning sunbeams, the dispersing mists, and lovely flowers seem to pay tribute to him. He passes through successive stages of ecstasy, and suddenly upon his opened mind bursts the knowledge of his previous births in different forms; of the causes of re-birth, — ignorance (the root of evil) and unsatisfied desires ; and of the way to extinguish desires by right thinking, speaking and living, not by outward observance of forms and ceremonies. He is emancipated from the thraldom of those austerities which have formed the basis of religious life for generations unknown, and he resolves to teach.

Buddha travels slowly to the sacred city of Benares, converting by the way even Brahmans themselves. He claims to have reached perfect wisdom. He is followed by disciples, for there was something attractive and extraordinary about him; his person was beautiful and commanding. While he shows that painful austerities will not produce wisdom, he also teaches that wisdom is not reached by self-indulgence; that there is a middle path between penance and pleasures, even *temperance*, — the use, but not abuse, of the good things of earth. In his first sermon he declares that sorrow is in self; therefore to get rid of sorrow is to get rid of self. The means to this end is to forget self in deeds of mercy and kindness to others; to crucify demoralizing desires; to live in the realm of devout contemplation.

The active life of Buddha now begins, and for fifty years he travels from place to place as a teacher, gathers around him disciples, frames rules for his society, and brings within his community both the rich and poor. He even allows women to enter it. He thus matures his system, which is destined to be embraced by so large a part of the human race, and finally dies at the age of eighty, surrounded by reverential followers, who see in him an incarnation of the Deity.

Thus Buddha devoted his life to the welfare of men, moved by an exceeding tenderness and pity for the objects of misery which he beheld on every side. He attempted to point out a higher life, by which sorrow would be forgotten. He could not prevent sorrow culminating in old age, disease, and death; but he hoped to make men ignore their miseries, and thus rise above them to a beatific state of devout contemplation and the practice of virtues, for which he laid down certain rules and regulations.

It is astonishing how the new doctrines spread, — from India to China, from China to Japan and Ceylon, until Eastern Asia was filled with pagodas, temples, and monasteries to attest his influence; some eighty-five thousand existed in China alone. Buddha probably had as many converts in China as Confucius himself. The Buddhists from time to time were subjected to great persecution from the emperors of China, in which their sacred books were destroyed; and in India the Brahmans at last regained their power, and expelled Buddhism from the country. In the year 845 A.D. two hundred and sixty thousand monks and nuns were made to return to secular life in China, being regarded as mere drones, — lazy and useless members of the community. But the policy of persecution was reversed by succeeding emperors. In the thirteenth century there were in China nearly fifty thousand Buddhist temples and two hundred and thirteen thousand monks; and these represented but a fraction of the professed adherents of the religion. Under the present dynasty the Buddhists are proscribed, but still they flourish.

Now, what has given to the religion of Buddha such an extraordinary attraction for the people of Eastern Asia?

Buddhism has a twofold aspect, — *practical* and *speculative*. In its most definite form it was a moral and philanthropic movement, — the reaction against Brahmanism, which had no humanity, and which was as repulsive and oppressive as Roman Catholicism was when loaded down with ritualism and sacerdotal rites, when Europe was governed by priests, when churches were damp, gloomy crypts, before the tall cathedrals arose in their artistic beauty.

From a religious and philosophical point of view, Buddhism at first did not materially differ from Brahmanism. The same dreamy pietism, the same belief in the transmigration of souls, the same pantheistic ideas of God and Nature, the same desire for rest and final absorption in the divine essence characterized both. In both there was a certain principle of faith, which was a feeling of reverence rather than the recognition of the unity and personality and providence of God. The prayer of the Buddhist was a yearning for deliverance from sorrow, a hope of final rest; but this was not to be attained until desires and passions were utterly suppressed in the soul, which could be effected only by prayer, devout meditations, and a rigorous self-discipline. In order to be purified and fitted for Nirvana the soul, it was supposed, must pass through successive stages of existence in mortal forms, without conscious recollection, — innumerable births and deaths, with sorrow and disease. And the final state of supreme blessedness, the ending of the long and weary transmigration, would be attained only with the extinction of all desires, even the instinctive desire for existence.

Buddha had no definite ideas of the deity, and the worship of a personal God is nowhere to be found in his teachings, which exposed him to the charge of atheism. He even supposed that gods were subject to death, and must return to other forms of life before they obtained final rest in Nirvana. Nirvana means that state which admits of neither birth nor death, where there is no sorrow or disease, — an impassive state of existence, absorption in the Spirit of the Universe. In the Buddhist catechism Nirvana is defined as the "total cessation of changes; a perfect rest; the absence of desire, illusion, and sorrow; the total obliteration of everything that goes to make up the physical man." This theory of re-births, or transmigration of souls, is very strange and unnatural to our less imaginative and subtile Occidental minds; but to the speculative Orientals it is an attractive and reasonable belief. They make the "spirit" the immortal part of man, the "soul" being its emotional embodiment, its "spiritual body," whose unsatisfied desires cause its birth and re-birth into the fleshly form of the physical "body," — a very brief and temporary incarnation. When by the progressive enlightenment of the spirit its longings and desires have been gradually conquered, it no longer needs or has embodiment either of soul or of body; so that, to quote Elliott Coues in Olcott's "Buddhist Catechism," "a spirit in a state of conscious formlessness, subject to no further modification by embodiment, yet in full knowledge of its experiences [during its various incarnations], is Nirvanic."

Buddhism, however, viewed in any aspect, must be regarded as a gloomy religion. It is hard enough to crucify all natural desires and lead a life of self-abnegation; but for the spirit, in order to be purified, to be obliged to enter into body after body, each subject to disease, misery, and death, and then after a long series of migrations to be virtually annihilated as the highest consummation of happiness, gives one but a poor conception of the efforts of the proudest unaided intellect to arrive at a knowledge of God and immortal bliss. It would thus seem that the true idea of God, or even that of immortality, is not an innate conception revealed by consciousness; for why should good and intellectual men, trained to study and reflection all their lives, gain no clearer or more inspiring notions of the Being of infinite love and power, or of the happiness which He is able and willing to impart? What a feeble conception of God is a being without the oversight of the worlds that he created, without volition or purpose or benevolence, or anything corresponding to our notion of personality! What a poor conception of supernal bliss, without love or action or thought or holy companionship, — only rest, unthinking repose, and absence from disease, misery, and death, a state of endless impassiveness! What is Nirvana but an escape from death and deliverance from mortal desires, where there are neither ideas nor the absence of ideas; no changes or hopes or fears, it is true, but also no joy, no aspiration, no growth, no life, — a state of nonentity, where even consciousness is practically extinguished, and individuality merged into absolute stillness and a dreamless rest? What a poor reward for ages of struggle and the final achievement of exalted virtue!

But if Buddhism failed to arrive at what we believe to be a true knowledge of God and the destiny of the soul, — the forgiveness and remission, or doing-away, of sin, and a joyful and active immortality, all which I take to be revelations rather than intuitions, — yet there were some great certitudes in its teachings which did appeal to consciousness, — certitudes recognized by the noblest teachers of all ages and nations. These were such realities as truthfulness, sincerity, purity, justice, mercy, benevolence, unselfishness, love. The human mind arrives at ethical truths, even when all speculation about God and immortality has failed. The idea of God may be lost, but not that of moral obligation, — the mutual social duties of mankind. There is a sense of duty even among savages; in the lowest civilization there is true admiration of virtue. No sage that I ever read of enjoined immorality. No ignorance can prevent the sense of shame, of honor, or of duty. Everybody detests a liar and despises a thief. Thou shalt not bear false witness; thou shalt not commit adultery; thou shalt not kill, — these are laws written in human consciousness as well as in the code of Moses. Obedience and respect to parents are instincts as well as obligations.

Hence the prince Siddârtha, as soon as he had found the wisdom of inward motive and the folly of outward rite, shook off the yoke of the priests, and denounced caste and austerities and penances and sacrifices as of no avail in securing the welfare and peace of the soul or the favor of deity. In all this he showed an enlightened mind, governed by wisdom and truth, and even a bold and original genius, — like Abraham when he disowned the gods of his fathers. Having thus himself gained the security of the heights, Buddha longed to help others up, and turned his attention to the moral instruction of the people of India. He was emphatically a missionary of ethics, an apostle of righteousness, a reformer of abuses, as well as a tender and compassionate man, moved to tears in view of human sorrows and sufferings. He gave up metaphysical speculations for practical philanthropy. He wandered from city to city and village to village to relieve misery and teach duties rather than theological philosophies. He did not know that God is love, but he did know that peace and rest are the result of virtuous thoughts and acts.

"Let us then," said he, "live happily, not hating those who hate us; free from greed among the greedy. . . . Proclaim mercy freely to all men; it is as large as the spaces of heaven. . . . Whoever loves will feel the longing to save not himself alone, but all others." He compares himself to a father who rescues his children from a burning house, to a physician who cures the blind. He teaches the equality of the sexes as well as the injustice of castes. He enjoins kindness to servants and emancipation of slaves. "As a mother, as long as she lives, watches over her child, so among all beings," said Gautama, "let boundless good-will prevail. . . . Overcome evil with good, the avaricious with generosity, the false with truth. . . . Never forget thy own duty for the sake of another's. . . . If a man speaks or acts with evil thoughts pain follows, as the wheel the foot of him who draws the carriage. . . . He who lives seeking pleasure, and uncontrolled, the tempter will overcome. . . . The true sage dwells on earth, as the bee gathers sweetness with his mouth and wings. . . . One may conquer a thousand men in battle, but he who conquers himself alone is the greatest victor. . . . Let no man think lightly of sin, saying in his heart, 'It cannot overtake me.' . . . Let a man make himself what he preaches to others. . . . He who holds back rising anger as one might a rolling chariot, him, indeed, I call a driver; others may hold the reins. . . . A man who foolishly does me wrong, I will return to him the protection of my ungrudging love; the more evil comes from him, the more good shall go from me."

These are some of the sayings of the Indian reformer, which I quote from extracts of his writings as translated by Sanskrit scholars. Some of these sayings rise to a height of moral beauty surpassed only by the precepts of the great Teacher, whom many are too fond of likening to Buddha himself. The religion of Buddha is founded on a correct and virtuous life, as the only way to avoid sorrow and reach Nirvana. Its essence, theologically, is "Quietism," without firm belief in anything reached by metaphysic speculation; yet morally and practically it inculcates ennobling, active duties.

Among the rules that Buddha laid down for his disciples were — to keep the body pure; not to enter upon affairs of trade; to have no lands and cattle, or houses, or money, to abhor all hypocrisy and dissimulation; to be kind to everything that lives; never to take the life of any living being; to control the passions; to eat food only to satisfy hunger; not to feel resentment from injuries; to be patient and forgiving; to avoid covetousness, and never to tire of self-reflection. His fundamental principles are purity of mind, chastity of life, truthfulness, temperance, abstention from the wanton destruction of animal life, from vain pleasures, from envy, hatred, and malice. He does not enjoin sacrifices, for he knows no god to whom they can be offered; but "he proclaimed the brotherhood of man, if he did not reveal the fatherhood of God." He insisted on the natural equality of all men, — thus giving to caste a mortal wound, which offended the Brahmans, and finally led to the expulsion of his followers from India. He protested against all absolute authority, even that of the Vedas. Nor did he claim, any more than Confucius, originality of doctrines, only the revival of forgotten or neglected truths. He taught that Nirvana was not attained by Brahmanical rites, but by individual virtues; and that punishment is the inevitable result of evil deeds by the inexorable law of cause and effect.

Buddhism is essentially rationalistic and ethical, while Brahmanism is a pantheistic tendency to polytheism, and ritualistic even to the most offensive sacerdotalism. The Brahman reminds me of a Dunstan, — the Buddhist of a Benedict; the former of the gloomy, spiritual despotism of the Middle Ages, — the latter of self-denying monasticism in its best ages. The Brahman is like Thomas Aquinas with his dogmas and metaphysics; the Buddhist is more like a mediæval freethinker, stigmatized as an atheist. The Brahman was so absorbed with his theological speculation that he took no account of the sufferings of humanity; the Buddhist was so absorbed with the miseries of man that the greatest blessing seemed to be entire and endless rest, the cessation of existence itself,—since existence brought desire, desire sin, and sin misery. As a religion Buddhism is an absurdity; in fact, it is no religion at all, only a system of moral philosophy. Its weak points, practically, are the abuse of philanthropy, its system of organized idleness and mendicancy, the indifference to thrift and industry, the multiplication of lazy fraternities and useless retreats, reminding us of monastic institutions in the days of Chaucer and Luther. The Buddhist priest is a mendicant and a pauper, clothed in rags, begging his living from door to door, in which he sees no disgrace and no impropriety. Buddhism failed to ennoble the daily occupations of life, and produced drones and idlers and religious vagabonds. In its corruption it lent itself to idolatry, for the Buddhist temples are filled with hideous images of all sorts of repulsive deities, although Buddha himself did not hold to idol worship any more than to the belief in a personal God.

"Buddhism," says the author of its accepted catechism, "teaches goodness without a God, existence without a soul, immortality without life, happiness without a heaven, salvation without a saviour, redemption without a redeemer, and worship without rites." The failure of Buddhism, both as a philosophy and a religion, is a confirmation of the great historical fact, that in the ancient Pagan world no efforts of reason enabled man unaided to arrive at a true — that is, a helpful and practically elevating — knowledge of deity. Even Buddha, one of the most gifted and excellent of all the sages who have enlightened the world, despaired of solving the great mysteries of existence, and turned his attention to those practical duties of life which seemed to promise a way of escaping its miseries. He appealed to human consciousness; but lacking the inspiration and aid which come from a sense of personal divine influence, Buddhism has failed, on the large scale, to raise its votaries to higher planes of ethical accomplishment. And hence the necessity of that new revelation which Jesus declared amid the moral ruins of a crumbling world, by which alone can the debasing superstitions of India and the godless materialism of China be replaced with a vital spirituality, — even as the elaborate mythology of Greece and Rome gave way before the fervent earnestness of Christian apostles and martyrs

It does not belong to my subject to present the condition of Buddhism as it exists to-day in Thibet, in Siam, in China, in Japan, in Burmah, in Ceylon, and in various other Eastern countries. It spread by reason of its sympathy with the poor and miserable, by virtue of its being a great system of philanthropy and morals which appealed to the consciousness of the lower classes. Though a proselyting religion it was never a persecuting one, and is still distinguished, in all its corruption, for its toleration.

AUTHORITIES.

THE chief authorities that I would recommend for this chapter are Max Müller's History of Ancient Sanskrit Literature; Rev. S. Beal's Buddhism in China; Buddhism, by T. W. Rhys-Davids; Monier Williams's Sákoontalá; I. Muir's Sanskrit Texts; Burnouf's Essai sur la Véda; Sir William Jones's Works; Colebrook's Miscellaneous Essays; Joseph Muller's Religious Aspects of Hindu Philosophy; Manual of Buddhism, by R. Spence Hardy; Dr. H. Clay Trumbull's The Blood Covenant; Orthodox Buddhist Catechism, by H. S. Olcott, edited by Prof. Elliott C. Coues. I have derived some instruction from Samuel Johnson's bulky and diffuse books, but more from James Freeman Clarke's Ten Great Religions and Rawlinson's Religions of the Ancient World.

RELIGION OF THE GREEKS AND ROMANS.

CLASSIC MYTHOLOGY.

RELIGION OF THE GREEKS AND ROMANS.

CLASSIC MYTHOLOGY.

RELIGION among the lively and imaginative Greeks took a different form from that of the Aryan race in India or Persia. However the ideas of their divinities originated in their relations to the thought and life of the people, their gods were neither abstractions nor symbols. They were simply men and women, immortal, yet having a beginning, with passions and appetites like ordinary mortals. They love, they hate, they eat, they drink, they have adventures and misfortunes like men, — only differing from men in the superiority of their gifts, in their miraculous endowments, in their stupendous feats, in their more than gigantic size, in their supernal beauty, in their intensified pleasures. It was not their aim "to raise mortals to the skies," but to enjoy themselves in feasting and love-making; not even to govern the world, but to protect their particular worshippers, — taking part and interest in human quarrels, without reference to justice or right, and without communicating any great truths for the guidance of mankind.

The religion of Greece consisted of a series of myths, — creations for the most part of the poets, — and therefore properly called a mythology. Yet in some respects the gods of Greece resembled those of Phœnicia and Egypt, being the powers of Nature, and named after the sun, moon, and planets. Their priests did not form a sacerdotal caste, as in India and Egypt; they were more like officers of the state, to perform certain functions or duties pertaining to rites, ceremonies, and sacrifices. They taught no moral or spiritual truths to the people, nor were they held in extraordinary reverence. They were not ascetics or enthusiasts; among them were no great reformers or prophets, as among the sacerdotal class of the Jews or the Hindus. They had even no sacred books, and claimed no esoteric knowledge. Nor was their office hereditary. They were appointed by the rulers of the state, or elected by the people themselves; they imposed no restraints on the conscience, and apparently cared little for morals, leaving the people to an unbounded freedom to act and think for themselves, so far as they did not interfere with prescribed usages and laws. The real objects of Greek worship were beauty, grace, and heroic strength. The people worshipped no supreme creator, no providential governor, no ultimate judge of human actions. They had no aspirations for heaven and no fear of hell. They did not feel accountable for their deeds or thoughts or words to an irresistible Power working for righteousness or truth. They had no religious sense, apart from wonder or admiration of the glories of Nature, or the good or evil which might result from the favor or hatred of the divinities they accepted.

These divinities, moreover, were not manifestations of supreme power and intelligence, but were creations of the fancy, as they came from popular legends, or the brains of poets, or the hands of artists, or the speculations of philosophers. And as everything in Greece was beautiful and radiant, — the sea, the sky, the mountains, and the valleys, — so was religion cheerful, seen in all the festivals which took the place of the Sabbaths and holy-days of more spiritually minded peoples. The worshippers of the gods danced and played and sported to the sounds of musical instruments, and revelled in joyous libations, in feasts and imposing processions, — in whatever would amuse the mind or intoxicate the senses. The gods were rather unseen companions in pleasures, in sports, in athletic contests and warlike enterprises, than beings to be adored for moral excellence or supernal knowledge. "Heaven was so near at hand that their own heroes climbed to it and became demigods." Every grove, every fountain, every river, every beautiful spot, had its presiding deity; while every wonder of Nature, — the sun, the moon, the stars, the tempest, the thunder, the lightning, — was impersonated as an awful power for good or evil. To them temples were erected, within which were their shrines and images in human shape, glistening with gold and gems, and wrought in every form of grace or strength or beauty, and by artists of marvellous excellence.

This polytheism of Greece was exceedingly complicated, but was not so degrading as that of Egypt, since the gods were not represented by the forms of hideous animals, and the worship of them was not attended by revolting ceremonies; and yet it was divested of all spiritual aspirations, and had but little effect on personal struggles for truth or holiness. It was human and worldly, not lofty nor even reverential, except among the few who had deep religious wants. One of its characteristic features was the acknowledged impotence of the gods to secure future happiness. In fact, the future was generally ignored, and even immortality was but a dream of philosophers. Men lived not in view of future rewards and punishments, or future existence at all, but for the enjoyment of the present; and the gods themselves set the example of an immoral life. Even Zeus, " the Father of gods and men," to whom absolute supremacy was ascribed, the work of creation, and all majesty and serenity, took but little interest in human affairs, and lived on Olympian heights like a sovereign surrounded with the instruments of his will, freely indulging in those pleasures which all lofty moral codes have forbidden, and taking part in the quarrels, jealousies, and enmities of his divine associates.

Greek mythology had its source in the legends of a remote antiquity, — probably among the Pelasgians, the early inhabitants of Greece, which they brought with them in their migration from their original settlement, or perhaps from Egypt and Phœnicia. Herodotus — and he is not often wrong — ascribes a great part of the mythology which the Greek poets elaborated to a Phœnician or Egyptian source. The legends have also some similarity to the poetic creations of the ancient Persians, who delighted in fairies and genii and extravagant exploits, like the labors of Hercules The faults and foibles of deified mortals were transmitted to posterity and incorporated with the attributes of the supreme divinity, and hence the mixture of the mighty and the mean which marks the characters of the Iliad and Odyssey. The Greeks adopted Oriental fables, and accommodated them to those heroes who figured in their own country in the earliest times. "The labors of Hercules originated in

Egypt, and relate to the annual progress of the sun in the zodiac. The rape of Proserpine, the wanderings of Ceres, the Eleusinian mysteries, and the orgies of Bacchus were all imported from Egypt or Phœnicia, while the wars between the gods and the giants were celebrated in the romantic annals of Persia. The oracle of Dodona was copied from that of Ammon in Thebes, and the oracle of Apollo at Delphos has a similar source."

Behind the Oriental legends which form the basis of Grecian mythology there was, in all probability, in those ancient times before the Pelasgians were known as Ionians and the Hellenes as Dorians, a mystical and indefinite idea of supreme power, — as among the Persians, the Hindus, and the esoteric priests of Egypt. In all the ancient religions the farther back we go the purer and loftier do we find the popular religion. Belief in supreme deity underlies all the Eastern theogonies, which belief, however, was soon perverted or lost sight of. There is great difference of opinion among philosophers as to the origin of myths, — whether they began in fable and came to be regarded as history, or began as human history and were poetized into fable. My belief is that in the earliest ages of the world there were no mythologies. Fables were the creations of those who sought to amuse or control the people, who have ever delighted in the marvellous. As the magnificent, the vast, the sublime, which was seen in Nature, impressed itself on the imagination of the Orientals and ended in legends, so did allegory in process of time multiply fictions and fables to an indefinite extent; and what were symbols among Eastern nations became impersonations in the poetry of Greece. Grecian mythology was a vast system of impersonated forces, beginning with the legends of heroes and ending with the personification of the faculties of the mind and the manifestations of Nature, in deities who presided over festivals, cities, groves, and mountains, with all the infirmities of human nature, and without calling out exalted sentiments of love or reverence. They are all creations of the imagination, invested with human traits and adapted to the genius of the people, who were far from being religious in the sense that the Hindus and Egyptians were. It was the natural and not the supernatural that filled their souls. It was art they worshipped, and not the God who created the heavens and the earth, and who exacts of his creatures obedience and faith.

In regard to the gods and goddesses of the Grecian Pantheon, we observe that most of them were immoral; at least they had the usual infirmities of men. They are thus represented by the poets, probably to please the people, who like all other peoples had to make their own conceptions of God; for even a miraculous revelation of deity must be interpreted by those who receive it, according to their own understanding of the qualities revealed. The ancient Romans, themselves stern, earnest, practical, had an almost Oriental reverence for their gods, so that their Jupiter (Father of Heaven) was a majestic, powerful, all-seeing, severely just national deity, regarded by them much as the Jehovah of the Hebrews was by that nation. When in later times the conquest of Eastern countries and of Macedon and Greece brought in luxury, works of art, foreign literature, and all the delightful but enervating influences of æstheticism, the Romans became corrupted, and gradually began to identify their own more noble deities with the beautiful but unprincipled, self-indulgent, and tricky set of gods and goddesses of the Greek mythology.

The Greek Zeus, with whom were associated majesty and dominion, and who reigned supreme in the celestial hierarchy, — who as the chief god of the skies, the god of storms, ruler of the atmosphere, was the favorite deity of the Aryan race, the Indra of the Hindus, the Jupiter of the Romans, — was in his Grecian presentment a rebellious son, a faithless husband, and sometimes an unkind father. His character was a combination of weakness and strength, — anything but a pattern to be imitated, or even to be reverenced. He was the impersonation of power and dignity, represented by the poets as having such immense strength that if he had hold of one end of a chain, and all the gods held the other, with the earth fastened to it, he would be able to move them all.

Poseidon (Roman Neptune), the brother of Zeus, was represented as the god of the ocean, and was worshipped chiefly in maritime States. His morality was no higher than that of Zeus; moreover, he was rough, boisterous, and vindictive. He was hostile to Troy, and yet persecuted Ulysses.

Apollo, the next great personage of the Olympian divinities, was more respectable morally than his father. He was the sun-god of the Greeks, and was the embodiment of divine prescience, of healing skill, of musical and poetical productiveness, and hence the favorite of the poets. He had a form of ideal beauty, grace, and vigor, inspired by unerring wisdom and insight into futurity. He was obedient to the will of Zeus, to whom he was not much inferior in power. Temples were erected to this favorite deity in every part of Greece, and he was supposed to deliver oracular responses in several cities, especially at Delphos.

Hephæstus (Roman Vulcan), the god of fire, was a sort of jester at the Olympian court, and provoked perpetual laughter from his awkwardness and lameness. He forged the thunderbolts for Zeus, and was the armorer of heaven. It accorded with the grim humor of the poets to make this clumsy blacksmith the husband of Aphrodite, the queen of beauty and of love.

Ares (Roman Mars), the god of war, was represented as cruel, lawless, and greedy of blood, and as occupying a subordinate position, receiving orders from Apollo and Athene.

Hermes (Roman Mercury) was the impersonation of commercial dealings, and of course was full of tricks and thievery, — the Olympian man of business, industrious, inventive, untruthful, and dishonest. He was also the god of eloquence.

Besides these six great male divinities there were six goddesses, the most important of whom was Hera (Roman Juno), wife of Zeus, and hence the Queen of Heaven. She exercised her husband's prerogatives, and thundered and shook Olympus; but she was proud, vindictive, jealous, unscrupulous, and cruel, — a poor model for women to imitate. The Greek poets, however, had a poor opinion of the female sex, and hence represent this deity without those elements of character which we most admire in woman, — gentleness, softness, tenderness, and patience. She scolded her august husband so perpetually that he gave way to complaints before the assembled deities, and that too with a bitterness hardly to be reconciled with our notions of dignity.

The Roman Juno, before the identification of the two goddesses, was a nobler character, being the queen of heaven, the protectress of virgins and of matrons, and was also the celestial housewife of the nation, watching over its revenues and its expenses. She was the especial goddess of chastity, and loose women were forbidden to touch her altars.

Athene (Roman Minerva) however, the goddess of wisdom, had a character without a flaw, and ranked with Apollo in wisdom. She even expostulated with Zeus himself when he was wrong. But on the other hand she had few attractive feminine qualities, and no amiable weaknesses.

Artemis (Roman Diana) was "a shadowy divinity, a pale reflection of her brother Apollo." She presided over the pleasures of the chase, in which the Greeks delighted, — a masculine female who took but little interest in anything intellectual.

Aphrodite (Roman Venus) was the impersonation of all that was weak and erring in the nature of woman, — the goddess of sensual desire, of mere physical beauty, silly, childish, and vain, utterly odious in a moral point of view, and mentally contemptible. This goddess was represented as exerting a great influence even when despised, fascinating yet revolting, admired and yet corrupting. She was not of much importance among the Romans, — who were far from being sentimental or passionate, — until the growth of the legend of their Trojan origin. Then, as mother of Æneas, their progenitor, she took a high rank, and the Greek poets furnished her character.

Hestia (Roman Vesta) presided over the private hearths and homesteads of the Greeks, and imparted to them a sacred character. Her personality was vague, but she represented the purity which among both Greeks and Romans is attached to home and domestic life.

Demeter (Roman Ceres) represented Mother Earth, and thus was closely associated with agriculture and all operations of tillage and bread-making. As agriculture is the primitive and most important of all human vocations, this deity presided over civilization and law-giving, and occupied an important position in the Eleusinian mysteries.

These were the twelve Olympian divinities, or greater gods; but they represent only a small part of the Grecian Pantheon. There was Dionysus (Roman Bacchus), the god of drunkenness. This deity presided over vineyards, and his worship was attended with disgraceful orgies, — with wild dances, noisy revels, exciting music, and frenzied demonstrations.

Leto (Roman Latona), another wife of Zeus, and mother of Apollo and Diana, was a very different personage from Hera, being the impersonation of all those womanly qualities which are valued in woman, — silent, unobtrusive, condescending, chaste, kindly, ready to help and tend, and subordinating herself to her children.

Persephone (Roman Proserpina) was the queen of the dead, ruling the infernal realm even more distinctly than her husband Pluto, severely pure as she was awful and terrible; but there were no temples erected to her, as the Greeks did not trouble themselves much about the future state.

The minor deities of the Greeks were innumerable, and were identified with every separate thing which occupied their thoughts, — with mountains, rivers, capes, towns, fountains, rocks; with domestic animals, with monsters of the deep, with demons and departed heroes, with water-nymphs and wood-nymphs, with the qualities of mind and attributes of the body; with sleep and death, old age and pain, strife and victory; with hunger, grief, ridicule, wisdom, deceit, grace; with night and day, the hours, the thunder the rainbow, — in short, all the wonders of Nature, all the affections of the soul, and all the qualities of the mind; everything they saw, everything they talked about, everything they felt. All these wonders and sentiments they impersonated; and these impersonations were supposed to preside over the things they represented, and to a certain extent were worshipped. If a man wished the winds to be propitious, he prayed to Zeus; if he wished to be prospered in his bargains, he invoked Hermes; if he wished to be successful in war, he prayed to Ares.

He never prayed to a supreme and eternal deity, but to some special manifestation of deity, fancied or real; and hence his religion was essentially pantheistic, though outwardly polytheistic. The divinities whom he invoked he celebrated with rites corresponding with those traits which they represented. Thus, Aphrodite was celebrated with lascivious dances, and Dionysus with drunken revels. Each deity represented the Grecian ideal, — of majesty or grace or beauty or strength or virtue or wisdom or madness or folly. The character of Hera was what the poets supposed should be the attributes of the Queen of heaven; that of Leto, what should distinguish a disinterested housewife; that of Hestia, what should mark the guardian of the fireside; that of Demeter, what should show supreme benevolence and thrift; that of Athene, what would naturally be associated with wisdom, and that of Aphrodite, what would be expected from a sensual beauty. In the main, Zeus was serene, majestic, and benignant, as became the king of the gods, although he was occasionally faithless to his wife; Poseidon was boisterous, as became the monarch of the seas; Apollo was a devoted son and a bright companion, which one would expect in a gifted poet and wise prophet, beautiful and graceful as a sun-god should be ; Hephæstus, the god of fire and smiths, showed naturally the awkwardness to which manual labor leads ; Ares was cruel and bloodthirsty, as the god of war should be; Hermes, as the god of trade and business, would of course be sharp and tricky; and Dionysus, the father of the vine, would naturally become noisy and rollicking in his intoxication.

Thus, whatever defects are associated with the principal deities, these are all natural and consistent with the characters they represent, or the duties and business in which they engage. Drunkenness is not associated with Zeus, or unchastity with Hera or Athene. The poets make each deity consistent with himself, and in harmony with the interests he represents. Hence the mythology of the poets is elaborate and interesting. Who has not devoured the classical dictionary before he has learned to scan the lines of Homer or of Virgil ? As varied and romantic as the "Arabian Nights," it shines in the beauty of nature. In the Grecian creations of gods and goddesses there is no insult to the understanding, because these creations are in harmony with Nature, are consistent with humanity. There is no hatred and no love, no jealousy and no fear, which has not a natural cause. The poets proved themselves to be great artists in the very characters they gave to their divinities. They did not aim to excite reverence or stimulate to duty or point out the higher life, but to amuse a worldly, pleasure-seeking, good-natured, joyous, art-loving, poetic people, who lived in the present and for themselves alone.

As a future state of rewards and punishments seldom entered into the minds of the Greeks, so the gods are never represented as conferring future salvation. The welfare of the soul was rarely thought of where there was no settled belief in immortality. The gods themselves were fed on nectar and ambrosia, that they might not die like ordinary mortals. They might prolong their own existence indefinitely, but they were impotent to confer eternal life upon their worshippers; and as eternal life is essential to perfect happiness, they could not confer even happiness in its highest sense.

On this fact Saint Augustine erected the grand fabric of his theological system. In his most celebrated work, "The City of God," he holds up to derision the gods of antiquity, and with blended logic and irony makes them contemptible as objects of worship, since they were impotent to save the soul. In his view the grand and distinguishing feature of Christianity, in contrast with Paganism, is the gift of eternal life and happiness. It is not the morality which Christ and his Apostles taught, which gave to

Christianity its immeasurable superiority over all other religions, but the promise of a future felicity in heaven. And it was this promise which gave such comfort to the miserable people of the old Pagan world, ground down by oppression, injustice, cruelty, and poverty. It was this promise which filled the converts to Christianity with joy, enthusiasm, and hope, — yea, more than this, even boundless love that salvation was the gift of God through the self-sacrifice of Christ. Immortality was brought to light by the gospel alone, and to miserable people the idea of eternal bliss after the trials of mortal life were passed was the source of immeasurable joy. No sooner was this sublime expectation of happiness planted firmly in the minds of pagans, than they threw their idols to the moles and the bats.

But even in regard to morality, Augustine showed that the gods were no examples to follow. He ridicules their morals and their offices as severely as he points out their impotency to bestow happiness. He shows the absurdity and inconsistency of tolerating players in their delineation of the vices and follies of deities for the amusement of the people in the theatre, while the priests performed the same obscenities as religious rites in the temples which were upheld by the State; so that philosophers like Varro could pour contempt on players with impunity, while he dared not ridicule priests for doing in the temples the same things. No wonder that the popular religion at last was held in contempt by philosophers, since it was not only impotent to save, but did not stimulate to ordinary morality, to virtue, or to lofty sentiments. A religion which was held sacred in one place and ridiculed in another, before the eyes of the same people, could not in the end but yield to what was better.

If we ascribe to the poets the creation of the elaborate mythology of the Greeks, — that is, a system of gods made by men, rather than men made by gods, — whether as symbols or objects of worship, whether the religion was pantheistic or idolatrous, we find that artists even surpassed the poets in their conceptions of divine power, goodness, and beauty, and thus riveted the chains which the poets forged.

The temple of Zeus at Olympia in Elis, where the intellect and the culture of Greece assembled every four years to witness the games instituted in honor of the Father of the gods, was itself calculated to impose on the senses of the worshippers by its grandeur and beauty. The image of the god himself, sixty feet high, made of ivory, gold, and gems by the greatest of all the sculptors of antiquity, must have impressed spectators with ideas of strength and majesty even more than any poetical descriptions could do. If it was art which the Greeks worshipped rather than an unseen deity who controlled their destinies, and to whom supreme homage was due, how nobly did the image before them represent the highest conceptions of the attributes to be ascribed to the King of Heaven! Seated on his throne, with the emblems of sovereignty in his hands and attendant deities around him, his head, neck, breast, and arms in massive proportions, and his face expressive of majesty and sweetness, power in repose, benevolence blended with strength, — the image of the Olympian deity conveyed to the minds of his worshippers everything that could inspire awe, wonder, and goodness, as well as power. No fear was blended with admiration, since his favor could be won by the magnificent rites and ceremonies which were instituted in his honor.

Clarke alludes to the sculptured Apollo Belvedere as giving a still more elevated idea of the sun-god than the poets themselves, — a figure expressive of the highest thoughts of the Hellenic mind, — and quotes Milman in support of his admiration: —

> " All, all divine! no struggling muscle glows,
> Through heaving vein no mantling life-blood flows;
> But, animate with deity alone,
> In deathless glory lives the breathing stone."

If a Christian poet can see divinity in the chiselled stone, why should we wonder at the worship of art by the pagan Greeks? The same could be said of the statues of Artemis, of Pallas-Athene, of Aphrodite, and other "divine" productions of Grecian artists, since they represented the highest ideal the world has seen of beauty, grace, loveliness, and majesty, which the Greeks adored. Hence, though the statues of the gods are in human shape, it was not men that the Greeks worshipped, but those qualities of mind and those forms of beauty to which the cultivated intellect instinctively gave the highest praise. No one can object to this boundless admiration which the Greeks had for art in its highest forms, in so far as that admiration became worship. It was the divorce of art from morals which called out the indignation and censure of the Christian fathers, and even undermined the religion of philosophers so far as it had been directed to the worship of the popular deities, which were simply creations of poets and artists.

It is difficult to conceive how the worship of the gods could have been kept up for so long a time, had it not been for the festivals. This wise provision for providing interest and recreation for the people was also availed of by the Mosaic ritual among the Hebrews, and has been a part of most well-organized religious systems. The festivals were celebrated in honor not merely of deities, but of useful inventions, of the seasons of the year, of great national victories, — all which were religious in the pagan sense, and constituted the highest pleasures of Grecian life. They were observed with great pomp and splendor in the open air in front of temples, in sacred groves, wherever the people could conveniently assemble to join in jocund dances, in athletic sports, and whatever could animate the soul with festivity and joy. Hence the religious worship of the Greeks was cheerful, and adapted itself to the tastes and pleasures of the people; it was, however, essentially worldly, and sometimes degrading. It was similar in its effects to the rural sports of the yeomanry of the Middle Ages, and to the theatrical representations sometimes held in mediæval churches, — certainly to the processions and pomps which the Catholic clergy instituted for the amusement of the people. Hence the sneering but acute remark of Gibbon, that all religions were equally true to the people, equally false to philosophers, and equally useful to rulers. The State encouraged and paid for sacrifices, rites, processions, and scenic dances on the same principle that they gave corn to the people to make them contented in their miseries, and severely punished those who ridiculed the popular religion when it was performed in temples, even though it winked at the ridicule of the same performances in the theatres.

Among the Greeks there were no sacred books like the Hindu Vedas or Hebrew Scriptures, in which the people could learn duties and religious truths. The priests taught nothing; they merely officiated at rites and ceremonies. It is difficult to find out what were the means and forms of religious instruction, so far as pertained to the heart and conscience. Duties were certainly not learned from the ministers of religion. From what source did the people learn the necessity of obedience to parents, of conjugal fidelity, of truthfulness, of chastity, of honesty? It is difficult to tell. The poets and artists taught ideas of beauty, of grace, of strength; and Nature in her grandeur and loveliness taught the same things. Hence a severe taste was cultivated, which excluded vulgarity and grossness in the intercourse of life. It was the rule to be courteous, affable, gentlemanly, for all this was in harmony with the severity of art. The comic poets ridiculed pretension, arrogance, quackery, and lies. Patriotism, which was learned from the dangers of the State, amid warlike and unscrupulous neighbors, called out many manly virtues, like courage, fortitude, heroism, and self-sacrifice. A hard and rocky soil necessitated industry, thrift, and severe punishment on those who stole the fruits of labor, even as miners in the Rocky Mountains sacredly abstain from appropriating the gold of their fellow-laborers. Self-interest and self-preservation dictated many laws which secured the welfare of society. The natural sacredness of home guarded the virtue of wives and children; the natural sense of justice raised indignation against cheating and tricks in trade. Men and women cannot live together in peace and safety without observing certain conditions, which may be ranked with virtues even among savages and barbarians, — much more so in cultivated and refined communities.

The graces and amenities of life can exist without reference to future rewards and punishments. The ultimate law of self-preservation will protect men in ordinary times against murder and violence, and will lead to public and social enactments which bad men fear to violate. A traveller ordinarily feels as safe in a highly-civilized pagan community as in a Christian city. The "heathen Chinee" fears the officers of the law as much as does a citizen of London.

The great difference between a Pagan and a Christian people is in the power of conscience, in the sense of a moral accountability to a spiritual Deity, in the hopes or fears of a future state, — motives which have a powerful influence on the elevation of individual character and the development of higher types of social organization. But whatever laws are necessary for the maintenance of order, the repression of violence, of crimes against person and the State and the general material welfare of society, are found in Pagan as well as in Christian States; and the natural affections, — of paternal and filial love, friendship, patriotism, generosity, etc., — while strengthened by Christianity, are also an inalienable part of the God-given heritage of all mankind. We see many heroic traits, many manly virtues, many domestic amenities, and many exalted sentiments in pagan Greece, even if these were not taught by priests or sages. Every man instinctively clings to life, to property, to home, to parents, to wife and children; and hence these are guarded in every community, and the violation of these rights is ever punished with greater or less severity for the sake of general security and public welfare, even if there be no belief in God. Religion, loftily considered, has but little to do with the temporal interests of men. Governments and laws take these under their protection, and it is men who make governments and laws. They are made from the instinct of self-preservation, from patriotic aspirations, from the necessities of civilization. Religion, from the Christian standpoint, is unworldly, having reference to the life which is to come, to the enlightenment of the conscience, to restraint from sins not punishable by the laws, and to the inspiration of virtues which have no worldly reward.

This kind of religion was not taught by Grecian priests or poets or artists, and did not exist in Greece, with all its refinements and glories, until partially communicated by those philosophers who meditated on the secrets of Nature, the mighty mysteries of life.

and the duties which reason and reflection reveal. And it may be noticed that the philosophers themselves, who began with speculations on the origin of the universe, the nature of the gods, the operations of the mind, and the laws of matter, ended at last with ethical inquiries and injunctions. We see this illustrated in Socrates and Zeno. They seemed to despair of finding out God, of explaining the wonders of his universe, and came down to practical life in its sad realities, — like Solomon himself when he said, "Fear God and keep his commandments, for this is the whole duty of man." In ethical teachings and inquiries some of these philosophers reached a height almost equal to that which Christian sages aspired to climb; and had the world practised the virtues which they taught, there would scarcely have been need of a new revelation, so far as the observance of rules to promote happiness on earth is concerned. But these Pagan sages did not hold out hopes beyond the grave They even doubted whether the soul was mortal or immortal. They did teach many ennobling and lofty truths for the enlightenment of thinkers; but they held out no divine help, nor any hope of completing in a future life the failures of this one; and hence they failed in saving society from a persistent degradation, and in elevating ordinary men to those glorious heights reached by the Christian converts.

That was the point to which Augustine directed his vast genius and his unrivalled logic. He admitted that arts might civilize, and that the elaborate mythology which he ridiculed was interesting to the people, and was, as a creation of the poets, ingenious and beautiful; but he showed that it did not reveal a future state, that it did not promise eternal happiness, that it did not restrain men from those sins which human laws could not punish, and that it did not exalt the soul to lofty communion with the Deity, or kindle a truly spiritual life, and therefore was worthless as a religion, imbecile to save, and only to be classed with those myths which delight an ignorant or sensuous people, and with those rites which are shrouded in mystery and gloom. Nor did he, in his matchless argument against the gods of Greece and Rome, take for his attack those deities whose rites were most degrading and senseless, and which the thinking world despised, but the most lofty forms of pagan religion, such as were accepted by moralists and philosophers like Seneca and Plato. And thus he reached the intelligence of the age, and gave a final blow to all the gods of antiquity.

It would be instructive to show that the religion of Greece, as embraced by the people, did not prevent or even condemn those social evils that are the greatest blot on enlightened civilization. It did not discourage slavery, the direst evil which ever afflicted humanity; it did not elevate woman to her true position at home or in public; it ridiculed those passive virtues that are declared and commended in the Sermon on the Mount; it did not pronounce against the wickedness of war, or the vanity of military glory; it did not dignify home, or the virtues of the family circle; it did not declare the folly of riches, or show that the love of money is a root of all evil. It made sensual pleasure and outward prosperity the great aims of successful ambition, and hid with an impenetrable screen from the eyes of men the fatal results of a worldly life, so that suicide itself came to be viewed as a justifiable way to avoid evils that are hard to be borne; in short, it was a religion which, though joyous, was without hope, and with innumerable deities was without God in the world,—which was no religion at all, but a fable, a delusion, and a superstition, as Paul argued before the assembled intellect of the most fastidious and cultivated city of the world

And yet we see among those who worshipped the gods of Greece a sense of dependence on supernatural power; and this dependence stands out, both in the Iliad and the Odyssey, among the boldest heroes. They seem to be reverential to the powers above them, however indefinite their views. In the best ages of Greece the worship of the various deities was sincere and universal, and was attended with sacrifices to propitiate favor or avert their displeasure.

It does not appear that these sacrifices were always offered by priests. Warriors, kings, and heroes themselves sacrificed oxen, sheep, and goats, and poured out libations to the gods. Homer's heroes were very strenuous in the exercise of these duties; and they generally traced their calamities and misfortunes to the neglect of sacrifices, which was a great offence to the deities, from Zeus down to inferior gods. We read, too, that the gods were supplicated in fervent prayer. There was universally felt, in earlier times, a need of divine protection. If the gods did not confer eternal life, they conferred, it was supposed, temporal and worldly good. People prayed for the same blessings that the ancient Jews sought from Jehovah. In this sense the early Greeks were religious. Irreverence toward the gods was extremely rare. The people, however, did not pray for divine guidance in the discharge of duty, but for the blessings which would give them health and prosperity. We seldom see a proud self-reliance even among the heroes of the Iliad, but great solicitude to secure aid from the deities they worshipped.

The religion of the Romans differed in some respects from that of the Greeks, inasmuch as it was emphatically a state religion. It was more of a ritual and a ceremony. It included most of the deities of the Greek Pantheon, but was more comprehensive. It accepted the gods of all the nations that composed the empire, and placed them in the Pantheon, — even Mithra, the Persian sun-god, and the Isis and Osiris of the Egyptians, to whom sacrifices were made by those who worshipped them at home. It was also a purer mythology, and rejected many of the blasphemous myths concerning the loves and quarrels of the Grecian deities. It was more practical and less poetical. Every Roman god had something to do, some useful office to perform. Several divinities presided over the birth and nursing of an infant, and they were worshipped for some fancied good, for the benefits which they were supposed to bestow. There was an elaborate "division of labor" among them. A divinity presided over bakers, another over ovens, — every vocation and every household transaction had its presiding deities.

There were more superstitious rites practised by the Romans than by the Greeks, — such as examining the entrails of beasts and birds for good or bad omens. Great attention was given to dreams and rites of divination. The Roman household gods were of great account, since there was a more defined and general worship of ancestors than among the Greeks. These were the *Penates*, or familiar household gods, the guardians of the home, whose fire on the sacred hearth was perpetually burning, and to whom every meal was esteemed a sacrifice. These included a *Lar*, or ancestral family divinity, in each house. There were Vestal virgins to guard the most sacred places. There was a college of pontiffs to regulate worship and perform the higher ceremonies, which were complicated and minute. The pontiffs were presided over by one called Pontifex Maximus, — a title shrewdly assumed by Cæsar to gain control of the popular worship, and still surviving in the title of the Pope of Rome with his college of cardinals. There were augurs and haruspices to discover the will of the gods, according to entrails and the flight of birds.

The festivals were more numerous in Rome than in Greece, and perhaps were more piously observed. About one day in four was set apart for the worship of particular gods, celebrated by feasts and games and sacrifices. The principal feast days were in honor of Janus, the great god of the Sabines, the god of beginnings, celebrated on the first of January, to which month he gave his name; also the feasts in honor of the Penates, of Mars, of Vesta, of Minerva, of Venus, of Ceres, of Juno, of Jupiter, and of Saturn. The Saturnalia, December 19, in honor of Saturn, the annual Thanksgiving, lasted seven days, when the rich kept open house and slaves had their liberty. —

the most joyous of the festivals. The feast of Minerva lasted five days, when offerings were made by all mechanics, artists, and scholars. The feast of Cybele, analogous to that of Ceres in Greece and Isis in Egypt, lasted six days. These various feasts imposed great contributions on the people, and were managed by the pontiffs with the most minute observances and legalities.

The principal Roman divinities were the Olympic gods under Latin names, like Jupiter, Juno, Mars, Minerva Neptune, Vesta, Apollo, Venus, Ceres, and Diana; but the secondary deities were almost innumerable. Some of the deities were of Etruscan, some of Sabine, and some of Latin origin; but most of them were imported from Greece or corresponded with those of the Greek mythology. Many were manufactured by the pontiffs for utilitarian purposes, and were mere abstractions, like Hope, Fear, Concord, Justice, Clemency, etc., to which temples were erected. The powers of Nature were also worshipped, like the sun, the moon, and stars. The best side of Roman life was represented in the worship of Vesta, who presided over the household fire and home, and was associated with the Lares and Penates. Of these household gods the head of the family was the officiating minister who offered prayers and sacrifices. The Vestal virgins received especial honor, and were appointed by the Pontifex Maximus.

Thus the Romans accounted themselves very religious, and doubtless are to be so accounted, certainly in the same sense as were the Athenians by the Apostle Paul, since altars, statues, and temples in honor of gods were everywhere present to the eye, and rites and ceremonies were most systematically and mechanically observed according to strict rules laid down by the pontiffs. They were grave and decorous in their devotions, and seemed anxious to learn from their augurs and haruspices the will of the gods; and their funeral ceremonies were held with great pomp and ceremony. As faith in the gods declined, ceremonies and pomps were multiplied, and the ice of ritualism accumulated on the banks of piety. Superstition and unbelief went hand in hand. Worship in the temples was most imposing when the amours and follies of the gods were most ridiculed in the theatres; and as the State was rigorous in its religious observances, hypocrisy became the vice of the most prominent and influential citizens. What sincerity was there in Julius Cæsar when he discharged the duties of high-priest of the Republic? It was impossible for an educated Roman who read Plato and Zeno to believe in Janus and Juno. It was all very well for the people so to believe, he said. who must be kept in order; but scepticism increased in the higher classes until the prevailing atheism culminated in the poetry of Lucretius, who had the boldness to declare that faith in the gods had been the curse of the human race.

If the Romans were more devoted to mere external and ritualistic services than the Greeks, — more outwardly religious, — they were also more hypocritical. If they were not professed freethinkers, — for the State did not tolerate opposition or ridicule of those things which it instituted or patronized, — religion had but little practical effect on their lives. The Romans were more immoral yet more observant of religious ceremonies than the Greeks, who acted and thought as they pleased. Intellectual independence was not one of the characteristics of the Roman citizen. He professed to think as the State prescribed, for the masters of the world were the slaves of the State in religion as in war. The Romans were more gross in their vices as they were more pharisaical in their profession than the Greeks, whom they conquered and imitated. Neither the sincere worship of ancestors, nor the ceremonies and rites which they observed in honor of their innumerable divinities, softened the severity of their character, or weakened their passion for war and bloody sports. Their hard and rigid wills were rarely moved by the cries of agony or the shrieks of despair. Their slavery was more cruel than among any nation of antiquity. Butchery and legalized murder were the delight of Romans in their conquering days, as were inhuman sports in the days of their political decline. Where was the spirit of religion, as it was even in India and Egypt, when women were debased; when every man and woman held a human being in cruel bondage; when home was abandoned for the circus and the amphitheatre; when the cry of the mourner was unheard in shouts of victory; when women sold themselves as wives to those who would pay the highest price, and men abstained from marriage unless they could fatten on rich dowries; when utility was the spring of every action, and demoralizing pleasure was the universal pursuit; when feastings and banquets were riotous and expensive, and violence and rapine were restrained only by the strong arm of law dictated by instincts of self-preservation? Where was the ennobling influence of the gods, when nobody of any position finally believed in them? How powerless the gods, when the general depravity was so glaring as to call out the terrible invective of Paul, the cosmopolitan traveller, the shrewd observer, the pure-hearted Christian missionary, indicting not a few, but a whole people: "Who exchanged the truth of God for a lie, and worshipped and served the creature rather than the Creator, . . . being filled with all unrighteousness, fornication, wickedness, covetousness, maliciousness; full of envy, murder, strife, deceit.

malignity; whisperers, backbiters, haters of God, insolent, haughty, boastful, inventors of evil things, disobedient to parents, without understanding, covenant breakers, without natural affections, unmerciful." An awful picture, but sustained by the evidence of the Roman writers of that day as certainly no worse than the hideous reality.

If this was the outcome of the most exquisitely poetical and art-inspiring mythology the world has ever known, what wonder that the pure spirituality of Jesus the Christ, shining into that blackness of darkness, should have been hailed by perishing millions as the "light of the world"!

AUTHORITIES.

Rawlinson's Religions of the Ancient World; Grote's History of Greece; Thirlwall's History of Greece; Homer's Iliad and Odyssey; Max Müller's Chips from a German Workshop; Curtius's History of Greece; Mr. Gladstone's Homer and the Homeric Age; Rawlinson's Herodotus; Döllinger's Jew and Gentile; Fenton's Lectures on Ancient and Modern Greece; Smith's Dictionary of Greek and Roman Mythology; Clarke's Ten Great Religions; Dwight's Mythology; Saint Augustine's City of God.

CONFUCIUS:

SAGE AND MORALIST.

550–478 B. C.

CONFUCIUS:

SAGE AND MORALIST.

550–478 B.C.

CONFUCIUS.

SAGE AND MORALIST.

ABOUT one hundred years after the great religious movement in India under Buddha, a man was born in China who inaugurated a somewhat similar movement there, and who impressed his character and principles on three hundred millions of people. It cannot be said that he was the founder of a new religion, since he aimed only to revive what was ancient. To quote his own words, he was "a transmitter, and not a maker." But he was, nevertheless, a very extraordinary character; and if greatness is to be measured by results, I know of no heathen teacher whose work has been so permanent. In genius, in creative power, he was inferior to many; but in influence he has had no equal among the sages of the world.

"Confucius" is a Latin name given him by Jesuit missionaries in China; his real name was K'ung-foo-tseu. He was born about 550 B. C., in the province of Loo, and was the contemporary of Belshazzar, of Cyrus, of Crœsus, and of Pisistratus. It is claimed that Confucius was a descendant of one of the early emperors of China, of the Chow dynasty, 1121 B. C.; but he was simply of an upper-class family of the State of Loo, one of the provinces of the empire, — his father and grandfather having been prime ministers to the reigning princes or dukes of Loo, which State resembled a feudal province of France in the Middle Ages, acknowledging only a nominal fealty to the Emperor.

We know but little of the early condition of China. The earliest record of events which can be called history takes us back to about 2350 B. C., when Yaou was emperor, — an intelligent and benignant prince, uniting under his sway the different States of China, which had even then reached a considerable civilization, for the legendary or mythical history of the country dates back about five thousand years. Yaou's son Shun was an equally remarkable man, wise and accomplished, who lived only to advance the happiness of his subjects. At that period the religion of China was probably monotheistic. The supreme being was called Shang-te, to whom sacrifices were made, a deity who exercised a superintending care of the universe; but corruptions rapidly crept in, and a worship of the powers of Nature and of the spirits of departed ancestors, who were supposed to guard the welfare of their descendants, became the prevailing religion. During the reigns of these good emperors the standard of morality was high throughout the empire.

But morals declined, — the old story in all the States of the ancient world. In addition to the decline in morals, there were political discords and endless wars between the petty princes of the empire.

To remedy the political and moral evils of his time was the great desire and endeavor of Confucius. The most marked feature in the religion of the Chinese, before his time, was the worship of ancestors, and this worship he did not seek to change. "Confucius taught three thousand disciples, of whom the more eminent became influential authors. Like Plato and Xenophon, they recorded the sayings of their master, and his maxims and arguments preserved in their works were afterward added to the national collection of the sacred books called the 'Nim Classes.'"

Confucius was a mere boy when his father died, and we know next to nothing of his early years. At fifteen years of age, however, we are told that he devoted himself to learning, pursuing his studies under considerable difficulties, his family being poor. He married when he was nineteen years of age; and in the following year was born his son Le, his only child, of whose descendants eleven thousand males were living one hundred and fifty years ago, constituting the only hereditary nobility of China, — a class who for seventy generations were the recipients of the highest honors and privileges. On the birth of Le, the duke Ch'aou of Loo sent Confucius a present of a carp, which seems to indicate that he was already distinguished for his attainments.

At twenty years of age Confucius entered upon political duties, being the superintendent of cattle, from which, for his fidelity and ability, he was promoted to the higher office of distributer of grain, having attracted the attention of his sovereign. At twenty-two he began his labors as a public teacher, and his house became the resort of enthusiastic youth who wished to learn the doctrines of antiquity. These were all that the sage undertook to teach, — not new and original doctrines of morality or political economy, but only such as were established from a remote antiquity, going back two thousand years before he was born. There is no improbability in this alleged antiquity of the Chinese Empire, for Egypt at this time was a flourishing State.

At twenty-nine years of age Confucius gave his attention to music, which he studied under a famous master; and to this art he devoted no small part of his life, writing books and treatises upon it. Six years afterward, at thirty-five, he had a great desire to travel; and the reigning duke, in whose service he was as a high officer of state, put at his disposal a carriage and two horses, to visit the court of the Emperor, whose sovereignty, however, was only nominal. It does not appear that Confucius was received with much distinction, nor did he have much intercourse with the court or the ministers. He was a mere seeker of knowledge, an inquirer about the ceremonies and maxims of the founder of the dynasty of Chow, an observer of customs, like Herodotus. He wandered for eight years among the various provinces of China, teaching as he went, but without making a great impression. Moreover, he was regarded with jealousy by the different ministers of princes; one of them, however, struck with his wisdom and knowledge, wished to retain him in his service.

On the return of Confucius to Loo, he remained fifteen years without official employment, his native province being in a state of anarchy. But he was better employed than in serving princes, prosecuting his researches into poetry, history, ceremonies, and music,— a born scholar, with insatiable desire of knowledge. His great gifts and learning, however, did not allow him to remain without public employment. He was made governor of an important city. As chief magistrate of this city, he made a marvellous change in the manners of the people. The duke, surprised at what he saw, asked if his rules could be employed to govern a whole State; and Confucius told him that they could be applied to the government of the Empire. On this the duke appointed him assistant superintendent of Public Works, — a great office, held only by members of the ducal family. So many improvements did Confucius make in agriculture that he was made minister of Justice; and so wonderful was his management, that soon there was no necessity to put the penal laws in execution, since no offenders could be found. Confucius held his high office as minister of Justice for two years longer, and some suppose he was made prime minister. His authority certainly continued to increase. He exalted the sovereign, depressed the ministers, and weakened private families, — just as Richelieu did in France, strengthening the throne at the expense of the nobility. It would thus seem that his political reforms were in the direction of absolute monarchy, a needed force in times of anarchy and demoralization. So great was his fame as a statesman that strangers came from other States to see him.

These reforms in the state of Loo gave annoyance to the neighboring princes; and to undermine the influence of Confucius with the duke, these princes sent the duke a present of eighty beautiful girls, possessing musical and dancing accomplishments, and also one hundred and twenty splendid horses. As the duke soon came to think more of his girls and horses than of his reforms, Confucius became disgusted, resigned his office, and retired to private life. Then followed thirteen years of homeless wandering. He was now fifty-six years of age, depressed and melancholy in view of his failure with princes. He was accompanied in his travels by some of his favorite disciples, to whom he communicated his wisdom.

But his fame preceded him wherever he journeyed, and such was the respect for his character and teachings that he was loaded with presents by the people, and was left unmolested to do as he pleased. The dissoluteness of courts filled him with indignation and disgust; and he was heard to exclaim on one occasion, "I have not seen one who loves virtue as he loves beauty,"— meaning the beauty of women. The love of the beautiful, in an artistic sense, is a Greek and not an Oriental idea.

In the meantime Confucius continued his wanderings from city to city and State to State, with a chosen band of disciples all of whom became famous. He travelled for the pursuit of knowledge, and to impress the people with his doctrines. A certain one of his followers was questioned by a prince as to the merits and peculiarities of his master, but was afraid to give a true answer. The sage hearing of it, said, "You should have told him, He is simply a man who in his eager pursuit of knowledge forgets his food, who in the joy of his attainments forgets his sorrows, and who does not perceive that old age is coming on." How seldom is it that any man reaches such a height! In a single sentence the philosopher describes himself truly and impressively.

At last, in the year 491 B.C., a new sovereign reigned in Loo, and with costly presents invited Confucius to return to his native State. The philosopher was now sixty-nine years of age, and notwithstanding the respect in which he was held, the world cannot be said to have dealt kindly with him. It is the fate of prophets and sages to be rejected. The world will not bear rebukes. Even a friend, if discreet, will rarely venture to tell another friend his faults. Confucius told the truth when pressed, but he does not seem to have courted martyrdom; and his manners and speech were too bland, too proper, too unobtrusive to give much offence. Luther was aided in his reforms by his very roughness and boldness, but he was surrounded by a different class of people from those whom Confucius sought to influence. Conventional, polite, considerate, and a great respecter of persons in authority was the Chinese sage. A rude, abrupt, and fierce reformer would have had no weight with the most courteous and polite people of whom history speaks ; whose manners twenty-five hundred years ago were substantially the same as they are at the present day, — a people governed by the laws of propriety alone.

The few remaining years of Confucius' life were spent in revising his writings; but his latter days were made melancholy by dwelling on the evils of the world that he could not remove. Disappointment also had made him cynical and bitter, like Solomon of old, although from different causes. He survived his son and his most beloved disciples. As he approached the dark valley he uttered no prayer, and betrayed no apprehension. Death to him was a rest. He died at the age of seventy-three.

In the tenth book of his Analects we get a glimpse of the habits of the philosopher. He was a man of rule and ceremony. He was particular about his dress and appearance. He was no ascetic, but moderate and temperate. He lived chiefly on rice, like the rest of his countrymen, but required to have his rice cooked nicely, and his meat cut properly. He drank wine freely, but was never known to have obscured his faculties by this indulgence. I do not read that tea was then in use. He was charitable and hospitable, but not ostentatious. He generally travelled in a carriage with two horses, driven by one of his disciples; but a carriage in those days was like one of our carts. In his village, it is said, he looked simple and sincere, as if he were one not able to speak; when waiting at court, or speaking with officers of an inferior grade, he spoke freely, but in a straightforward manner; with officers of a higher grade he spoke blandly, but precisely; with the prince he was grave, but self-possessed. When eating he did not converse; when in bed he did not speak. If his mat were not straight he did not sit on it. When a friend sent him a present he did not bow; the only present for which he bowed was that of the flesh of sacrifice. He was capable of excessive grief, with all his placidity. When his favorite pupil died, he exclaimed, "Heaven is destroying me!" His disciples on this said, "Sir, your grief is excessive." "It is excessive," he replied. "If I am not to mourn bitterly for this man, for whom should I mourn?"

The reigning prince of Loo caused a temple to be erected over the remains of Confucius, and the number of his disciples continually increased. The emperors of the falling dynasty of Chow had neither the intelligence nor the will to do honor to the departed philosopher, but the emperors of the succeeding dynasties did all they could to perpetuate his memory. During his life Confucius found ready acceptance for his doctrines, and was everywhere revered among the people, though not uniformly appreciated by the rulers, nor able permanently to establish the reforms he inaugurated. After his death, however, no honor was too great to be rendered him. The most splendid temple in China was built over his grave, and he received a homage little removed from worship. His writings became a sacred rule of faith and practice; schools were based upon them, and scholars devoted themselves to their interpretation. For two thousand years Confucius has reigned supreme, — the undisputed teacher of a population of three or four hundred millions.

Confucius must be regarded as a man of great humility, conscious of infirmities and faults, but striving after virtue and perfection. He said of himself, "I have striven to become a man of perfect virtue, and to teach others without weariness; but the character of the superior man, carrying out in his conduct what he professes is what I have not attained to. I am not one born in the possession of knowledge, but I am one who is fond of antiquity, and earnest in seeking it there. I am a transmitter, and not a maker." If he did not lay claim to divine illumination, he felt that he was born into the world for a special purpose; not to declare new truths, not to initiate any new ceremony, but to confirm what he felt was in danger of being lost, — the most conservative of all known reformers.

Confucius left behind voluminous writings, of which his Analects, his book of Poetry, his book of History, and his Rules of Propriety are the most important. It is these which are now taught, and have been taught for two thousand years, in the schools and colleges of China. The Chinese think that no man so great and perfect as he has ever lived. His writings are held in the same veneration that Christians attach to their own sacred literature. There is this one fundamental difference between the authors of the Bible and the Chinese sage, — that he did not like to talk of spiritual things; indeed, of them he was ignorant, professing no interest in relation to the working out of abstruse questions, either of philosophy or theology. He had no taste or capacity for such inquiries. Hence, he did not aspire to throw any new light on the great problems of human condition and destiny; nor did he speculate, like the Ionian philosophers, on the creation or end of things. He was not troubled about the origin or destiny of man. He meddled neither with physics nor metaphysics, but he earnestly and consistently strove to bring to light and to enforce those principles which had made remote generations wise and virtuous. He confined his attention to outward phenomena, — to the world of sense and matter; to forms, precedents, ceremonies, proprieties, rules of conduct, filial duties.

and duties to the State; enjoining temperance, honesty, and sincerity as the cardinal and fundamental laws of private and national prosperity. He was no prophet of wrath, though living in a corrupt age. He utters no anathemas on princes, and no woes on peoples. Nor does he glow with exalted hopes of a millennium of bliss, or of the beatitudes of a future state. He was not stern and indignant like Elijah, but more like the courtier and counsellor Elisha. He was a man of the world, and all his teachings have reference to respectability in the world's regard. He doubted more than he believed.

And yet in many of his sayings Confucius rises to an exalted height, considering his age and circumstances. Some of them remind us of some of the best Proverbs of Solomon. In general, we should say that to his mind filial piety and fraternal submission were the foundation of all virtuous practices, and absolute obedience to rulers the primal principle of government. He was eminently a peace man, discouraging wars and violence. He was liberal and tolerant in his views. He said that the " superior man is catholic and no partisan." Duke Gae asked, " What should be done to secure the submission of the people?" The sage replied, "Advance the upright, and set aside the crooked; then the people will submit. But advance the crooked, and set aside the upright, and the people will not submit." Again he said, "It is virtuous manners which constitute the excellence of a neighborhood; therefore fix your residence where virtuous manners prevail." The following sayings remind me of Epictetus: "A scholar whose mind is set on truth, and who is ashamed of bad clothes and bad food, is not fit to be discoursed with. A man should say, 'I am not concerned that I have no place,— I am concerned how I may fit myself for one. I am not concerned that I am not known; I seek to be worthy to be known.'" Here Confucius looks to the essence of things, not to popular desires. In the following, on the other hand, he shows his prudence and policy: "In serving a prince, frequent remonstrances lead to disgrace; between friends, frequent reproofs make the friendship distant." Thus he talks like Solomon. "Tsae-yu, one of his disciples, being asleep in the day-time, the master said, 'Rotten wood cannot be carved. This Yu — what is the use of my reproving him?'" Of a virtuous prince, he said: "In his conduct of himself, he was humble; in serving his superiors, he was respectful; in nourishing the people, he was kind; in ordering the people, he was just."

It was discussed among his followers what it is to be distinguished. One said: "It is to be heard of through the family and State." The master replied: "That is notoriety, not distinction." Again he said: "Though a man may be able to recite three hundred odes, yet if when intrusted with office he does not know how to act, of what practical use is his poetical knowledge?" Again, "If a minister cannot rectify himself, what has he to do with rectifying others?" There is great force in this saying: "The superior man is easy to serve and difficult to please, since you cannot please him in any way which is not accordant with right; but the mean man is difficult to serve and easy to please. The superior man has a dignified ease without pride; the mean man has pride without a dignified ease." A disciple asked him what qualities a man must possess to entitle him to be called a scholar. The master said: "He must be earnest, urgent, and bland, — among his friends earnest and urgent, among his brethren bland." And, "The scholar who cherishes a love of comfort is not fit to be deemed a scholar." "If a man," he said, "take no thought about what is distant, he will find sorrow near at hand." And again, "He who requires much from himself and little from others, he will keep himself from being an object of resentment." These proverbs remind us of Bacon: "Specious words confound virtue." "Want of forbearance in small matters confound great plans." "Virtue," the master said, "is more to man than either fire or water. I have seen men die from treading on water or fire, but I have never seen a man die from treading the course of virtue." This is a lofty sentiment, but I think it is not in accordance with the records of martyrdom. "There are three things," he continued, "which the superior man guards against: In youth he guards against his passions, in manhood against quarrelsomeness, and in old age against covetousness."

I do not find anything in the sayings of Confucius that can be called cynical, such as we find in some of the Proverbs of Solomon, even in reference to women, where women were, as in most Oriental countries, despised. The most that approaches cynicism is in such a remark as this: "I have not yet seen one who could perceive his faults and inwardly accuse himself." His definition of perfect virtue is above that of Paley: "The man of virtue makes the difficulty to be overcome his first business, and success only a secondary consideration." Throughout his writings there is no praise of success without virtue, and no disparagement of want of success with virtue. Nor have I found in his sayings a sentiment which may be called demoralizing. He always takes the higher ground, and with all his ceremony ever exalts inward purity above all external appearances. There is a quaint common-sense in some of his writings which reminds one of the sayings of Abraham Lincoln. For instance: One of his disciples asked. "If you had the conduct of armies, whom would you have to act with you?" The master replied: "I would not have him to act with me who will unarmed attack a tiger, or cross a river without a boat." Here something like wit and irony break out: "A man of the village said, 'Great is K'ung the philosopher; his learning is extensive, and yet he does not render his name famous by any particular thing.' The master heard this observation, and said to his disciples: 'What shall I practise, charioteering or archery? I will practise charioteering.'"

When the Duke of Loo asked about government, the master said: "Good government exists when those who are near are made happy, and when those who are far off are attracted." When the Duke questioned him again on the same subject, he replied: "Go before the people with your example, and be laborious in their affairs. . . . Pardon small faults, and raise to office men of virtue and talents." "But how shall I know the men of virtue?" asked the duke. "Raise to office those whom you do know." The key to his political philosophy seems to be this: "A man who knows how to govern himself, knows how to govern others; and he who knows how to govern other men, knows how to govern an empire." "The art of government," he said, "is to keep its affairs before the mind without weariness, and to practise them with undeviating constancy. . . . To govern means to rectify. If you lead on the people with correctness, who will not dare to be correct?" This is one of his favorite principles; namely, the force of a good example, — as when the reigning prince asked him how to do away with thieves, he replied: "If you, Sir, were not covetous, although you should reward them to do it, they would not steal." This was not intended as a rebuke to the prince, but an illustration of the force of a great example. Confucius rarely openly rebuked any one, especially a prince, whom it was his duty to venerate for his office. He contented himself with enforcing principles. Here his moderation and great courtesy are seen.

Confucius sometimes soared to the highest morality known to the Pagan world. 'Chung-kung asked about perfect virtue. The master said: "It is when you go abroad, to behave to every one as if you were receiving a great guest, to have no murmuring against you in the country and family, and not to do to others as you would not wish done to yourself. . . . The superior man has neither anxiety nor fear. Let him never fail reverentially to order his own conduct, and let him be respectful to others and observant of propriety; then all within the four seas will be brothers. . . . Hold faithfulness and sincerity as first principles, and be moving continually to what is right." Fan-Chi asked about benevolence; the master said: "It is to love all men." Another asked about friendship. Confucius replied: "Faithfully admonish your friend, and kindly try to lead him. If you find him impracticable, stop. Do not disgrace yourself." This saying reminds us of that of our great Master: "Cast not your pearls before swine." There is no greater folly than in making oneself disagreeable without any probability of reformation. Some one asked: "What do you say about the treatment of injuries?" The master answered: "Recompense injury with justice, and recompense kindness with kindness." Here again he was not far from the greater Teacher on the Mount. "When a man's knowledge is sufficient to attain and his virtue is not sufficient to hold, whatever he may have gained he will lose again." One of the favorite doctrines of Confucius was the superiority of the ancients to the men of his day. Said he: "The high-mindedness of antiquity showed itself in a disregard of small things; that of the present day shows itself in license. The stern dignity of antiquity showed itself in grave reserve; that of the present shows itself in quarrelsome perverseness. The policy of antiquity showed itself in straightforwardness; that of the present in deceit." The following is a saying worthy of Montaigne: "Of all people, girls and servants are the most difficult to behave to. If you are familiar with them, they lose their humility; if you maintain reserve to them, they are discontented."

Such are some of the sayings of Confucius, on account of which he was regarded as the wisest of his countrymen; and as his conduct was in harmony with his principles, he was justly revered as a pattern of morality. The greatest virtues which he enjoined were sincerity, truthfulness, and obedience to duty whatever may be the sacrifice; to do right because it is right and not because it is expedient; filial piety extending to absolute reverence; and an equal reverence for rulers. He had no theology; he confounded God with heaven and earth. He says nothing about divine providence; he believed in nothing supernatural. He thought little and said less about a future state of rewards and punishments. His morality was elevated, but not supernal. We infer from his writings that his age was degenerate and corrupt, but, as we have already said, his reproofs were gentle. Blandness of speech and manners was his distinguishing outward peculiarity; and this seems to characterize his nation, — whether learned from him, or whether an inborn national peculiarity, I do not know. He went through great trials most creditably, but he was no martyr. He constantly complained that his teachings fell on listless ears, which made him sad and discouraged; but he never flagged in his labors to improve his generation. He had no egotism, but great self-respect, reminding us of Michael Angelo. He was humble but full of dignity, serene though distressed, cheerful but not hilarious. Were he to live among us now, we should call him a perfect gentleman, with aristocratic sympathies, but more autocratic in his views of government and society than aristocratic. He seems to have loved the people, and was kind, even respectful, to everybody. When he visited a school, it is said that he arose in quiet deference to speak to the children, since some of the boys, he thought, would probably be distinguished and powerful at no distant day. He was also remarkably charitable, and put a greater value on virtues and abilities than upon riches and honors. Though courted by princes he would not serve them in violation of his self-respect, asked no favors, and returned their presents. If he did not live above the world, he adorned the world. We cannot compare his teachings with those of Christ; they are immeasurably inferior in loftiness and spirituality; but they are worldly wise and decorous, and are on an equality with those of Solomon in moral wisdom. They are wonderfully adapted to a people who are conservative of their institutions, and who have more respect for tradition than for progress.

The worship of ancestors is closely connected with veneration for parental authority; and with absolute obedience to parents is allied absolute obedience to the

Emperor as head of the State. Hence, the writings of Confucius have tended to cement the Chinese imperial power, — in which fact we may perhaps find the secret of his extraordinary posthumous influence. No wonder that emperors and rulers have revered and honored his memory, and used the power of the State to establish his doctrines. Moreover, his exaltation of learning as a necessity for rulers has tended to put all the offices of the realm into the hands of scholars. There never was a country where scholars have been and still are so generally employed by Government. And as men of learning are conservative in their sympathies, so they generally are fond of peace and detest war. Hence, under the influence of scholars the policy of the Chinese Government has always been mild and pacific. It is even paternal. It has more similarity to the governments of a remote antiquity than that of any existing nation. Thus is the influence of Confucius seen in the stability of government and of conservative institutions, as well as in decency in the affairs of life, and gentleness and courtesy of manners. Above all is his influence seen in the employment of men of learning and character in the affairs of state and in all the offices of government, as the truest guardians of whatever tends to exalt a State and make it respectable and stable, if not powerful for war or daring in deeds of violence.

Confucius was essentially a statesman as well as a moralist; but his political career was an apparent failure, since few princes listened to his instructions. Yet if he was lost to his contemporaries, he has been preserved by posterity. Perhaps there never lived a man so worshipped by posterity who had so slight a following by the men of his own time, — unless we liken him to that greatest of all Prophets, who, being despised and rejected, is, and is to be, the "headstone of the corner" in the rebuilding of humanity. Confucius says so little about the subjects that interested the people of China that some suppose he had no religion at all. Nor did he mention but once in his writings Shang-te, the supreme deity of his remote ancestors; and he deduced nothing from the worship of him. And yet there are expressions in his sayings which seem to show that he believed in a supreme power. He often spoke of Heaven, and loved to walk in the heavenly way. Heaven to him was Destiny, by the power of which the world was created. By Heaven the virtuous are rewarded, and the guilty are punished. Out of love for the people, Heaven appoints rulers to protect and instruct them. Prayer is unnecessary, because Heaven does not actively interfere with the soul of man.

Confucius was philosophical and consistent in the all-pervading principle by which he insisted upon the common source of power in government, — of the State, of the family, and of one's self. Self-knowledge and self-control he maintained to be the fountain of all personal virtue and attainment in performance of the moral duties owed to others, whether above or below in social standing. He supposed that all men are born equally good, but that the temptations of the world at length destroy the original rectitude. The "superior man," who next to the "sage" holds the highest place in the Confucian humanity, conquers the evil in the world, though subject to infirmities; his acts are guided by the laws of propriety, and are marked by strict sincerity. Confucius admitted that he himself had failed to reach the level of the superior man. This admission may have been the result of his extraordinary humility and modesty.

In "The Great Learning" Confucius lays down the rules to enable one to become a superior man. The foundation of his rules is in the investigation of things, or *knowledge*, with which virtue is indissolubly connected, — as in the ethics of Socrates. He maintained that no attainment can be made, and no virtue can remain untainted, without learning. "Without this, benevolence becomes folly, sincerity recklessness, straightforwardness rudeness, and firmness foolishness." But mere accumulation of facts was not knowledge, for "learning without thought is labor lost; and thought without learning is perilous." Complete wisdom was to be found only among the ancient sages; by no mental endeavor could any man hope to equal the supreme wisdom of Yaou and of Shun. The object of learning, he said, should be truth; and the combination of learning with a firm will, will surely lead a man to virtue. Virtue must be free from all hypocrisy and guile.

The next step towards perfection is the *cultivation of the person*, — which must begin with introspection, and ends in harmonious outward expression. Every man must guard his thoughts, words, and actions; and conduct must agree with words. By words the superior man directs others; but in order to do this his words must be sincere. It by no means follows, however, that virtue is the invariable concomitant of plausible speech.

The height of virtue is *filial piety;* for this is connected indissolubly with loyalty to the sovereign, who is the father of his people and the preserver of the State. Loyalty to the sovereign is synonymous with duty, and is outwardly shown by obedience. Next to parents, all superiors should be the object of reverence. This reverence, it is true, should be reciprocal; a sovereign forfeits all right to reverence and obedience when he ceases to be a minister of good. But then, only the man who has developed virtues in himself is considered competent to rule a family or a State; for the same virtues which enable a man to rule the one will enable him to rule the other. No man can teach others who cannot teach his own family. The greatest stress, as we have seen, is laid by Confucius on filial piety, which consists in obedience to authority, — in serving parents according to propriety, that is, with the deepest affection, and the father of the State with loyalty. But while it is incumbent on a son to obey the wishes of his parents, it is also a part of his duty to remonstrate with them should they act contrary to the rules of propriety. All remonstrances, however, must be made humbly. Should these remonstrances fail, the son must mourn in silence the obduracy of the parents. He carried the obligations of filial piety so far as to teach that a son should conceal the immorality of a father, forgetting the distinction of right and wrong. Brotherly love is the sequel of filial piety. "Happy," says he, "is the union with wife and children; it is like the music of lutes and harps. The love which binds brother to brother is second only to that which is due from children to parents. It consists in mutual friendship, joyful harmony, and dutiful obedience on the part of the younger to the elder brothers."

While obedience is exacted to an elder brother and to parents, Confucius said but little respecting the ties which should bind husband and wife. He had but

SAGE AND MORALIST.

little respect for woman, and was divorced from his wife after living with her for a year. He looked on women as every way inferior to men, and only to be endured as necessary evils. It was not until a woman became a mother, that she was treated with respect in China. Hence, according to Confucius, the great object of marriage is to increase the family, especially to give birth to sons. Women could be lawfully and properly divorced who had no children, — which put women completely in the power of men, and reduced them to the condition of slaves. The failure to recognize the sanctity of marriage is the great blot on the system of Confucius as a scheme of morals.

But the sage exalts friendship. Everybody, from the Emperor downward, must have friends; and the best friends are those allied by ties of blood. "Friends," said he, "are wealth to the poor, strength to the weak, and medicine to the sick." One of the strongest bonds to friendship is literature and literary exertion. Men are enjoined by Confucius to make friends among the most virtuous of scholars, even as they are enjoined to take service under the most worthy of great officers. In the intercourse of friends, the most unbounded sincerity and frankness is imperatively enjoined. "He who is not trusted by his friends will not gain the confidence of the sovereign, and he who is not obedient to parents will not be trusted by friends'

Everything is subordinated to the State; but, on the other hand, the family, friends, culture, virtue, — the good of the people, — is the main object of good government. "No virtue," said Emperor Kuh, 2435 B. C., "is higher than love to all men, and there is no loftier aim in government than to profit all men." When he was asked what should be done for the people, he replied, "Enrich them;" and when asked what more should be done, he replied, "Teach them." On these two principles the whole philosophy of the sage rested, — the temporal welfare of the people, and their education. He laid great stress on knowledge, as leading to virtue; and on virtue, as leading to prosperity. He made the profession of a teacher the most honorable calling to which a citizen could aspire. He himself was a teacher. All sages are teachers, though all teachers are not sages.

Confucius enlarged upon the necessity of having good men in office. The officials of his day excited his contempt, and reciprocally scorned his teachings. It was in contrast to these officials that he painted the ideal times of Kings Wan and Woo. The two motive-powers of government, according to Confucius, are righteousness and the observance of ceremonies. Righteousness is the law of the world, as ceremonies form a rule to the heart. What he meant by ceremonies was rules of propriety, intended to keep all unruly passions in check, and produce a reverential manner among all classes. Doubtless he over-estimated the force of example, since there are men in every country and community who will be lawless and reckless, in spite of the best models of character and conduct.

The ruling desire of Confucius was to make the whole empire peaceful and happy. The welfare of the people, the right government of the State, and the prosperity of the empire were the main objects of his solicitude. As conducive to these, he touched on many other things incidentally, — such as the encouragement of music, of which he was very fond. He himself summed up the outcome of his rules for conduct in this prohibitive form: "Do not unto others that which you would not have them do to you." Here we have the negative side of the positive "golden rule." Reciprocity, and that alone, was his law of life. He does not inculcate forgiveness of injuries, but exacts a tooth for a tooth, and an eye for an eye.

As to his own personal character, it was nearly faultless. His humility and patience were alike remarkable, and his sincerity and candor were as marked as his humility. He was the most learned man in the empire, yet lamented the deficiency of his knowledge. He even disclaimed the qualities of the superior man, much more those of the sage. "I am," said he, "not virtuous enough to be free from cares, nor wise enough to be free from anxieties, nor bold enough to be free from fear." He was always ready to serve his sovereign or the State; but he neither grasped office, nor put forward his own merits, nor sought to advance his own interests. He was grave, generous, tolerant, and sincere. He carried into practice all the rules he taught. Poverty was his lot in life, but he never repined at the absence of wealth, or lost the severe dignity which is ever to be associated with wisdom and the force of personal character. Indeed, his greatness was in his character rather than in his genius; and yet I think his genius has been underrated. His greatness is seen in the profound devotion of his followers to him, however lofty their merits or exalted their rank. No one ever disputed his influence and fame; and his moral excellence shines all the brighter in view of the troublous times in which he lived, when warriors occupied the stage, and men of letters were driven behind the scenes.

The literary labors of Confucius were very great, since he made the whole classical literature of China accessible to his countrymen. The fame of all preceding writers is merged in his own renown. His works have had the highest authority for more than two thousand years. They have been regarded as the exponents of supreme wisdom, and adopted as text-books by all scholars and in all schools in that vast empire, which includes one-fourth of the human race. To all educated men the "Book of Changes" (Yih-King), the "Book of Poetry" (She-King), the "Book of History" (Shoo-King), the "Book of Rites" (Le-King), the "Great Learning" (Ta-heo), showing the parental essence of all government, the "Doctrine of the Mean" (Chung-yung), teaching the "golden mean" of conduct, and the "Confucian Analects" (Lun-yu), recording his conversations, are supreme authorities; to which must be added the Works of Mencius, the greatest of his disciples. There is no record of any books that have exacted such supreme reverence in any nation as the Works of Confucius, except the Koran of the Mohammedans, the Book of the Law among the Hebrews, and the Bible among the Christians. What an influence for one man to have exerted on subsequent ages, who laid no claim to divinity or even originality, — recognized as a man, worshipped as a god!

No sooner had the sun of Confucius set under a cloud (since sovereigns and princes had neglected if they had not scorned his precepts), than his memory and principles were duly honored. But it was not until the accession of the Han dynasty, 206 B. C., that the reigning emperor collected the scattered writings of the sage, and exerted his vast power to secure the study of them throughout the schools of China. It must be borne in mind that a hostile emperor of the preceding dynasty had ordered the books of Confucius to be burned; but they were secreted by his faithful admirers in the walls of houses and beneath the ground. Succeeding emperors heaped additional honors on the memory of the sage, and in the early part of the sixteenth century an emperor of the Ming dynasty gave him the title which he at present bears in China, — "The perfect sage, the ancient teacher, Confucius." No higher title could be conferred upon him in a land where to be " ancient " is to be revered. For more than twelve hundred years temples have been erected to his honor, and his worship has been universal throughout the empire. His maxims of morality have appealed to human consciousness in every succeeding generation, and carry as much weight to-day as they did when the Han dynasty made them the standard of human wisdom. They were especially adapted to the Chinese intellect, which although shrewd and ingenious is phlegmatic, unspeculative, matter-of-fact, and unspiritual. Moreover, as we have said, it was to the interest of rulers to support his doctrines, from the constant exhortations to loyalty which Confucius enjoined. And yet there is in his precepts a democratic influence also, since he recognized no other titles or ranks but such as are won by personal merit. — thus opening every office in the State to the learned, whatever their original social rank. The great political truth that the welfare of the people is the first duty and highest aim of rulers, has endeared the memory of the sage to the unnumbered millions who toil upon the scantiest means of subsistence that have been known in any nation's history.

This essay on the religion of the Chinese would be incomplete without some allusion to one of the contemporaries of Confucius, who spiritually and intellectually was probably his superior, and to whom even Confucius paid extraordinary deference. This man was called Lao-tse, a recluse and philosopher, who was already an old man when Confucius began his travels. He was the founder of Tao-tze, a kind of rationalism, which at present has millions of adherents in China. This old philosopher did not receive Confucius very graciously, since the younger man declared nothing new, only wishing to revive the teachings of ancient sages, while he himself was a great awakener of thought. He was, like Confucius, a politico-ethical teacher, but unlike him sought to lead people back to a state of primitive society before forms and regulations existed. He held that man's nature was good, and that primitive pleasures and virtues were better than worldly wisdom. He maintained that spiritual weapons cannot be formed by laws and regulations, and that prohibiting enactments tended to increase the evils they were meant to avert. While this great and profound man was in some respects superior to Confucius, his influence has been most seen on the inferior people of China. Taoism rivals Buddhism as the religion of the lower classes, and Taoism combined with Buddhism has more adherents than Confucianism. But the wise, the mighty, and the noble still cling to Confucius as the greatest man whom China has produced.

Of spiritual religion, indeed, the lower millions of Chinese have now but little conception; their nearest approach to any supernaturalism is the worship of deceased ancestors, and their religious observances are the grossest formalism. But as a practical system of morals in the days of its early establishment, the religion of Confucius ranks very high among the best developments of Paganism. Certainly no man ever had a deeper knowledge of his countrymen than he, or adapted his doctrines to the peculiar needs of their social organism with such amazing tact.

It is a remarkable thing that all the religions of antiquity have practically passed away, with their cities and empires, except among the Hindus and Chinese; and it is doubtful if these religions can withstand the changes which foreign conquest and Christian missionary enterprise and civilization are producing. In the East the old religions gave place to Mohamedanism, as in the West they disappeared before the power of Christianity. And these conquering religions retain and extend their hold upon the human mind and human affections by reason of their fundamental principles, — the fatherhood of a personal God, and the brotherhood of universal man. With the ideas prevalent among all sects that God is not only supreme in power, but benevolent in his providence, and that every man has claims and rights which cannot be set aside by kings or rulers or priests, — nations must indefinitely advance in virtue and happiness, as they receive and live by the inspiration of this elevating faith.

AUTHORITIES.

RELIGION in China, by Joseph Edkins, D.D.; Rawlinson's Religions of the Ancient World; Freeman Clarke's Ten Great Religions; Johnson's Oriental Religions; Davis's Chinese; Nevins's China and the Chinese; Giles's Chinese Sketches; Lenormant's Ancient History of the East; Huc's Christianity in China; Legge's Prolegomena to the Shoo-King; Lecomte's China; Dr. S. Wells Williams's Middle Kingdom; China, by Professor Douglas; The Religions of China, by James Legge.

ANCIENT PHILOSOPHY

SEEKING AFTER TRUTH.

ANCIENT PHILOSOPHY.

SEEKING AFTER TRUTH.

WHATEVER may be said of the inferiority of the ancients to the moderns in natural and mechanical science, which no one is disposed to question, or even in the realm of literature, which may be questioned, there was one department of knowledge to which we have added nothing of consequence. In the realm of art they were our equals, and probably our superiors; in philosophy, they carried logical deduction to its utmost limit. They advanced from a few crude speculations on material phenomena to an analysis of all the powers of the mind, and finally to the establishment of ethical principles which even Christianity did not supersede.

The progress of philosophy from Thales to Plato is the most stupendous triumph of the human intellect. The reason of man soared to the loftiest flights that it has ever attained. It cast its searching eye into the most abstruse inquiries which ever tasked the famous minds of the world. It exhausted all the subjects which dialectical subtlety ever raised. It originated and carried out the boldest speculations respecting the nature of the soul and its future existence. It established important psychological truths and created a method for the solution of abstruse questions. It went on from point to point, until all the faculties of the mind were severely analyzed, and all its operations were subjected to a rigid method. The Romans never added a single principle to the philosophy which the Greeks elaborated; the ingenious scholastics of the Middle Ages merely reproduced Greek ideas; and even the profound and patient Germans have gone round in the same circles that Plato and Aristotle marked out more than two thousand years ago. Only the Brahmans of India have equalled them in intellectual subtilty and acumen. It was Greek philosophy in which noble Roman youths were educated; and hence, as it was expounded by a Cicero, a Marcus Aurelius, and an Epictetus, it was as much the inheritance of the Romans as it was of the Greeks themselves, after Grecian liberties were swept away and Greek cities became a part of the Roman empire. The Romans learned what the Greeks created and taught; and philosophy, as well as art, became identified with the civilization which extended from the Rhine and the Po to the Nile and the Tigris

Greek philosophy was one of the distinctive features of ancient civilization long after the Greeks had ceased to speculate on the laws of mind or the nature of the soul, on the existence of God or future rewards and punishments. Although it was purely Grecian in its origin and development, it became one of the grand ornaments of the Roman schools. The Romans did not originate medicine, but Galen was one of its greatest lights; they did not invent the hexameter verse, but Virgil sang to its measure; they did not create Ionic capitals, but their cities were ornamented with marble temples on the same principles as those which called out the admiration of Pericles. So, if they did not originate philosophy, and generally had but little taste for it, still its truths were systematized and explained by Cicero, and formed no small accession to the treasures with which cultivated intellects sought everywhere to be enriched. It formed an essential part of the intellectual wealth of the civilized world, when civilization could not prevent the world from falling into decay and ruin. And as it was the noblest triumph which the human mind, under Pagan influences, ever achieved, so it was followed by the most degrading imbecility into which man, in civilized countries, was ever allowed to fall. Philosophy, like art, like literature, like science, arose, shone, grew dim, and passed away, leaving the world in night. Why was so bright a glory followed by so dismal a shame? What a comment is this on the greatness and littleness of man!

In all probability the development of Greek philosophy originated with the Ionian Sophoi, though many suppose it was derived from the East. It is questionable whether the Oriental nations had any philosophy distinct from religion. The Germans are fond of tracing resemblances in the early speculations of the Greeks to the systems which prevailed in Asia from a very remote antiquity. Gladish sees in the Pythagorean system an adoption of Chinese doctrines; in the Heraclitic system, the influence of Persia; in the Empedoclean, Egyptian speculations; and in the Anaxagorean, the Jewish creeds. But the Orientals had theogonies, not philosophies. The Indian speculations aim at an exposition of ancient revelation. They profess to liberate the soul from the evils of mortal life, — to arrive at eternal beatitudes. But the state of perfectibility could be reached only by religious ceremonial observances and devout contemplation. The Indian systems do not disdain logical discussions, or a search after the principles of which the universe is composed; and hence we find great refinements in sophistry, and a wonderful subtilty of logical discussion, though these are directed to unattainable ends, — to the connection of good with evil, and the union of the Supreme with Nature. Nothing seemed to come out of these specula tions but an occasional elevation of mind among the learned, and a profound conviction of the misery of man and the obstacles to his perfection. The Greeks, starting from physical phenomena, went on in successive series of inquiries, elevating themselves above matter, above experience, even to the loftiest abstractions, until they classified the laws of thought. It is curious how speculation led to demonstration, and how inquiries into the world of matter prepared the way for the solution of intellectual phenomena. Philosophy kept pace with geometry, and those who observed Nature also gloried in abstruse calculations. Philosophy and mathematics seem to have been allied with the worship of art among the same men, and it is difficult to say which more distinguished them, — æsthetic culture or power of abstruse reasoning.

We do not read of any remarkable philosophical inquirer until Thales arose, the first of the Ionian school. He was born at Miletus, a Greek colony in Asia Minor, about the year 636 B.C., when Ancus Martius was king of Rome, and Josiah reigned at Jerusalem. He has left no writings behind him, but was numbered as one of the seven wise men of Greece on account of his political sagacity and wisdom in public affairs. I do not here speak of his astronomical and geometrical labors, which were great, and which have left their mark even upon our own daily life, — as for instance, in the fact that he was the first to have divided the year into three hundred and sixty-five days.

> "And he, 'tis said, did first compute the stars
> Which beam in Charles's wain, and guide the bark
> Of the Phœnecian sailor o'er the sea."

He is celebrated also for practical wisdom. "Know thyself," is one of his remarkable sayings. The chief claim of Thales to a lofty rank among sages, however, is that he was the first who attempted a logical solution of material phenomena, without resorting to mythical representations. Thales felt that there was a grand question to be answered relative to the *beginning of things*. "Philosophy," it has been well said, "may be a history of *errors*, but not of *follies*." It was not a folly, in a rude age, to speculate on the first or fundamental principle of things. Thales looked around him upon Nature, upon the sea and earth and sky, and concluded that water or moisture was the vital principle. He felt it in the air, he saw it in the clouds above and in the ground beneath his feet. He saw that plants were sustained by rain and by the dew, that neither animal nor man could live without water, and that to fishes it was the native element. What more important or vital than water? It was the *prima materia*, the ἀρχή, the beginning of all things, —the origin of the world. How so crude a speculation could have been maintained by so wise a man it is difficult to conjecture. It is not, however, the cause which he assigns for the beginning of things which is noteworthy, so much as the fact that his mind was directed to any solution of questions pertaining to the origin of the universe. It was these questions, and the solution of them, which marked the Ionian philosophers, and which showed the inquiring nature of their minds. What is the great first cause of all things? Thales saw it in one of the four elements of Nature as the ancients divided them; and this is the earliest recorded theory among the Greeks of the origin of the world. It is an induction from one of the phenomena of animated Nature, — the nutrition and production of a seed. He regarded the entire world in the light of a living being gradually maturing and forming itself from an imperfect seed-state, which was of a moist nature. This moisture endues the universe with vitality. The world, he thought, was full of gods, but they had their origin in water. He had no conception of God as *intelligence,* or as a *creative* power. He had a great and inquiring mind, but it gave him no knowledge of a spiritual, controlling, and personal deity.

Anaximenes, the disciple of Thales, pursued his master's inquiries and adopted his method. He also was born in Miletus, but at what time is unknown, —

probably 500 B. C. Like Thales, he held to the eternity of matter. Like him, he disbelieved in the existence of anything immaterial, for even a human soul is formed out of matter. He, too, speculated on the origin of the universe, but thought that *air*, not water, was the primal cause. This element seems to be universal. We breathe it; all things are sustained by it. It is Life, — that is, pregnant with vital energy, and capable of infinite transmutations. All things are produced by it; all is again resolved into it; it supports all things; it surrounds the world; it has infinitude; it has eternal motion. Thus did this philosopher reason, comparing the world with our own living existence, — which he took to be air, — an imperishable principle of life. He thus advanced a step beyond Thales, since he regarded the world not after the analogy of an imperfect seed-state, but after that of the highest condition of life, — the human soul. And he attempted to refer to one general law all the transformations of the first simple substance into its successive states, in that the cause of change is the eternal motion of the air.

Diogenes of Apollonia, in Crete, one of the disciples of Anaximenes, born 500 B. C., also believed that air was the principle of the universe, but he imputed to it an intellectual energy, yet without recognizing any distinction between mind and matter. He made air and the soul identical. "For," says he, "man and all other animals breathe and live by means of the air, and therein consists their soul." And as it is the primary being from which all is derived, it is necessarily an eternal and imperishable body; but as *soul* it is also endued with consciousness. Diogenes thus refers the origin of the world to an intelligent being, — to a soul which knows and vivifies. Anaximenes regarded air as having life; Diogenes saw in it also intelligence. Thus philosophy advanced step by step, though still groping in the dark; for the origin of all things, according to Diogenes, must exist in *intelligence.* According to Diogenes Laertius, he said: "It appears to me that he who begins any treatise ought to lay down principles about which there can be no dispute."

Heraclitus of Ephesus, classed by Ritter among the Ionian philosophers, was born 503 B. C. Like others of his school, he sought a physical ground for all phenomena. The elemental principle he regarded as *fire*, since all things are convertible into it. In one of its modifications this fire, or fluid, self-kindled, permeating everything as the soul or principle of life, is endowed with intelligence and powers of ceaseless activity. "If Anaximenes," says Maurice, not very clearly, "discovered that he had within him a power and principle which ruled over all the acts and functions of his bodily frame, Heraclitus found that there was life within him which he could not call his own, and yet it was, in the very highest sense, *himself,* so that without it he would have been a poor, helpless, isolated creature, — a universal life which connected him with his fellow-men, with the absolute source and original fountain of life. . . . He proclaimed the absolute vitality of Nature, the endless change of matter, the mutability and perishability of all individual things in contrast with the eternal Being, — the supreme harmony which rules over all." To trace the divine energy of life in all things was the general problem of the philosophy of Heraclitus, and this spirit was akin to the pantheism of the East. But he was one of the greatest speculative intellects that preceded Plato, and of all the physical theorists arrived nearest to spiritual truth. He taught the germs of what was afterward more completely developed. "From his theory of perpetual fluxion," says Archer Butler, "Plato derived the necessity of seeking a stable basis for the universal system in his world of ideas." Heraclitus was, however, an obscure writer, and moreover cynical and arrogant.

Anaxagoras, the most famous of the Ionian philosophers, was born 500 B. C., and belonged to a rich and noble family. Regarding philosophy as the noblest pursuit of earth, he abandoned his inheritance for the study of Nature. He went to Athens in the most brilliant period of her history, and had Pericles, Euripides, and Socrates for pupils. He taught that the great moving force of Nature was intellect ($νοῦς$). Intelligence was the cause of the world and of order, and mind was the principle of motion; yet this intelligence was not a moral intelligence, but simply the *primum mobile*, — the all-knowing motive force by which the order of Nature is effected. He thus laid the foundation of a new system, under which the Attic philosophers sought to explain Nature, by regarding as the cause of all things, not *matter* in its different elements, but rather *mind*, thought, intelligence, which both knows and acts, — a grand conception, unrivalled in ancient speculation. This explanation of material phenomena by intellectual causes was the peculiar merit of Anaxagoras, and places him in a very high rank among the thinkers of the world. Moreover, he recognized the reason as the only faculty by which we become cognizant of truth, the senses being too weak to discover the real component particles of things. Like all the great inquirers, he was impressed with the limited degree of positive knowledge compared with what there is to be learned. "Nothing," says he, "can be known; nothing is certain; sense is limited, intellect is weak, life is short," — the complaint, not of a sceptic, but of a man overwhelmed with the sense of his incapacity to solve the problems which arose before his active mind. Anaxagoras thought that this spirit (νοῦς) gave to all those material atoms which in the beginning of the world lay in disorder the impulse by which they took the forms of individual things, and that this impulse was given in a circular direction. Hence that the sun, moon, and stars, and even the air, are constantly moving in a circle.

In the mean time another sect of philosophers had arisen, who, like the Ionians, sought to explain Nature, but by a different method. Anaximander, born 610 B.C., was one of the original mathematicians of Greece, yet, like Pythagoras and Thales, speculated on the beginning of things. His principle was that *The Infinite* is the origin of all things. He used the word ἀρχή (*beginning*) to denote the material out of which all things were formed, as the Everlasting, the Divine. The idea of elevating an abstraction into a great first cause was certainly a long stride in philosophic generalization to be taken at that age of the world, following as it did so immediately upon such partial and childish ideas as that any single one of the familiar "elements" could be the primal cause of all things. It seems almost like the speculations of our own time, when philosophers seek to find the first cause in impersonal Force, or infinite Energy. Yet it is not really easy to understand Anaximander's meaning, other than that the abstract has a higher significance than the concrete. The speculations of Thales had tended toward discovering the material constitution of the universe upon an *induction* from observed facts, and thus made water to be the origin of all things. Anaximander, accustomed to view things in the abstract, could not accept so concrete a thing as water; his speculations tended toward mathematics, to the science of pure *deduction*. The primary Being is a unity, one in all, comprising within itself the multiplicity of elements from which all mundane things are composed. It is only in infinity that the perpetual changes of things can take place. Thus Anaximander, an original but vague thinker, prepared the way for Pythagoras.

This later philosopher and mathematician, born about the year 600 B. C., stands as one of the great names of antiquity; but his life is shrouded in dim magnificence. The old historians paint him as "clothed in robes of white, his head covered with gold, his aspect grave and majestic, rapt in the contemplation of the mysteries of existence, listening to the music of Homer and Hesiod, or to the harmony of the spheres."

Pythagoras was supposed to be a native of Samos. When quite young, being devoted to learning, he quitted his country and went to Egypt, where he learned its language and all the secret mysteries of the priests. He then returned to Samos, but finding the island under the dominion of a tyrant he fled to Crotona, in Italy, where he gained great reputation for wisdom, and made laws for the Italians. His pupils were about three hundred in number. He wrote three books, which were extant in the time of Diogenes Laertius, — one on Education, one on Politics, and one on Natural Philosophy. He also wrote an epic poem on the universe, to which he gave the name of *Kosmos.*

Among the ethical principles which Pythagoras taught was that men ought not to pray for anything in particular, since they do not know what is good for them; that drunkenness was identical with ruin; that no one should exceed the proper quantity of meat and drink; that the property of friends is common; that men should never say or do anything in anger. He forbade his disciples to offer victims to the gods, ordering them to worship only at those altars which were unstained with blood.

Pythagoras was the first person who introduced measures and weights among the Greeks. But it is his philosophy which chiefly claims our attention. His main principle was that *number* is the essence of things, — probably meaning by number order and harmony and conformity to law. The order of the universe, he taught, is only a harmonical development of the first principle of all things to virtue and wisdom. He attached much value to music, as an art which has great influence on the affections; hence his doctrine of the music of the spheres. Assuming that number is the essence of the world, he deduced the idea that the world is regulated by numerical proportions, or by a system of laws which are regular and harmonious in their operations. Hence the necessity for an intelligent creator of the universe. The Infinite of Anaximander became the One of Pythagoras. He believed that the soul is incorporeal, and is put into the body subject to numerical and harmonical relation, and thus to divine regulation. Hence the tendency of his speculations was to raise the soul to the contemplation of law and order, — of a supreme Intelligence reigning in justice and truth. Justice and truth became thus paramount virtues, to be practised and sought as the end of life. "It is impossible not to see in these lofty speculations the effect of the Greek mind, according to its own genius, seeking after God, if haply it might find Him."

We now approach the second stage of Greek philosophy. The Ionic philosophers had sought to find the first principle of all things in the elements, and the Pythagoreans in number, or harmony and law, implying an intelligent creator. The Eleatics, who now arose, went beyond the realm of physics to pure metaphysical inquiries, to an idealistic pantheism, which disregarded the sensible, maintaining that the source of truth is independent of the senses. Here they were forestalled by the Hindu sages.

The founder of this school was Xenophanes, born in Colophon, an Ionian city of Asia Minor, from which being expelled he wandered over Sicily as a rhapsodist, or minstrel, reciting his elegiac poetry on the loftiest truths, and at last, about the year 536 B. C., came to Elea, where he settled. The principal subject of his inquiries was deity itself, — the great First Cause, the supreme Intelligence of the universe. From the principle *ex nihilo nihil fit* he concluded that nothing could pass from non-existence to existence. All things that exist are created by supreme Intelligence, who is eternal and immutable. From this truth that God must be from all eternity, he advances to deny all multiplicity. A plurality of gods is impossible. With these sublime views, — the unity and eternity and omnipotence of God, — Xenophanes boldly attacked the popular errors of his day. He denounced the transference to the deity of the human form; he inveighed against Homer and Hesiod; he ridiculed the doctrine of migration of souls. Thus he sings, —

"Such things of the gods are related by Homer and Hesiod
 As would be shame and abiding disgrace to mankind, —
 Promises broken, and thefts, and the one deceiving the other."

And again, respecting anthropomorphic representations of the deity —

> "But men foolishly think that gods are born like as men are,
> And have too a dress like their own, and their voice and their figure;
> But there's but one God alone, the greatest of gods and of mortals,
> Neither in body to mankind resembling, neither in ideas."

Such were the sublime meditations of Xenophanes. He believed in the *One*, which is God; but this all-pervading, unmoved, undivided being was not a personal God, nor a moral governor, but deity pervading all space. He could not separate God from the world, nor could he admit the existence of world which is not God. He was a monotheist, but his monotheism was pantheism. He saw God in all the manifestations of Nature. This did not satisfy him nor resolve his doubts, and he therefore confessed that reason could not compass the exalted aims of philosophy. But there was no cynicism in his doubt. It was the soul-sickening consciousness that reason was incapable of solving the mighty questions that he burned to know. There was no way to arrive at the truth, "for," said he, "error is spread over all things." It was not disdain of knowledge, it was the combat of contradictory opinions that oppressed him. He could not solve the questions pertaining to God. What uninstructed reason can? "Canst thou by searching find out God? canst thou know the Almighty unto perfection?" What was impossible to Job was not possible to Xenophanes. But he had attained a recognition of the unity and perfections of God; and this conviction he would spread abroad, and tear down the superstitions which hid the face of truth. I have great admiration for this philosopher, so sad, so earnest, so enthusiastic, wandering from city to city, indifferent to money, comfort, friends, fame, that he might kindle the knowledge of God. This was a lofty aim indeed for philosophy in that age. It was a higher mission than that of Homer, great as his was, though not so successful.

Parmenides of Elea, born about the year 530 B. C., followed out the system of Xenophanes, the central idea of which was the existence of God. With Parmenides the main thought was the notion of *being*. Being is uncreated and unchangeable; the fulness of all being is *thought*; the *All* is thought and intelligence. He maintained the uncertainty of knowledge, meaning the knowledge derived through the senses He did not deny the certainty of reason. He was the first who drew a distinction between knowledge obtained by the senses and that obtained through the reason; and thus he anticipated the doctrine of innate ideas. From the uncertainty of knowledge derived through the senses, he deduced the twofold system of true and apparent knowledge.

Zeno of Elea, the friend and pupil of Parmenides, born 500 B. C., brought nothing new to the system, but invented *Dialectics*, the art of disputation, — that department of logic which afterward became so powerful in the hands of Plato and Aristotle, and so generally admired among the schoolmen. It seeks to establish truth by refuting error through the *reductio ad absurdum*. While Parmenides sought to establish the doctrine of the *One*, Zeno proved the non-existence of the *Many*. He did not deny existences, but denied that appearances were real existences. It was the mission of Zeno to establish the doctrines of his master. But in order to convince his listeners, he was obliged to use a new method of argument. So he carried on his argumentation by question and answer, and was therefore the first who used dialogue, which he called dialectics, as a medium of philosophical communication.

Empedocles, born 444 B. C., like others of the Eleatics, complained of the imperfection of the senses, and looked for truth only in reason. He regarded truth as a perfect unity, ruled by love, — the only true force, the one moving cause of all things, — the first creative power by which or whom the world was formed. Thus "God is love" is a sublime doctrine which philosophy revealed to the Greeks, and the emphatic and continuous and assured declaration of which was the central theme of the revelation made by Jesus, the Christ, who resolved all the Law and the Gospel into the element of Love, — fatherly on the part of God, filial and fraternal on the part of men.

Thus did the Eleatic philosophers speculate almost contemporaneously with the Ionians on the beginning of things and the origin of knowledge, taking different grounds, and attempting to correct the representations of sense by the notions of reason. But both schools, although they did not establish many truths, raised an inquisitive spirit, and awakened freedom of thought and inquiry. They raised up workmen for more enlightened times, even as scholastic inquirers in the Middle Ages prepared the way for the revival of philosophy on sounder principles. They were all men of remarkable elevation of character as well as genius. They hated superstitions, and attacked the anthropomorphism of their day. They handled gods and goddesses with allegorizing boldness, and hence were often persecuted by the people. They did not establish moral truths by scientific processes, but they set examples of lofty disdain of wealth and factitious advantages, and devoted themselves with holy enthusiasm to the solution of the great questions which

SEEKING AFTER TRUTH.

pertain to God and Nature. Thales won the respect of his countrymen by devotion to studies. Pythagoras spent twenty-two years in Egypt to learn its science. Xenophanes wandered over Sicily as a rhapsodist of truth. Parmenides, born to wealth and splendor, forsook the feverish pursuit of sensual enjoyments that he might "behold the bright countenance of truth in the quiet and still air of delightful studies." Zeno declined all worldly honors in order that he might diffuse the doctrines of his master. Heraclitus refused the chief magistracy of Ephesus that he might have leisure to explore the depths of his own nature. Anaxagoras allowed his patrimony to run to waste in order to solve problems. "To philosophy," said he, "I owe my worldly ruin, and my soul's prosperity." All these men were, without exception, the greatest and best men of their times. They laid the foundation of the beautiful temple which was constructed after they were dead, in which both physics and psychology reached the dignity of science. They too were prophets, although unconscious of their divine mission, — prophets of that day when the science which explores and illustrates the works of God shall enlarge, enrich, and beautify man's conceptions of the great creative Father.

Nevertheless, these great men, lofty as were their inquiries and blameless their lives, had not established any system, nor any theories which were incontrovertible. They had simply speculated, and the world ridiculed their speculations. Their ideas were one-sided, and when pushed out to their extreme logical sequence were antagonistic to one another; which had a tendency to produce doubt and scepticism. Men denied the existence of the gods, and the grounds of certainty fell away from the human mind.

This spirit of scepticism was favored by the tide of worldliness and prosperity which followed the Persian War. Athens became a great centre of art, of taste, of elegance, and of wealth. Politics absorbed the minds of the people. Glory and splendor were followed by corruption of morals and the pursuit of material pleasures. Philosophy went out of fashion, since it brought no outward and tangible good. More scientific studies were pursued, — those which could be applied to purposes of utility and material gains; even as in our day geology, chemistry, mechanics, engineering, having reference to the practical wants of men, command talent, and lead to certain reward. In Athens, rhetoric, mathematics, and natural history supplanted rhapsodies and speculations on God and Providence. Renown and wealth could be secured only by readiness and felicity of speech, and that was most valued which brought immediate recompense, like eloquence. Men began to practise eloquence as an art, and to employ it in furthering their interests.

They made special pleadings, since it was their object to gain their point at any expense of law and justice. Hence they taught that nothing was immutably right, but only so by convention. They undermined all confidence in truth and religion by teaching its uncertainty. They denied to men even the capability of arriving at truth. They practically affirmed the cold and cynical doctrine that there is nothing better for a man than that he should eat and drink. *Cui bono?* this, the cry of most men in periods of great outward prosperity, was the popular inquiry. Who will show us any good? — how can we become rich, strong, honorable? — this was the spirit of that class of public teachers who arose in Athens when art and eloquence and wealth and splendor were at their height in the fifth century before Christ, and when the elegant Pericles was the leader of fashion and of political power.

These men were the Sophists, — rhetorical men, who taught the children of the rich; worldly men, who sought honor and power; frivolous men, trifling with philosophical ideas; sceptical men, denying all certainty in truth; men who as teachers added nothing to the realm of science, but who yet established certain dialectical rules useful to later philosophers. They were a wealthy, powerful, honored class, not much esteemed by men of thought, but sought out as very successful teachers of rhetoric, and also generally selected as ambassadors on difficult missions. They were full of logical tricks, and contrived to throw ridicule upon profound inquiries. They taught also mathematics, astronomy, philology, and natural history with success. They were polished men of society; not profound nor religious, but very brilliant as talkers, and very ready in wit and sophistry. And some of them were men of great learning and talent, like Democritus, Leucippus, and Gorgias. They were not pretenders and quacks; they were sceptics who denied subjective truths, and labored for outward advantage. They taught the art of disputation, and sought systematic methods of proof. They thus prepared the way for a more perfect philosophy than that taught by the Ionians, the Pythagoreans, or the Eleatics, since they showed the vagueness of such inquiries, conjectural rather than scientific. They had no doctrines in common. They were the barristers of their age, *pail* to make the " worse appear the better reason;" yet not teachers of immorality any more than the lawyers of our day, — men of talents, the intellectual leaders of society. If they did not advance positive truths, they were useful in the method they created. They had no hostility to truth, as such; they only doubted whether it could be reached in the realm of psychological inquiries, and sought to apply knowledge to their own purposes, or rather to distort it in order to gain a case. They are not a class of men whom I admire, as I do the old sages they ridiculed, but they were not without their use in the development of philosophy. The Sophists also rendered a service to literature by giving definiteness to language, and creating style in prose writing. Protagoras investigated the principles of accurate composition; Prodicus busied himself with inquiries into the significance of words; Gorgias, like Voltaire, gloried in a captivating style, and gave symmetry to the structure of sentences.

The ridicule and scepticism of the Sophists brought out the great powers of Socrates, to whom philosophy is probably more indebted than to any man who ever lived, not so much for a perfect system as for the impulse he gave to philosophical inquiries, and for his successful exposure of error. He inaugurated a new era. Born in Athens in the year 470 B.C., the son of a poor sculptor, he devoted his life to the search after truth for its own sake, and sought to base it on immutable foundations. He was the mortal enemy of the Sophists, whom he encountered, as Pascal did the Jesuits, with wit, irony, puzzling questions, and remorseless logic. It is true that Socrates and his great successors Plato and Aristotle were called "Sophists," but only as all philosophers or wise men were so called. The Sophists as a class had incurred the odium of being the first teachers who received pay for the instruction they imparted. The philosophers generally taught for the love of truth. The Sophists were a natural and necessary and very useful development of their time, but they were distinctly on a lower level than the Philosophers, or *lovers* of wisdom.

Like the earlier philosophers, Socrates disdained wealth, ease, and comfort, — but with greater devotion than they, since he lived in a more corrupt age, when poverty was a disgrace and misfortune a crime, when success was the standard of merit, and every man was supposed to be the arbiter of his own fortune, ignoring that Providence who so often refuses the race to the swift, and the battle to the strong. He was what in our time would be called eccentric. He walked barefooted, meanly clad, and withal not over cleanly, seeking public places, disputing with everybody willing to talk with him, making everybody ridiculous, especially if one assumed airs of wisdom or knowledge, — an exasperating opponent, since he wove a web around a man from which he could not be extricated, and then exposed him to ridicule in the wittiest city of the world. He attacked everybody, and yet was generally respected, since it was *errors* rather than persons, *opinions* rather than vices, that he attacked; and this he did with bewitching eloquence and irresistible fascination, so that though he was poor and barefooted, a Silenus in appearance, with thick lips, upturned nose, projecting eyes, unwieldy belly, he was sought by Alcibiades and admired by Aspasia. Even Xanthippe, a beautiful young woman, very much younger than he, a woman fond of the comforts and pleasures of life, was willing to marry him, although it is said that she turned out a "scolding wife" after the *res angusta domi* had disenchanted her from the music of his voice and the divinity of his nature. "I have heard Pericles," said the most dissipated and voluptuous man in Athens, "and other excellent orators, but was not moved by them; while this Marsyas — this Satyr — so affects me that the life I lead is hardly worth living, and I stop my ears as from the Sirens, and flee as fast as possible, that I may not sit down and grow old in listening to his talk."

Socrates learned his philosophy from no one, and struck out an entirely new path. He declared his own ignorance, and sought to convince other people of theirs. He did not seek to reveal truth so much as to expose error. And yet it was his object to attain correct ideas as to moral obligations. He proclaimed the sovereignty of virtue and the immutability of justice. He sought to delineate and enforce the practical duties of life. His great object was the elucidation of morals; and he was the first to teach ethics systematically from the immutable principles of moral obligation. Moral certitude was the lofty platform from which he surveyed the world, and upon which, as a rock, he rested in the storms of life. Thus he was a reformer and a moralist. It was his ethical doctrines which were most antagonistic to the age and the least appreciated. He was a profoundly religious man, recognized Providence, and believed in the immortality of the soul. He did not presume to inquire into the Divine essence, yet he believed that the gods were omniscient and omnipresent, that they ruled by the law of goodness, and that in spite of their multiplicity there was unity, — a supreme Intelligence that governed the world. Hence he was hated by the Sophists, who denied the certainty of arriving at any knowledge of God. From the comparative worthlessness of the body he deduced the immortality of the soul. With him the end of life was reason and intelligence. He deduced the existence of God from the order and harmony of Nature, belief in which was irresistible. He endeavored to connect the moral with the religious consciousness, and thus to promote the practical welfare of society. In this light Socrates stands out the grandest personage of Pagan antiquity, — as a moralist, as a teacher of ethics, as a man who recognized the Divine.

So far as he was concerned in the development of Greek philosophy proper, he was inferior to some of his disciples. Yet he gave a turning-point to a new period when he awakened the *idea* of knowledge, and was the founder of the method of scientific inquiry, since he pointed out the legitimate bounds of inquiry, and was thus the precursor of Bacon and Pascal. He did not attempt to make physics explain metaphysics, nor metaphysics the phenomena of the natural world; and he reasoned only from what was generally assumed to be true and invariable. He was a great pioneer of philosophy, since he resorted to inductive methods of proof, and gave general definiteness to ideas. Although he employed induction, it was his aim to withdraw the mind from the contemplation of Nature, and to fix it on its own phenomena, — to look inward rather than outward; a method carried out admirably by his pupil Plato. The previous philosophers had given their attention to external nature; Socrates gave up speculations about material phenomena, and directed his inquiries solely to the nature of knowledge. And as he considered knowledge to be identical with virtue, he speculated on ethical questions mainly, and the method which he taught was that by which alone man could become better and wiser. To know one's self, — in other words, that "the proper study of mankind is man," — he proclaimed with Thales. Cicero said of him, "Socrates brought down philosophy from the heavens to the earth." He did not disdain the subjects which chiefly interested the Sophists, — astronomy, rhetoric, physics, — but he chiefly discussed moral questions, such as, What is piety? What is the just and the unjust? What is temperance? What is courage? What is the character fit for a citizen? — and other ethical points, involving practical human relationships.

These questions were discussed by Socrates in a striking manner, and by a method peculiarly his own. " Professing ignorance, he put perhaps this question: What is law? It was familiar, and was answered offhand. Socrates, having got the answer, then put fresh questions applicable to specific cases, to which the respondent was compelled to give an answer inconsistent with the first, thus showing that the definition was too narrow or too wide, or defective in some essential condition. The respondent then amended his answer; but this was a prelude to other questions, which could only be answered in ways inconsistent with the amendment; and the respondent, after many attempts to disentangle himself, was obliged to plead guilty to his inconsistencies, with an admission that he could make no satisfactory answer to the original inquiry which had at first appeared so easy." Thus, by this system of cross-examination, he showed the intimate connection between the dialectic method and the logical distribution of particulars into species and genera. The discussion first turns upon the meaning of some generic term; the queries bring the answers into collision with various particulars which it ought not to comprehend, or which it ought to comprehend, but does not. Socrates broke up the one into many by his analytical string of questions, which was a mode of argument by which he separated *real* knowledge from the *conceit* of knowledge, and led to precision in the use of definitions. It was thus that he exposed the false, without aiming even to teach the true; for he generally professed ignorance on his part, and put himself in the attitude of a learner, while by his cross-examinations he made the man from whom he apparently sought knowledge to appear as ignorant as himself, or, still worse, absolutely ridiculous.

Thus Socrates pulled away all the foundations on which a false science had been erected, and indicated the mode by which alone the true could be established. Here he was not unlike Bacon, who pointed out the way whereby science could be advanced, without founding any school or advocating any system; but the Athenian was unlike Bacon in the object of his inquiries. Bacon was disgusted with ineffective *logical* speculations, and Socrates with ineffective *physical* researches. He never suffered a general term to remain undetermined, but applied it at once to particulars, and by questions the purport of which was not comprehended. It was not by positive teaching, but by exciting scientific impulse in the minds of others, or stirring up the analytical faculties, that Socrates manifested originality. It was his aim to force the seekers after truth into the path of inductive generalization, whereby alone trustworthy conclusions could be formed. He thus struck out from his own and other minds that fire which sets light to original thought and stimulates analytical inquiry. He was a religious and intellectual missionary, preparing the way for the Platos and Aristotles of the succeeding age by his severe dialectics. This was his mission, and he declared it by talking. He did not lecture; he conversed. For more than thirty years he discoursed on the principles of morality, until he arrayed against himself enemies who caused him to be put to death, for his teachings had undermined the popular system which the Sophists accepted and practised. He probably might have been acquitted if he had chosen to be, but he did not wish to live after his powers of usefulness had passed away.

The services which Socrates rendered to philosophy, as enumerated by Tennemann, "are twofold, — negative and positive. *Negative,* inasmuch as he avoided all vain discussions; combated mere speculative reasoning on substantial grounds; and had the wisdom to acknowledge ignorance when necessary, but without attempting to determine accurately what is capable and what is not of being accurately known. *Positive*, inasmuch as he examined with great ability the ground directly submitted to our understanding, and of which man is the centre."

Socrates cannot be said to have founded a school, like Xenophanes. He did not bequeath a system of doctrines. He had however his disciples, who followed in the path which he suggested. Among these were Aristippus, Antisthenes, Euclid of Megara, Phædo of Elis, and Plato, all of whom were pupils of Socrates and founders of schools. Some only partially adopted his method, and each differed from the other. Nor can it be said that all of them advanced science. Aristippus, the founder of the Cyreniac school, was a sort of philosophic voluptuary, teaching that pleasure is the end of life. Antisthenes, the founder of the Cynics, was both virtuous and arrogant, placing the supreme good in virtue, but despising speculative science, and maintaining that no man can refute the opinions of another. He made it a virtue to be ragged, hungry, and cold, like the ancient monks; an austere, stern, bitter, reproachful man, who affected to despise all pleasures, — like his own disciple Diogenes, who lived in a tub, and carried on a war between the mind and body, brutal, scornful, proud. To men who maintained that science was impossible, philosophy is not much indebted, although they were disciples of Socrates. Euclid — not the mathematician, who was about a century later — merely gave a new edition of the Eleatic doctrines, and Phædo speculated on the oneness of "the good."

It was not till Plato arose that a more complete system of philosophy was founded. He was born of noble Athenian parents, 429 B. C., the year that Pericles died, and the second year of the Peloponnesian War, — the most active period of Grecian thought. He had a severe education, studying mathematics, poetry, music, rhetoric, and blending these with philosophy. He was only twenty when he found out Socrates, with whom he remained ten years, and from whom he was separated only by death. He then went on his travels, visiting everything worth seeing in his day, especially in Egypt. When he returned he began to teach the doctrines of his master, which he did, like him, gratuitously, in a garden near Athens, planted with lofty plane-trees and adorned with temples and statues. This was called the Academy, and gave a name to his system of philosophy. It is this only with which we have to do. It is not the calm, serious, meditative, isolated man that I would present, but *his contribution* to the developments of philosophy on the principles of his master. Surely no man ever made a richer contribution to this department of human inquiry than Plato. He may not have had the originality or keenness of Socrates, but he was more profound. He was pre-eminently a great thinker, a great logician, skilled in dialectics; and his "Dialogues" are such perfect exercises of dialectical method that the ancients were divided as to whether he was a sceptic or a dogmatist. He adopted the Socratic method and enlarged it. Says Lewes:—

"Analysis, as insisted on by Plato, is the decomposition of the whole into its separate parts,— is seeing the one in many. . . . The individual thing was transitory; the abstract idea was eternal. Only concerning the latter could philosophy occupy itself. Socrates, insisting on proper definitions, had no conception of the classification of those definitions which must constitute philosophy. Plato, by the introduction of this process, shifted philosophy from the ground of inquiries into man and society, which exclusively occupied Socrates, to that of dialectics."

Plato was also distinguished for skill in composition. Dionysius of Halicarnassus classes him with Herodotus and Demosthenes in the perfection of his style, which is characterized by great harmony and rhythm, as well as by a rich variety of elegant metaphors.

Plato made philosophy to consist in the discussion of general terms, or abstract ideas. General terms were synonymous with real existences, and these were the only objects of philosophy. These were called *Ideas*;

and ideas are the basis of his system, or rather the subject-matter of dialectics. He maintained that every general term, or abstract idea, has a real and independent existence; nay, that the mental power of conceiving and combining ideas, as contrasted with the mere impressions received from matter and external phenomena, is the only real and permanent existence. Hence his writings became the great fountain-head of the Ideal philosophy. In his assertion of the real existence of so abstract and supersensuous a thing as an idea, he probably was indebted to Pythagoras, for Plato was a master of the whole realm of philosophical speculation; but his conception of *ideas* as the essence of being is a great advance on that philosopher's conception of *numbers*. He was taught by Socrates that beyond this world of sense there is the world of eternal truth, and that there are certain principles concerning which there can be no dispute. The soul apprehends the idea of goodness, greatness, etc. It is in the celestial world that we are to find the realm of ideas. Now, God is the supreme idea. To know God, then, should be the great aim of life. We know him through the desire which like feels for like. The divinity within feels its affinity with the divinity revealed in beauty, or any other abstract idea. The longing of the soul for beauty is *love*. Love, then, is the bond which unites the human with the divine.

SEEKING AFTER TRUTH.

Beauty is not revealed by harmonious outlines that appeal to the senses, but is *truth;* it is divinity. Beauty, truth, love, these are God, whom it is the supreme desire of the soul to comprehend, and by the contemplation of whom the mortal soul sustains itself. Knowledge of God is the great end of life; and this knowledge is effected by dialectics, for only out of dialectics can correct knowledge come. But man, immersed in the flux of sensualities, can never fully attain this knowledge of God, the object of all rational inquiry. Hence the imperfection of all human knowledge. The supreme good is attainable; it is not attained. God is the immutable good, and justice the rule of the universe. "The vital principle of Plato's philosophy," says Ritter, "is to show that true science is the knowledge of the good, is the eternal contemplation of truth, or ideas; and though man may not be able to apprehend it in its unity, because he is subject to the restraints of the body, he is nevertheless permitted to recognize it imperfectly by calling to mind the eternal measure of existence by which he is in his origin connected." To quote from Ritter again: —

"When we review the doctrines of Plato, it is impossible to deny that they are pervaded with a grand view of life and the universe. This is the noble thought which inspired him to say that God is the constant and immutable good;

the world is good in a state of becoming, and the human soul that in and through which the good in the world is to be consummated. In his sublimer conception he shows himself the worthy disciple of Socrates. . . . While he adopted many of the opinions of his predecessors, and gave due consideration to the results of the earlier philosophy, he did not allow himself to be disturbed by the mass of conflicting theories, but breathed into them the life-giving breath of unity. He may have erred in his attempts to determine the nature of good; still he pointed out to all who aspire to a knowledge of the divine nature an excellent road by which they may arrive at it."

That Plato was one of the greatest lights of the ancient world there can be no reasonable doubt. Nor is it probable that as a dialectician he has ever been surpassed, while his purity of life and his lofty inquiries and his belief in God and immortality make him, in an ethical point of view, the most worthy of the disciples of Socrates. He was to the Greeks what Kant was to the Germans; and these two great thinkers resemble each other in the structure of their minds and their relations to society.

The ablest part of the lectures of Archer Butler, of Dublin, is devoted to the Platonic philosophy. It is at once a criticism and a eulogium. No modern writer has written more enthusiastically of what he considers the crowning excellence of the Greek philosophy. The dialectics of Plato, his ideal theory, his physics, his psychology, and his ethics are most ably discussed, and in the spirit of a loving and eloquent disciple. Butler represents the philosophy which he so much admires as a contemplation of, and a tendency to, the absolute and eternal good. As the admirers of Ralph Waldo Emerson claim that he, more than any other man of our times, entered into the spirit of the Platonic philosophy, I introduce some of his most striking paragraphs of subdued but earnest admiration of the greatest intellect of the ancient Pagan world, hoping that they may be clearer to others than they are to me: —

"These sentences [of Plato] contain the culture of nations; these are the corner-stone of schools; these are the fountain-head of literatures. A discipline it is in logic, arithmetic, taste, symmetry, poetry, language, rhetoric, ontology, morals, or practical wisdom. There never was such a range of speculation. Out of Plato come all things that are still written and debated among men of thought. Great havoc makes he among our originalities. We have reached the mountain from which all these drift-bowlders were detached. . . . Plato, in Egypt and in Eastern pilgrimages, imbibed the idea of one Deity, in which all things are absorbed. The unity of Asia and the detail of Europe, the infinitude of the Asiatic soul and the defining, result-loving, machine-making, surface-seeking, opera-going Europe

Plato came to join, and by contact to enhance the energy of each. The excellence of Europe and Asia is in his brain. Metaphysics and natural philosophy expressed the genius of Europe; he substricts the religion of Asia as the base. In short, a balanced soul was born, perceptive of the two elements. . . . The physical philosophers had sketched each his theory of the world; the theory of atoms, of fire, of flux, of spirit, — theories mechanical and chemical in their genius. Plato, a master of mathematics, studious of all natural laws and causes, feels these, as second causes, to be no theories of the world, but bare inventories and lists. To the study of Nature he therefore prefixes the dogma, — ' Let us declare the cause which led the Supreme Ordainer to produce and compose the universe. He was good; . . . he wished that all things should be as much as possible like himself.' . . .

"Plato . . . represents the privilege of the intellect, — the power, namely, of carrying up every fact to successive platforms, and so disclosing in every fact a germ of expansion. . . . These expansions, or extensions, consist in continuing the spiritual sight where the horizon falls on our natural vision, and by this second sight discovering the long lines of law which shoot in every direction. . . . His definition of ideas as what is simple, permanent, uniform, and self-existent, forever discriminating them from the notions of the understanding, marks an era in the world.

The great disciple of Plato was Aristotle, and he carried on the philosophical movement which Socrates had started to the highest limit that it ever reached in the ancient world. He was born at Stagira, 384 B. C., and early evinced an insatiable thirst for knowledge. When Plato returned from Sicily Aristotle joined his disciples at Athens, and was his pupil for seventeen years. On the death of Plato, he went on his travels and became the tutor of Alexander the Great, and in 335 B. C. returned to Athens after an absence of twelve years, and set up a school in the Lyceum. He taught while walking up and down the shady paths which surrounded it, from which habit he obtained the name of the Peripatetic, which has clung to his name and philosophy. His school had a great celebrity, and from it proceeded illustrious philosophers, statesmen, historians, and orators. Aristotle taught for thirteen years, during which time he composed most of his greater works. He not only wrote on dialectics and logic, but also on physics in its various departments. His work on "The History of Animals" was deemed so important that his royal pupil Alexander presented him with eight hundred talents — an enormous sum — for the collection of materials. He also wrote on ethics and politics, history and rhetoric, — pouring out letters, poems, and speeches, three-fourths of which are lost. He was one of the most voluminous writers of antiquity, and probably is the most learned man whose writings have come down to us. Nor has any one of the ancients exercised upon the thinking of succeeding ages so wide an influence. He was an oracle until the revival of learning. Hegel says: —

"Aristotle penetrated into the whole mass, into every department of the universe of things, and subjected to the comprehension its scattered wealth; and the greater number of the philosophical sciences owe to him their separation and commencement."

He is also the father of the history of philosophy, since he gives an historical review of the way in which the subject has been hitherto treated by the earlier philosophers. Says Adolph Stahr: —

"Plato made the external world the region of the incomplete and bad, of the contradictory and the false, and recognized absolute truth only in the eternal immutable ideas. Aristotle laid down the proposition that the idea, which cannot of itself fashion itself into reality, is powerless, and has only a potential existence; and that it becomes a living reality only by realizing itself in a creative manner by means of its own energy."

There can be no doubt as to Aristotle's marvellous power of systematizing. Collecting together all the results of ancient speculation, he so combined them into a co-ordinate system that for a thousand years he reigned supreme in the schools. From a literary point of view, Plato was doubtless his superior; but Plato was a poet, making philosophy divine and musical, while Aristotle's investigations spread over a far wider range. He differed from Plato chiefly in relation to the doctrine of ideas, without however resolving the difficulty which divided them. As he made matter to be the eternal ground of phenomena, he reduced the notion of it to a precision it never before enjoyed, and established thereby a necessary element in human science. But being bound to matter, he did not soar, as Plato did, into the higher regions of speculation; nor did he entertain as lofty views of God or of immortality. Neither did he have as high an ideal of human life; his definition of the highest good was a perfect practical activity in a perfect life.

With Aristotle closed the great Socratic movement in the history of speculation. When Socrates appeared there was a general prevalence of scepticism, arising from the unsatisfactory speculations respecting Nature. He removed this scepticism by inventing a new method of investigation, and by withdrawing the mind from the contemplation of Nature to the study of man himself. He bade men to look inward. Plato accepted his method, but applied it more universally. Like Socrates, however, ethics were the great subject of his inquiries, to which physics were only subordinate.

The problem he sought to solve was the way to live like the Deity; he would contemplate truth as the great aim of life. With Aristotle, ethics formed only one branch of attention; his main inquiries were in reference to physics and metaphysics. He thus, by bringing these into the region of inquiry, paved the way for a new epoch of scepticism.

Both Plato and Aristotle taught that reason alone can form science; but, as we have said, Aristotle differed from his master respecting the theory of ideas. He did not deny to ideas a *subjective* existence, but he did deny that they have an objective existence. He maintained that individual things alone *exist;* and if individuals alone exist, they can be known only by *sensation*. Sensation thus becomes the basis of knowledge. Plato made *reason* the basis of knowledge, but Aristotle made *experience* that basis. Plato directed man to the contemplation of Ideas; Aristotle, to the observation of Nature. Instead of proceeding synthetically and dialectically like Plato, he pursues an analytic course. His method is hence inductive, — the derivation of certain principles from a sum of given facts and phenomena. It would seem that positive science began with Aristotle, since he maintained that experience furnishes the principles of every science; but while his conception was just, there was not at that time a sufficient amount of experience from which to generalize with effect. It is only a most extensive and exhaustive examination of the accuracy of a proposition which will warrant secure reasoning upon it. Aristotle reasoned without sufficient certainty of the major premise of his syllogisms.

Aristotle was the father of logic, and Hegel and Kant think there has been no improvement upon it since his day. This became to him the real organon of science. "He supposed it was not merely the instrument of thought, but the instrument of investigation." Hence it was futile for purposes of discovery, although important to aid processes of thought. Induction and syllogism are the two great features of his system of logic. The one sets out from particulars already known to arrive at a conclusion; the other sets out from some general principle to arrive at particulars. The latter more particularly characterized his logic, which he presented in sixteen forms, the whole evincing much ingenuity and skill in construction, and presenting at the same time a useful dialectical exercise. This syllogistic process of reasoning would be incontrovertible, if the *general* were better known than the *particular*; but it is only by induction, which proceeds from the world of experience, that we reach the higher world of cognition. Thus Aristotle made speculation subordinate to logical distinctions, and his system, when carried out by the mediæval Schoolmen, led to a spirit of useless quibbling. Instead of interrogating Nature they interrogated their own minds, and no great discoveries were made. From want of proper knowledge of the conditions of scientific inquiry, the method of Aristotle became fruitless for him; but it was the key by which future investigators were enabled to classify and utilize their vastly greater collection of facts and materials.

Though Aristotle wrote in a methodical manner, his writings exhibit great parsimony of language. There is no fascination in his style. It is without ornament, and very condensed. His merit consisted in great logical precision and scrupulous exactness in the employment of terms.

Philosophy, as a great system of dialectics, as an analysis of the power and faculties of the mind, as a method to pursue inquiries, culminated in Aristotle. He completed the great fabric of which Thales laid the foundation. The subsequent schools of philosophy directed attention to ethical and practical questions, rather than to intellectual phenomena. The Sceptics, like Pyrrho, had only negative doctrines, and held in disdain those inquiries which sought to penetrate the mysteries of existence. They did not believe that absolute truth was attainable by man; and they attacked the prevailing systems with great plausibility. They pointed out the uncertainty of things, and the folly of striving to comprehend them.

The Epicureans despised the investigations of philosophy, since in their view these did not contribute to happiness. The subject of their inquiries was happiness, not truth. What will promote this? was the subject of their speculation. Epicurus, born 342 B. C., contended that pleasure was happiness; that pleasure should be sought not for its own sake, but with a view to the happiness of life obtained by it. He taught that happiness was inseparable from virtue, and that its enjoyments should be limited. He was averse to costly pleasures, and regarded contentedness with a little to be a great good. He placed wealth not in great possessions, but in few wants. He sought to widen the domain of pleasure and narrow that of pain, and regarded a passionless state of life as the highest. Nor did he dread death, which was deliverance from misery, as the Buddhists think. Epicurus has been much misunderstood, and his doctrines were subsequently perverted, especially when the arts of life were brought into the service of luxury, and a gross materialism was the great feature of society. Epicurus had much of the spirit of a practical philosopher, although very little of the earnest cravings of a religious man. He himself led a virtuous life, because he thought it was wiser and better and more productive of happiness to be virtuous, not because it was his duty. His writings were very voluminous, and in his tranquil garden he led a peaceful life of study and enjoyment. His followers, and they were numerous, were led into luxury and effeminacy, — as was to be expected from a sceptical and irreligious philosophy, the great principle of which was that whatever is pleasant should be the object of existence. Sir James Mackintosh says : —

"To Epicurus we owe the general concurrence of reflecting men in succeeding times in the important truth that men cannot be happy without a virtuous frame of mind and course of life, — a truth of inestimable value, not peculiar to the Epicureans, but placed by their exaggerations in a stronger light; a truth, it must be added, of less importance as a motive to right conduct than to the completeness of moral theory, which, however, it is very far from solely constituting. With that truth the Epicureans blended another position, — that because virtue promotes happiness, every act of virtue must be done in order to promote the happiness of the agent. Although, therefore, he has the merit of having more strongly inculcated the connection of virtue with happiness, yet his doctrine is justly charged with indisposing the mind to those exalted and generous sentiments without which no pure, elevated, bold, or tender virtues can exist."

SEEKING AFTER TRUTH.

The Stoics were a large and celebrated sect of philosophers; but they added nothing to the domain of thought, — they created no system, they invented no new method, they were led into no new psychological inquiries. Their inquiries were chiefly ethical; and since ethics are a great part of the system of Greek philosophy, the Stoics are well worthy of attention. Some of the greatest men of antiquity are numbered among them, — like Seneca, Epictetus, and Marcus Aurelius. The philosophy they taught was morality, and this was eminently practical and also elevated.

The founder of this sect, Zeno, was born, it is supposed, on the island of Cyprus, about the year 350 B. C. He was the son of wealthy parents, but was reduced to poverty by misfortune. He was so good a man, and so profoundly revered by the Athenians, that they intrusted to him the keys of their citadel. He lived in a degenerate age, when scepticism and sensuality were eating out the life and vigor of Grecian society, when Greek civilization was rapidly passing away, when ancient creeds had lost their majesty, and general levity and folly overspread the land. Deeply impressed with the prevailing laxity of morals and the absence of religion, he lifted up his voice more as a reformer than as an inquirer after truth, and taught for more than fifty years in a place called the *Stoa*, "the Porch," which had once been the resort of the poets. Hence the name of his school. He was chiefly absorbed with ethical questions, although he studied profoundly the systems of the old philosophers. "The Sceptics had attacked both perception and reason. They had shown that perception is after all based upon appearance, and appearance is not a certainty; and they showed that reason is unable to distinguish between appearance and certainty, since it had nothing but phenomena to build upon, and since there is no criterion to apply to reason itself." Then they proclaimed philosophy a failure, and without foundation. But Zeno, taking a stand on commonsense, fought for morality, as did Buddha before him, and long after him Reid and Beattie, when they combated the scepticism of Hume.

Philosophy, according to Zeno and other Stoics, was intimately connected with the duties of practical life. The contemplation, meditation, and thought recommended by Plato and Aristotle seemed only a covert recommendation of selfish enjoyment. The wisdom which it should be the aim of life to attain is virtue; and virtue is to live harmoniously with Nature. To live harmoniously with Nature is to exclude all personal ends; hence pleasure is to be disregarded, and pain is to be despised. And as all moral action must be in harmony with Nature the law of destiny is supreme, and all things move according to immutable fate. With the predominant tendency to the universal which characterized their system, the Stoics taught that the sage ought to regard himself as a citizen of the world rather than of any particular city or state. They made four things to be indispensable to virtue, — a knowledge of *good* and *evil*, which is the province of the reason; *temperance*, a knowledge of the due regulation of the sensual passions; *fortitude*, a conviction that it is good to suffer what is necessary; and *justice*, or acquaintance with what ought to be to every individual. They made *perfection* necessary to virtue; hence the severity of their system. The perfect sage, according to them, is raised above all influence of external events; he submits to the law of destiny; he is exempt from desire and fear, joy or sorrow; he is not governed even by what he is exposed to necessarily, like sorrow and pain; he is free from the restraints of passion; he is like a god in his mental placidity. Nor must the sage live only for himself, but for others also; he is a member of the whole body of mankind. He ought to marry, and to take part in public affairs; but he is to attack error and vice with uncompromising sternness, and will never weakly give way to compassion or forgiveness. Yet with this ideal the Stoics were forced to admit that virtue, like true knowledge, although theoretically attainable is practically beyond the reach of man. They were discontented with themselves and with all around them, and looked upon all institutions as corrupt. They had a profound contempt for their age, and for what modern society calls "success in life;" but it cannot be denied that they practised a lofty and stern virtue in their degenerate times. Their God was made subject to Fate; and he was a material god, synonymous with Nature. Thus their system was pantheistic. But they maintained the dignity of reason, and sought to attain to virtues which it is not in the power of man fully to reach.

Zeno lived to the extreme old age of ninety-eight, although his constitution was not strong. He retained his powers by great abstemiousness, living chiefly on figs, honey, and bread. He was a modest and retiring man, seldom mingling with a crowd, or admitting the society of more than two or three friends at a time. He was as plain in his dress as he was frugal in his habits, — a man of great decorum and propriety of manners, resembling noticeably in his life and doctrines the Chinese sage Confucius. And yet this good man, a pattern to the loftiest characters of his age, strangled himself. Suicide was not deemed a crime by his followers, among whom were some of the most faultless men of antiquity, especially among the Romans. The doctrines of Zeno were never popular, and were confined to a small though influential party.

With the Stoics ended among the Greeks all inquiry of a philosophical nature worthy of especial mention, until centuries later, when philosophy was revived in the Christian schools of Alexandria, where the Hebrew element of faith was united with the Greek ideal of reason. The struggles of so many great thinkers, from Thales to Aristotle, all ended in doubt and in despair. It was discovered that all of them were wrong, or rather partial; and their error was without a remedy, until "the fulness of time" should reveal more clearly the plan of the great temple of Truth, in which they were laying foundation stones.

The bright and glorious period of Greek philosophy was from Socrates to Aristotle. Philosophical inquiries began about the origin of things, and ended with an elaborate systematization of the forms of thought, which was the most magnificent triumph that the unaided intellect of man ever achieved. Socrates does not found a school, nor elaborate a system. He reveals most precious truths, and stimulates the youth who listen to his instructions by the doctrine that it is the duty of man to pursue a knowledge of himself which is to be sought in that divine reason which dwells within him, and which also rules the world. He believes in science; he loves truth for its own sake; he loves virtue, which consists in the knowledge of the good.

Plato seizes the weapons of his great master, and is imbued with his spirit. He is full of hope for science and humanity. With soaring boldness he directs his inquiries to futurity, dissatisfied with the present, and cherishing a fond hope of a better existence. He speculates on God and the soul. He is not much interested in physical phenomena; he does not, like Thales, strive to find out the beginning of all things, but the highest good, by which his immortal soul may be refreshed and prepared for the future life, in which he firmly believes. The sensible is an impenetrable empire; but ideas are certitudes, and upon these he dwells with rapt and mystical enthusiasm, — a great poetical rhapsodist, severe dialectician as he is, believing in truth and beauty and goodness.

Then Aristotle, following out the method of his teachers, attempts to exhaust experience, and directs his inquiries into the outward world of sense and observation, but all with the view of discovering from phenomena the unconditional truth, in which he too believes. But everything in this world is fleeting and transitory, and therefore it is not easy to arrive at truth. A cold doubt creeps into the experimental mind of Aristotle, with all his learning and his logic.

The Epicureans arise. Misreading or corrupting the purer teaching of their founder, they place their hopes in sensual enjoyment. They despair of truth.

But the world will not be abandoned to despair. The Stoics rebuke the impiety which is blended with sensualism, and place their hopes on virtue. Yet it is unattainable virtue, while their God is not a moral governor, but subject to necessity.

Thus did those old giants grope about, for they did not know the God who was revealed unto the more spiritual sense of Abraham, Moses, David, and Isaiah. And yet with all their errors they were the greatest benefactors of the ancient world. They gave dignity to intellectual inquiries, while by their lives they set examples of a pure morality.

The Romans added absolutely nothing to the philosophy of the Greeks. Nor were they much interested in any speculative inquiries. It was only the ethical views of the old sages which had attraction or force to them. They were too material to love pure subjective inquiries. They had conquered the land; they disdained the empire of the air.

There were doubtless students of the Greek philosophy among the Romans, perhaps as early as Cato the Censor. But there were only two persons of note in Rome who wrote philosophy, till the time of Cicero, — Aurafanius and Rubinus, — and these were Epicureans.

Cicero was the first to systematize the philosophy which contributed so greatly to his intellectual culture.

But even he added nothing; he was only a commentator and expositor. Nor did he seek to found a system or a school, but merely to influence and instruct men of his own rank. Those subjects which had the greatest attraction for the Grecian schools Cicero regarded as beyond the power of human cognition, and therefore looked upon the practical as the proper domain of human inquiry. Yet he held logic in great esteem, as furnishing rules for methodical investigation. He adopted the doctrine of Socrates as to the pursuit of moral good, and regarded the duties which grow out of the relations of human society as preferable to those of pursuing scientific researches. He had a great contempt for knowledge which could lead neither to the clear apprehension of certitude nor to practical applications. He thought it impossible to arrive at a knowledge of God, or the nature of the soul, or the origin of the world; and thus he was led to look upon the sensible and the present as of more importance than inconclusive inductions, or deductions from a truth not satisfactorily established.

Cicero was an eclectic, seizing on what was true and clear in the ancient systems, and disregarding what was simply a matter of speculation. This is especially seen in his treatise "De Finibus Bonorum et Malorum," in which the opinions of all the Grecian schools concerning the supreme good are expounded and compared. Nor does he hesitate to declare that the highest happiness consists in the knowledge of Nature and science which is the true source of pleasure both to gods and men. Yet these are but hopes, in which it does not become us to indulge. It is the actual, the real, the practical, which pre-eminently claims attention, — in other words, the knowledge which will furnish man with a guide and rule of life. Even in the consideration of moral questions Cicero is pursued by the conflict of opinions, although in this department he is most at home. The points he is most anxious to establish are the doctrines of God and the soul. These are most fully treated in his essay "De Natura Deorum," in which he submits the doctrines of the Epicureans and the Stoics to the objections of the Academy. He admits that man is unable to form true conceptions of God, but acknowledges the necessity of assuming one supreme God as the creator and ruler of all things, moving all things, remote from all mortal mixture, and endued with eternal motion in himself. He seems to believe in a divine providence ordering good to man, in the soul's immortality, in free-will, in the dignity of human nature, in the dominion of reason, in the restraint of the passions as necessary to virtue, in a life of public utility, in an immutable morality, in the imitation of the divine.

Thus there is little of original thought in the moral theories of Cicero, which are the result of observation rather than of any philosophical principle. We might enumerate his various opinions, and show what an enlightened mind he possessed; but this would not be the development of philosophy. His views, interesting as they are, and generally wise and lofty, do not indicate any progress of the science. He merely repeats earlier doctrines. These were not without their utility, since they had great influence on the Latin fathers of the Christian Church. He was esteemed for his general enlightenment. He softened down the extreme views of the great thinkers before his day, and clearly unfolded what had become obscured. He was a critic of philosophy, an expositor whom we can scarcely spare.

If anybody advanced philosophy among the Romans it was Epictetus, and even he only in the realm of ethics. Quintius Sextius, in the time of Augustus, had revived the Pythagorean doctrines. Seneca had recommended the severe morality of the Stoics, but added nothing that was not previously known.

The greatest light among the Romans was the Phrygian slave Epictetus, who was born about fifty years after the birth of Jesus Christ, and taught in the time of the Emperor Domitian. Though he did not leave any written treatises, his doctrines were preserved and handed down by his disciple Arrian, who had for him the reverence that Plato had for Socrates. The loftiness of his recorded views has made some to think that he must have been indebted to Christianity, for no one before him revealed precepts so much in accordance with its spirit. He was a Stoic, but he held in the highest estimation Socrates and Plato. It is not for the solution of metaphysical questions that he was remarkable. He was not a dialectician, but a moralist, and as such takes the highest ground of all the old inquirers after truth. With him, as to Cicero and Seneca, philosophy is the wisdom of life. He sets no value on logic, nor much on physics; but he reveals sentiments of great simplicity and grandeur. His great idea is the purification of the soul. He believes in the severest self-denial; he would guard against the siren spells of pleasure; he would make men feel that in order to be good they must first feel that they are evil. He condemns suicide, although it had been defended by the Stoics. He would complain of no one, not even as to injustice; he would not injure his enemies; he would pardon all offences; he would feel universal compassion, since men sin from ignorance; he would not easily blame, since we have none to condemn but ourselves. He would not strive after honor or office, since we put ourselves in subjection to that we seek or prize; he would constantly bear in mind that all things are transitory, and that they are not our own. He would bear evils with patience, even as he would practise self-denial of pleasure. He would, in short, be calm, free, keep in subjection his passions, avoid self-indulgence, and practise a broad charity and benevolence. He felt that he owed all to God, — that all was his gift, and that we should thus live in accordance with his will; that we should be grateful not only for our bodies, but for our souls and reason, by which we attain to greatness. And if God has given us such a priceless gift, we should be contented, and not even seek to alter our external relations, which are doubtless for the best. We should wish, indeed, for only what God wills and sends, and we should avoid pride and haughtiness as well as discontent, and seek to fulfil our allotted part.

Such were the moral precepts of Epictetus, in which we see the nearest approach to Christianity that had been made in the ancient world, although there is no proof or probability that he knew anything of Christ or the Christians. And these sublime truths had a great influence, especially on the mind of the most lofty and pure of all the Roman emperors, Marcus Aurelius, who *lived* the principles he had learned from the slave, and whose "Thoughts" are still held in admiration.

Thus did the philosophic speculations about the beginning of things lead to elaborate systems of thought, and end in practical rules of life, until in spirit they had, with Epictetus, harmonized with many of the revealed truths which Christ and his Apostles laid down for the regeneration of the world. Who cannot see in the inquiries of the old Philosopher, — whether into Nature, or the operations of mind, or the existence of God, or the immortality of the soul, or the way to happiness and virtue, — a magnificent triumph of human genius, such as has been exhibited in no other department of human science? Nay, who does not rejoice to see in this slow but ever-advancing development of man's comprehension of the truth the inspiration of that Divine Teacher, that Holy Spirit, which shall at last lead man into all truth?

We regret that our limits preclude a more extended view of the various systems which the old sages propounded, — systems full of errors yet also marked by important gains, but, whether false or true, showing a marvellous reach of the human understanding. Modern researches have discarded many opinions that were highly valued in their day, yet philosophy in its methods of reasoning is scarcely advanced since the time of Aristotle, while the subjects which agitated the Grecian schools have been from time to time revived and rediscussed, and are still unsettled. If any intellectual pursuit has gone round in perpetual circles, incapable apparently of progression or rest, it is that glorious study of philosophy which has tasked more than any other the mightiest intellects of this world, and which, progressive or not, will never be relinquished without the loss of what is most valuable in human culture.

AUTHORITIES.

For original authorities in reference to the matter of this chapter, read Diogenes Laertius's Lives of the Philosophers; the Writings of Plato and Aristotle; Cicero, De Natura Deorum, De Oratore, De Officiis, De Divinatione, De Finibus, Tusculanæ Disputationes; Xenophon, Memorabilia; Boethius, De Consolatione Philosophiæ; Lucretius.

The great modern authorities are the Germans, and these are very numerous. Among the most famous writers on the history of philosophy are Brucker, Hegel, Brandis, I. G. Buhle, Tennemann, Ritter, Plessing, Schwegler, Hermann, Meiners, Stallbaum, and Spiegel. The History of Ritter is well translated, and is always learned and suggestive. Tennemann, translated by Morell, is a good manual, brief but clear. In connection with the writings of the Germans, the great work of the French Cousin should be consulted.

The English historians of ancient philosophy are not so numerous as the Germans. The work of Enfield is based on Brucker, or is rather an abridgment. Archer Butler's Lectures are suggestive and able, but discursive and vague. Grote has written learnedly on Socrates and the other great lights. Lewes's Biographical History of Philosophy has the merit of clearness, and is very interesting, but rather superficial. See also Thomas Stanley's History of Philosophy, and the articles in Smith's Dictionary on the leading ancient philosophers. J. W. Donaldson's continuation of K. O. Müller's History of the Literature of Ancient Greece is learned, and should be consulted with Thompson's Notes on Archer Butler. Schleiermacher, on Socrates, translated by Bishop Thirlwall, is well worth attention. There are also fine articles in the Encyclopædias Britannica and Metropolitana.

SOCRATES.

470–399 B.C.

GREEK PHILOSOPHY.

SOCRATES.

GREEK PHILOSOPHY.

TO Socrates the world owes a new method in philosophy and a great example in morals: and it would be difficult to settle whether his influence has been greater as a sage or as a moralist. In either light he is one of the august names of history. He has been venerated for more than two thousand years as a teacher of wisdom, and as a martyr for the truths he taught. He did not commit his precious thoughts to writing; that work was done by his disciples, even as his exalted worth has been published by them, especially by Plato and Xenophon. And if the Greek philosophy did not culminate in him, yet he laid down those principles by which only it could be advanced. As a system-maker, both Plato and Aristotle were greater than he; yet for original genius he was probably their superior, and in important respects he was their master. As a good man, battling with infirmities and temptations and coming off triumphantly, the ancient world has furnished no prouder example.

He was born about 470 or 469 years B. C., and therefore may be said to belong to that brilliant age of Grecian literature and art when Prodicus was teaching rhetoric, and Democritus was speculating about the doctrine of atoms, and Phidias was ornamenting temples, and Alcibiades was giving banquets, and Aristophanes was writing comedies, and Euripides was composing tragedies, and Aspasia was setting fashions, and Cimon was fighting battles, and Pericles was making Athens the centre of Grecian civilization. But he died thirty years after Pericles; so that what is most interesting in his great career took place during and after the Peloponnesian war, — an age still interesting, but not so brilliant as the one which immediately preceded it. It was the age of the Sophists, — those popular but superficial teachers who claimed to be the most advanced of their generation; men who were doubtless accomplished, but were cynical, sceptical, and utilitarian, placing a high estimate on popular favor and an outside life, but very little on pure subjective truth or the wants of the soul. They were paid teachers, and sought pupils from the sons of the rich, — the more eminent of them being Protagoras, Gorgias, Hippias, and Prodicus; men who travelled from city to city, exciting great admiration for their rhetorical skill, and really improving the public speaking of popular orators. They also taught science to a limited extent, and it was through them that Athenian youth mainly acquired what little knowledge they had of arithmetic and geometry. In loftiness of character they were not equal to those Ionian philosophers, who, prior to Socrates, in the fifth century B. C., speculated on the great problems of the material universe,— the origin of the world, the nature of matter, and the source of power, — and who, if they did not make discoveries, yet evinced great intellectual force.

It was in this sceptical and irreligious age, when all classes were devoted to pleasure and money-making, but when there was great cultivation, especially in arts, that Socrates arose, whose "appearance," says Grote, "was a moral phenomenon."

He was the son of a poor sculptor, and his mother was a midwife. His family was unimportant, although it belonged to an ancient Attic *gens*. Socrates was rescued from his father's workshop by a wealthy citizen who perceived his genius, and who educated him at his own expense. He was twenty when he conversed with Parmenides and Zeno; he was twenty-eight when Phidias adorned the Parthenon; he was forty when he fought at Potidæa and rescued Alcibiades. At this period he was most distinguished for his physical strength and endurance, — a brave and patriotic soldier, insensible to heat and cold, and, though temperate in his habits, capable of drinking more wine, without becoming intoxicated, than anybody in Athens. His powerful physique and sensual nature inclined him to self-indulgence, but he early learned to restrain both appetites and passions. His physiognomy was ugly and his person repulsive; he was awkward, obese, and ungainly; his nose was flat, his lips were thick, and his neck large; he rolled his eyes, went barefooted, and wore a dirty old cloak. He spent his time chiefly in the market-place, talking with everybody, old or young, rich or poor, — soldiers, politicians, artisans, or students; visiting even Aspasia, the cultivated, wealthy courtesan, with whom he formed a friendship; so that, although he was very poor, — his whole property being only five minæ (about fifty dollars) a year, — it would seem he lived in "good society."

The ancient Pagans were not so exclusive and aristocratic as the Christians of our day, who are ambitious of social position. Socrates never seemed to think about his social position at all, and uniformly acted as if he were well known and prominent. He was listened to because he was eloquent. His conversation is said to have been charming, and even fascinating. He was an original and ingenious man, different from everybody else, and was therefore what we call "a character."

But there was nothing austere or gloomy about him. Though lofty in his inquiries, and serious in his mind he resembled neither a Jewish prophet nor a mediæval sage in his appearance. He looked rather like a Silenus, — very witty, cheerful, good-natured, jocose, and disposed to make people laugh. He enjoined no austerities or penances. He was very attractive to the young, and tolerant of human infirmities, even when he gave the best advice. He was the most human of teachers. Alcibiades was completely fascinated by his talk, and made good resolutions.

His great peculiarity in conversation was to ask questions, — sometimes to gain information, but oftener to puzzle and raise a laugh. He sought to expose ignorance, when it was pretentious; he made all the quacks and shams appear ridiculous. His irony was tremendous; nobody could stand before his searching and unexpected questions, and he made nearly every one with whom he conversed appear either as a fool or an ignoramus. He asked his questions with great apparent modesty, and thus drew a mesh over his opponents from which they could not extricate themselves. His process was the *reductio ad absurdum*. Hence he drew upon himself the wrath of the Sophists He had no intellectual arrogance, since he professed to know nothing himself, although he was conscious of his own intellectual superiority. He was contented to show that others knew no more than he. He had no passion for admiration, no political ambition, no desire for social distinction; and he associated with men not for what they could do for him, but for what he could do for them. Although poor, he charged nothing for his teachings. He seemed to despise riches since riches could only adorn or pamper the body. He did not live in a cell or a cave or a tub, but among the people, as an apostle. He must have accepted gifts, since his means of living were exceedingly small, even for Athens.

He was very practical, even while he lived above the world, absorbed in lofty contemplations. He was always talking with such as the skin-dressers and leather-dealers, using homely language for his illustrations, and uttering plain truths. Yet he was equally at home with poets and philosophers and statesmen. He did not take much interest in that knowledge which was applied merely to rising in the world. Though plain, practical, and even homely in his conversation, he was not utilitarian. Science had no charm to him, since it was directed to utilitarian ends and was uncertain. His sayings had such a lofty, hidden wisdom that very few people understood him: his utterances seemed either paradoxical, or unintelligible, or sophistical. "To the mentally proud and mentally feeble he was equally a bore." Most people probably thought him a nuisance, since he was always about with his questions, puzzling some, confuting others, and reproving all, — careless of love or hatred, and contemptuous of all conventionalities. So severely dialectical was he that he seemed to be a hair-splitter. The very Sophists, whose ignorance and pretension he exposed, looked upon him as a quibbler; although there were some — so severely trained was the Grecian mind — who saw the drift of his questions, and admired his skill. Probably there are few educated people in these times who could have understood him any more easily than a modern audience, even of scholars, could take in one of the orations of Demosthenes, although they might laugh at the jokes of the sage, and be impressed with the invectives of the orator.

And yet there were defects in Socrates. He was most provokingly sarcastic; he turned everything to ridicule; he remorselessly punctured every gas-bag he met; he heaped contempt on every snob; he threw stones at every glass house, — and everybody lived in one. He was not quite just to the Sophists, for they did not pretend to teach the higher life, but chiefly rhetoric, which is useful in its way. And if they loved applause and riches, and attached themselves to those whom they could utilize, they were not different from most fashionable teachers in any age. And then Socrates was not very delicate in his tastes. He was too much carried away by the fascinations of Aspasia, when he knew that she was not virtuous. — although it was doubtless her remarkable intellect which most attracted him, not her physical beauty; since in the "Menexenus" (by many ascribed to Plato) he is made to recite at length one of her long orations, and in the "Symposium" he is made to appear absolutely indelicate in his conduct with Alcibiades, and to make what would be abhorrent to us a matter of irony, although there was the severest control of the passions.

To me it has always seemed a strange thing that such an ugly, satirical, provoking man could have won and retained the love of Xanthippe, especially since he was so careless of his dress, and did so little to provide for the wants of the household. I do not wonder that she scolded him, or became very violent in her temper; since, in her worst tirades, he only provokingly laughed at her. A modern Christian woman of society would have left him. But perhaps in Pagan Athens she could not have got a divorce. It is only in these enlightened and progressive times that women desert their husbands when they are tantalizing, or when they do not properly support the family, or spend their time at the clubs or in society,— into which it would seem that Socrates was received, even the best, barefooted and dirty as he was, and for his intellectual gifts alone. Think of such a man being the oracle of a modern salon, either in Paris, London, or New York, with his repulsive appearance, and tantalizing and provoking irony. But in artistic Athens, at one time, he was all the fashion. Everybody liked to hear him talk. Everybody was both amused and instructed. He provoked no envy, since he affected modesty and ignorance, apparently asking his questions for information, and was so meanly clad, and lived in such a poor way. Though he provoked animosities, he had many friends. If his language was sarcastic, his affections were kind. He was always surrounded by the most gifted men of his time. The wealthy Crito constantly attended him; Plato and Xenophon were enthusiastic pupils; even Alcibiades was charmed by his conversation; Apollodorus and Antisthenes rarely quitted his side; Cebes and Simonides came from Thebes to hear him; Isocrates and Aristippus followed in his train; Euclid of Megara sought his society, at the risk of his life; the tyrant Critias, and even the Sophist Protagoras, acknowledged his marvellous power.

But I cannot linger longer on the man, with his gifts and peculiarities. More important things demand our attention. I propose briefly to show his contributions to philosophy and ethics.

In regard to the first, I will not dwell on his method, which is both subtle and dialectical. We are not Greeks. Yet it was his method which revolutionized philosophy. That was original. He saw this, — that the theories of his day were mere opinions; even the lofty speculations of the Ionian philosophers were dreams, and the teachings of the Sophists were mere words. He despised both dreams and words. Speculations ended in the indefinite and insoluble; words ended in rhetoric. Neither dreams nor words revealed the true, the beautiful, and the good,—which, to his mind, were the only realities, the only sure foundation for a philosophical system.

So he propounded certain questions, which, when answered, produced glaring contradictions, from which disputants shrank. Their conclusions broke down their assumptions. They stood convicted of ignorance, to which all his artful and subtle questions tended, and which it was his aim to prove. He showed that they did not know what they affirmed. He proved that their definitions were wrong or incomplete, since they logically led to contradictions; and he showed that for purposes of disputation the same meaning must always attach to the same word, since in ordinary language terms have different meanings, partly true and partly false, which produce confusion in argument. He would be precise and definite, and use the utmost rigor of language, without which inquirers and disputants would not understand each other. Every definition should include the whole thing, and nothing else; otherwise, people would not know what they were talking about, and would be forced into absurdities.

Thus arose the celebrated "definitions," — the first step in Greek philosophy, — intending to show what *is*, and what *is not*. After demonstrating what is not, Socrates advanced to the demonstration of what is, and thus laid a foundation for certain knowledge: thus he arrived at clear conceptions of justice, friendship, patriotism, courage, and other certitudes, on which truth is based. He wanted only positive truth, — something to build upon, — like Bacon and all great inquirers. Having reached the certain, he would apply it to all the relations of life, and to all kinds of knowledge. Unless knowledge is certain, it is worthless, — there is no foundation to build upon. Uncertain or indefinite knowledge is no knowledge at all; it may be very pretty, or amusing, or ingenious, but no more valuable for philosophical research than poetry or dreams or speculations.

How far the "definitions" of Socrates led to the solution of the great problems of philosophy, in the hands of such dialecticians as Plato and Aristotle, I will not attempt to enter upon here; but this I think I am warranted in saying, that the main object and aim of Socrates, as a teacher of philosophy, were to establish certain elemental truths, concerning which there could be no dispute, and then to reason from them, — since they were not mere assumptions, but certitudes, and certitudes also which appealed to human consciousness, and therefore could not be overthrown. If I were teaching metaphysics, it would be necessary for me to make clear this method, — the questions and definitions by which Socrates is thought to have laid the foundation of true knowledge, and therefore of all healthful advance in philosophy. But for my present purpose I do not care so much what his *method* was as what his *aim* was.

The aim of Socrates, then, being to find out and teach what is definite and certain, as a foundation of knowledge, — having cleared away the rubbish of ignorance, — he attached very little importance to what is called physical science. And no wonder, since science in his day was very imperfect. There were not facts enough known on which to base sound inductions: better, deductions from established principles. What is deemed most certain in this age was the most uncertain of all knowledge in his day. Scientific knowledge, truly speaking, there was none. It was all speculation. Democritus might resolve the material universe — the earth, the sun, and the stars — into combinations produced by the motion of atoms. But whence the original atoms, and what force gave to them motion? The proudest philosopher, speculating on the origin of the universe, is convicted of ignorance.

Much has been said in praise of the Ionian philosophers; and justly, so far as their genius and loftiness of character are considered. But what did they discover? What truths did they arrive at to serve as foundation-stones of science? They were among the greatest intellects of antiquity. But their method was a wrong one. Their philosophy was based on assumptions and speculations, and therefore was worthless, since they settled nothing. Their science was based on inductions which were not reliable, because of a lack of facts. They drew conclusions as to the origin of the universe from material phenomena. Thales, seeing that plants are sustained by dew and rain, concluded that water was the first beginning of things. Anaximenes, seeing that animals die without air, thought that air was the great primal cause. Then Diogenes of Crete, making a fanciful speculation, imparted to air an intellectual energy. Heraclitus of Ephesus substituted fire for air. None of the illustrious Ionians reached anything higher, than that the first cause of all things must be intelligent. The speculations of succeeding philosophers, living in a more material age, all pertained to the world of matter which they could see with their eyes. And in close connection with speculations about matter, the cause of which they could not settle, was indifference to the spiritual nature of man, which they could not see, and all the wants of the soul, and the existence of the future state, where the soul alone was of any account. So atheism, and the disbelief of the existence of the soul after death, characterized that materialism. Without God and without a future, there was no stimulus to virtue and no foundation for anything. They said, "Let us eat and drink, for to-morrow we die," — the essence and spirit of all paganism.

Socrates, seeing how unsatisfactory were all physical inquiries, and what evils materialism introduced into society, making the body everything and the soul nothing, turned his attention to the world within, and "for physics substituted morals." He knew the uncertainty of physical speculation, but believed in the certainty of moral truths. He knew that there was a reality in justice, in friendship, in courage. Like Job, he reposed on consciousness. He turned his attention to what afterwards gave immortality to Descartes. To the scepticism of the Sophists he opposed self-evident truths. He proclaimed the sovereignty of virtue, the universality of moral obligation. "Moral certitude was the platform from which he would survey the universe." It was the ladder by which he would ascend to the loftiest regions of knowledge and of happiness. "Though he was negative in his means, he was positive in his ends." He was the first who had glimpses of the true mission of philosophy, — even to sit in judgment on all knowledge, whether it pertains to art, or politics, or science; eliminating the false and retaining the true. It was his mission to separate truth from error. He taught the world how to weigh evidence. He would discard any doctrine which, logically carried out, led to absurdity. Instead of turning his attention to outward phenomena, he dwelt on the truths which either God or consciousness reveals. Instead of the creation, he dwelt on the Creator. It was not the body he cared for so much as the soul. Not wealth, not power, not the appetites were the true source of pleasure, but the peace and harmony of the soul. The inquiry should be, not what we shall eat, but how shall we resist temptation; how shall we keep the soul pure; how shall we arrive at virtue; how shall we best serve our country; how shall we best educate our children; how shall we expel worldliness and deceit and lies; how shall we walk with God?—for there is a God, and there is immortality and eternal justice: these are the great certitudes of human life, and it is only by these that the soul will expand and be happy forever.

Thus there was a close connection between his philosophy and his ethics. But it was as a moral teacher that he won his most enduring fame. The teacher of wisdom became subordinate to the man who lived it. As a living Christian is nobler than merely an acute theologian, so he who practises virtue is greater than the one who preaches it. The dissection of the passions is not so difficult as the regulation of the passions. The moral force of the soul is superior to the utmost grasp of the intellect. The "Thoughts" of Pascal are all the more read because the religious life of Pascal is known to have been lofty. Augustine was the oracle of the Middle Ages, from the radiance of his character as much as from the brilliancy and originality of his intellect. Bernard swayed society more by his sanctity than by his learning. The useful life of Socrates was devoted not merely to establish the grounds of moral obligation, in opposition to the false and worldly teaching of his day, but to the practice of temperance, disinterestedness, and patriotism. He found that the ideas of his contemporaries centred in the pleasure of the body: he would make his body subservient to the welfare of the soul. No writer of antiquity says so much of the soul as Plato, his chosen disciple, and no other one placed so much value on pure subjective knowledge. His longings after love were scarcely exceeded by Augustine or St. Theresa, — not for a divine Spouse, but for the harmony of the soul. With longings after love were united longings after immortality, when the mind would revel forever in the contemplation of eternal ideas and the solution of mysteries, — a sort of Dantean heaven. Virtue became the foundation of happiness, and almost a synonym for knowledge. He discoursed on knowledge in its connection with virtue, after the fashion of Solomon in his Proverbs. Happiness, virtue, knowledge: this was the Socratic trinity, the three indissolubly connected together, and forming the life of the soul, — the only precious thing a man has, since it is immortal, and therefore to be guarded beyond all bodily and mundane interests. But human nature is frail. The soul is fettered and bewildered; hence the need of some outside influence, some illumination, to guard, or to restrain, or guide. "This inspiration, he was persuaded, was imparted to him from time to time, as he had need, by the monitions of an internal voice which he called δαιμόνιον, or dæmon, — not a personification, like an angel or devil, but a divine sign or supernatural voice." From youth he was accustomed to obey this prohibitory voice, and to speak of it, — a voice "which forbade him to enter on public life," or to take any thought for a prepared defence on his trial. The Fathers of the Church regarded this dæmon as a devil, probably from the name; but it is not far, in its real meaning, from the "divine grace" of St. Augustine and of all men famed for Christian experience, — that restraining grace which keeps good men from folly or sin.

Socrates, again, divorced happiness from pleasure, — identical things, with most pagans. Happiness is the peace and harmony of the soul; pleasure comes from animal sensations, or the gratification of worldly and ambitious desires, and therefore is often demoralizing. Happiness is an elevated joy, — a beatitude, existing with pain and disease, when the soul is triumphant over the body; while pleasure is transient, and comes from what is perishable. Hence but little account should be made of pain and suffering, or even of death. The life is more than meat, and virtue is its own reward. There is no reward of virtue in mere outward and worldly prosperity; and, with virtue, there is no evil in adversity. One must do right because it is right, not because it is expedient: he must do right, whatever advantages may appear by not doing it. A good citizen must obey the laws, because they are laws: he may not violate them because temporal and immediate advantages are promised. A wise man, and therefore a good man, will be temperate. He must neither eat nor drink to excess. But temperance is not abstinence. Socrates not only enjoined temperance as a great virtue, but he practised it. He was a model of sobriety, and yet he drank wine at feasts, — at those glorious symposia where he discoursed with his friends on the highest themes. While he controlled both appetites and passions, in order to promote true happiness, — that is, the welfare of the soul, — he was not solicitous, as others were, for outward prosperity, which could not extend beyond mortal life. He would show, by teaching and example, that he valued future good beyond any transient joy. Hence he accepted poverty and physical discomfort as very trifling evils. He did not lacerate the body, like Brahmans and monks, to make the soul independent of it. He was a Greek, and a practical man, — anything but visionary, — and regarded the body as a sacred temple of the soul, to be kept beautiful; for beauty is as much an eternal idea as friendship or love. Hence he threw no contempt on art, since art is based on beauty. He approved of athletic exercises, which strengthened and beautified the body; but he would not defile the body or weaken it, either by lusts or austerities. Passions were not to be exterminated but controlled; and controlled by reason, the light within us, — that which guides to true knowledge, and hence to virtue, and hence to happiness. The law of temperance, therefore, is self-control.

Courage was another of his certitudes, — that which animated the soldier on the battlefield with patriotic glow and lofty self-sacrifice. Life is subordinate to patriotism. It was of but little consequence whether a man died or not, in the discharge of duty. To do right was the main thing, because it was right. "Like George Fox, he would do right if the world were blotted out."

The weak point, to my mind, in the Socratic philosophy, considered in its ethical bearings, was the confounding of virtue with knowledge, and making them identical. Socrates could probably have explained this difficulty away, for no one more than he appreciated the tyranny of passion and appetite, which thus fettered the will; according to St. Paul, "The evil that I would not, that I do." Men often commit sin when the consequences of it and the nature of it press upon the mind. The knowledge of good and evil does not always restrain a man from doing what he knows will end in grief and shame. The restraint comes, not from knowledge, but from divine aid, which was probably what Socrates meant by his dæmon, — a warning and a constraining power.

"Est Deus in nobis, agitante calescimus illo."

But this is not exactly the knowledge which Socrates meant, or Solomon. Alcibiades was taught to see the loveliness of virtue and to admire it; but *he* had not the divine and restraining power, which Socrates called an "inspiration," and others would call "grace." Yet Socrates himself, with passions and appetites as great as Alcibiades, restrained them, — was assisted to do so by that divine Power which he recognized, and probably adored. How far he felt his personal responsibility to this Power I do not know. The sense of personal responsibility to God is one of the highest manifestations of Christian life, and implies a recognition of God as a personality, as a moral governor whose eye is everywhere, and whose commands are absolute. Many have a vague idea of Providence as pervading and ruling the universe, without a sense of personal responsibility to Him; in other words, without a "fear" of Him, such as Moses taught, and which is represented by David as "the beginning of wisdom,"— the fear to do wrong, not only because it is wrong, but also because it is displeasing to Him who can both punish and reward. I do not believe that Socrates had this idea of God; but I do believe that he recognized His existence and providence. Most people in Greece and Rome had religious instincts, and believed in supernatural forces, who exercised an influence over their destiny, — although they called them "gods," or divinities, and not *the* "God Almighty" whom Moses taught. The existence of temples, the offices of priests, and the consultation of oracles and soothsayers, all point to this. And the people not only believed in the existence of these supernatural powers, to whom they erected temples and statues, but many of them believed in a future state of rewards and punishments,— otherwise the names of Minos and Rhadamanthus and other judges of the dead are unintelligible. Paganism and mythology did not deny the existence and power of gods, — yea, the immortal gods; they only multiplied their number, representing them as avenging deities with human passions and frailties, and offering to them gross and superstitious rites of worship. They had imperfect and even degrading ideas of the gods, but acknowledged their existence and their power. Socrates emancipated himself from these degrading superstitions, and had a loftier idea of God than the people, or he would not have been accused of impiety, — that is, a dissent from the popular belief; although there is one thing which I cannot understand in his life, and cannot harmonize with his general teachings, — that in his last hours his last act was to command the sacrifice of a cock to Æsculapius.

But whatever may have been his precise and definite ideas of God and immortality, it is clear that he soared beyond his contemporaries in his conceptions of Providence and of duty. He was a reformer and a missionary, preaching a higher morality and revealing loftier truths than any other person that we know of in pagan antiquity; although there lived in India, about two hundred years before his day, a sage whom they called Buddha, whom some modern scholars think approached nearer to Christ than did Socrates or Marcus Aurelius. Very possibly. Have we any reason to adduce that God has ever been without his witnesses on earth, or ever will be? Why could he not have imparted wisdom both to Buddha and Socrates, as he did to Abraham, Moses, and Paul? I look upon Socrates as one of the witnesses and agents of Almighty power on this earth to proclaim exalted truth and turn people from wickedness. He himself — not indistinctly — claimed this mission.

Think what a man he was: truly was he a "moral phenomenon." You see a man of strong animal propensities, but with a lofty soul, appearing in a wicked and materialistic — and possibly atheistic — age, overturning all previous systems of philosophy, and inculcating a new and higher law of morals. You see him spending his whole life, — and a long life, — in disinterested teachings and labors; teaching without pay, attaching himself to youth, working in poverty and discomfort, indifferent to wealth and honor, and even power, inculcating incessantly the worth and dignity of the soul, and its amazing and incalculable superiority to all the pleasures of the body and all the rewards of a worldly life. Who gave to him this wisdom and this almost superhuman virtue? Who gave to him this insight into the fundamental principles of morality? Who, in this respect, made him a greater light and a clearer expounder than the Christian Paley? Who made him, in all spiritual discernment, a wiser man than the gifted John Stuart Mill, who seems to have been a candid searcher after truth? In the wisdom of Socrates you see some higher force than intellectual hardihood or intellectual clearness. How much this pagan did to emancipate and elevate the soul! How much he did to present the vanities and pursuits of worldly men in their true light! What a rebuke were his life and doctrines to the Epicureanism which was pervading all classes of society, and preparing the way for ruin! Who cannot see in him a forerunner of that greater Teacher who was the friend of publicans and sinners; who rejected the leaven of the Pharisees and the speculations of the Sadducees; who scorned the riches and glories of the world; who rebuked everything pretentious and arrogant; who enjoined humility and self-abnegation; who exposed the ignorance and sophistries of ordinary teachers; and who propounded to *his* disciples no such "miserable interrogatory" as "Who shall show us any good?" but a higher question for their solution and that of all pleasure-seeking and money-hunting people to the end of time, — "What shall a man give in exchange for his soul?"

It very rarely happens that a great benefactor escapes persecution, especially if he is persistent in denouncing false opinions which are popular, or prevailing follies and sins. As the Scribes and Pharisees, who had been so severely and openly exposed in all their hypocrisies by our Lord, took the lead in causing his crucifixion, so the Sophists and tyrants of Athens headed the fanatical persecution of Socrates because he exposed their shallowness and worldliness, and stung them to the quick by his sarcasms and ridicule. His elevated morality and lofty spiritual life do not alone account for the persecution. If he had let persons alone, and had not ridiculed their opinions and pretensions, they would probably have let him alone. Galileo aroused the wrath of the Inquisition not for his scientific discoveries, but because he ridiculed the Dominican and Jesuit guardians of the philosophy of the Middle Ages, and because he seemed to undermine the authority of the Scriptures and of the Church; his boldness, his sarcasms, and his mocking spirit were more offensive than his doctrines. The Church did not persecute Kepler or Pascal. The Athenians may have condemned Xenophanes and Anaxagoras, yet not the other Ionian philosophers, nor the lofty speculations of Plato; but they murdered Socrates because they hated him. It was not pleasant to the gay leaders of Athenian society to hear the utter vanity of their worldly lives painted with such unsparing severity, nor was it pleasant to the Sophists and rhetoricians to see their idols overthrown, and they themselves exposed as false teachers and shallow pretenders. No one likes to see himself held up to scorn and mockery; nobody is willing to be shown up as ignorant and conceited. The people of Athens did not like to see their gods ridiculed, for the logical sequence of the teachings of Socrates was to undermine the popular religion. It was very offensive to rich and worldly people to be told that their riches and pleasures were transient and worthless. It was impossible that those rhetoricians who gloried in words those Sophists who covered up the truth, those pedants who prided themselves on their technicalities, those politicians who lived by corruption, those worldly fathers who thought only of pushing the fortunes of their children, should not see in Socrates their uncompromising foe; and when he added mockery and ridicule to contempt, and piqued their vanity, and offended their pride, they bitterly hated him and wished him out of the way. My wonder is that he should have been tolerated until he was seventy years of age. Men less offensive than he have been burned alive, and stoned to death, and tortured on the rack, and devoured by lions in the amphitheatre. It is the fate of prophets to be exiled, or slandered, or jeered at, or stigmatized, or banished from society, — to be subjected to some sort of persecution; but when prophets denounce woes, and utter invectives, and provoke by stinging sarcasms, they have generally been killed. No matter how enlightened society is, or tolerant the age, he who utters offensive truths will be disliked, and in some way punished.

So Socrates must meet the fate of all benefactors who make themselves disliked and hated. First the great comic poet Aristophanes, in his comedy called the "Clouds," held him up to ridicule and reproach, and thus prepared the way for his arraignment and trial. He is made to utter a thousand impieties and impertinences.

He is made to talk like a man of the greatest vanity and conceit, and to throw contempt and scorn on everybody else. It is not probable that the poet entered into any formal conspiracy against him, but found him a good subject of raillery and mockery, since Socrates was then very unpopular, aside from his moral teachings, for being declared by the oracle of Delphi the wisest man in the world, and for having been intimate with the two men whom the Athenians above all men justly execrated, — Critias, the chief of the Thirty Tyrants whom Lysander had imposed, or at least consented to, after the Peloponnesian war; and Alcibiades, whose evil counsels had led to an unfortunate expedition, and who in addition had proved himself a traitor to his country.

Public opinion being now against him, on various grounds he is brought to trial before the Dikastery, — a board of some five hundred judges, leading citizens of Athens. One of his chief accusers was Anytus, — a rich tradesman, of very narrow mind, personally hostile to Socrates because of the influence the philosopher had exerted over his son, yet who then had considerable influence from the active part he had taken in the expulsion of the Thirty Tyrants. The more formidable accuser was Meletus, — a poet and a rhetorician, who had been irritated by Socrates' terrible cross-examinations. The principal charges against him were, that he did not admit the gods acknowledged by the republic, and that he corrupted the youth of Athens.

In regard to the first charge, it could not be technically proved that he had assailed the gods, for he was exact in his legal worship; but really and virtually there was some foundation for the accusation, since Socrates was a religious innovator if ever there was one. His lofty realism *was* subversive of popular superstitions, when logically carried out. As to the second charge, of corrupting youth, this was utterly groundless; for he had uniformly enjoined courage, and temperance, and obedience to the laws, and patriotism, and the control of the passions, and all the higher sentiments of the soul. But the tendency of his teachings was to create in young men contempt for all institutions based on falsehood or superstition or tyranny, and he openly disapproved some of the existing laws, — such as choosing magistrates by lot, — and freely expressed his opinions. In a narrow and technical sense there was some reason for this charge; for if a young man came to combat his father's business or habits of life or general opinions, in consequence of his own superior enlightenment, it might be made out that he had not sufficient respect for his father, and thus was failing in the virtues of reverence and filial obedience.

Considering the genius and innocence of the accused

he did not make an able defence; he might have done better. It appeared as if he did not wish to be acquitted. He took no thought of what he should say; he made no preparation for so great an occasion. He made no appeal to the passions and feelings of his judges. He refused the assistance of Lysias, the greatest orator of the day. He brought neither his wife nor children to incline the judges in his favor by their sighs and tears. His discourse was manly, bold, noble, dignified, but without passion and without art. His unpremeditated replies seemed to scorn an elaborate defence. He even seemed to rebuke his judges, rather than to conciliate them. On the culprit's bench he assumed the manners of a teacher. He might easily have saved himself, for there was but a small majority (only five or six at the first vote) for his condemnation. And then he irritated his judges unnecessarily. According to the laws he had the privilege of proposing a substitution for his punishment, which would have been accepted, — exile for instance; but, with a provoking and yet amusing irony, he asked to be supported at the public expense in the Prytaneum: that is, he asked for the highest honor of the republic. For a condemned criminal to ask this was audacity and defiance.

We cannot otherwise suppose than that he did not wish to be acquitted. He wished to die. The time had come; he had fulfilled his mission; he was old and poor; his condemnation would bring his truths before the world in a more impressive form. He knew the moral greatness of a martyr's death. He reposed in the calm consciousness of having rendered great services, of having made important revelations. He never had an ignoble love of life; death had no terrors to him at any time. So he was perfectly resigned to his fate. Most willingly he accepted the penalty of plain speaking, and presented no serious remonstrances and no indignant denials. Had he pleaded eloquently for his life, he would not have fulfilled his mission. He acted with amazing foresight; he took the only course which would secure a lasting influence. He knew that his death would evoke a new spirit of inquiry, which would spread over the civilized world. It was a public disappointment that he did not defend himself with more earnestness. But he was not seeking applause for his genius, — simply the final triumph of his cause, best secured by martyrdom.

So he received his sentence with evident satisfaction; and in the interval between it and his execution he spent his time in cheerful but lofty conversations with his disciples. He unhesitatingly refused to escape from his prison when the means would have been provided. His last hours were of immortal beauty. His friends were dissolved in tears, but he was calm, composed, triumphant: and when he lay down to die he prayed that his migration to the unknown land might be propitious. He died without pain, as the hemlock produced only torpor.

His death, as may well be supposed, created a profound impression. It was one of the most memorable events of the pagan world, whose greatest light was extinguished, — no, not extinguished, since it has been shining ever since in the "Memorabilia" of Xenophon and the "Dialogues" of Plato. Too late the Athenians repented of their injustice and cruelty. They erected to his memory a brazen statue, executed by Lysippus. His character and his ideas are alike immortal. The schools of Athens properly date from his death, about the year 400 B. C., and these schools redeemed the shame of her loss of political power. The Socratic philosophy, as expounded by Plato, survived the wrecks of material greatness. It entered even into the Christian schools, especially at Alexandria; it has ever assisted and animated the earnest searchers after the certitudes of life; it has permeated the intellectual world, and found admirers and expounders in all the universities of Europe and America. "No man has ever been found," says Grote, "strong enough to bend the bow of Socrates, the father of philosophy, the most original thinker of antiquity." His teachings gave an immense impulse to civilization, but they could not reform or save the world; it was too deeply sunk in the infamies and immoralities of an Epicurean life. Nor was his philosophy ever popular in any age of our world. It never will be popular until the light which men hate shall expel the darkness which they love. But it has been the comfort and the joy of an esoteric few,—the witnesses of truth whom God chooses, to keep alive the virtues and the ideas which shall ultimately triumph over all the forces of evil.

AUTHORITIES.

The direct sources are chiefly Plato (Jowett's translation) and Xenophon. Indirect sources: chiefly Aristotle, Metaphysics; Diogenes Laertius's Lives of Philosophers; Grote's History of Greece; Brandis's Plato, in Smith's Dictionary; Ralph Waldo Emerson's Representative Men; Cicero on Immortality; J. Martineau, Essay on Plato; Thirlwall's History of Greece. See also the late work of Curtius; Ritter's History of Philosophy; F. D. Maurice's History of Moral Philosophy; G. H. Lewes' Biographical History of Philosophy; Hampden's Fathers of Greek Philosophy; J. S. Blackie's Wise Men of Greece; Starr King's Lecture on Socrates; Smith's Biographical Dictionary; Ueberweg's History of Philosophy; W. A. Butler's History of Ancient Philosophy; Grote's Aristotle.

PHIDIAS

500–430 B.C.

GREEK ART.

PHIDIAS.

GREEK ART.

I SUPPOSE there is no subject, at this time, which interests cultivated people in favored circumstances more than Art. They travel in Europe, they visit galleries, they survey cathedrals, they buy pictures, they collect old china, they learn to draw and paint, they go into ecstasies over statues and bronzes, they fill their houses with bric-à-brac, they assume a cynical criticism, or gossip pedantically, whether they know what they are talking about or not. In short, the contemplation of Art is a fashion, concerning which it is not well to be ignorant, and about which there is an amazing amount of cant, pretension, and borrowed opinions. Artists themselves differ in their judgments, and many who patronize them have no severity of discrimination. We see bad pictures on the walls of private palaces, as well as in public galleries, for which fabulous prices are paid because they are, or are supposed to be, the creation of great masters, or because they are rare like old books in an antiquarian library, or because fashion has given them a fictitious value, even when these pictures fail to create pleasure or emotion in those who view them. And yet there is great enjoyment, to some people, in the contemplation of a beautiful building or statue or painting, — as of a beautiful landscape or of a glorious sky. The ideas of beauty, of grace, of grandeur, which are eternal, are suggested to the mind and soul, and these cultivate and refine in proportion as the mind and soul are enlarged, especially among the rich, the learned, and the favored classes. So, in high civilizations, especially material, Art is not only a fashion but a great enjoyment, a lofty study, and a theme of general criticism and constant conversation.

It is my object, of course, to present the subject historically, rather than critically. My criticisms would be mere opinions, worth no more than those of thousands of other people. As a public teacher to those who may derive some instruction from my labors and studies, I presume to offer only reflections on Art as it existed among the Greeks, and to show its developments in an historical point of view.

The reader may be surprised that I should venture to present Phidias as one of the benefactors of the world, when so little is known about him, or can be known about him. So far as the man is concerned, I might as well lecture on Melchizedek, or Pharaoh, or one of the dukes of Edom. There are no materials to construct a personal history which would be interesting, such as abound in reference to Michael Angelo or Raphael. Thus he must be made the mere text of a great subject. The development of Art is an important part of the history of civilization. The influence of Art on human culture and happiness is prodigious. Ancient Grecian art marks one of the stepping-stones of the race. Any man who largely contributed to its development was a world-benefactor.

Now, history says this much of Phidias: that he lived in the time of Pericles, — in the culminating period of Grecian glory, — and ornamented the Parthenon with his unrivalled statues; which Parthenon was to Athens what Solomon's Temple was to Jerusalem, — a wonder, a pride, and a glory. His great contribution to that matchless edifice was the statue of Minerva, made of gold and ivory, forty feet in height, the gold of which alone was worth forty-four talents, — about fifty thousand dollars, — an immense sum when gold was probably worth more than twenty times its present value. All antiquity was unanimous in its praise of this statue, and the exactness and finish of its details were as remarkable as the grandeur and majesty of its proportions. Another of the famous works of Phidias was the bronze statue of Minerva, which was the glory of the Acropolis. This was sixty feet in height. But even this yielded to the colossal statue of Zeus or Jupiter in his great temple at Olympia, representing the figure in a sitting posture, forty feet high, on a throne made of gold, ebony, ivory, and precious stones. In this statue the immortal artist sought to represent power in repose, as Michael Angelo did in his statue of Moses. So famous was this majestic statue, that it was considered a calamity to die without seeing it; and it served as a model for all subsequent representations of majesty and repose among the ancients. This statue, removed to Constantinople by Theodosius the Great, remained undestroyed until the year 475 A. D.

Phidias also executed various other works, — all famous in his day, — which have, however, perished; but many executed under his superintendence still remain, and are universally admired for their grace and majesty of form. The great master himself was probably vastly superior to any of his disciples, and impressed his genius on the age, having, so far as we know, no rival among his contemporaries, as he has had no successor among the moderns of equal originality and power, unless it be Michael Angelo. His distinguished excellence was simplicity and grandeur; and he was to sculpture what Æschylus was to tragic poetry, — sublime and grand, representing ideal excellence.

Though his works have perished, the ideas he represented still live. His fame is immortal, though we know so little about him. It is based on the admiration of antiquity, on the universal praise which his creations extorted even from the severest critics in an age of Art, when the best energies of an ingenious people were directed to it with the absorbing devotion now given to mechanical inventions and those pursuits which make men rich and comfortable. It would be interesting to know the private life of this great artist, his ardent loves and fierce resentments, his social habits, his public honors and triumphs, — but this is mere speculation. We may presume that he was rich, flattered, and admired, — the companion of great statesmen, rulers, and generals; not a persecuted man like Dante, but honored like Raphael; one of the fortunate of earth, since he was a master of what was most valued in his day.

But it is the work which he represents — and still more comprehensively Art itself in the ancient world — to which I would call your attention, especially the expression of Art in buildings, in statues, and in pictures.

"Art" is itself a very great word, and means many things; it is applied to style in writing, to musical compositions, and even to effective eloquence, as well as to architecture, sculpture, and painting. We speak of music as artistic, — and not foolishly; of an artistic poet, or an artistic writer like Voltaire or Macaulay; of an artistic preacher,—by which we mean that each and all move the sensibilities and souls and minds of men by adherence to certain harmonies which accord with fixed ideas of grace, beauty, and dignity. Eternal ideas which the mind conceives are the foundation of Art, as they are of Philosophy. Art claims to be creative, and is in a certain sense inspired, like the genius of a poet. However material the creation, the spirit which gives beauty to it is of the mind and soul. Imagination is tasked to its utmost stretch to portray sentiments and passions in the way that makes the deepest impression. The marble bust becomes animated, and even the temple consecrated to the deity becomes religious, in proportion as these suggest the ideas and sentiments which kindle the soul to admiration and awe. These feelings belong to every one by nature, and are most powerful when most felicitously called out by the magic of the master, who requires time and labor to perfect his skill. Art is therefore popular, and appeals to every one, but to those most who live in the great ideas on which it is based. The peasant stands awe-struck before the majestic magnitude of a cathedral; the man of culture is roused to enthusiasm by the contemplation of its grand proportions, or graceful outlines, or bewitching details, because he sees in them the realization of his ideas of beauty, grace, and majesty, which shine forever in unutterable glory, — indestructible ideas which survive all thrones and empires, and even civilizations. They are as imperishable as stars and suns and rainbows and landscapes, since these unfold new beauties as the mind and soul rest upon them. Whenever, then, man creates an image or a picture which reveals these eternal but indescribable beauties, and calls forth wonder or enthusiasm, and excites refined pleasures, he is an artist. He impresses, to a greater or less degree, every order and class of men. He becomes a benefactor, since he stimulates exalted sentiments, which, after all, are the real glory and pride of life, and the cause of all happiness and virtue, — in cottage or in palace, amid hard toils as well as in luxurious leisure. He is a self-sustained man, since he revels in ideas rather than in praises and honors. Like the man of virtue, he finds in the adoration of the deity he worships his highest reward. Michael Angelo worked preoccupied and rapt, without even the stimulus of praise, to advanced old age, even as Dante lived in the visions to which his imagination gave form and reality. Art is therefore not only self-sustained, but lofty and unselfish. It is indeed the exalted soul going forth triumphant over external difficulties, jubilant and melodious even in poverty and neglect, rising above all the evils of life, revelling in the glories which are impenetrable, and living — for the time — in the realm of deities and angels. The accidents of earth are no more to the true artist striving to reach and impersonate his ideal of beauty and grace, than furniture and tapestries are to a true woman seeking the beatitudes of love. And it is only when there is this soul longing to reach the excellence conceived, for itself alone, that great works have been produced. When Art has been prostituted to pander to perverted tastes, or has been stimulated by thirst for gain, then inferior works only have been created. Fra Angelico lived secluded in a convent when he painted his exquisite Madonnas. It was the exhaustion of the nervous energies consequent on superhuman toils, rather than the luxuries and pleasures which his position and means afforded, which killed Raphael at thirty-seven.

The artists of Greece did not live for utilities any more than did the Ionian philosophers, but in those glorious thoughts and creations which were their chosen joy. Whatever can be reached by the unaided powers of man was attained by them. They represented all that the mind can conceive of the beauty of the human form, and the harmony of architectural proportions. In the realm of beauty and grace modern civilization has no prouder triumphs than those achieved by the artists of Pagan antiquity. Grecian artists have been the teachers of all nations and all ages in architecture, sculpture, and painting. How far they were themselves original we cannot tell. We do not know how much they were indebted to Egyptians, Phœnicians, and Assyrians, but in real excellence they have never been surpassed. In some respects, their works still remain objects of hopeless imitation: in the realization of ideas of beauty and form, they reached absolute perfection. Hence we have a right to infer that Art can flourish under Pagan as well as Christian influences. It was a comparatively Pagan age in Italy when the great artists arose who succeeded Da Vinci, especially under the patronage of the Medici and the Medicean popes. Christianity has only modified Art by purifying it from sensual attractions. Christianity added very little to Art, until cathedrals arose in their grand proportions and infinite details, and until artists sought to portray in the faces of their Saints and Madonnas the seraphic sentiments of Christian love and angelic purity. Art even declined in the Roman world from the second century after Christ, in spite of all the efforts of Christian emperors. In fact neither Christianity nor Paganism creates it; it seems to be independent of both, and arises from the peculiar genius and circumstances of an age. Make Art a fashion, honor and reward it, crown its great masters with Olympic leaves, direct the energies of an age or race upon it, and we probably shall have great creations, whether the people are Christian or Pagan. So that Art seems to be a human creation, rather than a divine inspiration. It is the result of genius, stimulated by circumstances and directed to the contemplation of ideal excellence.

Much has been written on those principles upon which Art is supposed to be founded, but not very satisfactorily, although great learning and ingenuity have been displayed. It is difficult to conceive of beauty or grace by definitions, — as difficult as it is to define love or any other ultimate sentiment of the soul. "Metaphysics, mathematics, music, and philosophy," says Cleghorn, "have been called in to analyze, define, demonstrate, or generalize." Great critics, like Burke, Alison, and Stewart, have written interesting treatises on beauty and taste. "Plato represents beauty as the contemplation of the mind. Leibnitz maintained that it consists in perfection. Diderot referred beauty to the idea of relation. Blondel asserted that it was in harmonic proportions. Leigh speaks of it as the music of the age." These definitions do not much assist us. We fall back on our own conceptions or intuitions, as probably did Phidias, although Art in Greece could hardly have attained such perfection without the aid which poetry and history and philosophy alike afforded

Art can flourish only as the taste of the people becomes cultivated, and by the assistance of many kinds of knowledge. The mere contemplation of Nature is not enough. Savages have no art at all, even when they live amid grand mountains and beside the ever-changing sea. When Phidias was asked how he conceived his Olympian Jove, he referred to Homer's poems. Michael Angelo was enabled to paint the saints and sibyls of the Sistine Chapel from familiarity with the writings of the Jewish prophets. Isaiah inspired him as truly as Homer inspired Phidias. The artists of the age of Phidias were encouraged and assisted by the great poets, historians, and philosophers who basked in the sunshine of Pericles, even as the great men in the Court of Elizabeth derived no small share of their renown from her glorious appreciation. Great artists appear in clusters, and amid the other constellations that illuminate the intellectual heavens. They all mutually assist each other. When Rome lost her great men, Art declined. When the egotism of Louis XIV. extinguished genius, the great lights in all departments disappeared. So Art is indebted not merely to the contemplation of ideal beauty, but to the influence of great ideas permeating society, — such as when the age of Phidias was kindled with the great thoughts of Socrates, Democritus, Thucydides, Euripides, Aristophanes, and others, whether contemporaries or not; a sort of Augustan or Elizabethan age, never to appear but once among the same people.

Now, in reference to the history or development of ancient Art, until it culminated in the age of Pericles, we observe that its first expression was in architecture, and was probably the result of religious sentiments, when nations were governed by priests, and not distinguished for intellectual life. Then arose the temples of Egypt, of Assyria, of India. They are grand, massive, imposing, but not graceful or beautiful. They arose from blended superstition and piety, and were probably erected before the palaces of kings, and in Egypt by the dynasty that builded the older pyramids. Even those ambitious and prodigious monuments, which have survived every thing contemporaneous, indicate the reign of sacerdotal monarchs and artists who had no idea of beauty, but only of permanence. They do not indicate civilization, but despotism, — unless it be that they were erected for astronomical purposes, as some maintain, rather than as sepulchres for kings. But this supposition involves great mathematical attainments. It is difficult to conceive of such a waste of labor by enlightened princes, acquainted with astronomical and mathematical knowledge and mechanical forces, for Herodotus tells us that one hundred thousand men toiled on the Great Pyramid during forty years. What for? Surely it is hard to suppose that such a pile was necessary for the observation of the polar star; and still less probably was it built as a sepulchre for a king, since no covered sarcophagus has ever been found in it, nor have even any hieroglyphics. The mystery seems impenetrable.

But the temples are not mysteries. They were built also by sacerdotal monarchs, in honor of the deity. They must have been enormous, perhaps the most imposing ever built by man: witness the ruins of Karnac — a temple designated by the Greeks as that of Jupiter Ammon — with its large blocks of stone seventy feet in length, on a platform one thousand feet long and three hundred wide, its alleys over a mile in length lined with colossal sphinxes, and all adorned with obelisks and columns, and surrounded with courts and colonnades, like Solomon's temple, to accommodate the crowds of worshippers as well as priests. But these enormous structures were not marked by beauty of proportion or fitness of ornament; they show the power of kings, not the genius of a nation. They may have compelled awe; they did not kindle admiration. The emotion they called out was such as is produced now by great engineering exploits, involving labor and mechanical skill, not suggestive of grace or harmony, which require both taste and genius. The same is probably true of Solomon's temple, built at a much later period, when Art had been advanced somewhat by the Phœnicians, to whose assistance it seems he was much indebted. We cannot conceive how that famous structure should have employed one hundred and fifty thousand men for eleven years, and have cost what would now be equal to $200,000,000, from any description which has come down to us, or any ruins which remain, unless it were surrounded by vast courts and colonnades, and ornamented by a profuse expenditure of golden plates,— which also evince both power and money rather than architectural genius.

After the erection of temples came the building of palaces for kings, equally distinguished for vast magnitude and mechanical skill, but deficient in taste and beauty, showing the infancy of Art. Yet even these were in imitation of the temples. And as kings became proud and secular, probably their palaces became grander and larger, — like the palaces of Nebuchadnezzar and Rameses the Great and the Persian monarchs at Susa, combining labor, skill, expenditure, dazzling the eye by the number of columns and statues and vast apartments, yet still deficient in beauty and grace.

It was not until the Greeks applied their wonderful genius to architecture that it became the expression of a higher civilization. And, as among Egyptians, Art in Greece is first seen in temples; for the earlier Greeks were religious, although they worshipped the deity under various names, and in the forms which their own hands did make.

The Dorians, who descended from the mountains of northern Greece, eighty years after the fall of Troy, were the first who added substantially to the architectural art of Asiatic nations, by giving simplicity and harmony to their temples. We see great thickness of columns, a fitting proportion to the capitals, and a beautiful entablature. The horizontal lines of the architrave and cornice predominate over the vertical lines of the columns. The temple arises in the severity of geometrical forms. The Doric column was not entirely a new creation, but was an improvement on the Egyptian model, — less massive, more elegant, fluted, increasing gradually towards the base, with a slight convexed swelling downward, about six diameters in height, superimposed by capitals. "So regular was the plan of the temple, that if the dimensions of a single column and the proportion the entablature should bear to it were given to two individuals acquainted with this style, with directions to compose a temple, they would produce designs exactly similar in size, arrangement, and general proportions." And yet while the style of all the Doric temples is the same, there are hardly two temples alike, being varied by the different proportions of the *column*, which is the peculiar mark of Grecian architecture, even as the *arch* is the feature of Gothic architecture. The later Doric was less massive than the earlier. but more rich in sculptured ornaments. The pedestal was from two thirds to a whole diameter of a column in height, built in three courses, forming as it were steps to the platform on which the pillar rested. The pillar had twenty flutes, with a capital of half a diameter, supporting the entablature. This again, two diameters in height, was divided into architrave, frieze, and cornice. But the great beauty of the temple was the portico in front, — a forest of columns, supporting the pediment above, which had at the base an angle of about fourteen degrees. From the pediment the beautiful cornice projects with various mouldings, while at the base and at the apex are sculptured monuments representing both men and animals. The graceful outline of the columns, and the variety of light and shade arising from the arrangement of mouldings and capitals, produced an effect exceedingly beautiful. All the glories of this order of architecture culminated in the Parthenon, — built of Pentelic marble, resting on a basement of limestone, surrounded with forty-eight fluted columns of six feet and two inches diameter at the base and thirty-four feet in height, the frieze and pediment elaborately ornamented with reliefs and statues, while within the cella or interior was the statue of Minerva, forty feet high, built of gold and ivory. The walls were decorated with the rarest paintings, and the cella itself contained countless treasures. This unrivalled temple was not so large as some of the cathedrals of the Middle Ages, but it covered twelve times the ground of the temple of Solomon, and from the summit of the Acropolis it shone as a wonder and a glory. The marbles have crumbled and its ornaments have been removed, but it has formed the model of the most beautiful buildings of the world, from the Quirinus at Rome to the Madeleine at Paris, stimulating alike the genius of Michael Angelo and Christopher Wren, immortal in the ideas it has perpetuated, and immeasurable in the influence it has exerted. Who has copied the Flavian amphitheatre except as a convenient form for exhibitors on the stage, or for the rostrum of an orator? Who has not copied the Parthenon as the severest in its proportions for public buildings for civic purposes?

The Ionic architecture is only a modification of the Doric, — its columns more slender and with a greater number of flutes, and capitals more elaborate, formed with volutes or spiral scrolls, while its pediment, the triangular facing of the portico, is formed with a less angle from the base, — the whole being more suggestive of grace than strength. Vitruvius, the greatest authority among the ancients, says that "the Greeks, in inventing these two kinds of columns, imitated in the one the naked simplicity and aspects of a man, and in the other the delicacy and ornaments of a woman, whose ringlets appear in the volutes of the capital."

The Corinthian order, which was the most copied by the Romans, was still more ornamented, with foliated capitals, greater height, and a more decorated entablature.

But the principles of all these three orders are substantially the same, — their beauty consisting in the column and horizontal lines, even as vertical lines marked the Gothic. We see the lintel and not the arch; huge blocks of stone perfectly squared, and not small stones irregularly laid; external rather than internal pillars, the cella receiving light from the open roof above, rather than from windows; a simple outline uninterrupted, — generally in the form of a parallelogram, — rather than broken by projections. There is no great variety; but the harmony, the severity, and beauty of proportion will eternally be admired, and can never be improved, — a temple of humanity, cheerful, useful, complete, not aspiring to reach what on earth can never be obtained, with no gloomy vaults speaking of maceration and grief, no lofty towers and spires soaring to the sky, no emblems typical of consecrated sentiments and of immortality beyond the grave, but rich in ornaments drawn from the living world, — of plants and animals, of man in the perfection of physical strength, of woman in the unapproachable loveliness of grace of form. As the world becomes pagan, intellectual, thrifty, we see the architecture of the Greeks in palaces, banks, halls, theatres, stores, libraries; when it is emotional, poetic, religious, fervent, aspiring, we see the restoration of the Gothic in churches, cathedrals, schools, — for Philosophy and Art did all they could to civilize the world before Christianity was sent to redeem it and prepare mankind for the life above. Such was the temple of the Greeks, reappearing in all the architectures of nations, from the Romans to our own times, — so perfect that no improvements have subsequently been made, no new principles discovered which were not known to Vitruvius. What a creation, to last in its simple beauty for more than two thousand years, and forever to remain a perfect model of its kind! Ah, that was a triumph of Art, the praises of which have been sung for more than sixty generations, and will be sung for hundreds yet to come. But how hidden and forgotten the great artists who invented all this, showing the littleness of man and the greatness of Art itself. How true that old Greek saying, "Life is short, but Art is long."

But the genius displayed in sculpture was equally remarkable, and was carried to the same perfection. The Greeks did not originate sculpture. We read of sculptured images from remotest antiquity. Assyria, Egypt, and India are full of relics. But these are rude, unformed, without grace, without expression, though often colossal and grand. There are but few traces of emotion, or passion, or intellectual force. Everything which has come down from the ancient monarchies is calm, impassive, imperturbable. Nor is there a severe beauty of form. There is no grace, no loveliness, that we should desire them. Nature was not severely studied. We see no aspiration after what is ideal. Sometimes the sculptures are grotesque, unnatural, and impure. They are emblematic of strange deities, or are rude monuments of heroes and kings. They are curious, but they do not inspire us. We do not copy them; we turn away from them. They do not live, and they are not reproduced. Art could spare them all, except as illustrations of its progress. They are merely historical monuments, to show despotism and superstition, and the degradation of the people.

But this cannot be said of the statues which the Greeks created, or improved from ancient models. In the sculptures of the Greeks we see the utmost perfection of the human form, both of man and woman, learned by the constant study of anatomy and of nude figures of the greatest beauty. A famous statue represented the combined excellences of perhaps one hundred different persons. The study of the human figure became a noble object of ambition, and led to conceptions of ideal grace and loveliness such as no one human being perhaps ever possessed in all respects. And not merely grace and beauty were thus represented in marble or bronze, but dignity, repose, majesty. We see in those figures which have survived the ravages of time suggestions of motion, rest, grace, grandeur, — every attitude, every posture, every variety of form. We see also every passion which moves the human soul, — grief, rage, agony, shame, joy, peace. But it is the perfection of form which is most wonderful and striking. Nor did the artists work to please the vulgar rich, but to realize their own highest conceptions, and to represent sentiments in which the whole nation shared. They sought to instruct; they appealed to the highest intelligence. "Some sought to represent tender beauty, others daring power, and others again heroic grandeur." Grecian statuary began with ideal representations of deities; then it produced the figures of gods and goddesses in mortal forms; then the portrait-statues of distinguished men. This art was later in its development than architecture, since it was directed to ornamenting what had already nearly reached perfection. Thus Phidias ornamented the Parthenon in the time of Pericles, when sculpture was purest and most ideal. In some points of view it declined after Phidias, but in other respects it continued to improve until it culminated in Lysippus, who was contemporaneous with Alexander. He is said to have executed fifteen hundred statues, and to have displayed great energy of execution. He idealized human beauty, and imitated Nature to the minutest details. He alone was selected to make the statue of Alexander, which is lost. None of his works, which were chiefly in bronze, are extant; but it is supposed that the famous *Hercules* and the *Torso Belvedere* are copies from his works, since his favorite subject was Hercules. We only can judge of his great merits from his transcendent reputation and the criticism of classic writers, and also from the works that have come down to us which are supposed to be imitations of his masterpieces. It was his scholars who sculptured the *Colossus of Rhodes*, the *Laocoön*, and the *Dying Gladiator*. After him plastic art rapidly degenerated, since it appealed to passion, especially under Praxiteles, who was famous for his undraped Venuses and the expression of sensual charms. The decline of Art was rapid as men became rich, and Epicurean life was sought as the highest good. Skill of execution did not decline, but ideal beauty was lost sight of, until the art itself was prostituted — as among the Romans — to please perverted tastes or to flatter senatorial pride.

But our present theme is not the history of decline.

but of the original creations of genius, which have been copied in every succeeding age, and which probably will never be surpassed, except in some inferior respects, — in mere mechanical skill. The *Olympian Jove* of Phidias lives perhaps in the *Moses* of Michael Angelo, great as was his original genius, even as the *Venus* of Praxiteles may have been reproduced in Powers's *Greek Slave*. The great masters had innumerable imitators not merely in the representation of man but of animals. What a study did these artists excite, especially in their own age, and how honorable did they make their noble profession even in degenerate times! They were the schoolmasters of thousands and tens of thousands, perpetuating their ideas to remotest generations. Their instructions were not lost, and never can be lost in a realm which constitutes one of the proudest features of our own civilization. It is true that Christianity does not teach æsthetic culture, but it teaches the duties which prevent the eclipse of Art. In this way it comes to the rescue of Art when in danger of being perverted. Grecian Art was consecrated to Paganism, — but, revived, it may indirectly be made tributary to Christianity, like music and eloquence. It will not conserve Christianity, but may be purified by it, even if able to flourish without it.

I can now only glance at the third development of Grecian Art, as seen in painting.

It is not probable that such perfection was reached in this art as in sculpture and architecture. We have no means of forming incontrovertible opinions. Most of the ancient pictures have perished; and those that remain, while they show correctness of drawing and brilliant coloring, do not give us as high conceptions of ideal beauties as do the pictures of the great masters of modern times. But we have the testimony of the ancients themselves, who were as enthusiastic in their admiration of pictures as they were of statues. And since their taste was severe, and their sensibility as to beauty unquestioned, we have a right to infer that even painting was carried to considerable perfection among the Greeks. We read of celebrated schools,— like the modern schools of Florence, Rome, Bologna, Venice, and Naples. The schools of Sicyon, Corinth, Athens, and Rhodes were as famous in their day as the modern schools to which I have alluded.

Painting, being strictly a decoration, did not reach a high degree of art, like sculpture, until architecture was perfected. But painting is very ancient. The walls of Babylon, it is asserted by the ancient historians, were covered with paintings. Many survive amid the ruins of Egypt and on the chests of mummies; though these are comparatively rude, without regard to light and shade, like Chinese pictures. Nor do they represent passions and emotions. They aimed to perpetuate historical events, not ideas. The first paintings of the Greeks simply marked out the outline of figures. Next appeared the inner markings, as we see in ancient vases, on a white ground. The effects of light and shade were then introduced; and then the application of colors in accordance with Nature. Cimon of Cleonæ, in the eightieth Olympiad, invented the art of "fore-shortening," and hence was the first painter of perspective. Polygnotus, a contemporary of Phidias, was nearly as famous for painting as he was for sculpture. He was the first who painted woman with brilliant drapery and variegated head-dresses. He gave to the cheek the blush and to his draperies gracefulness. He is said to have been a great epic painter, as Phidias was an epic sculptor and Homer an epic poet. He expressed, like them, ideal beauty. But his pictures had no elaborate grouping, which is one of the excellences of modern art. His figures were all in regular lines, like the bas-reliefs on a frieze. He took his subjects from epic poetry. He is celebrated for his accurate drawing, and for the charm and grace of his female figures. He also gave great grandeur to his figures, like Michael Angelo. Contemporary with him was Dionysius, who was remarkable for expression, and Micon, who was skilled in painting horses.

With Apollodorus of Athens, who flourished toward the close of the fifth century before Christ, there was a new development, — that of dramatic effect. His aim was to deceive the eye of the spectator by the appearance of reality. He painted men and things as they appeared. He also improved coloring, invented *chiaroscuro* (or the art of relief by a proper distribution of the lights and shadows), and thus obtained what is called "tone." He prepared the way for Zeuxis, who surpassed him in the power to give beauty to forms. The *Helen* of Zeuxis was painted from five of the most beautiful women of Croton. He aimed at complete illusion of the senses, as in the instance recorded of his grape picture. His style was modified by the contemplation of the sculptures of Phidias, and he taught the true method of grouping. His marked excellence was in the contrast of light and shade. He did not paint ideal excellence; he was not sufficiently elevated in his own moral sentiments to elevate the feelings of others: he painted sensuous beauty as it appeared in the models which he used. But he was greatly extolled, and accumulated a great fortune, like Rubens, and lived ostentatiously, as rich and fortunate men ever have lived who do not possess elevation of sentiment. His headquarters were not at Athens, but at Ephesus, — a city which also produced Parrhasius, to whom Zeuxis himself gave the palm, since he deceived the painter by his curtain, while Zeuxis only deceived birds by his grapes. Parrhasius established the rule of proportions, which was followed by succeeding artists. He was a very luxurious and arrogant man, and fancied he had reached the perfection of his art.

But if that was ever reached among the ancients it was by Apelles, — the Titian of that day, — who united the rich coloring of the Ionian school with the scientific severity of the school of Sicyonia. He alone was permitted to paint the figure of Alexander, as Lysippus only was allowed to represent him in bronze. He invented ivory black, and was the first to cover his pictures with a coating of varnish, to bring out the colors and preserve them. His distinguishing excellency was grace, — "that artless balance of motion and repose," says Fuseli, "springing from character and founded on propriety." Others may have equalled him in perspective, accuracy, and finish, but he added a refinement of taste which placed him on the throne which is now given to Raphael. No artists could complete his unfinished pictures. He courted the severest criticism, and, like Michael Angelo, had no jealousy of the fame of other artists; he reposed in the greatness of his own self-consciousness. He must have made enormous sums of money, since one of his pictures — a Venus rising out of the sea, painted for a temple in Cos, and afterwards removed by Augustus to Rome — cost one hundred talents (equal to about one hundred thousand dollars), — a greater sum, I apprehend, than was ever paid to a modern artist for a single picture, certainly in view of the relative value of gold. In this picture female grace was impersonated.

After Apelles the art declined, although there were distinguished artists for several centuries. They generally flocked to Rome, where there was the greatest luxury and extravagance, and they pandered to vanity and a vitiated taste. The masterpieces of the old artists brought enormous sums, as the works of the old masters do now; and they were brought to Rome by the conquerors, as the masterpieces of Italy and Spain and Flanders were brought to Paris by Napoleon. So Rome gradually possessed the best pictures of the world, without stimulating the art or making new creations; it could appreciate genius, but creative genius expired with Grecian liberties and glories. Rome multiplied and rewarded painters, but none of them were famous. Pictures were as common as statues. Even Varro, a learned writer, had a gallery of seven hundred portraits. Pictures were placed in all the baths, theatres, temples, and palaces, as were statues.

We are forced, therefore, to believe that the Greeks carried painting to the same perfection that they did sculpture, not only from the praises of critics like Cicero and Pliny, but from the universal enthusiasm which the painters created and the enormous prices they received.

Whether Polygnotus was equal to Michael Angelo, Zeuxis to Titian, and Apelles to Raphael, we cannot tell. Their works have perished. What remains to us, in the mural decorations of Pompeii and the designs on vases, seem to confirm the criticisms of the ancients. We cannot conceive how the Greek painters could have equalled the great Italian masters, since they had fewer colors, and did not make use of oil, but of gums mixed with the white of eggs, and resin and wax, which mixture we call "encaustic." Yet it is not the perfection of colors or of design, or mechanical aids, or exact imitations, or perspective skill, which constitute the highest excellence of the painter, but his power of creation, — the power of giving ideal beauty and grandeur and grace, inspired by the contemplation of eternal ideas, an excellence which appears in all the masterworks of the Greeks, and such as has not been surpassed by the moderns.

But Art was not confined to architecture, sculpture, and painting alone. It equally appears in all the literature of Greece. The Greek poets were artists, as also the orators and historians, in the highest sense. They were the creators of *style* in writing, which we do not see in the literature of the Jews or other Oriental nations, marvellous and profound as were their thoughts. The Greeks had the power of putting things so as to make the greatest impression on the mind. This especially appears among such poets as Sophocles and Euripides, such orators as Pericles and Demosthenes, such historians as Xenophon and Thucydides, such philosophers as Plato and Aristotle. We see in their finished productions no repetitions, no useless expressions, no superfluity or redundancy, no careless arrangement, no words even in bad taste, save in the abusive epithets in which the orators indulged. All is as harmonious in their literary style as in plastic art; while we read, unexpected pleasures arise in the mind, based on beauty and harmony, somewhat similar to the enjoyment of artistic music, or as when we read Voltaire, Rousseau, or Macaulay. We perceive art in the arrangement of sentences, in the rhythm, in the symmetry of construction. We see means adapted to an end. The Latin races are most marked for artistic writing, especially the French, who seem to be copyists of Greek and Roman models. We see very little of this artistic writing among the Germans, who seem to disdain it as much as an English lawyer or statesman does rhetoric. It is in rhetoric and poetry that Art most strikingly appears in the writings of the Greeks, and this was perfected by the Athenian Sophists. But all the Greeks, and after them the Romans, especially in the time of Cicero, sought the graces and fascinations of style. Style is an art, and all art is eternal.

It is probable also that Art was manifested to a high degree in the conversation of the Greeks, as they were brilliant talkers,— like Brougham, Mackintosh, Madame de Staël, and Macaulay, in our times.

But I may not follow out, as I could wish, this department of Art, — generally overlooked, certainly not dwelt upon like pictures and statues. An interesting and captivating writer or speaker is as much an artist as a sculptor or musician; and unless authors possess art their works are apt to perish, like those of Varro, the most learned of the Romans. It is the exquisite art seen in all the writings of Cicero which makes them classic; it is the style rather than the ideas. The same may be said of Horace: it is his elegance of style and language which makes him immortal. It is this singular fascination of language and style which keeps Hume on the list of standard and classic writers, like Pascal, Goldsmith, Voltaire, and Fénelon. It is on account of these excellences that the classical writers of antiquity will never lose their popularity, and for which they will be imitated, and by which they have exerted their vast influence.

Art, therefore, in every department, was carried to high excellence by the Greeks, and they thus became the teachers of all succeeding races and ages. Artists are great exponents of civilization. They are generally learned men, appreciated by the cultivated classes, and usually associating with the rich and proud. The Popes rewarded artists while they crushed reformers. I never read of an artist who was persecuted. Men do not turn with disdain or anger in disputing with them, as they do from great moral teachers; artists provoke no opposition and stir up no hostile passions. It is the men who propound agitating ideas and who revolutionize the character of nations, that are persecuted. Artists create no revolutions, not even of thought. Savonarola kindled a greater fire in Florence than all the artists whom the Medici ever patronized. But if the artists cannot wear the crown of apostles and reformers and sages, — the men who save nations, men like Socrates, Luther, Bacon, Descartes, Burke, — yet they have fewer evils to contend with in their progress, and they still leave a mighty impression behind them, not like that of Moses and Paul, but still an influence; they kindle the enthusiasm of a class that cannot be kindled by ideas, and furnish inexhaustible themes of conversation to cultivated people and make life itself graceful and beautiful, enriching our houses and adorning our consecrated temples and elevating our better sentiments. The great artist is himself immortal, even if he contributes very little to save the world. Art seeks only the perfection of outward form; it is mundane in its labors; it does not aspire to those beatitudes which shine beyond the grave. And yet it

GREEK ART. 315

is a great and invaluable assistance to those who would communicate great truths, since it puts them in attractive forms and increases the impression of the truths themselves. To the orator, the historian, the philosopher, and the poet, a knowledge of the principles of Art is as important as to the architect, the sculptor, and the painter; and these principles are learned only by study and labor, while they cannot be even conceived of by ordinary men.

Thus it would appear that in all departments and in all the developments of Art the Greeks were the teachers of the modern European nations, as well of the ancient Romans; and their teachings will be invaluable to all the nations which are yet to arise, since no great improvement has been made on the models which have come down to us, and no new principles have been discovered which were not known to them. In everything which pertains to Art they were benefactors of the human race, and gave a great impulse to civilization.

AUTHORITIES.

Müller's De Phidiæ Vita, Vitruvius, Aristotle. Pliny, Ovid, Martial, Lucian, and Cicero have made criticisms on ancient Art. The modern writers are very numerous, especially among the Germans and the French. From these may be selected Winckelmann's History of Ancient Art; Müller's Remains of Ancient Art; Donaldson's Antiquities of Athens; Sir W. Gill's Pompeiana; Montfauçon's Antiquité Expliquée en Figures; Ancient Marbles of the British Museum, by Taylor Combe; Mayer's Kunstgeschicte; Cleghorn's Ancient and Modern Art; Wilkinson's Topography of Thebes; Dodwell's Classical Tour; Wilkinson's Ancient Egyptians; Flaxman's Lectures on Sculpture; Fuseli's Lectures; Sir Joshua Reynolds's Lectures; also see five articles on Painting, Sculpture, and Architecture, in the Encyclopædia Britannica, and in Smith's Dictionary.

LITERARY GENIUS:

THE GREEK AND ROMAN CLASSICS.

LITERARY GENIUS:

THE GREEK AND ROMAN CLASSICS.

WE know but little of the literature of antiquity until the Greeks applied to it the principles of art. The Sanskrit language has revealed the ancient literature of the Hindus, which is chiefly confined to mystical religious poetry, and which has already been mentioned in the chapter on "Ancient Religions." There was no history worthy the name in India. The Egyptians and Babylonians recorded the triumphs of warriors and domestic events, but those were mere annals without literary value. It is true that the literary remains of Egypt show a reading and writing people as early as three thousand years before Christ, and in their various styles of pen-language reveal a remarkable variety of departments and topics treated, — books of religion, of theology, of ethics, of medicine, of astronomy, of magic, of mythic poetry, of fiction, of personal correspondence, etc. The difficulties of deciphering them, however, and their many peculiarities and for malisms of style, render them rather of curious historical and archæological than of literary interest. The Chinese annals also extend back to a remote period for Confucius wrote history as well as ethics; but Chinese literature has comparatively little interest for us, as also that of all Oriental nations, except the Hindu Vedas and the Persian Zend-Avesta, and a few other poems showing great fertility of the imagination, with a peculiar tenderness and pathos.

Accordingly, as I wish to show chiefly the triumphs of ancient genius when directed to literature generally, and especially such as has had a direct influence upon our modern literature, I confine myself to that of Greece and Rome. Even our present civilization delights in the masterpieces of the classical poets, historians, orators, and essayists, and seeks to rival them. Long before Christianity became a power the great literary artists of Greece had reached perfection in style and language, especially in Athens, to which city youths were sent to be educated, as to a sort of university town where the highest culture was known. Educated Romans were as familiar with the Greek classics as they were with those of their own country, and could talk Greek as the modern cultivated Germans talk French. Without the aid of Greece, Rome could never have reached the civilization to which she attained.

How rich in poetry was classical antiquity, whether sung in the Greek or Latin language! In all those qualities which give immortality classical poetry has never been surpassed, whether in simplicity, in passion, in fervor, in fidelity to nature, in wit, or in imagination. It existed from the early times of Greek civilization, and continued to within a brief period of the fall of the Roman empire. With the rich accumulation of ages the Romans were familiar. They knew nothing indeed of the solitary grandeur of the Jewish muse, or the Nature-myths of the ante-Homeric singers; but they possessed the Iliad and the Odyssey, with their wonderful truthfulness, their clear portraiture of character, their absence of all affectation, their serenity and cheerfulness, their good sense and healthful sentiments, withal so original that the germ of almost every character which has since figured in epic poetry can be found in them.

We see in Homer a poet of the first class, holding the same place in literature that Plato holds in philosophy or Newton in science, and exercising a mighty influence on all the ages which have succeeded him. He was born, probably, at Smyrna, an Ionian city; the dates attributed to him range from the seventh to the twelfth century before Christ. Herodotus puts him at 850 B. C. For nearly three thousand years his immortal creations have been the delight and the inspiration of men of genius; and they are as marvellous to us as they were to the Athenians, since they are exponents of the learning as well as of the consecrated sentiments of the heroic ages. We find in them no pomp of words, no far-fetched thoughts, no theatrical turgidity, no ambitious speculations, no indefinite longings; but we see the manners and customs of the primitive nations, the sights and wonders of the external world, the marvellously interesting traits of human nature as it was and is; and with these we have lessons of moral wisdom, — all recorded with singular simplicity yet astonishing artistic skill. We find in the Homeric narrative accuracy, delicacy, naturalness, with grandeur, sentiment, and beauty, such as Phidias represented in his statues of Zeus. No poems have ever been more popular, and none have extorted greater admiration from critics. Like Shakspeare, Homer is a kind of Bible to both the learned and unlearned among all peoples and ages, — one of the prodigies of the world. His poems form the basis of Greek literature, and are the best understood and the most widely popular of all Grecian compositions. The unconscious simplicity of the Homeric narrative, its high moral tone, its vivid pictures, its graphic details, and its religious spirit create an enthusiasm such as few works of genius can claim. Moreover it presents a painting of society, with its simplicity

and ferocity, its good and evil passions, its tenderness
and its fierceness, such as no other poem affords.
Its influence on the popular mythology of the Greeks
has been already alluded to. If Homer did not create
the Grecian theogony, he gave form and fascination
to it. Nor is it necessary to speak of any other Grecian epic, when the Iliad and the Odyssey attest
the perfection which was attained one hundred and
twenty years before Hesiod was born. Grote thinks
that the Iliad and the Odyssey were produced at
some period between 850 B. C. and 776 B. C.

In lyrical poetry the Greeks were no less remarkable; indeed they attained to what may be called
absolute perfection, owing to the intimate connection
between poetry and music, and the wonderful elasticity
and adaptiveness of their language. Who has surpassed Pindar in artistic skill? His triumphal odes
are pæans, in which piety breaks out in expressions of
the deepest awe and the most elevated sentiments of
moral wisdom. They alone of all his writings have
descended to us, but these, made up as they are of
odic fragments, songs, dirges, and panegyrics, show
the great excellence to which he attained. He was
so celebrated that he was employed by the different
States and princes of Greece to compose choral songs
for special occasions, especially for the public games.
Although a Theban, he was held in the highest esti-

mation by the Athenians, and was courted by kings and princes. Born in Thebes 522 B. C., he died probably in his eightieth year, being contemporary with Æschylus and the battle of Marathon. We possess also fragments of Sappho, Simonides, Anacreon, and others, enough to show that could the lyrical poetry of Greece be recovered, we should probably possess the richest collection that the world has produced.

Greek dramatic poetry was still more varied and remarkable. Even the great masterpieces of Sophocles and Euripides now extant were regarded by their contemporaries as inferior to many other Greek tragedies utterly unknown to us. The great creator of the Greek drama was Æschylus, born at Eleusis 525 B. C. It was not till the age of forty-one that he gained his first prize. Sixteen years afterward, defeated by Sophocles, he quitted Athens in disgust and went to the court of Hiero, king of Syracuse. But he was always held, even at Athens, in the highest honor, and his pieces were frequently reproduced upon the stage. It was not so much the object of Æschylus to amuse an audience as to instruct and elevate it. He combined religious feeling with lofty moral sentiment, and had unrivalled power over the realm of astonishment and terror. "At his summons," says Sir Walter Scott, "the mysterious and tremendous volume of destiny, in which is inscribed the doom of gods and men, seemed to display its leaves of iron before the appalled spectators; the more than mortal voices of Deities, Titans, and departed heroes were heard in awful conference; heaven bowed, and its divinities descended; earth yawned, and gave up the pale spectres of the dead and yet more undefined and ghastly forms of those infernal deities who struck horror into the gods themselves." His imagination dwells in the loftiest regions of the old mythology of Greece; his tone is always pure and moral, though stern and harsh; he appeals to the most violent passions, and is full of the boldest metaphors. In sublimity Æschylus has never been surpassed. He was in poetry what Phidias and Michael Angelo were in art. The critics say that his sublimity of diction is sometimes carried to an extreme, so that his language becomes inflated. His characters, like his sentiments, were sublime, — they were gods and heroes of colossal magnitude. His religious views were Homeric, and he sought to animate his countrymen to deeds of glory, as it became one of the generals who fought at Marathon to do. He was an unconscious genius, and worked like Homer without a knowledge of artistic laws. He was proud and impatient, and his poetry was religious rather than moral. He wrote seventy plays, of which only seven are extant; but these are immortal, among the greatest creations of humar genius, like the dramas of Shakspeare. He died in Sicily, in the sixty-ninth year of his age.

The fame of Sophocles is scarcely less than that of Æschylus. He was twenty-seven years of age when he publicly appeared as a poet. He was born in Colonus, in the suburbs of Athens, 495 B. C., and was the contemporary of Herodotus, of Pericles, of Pindar, of Phidias, of Socrates, of Cimon, of Euripides, — the era of great men, the period of the Peloponnesian War, when everything that was elegant and intellectual culminated at Athens. Sophocles had every element of character and person to fascinate the Greeks, — beauty of face, symmetry of form, skill in gymnastics, calmness and dignity of manner, a cheerful and amiable temper, a ready wit, a meditative piety, a spontaneity of genius, an affectionate admiration for talent, and patriotic devotion to his country. His tragedies, by the universal consent of the best critics, are the perfection of the Greek drama; and they moreover maintain that he has no rival, Æschylus and Shakspeare alone excepted, in the whole realm of dramatic poetry. It was the peculiarity of Sophocles to excite emotions of sorrow and compassion. He loved to paint forlorn heroes. He was human in all his sympathies, perhaps not so religious as Æschylus, but as severely ethical; not so sublime, but more perfect in art. His sufferers are not the victims of an inexorable destiny, but of their own follies. Nor does he even excite emotion apart from a moral end. He lived to be ninety years old, and produced the most beautiful of his tragedies in his eightieth year, the "Œdipus at Colonus." Sophocles wrote the astonishing number of one hundred and thirty plays, and carried off the first prize twenty-four times. His "Antigone" was written when he was forty-five, and when Euripides had already gained a prize. Only seven of his tragedies have survived, but these are priceless treasures.

Euripides, the last of the great triumvirate of the Greek tragic poets, was born at Athens, 485 B. C. He had not the sublimity of Æschylus, nor the touching pathos of Sophocles, nor the stern simplicity of either, but in seductive beauty and successful appeal to passion was superior to both. In his tragedies the passion of love predominates, but it does not breathe the purity of sentiment which marked the tragedies of Æschylus and Sophocles; it approaches rather to the tone of the modern drama. He paints the weakness and corruptions of society, and brings his subjects to the level of common life. He was the pet of the Sophists, and was pantheistic in his views. He does not attempt to show ideal excellence, and his characters represent men not as they ought to be, but as they are, especially in corrupt states of society

Euripides wrote ninety-five plays, of which eighteen are extant. Whatever objection may be urged to his dramas on the score of morality, nobody can question their transcendent art or their great originality.

With the exception of Shakspeare, all succeeding dramatists have copied the three great Greek tragic poets whom we have just named, — especially Racine, who took Sophocles for his model, — even as the great epic poets of all ages have been indebted to Homer.

The Greeks were no less distinguished for comedy than for tragedy. Both tragedy and comedy sprang from feasts in honor of Bacchus; and as the jests and frolics were found misplaced when introduced into grave scenes, a separate province of the drama was formed, and comedy arose. At first it did not derogate from the religious purposes which were at the foundation of the Greek drama; it turned upon parodies in which the adventures of the gods were introduced by way of sport, — as in describing the appetite of Hercules or the cowardice of Bacchus. The comic authors entertained spectators by fantastic and gross displays, by the exhibition of buffoonery and pantomime. But the taste of the Athenians was too severe to relish such entertainments, and comedy passed into ridicule of public men and measures and the fashions of the day. The people loved to see their great men brought down to their own level. Comedy, however, did not flourish until the morals of society were degenerated, and ridicule had become the most effective weapon wherewith to assail prevailing follies. In modern times, comedy reached its culminating point when society was both the most corrupt and the most intellectual, — as in France, when Molière pointed his envenomed shafts against popular vices. In Greece it flourished in the age of Socrates and the Sophists, when there was great bitterness in political parties and an irrepressible desire for novelties. Comedy first made itself felt as a great power in Cratinus, who espoused the side of Cimon against Pericles with great bitterness and vehemence.

Many were the comic writers of that age of wickedness and genius, but all yielded precedence to Aristophanes, of whose writings only his plays have reached us. Never were libels on persons of authority and influence uttered with such terrible license. He attacked the gods, the politicians, the philosophers, and the poets of Athens; even private citizens did not escape from his shafts, and women were the subjects of his irony. Socrates was made the butt of his ridicule when most revered, Cleon in the height of his power, and Euripides when he had gained the highest prizes. Aristophanes has furnished jests for Rabelais, hints to Swift and humor for Molière. In satire, in derision, in invective, as bitter scorn he has never been surpassed. No modern capital would tolerate such unbounded license; yet no plays in their day were ever more popular, or more fully exposed follies which could not otherwise be reached. Aristophanes is called the Father of Comedy, and his comedies are of great historical importance, although his descriptions are doubtless caricatures. He was patriotic in his intentions, even setting up as a reformer. His peculiar genius shines out in his "Clouds," the greatest of his pieces, in which he attacks the Sophists. He wrote fifty-four plays. He was born 444 B. C., and died 380 B. C.

Thus it would appear that in the three great departments of poetry, — the epic, the lyric, and the dramatic, — the old Greeks were great masters, and have been the teachers of all subsequent nations and ages.

The Romans in these departments were not the equals of the Greeks, but they were very successful copyists, and will bear comparison with modern nations. If the Romans did not produce a Homer, they can boast of a Virgil; if they had no Pindar, they furnished a Horace; and in satire they transcended the Greeks.

The Romans produced no poetry worthy of notice until the Greek language and literature were introduced among them. It was not till the fall of Tarentum that we read of a Roman poet. Livius Andronicus, a Greek slave, 240 B.C., rudely translated the Odyssey into Latin, and was the author of various plays, all of which have perished, and none of which, according to Cicero, were worth a second perusal. Still, Andronicus was the first to substitute the Greek drama for the old lyrical stage poetry. One year after the first Punic War, he exhibited the first Roman play. As the creator of the drama he deserves historical notice, though he has no claim to originality, but, like a schoolmaster as he was, pedantically labored to imitate the culture of the Greeks. His plays formed the commencement of Roman translation-literature, and naturalized the Greek metres in Latium, even though they were curiosities rather than works of art.

Nævius, 235 B.C., produced a play at Rome, and wrote both epic and dramatic poetry, but so little has survived that no judgment can be formed of his merits. He was banished for his invectives against the aristocracy, who did not relish severity of comedy. Mommsen regards Nævius as the first of the Romans who deserves to be ranked among the poets. His language was free from stiffness and affectation, and his verses had a graceful flow. In metres he closely adhered to Andronicus.

Plautus was perhaps the first great dramatic poet whom the Romans produced, and his comedies are still admired by critics as both original and fresh. He was born in Umbria, 257 B. C., and was contemporaneous with Publius and Cneius Scipio. He died 184 B. C. The first development of Roman genius in the field of poetry seems to have been the dramatic, in which still the Greek authors were copied. Plautus might be mistaken for a Greek, were it not for the painting of Roman manners, for his garb is essentially Greek. Plautus wrote one hundred and thirty plays, not always for the stage, but for the reading public. He lived about the time of the second Punic War, before the theatre was fairly established at Rome. His characters, although founded on Greek models, act, speak, and joke like Romans. He enjoyed great popularity down to the latest times of the empire, while the purity of his language, as well as the felicity of his wit, was celebrated by the ancient critics. Cicero places his wit on a par with the old Attic comedy; while Jerome spent much time in reading his comedies, even though they afterward cost him tears of bitter regret. Modern dramatists owe much to Plautus. Molière has imitated him in his "Avare," and Shakspeare in his "Comedy of Errors." Lessing pronounces the "Captivi" to be the finest comedy ever brought upon the stage; he translated this play into German, and it has also been admirably translated into English. The great excellence of Plautus was the masterly handling of language, and the adjusting the parts for dramatic effect.

His humor, broad and fresh, produced irresistible comic effects. No one ever surpassed him in his vocabulary of nicknames and his happy jokes. Hence he maintained his popularity in spite of his vulgarity.

Terence shares with Plautus the throne of Roman comedy. He was a Carthaginian slave, born 185 B. C., but was educated by a wealthy Roman into whose hands he fell, and ever after associated with the best society and travelled extensively in Greece. He was greatly inferior to Plautus in originality, and has not exerted a like lasting influence; but he wrote comedies characterized by great purity of diction, which have been translated into all modern languages. Terence, whom Mommsen regards as the most polished, elegant, and chaste of all the poets of the newer comedy, closely copied the Greek Menander. Unlike Plautus, he drew his characters from good society, and his comedies, if not moral, were decent. Plautus wrote for the multitude, Terence for the few; Plautus delighted in noisy dialogue and slang expressions; Terence confined himself to quiet conversation and elegant expressions, for which he was admired by Cicero and Quintilian and other great critics. He aspired to the approval of the cultivated, rather than the applause of the vulgar; and it is a remarkable fact that his comedies supplanted the more original productions of Plautus in the later years of the republic, showing that the literature of the aristocracy was more prized than that of the people, even in a degenerate age.

The "Thyestes" of Varius was regarded in its day as equal to Greek tragedies. Ennius composed tragedies in a vigorous style, and was regarded by the Romans as the parent of their literature, although most of his works have perished. Virgil borrowed many of his thoughts, and was regarded as the prince of Roman song in the time of Cicero. The Latin language is greatly indebted to him. Pacuvius imitated Æschylus in the loftiness of his style. From the times before the Augustan age no tragic production has reached us, although Quintilian speaks highly of Accius, especially of the vigor of his style; but he merely imitated the Greeks. The only tragedy of the Romans which has reached us was written by Seneca the philosopher.

In epic poetry the Romans accomplished more, though even here they are still inferior to the Greeks. The Æneid of Virgil has certainly survived the material glories of Rome. It may not have come up to the exalted ideal of its author; it may be defaced by political flatteries; it may not have the force and originality of the Iliad, — but it is superior in art, and delineates the passion of love with more delicacy than can be found in any Greek author. In soundness of judgment, in tenderness of feeling, in chastened fancy, in picturesque description, in delineation of character, in matchless beauty of diction, and in splendor of versification, it has never been surpassed by any poem in any language, and proudly takes its place among the imperishable works of genius. Henry Thompson, in his "History of Roman Literature," says:—

"Availing himself of the pride and superstition of the Roman people, the poet traces the origin and establishment of the 'Eternal City' to those heroes and actions which had enough in them of what was human and ordinary to excite the sympathies of his countrymen, intermingled with persons and circumstances of an extraordinary and superhuman character to awaken their admiration and awe. No subject could have been more happily chosen. It has been admired also for its perfect unity of action; for while the episodes command the richest variety of description, they are always subordinate to the main object of the poem, which is to impress the divine authority under which Æneas first settled in Italy. The wrath of Juno, upon which the whole fate of Æneas seems to turn, is at once that of a woman and a goddess; the passion of Dido and her general character bring us nearer to the present world, — but the poet is continually introducing higher and more effectual influences, until, by the intervention of gods and men, the Trojan name is to be continued in the Roman, and thus heaven and earth are appeased."

Probably no one work of man has had such a wide and profound influence as this poem of Virgil, — a textbook in all schools since the revival of learning, the model of the Carlovingian poets, the guide of Dante, the oracle of Tasso. Virgil was born seventy years before Christ, and was seven years older than Augustus. His parentage was humble, but his facilities of education were great. He was a most fortunate man, enjoying the friendship of Augustus and Mæcenas, fame in his own lifetime, leisure to prosecute his studies, and ample rewards for his labors. He died at Brundusium at the age of fifty.

In lyrical poetry, the Romans can boast of one of the greatest masters of any age or nation. The Odes of Horace have never been transcended, and will probably remain through all ages the delight of scholars. They may not have the deep religious sentiment and unity of imagination and passion which belong to the Greek lyrical poets, but as works of art, of exquisite felicity of expression, of agreeable images, they are unrivalled. Even in the time of Juvenal his poems were the common school-books of Roman youth. Horace, born 65 B. C., like Virgil was also a favored man, enjoying the friendship of the great, and possessing ease, fame, and fortune; but his longings for retirement and his disgust at the frivolities around him are a sad commentary on satisfied desires. His Odes composed but a small part of his writings. His Epistles are the most perfect of his productions, and rank with the "Georgics" of Virgil and the "Satires" of Juvenal as the most perfect form of Roman verse. His satires are also admirable, but without the fierce vehemence and lofty indignation that characterized those of Juvenal. It is the folly rather than the wickedness of vice which Horace describes with such playful skill and such keenness of observation. He was the first to mould the Latin tongue to the Greek lyric measures. Quintilian's criticism is indorsed by all scholars, — *Lyricorum Horatius fere solus legi dignus, in verbis felicissime audax.* No poetry was ever more severely elaborated than that of Horace, and the melody of the language imparts to it a peculiar fascination. If inferior to Pindar in passion and loftiness, it glows with a more genial humanity and with purer wit. It cannot be enjoyed fully except by those versed in the experiences of life, who perceive in it a calm wisdom, a penetrating sagacity, a sober enthusiasm, and a refined taste, which are unusual even among the masters of human thought.

It is the fashion to depreciate the original merits of this poet, as well as those of Virgil, Plautus, and Terence, because they derived so much assistance from the Greeks. But the Greeks also borrowed from one another. Pure originality is impossible. It is the mission of art to add to its stores, without hoping to monopolize the whole realm. Even Shakspeare, the most original of modern poets, was vastly indebted to those who went before him, and he has not escaped the hypercriticism of minute observers.

In this mention of lyrical poetry I have not spoken of Catullus, unrivalled in tender lyric, the greatest poet before the Augustan era. He was born 87 B. C., and enjoyed the friendship of the most celebrated characters. One hundred and sixteen of his poems have come down to us, most of which are short, and many of them defiled by great coarseness and sensuality. Critics say, however, that whatever he touched he adorned; that his vigorous simplicity, pungent wit, startling invective, and felicity of expression make him one of the great poets of the Latin language.

In didactic poetry Lucretius was pre-eminent, and is regarded by Schlegel as the first of Roman poets in native genius. He was born 95 B. C., and died at the age of forty-two by his own hand. His principal poem "De Rerum Natura" is a delineation of the Epicurean philosophy, and treats of all the great subjects of thought with which his age was conversant. Somewhat resembling Pope's "Essay on Man" in style and subject, it is immeasurably superior in poetical genius. It is a lengthened disquisition, in seven thousand four hundred lines, upon the great phenomena of the outward world. As a painter and worshipper of Nature, Lucretius was superior to all the poets of antiquity.

His skill in presenting abstruse speculations is marvellous, and his outbursts of poetic genius are matchless in power and beauty. Into all subjects he casts a fearless eye, and writes with sustained enthusiasm. But he was not fully appreciated by his countrymen, although no other poet has so fully brought out the power of the Latin language. Professor Ramsay, while alluding to the melancholy tenderness of Tibullus, the exquisite ingenuity of Ovid, the inimitable felicity and taste of Horace, the gentleness and splendor of Virgil, and the vehement declamation of Juvenal, thinks that had the verse of Lucretius perished we should never have known that the Latin could give utterance to the grandest conceptions, with all that self-sustained majesty and harmonious swell in which the Grecian muse rolls forth her loftiest outpourings. The eulogium of Ovid is —

> "Carmina sublimis tunc sunt peritura Lucreti,
> Exitio terras quum dabit una dies."

Elegiac poetry has an honorable place in Roman literature. To this school belongs Ovid, born 43 B. C., died 18 A. D., whose "Tristia," a doleful description of the evils of exile, were much admired by the Romans. His most famous work was his "Metamorphoses," mythologic legends involving transformations, — a most poetical and imaginative production. He, with that self-conscious genius common to poets, declares that his poem would be proof against sword, fire, thunder, and time, — a prediction, says Bayle, which has not yet proved false. Niebuhr thinks that Ovid next to Catullus was the most poetical of his countrymen. Milton thinks he might have surpassed Virgil, had he attempted epic poetry. He was nearest to the romantic school of all the classical authors; and Chaucer, Ariosto, and Spenser owe to him great obligations. Like Pope, his verses flowed spontaneously. His "Tristia" were more highly praised than his "Amores" or his "Metamorphoses," a fact which shows that contemporaries are not always the best judges of real merit. His poems, great as was their genius, are deficient in the severe taste which marked the Greeks, and are immoral in their tendency. He had great advantages, but was banished by Augustus for his description of licentious love. Nor did he support exile with dignity; he languished like Cicero when doomed to a similar fate, and died of a broken heart. But few intellectual men have ever been able to live at a distance from the scene of their glories, and without the stimulus of high society. Chrysostom is one of the few exceptions. Ovid, as an immoral writer, was justly punished.

Tibullus, also a famous elegiac poet, was born the same year as Ovid, and was the friend of the poet Horace. He lived in retirement, and was both gentle and amiable. At his beautiful country-seat he soothed his soul with the charms of literature and the simple pleasures of the country. Niebuhr pronounces the elegies of Tibullus to be doleful, but Merivale thinks that "the tone of tender melancholy in which he sung his unprosperous loves had a deeper and purer source than the caprices of three inconstant paramours. . . . His spirit is eminently religious, though it bids him fold his hands in resignation rather than open them in hope. He alone of all the great poets of his day remained undazzled by the glitter of the Cæsarian usurpation, and pined away in unavailing despondency while beholding the subjugation of his country."

Propertius, the contemporary of Tibullus, born 51 B. C., was on the contrary the most eager of all the flatterers of Augustus, — a man of wit and pleasure, whose object of idolatry was Cynthia, a poetess and a courtesan. He was an imitator of the Greeks, but had a great contemporary fame. He showed much warmth of passion, but never soared into the sublime heights of poetry like his rival.

Such were among the great elegiac poets of Rome, who were generally devoted to the delineation of the passion of love. The older English poets resembled them in this respect, but none of them have risen to such lofty heights as the later ones, — for instance, Wordsworth and Tennyson. It is in lyric poetry that the moderns have chiefly excelled the ancients, in variety, in elevation of sentiment, and in imagination. The grandeur and originality of the ancients were displayed rather in epic and dramatic poetry.

In satire the Romans transcended both the Greeks and the moderns. Satire arose with Lucilius, 148 B. C., in the time of Marius, an age when freedom of speech was tolerated. Horace was the first to gain immortality in this department. Next Persius comes, born 34 A. D., the friend of Lucian and Seneca in the time of Nero, who painted the vices of his age as it was passing to that degradation which marked the reign of Domitian, when Juvenal appeared. The latter, disdaining fear, boldly set forth the abominations of the times, and struck without distinction all who departed from duty and conscience. There is nothing in any language which equals the fire, the intensity, and the bitterness of Juvenal, not even the invectives of Swift and Pope. But he flourished during the decline of literature, and had neither the taste nor the elegance of the Augustan writers. He was born 60 A. D., the son of a freedman, and was the contemporary of Martial. He was banished by Domitian on account of a lampoon against a favorite dancer, but under the reign of Nerva he returned to Rome, and the imperial tyranny was the subject of his bitterest denunciation next to the degradation of public morals. His great rival in satire was Horace, who laughed at follies; but Juvenal, more austere, exaggerated and denounced them. His sarcasms on women have never been equalled in severity, and we cannot but hope that they were unjust. From an historical point of view, as a delineation of the manners of his age, his satires are priceless, even like the epigrams of Martial. This uncompromising poet, not pliant and easy like Horace, animadverted like an incorruptible censor on the vices which were undermining the moral health and preparing the way for violence; on the hypocrisy of philosophers and the cruelty of tyrants; on the frivolity of women and the debauchery of men. He discoursed on the vanity of human wishes with the moral wisdom of Dr. Johnson, and urged self-improvement like Socrates and Epictetus.

I might speak of other celebrated poets, — of Lucan, of Martial, of Petronius; but I only wish to show that the great poets of antiquity, both Greek and Roman, have never been surpassed in genius, in taste, and in art, and that few were ever more honored in their lifetime by appreciating admirers, — showing the advanced state of civilization which was reached in those classic countries in everything pertaining to the realm of thought and art.

The genius of the ancients was displayed in prose composition as well as in poetry, although perfection was not so soon attained. The poets were the great creators of the languages of antiquity. It was not until they had produced their immortal works that the languages were sufficiently softened and refined to admit of great beauty in prose. But prose requires art as well as poetry. There is an artistic rhythm in the writings of the classical authors — like those of Cicero, Herodotus, and Thucydides — as marked as in the beautiful measure of Homer and Virgil. Plato did not write poetry, but his prose is as "musical as Apollo's lyre." Burke and Macaulay are as great artists in style as Tennyson himself. And it is seldom that men, either in ancient or modern times, have been distinguished for both kinds of composition, although Voltaire, Schiller, Milton, Swift, and Scott are among the exceptions. Cicero, the greatest prose writer of antiquity, produced in poetry only a single inferior work, which was laughed at by his contemporaries. Bacon, with all his affluence of thought, vigor of imagination, and command of language, could not write poetry any easier than Pope could write prose, — although it is asserted by some modern writers, of no great reputation, that Bacon wrote Shakspeare's plays.

All sorts of prose compositions were carried to perfection by both Greeks and Romans, in history, in criticism, in philosophy, in oratory, in epistles.

The earliest great prose writer among the Greeks was Herodotus, 484 B. C., from which we may infer that History was the first form of prose composition to attain development. But Herodotus was not born until Æschylus had gained a prize for tragedy, nor for more than two hundred years after Simonides the lyric poet flourished, and probably five or six hundred years after Homer sang his immortal epics; yet though two thousand years and more have passed since he wrote, the style of this great "Father of History" is admired by every critic, while his history as a work of art is still a study and a marvel. It is difficult to understand why no work in prose anterior to Herodotus is worthy of note, since the Greeks had attained a high civilization two hundred years before he appeared, and the language had reached a high point of development under Homer for more than five hundred years. The History of Herodotus was probably written in the decline of life, when his mind was enriched with great attainments in all the varied learning of his age, and when he had conversed with most of the celebrated men of the various countries he had visited. It pertains chiefly to the wars of the Greeks with the Persians; but in his frequent episodes, which do not impair the unity of the work, he is led to speak of the manners and customs of the Oriental nations. It was once the fashion to speak of

Herodotus as a credulous man, who embodied the most improbable though interesting stories. But now it is believed that no historian was ever more profound, conscientious, and careful; and all modern investigations confirm his sagacity and impartiality. He was one of the most accomplished men of antiquity, or of any age, — an enlightened and curious traveller, a profound thinker; a man of universal knowledge, familiar with the whole range of literature, art, and science in his day; acquainted with all the great men of Greece and at the courts of Asiatic princes; the friend of Sophocles, of Pericles, of Thucydides, of Aspasia, of Socrates, of Damon, of Zeno, of Phidias, of Protagoras, of Euripides, of Polygnotus, of Anaxagoras, of Xenophon, of Alcibiades, of Lysias, of Aristophanes, — the most brilliant constellation of men of genius who were ever found together within the walls of a Grecian city, — respected and admired by these great lights, all of whom were inferior to him in knowledge. Thus was he fitted for his task by travel, by study, and by intercourse with the great, to say nothing of his original genius. The greatest prose work which had yet appeared in Greece was produced by Herodotus, — a prose epic, severe in taste, perfect in unity, rich in moral wisdom, charming in style, religious in spirit, grand in subject, without a coarse passage; simple, unaffected, and beautiful, like the narratives of the Bible, amusing yet instructive, easy to understand, yet extending to the utmost boundaries of human research, — a model for all subsequent historians. So highly was this historic composition valued by the Athenians when their city was at the height of its splendor that they decreed to its author ten talents (about twelve thousand dollars) for reciting it. He even went from city to city, a sort of prose rhapsodist, or like a modern lecturer, reciting his history, — an honored and extraordinary man, a sort of Humboldt, having mastered everything. And he wrote, not for fame, but to communicate the results of inquiries made to satisfy his craving for knowledge, which he obtained by personal investigation at Dodona, at Delphi, at Samos, at Athens, at Corinth, at Thebes, at Tyre; he even travelled into Egypt, Scythia, Asia Minor, Palestine, Babylonia, Italy, and the islands of the sea. His episode on Egypt is worth more, from an historical point of view, than all things combined which have descended to us from antiquity. Herodotus was the first to give dignity to history; nor in truthfulness, candor, and impartiality has he ever been surpassed. His very simplicity of style is a proof of his transcendent art, even as it is the evidence of his severity of taste. The translation of this great history by Rawlinson, with notes, is invaluable.

To Thucydides, as an historian, the modern world

also assigns a proud pre-eminence. He was born 471 B. C., and lived twenty years in exile on account of a military failure. He treated only of a short period, during the Peloponnesian War; but the various facts connected with that great event could be known only by the most minute and careful inquiries. He devoted twenty-seven years to the composition of his narrative, and weighed his evidence with the most scrupulous care. His style has not the fascination of Herodotus, but it is more concise. In a single volume Thucydides relates what could scarcely be compressed into eight volumes of a modern history. As a work of art, of its kind it is unrivalled. In his description of the plague of Athens this writer is as minute as he is simple. He abounds with rich moral reflections, and has a keen perception of human character. His pictures are striking and tragic. He is vigorous and intense, and every word he uses has a meaning, but some of his sentences are not always easily understood. One of the greatest tributes which can be paid to him is the estimate of an able critic, George Long, that we have a more exact history of a protracted and eventful period by Thucydides than we have of any period in modern history equally extended and eventful; and all this is compressed into a volume.

Xenophon is the last of the trio of the Greek historians whose writings are classic and inimitable. He was born probably about 444 B. C. He is characterized by great simplicity and absence of affectation. His "Anabasis," in which he describes the expedition of the younger Cyrus and the retreat of the ten thousand Greeks, is his most famous book. But his "Cyropædia," in which the history of Cyrus is the subject, although still used as a classic in colleges for the beauty of its style, has no value as a history, since the author merely adopted the current stories of his hero without sufficient investigation. Xenophon wrote a variety of treatises and dialogues, but his "Memorabilia" of Socrates is the most valuable. All antiquity and all modern writers unite in ascribing to Xenophon great merit as a writer and great moral elevation as a man.

If we pass from the Greek to the Latin historians, — to those who were as famous as the Greek, and whose merit has scarcely been transcended in our modern times, if indeed it has been equalled, — the great names of Sallust, of Cæsar, of Livy, of Tacitus rise up before us, together with a host of other names we have not room or disposition to present, since we only aim to show that the ancients were at least our equals in this great department of prose composition. The first great masters of the Greek language in prose were the historians, so far as we can judge by the writings that have descended to us, although it is probable that the orators may have shaped the language before them, and given it flexibility and refinement The first great prose writers of Rome were the orators; nor was the Latin language fully developed and polished until Cicero appeared. But we do not here write a history of the language; we speak only of those who wrote immortal works in the various departments of learning.

As Herodotus did not arise until the Greek language had been already formed by the poets, so no great prose writer appeared among the Romans for a considerable time after Plautus, Terence, Ennius, and Lucretius flourished. The first great historian was Sallust, the contemporary of Cicero, born 86 B. C., the year that Marius died. Q. Fabius Pictor, M. Portius Cato, and L. Cal. Piso had already written works which are mentioned with respect by Latin authors, but they were mere annalists or antiquarians, like the chroniclers of the Middle Ages, and had no claim as artists. Sallust made Thucydides his model, but fell below him in genius and elevated sentiment. He was born a plebeian, and rose to distinction by his talents, but was ejected from the senate for his profligacy. Afterward he made a great fortune as prætor and governor of Numidia, and lived in magnificence on the Quirinal, — one of the most profligate of the literary men of antiquity. We possess but a small portion of his works, but the fragments which have come down to us show peculiar merit. He sought to penetrate the human heart, and to reveal the secret motives which actuate the conduct of men. The style of Sallust is brilliant, but his art is always apparent; he is clear and lively, but rhetorical. Like Voltaire, who inaugurated modern history, Sallust thought more of style than of accuracy as to facts. He was a party man, and never soared beyond his party. He aped the moralist, but exalted egoism and love of pleasure into proper springs of action, and honored talent disconnected with virtue. Like Carlyle, Sallust exalted *strong* men, and *because* they were strong. He was not comprehensive like Cicero, or philosophical like Thucydides, although he affected philosophy as he did morality. He was the first who deviated from the strict narratives of events, and also introduced much rhetorical declamation, which he puts into the mouths of his heroes. He wrote for *éclat*.

Julius Cæsar, born 100 or 102 B. C., as an historian ranks higher than Sallust, and no Roman ever wrote purer Latin. Yet his historical works, however great their merit, but feebly represent the transcendent genius of the most august name of antiquity. He was mathematician, architect, poet, philologist, orator, jurist, general, statesman, and imperator. In eloquence he was second only to Cicero. The great value of Cæsar's history is in the sketches of the productions, the manners, the customs, and the political conditions of Gaul, Britain, and Germany. His observations on military science, on the operation of sieges and the construction of bridges and military engines are valuable; but the description of his military career is only a studied apology for his crimes, — even as the bulletins of Napoleon were set forth to show his victories in the most favorable light. Cæsar's fame rests on his victories and successes as a statesman rather than on his merits as an historian, — even as Louis Napoleon will live in history for his deeds rather than as the apologist of his great usurping prototype. Cæsar's "Commentaries" resemble the history of Herodotus more than any other Latin production, at least in style; they are simple and unaffected, precise and elegant, plain and without pretension.

The Augustan age which followed, though it produced a constellation of poets who shed glory upon the throne before which they prostrated themselves in abject homage, like the courtiers of Louis XIV., still was unfavorable to prose composition, — to history as well as eloquence. Of the historians of that age, Livy, born 59 B. C., is the only one whose writings are known to us, in the shape of some fragments of his history. He was a man of distinction at court, and had a great literary reputation, — so great that a Spaniard travelled from Cadiz on purpose to see him. Most of the great historians of the world have occupied places of honor and rank, which were given to them not as prizes for literary successes, but for the experience, knowledge, and culture which high social position and ample means secure. Herodotus lived in courts; Thucydides was a great general, as also was Xenophon; Cæsar was the first man of his times; Sallust was prætor and governor; Livy was tutor to Claudius; Tacitus was prætor and consul; Eusebius was bishop and favorite of Constantine; Ammianus was the friend of the Emperor Julian; Gregory of Tours was one of the leading prelates of the West; Froissart attended in person, as a man of rank, the military expeditions of his day; Clarendon was Lord Chancellor; Burnet was a bishop and favorite of William III.; Thiers and Guizot both were prime ministers; while Gibbon, Hume, Robertson, Macaulay, Grote, Milman, Froude, Neander, Niebuhr, Müller Dahlman, Buckle, Prescott, Irving, Bancroft, Motley, have all been men of wealth or position. Nor do I remember a single illustrious historian who has been poor and neglected.

The ancients regarded Livy as the greatest of historians, — an opinion not indorsed by modern critics, on account of his inaccuracies. But his narrative is always interesting, and his language pure. He did not sift evidence like Grote, nor generalize like Gibbon;

but like Voltaire and Macaulay, he was an artist in style, and possessed undoubted genius. His Annals are comprised in one hundred and forty-two books, extending from the foundation of the city to the death of Drusus, 9 B.C., of which only thirty-five have come down to us.

Livy, unlike most of the Roman historians who preceded him, was not merely a narrator of facts. "His story flows in a calm, clear, sparkling current, with every charm which simplicity and ease can give." He delineates character with great clearness and power; his speeches are noble rhetorical compositions; his sentences are rhythmical cadences. Livy was not a critical historian like Herodotus, for he took his materials second-hand, and was ignorant of geography, nor did he write with the exalted ideal of Thucydides; but as a painter of beautiful forms, which only a rich imagination could conjure, he is unrivalled in the history of literature. Moreover, he was honest and sound in heart, and was just and impartial in reference to those facts with which he was conversant.

In the estimation of modern critics the highest rank as an historian is assigned to Tacitus, and it would indeed be difficult to find his superior in any age or country. He was born 57 A.D., about forty-three years after the death of Augustus. He belonged to the equestrian rank, and was a man of consular dignity.

He had every facility for literary labors that leisure, wealth, friends, and social position could give, and lived under a reign when truth might be told. The extant works of this great writer are the "Life of Agricola," his father-in-law; his "Annales," which begin with the death of Augustus, 14 A. D., and close with the death of Nero, 68 A. D.; the "Historiæ," which comprise the period from the second consulate of Galba, 68 A. D., to the death of Domitian; and a treatise on the Germans. His histories describe Rome in the fulness of imperial glory, when the will of one man was the supreme law of the empire. He also wrote of events that occurred when liberty had fled, and the yoke of despotism was nearly insupportable. He describes a period of great moral degradation, nor does he hesitate to lift the veil of hypocrisy in which his generation had wrapped itself. He fearlessly exposes the cruelties and iniquities of the early emperors, and writes with judicial impartiality respecting all the great characters he describes. No ancient writer shows greater moral dignity and integrity of purpose than Tacitus. In point of artistic unity he is superior to Livy and equal to Thucydides, whom he resembles in conciseness of style. His distinguishing excellence as an historian is his sagacity and impartiality. Nothing escapes his penetrating eye; and he inflicts merited chastisement on the tyrants who revelled in the prostrated liberties of his country, while he immortalizes those few who were faithful to duty and conscience in a degenerate age. But the writings of Tacitus were not so popular as those of Livy, since neither princes nor people relished his intellectual independence and moral elevation. He does not satisfy Dr. Arnold, who thinks he ought to have been better versed in the history of the Jews, and who dislikes his speeches because they were fictitious.

Neither the Latin nor Greek historians are admired by those dry critics who seek to give to rare antiquarian matter a disproportionate importance, and to make this matter as fixed and certain as the truths of natural science. History can never be other than an approximation to the truth, even when it relates to the events and characters of its own age. History does not give positive, indisputable knowledge. We know that Cæsar was ambitious; but we do not know whether he was more or less so than Pompey, nor do we know how far he was justified in his usurpation. A great history must have other merits besides accuracy, antiquarian research, and presentation of authorities and notes. It must be a work of art; and art has reference to style and language, to grouping of details and richness of illustration, to eloquence and poetry and beauty. A dry history, however learned, will never be read; it will only be consulted, like a law-book, or Mosheim's "Commentaries." We require *life* in history, and it is for their vividness that the writings of Livy and Tacitus will be perpetuated. Voltaire and Schiller have no great merit as historians in a technical sense, but the "Life of Charles XII." and the "Thirty Years' War" are still classics. Neander has written one of the most searching and recondite histories of modern times; but it is too dry, too deficient in art, to be cherished, and may pass away like the voluminous writings of Varro, the most learned of the Romans. It is the *art* which is immortal in a book, — not the knowledge, nor even the thoughts. What keeps alive the "Provincial Letters" of Pascal? It is the style, the irony, the elegance that characterize them. The exquisite delineation of character, the moral wisdom, the purity and force of language, the artistic arrangement, and the lively and interesting narrative appealing to all minds, like the "Arabian Nights" or Froissart's "Chronicles," are the elements which give immortality to the classic authors. We will not let them perish, because they amuse and interest and inspire us.

A remarkable example is that of Plutarch, who, although born a Greek and writing in the Greek language, was a contemporary of Tacitus, lived long in Rome, and was one of the "immortals" of the imperial age. A teacher of philosophy during his early manhood, he spent his last years as archon and priest of Apollo in his native town. His most famous work is his "Parallel Lives" of forty-six historic Greeks and Romans, arranged in pairs, depicted with marvellous art and all the fascination of anecdote and social wit, while presenting such clear conceptions of characters and careers, and the whole so restrained within the bounds of good taste and harmonious proportion, as to have been even to this day regarded as forming a model for the ideal biography.

But it is taking a narrow view of history to make all writers after the same pattern, even as it would be bigoted to make all Christians belong to the same sect. Some will be remarkable for style, others for learning, and others again for moral and philosophical wisdom; some will be minute, and others generalizing; some will dig out a multiplicity of facts without apparent object, and others induce from those facts; some will make essays, and others chronicles. We have need of all styles and all kinds of excellence. A great and original thinker may not have the time or opportunity or taste for a minute and searching criticism of original authorities; but he may be able to generalize previously established facts so as to draw most valuable moral instruction from them for the benefit of his readers. History is a boundless field of inquiry; no man can master it in all its departments and periods. It will not do to lay great emphasis on minute details, and neglect the art of generalization. If an historian attempts to embody too much learning, he is likely to be deficient in originality; if he would say everything, he is apt to be dry; if he elaborates too much, he loses animation. Moreover, different classes of readers require different kinds and styles of histories; there must be histories for students, histories for old men, histories for young men, histories to amuse, and histories to instruct. If all men were to write history according to Dr. Arnold's views, we should have histories of interest only to classical scholars. The ancient historians never quoted their sources of knowledge, but were valued for their richness of thoughts and artistic beauty of style. The ages in which they flourished attached no value to pedantic displays of learning paraded in foot-notes.

Thus the great historians whom I have mentioned, both Greek and Latin, have few equals and no superiors in our own times in those things that are most to be admired. They were not pedants, but men of immense genius and genuine learning, who blended the profoundest principles of moral wisdom with the most fascinating narrative,— men universally popular among learned and unlearned, great artists in style, and masters of the language in which they wrote.

Rome can boast of no great historian after Tacitus,

who should have belonged to the Ciceronian epoch. Suetonius, born about the year 70 A. D., shortly after Nero's death, was rather a biographer than an historian; nor as a biographer does he take a high rank. His "Lives of the Cæsars," like Diogenes Laertius's "Lives of the Philosophers," are rather anecdotical than historical. L. Anneus Florus, who flourished during the reign of Trajan, has left a series of sketches of the different wars from the days of Romulus to those of Augustus. Frontinus epitomized the large histories of Pompeius. Ammianus Marcellinus wrote a history from Nerva to Valens, and is often quoted by Gibbon. But none wrote who should be adduced as examples of the triumph of genius, except Sallust, Cæsar, Livy, Plutarch, and Tacitus.

There is another field of prose composition in which the Greeks and Romans gained great distinction, and proved themselves equal to any nation of modern times, — that of eloquence. It is true, we have not a rich collection of ancient speeches; but we have every reason to believe that both Greeks and Romans were most severely trained in the art of public speaking, and that forensic eloquence was highly prized and munificently rewarded. It began with democratic institutions, and flourished as long as the People were a great power in the State; it declined whenever and wherever tyrants bore rule. Eloquence and liberty flourish together; nor can there be eloquence where there is not freedom of debate. In the fifth century before Christ — the first century of democracy — great orators arose, for without the power and the opportunity of defending himself against accusation no man could hold an ascendent position. Socrates insisted upon the gift of oratory for a general in the army as well as for a leader in political life. In Athens the courts of justice were numerous, and those who could not defend themselves were obliged to secure the services of those who were trained in the use of public speaking. Thus arose the lawyers, among whom eloquence was more in demand and more richly paid than in any other class. Rhetoric became connected with dialectics, and in Greece, Sicily, and Italy both were extensively cultivated. Empedocles was distinguished as much for rhetoric as for philosophy. It was not, however, in the courts of law that eloquence displayed the greatest fire and passion, but in political assemblies. These could only coexist with liberty; for a democracy is more favorable than an aristocracy to large assemblies of citizens. In the Grecian republics eloquence as an art may be said to have been born. It was nursed and fed by political agitation, by the strife of parties. It arose from appeals to the people as a source of power when the people were not cultivated, it addressed chiefly popular passions and prejudices; when they were enlightened, it addressed interests.

It was in Athens, where there existed the purest form of democratic institutions, that eloquence rose to the loftiest heights in the ancient world, so far as eloquence appeals to popular passions. Pericles, the greatest statesman of Greece, 495 B. C., was celebrated for his eloquence, although no specimens remain to us. It was conceded by the ancient authors that his oratory was of the highest kind, and the epithet of "Olympian" was given him, as carrying the weapons of Zeus upon his tongue. His voice was sweet, and his utterance distinct and rapid. Peisistratus was also famous for his eloquence, although he was a usurper and a tyrant. Isocrates, 436 B. C., was a professed rhetorician, and endeavored to base his art upon sound moral principles, and rescue it from the influence of the Sophists. He was the great teacher of the most eminent statesmen of his day. Twenty-one of his orations have come down to us, and they are excessively polished and elaborated; but they were written to be read, they were not extemporary. His language is the purest and most refined Attic dialect. Lysias, 458 B. C., was a fertile writer of orations also, and he is reputed to have produced as many as four hundred and twenty-five; of these only thirty-five are extant.

They are characterized by peculiar gracefulness and elegance, which did not interfere with strength. So able were these orations that only two were unsuccessful. They were so pure that they were regarded as the best canon of the Attic idiom.

But all the orators of Greece — and Greece was the land of orators — gave way to Demosthenes, born 385 B. C. He received a good education, and is said to have been instructed in philosophy by Plato and in eloquence by Isocrates; but it is more probable that he privately prepared himself for his brilliant career. As soon as he attained his majority, he brought suits against the men whom his father had appointed his guardians, for their waste of property, and after two years was successful, conducting the prosecution himself. It was not until the age of thirty that he appeared as a speaker in the public assembly on political matters, where he rapidly attained universal respect, and became one of the leading statesmen of Athens. Henceforth he took an active part in every question that concerned the State. He especially distinguished himself in his speeches against Macedonian aggrandizements, and his Philippics are perhaps the most brilliant of his orations. But the cause which he advocated was unfortunate; the battle of Cheronæa, 338 B. C., put an end to the independence of Greece, and Philip of Macedon was all-powerful. For this catastrophe Demosthenes was somewhat responsible, but as his motives were conceded to be pure and his patriotism lofty, he retained the confidence of his countrymen. Accused by Æschines, he delivered his famous Oration on the Crown. Afterward, during the supremacy of Alexander, Demosthenes was again accused, and suffered exile. Recalled from exile on the death of Alexander, he roused himself for the deliverance of Greece, without success; and hunted by his enemies he took poison in the sixty-third year of his age, having vainly contended for the freedom of his country, — one of the noblest spirits of antiquity, and lofty in his private life.

As an orator Demosthenes has not probably been equalled by any man of any country. By his contemporaries he was regarded as faultless in this respect; and when it is remembered that he struggled against physical difficulties which in the early part of his career would have utterly discouraged any ordinary man, we feel that he deserves the highest commendation. He never spoke without preparation, and most of his orations were severely elaborated. He never trusted to the impulse of the occasion; he did not believe in extemporary eloquence any more than Daniel Webster, who said there is no such thing. All the orations of Demosthenes exhibit him as a pure and noble patriot, and are full of the loftiest sentiments. He was a great artist, and his oratorical successes were greatly owing to the arrangement of his speeches and the application of the strongest arguments in their proper places. Added to this moral and intellectual superiority was the "magic power of his language, majestic and simple at the same time, rich yet not bombastic, strange and yet familiar, solemn and not too ornate, grave and yet pleasing, concise and yet fluent, sweet and yet impressive, which altogether carried away the minds of his hearers." His orations were most highly prized by the ancients, who wrote innumerable commentaries on them, most of which are lost. Sixty of the great productions of his genius have come down to us.

Demosthenes, like other orators, first became known as the composer of speeches for litigants; but his fame was based on the orations he pronounced in great political emergencies. His rival was Æschines, who was vastly inferior to Demosthenes, although bold, vigorous, and brilliant. Indeed, the opinions of mankind for two thousand years have been unanimous in ascribing to Demosthenes the highest position as an orator among all the men of ancient and modern times. David Hume says of him that "could his manner be copied, its success would be infallible over a modern audience." Says Lord Brougham, "It is rapid harmony exactly adjusted to the sense. It is vehement reasoning, without any appearance of art. It is disdain, anger, boldness, freedom involved in a continual stream of argument; so that of all human productions his orations present to us the models which approach the nearest to perfection."

It is probable that the Romans were behind the Athenians in all the arts of rhetoric; yet in the days of the republic celebrated orators arose among the lawyers and politicians. It was in forensic eloquence that Latin prose first appeared as a cultivated language; for the forum was to the Romans what libraries are to us. The art of public speaking in Rome was early developed. Cato, Lælius, Carbo, and the Gracchi are said to have been majestic and harmonious in speech, yet excelled by Antonius, Crassus, Cotta, Sulpitius, and Hortensius. The last had a very brilliant career as an orator, though his orations were too florid to be read. Cæsar was also distinguished for his eloquence, its characteristics being force and purity. "Cœlius was noted for lofty sentiment, Brutus for philosophical wisdom, Calidius for a delicate and harmonious style, and Calvus for sententious force."

But all the Roman orators yielded to Cicero, as the Greeks did to Demosthenes. These two men are always coupled together when allusion is made to eloquence. They were pre-eminent in the ancient world, and have never been equalled in the modern.

Cicero, 106 B. C., was probably not equal to his great Grecian rival in vehemence, in force, in fiery argument which swept everything away before him, nor generally in original genius; but he was his superior in learning, in culture, and in breadth. Cicero distinguished himself very early as an advocate, but his first great public effort was made in the prosecution of Verres for corruption. Although Verres was defended by Hortensius and backed by the whole influence of the Metelli and other powerful families, Cicero gained his cause, — more fortunate than Burke in his prosecution of Warren Hastings, who also was sustained by powerful interests and families. The speech on the Manilian Law, when Cicero appeared as a political orator, greatly contributed to his popularity. I need not describe his memorable career, — his successive elections to all the highest offices of state, his detection of Catiline's conspiracy, his opposition to turbulent and ambitious partisans, his alienations and friendships, his brilliant career as a statesman, his misfortunes and sorrows, his exile and recall, his splendid services to the State, his greatness and his defects, his virtues and weaknesses, his triumphs and martyrdom. These are foreign to my purpose. No man of heathen antiquity is better known to us, and no man by pure genius ever won more glorious laurels. His life and labors are immortal. His virtues and services are embalmed in the heart of the world. Few men ever performed greater literary labors, and in so many of its departments. Next to Aristotle and Varro, Cicero was the most learned man of antiquity, but performed more varied labors than either, since he was not only great as a writer and speaker, but also as a statesman, being the most conspicuous man in Rome after Pompey and Cæsar. He may not have had the moral greatness of Socrates, nor the philosophical genius of Plato, nor the overpowering eloquence of Demosthenes, but he was a master of all the wisdom of antiquity. Even civil law, the great science of the Romans, became interesting in his hands, and was divested of its dryness and technicality. He popularized history, and paid honor to all art, even to the stage; he made the Romans conversant with the philosophy of Greece, and systematized the various speculations. He may not have added to philosophy, but no Roman after him understood so well the practical bearing of all its various systems. His glory is purely intellectual, and it was by sheer genius that he rose to his exalted position and influence.

But it was in forensic eloquence that Cicero was pre-eminent, in which he had but one equal in ancient times. Roman eloquence culminated in him. He composed about eighty orations, of which fifty-nine are preserved. Some were delivered from the rostrum to the people, and some in the senate; some were mere philippics, as severe in denunciation as those of Demosthenes; some were laudatory; some were judicial; but all were severely logical, full of historical allusion, profound in philosophical wisdom, and pervaded with the spirit of patrictism. Francis W. Newman, in his "Regal Rome," thus describes Cicero's eloquence: —

"He goes round and round his object, surveys it in every light, examines it in all its parts, retires and then advances, compares and contrasts it, illustrates, confirms, and enforces it, till the hearer feels ashamed of doubting a position which seems built on a foundation so strictly argumentative. And having established his case, he opens upon his opponent a discharge of raillery so delicate and good-natured that it is impossible for the latter to maintain his ground against it; or, when the subject is too grave, he colors his exaggerations with all the bitterness of irony and vehemence of passion."

Critics have uniformly admired Cicero's style as peculiarly suited to the Latin language, which, being scanty and unmusical, requires more redundancy than the Greek. The simplicity of the Attic writers would make Latin composition bald and tame. To be perspicuous, the Latin must be full. Thus Arnold thinks that what Tacitus gained in energy he lost in elegance and perspicuity. But Cicero, dealing with a barren and unphilosophical language, enriched it with circumlocutions and metaphors, while he freed it of harsh and uncouth expressions, and thus became the greatest master of composition the world has seen. He was a great artist, making use of his scanty materials to the best effect; he had absolute control over the resources of his vernacular tongue, and not only unrivalled skill in composition, but tact and judgment. Thus he was generally successful, in spite of the venality and corruption of the times. The courts of justice were the scenes of his earliest triumphs; nor until he was prætor did he speak from the rostrum on mere political questions, as in reference to the Manilian and Agrarian laws. It is in his political discourses that Cicero rises to the highest ranks. In his speeches against Verres, Catiline, and Antony he kindles in his countrymen lofty feelings for the honor of his country, and abhorrence of tyranny and corruption. Indeed, he hated bloodshed, injustice, and strife, and beheld the downfall of liberty with indescribable sorrow.

Thus in oratory as in history the ancients can boast of most illustrious examples, never even equalled. Still, we cannot tell the comparative merits of the great classical orators of antiquity with the more distinguished of our times; indeed only Mirabeau, Pitt, Fox, Burke, Brougham, Webster, and Clay can even be compared with them. In power of moving the people, some of our modern reformers and agitators may be mentioned favorably; but their harangues are comparatively tame when read.

In philosophy the Greeks and Romans distinguished themselves more even than in poetry, or history, or eloquence. Their speculations pertained to the loftiest subjects that ever tasked the intellect of man. But this great department has already been presented. There were respectable writers in various other departments of literature, but no very great names whose writings have descended to us. Contemporaries had an exalted opinion of Varro, who was considered the most learned of the Romans, as well as their most voluminous author. He was born ten years before Cicero, and is highly commended by Augustine. He was entirely devoted to literature, took no interest in passing events, and lived to a good old age. Saint Augustine says of him that "he wrote so much that one wonders how he had time to read; and he read so much, we are astonished how he found time to write." He composed four hundred and ninety books. Of these only one has descended to us entire, — " De Re Rustica," written at the age of eighty; but it is the best treatise which has come down from antiquity on ancient agriculture. We have parts of his other books, and we know of still others that have entirely perished which for their information would be invaluable, especially his " Divine Antiquities," in sixteen books, — his great work, from which Saint Augustine drew materials for his "City of God." Varro wrote treatises on language, on the poets, on philosophy, on geography, and on various other subjects; he also wrote satire and criticism. But although his writings were learned, his style was so bad that the ages have failed to preserve him. The truly immortal books are most valued for their artistic excellences. No man, however great his genius, can afford to be dull. Style is to written composition what delivery is to a public speaker. The multitude do not go to hear the man of thoughts, but to hear the man of words, being repelled or attracted by *manner*.

Seneca was another great writer among the Romans, but he belongs to the domain of philosophy, although it is his ethical works which have given him immortality, — as may be truly said of Socrates and Epictetus, although they are usually classed among the philosophers. Seneca was a Spaniard, born but a few years before the Christian era; he was a lawyer and a rhetorician, also a teacher and minister of Nero. It was his misfortune to know one of the most detestable princes that ever scandalized humanity, and it is not to his credit to have accumulated in four years one of the largest fortunes in Rome while serving such a master; but since he lived to experience Nero's ingratitude, Seneca is more commonly regarded as a martyr. Had he lived in the republican period, he would have been a great orator. He wrote voluminously, on many subjects, and was devoted to a literary life. He rejected the superstitions of his country, and looked upon the ritualism of religion as a mere fashion. In his own belief he was a deist; but though he wrote fine ethical treatises, he dishonored his own virtues by a compliance with the vices of others. He saw much of life, and died at fifty-three. What is remarkable in Seneca's writings, which are clear but labored, is that under Pagan influences and imperial tyranny he should have presented such lofty moral truth; and it is a mark of almost transcendent talent that he should, unaided by Christianity, have soared so high in the realm of ethical inquiry. Nor is it easy to find any modern author who has treated great questions in so attractive a way.

Quintilian is a Latin classic, and belongs to the class of rhetoricians. He should have been mentioned among the orators, yet, like Lysias the Greek, Quintilian was a teacher of eloquence rather than an orator. He was born 40 A. D., and taught the younger Pliny, also two nephews of Domitian, receiving a regular salary from the imperial treasury. His great work is a complete system of rhetoric. "Institutiones Oratoriæ" is one of the clearest and fullest of all rhetorical manuals ever written in any language, although, as a literary production, it is inferior to the "De Oratore" of Cicero. It is very practical and sensible, and a complete compendium of every topic likely to be useful in the education of an aspirant for the honors of eloquence. In systematic arrangement it falls short of a similar work by Aristotle; but it is celebrated for its sound judgment and keen discrimination, showing great reading and reflection. Quintilian should be viewed as a critic rather than as a rhetorician, since he entered into the merits and defects of the great masters of Greek and Roman literature. In his peculiar province he has had no superior. Like Cicero or Demosthenes or Plato or Thucydides or Tacitus, Quintilian would be a great man if he lived in our times, and could proudly challenge the modern world to produce a better teacher than he in the art of public speaking.

There were other classical writers of immense fame, but they do not represent any particular class in the field of literature which can be compared with the modern. I can only draw attention to Lucian, — a witty and voluminous Greek author, who lived in the reign of Commodus, and who wrote rhetorical, critical, and biographical works, and even romances which have given hints to modern authors. His fame rests on his "Dialogues," intended to ridicule the heathen philosophy and religion, and which show him to have been one of the great masters of ancient satire and mockery. His style of dialogue — a combination of Plato and Aristophanes — is not much used by modern writers, and his peculiar kind of ridicule is reserved now for the stage. Yet he cannot be called a writer of comedy, like Molière. He resembles Rabelais and Swift more than any other modern writers, having their indignant wit, indecent jokes, and pungent sarcasms. Like Juvenal, Lucian paints the vices and follies of his time, and exposes the hypocrisy that reigns in the high places of fashion and power. His dialogues have been imitated by Fontanelle and Lord Lyttleton, but these authors do not possess his humor or pungency. Lucian does not grapple with great truths, but contents himself with ridiculing those who have proclaimed them, and in his cold cynicism depreciates human knowledge and all the great moral teachers of mankind. He is even shallow and flippant upon Socrates; but he was well read in human nature, and superficially acquainted with all the learning of antiquity. In wit and sarcasm he may be compared with Voltaire, and his object was the same, — to demolish and pull down without substituting anything instead. His scepticism was universal, and extended to religion, to philosophy, and to everything venerated and ancient. His purity of style was admired by Erasmus, and his works have been translated into most European languages. In strong contrast to the "Dialogues" of Lucian is the "City of God" by Saint Augustine, in which he demolishes with keener ridicule all the gods of antiquity, but substitutes instead the knowledge of the true God.

Thus the Romans, as well as Greeks, produced works in all departments of literature that will bear comparison with the masterpieces of modern times. And where would have been the literature of the early Church, or of the age of the Reformation, or of modern nations, had not the great original writers of Athens and Rome been our school-masters? When we further remember that their glorious literature was created by native genius, without the aid of Christianity, we are filled with amazement, and may almost be excused if we deify the reason of man. Nor, indeed, have greater triumphs of intellect been witnessed in these our Christian times than are produced among that class which is the least influenced by Christian ideas. Some of the proudest trophies of genius have been won by infidels, or by men stigmatized as such. Witness Voltaire, Rousseau, Diderot, Hegel, Fichte, Gibbon, Hume, Buckle. May there not be the greatest practical infidelity with the most artistic beauty and native reach of thought? Milton ascribes the most sublime intelligence to Satan and his angels on the point of rebellion against the majesty of

Heaven. A great genius may be kindled even by the fires of discontent and ambition, which may quicken the intellectual faculties while consuming the soul, and spread their devastating influence on the homes and hopes of man.

Since, then, we are assured that literature as well as art may flourish under Pagan influences, it seems certain that Christianity has a higher mission than the culture of the mind. Religious scepticism cannot be disarmed if we appeal to Christianity as the test of intellectual culture. The realm of reason has no fairer fields than those that are adorned by Pagan achievements.

AUTHORITIES.

There are no better authorities than the classical authors themselves, and their works must be studied in order to comprehend the spirit of ancient literature. Modern historians of Roman literature are merely critics, like Dalhmann, Schlegel, Niebuhr, Muller, Mommsen, Mure, Arnold, Dunlap, and Thompson. Nor do I know of an exhaustive history of Roman literature in the English language; yet nearly every great writer has occasional criticisms upon the subject which are entitled to respect. The Germans, in this department, have no equals.

PART II.

JEWISH HEROES AND PROPHETS.

PART II.

JEWISH HEROES AND PROPHETS.

CONTENTS.

ABRAHAM.

Religious Faith.

	Page
Abraham the spiritual father of nations	27
General forgetfulness of God when Abraham arose	28
Civilization in his age	28
Ancestors of Abram	30
His settlement in Haran	31
His moral courage	32
The call of Abram	32
His migrations	34
The Canaanites	34
Abram in Egypt	35
Separation between Abram and Lot	36
Melchizedek	36
Abram covenants with God	37
The mission of the Hebrews	38
The faith of Abram	39
Its peculiarities	40
Trials of faith	40
God's covenant with Abram	41
The sacrifice of Isaac	42
Paternal rights among Oriental nations	43

	PAGE
Universality of sacrifice	44
Had Abram a right to sacrifice Isaac?	46
Supreme test of his faith	47
His obedience to God	48
His righteousness	49
Supremacy of religious faith	50
Abraham's defects	51
The most favored of mortals	52
The boons he bestowed	53

JOSEPH.

ISRAEL IN EGYPT.

Early days of Joseph	57
Envy of his brethren	58
Sale of Joseph	59
Its providential results	60
Fortunes of Joseph in Egypt	62
The imprisonment of Joseph	63
Favor with the king	63
Joseph prime minister	64
The Shepherd kings	65
The service of Joseph to the king	66
Famine in Egypt	67
Power of Pharaoh	68
Power of the priests	69
Character of the priests	69
Knowledge of the priests	70
Teachings of the priests	71
Egyptian gods	72
Antiquity of sacrifices	73

CONTENTS.

	PAGE
Civilization of Egypt	74
Initiation of Joseph in Egyptian knowledge	76
Austerity to his brethren	77
Grief of Jacob	78
Severity of the famine in Canaan	78
Jacob allows the departure of Benjamin	79
Joseph's partiality to Benjamin	80
His continued austerity to his brethren	81
Joseph at length reveals himself	81
The kindness of Pharaoh	82
Israel in Egypt	83
Prosperity of the Israelites	84
Old age of Jacob	84
His blessing to Joseph's sons	84
Jacob's predictions	85
Death of Jacob	85
Death of Joseph	86
Character of Joseph	87
Condition of the Israelites in Egypt	88
Rameses the Great	89
Acquisitions of the Israelites in Egypt	90
Influence of Egyptian civilization on the Israelites	92

MOSES.

JEWISH JURISPRUDENCE

Exalted mission of Moses	97
His appearance at a great crisis	98
His early advantages and education	99
His premature ambition	101
His retirement to the wilderness	101

CONTENTS.

	PAGE
Description of the land of Midian	101
Studies and meditations of Moses	102
The Book of Genesis	103
Call of Moses and return to Egypt	104
Appearance before Pharaoh	104
Miraculous deliverance of the Israelites	105
Their sojourn in the wilderness	106
The labors of Moses	106
His Moral Code	107
Universality of the obligations	108
General acceptance of the Ten Commandments	109
The foundation of the ritualistic laws	110
Utility of ritualism in certain states of society	113
Immortality seemingly ignored	116
The possible reason of Moses	116
Its relation to the religion of Egypt	118
The Civil Code of Moses	118
Reasons for the isolation of the Israelites	119
The wisdom of the Civil Code	120
Source of the wisdom of Moses	122
The divine legation of Moses	123
Logical consequences of its denial	124
General character of Moses	128
His last days	129
His influence	130

SAMUEL.

ISRAEL UNDER JUDGES.

Condition of the Israelites on the death of Joshua	136
The Judges	137
Birth and youth of Samuel	138

CONTENTS.

	PAGE
The Jewish Theocracy	140
Eli and his sons	141
Samuel called to be judge	142
His efforts to rekindle religious life	143
The school of the prophets	144
The people want a king	146
Views of Samuel as to a change of government	147
He tells the people the consequences	148
Persistency of the Israelites	149
Condition of the nation	151
Saul privately anointed king	153
Clothed with regal power	154
Mistakes and wars of Saul	155
Spares Agag	156
Rebuked by Samuel	157
Samuel withdraws into retirement	157
Seeks a successor to Saul	158
Jehovah indicates the selection of David	158
Saul becomes proud and jealous	159
His wars with the Philistines	160
Great victory at Michmash	161
Death of Samuel	162
Universal mourning	162
His character as Prophet	164
His moral greatness	165
His transcendent influence	165

DAVID.

ISRAELITISH CONQUESTS.

David as an historical study	170
Early days of David	171

CONTENTS.

	PAGE
His accomplishments	172
His connection with Saul	173
His love for Jonathan	173
Death of Saul	173
David becomes king	174
Death of Abner	175
David generally recognized as king	176
Makes Jerusalem his capital	176
Alliance with Hiram	177
Transfer of the Sacred Ark	177
Folly of David's Wife	178
Organization of the kingdom	179
Joab commander-in-chief of the army	179
The court of David	179
His polygamy	180
War with Moab	181
War with the Ammonites	181
Conquest of the Edomites	182
Bathsheba	183
David's shame and repentence	184
Edward Irving on David's fall	185
Its causes	185
Census of the people	186
Why this was a folly	186
Wickedness of David's children	187
Amnon	187
Alienation of David's subjects	188
The famine in Judah	188
Revolt of Sheba	188
Adonijah seeks to steal the sceptre	189
Troubles and trials of David	190
Preparation for building the Temple	190
David's wealth	190

	PAGE
His premature old age	191
Absalom's rebellion and death	192
David's final labors	192
His character as a man and a monarch	193
Why he was a man after God's own heart	194
David's services	195
His Psalms	196
Their mighty influence	198

SOLOMON.

GLORY OF THE MONARCHY.

Early years of Solomon	204
His first acts as monarch	204
The prosperity of his kingdom	205
Glory of Solomon	206
His mistakes	208
His marriage with an Egyptian princess	208
His harem	208
Building of the Temple	210
Its magnificence	210
The treasures accumulated in it	211
Its dedication	213
The sacrifices in its honor	214
Extraordinary celebration of the Festivals	214
The royal palace in Jerusalem	215
The royal palace on Mount Lebanon	216
Excessive taxation of the people	217
Forced labor	218
Change of habits and pursuits	219
Solomon's effeminacy and luxury	219
His unpopularity	219
His latter days of shame	220

	PAGE
His death	220
Character	220
Influence of his reign	221
His writings	223
Their great value	223
The Canticles	225
The Proverbs	226
Praises of wisdom and knowledge	228
Ecclesiastes contrasted with Proverbs	229
Cynicism of Ecclesiastes	230
Hidden meaning of the book	231
The writing of Solomon rich in moral wisdom	235
His wisdom confirmed by experience	235
Lessons to be learned by the career of Solomon	236

ELIJAH.

DIVISION OF THE KINGDOM.

Evil days fall on Israel	239
Division of the kingdom under Rehoboam	240
Jeroboam of Israel sets up golden calves	240
Other innovations	241
Egypt attacks Jerusalem	241
City saved only by immense contribution	242
Interest centres in the northern kingdom	242
Ruled by bad kings	243
Given to idolatry under Ahab	244
Influence of Jezebel	245
The priests of Baal	245
The apostasy of Israel	246
The prophet Elijah	246
His extraordinary appearance	246

CONTENTS.

	Page
Appears before Ahab	247
Announces calamities	247
Flight of Elijah	248
The drought	249
The woman of Zarephath	250
Shields and feeds Elijah	250
He restores her son to life	251
Miseries of the drought	252
Elijah confronts Ahab	253
Assembly of the people at Mount Carmel	254
Presentation of choice between Jehovah and Baal	255
Elijah mocks the priests of Baal	256
Triumphs, and slays them	256
Elijah promises rain	257
The tempest	258
Ahab seeks Jezebel	259
She threatens Elijah in her wrath	259
Second flight of Elijah	260
His weakness and fear	260
The still small voice	261
Selection of Elisha to be prophet	263
He becomes the companion of Elijah	264
Character and appearance of Elisha	264
War between Ahab and Benhadad	266
Naboth and his vineyard	266
Chagrin and melancholy of Ahab	267
Wickedness and cunning of Jezebel	268
Murder of Naboth	269
Dreadful rebuke of Elijah	270
Despair of Ahab	271
Athaliah and Jehoshaphat	272
Death of Ahab	273
Regency of Jezebel	273

	PAGE
Ahaziah and Elijah	274
Fall of Ramoth-Gilead	275
Reaction to idolatry	275
Jehu	276
Death of Jezebel	278
Death of Ahaziah	278
The massacres and reforms of Jehu	279
Extermination of idolatry	281
Last days of Elijah	282
His translation	282

ISAIAH.

NATIONAL DEGENERACY.

Superiority of Judah to Israel	287
A succession of virtuous princes	288
Syrian wars	289
The prophet Joel	290
Outward prosperity of the kingdom of Judah	291
Internal decay	291
Assyrian conquests	292
Tiglath-pilneser	292
Fall of Damascus	293
Fall of Samaria	293
Demoralization of Jerusalem	294
Birth of Isaiah	294
His exalted character	295
Invasion of Judah by the Assyrians	297
Hezekiah submits to Sennacherib	297
Rebels anew	297
Renewed invasion of Judah	298

CONTENTS.

	PAGE
Signal deliverance	298
The warnings and preaching of Isaiah	299
His terrible denunciations of sin	300
Retribution the spirit of his preaching	301
Holding out hope by repentance	302
Absence of art in his writings	303
National wickedness ending in calamities	304
God's moral government	304
Isaiah's predictions fulfilled	305
Woes denounced on Judah	306
Fall of Babylon foretold	307
Predicted woes of Moab	309
Woes denounced on Egypt	310
Calamities of Tyre	312
General predictions of woe on other nations	313
End and purpose of chastisements	315
Isaiah the Prophet of Hope	316
The promised glories of the Chosen People	316
Messianic promises	317
Exultation of Isaiah	318
His catholicity	319
The promised reign of peace	320
The future glories of the righteous	321
Glad tidings declared to the whole world	322
Messianic triumphs	323

JEREMIAH.

FALL OF JERUSALEM.

Sadness and greatness of Jeremiah	327
Second as a prophet only to Isaiah	328

VOL. II. —

CONTENTS.

	Page
Jeremiah the Prophet of Despair	329
Evil days in which he was born	330
National misfortunes predicted	331
Idolatry the crying sin of the times	331
Discovery of the Book of Deuteronomy	332
Renewed study of the Law	333
The reforms of Josiah	333
The greatness of Josiah	335
Inability to stem prevailing wickedness	336
Incompleteness of Josiah's reforms	336
Necho II. extends his conquests	337
Death of Josiah	338
Lamentations on the death of Josiah	338
Rapid decline of the kingdom	339
The voice of Jeremiah drowned	340
Invasion of Assyria by Necho	341
Shallum succeeds Josiah	341
Eliakim succeeds Shallum	341
His follies	341
Judah's relapse into idolatry	342
Neglect of the Sabbath	343
Jeremiah announces approaching calamity	345
His voice unheeded	345
His despondency	349
Fall of Nineveh	350
Defeat and retreat of Necho	350
Greatness of Nebuchadnezzar	351
Appears before Jerusalem	353
Fall of Jerusalem, but destruction delayed	353
Folly and infatuation of the people of Jerusalem	356
Revolt of the city	356
Zedekiah the king temporizes	357
Expostulations of Jeremiah	359

	PAGE
Nebuchadnezzar loses patience	361
Second fall of Jerusalem	362
The captivity	363
Weeping by the river of Babylon	363

JUDAS MACCABÆUS.

RESTORATION OF THE JEWISH COMMONWEALTH.

Eventful career of Judas Maccabæus	368
Condition of the Jews after their return from Babylon	368
Condition of Jerusalem	368
Fanatical hatred of idolatry	369
Severe morality of the Jews after the captivity	370
The Pharisees	371
The Sadducees	371
Synagogues, their number and popularity	372
The Jewish Sanhedrim	373
Advance in sacred literature	374
Apocryphal Books	374
Isolation of the Jews	374
Dark age of Jewish history	375
Power of the high priests	376
The Persian Empire	376
Judæa a province of the Persian Empire	377
Jews at Alexandria	377
Judæa the battle-ground of Egyptians and Syrians	378
The Syrian kings	379
Antiochus Epiphanes	379
His persecution of the Jews	380
Helplessness of the Jews	380
Sack of Jerusalem	381

CONTENTS.

	PAGE
Desecration of the Temple	381
Mattathias	382
His piety and bravery	382
Revolt of Mattathias	383
Slaughter of the Jews	384
Death of Mattathias	385
His gallant sons	386
Judas Maccabæus	386
His military genius	386
The Syrian generals	387
Wrath of Antiochus	388
Desolation of Jerusalem	389
Judas defeats the Syrian general	390
Judas cleanses and dedicates the Temple	391
Fortifies Jerusalem	391
The Feast of Dedication	391
Renewed hostilities	392
Successes of Judas	393
Death of Antiochus	393
Deliverance of the Jews	394
Rivalry between Lysias and Philip	394
Death of Eleazer	395
Bacchides	396
Embassy to Rome	396
Death of Judas Maccabæus	398
Judas succeeded by his brother Jonathan	399
Heroism of Jonathan	399
His death by treachery	399
Jonathan succeeded by his brother Simon	399
Simon's military successes	400
His prosperous administration	400
Succeeded by John Hyrcanus	401
The great talents and success of John Hyrcanus	402

CONTENTS.

The Asmonean princes	402
Pompey takes Jerusalem	403
Accession of Herod the Great	403
He destroys the Asmonean princes	404
His prosperous reign	405
Foundation of Cæsarea	405
Latter days of Herod	406
Loathsome death of Herod	406
Birth of Jesus, the Christ	407

SAINT PAUL.

The Spread of Christianity.

Birth and early days of Saul	411
His Phariseeism	412
His persecution of the Christians	412
His wonderful conversion	413
His leading idea	413
Saul a preacher at Damascus	414
Saul's visit to Jerusalem	414
Saul in Tarsus	415
Saul and Barnabas at Antioch	416
Description of Antioch	416
Contribution of the churches for Jerusalem	417
Saul and Barnabas at Jerusalem	417
Labors and discouragements	418
Saul and Barnabas at Cyprus	418
Saul smites Elymas the sorcerer	419
Missionary travels of Paul	420
Paul converts Timothy	421
Paul at Lystra and Derbe	421
Return of Paul to Antioch	422
Controversy about circumcision	422

CONTENTS.

	Page
Bigotry of the Jewish converts	423
Paul again visits Jerusalem	424
Paul and Barnabas quarrel	425
Paul chooses Silas for a companion	425
Paul and Silas visit the infant churches	426
Tact of Paul	426
Paul and Luke	427
The missionaries at Philippi	427
Paul and Silas at Thessalonica	428
Paul at Athens	429
Character of the Athenians	430
The success of Paul at Athens	431
Paul goes to Corinth	432
Paul led before Gallio	432
Mistake of Gallio	433
Paul's Epistle to the Thessalonians	433
Paul at Ephesus	435
The Temple of Diana	436
Excessive labors of Paul at Ephesus	437
Paul's first Epistle to the Corinthians	437
Popularity of Apollos	437
Second Epistle to the Corinthians	438
Paul again at Corinth	439
Epistles to the Galatians and to the Romans	439
The Pauline theology	440
Paul's last visit to Jerusalem	440
His cold reception	441
His arrest and imprisonment	442
The trial of Paul before Felix	443
Character of Felix	443
Paul kept a prisoner by Felix	445
Paul's defence before Festus	445
Paul appeals to Cæsar	445

CONTENTS.

	PAGE
Paul preaches before Agrippa	446
His voyage to Italy	447
Paul's life at Rome	449
Character of Paul	450
His magnificent services	451
His triumphant death	453

ABRAHAM.
RELIGIOUS FAITH.

ABRAHAM.

RELIGIOUS FAITH.

BEACON LIGHTS OF HISTORY.

ABRAHAM.

RELIGIOUS FAITH.

FROM a religious point of view, Abraham appears to us, after the lapse of nearly four thousand years, as the most august character in history. He may not have had the genius and learning of Moses, nor his executive ability; but as a religious thinker, inspired to restore faith in the world and the worship of the One God, it would be difficult to find a man more favored or more successful. He is the spiritual father equally of Jews, Christians, and Mohammedans, in their warfare with idolatry. In this sense, he is the spiritual progenitor of all those nations, tribes, and peoples who now acknowledge, or who may hereafter acknowledge, a personal God, supreme and eternal in the universe which He created. Abraham is the religious father of all those who associate with this personal and supreme Deity a providential oversight of this world, — a being whom all are required to worship, and alone to worship, as the only true God whose right it is to reign, and who does reign, and will reign forever and ever over everything that exists, animate or inanimate, visible or invisible, known or unknown, in the mighty universe of whose glory and grandeur we have such overwhelming yet indefinite conceptions.

When Abraham appeared, whether four thousand or five thousand years ago, for chronologists differ in their calculations, it would seem that the nations then existing had forgotten or ignored this great cardinal and fundamental truth, and were more or less given to idolatry, worshipping the heavenly bodies, or the forces of Nature, or animals, or heroes, or graven images, or their own ancestors. There were but few and feeble remains of the primitive revelation, — that is, the faith cherished by the patriarchs before the flood, and which it would be natural to suppose Noah himself had taught to his children.

There was even then, however, a remarkable material civilization, especially in Egypt, Palestine, and Babylon; for some of the pyramids had been built, the use of the metals, of weights and measures, and of textile fabrics was known. There were also cities and fortresses, cornfields and vineyards, agricultural implements and weapons of war, commerce and arts, musical instruments, golden vessels, ornaments for the person, purple dyes, spices, hand-made pottery, stone-engravings, sun-dials, and glass-work, and even the use of letters, or something similar, possibly transmitted from the antediluvian civilization. Even the art of printing was almost discovered, as we may infer from the stamping of letters on tiles. With all this material progress, however, there had been a steady decline in spiritual religion as well as in morals, — from which fact we infer that men if left to themselves, whatever truth they may receive from ancestors, will, without supernatural influences, constantly decline in those virtues on which the strength of man is built, and without which the proudest triumphs of the intellect avail nothing. The grandest civilization, in its material aspects, may coexist with the utmost debasement of morals, — as seen among the Greeks and Romans, and in the wicked capitals of modern Europe. "There is no God!" or "Let there be no God!" has been the cry in all ages of the world, whenever and wherever an impious pride or a low morality has defied or silenced conscience. Tell me, ye rationalists and agnostics! with your pagan sympathies, what mean ye by laws of development, and by the *necessary* progress of the human race, except in the triumphs of that kind of knowledge which is entirely disconnected with virtue, and which has proved powerless to prevent the decline and fall of nations? Why did not art, science, philosophy, and literature save the most lauded nations of the ancient world? Why so rapid a degeneracy among people favored not only with a primitive revelation, but by splendid triumphs of reason and knowledge? Why did gross superstition so speedily obscure the intellect, and infamous vices so soon undermine the moral health, if man can elevate himself by his unaided strength? Why did error seemingly prove as vital as truth in all the varied forms of civilization in the ancient world? Why did even tradition fail to keep alive the knowledge of God, at least among the people?

Now, among pagans and idolaters Abram (as he was originally called) lived until he was seventy-five. His father, Terah, was a descendant of Shem, of the eleventh generation, and the original seat of his tribe was among the mountains of Southern Armenia, north of Assyria. From thence Terah migrated to the plains of Mesopotamia, probably with the desire to share the rich pastures of the lowlands, and settled in Ur of the Chaldeans. Ur was one of the most ancient of the Chaldean cities and one of the most splendid, where arts and sciences were cultivated, where astronomers watched the heavens, poets composed hymns, and scribes stamped on clay tablets books which, according to Geikie, have in part come down to our own times. It was in this pagan city that Abram was born, and lived until the "call." His father was a worshipper of the tutelary gods of his tribe, of which he was the head; but his idolatry was not so degrading as that of the Chaldéans, who belonged to a different race from his own, being the descendants of Ham, among whom the arts and sciences had made considerable progress, — as was natural, since what we call civilization arose, it is generally supposed, in the powerful monarchies founded by Assyrian and Egyptian warriors, although it is claimed that both China and India were also great empires at this period. With the growth of cities and the power of kings idolatry increased, and the knowledge of the true God declined. From such influences it was necessary that Abram should be removed if he was to found a nation with a monotheistic belief. So, in obedience to a call from God, he left the city of his birthplace, and went toward the land of Canaan and settled in Haran, where he remained until the death of his father, who it seems had accompanied him in his wanderings, but was probably too infirm to continue the fatiguing journey. Abram, now the head of his tribe and doubtless a powerful chieftain, received another call, and with it the promise that he should be the founder of a great nation, and that in him all the families of the earth should be blessed.

What was that call, coupled with such a magnificent and cheering promise? It was the voice of God commanding Abram to leave country and kindred and go to a country utterly unknown to him, not even indicated to him, but which in due time should be revealed to him. He is not called to repudiate idolatry, but by divine command to go to an unknown country. He must have been already a believer in the One Supreme God, or he would not have felt the command to be imperative. Unless his belief had been monotheistic, we must attribute to him a marvellous genius and striking originality of mind, together with an independence of character still more remarkable; for it requires not only original genius to soar beyond popular superstitions, but also great force of will and lofty intrepidity to break away from them, — as when Buddha renounced Brahmanism, or Socrates ridiculed the Sophists of Attica. Nothing requires more moral courage than the renunciation of a popular and generally received religious belief. It was a hard struggle for Luther to give up the ideas of the Middle Ages in reference to self-expiation. It is exceedingly rare for any one to be emancipated from the tyranny of prevailing dogmas.

So, if Abram was not divinely instructed in a way that implies supernatural illumination, he must have been the most remarkable sage of all antiquity to found a religion never abrogated by succeeding revelations, which has lasted from his time to ours, and is to-day embraced by so large a part of the human race, including Christians, Mohammedans, and Jews. Abram must have been more gifted than the whole school of Ionian philosophers united, from Thales downward, since after three hundred years of speculation and lofty inquiries they only arrived at the truth that the being who controls the universe must be intelligent. Even Socrates, Plato, and Cicero — the most gifted men of classical antiquity — had very indefinite notions of the unity and personality of God, while Abram distinctly recognized this great truth even amid universal idolatry and a degrading polytheism.

Yet the Bible recognizes in Abram moral rather than intellectual greatness. He was distinguished for his faith, and a faith so exalted and pure that it was accounted unto him for righteousness. His faith in God was so profound that it was followed by unhesitating obedience to God's commands. He was ready to go wherever he was sent, instantly, without conditions or remonstrance.

In obedience to the divine voice then, Abram, after the death of his father Terah, passed through the land of Canaan unto Sichem, or Shechem, afterward a city of Samaria. He then went still farther south, and pitched his tent on a mountain having Bethel

on the west and Hai on the east, and there he built
an altar unto the Lord. After this it would appear
that he proceeded still farther to the south, probably
near the northern part of Idumæa.

Wherever Abram journeyed he found the Canaanites — descendants of Ham — petty tribes or nations,
governed by kings no more powerful than himself.
They are supposed in their invasions to have conquered the aboriginal inhabitants, whose remote origin
is veiled in impenetrable obscurity, but who retained
some principles of the primitive religion. It is even
possible that Melchizedek, the unconquered King of
Salem, who blessed Abram, belonged to those original people who were of Semitic origin. Nevertheless
the Canaanites, or Hametic tribes, were at this time
the dominant inhabitants.

Of these tribes or nations the Sidonians, or Phœnicians, were the most powerful. Next to them, according to Ewald, "were three nations living toward the
South, — the Hittites, the Jebusites, and the Amorites; then two in the most northerly country conquered by Israel, — the Girgashites and the Hivites;
then four in Phœnicia; and lastly, the most northern
of all, the well known kingdom of Hamath on the
Orontes." The Jebusites occupied the country around
Jerusalem; the Amorites also dwelt in the mountain-
ous regions, and were warlike and savage, like the

ancient Highlanders of Scotland. They entrenched themselves in strong castles. The Hittites, or children of Heth, were on the contrary peaceful, having no fortified cities, but dwelling in the valleys, and living in well-ordered communities. The Hivites dwelt in the middle of the country, and were also peaceful, having reached a considerable civilization, and being in the possession of the most flourishing inland cities. The Philistines entered the land at a period subsequent to the other Canaanites, probably after Abram, coming it is supposed from Crete.

It would appear that Abram was not molested by these various petty Canaanitish nations, that he was hospitably received by them, that he had pleasant relations with them, and even entered into their battles as an ally or protector. Nor did Abram seek to conquer territory. Powerful as he was, he was still a pilgrim and a wanderer, journeying with his servants and flocks wherever the Lord called him; and hence he excited no jealousy and provoked no hostilities. He had not long been settled quietly with his flocks and herds before a famine arose in the land, and he was forced to seek subsistence in Egypt, then governed by the shepherd kings called Hyksos, who had driven the proud native monarch reigning at Memphis to the southern part of the kingdom, in the vicinity of Thebes. Abram was well received at the court of the

Pharaohs, until he was detected in a falsehood in regard to his wife, whom he passed as his sister. He was then sent away with all that he had, together with his nephew Lot.

Returning to the land of Canaan, Abram came to the place where he had before pitched his tent, between Bethel and Hai, unto the altar which he had some time before erected, and called upon the name of the Lord. But the land was not rich enough to support the flocks and herds of both Abram and Lot, and there arose a strife between their respective herdsmen; so the patriarch and his nephew separated, Lot choosing for his residence the fertile plain of the Jordan, and Abram remaining in the land of Canaan. It was while sojourning at Bethel that the Lord appeared again unto Abram, and promised to him the whole land as a future possession of his posterity. After that he removed his tent to the plain of Mamre, near or in Hebron, and again erected an altar to his God.

Here Abram remained in true patriarchal dignity without further migrations, abounding in wealth and power, and able to rescue his nephew Lot from the hands of Chedorlaomer the King of Elam, and from the other Oriental monarchs who joined his forces, pursuing them even to Damascus. For this signal act of heroism Abram was blessed by Melchizedek, in the name of their common lord the most high God. Who was this Prince of Salem? Was he an earthly potentate ruling an unconquered city of the aboriginal inhabitants; or was he a mysterious personage, without father, without mother, without descent, having neither beginning nor end of days, nor end of life, but made like unto the Son of God, an incarnation of the Deity, to repeat the blessing which the patriarch had already received?

The history of Abram until his supreme trial seems principally to have been repeated covenants with God, and the promises held out of the future greatness of his descendants. The greatness of the Israelitish nation, however, was not to be in political ascendency, nor in great attainments in the arts and sciences, nor in cities and fortresses and chariots and horses, nor in that outward splendor which would attract the gaze of the world, and thus provoke conquests and political combinations and grand alliances and colonial settlements, by which the capital on Zion's hill would become another Rome, or Tyre, or Carthage, or Athens, or Alexandria, — but quite another kind of greatness. It was to be moral and spiritual rather than material or intellectual, the centre of a new religious life, from which theistic doctrines were to go forth and spread for the healing of the nations, — all to culminate, when the proper time should come, in the mission of Jesus

Christ, and in his teachings as narrated and propagated by his disciples.

This was the grand destiny of the Hebrew race; and for the fulfilment of this end they were located in a favored country, separated from other nations by mountains, deserts, and seas, and yet capable by cultivation of sustaining a great population, while they were governed by a polity tending to keep them a distinct, isolated, and peculiar people. To the descendants of Ham and Japhet were given cities, political power, material civilization; but in the tents of Shem religion was to dwell. "From first to last," says Geikie, " the intellect of the Hebrew dwelt supremely on the matters of his faith. The triumphs of the pencil or the chisel he left with contemptuous indifference to Egypt, or Assyria, or Greece. Nor had the Jew any such interest in religious philosophy as has marked other people. The Aryan nations, both East and West, might throw themselves with ardor into those high questions of metaphysics, but he contented himself with the utterances of revelation. The world may have inherited no advances in political science from the Hebrew, no great epic, no school of architecture, no high lessons in philosophy, no wide extension of human thought or knowledge in any secular direction; but he has given it his religion. To other races we owe the splendid inheritance of modern civilization and secular culture, but the religious education of mankind has been the gift of the Jew alone."

For this end Abram was called to the land of Canaan. From this point of view alone we see the blessing and the promise which were given to him. In this light chiefly he became a great benefactor. He gave a religion to the world; at least he established its fundamental principle, — the worship of the only true God. "If we were asked," says Max Müller, "how it was that Abraham possessed not only the primitive conception of the Divinity, as he has revealed himself to all mankind, but passed, through the denial of all other gods, to the knowledge of the One God, we are content to answer that it was by a *special divine revelation*."[1]

If the greatness of the Jewish race was spiritual rather than temporal, so the real greatness of Abraham was in his faith. Faith is a sentiment or a principle not easily defined. But be it intuition, or induction, or deduction, — supported by reason, or without reason, — whatever it is, we know what it means.

The faith of Abraham, which Saint Paul so urgently commends, the same in substance as his own faith in Jesus Christ, stands out in history as so bright and perfect that it is represented as the foundation of re-

[1] Chips from a German Workshop, vol. i. p. 372.

ligion itself, without which it is impossible to please God, and with which one is assured of divine favor, with its attendant blessings. If I were to analyze it, I should say that it is a perfect trust in God, allied with obedience to his commands.

With this sentiment as the supreme rule of life, Abraham is always prepared to go wherever the way is indicated. He has no doubts, no questionings, no scepticism. He simply adores the Lord Almighty, as the object of his supreme worship, and is ready to obey His commands, whether he can comprehend the reason of them or not. He needs no arguments to confirm his trust or stimulate his obedience. And this is faith, — an ultimate principle that no reasonings can shake or strengthen. This faith, so sublime and elevated, needs no confirmation, and is not made more intelligent by any definitions. If the *Cogito, ergo sum*, is an elemental and ultimate principle of philosophy, so the faith of Abraham is the fundamental basis of all religion, which is weakened rather than strengthened by attempts to define it. All definitions of an ultimate principle are vain, since everybody understands what is meant by it.

No truly immortal man, no great benefactor, can go through life without trials and temptations, either to test his faith or to establish his integrity. Even Jesus Christ himself was subjected for forty days to the snares of the Devil. Abram was no exception to this moral discipline. He had two great trials to pass through before he could earn the title of "father of the faithful,"— first, in reference to the promise that he should have legitimate children; and secondly, in reference to the sacrifice of Isaac.

As to the first, it seemed impossible that Abram should have issue through his wife Sarah, she being ninety years of age, and he ninety-nine or one hundred. The very idea of so strange a thing caused Sarah to laugh incredulously, and it is recorded in the seventeenth chapter of Genesis that Abram also fell on his face and laughed, saying in his heart, "Shall a son be born unto him that is one hundred years old?" Evidently he at first received the promise with some incredulity. He could leave Ur of the Chaldees by divine command,— this was an act of obedience; but he did not fully believe in what seemed to be against natural law, which would be a sort of faith without evidence, blind, against reason. He requires some sign from God. "Whereby," said he, "shall I *know* that I shall inherit it,"— that is Canaan,— "and that my seed shall be in number as the stars of heaven?" Then followed the renewal of the covenant; and, according to the frequent custom of the times, when covenants were made between individual men, Abram took a new name: "And God talked with him, saying, As for me, behold my covenant is with thee, and thou shalt be a father of many nations. Neither shall thy name be any more Abram [Father of Elevation] but thy name shall be Abraham [Father of a Multitude], for a father of many nations have I made thee." We observe that the covenant was repeatedly renewed; in connection with which was the rite of circumcision, which Abraham and his posterity, and even his servants, were required scrupulously to observe, and which it would appear he unreluctantly did observe as an important condition of the covenant. Why this rite was so imperatively commanded we do not know, neither can we understand why it was so indissolubly connected with the covenant between God and Abraham. We only know that it was piously kept, not only by Abraham himself, but by his descendants from generation to generation, and became one of the distinctive marks and peculiarities of the Jewish nation, — the sign of the promise that in Abraham all the families of the earth should be blessed, — a promise fulfilled even in the patriarchal monotheism of Arabia, the distant tribes of which, under Mohammed, accepted the One Supreme God.

A still more serious test of the faith of Abraham was the sacrifice of Isaac, on whose life all his hopes naturally rested. We are told that God "tempted," or tested, the obedient faith of Abraham, by suggesting to him that it was his duty to sacrifice that only son as a burnt-offering, to prove how utterly he trusted the Lord's promise; for if Isaac were cut off, where was another legitimate heir to be found? Abraham was then one hundred and twenty years old, and his wife was one hundred and ten. Moreover, on principles of reason why should such a sacrifice be demanded? It was not only apparently against reason but against nature, against every sacred instinct, against humanity, even an act of cruelty, — yea, more, a crime, since it was homicide, without any seeming necessity. Besides, everybody has a right to his own life, unless he has forfeited it by crime against society. Isaac was a gentle, harmless, interesting youth of twenty, and what right, by any human standard, had Abraham to take his life? It is true that by patriarchal customs and laws Isaac belonged to Abraham as much as if he were a slave or an animal. He had the Oriental right to do with his son as he pleased. The head of a family had not only absolute control over wife and children, but the power of life and death. And this absolute power was not exercised alone by Semitic races, but also by the Aryan in their original settlements, in Greece and Italy, as well as in Northern India. All the early institutions of society recognized this paternal right. Hence the moral sense of Abraham was not apparently shocked at the command of God, since his son was his absolute property. Even Isaac made no resistance, since he knew that Abraham had a right to his life.

Moreover, we should remember that sacrifices to all objects of worship formed the basis of all the religious rites of the ancient world, in all periods of its history. Human sacrifices were offered in India at the very period when Abraham was a wanderer in Palestine; and though human nature ultimately revolted from this cruelty, the sacrifice of substitute-animals continued from generation to generation as oblations to the gods, and is still continued by Brahminical priests. In China, in Egypt, in Assyria, in Greece, no religious rites were perfected without sacrifices. Even in the Mosaic ritual, sacrifices by the priests formed no inconsiderable part of worship. Not until the time of Isaiah was it said that God took no delight in burnt offerings, — that the real sacrifices which He requires are a broken and a contrite heart. Nor were the Jews finally emancipated from sacrificial rites until Christ himself made his own body an offering for the sins of the world, and in God's providence the Romans destroyed their temple and scattered their nation. In antiquity there was no objective worship of the Deity without sacrificial rites, and when these were omitted or despised there was atheism, — as in the case of Buddha, who taught morals rather than religion. Perhaps the oldest and most prevalent religious idea of antiquity was the necessity of propitiatory sacrifice, — generally of animals, though in remotest ages the offering of the fruits of the earth.[1]

The inquiry might here arise, whether in our times anything would justify a man in committing a homicide on an innocent person. Would he not be called a fanatic? If so, we may infer that morality — the proper conduct of men as regards one another in social relations — is better understood among us than it was among the patriarchs four thousand years ago; and hence, that as nations advance in civilization they have a more enlightened sense of duty, and practically a higher morality. Men in patriarchal times may have committed what we regard as crimes, while their ordinary lives were more virtuous than ours. And if so, should we not be lenient to immoralities and crimes committed in darker ages, if the ordinary current of men's lives was lofty and religious? On this principle we should be slow to denounce Christian people who formerly held slaves without remorse, when this sin did not shock the age in which they lived, and was not discrepant with prevailing ideas as to

[1] Dr. Trumbull has made a learned and ingenious argument in his "Blood Covenant" to show that sacrifices were not to propitiate the deity, but to bring about a closer Spiritual union between the soul and God; that the blood covenant was a covenant of friendship and love among all primitive peoples.

right and wrong. It is clear that in patriarchal times men had, according to universally accepted ideas, the power of life and death over their families, which it would be absurd and wicked to claim in our day, with our increased light as to moral distinctions. Hence, on the command of God to slay his son, Abraham had no scruples on the ground of morality; that is, he did not feel that it was wrong to take his son's life if God commanded him to do so, any more than it would be wrong, if required, to slay a slave or an animal, since both were alike his property. Had he entertained more enlightened views as to the sacredness of life, he might have felt differently. With his views, God's command did not clash with his conscience.

Still, the sacrifice of Isaac was a terrible shock to Abraham's paternal affection. The anguish of his soul was none the less, whether he had the right of life and death or not. He was required to part with the learest thing he had on earth, in whom was bound up his earthly happiness. What had he to live for, but Isaac? He doubtless loved this child of his old age with exceeding tenderness, devotion, and intensity; and what was perhaps still more weighty, in that day of polygamous households, than mere paternal affection, with Isaac were identified all the hopes and promises which had been held out to Abraham by God himself of becoming the father of a mighty and favored race

His affection as a father was strained to its utmost tension, but yet more was his faith in being the progenitor of offspring that should inherit the land of Canaan. Nevertheless, at God's command he was willing to make the sacrifice, "accounting that God is able to raise up, even from the dead." Was there ever such a supreme act of obedience in the history of our race? Has there ever been from his time to ours such a transcendent manifestation of faith? By reason Abraham saw the foundation of his hopes utterly swept away; and yet his faith towers above reason, and he feels that the divine promises in some way will be fulfilled. Did any man of genius ever conceive such an illustration of blended piety and obedience? Has dramatic poetry ever created such a display of conflicting emotions? Is it possible for a human being to transcend so mighty a sacrifice, and all by the power of faith? Let those philosophers and theologians who aspire to define faith, and vainly try to reconcile it with reason, learn modesty and wisdom from the lesson of Abraham, who is its great exponent, and be content with the definition of Paul himself, that it is "the substance of things hoped for, the evidence of things not seen;" that reason was in Abraham's case subordinate to a loftier and grander principle, — even a firm conviction, which nothing could shake, of the accomplishment of an end against all probabilities and mortal calculations, resting solely on a divine promise.

Another remarkable thing about that memorable sacrifice is, that Abraham does not expostulate or hesitate, but calmly and resolutely prepares for the slaughter of the innocent and unresisting victim, suppressing all the while his feelings as a father in obedience and love to the Sovereign of heaven and earth, whose will is his supreme law.

"And Abraham took the wood of the burnt-offering, and laid it upon Isaac his son," who was compelled as it were to bear his own cross. And he took the fire in his hand and a knife, and Isaac said, "Behold the fire and the wood, but where is the lamb for a burnt offering?" yet suffered himself to be bound by his father on the altar. And Abraham then stretched forth his hand and took the knife to slay his son. At this supreme moment of his trial, he heard the angel of the Lord calling upon him out of heaven and saying, "Abraham! Abraham! lay not thine hand upon the lad, neither do thou anything unto him; for now I know that thou fearest God, seeing thou hast not withheld thy son, thine only son from me. . . . And Abraham lifted up his eyes and looked, and behold behind him was a ram caught in the thicket by his horns; and Abraham went and took the ram, and offered him up for a burnt-offering instead of his son. And the angel of the Lord called unto Abraham a second time out of heaven and said, By myself have I sworn, saith the Lord, for because thou hast done this thing, and hast not withheld thy son, thine only son, that in blessing I will bless thee, and in multiplying I will multiply thy seed as the stars of the heavens, and as the sand upon the seashore, and in thy seed shall all the nations of the earth be blessed, because thou hast obeyed my voice."

There are no more recorded promises to Abraham, no more trials of his faith. His righteousness was established, and he was justified before God. His subsequent life was that of peace, prosperity, and exaltation. He lives to the end in transcendent repose with his family and vast possessions. His only remaining solicitude is for a suitable wife for Isaac, concerning whom there is nothing remarkable in gifts or fortunes, but who maintains the faith of his father, and lives like him in patriarchal dignity and opulence.

The great interest we feel in Abraham is as "the father of the faithful," as a model of that exalted sentiment which is best defined and interpreted by his own trials and experiences; and hence I shall not dwell on the well known incidents of his life outside the varied calls and promises by which he became the most favored man in human annals. It was his faith which made him immortal, and with which his name is forever associated. It is his religious faith looming up, after four thousand years, for our admiration and veneration which is the true subject of our meditation. This, I think, is distinct from our ordinary conception of faith, such as a belief in the operation of natural laws, in the return of the seasons, in the rewards of virtue, in the assurance of prosperity with due regard to the conditions of success. Faith in a friend, in a nation's future, in the triumphs of a good cause, in our own energies and resources *is*, I grant, necessarily connected with reason, with wide observation and experience, with induction, with laws of nature and of mind. But religious faith is supreme trust in an unseen God and supreme obedience to his commands, without any other exercise of reason than the intuitive conviction that what he orders is right because he orders it, whether we can fathom his wisdom or not. " Canst thou by searching find out Him ? "

Yet notwithstanding the exalted faith of Abraham, by which all religious faith is tested, an eternal pattern and example for our reverence and imitation, the grand old man deceived both Pharaoh and Abimelech, and if he did not tell positive lies, he uttered only half truths, for Sarah was a half sister; and thus he put expediency and policy above moral rectitude, — to be palliated indeed in his case by the desire to preserve his wife from pollution. Yet this is the only blot on his otherwise reproachless character, marked by so many noble traits that he may be regarded as almost perfect. His righteousness was as memorable as his faith, living in the fear of God. How noble was his disinterestedness in giving to Lot the choice of lands for his family and his flocks and his cattle! How brave was he in rescuing his kinsman from the hands of conquering kings! How lofty in refusing any remuneration for his services! How fervent were his intercessions with the Almighty for the preservation of the cities of the plain! How hospitable his mode of life, as when he entertained angels unawares! How kind he was to Hagar when she had incurred the jealousy of Sarah! How serene and dignified and generous he was, the model of courtesy and kindness!

With Abraham we associate the supremest happiness which an old man can attain unto and enjoy. He was prosperous, rich, powerful, and favored in every way; but the chief source of his happiness was the superb consciousness that he was to be the progenitor of a mighty and numerous progeny, through whom all the nations of the earth should be blessed. How far his faith was connected with temporal prosperity we cannot tell. Prosperity seems to have been the blessing of the Old Testament, as adversity was the blessing of the New. But he was certain of this, — that his descendants would possess ultimately the land of Canaan, and would be as numerous as the stars of heaven. He was certain that in some mysterious way there would come from his race something that would be a blessing to mankind. Was it revealed to his exultant soul what this blessing should be? Did this old patriarch cast a prophetic eye beyond the ages, and see that the promise made to him was spiritual rather than material, pertaining to the final triumph of truth and righteousness? — that the unity of God, which he taught to Isaac and perhaps to Ishmael, was to be upheld by his race alone among prevailing idolatries, until the Saviour should come to reveal a new dispensation and finally draw all men unto him? Did Abraham fully realize what a magnificent nation the Israelites should become, — not merely the rulers of western Asia under David and Solomon, but that even after their final dispersion they should furnish ministers to kings, scholars to universities, and dictators to legislative halls, — an unconquerable race, powerful even after the vicissitudes and humiliations of four thousand years? Did he realize fully that from his descendants should arise the religious teachers of mankind, — not only the prophets and sages of the Old Testament, but the apostles and martyrs of the New, — planting in every land the seeds of the everlasting gospel, which should finally uproot all Brahminical self-expiations, all Buddhistic reveries, all the specu-

RELIGIOUS FAITH.

lations of Greek philosophers, all the countless forms of idolatry, polytheism, pantheism, and pharisaism on this earth, until every knee should bow, and every tongue confess that Jesus Christ is Lord, to the glory of God the Father?

Yet such were the boons granted to Abraham, as the reward of faith and obedience to the One true God, — the vital principle without which religion dies into superstition, with which his descendants were inspired not only to nationality and civil coherence, but to the highest and noblest teachings the world has received from any people, and by which his name is forever linked with the spiritual progress and happiness of mankind.

JOSEPH.

ISRAEL IN EGYPT.

JOSEPH.

ISRAEL IN EGYPT.

NO one in his senses would dream of adding anything to the story of Joseph, as narrated in Genesis, whether it came from the pen of Moses or from some subsequent writer. It is a masterpiece of historical composition, unequalled in any literature sacred or profane, in ancient or modern times, for its simplicity, its pathos, its dramatic power, and its sustained interest. Nor shall I attempt to paraphrase or re-tell it, save by way of annotation and illustration of subjects connected with it, having reference to the subsequent development of the Jewish nation and character.

Joseph, the great-grandson of Abraham, was born at Haran in Mesopotamia, probably during the XVIII. Century B. C., when his father Jacob was in the service of Laban the Syrian. There was nothing remarkable in his career until he was sold as a slave by his unnatural and jealous brothers. He was the favorite son of the patriarch Jacob, by his beloved Rachel, being the youngest, except Benjamin, of a large family of twelve sons, — a beautiful and promising youth, with qualities which peculiarly called out the paternal affections. In the inordinate love and partiality of Jacob for this youth he gave to him, by way of distinction, a decorated tunic, such as was worn only by the sons of princes. The half-brothers of Joseph were filled with envy in view of this unwise step on the part of their common father, — a proceeding difficult to be reconciled with his politic and crafty nature; and their envy ripened into hostility when Joseph, with the frankness of youth, narrated his dreams, which signified his future pre-eminence and the humiliation of his brothers. Nor were his dreams altogether pleasing to his father, who rebuked him with this indignant outburst of feeling: "Shall I and thy brethren indeed come to bow down ourselves to thee on the earth?" But while the father pondered, the brothers were consumed with hatred, for envy is one of the most powerful passions that move the human soul, and is malignant in its developments. Strange to say, it is most common in large families and among those who pass for friends. We do not envy prosperous enemies with the virulence we feel for prosperous relatives, who theoretically are our equals. Nor does envy cease until inequality has become so great as to make rivalry preposterous: a subject does not envy his king, or his generally acknowledged superior. Envy may even give place to respect and deference when the object of it has achieved fame and conceded power. Relatives who begin with jealousy sometimes end as worshippers, but not until extraordinary merit, vast wealth, or overtopping influence are universally conceded. Conceive of Napoleon's brothers envying the great Emperor, or Webster's the great statesman, or Grant's the great general, although the passion may have lurked in the bosoms of political rivals and military chieftains.

But one thing certainly extinguishes envy; and that is death. Hence the envy of Joseph's brothers, after they had sold him to a caravan of Ishmaelite merchants, was succeeded by remorse and shame. Their murmurings passed into lies. They could not tell their broken-hearted father of their crime: they never told him. Jacob was led to suppose that his favorite son was devoured by wild beasts; they added deceit and cowardice to a depraved heartlessness, and nearly brought down the gray hairs of their father to the grave. No subsequent humiliation or punishment could be too severe for such wickedness. Although they were destined to become the heads of powerful tribes, even of the chosen people of God, these men have incurred the condemnation of all ages. But Judah and Reuben do not come in for unlimited censure, since these sons of Leah sought to save their brother from a violent death; and subsequently in Egypt Judah looms up as a magnanimous character, whom we admire almost as much as we do Joseph himself. What can be more eloquent than his defence of Benjamin, and his appeal to what seemed to him to be an Egyptian potentate!

The sale of Joseph as a slave is one of the most signal instances of the providence of God working by natural laws recorded in all history, — more marked even than the elevation of Esther and Mordecai. In it we see permission of evil and its counteraction, — its conversion into good; victory over evil, over conspiracy, treachery, and murderous intent. And so marked is this lesson of a superintending Providence over all human action, that a wise and good man can see wars and revolutions and revolting crimes with almost philosophical complacency, knowing that out of destruction proceeds creation; that the wrath of man is always overruled; that the love of God is the brightest and clearest and most consoling thing in the universe. We cannot interpret history without the recognition of this fundamental truth. We cannot be unmoved amid the prevalence of evil without this feeling, that God is more powerful than all the combined forces of his enemies both on earth and in hell; and that no matter what the evil is, it will surely be made to praise Him who sitteth in the heavens. This is a sublime revelation of the omnipotence and benevolence of a personal God, of his constant oversight of the world which he has made.

The protection and elevation of Joseph, seemingly a natural event in view of his genius and character, is in some respects a type of that great sacrifice by which a sinful world has been redeemed. Little did the Jews suspect when they crucified Jesus that he would arise from his tomb and overturn the idolatries of nations, and found a religion which should go on from conquering to conquer. Little did the gifted Burke see in the atrocities of the French Revolution the overturning of a system of injustices which for centuries had cried to Heaven for vengeance. Still less did the proud and conservative citizens of New England recognize in the cruelties of Southern slaveholders a crime which would provoke one of the bloodiest wars of modern times, and lead to the constitutional and political equality of the whites and blacks. Evil appeared to triumph, but ended in the humiliation of millions and the enfranchisement of humanity, when the cause of the right seemed utterly hopeless. So let every one write upon all walls and houses and chambers, upon his conscience and his intellect, "The Lord God Omnipotent reigneth, and will bring good out of the severest tribulation!" And this great truth applies not to nations

alone, but to the humblest individual, as he bows down
in grief or wrath or penitence to unlooked-for chastisement, — like Job upon his heap of ashes, or the broken-
hearted mother when afflicted with disease or poverty,
or the misconduct or death of children. There is no
wisdom, no sound philosophy, no religion, and no happiness until this truth is recognized in all the changes
and relations of life.

The history of Joseph in Egypt in all his varied fortunes is, as I have said, a most memorable illustration
of this cardinal and fundamental truth. A favorite of
fortune, he is sold as a slave for less than twenty dollars of our money, and is brought to a foreign country,
— a land oppressed by kings and priests, yet in which
is a high civilization, in spite of social and political
degradation. He is resold to a high official of the
Egyptian court, probably on account of his beauty and
intelligence. He rises in the service of this official, —
captain of the royal guard, or, as the critics tell us,
superintendent of the police and prisons, — for he has
extraordinary abilities and great integrity, character
as well as natural genius, until he is unjustly accused
of a meditated crime by a wicked woman. It is evident that Potiphar, his master, only half believes in
Joseph's guilt, in spite of the protestations of his artful
and profligate wife, since instead of summarily execut-
ing him, as Ahasuerus did Haman, he simply sends

him to a mild and temporary imprisonment in the prison adjacent to his palace. Here Joseph wins the favor of his jailers and of his brother prisoners, as Paul did nearly two thousand years later, and shows remarkable gifts, even to the interpretation of dreams,— a wonderful faculty to superstitious people like the Egyptians, and in which he exceeds even their magicians and priests. The fame of his rare gifts, the most prized in Egypt, reaches at last the ears of Pharaoh, who is troubled by a singular dream which no one of his learned men can interpret. The Hebrew slave interprets it, and is magnificently rewarded, becoming the prime minister of an absolute monarch. The King gives him his signet ring, emblem of power, and a collar or chain of gold, the emblem of the highest rank; clothes him in a vestment of fine linen, makes him ride in his second chariot, and appoints him ruler over the land, second only to the King in power and rank. And, further, he gives to him in marriage the daughter of the High Priest of On, by which he becomes connected with the priesthood.

Joseph deserves all the honor and influence he receives, for he saves the kingdom from a great calamity. He predicts seven years of plenty and seven years of famine, and points out the remedy. According to tradition, the monarch whom he served was Apepi, the last Shepherd King, during whose reign slaves were very numerous. The King himself had a vast number, as well as the nobles. Foreign slaves were preferred to native ones, and wars were carried on for the chief purpose of capturing and selling captives.

The sacred narrative says but little of the government of Egypt by a Hebrew slave, or of his abilities as a ruler, — virtually supreme in the land, since Pharaoh delegates to him his own authority, persuaded both of his fidelity and his abilities. It is difficult to understand how Joseph arose at a single bound to such dignity and power, under a proud and despotic king, and in the face of all the prejudices of the Egyptian priesthood and nobility, except through the custom of all Oriental despots to gratify the whim of the moment, — like the one who made his horse prime minister. But nothing short of transcendent talents and transcendent services can account for his retention of office and his marked success. Joseph was then thirty years of age, having served Potiphar ten years, and spent two or three years in prison.

This all took place, as some now suppose, shortly after 1700 B. C., under the dynasty of the Hyksos or Shepherd Kings, who had conquered the kingdom about three hundred years before. Their capital was Memphis, near the pyramids, which had been erected several centuries earlier by the older and native dynasties. Rawlinson supposes that Tanis on the delta was the seat of their court. Conquered by the Hyksos, the old kings retreated to their other capital, Thebes, and were probably made tributary to the conquerors. It was by the earlier and later dynasties that the magnificent temples and palaces were built, whose ruins have so long been the wonder of travellers. The Shepherd Kings were warlike, and led their armies from Scythia, — that land of roving and emigrant warriors, — or, as Ewald thinks, from the land of Canaan: Aramæan chieftains, who sought the spoil of the richest monarchy in the world. Hence there was more affinity between these people and the Hebrews than between them and the ancient Egyptians, who were the descendants of Ham. Abraham, when he visited Egypt, found it ruled by these Scythian or Aramæan warriors, which accounts for the kind and generous treatment he received. It is not probable that a monarch of the ancient dynasties would have been so courteous to Abraham, or would have elevated Joseph to such an exalted rank, for they were jealous of strangers, and hated a pastoral people. It was only under the rule of the Hyksos that the Hebrews could have been tolerated and encouraged; for as soon as the Shepherd Kings were expelled by the Pharaohs who reigned at Thebes, as the Moors were expelled from Spain by the old Castilian princes, it fared ill with the descendants of Jacob, and they were bitterly and cruelly oppressed until the exodus under Moses. Prosperity probably led the Hyksos conquerors to that fatal degeneracy which is unfavorable to war, while adversity strengthened the souls of the descendants of the ancient kings, and enabled them to subdue and drive away their invaders and conquerors. And yet the Hyksos could not have ruled Egypt had they not adapted themselves to the habits, religion, and prejudices of the people they subdued. The Pharaoh who reigned at the time of Joseph belonged like his predecessors to the sacerdotal caste, and worshipped the gods of the Egyptians. But he was not jealous of the Hebrews, and fully appreciated the genius of Joseph.

The wisdom of Joseph as ruler of the land destined to a seven years' famine was marked by foresight as well as promptness in action. He personally visited the various provinces, advising the people to husband their harvests. But as all people are thoughtless and improvident, he himself gathered up and stored all the grain which could be spared, and in such vast quantities that he ceased to measure it. At last the predicted famine came, as the Nile had not risen to its usual height; but the royal granaries were full, since all the surplus wheat—about a fifth of the annual produce—had been stored away; not purchased by Joseph, but exacted as a tax. Nor was this exaction unreasonable in view of the emergency. Under the Bourbon kings of France more than one half of the produce of the land was taken by the Government and the feudal proprietors without compensation, and that not in provision for coming national trouble, but for the fattening of the royal purse. Joseph exacted only a fifth as a sort of special tax, less than the present Italian government exacts from all landowners.

Very soon the famine pressed upon the Egyptian people, for they had no corn in reserve; the reserve was in the hands of the government. But this reserve Joseph did not deal out gratuitously, as the Roman government, under the emperors, dealt out food to the citizens. He made the people pay for their bread, and took their money and deposited it in the royal treasury. When after two years their money was all spent, it was necessary to resort to barter, and cattle were given in exchange for corn, by which means the King became possessed of all the personal property of his subjects. As famine pressed, the people next surrendered their land to avoid starvation, — all but the priests. Pharaoh thus became absolute proprietor of the whole country; of money, cattle, and land, — an unprecedented surrender, which would have produced a wide-spread disaffection and revolt, had it not been that Joseph, after the famine was past and the earth yielded its accustomed harvest, exacted only one-fifth of the produce of the land for the support of the government, which could not be regarded as oppressive. As the King thus became absolute proprietor of Egypt by consent of the people, whom he had saved from starvation through the wisdom and energy of his prime minister, it is probable that later a new division of land took place, it being distributed among the people generally in small farms, for which they paid as rent a fifth of their produce. The gratitude of the people was marked: " Thou hast saved our lives: let us find grace in the eyes of my lord, and we will be Pharaoh's slaves." Since the time of Christ there have been two similar famines recorded, — one in the eleventh century, lasting, like Joseph's, seven years; and the other in the twelfth century, of which the most distressing details are given, even to the extreme desperation of cannibalism. The same cause originated both, — the failure of the Nile overflow. Out of the sacred river came up for Egypt its fat kine and its lean, — its blessings and its curses.

The price exacted by Joseph for the people's salvation made the King more absolute than before, since all were thus made dependent on the government.

This absolute rule of the kings, however, was somewhat modified by ancient customs, and by the vast influence of the priesthood, to which the King himself belonged. The priests of Egypt, under all the dynasties, formed the most powerful caste ever seen among the nations of the earth, if we except the Brahmanical caste of India. At the head of it was the King himself, who was chief of the religion and of the state. He regulated the sacrifices of the temples, and had the peculiar right of offering them to the gods upon grand occasions. He superintended the feasts and festivals in honor of the deities. The priests enjoyed privileges which extended to their whole family. They were exempt from taxes, and possessed one third of the landed property, which was entailed upon them, and of which they could not be deprived. Among them there were great distinctions of rank, but the high-priests held the most honorable station; they were devoted to the service of the presiding deities of the cities in which they lived,— such as the worship of Ammon at Thebes, of Phtha at Memphis, and of Ra at On, or Heliopolis. One of the principal grades of the priesthood was that of prophets, who were particularly versed in all matters pertaining to religion. They presided over the temple and the sacred rites, and directed the management of the priestly revenues; they bore a distinguished part in solemn processions, carrying the holy vase.

The priests not only regulated all spiritual matters and superintended the worship of the gods, but they were esteemed for their superior knowledge. They acquired an ascendency over the people by their supposed understanding of the sacred mysteries, only those priests being initiated in the higher secrets of religion who had proved themselves virtuous and discerning. "The honor of ascending from the less to the greater mysteries was as highly esteemed as it was difficult to obtain. The aspirant was required to go through the most severe ordeal, and show the greatest moral resignation." Those who aspired to know the profoundest secrets, imposed upon themselves duties more severe than those required by any other class. It was seldom that the priests were objects of scandal; they were reserved and discreet, practising the strictest purification of body and mind. Their life was so full of minute details that they rarely appeared in public. They thus obtained the sincere respect of the people, and ruled by the power of learning and sanctity as well as by privilege. They are most censured for concealing and withholding knowledge from the people.

How deep and profound was the knowledge of the Egyptian priests it is difficult to settle, since it was so carefully guarded. Pythagoras made great efforts and sacrifices to be initiated in their higher mysteries; but these, it is thought, were withheld, since he was a foreigner. What he did learn, however, formed a foundation of what is most valuable in Grecian philosophy. Herodotus declares that he knew the mysteries, but should not divulge them. Moses was skilled in all the knowledge of the sacred schools of Egypt, and perhaps incorporated in his jurisprudence some of its most valued truths. Possibly Plato obtained from the Egyptian priests his idea of the immortality of the soul, since this was one of their doctrines. It is even thought by Wilkinson that they believed in the unity, the eternal existence, and invisible power of God, but there is no definite knowledge on that point. Ammon, the concealed god, seems to have corresponded with the Zeus of the Greeks, as Sovereign Lord of Heaven. The priests certainly taught a state of future rewards and punishments, for the great doctrine of metempsychosis is based upon it, — the transmission of the soul after death into the bodies of various animals as an expiation for sin. But however lofty were the esoteric doctrines which the more learned of the initiated believed, they were carefully concealed from the people, who were deemed too ignorant to understand them; and hence the immense difference between the priests and people, and the universal prevalence of degrading superstitions and the vile polytheism which everywhere existed, — even the worship of the powers of Nature in those animals which were held sacred. Among all the ancient nations, however complicated were their theogonies, and however degraded the forms of worship assumed, — of men, or animals, or plants, — it was heat or light (the sun as the visible promoter of blessings) which was regarded as the *animus mundi*, to be worshipped as the highest manifestation of divine power and goodness. The sun, among all the ancient polytheists, was worshipped under various names, and was one of the supremest deities. The priestly city of On, a sort of university town, was consecrated to the worship of Ra, the sun. Baal was the sun-god among the polytheistic Canaanites, as Bel was among the Assyrians.

The Egyptian Pantheon, except perhaps that of Rome, was the most extensive among the ancient nations, and the most degraded, although that people were the most religious as well as superstitious of ancient pagans. The worship of the Deity, in some form, was as devout as it was universal, however degrading were the rites; and no expense was spared in sacrifices to propitiate the favor of the peculiar deity who presided over each of the various cities, for almost every city had a different deity. Notwithstanding the degrading fetichism — the lowest kind of Nature-worship, including the worship of animals — which formed the basis of the Egyptian religion, there were traces in it of pure monotheism, as in that of Babylonia and of ancient India. The distinguishing peculiarity of the Egyptian religion was the adoration of sacred animals as emblems of the gods, the chief of which were the bull, the cat, and the beetle.

The gods of the Egyptian Pantheon were almost innumerable, since they represented every form and power of Nature, and all the passions which move the human soul; but the most remarkable of the popular deities was Osiris, who was regarded as the personification of good. Isis, the consort of Osiris, who with him presided at the judgment of the dead, was scarcely less venerated. Set, or Typhon, the brother of Osiris, was the personification of evil. Between Osiris and Set, therefore, was perpetual antagonism. This belief, divested of names and titles and technicalities and fables, seems to have resembled, in this respect, the religion of the Persians, — the eternal conflict between good and evil. The esoteric doctrines of the priests initiated into the higher mysteries probably were the primeval truths, too abstract for the ignorant and sensual people to comprehend, and which were represented to them in visible forms that appealed to their senses, and which they worshipped with degrading rites.

The oldest of all the rites of the ancient pagans was in the form of sacrifice, to propitiate the deity. Abraham and Jacob offered sacrifices, but without degrading ceremonies, and both abhorred the representation of the deity in the form of animals; but there was scarcely an animal or reptile in Egypt that the people did not hold sacred, in fear or reverence. Moral evil was represented by the serpent, showing that something was retained, though in a distorted form, of the primitive revelation. The most celebrated forms of animal worship were the bulls at Memphis, sacred to Osiris, or, as some think, to the sun; the cat to Phtha, and the beetle to Re. The origin of these superstitions cannot be traced; they are shrouded in impenetrable mystery. All that we know is that they existed from the remotest period of which we have cognizance, long before the pyramids were built.

In spite, however, of the despotism of the kings, the privileges of the priests, and the degrading superstitions of the people, which introduced the most revolting form of religious worship ever seen on earth, there was in Egypt a high civilization in comparison with that of other nations, dating back to a mythical period. More than two thousand years before the Christian era, and six hundred before letters were introduced into Greece, one thousand years before the Trojan War, twelve hundred years before Buddha, and fifteen hundred years before Rome was founded, great architectural works existed in Egypt, the remains of which still astonish travellers for their vastness and grandeur. In the time of Joseph, before the eighteenth dynasty, there was in Egypt an estimated population of seven millions, with twenty thousand cities. The civilization of that country four thousand years ago was as high as that of the Chinese of the present day; and their literary and scientific accomplishments, their proficiency in the industrial and fine arts, remain to-day the wonder of history. But one thing is very remarkable, — that while there seems to have been no great progress for two thousand years, there was not any marked decline, thus indicating virtuous habits of life among the great body of the people from generation to generation. They were preserved from degeneracy by their simple habits and peaceful pursuits. Though the armies of the King numbered four hundred thousand men, there were comparatively few wars, and these mostly of a defensive character.

Such was the Egypt which Joseph governed with signal ability for more than half a century, nearly four thousand years ago, — the mother of inventions, the pioneer in literature and science, the home of learned men, the teacher of nations, communicating a knowledge which was never lost, making the first great stride in the civilization of the world. No one knows whether this civilization was indigenous, or derived from unknown races, or the remains of a primitive revelation, since it cannot be traced beyond Egypt itself, whose early inhabitants were more Asiatic than African, and apparently allied with Phœnicians and Assyrians.

But the civilization of Egypt is too extensive a subject to be entered upon in this connection. I hope to treat it more at length in subsequent volumes. I can only say now that in some things the Egyptians were never surpassed. Their architecture, as seen in the pyramids and the ruins of temples, was marvellous; while their industrial arts would not be disdained even in the 19th century.

Over this fertile, favored, and civilized nation Joseph reigned, — with delegated power indeed, but with power that was absolute, — when his starving brothers came to Egypt to buy corn, for the famine extended probably over western Asia. He is to be viewed, not as a prophet, or preacher, or reformer, or even a warrior like Moses, but as a merely executive ruler. As the son-in-law of the high-priest of Hieropolis, and delegated governor of the land, in the highest favor with the King, and himself a priest, it is probable that Joseph was initiated into the esoteric wisdom of the priesthood. He was undoubtedly stern, resolute, and inflexible in his relations with men, as great executive chieftains necessarily must be, whatever their private sympathies and friendships. To all appearance he was a born Egyptian, as he spoke the language of Egypt, had adopted its habits, and was clothed with the insignia of Egyptian power.

So that when the sons of Jacob, who during the

years of famine in Canaan had come down to Egypt to buy corn, were ushered into his presence, and bowed down to him, as had been predicted, he was harsh to them, although at once recognizing them. "Whence come ye?" he said roughly to them. They replied, "From the land of Canaan to buy corn." "Nay," continued he, "ye are spies." "Not so, my lord, but to buy food are thy servants come. We are all one man's sons; we are true men; thy servants are not spies." "Nay," he said, "to see the nakedness of the land are ye come," — for famine also prevailed in Egypt, and its governor naturally would not wish its weakness to be known, for fear of a hostile invasion. They replied, "Thy servants are twelve brothers, the sons of one man in the land of Canaan; the youngest is this day with our father, and one is not." But Joseph still persisted that they were spies, and put them in prison for three days; after which he demanded as the condition of their release that the younger brother should also appear before him. "If ye be true men," said he, "let one of your brothers be bound in the house of your prison, while you carry corn for the famine of your house; but bring your youngest brother unto me, and ye shall not die." There was apparently no alternative but to perish, or to bring Benjamin into Egypt; and the sons of Jacob were compelled to accept the condition.

Then their consciences were moved, and they saw a punishment for their crime in selling Joseph fifteen years before. Even Reuben accused them, and in the very presence of Joseph reminded them of their unnatural cruelty, not supposing that he understood them, since Joseph had spoken through an interpreter. This was too much for the stern governor; he turned aside and wept, but speedily returned and took from them Simeon and bound him before their eyes, and retained him for a surety. Then he caused their sacks to be filled with corn, putting also their money therein, and gave them in addition food for their return journey. But as one of them on that journey opened his sack to give his ass provender, he espied the money; and they were all filled with fear at this unlooked-for incident. They made haste to reach their home and report the strange intelligence to their father, including the demand for the appearance of Benjamin, which filled him with the most violent grief. "Joseph is not," cried he, "and Simeon is not, and ye will take Benjamin away!" Reuben here expostulated with frantic eloquence. Jacob, however, persisted: "My son shall not go down with you; if mischief befall him, ye will bring down my gray hairs in sorrow to the grave."

Meanwhile the famine pressed, as Joseph knew full well it would, and Jacob's family had eaten all their corn, and it became necessary to get a new supply from Egypt. But Judah refused to go without Benjamin. "The man," said he, "did solemnly protest unto us, saying, Ye shall not see my face, except your brother be with you." Then Jacob upbraided Judah for revealing the number and condition of his family; but Judah excused himself on account of the searching cross-examination of the austere governor which no one could resist, and persisted in the absolute necessity of Benjamin's appearance in Egypt, unless they all should yield to starvation. Moreover, he promised to be surety for his brother, that no harm should come to him. Jacob at last saw the necessity of allowing Benjamin to go, and reluctantly gave his consent; but in order to appease the terrible man of Egypt he ordered his sons to take with them a present of spices and balm and almonds, luxuries then in great demand, and a double amount of money in their sacks to repay what they had received. Then in pious resignation he said, "If I am bereaved of my children, I am bereaved," and hurried away his sons.

In due time they all safely arrived in Egypt, and with Benjamin stood before Joseph, and made obeisance, and then excused themselves to Joseph's steward, because of the money which had been returned in their sacks. The steward encouraged them, and brought Simeon to them, and led them into Joseph's house, where a feast was prepared by his orders. With great difficulty Joseph restrained his feelings at the sight of Benjamin, who was his own full brother, but asked kindly about the father. At last his pent-up affections gave way, and he sought his chamber and wept there in secret. He then sat down to the banquet with his attendants at a separate table,— for the Egyptian would not eat with foreigners, — still unrevealed to his brethren, but showed his partiality to Benjamin by sending him a mess five times greater than to the rest. They marvelled greatly that they were seated at the table according to their seniority, and questioned among themselves how the austere governor could know the ages of strangers.

Not yet did Joseph declare himself. His brothers were not yet sufficiently humbled ; a severe trial was still in store for them. As before, he ordered his steward to fill the sacks as full as they could carry, with every man's money in them, for he would not take his father's money; and further ordered that his silver drinking-cup should be put in Benjamin's sack. The brothers had scarcely left the city when they were overtaken by the steward on a charge of theft, and upbraided for stealing the silver cup. Of course they felt their innocence and protested it ; but it was of no avail, although they declared that if the cup should be found in any one of their sacks, he in whose sack it might be should die for the offence. The steward took them at their word, proceeded to search the sacks, and lo! what was their surprise and grief to see that the cup was found in Benjamin's sack! They rent their clothes in utter despair, and returned to the city. Joseph received them austerely, and declared that Benjamin should be retained in Egypt as his servant, or slave. Then Judah, forgetting in whose presence he was, cast aside all fear, and made the most eloquent and plaintive speech recorded in the Bible, offering to remain in Benjamin's place as a slave, for how could he face his father, who would surely die of grief at the loss of his favorite child.

Joseph could refrain his feelings no longer. He made every attendant leave his presence, and then declared himself to his brothers, whom God had sent to Egypt to be the means of saving their lives. The brothers, conscience stricken and ashamed, completely humbled and afraid, could not answer his questions. Then Joseph tenderly, in their own language, begged them to come near, and explained to them that it was not they who sent him to Egypt, but God, to work out a great deliverance to their posterity, and to be a father to Pharaoh himself, inasmuch as the famine was to continue five years longer. "Haste ye, and go up to my father, and say unto him that God hath made me lord of all Egypt: come down unto me, and thou shalt dwell in the land of Goshen near unto me, thou and thy children, and thy children's children, and thy flocks and thy herds, and all that thou hast, and there will I nourish thee. And ye shall tell my father of all my glory in Egypt, and of all that ye have seen; and ye shall haste, and bring down my father hither." And he fell on Benjamin's neck and wept, and kissed all his brothers. They then talked with him without further reserve.

The news that Joseph's brethren had come to Egypt pleased Pharaoh, so grateful was the King for the preservation of his kingdom. He could not do enough for such a benefactor. "Say to thy brethren, lade your beasts and go, and take your father and your households, and come unto me; and I will give you the good of the land of Egypt, and ye shall eat the fat of the land." And the King commanded them to take his wagons to transport their families and goods. Joseph also gave to each one of them changes of raiment, and to Benjamin three hundred pieces of silver and five changes of raiment, and ten asses laden with the good things of Egypt for their father, and ten she-asses laden with corn. As they departed, he archly said unto them, "See that ye fall not out by the way!"

And when they arrived at Canaan, and told their father all that had happened and all that they had seen, he fainted. The news was too good to be true; he would not believe them. But when he saw the wagons his spirit revived, and he said, "It is enough. Joseph my son is yet alive. I will go and see him before I die." The old man is again young in spirit. He is for going immediately; he could leap, — yea, fly.

To Egypt, then, Israel with his sons and his cattle and all his wealth hastened. His sons are astonished at the providence of God, so clearly and impressively demonstrated on their behalf. The reconciliation of the family is complete. All envy is buried in the unbounded prosperity of Joseph. He is now too great for envy. He is to be venerated as the instrument of God in saving his father's house and the land of Egypt. They all now bow down to him, father and sons alike, and the only strife now is who shall render him the most honor. He is the pride and glory of his family, as he is of the land of Egypt, and of the household of Pharaoh.

In the hospitality of the King, and his absence of jealousy of the nomadic people whom he settled in the most fertile of his provinces, we see additional confirmation of the fact that he was one of the Shepherd Kings. The Pharaoh of Joseph's time seems to have affiliated with the Israelites as natural friends, — to assist him in case of war. All the souls that came into Egypt with Jacob were seventy in number, although some historians think there was a much larger number. Rawlinson estimates it at two thousand, and Dean Payne Smith at three thousand.

Jacob was one hundred and thirty years of age when he came to dwell in the land of Goshen, and he lived seventeen years in Egypt. When he died, Joseph was about fifty years old, and was still in power.

It was the dying wish of the old patriarch to be buried with his fathers, and he made Joseph promise to carry his bones to the land of Canaan and bury them in the sepulchre which Abraham had bought, — even the cave of Machpelah.

Before Jacob died, Joseph brought his two sons to him to receive his blessing, — Manasseh and Ephraim, born in Egypt, whose grandfather was the high-priest of On, the city of the sun. As Manasseh was the oldest, he placed him at the right hand of Jacob, but the old man wittingly and designedly laid his right hand on Ephraim, which displeased Joseph. But Jacob, without giving his reason, persisted. While he prophesied that Manasseh should be great, Ephraim he said should be greater, — verified in the fact that the tribe of Ephraim was the largest of all the tribes, and the most powerful until the captivity. It was nearly as large as all the rest together, although in the time of Moses the tribe of Manasseh had become more numerous. We cannot penetrate the reason why Ephraim the younger son was preferred to the older, any more than why Jacob was preferred to Esau. After Jacob had blessed the sons of Joseph, he called his other sons around his dying bed to predict the future of their descendants. Reuben the oldest was told that he would not excel, because he had loved his father's concubine and committed a grievous sin. Simeon and Levi were the most active in seeking to compass the death of Joseph, and a curse was sent upon them. Judah was exalted above them all, for he had sought to save Joseph, and was eloquent in pleading for Benjamin,—the most magnanimous of the sons. So from him it was predicted that the sceptre should not depart from his house until Shiloh should come, — the Messiah, to whose appearance all the patriarchs looked. And all that Jacob predicted about his sons to their remote descendants came to pass; but the highest blessing was accorded to Joseph, as was realized in the future ascendency of Ephraim.

When Jacob had made an end of his blessings and predictions he gathered up his feet into his bed and gave up the ghost, and Joseph caused him to be embalmed, as was the custom in Egypt. When the days of public mourning were over (seventy days), Joseph obtained leave from Pharaoh to absent himself from the kingdom and his government, to bury his father according to his wish. And he departed in great pomp, with chariots and horses, together with his brothers and a great number, and deposited the remains of Jacob in the cave of the field of Machpelah, where Abraham himself was buried, and then returned to his duties in Egypt.

It is not mentioned in the Scriptures how long Joseph retained his power as prime minister of Pharaoh, but probably until a new dynasty succeeded the throne,— the eighteenth as it is supposed, for we are told that a new king arose who knew not Joseph. He lived to be one hundred and ten years of age, and when he died his body was embalmed and placed in a sarcophagus, and ultimately was carried to Canaan and buried with his fathers, according to the oath or promise he exacted of his brothers. His last recorded words were a prediction that God would bring the children of Israel out of Egypt to the land which he sware unto Abraham, Isaac, and Jacob. On his deathbed he becomes, like his father, a prophet. He had foretold his own future elevation when only a youth of seventeen, though only in the form of a dream, the full purport of which he did not comprehend; as an old man, about to die, he predicts the greatest blessing which could happen to his kindred,— their restoration to the land promised unto Abraham.

Joseph is one of the most interesting characters of

the Bible, one of the most fortunate, and one of the most faultless. He resisted the most powerful temptations, and there is no recorded act which sullies his memory. Although most of his life was spent among idolaters, and he married a pagan woman, he retained his allegiance to the God of his fathers. He ever felt that he was a stranger in a strange land, although its supreme governor, and looked to Canaan as the future and beloved home of his family and race. He regarded his residence in Egypt only as a means of preserving the lives of his kindred, and himself as an instrument to benefit both his family and the country which he ruled. His life was one of extraordinary usefulness. He had great executive talents, which he exercised for the good of others. Though stern and even hard in his official duties, he had unquenchable natural affections. His heart went out to his old father, his brother Benjamin, and to all his kindred with inexpressible tenderness. He was as free from guile as he was from false pride. In giving instructions to his brothers how they should appear before the King, and what they should say when questioned as to their occupations, he advised the utmost frankness, — to say that they were shepherds, although the occupation of a shepherd was an abomination to an Egyptian. He had exceeding tact in confronting the prejudices of the King and the priesthood. He took no pains to conceal his birth and lineage in the most aristocratic country of the world. Considering that he was only second in power and dignity to an absolute monarch, his life was unostentatious and his habits simple.

If we seek a parallel to him among modern statesmen, he most resembles Colbert as the minister of Louis XIV., or Prince Metternich, who in great simplicity ruled Continental Europe for a quarter of a century.

Nothing is said of his palaces, or pleasures, or wealth. He had not the austere and unbending pride of Mordecai, whose career as an instrument of Providence for the welfare of his countrymen was as remarkable as Joseph's. He was more like Daniel in his private life than any of those Jews who have arisen to great power in foreign lands, though he had not Daniel's exalted piety or prophetic gifts. He was faithful to the interests of his sovereign, and greatly increased the royal authority. He got possession of the whole property of the nation for the benefit of his master, but exacted only a fifth part of the produce of the land for the support of the government. He was a priest of a grossly polytheistic religion, but acknowledged only the One Supreme God, whose instrument he felt himself to be. His services to the state were transcendent, but his supremest mission was to preserve the Hebrew nation.

The condition of the Israelites in Egypt after the death of Joseph, and during the period of their sojourn, it is difficult to determine. There is a doubt among the critics as to the length of this sojourn, — the Bible in several places asserting that it lasted four hundred and thirty years, which, if true, would bring the Exodus to the end of the nineteenth dynasty. Some suppose that the residence in Egypt was only two hundred and fifteen years. The territory assigned to the Israelites was a small one, and hence must have been densely populated, if, as it is reckoned, two millions of people left the country under the leadership of Moses and Aaron. It is supposed that the reigning sovereign at that time was Menephtah, successor of Rameses II. It is, then, the great Rameses, who was the king from whom Moses fled, — the most distinguished of all the Egyptian monarchs as warrior and builder of monuments. He was the second king of the eighteenth dynasty, and reigned in conjunction with his father Seti for sixty years. Among his principal works was the completion of the city of Rameses (Raamses, or Tanis, or Zoan), one of the principal cities of Egypt, begun by his father and made a royal residence. He also, it appears from the monuments, built Pithon and other important towns, by the forced labor of the Israelites. Rameses and Pithon were called treasure-cities, the site of the latter having been lately discovered, to the east of Tanis. They were located in the midst of a fertile country, now dreary and desolate, which was the object of great panegyric. An Egyptian poet, quoted by Dr. Charles S. Robinson, paints the vicinity of Zoan, where Pharaoh resided at the time of the Exodus, as full of loveliness and fertility. "Her fields are verdant with excellent herbage; her bowers bloom with garlands; her pools are prolific in fish; and in the ponds are ducks. Each garden is perfumed with the smell of honey; the granaries are full of wheat and barley; vegetables and reeds and herbs are growing in the parks; flowers and nosegays are in the houses; lemons, citrons and figs are in the orchards." Such was the field of Zoan in ancient times, near Rameses, which the Israelites had built without straw to make their bricks, and from which place they set out for the general rendezvous at Succoth, under Moses. It will be noted that if Rameses, or Tanis, was the residence of the court when Moses made his demands on Menephtah, it was in the midst of the settlements of the Israelites, in the land of Goshen, which the last of the Shepherd Kings had assigned to them.

It is impossible to tell what advance in civilization was made by the Israelites in consequence of their sojourn in Egypt; but they must have learned many useful arts, and many principles of jurisprudence, and

ISRAEL IN EGYPT.

acquired a better knowledge of agriculture. They learned to be patient under oppression and wrong, to be frugal and industrious in their habits, and obedient to the voice of their leaders. But unfortunately they acquired a love of idolatrous worship, which they did not lose until their captivity in Babylon. The golden calves of the wilderness were another form of the worship of the sacred bulls of Memphis. They were easily led to worship the sun under the Egyptian and Canaanitish names. Had the children of Israel remained in the promised land, in the early part of their history, they would probably have perished by famine, or have been absorbed by their powerful Canaanitish neighbors. In Egypt they were well fed, rapidly increased in number, and became a nation to be feared even while in bondage. In the land of Canaan they would have been only a pastoral or nomadic people, unable to defend themselves in war, and unacquainted with the use of military weapons. They might have been exterminated, without constant miracles and perpetual supernatural aid, — which is not the order of Providence.

In Egypt, it is true, the Israelites lost their political independence; but even under slavery there is much to be learned from civilized masters. How rapid and marvellous the progress of the African races in the Southern States in their two hundred years of bondage!

When before in the history of the world has there been such a progress among mere barbarians, with fetichism for their native religion? Races have advanced in every element of civilization, and in those virtues which give permanent strength to character, under all the benumbing and degrading influences of slavery, while nations with wealth, freedom, and prosperity have declined and perished. The slavery of the Israelites in Egypt may have been a blessing in disguise, from which they emerged when they were able to take care of themselves. Moses led them out of bondage; but Moses also incorporated in his institutions the "wisdom of the Egyptians." He was indeed inspired to declare certain fundamental truths, but he also taught the lessons of experience which a great nation had acquired by two thousand years of prosperity. Who can tell, who can measure, the civilization which the Israelites must have carried out of Egypt, with the wealth of which they despoiled their masters? Where else at that period could they have found such teachers? The Persians at that time were shepherds like themselves in Canaan, the Assyrians were hunters, and the Greeks had no historical existence. Only the discipline of forty years in the wilderness, under Moses, was necessary to make them a nation of conquerors, for they had already learned the arts of agriculture, and knew how to protect themselves in walled cities. A nomadic people were they no longer, as in the time of Jacob, but small farmers, who had learned to irrigate their barren hills and till their fertile valleys; and they became a powerful though peaceful nation, unconquered by invaders for a thousand years, and unconquerable for all time in their traditions, habits, and mental characteristics. From one man — the patriarch Jacob — did this great nation rise, and did not lose its national unity and independence until from the tribe of Judah a deliverer arose who redeemed the human race. Surely, how favored was Joseph, in being the instrument under Providence of preserving this nation in its infancy, and placing its people in a rich and fertile country where they could grow and multiply, and learn principles of civilization which would make them a permanent power in the progress of humanity!

MOSES.

1571–1451 B. C. [USHER].

HEBREW JURISPRUDENCE.

MOSES.

HEBREW JURISPRUDENCE.

AMONG the great actors in the world's history must surely be presented the man who gave the first recorded impulse to civilization, and who is the most august character of antiquity. I think Moses and his legislation should be considered from the standpoint of the Scriptures rather than from that of science and criticism. It is very true that the legislation and ritualism we have been accustomed to ascribe to Moses are thought by many great modern critics, including Ewald, to be the work of writers whose names are unknown, in the time of Hezekiah and even later, as Jewish literature was developed. But I remain unconvinced by the modern theories, plausible as they are, and weighty as is their authority; and hence I have presented the greatest man in the history of the Jews as our fathers regarded him, and as the Bible represents him. Nor is there any subject which bears more directly on the elemental principles of theological belief and practical morality, or is more closely connected with the progress of modern religious and social thought, than a consideration of the Mosaic writings. Whether as a "man of God," or as a meditative sage, or as a sacred historian, or as an inspired prophet, or as an heroic liberator and leader of a favored nation, or as a profound and original legislator, Moses alike stands out as a wonderful man, not to the eyes of Jews merely, but to all enlightened nations and ages. He was evidently raised up for a remarkable and exalted mission, — not only to deliver a debased and superstitious people from bondage, but to impress his mind and character upon them and upon all other nations, and to link his name with the progress of the human race.

He arose at a great crisis, when a new dynasty reigned in Egypt, — not friendly, as the preceding one had been, to the children of Israel; but a dynasty which had expelled the Shepherd Kings, and looked with fear and jealousy upon this alien race, already powerful, in sympathy with the old régime, located in the most fertile sections of the land, and acquainted not merely with agriculture, but with the arts of the Egyptians, — a population of over two millions of souls; so that the reigning monarch, probably a son of the Sesostris of the Greeks, bitterly exclaimed to his courtiers, "The children of Israel are more and mightier than we!" And the consequence of this jealousy

HEBREW JURISPRUDENCE.

was a persecution based on the elemental principle of all persecution, — that of fear blended with envy, carried out with remorseless severity; for in case of war (and the new dynasty scarcely felt secure on the throne) it was feared the Hebrews might side with enemies. So the new Pharaoh (Rameses II., as is thought by Rawlinson) attempted to crush their spirit by hard toils and unjust exactions. And as they still continued to multiply, there came forth the dreadful edict that every male child of the Hebrews should be destroyed as soon as born.

It was then that Moses, descended from a family of the tribe of Levi, was born, — 1571 B. C., according to Usher. I need not relate in detail the beautiful story of his concealment for three months by his mother Jochebed, his exposure in a basket of papyrus on the banks of the Nile, his rescue by the daughter of Pharaoh, at that time regent of the kingdom in the absence of her father, — or, as Wilberforce thinks, the wife of the king of Lower Egypt, — his adoption by this powerful princess, his education in the royal household among those learned priests to whose caste even the King belonged. Moses himself, a great master of historical composition, has in six verses told that story, with singular pathos and beauty; yet he directly relates nothing further of his life until, at the age of forty, he killed an Egyptian overseer who was smiting one of his oppressed brethren, and buried him in the sands, — thereby showing that he was indignant at injustice, or clung in his heart to his race of slaves. But what a history might have been written of those forty years of luxury, study, power, and honor! — since Josephus speaks of his successful and brilliant exploits as a conqueror of the Ethiopians. What a career did the son of the Hebrew bondwoman probably lead in the palaces of Memphis, sitting at the monarch's table, fêted as a conqueror, adopted as grandson and perhaps as heir, a proficient in all the learning and arts of the most civilized nation of the earth, enrolled in the college of priests, discoursing with the most accomplished of his peers on the wonders of magical enchantment, the hidden meaning of religious rites, and even the being and attributes of a Supreme God, — the esoteric wisdom from which even a Pythagoras drew his inspiration; possibly tasting, with generals and nobles, all the pleasures of sin. But whether in pleasure or honor, the soul of Moses, fortified by the maternal instructions of his early days, — for his mother was doubtless a good as well as a brave woman, — soars beyond his circumstances, and he seeks to avenge the wrongs of his brethren. Not wisely, however, for he slays a government official, and is forced to flee, — a necessity which we can hardly comprehend in view of his rank and power, unless it revealed all at once to the astonished king his Hebrew birth, and his dangerous sympathies with an oppressed people, the act showing that he may have sought, in his earnest soul, to break their intolerable bonds.

Certainly Moses aspires prematurely to be a deliverer. He is not yet prepared for such a mighty task. He is too impulsive and inexperienced. It must need be that he pass through a period of preparation, learn patience, mature his knowledge, and gain moral force, which preparation could be best made in severe contemplation; for it is in retirement and study that great men forge the weapons which demolish principalities and powers, and master those *principia* which are the foundation of thrones and empires. So he retires to the deserts of Midian, among a scattered pastoral people, on the eastern shore of the Red Sea, and is received by Jethro, a priest of Midian, whose flocks he tends, and whose daughter he marries.

The land of Midian, to which he fled, is not fertile like Egypt, nor rich in unnumbered monuments of pride and splendor, with pyramids for mausoleums, and colossal statues to perpetuate kingly memories. It is not scented with flowers and variegated with landscapes of beauty and fertility, but is for the most part, with here and there a patch of verdure, a land of utter barrenness and dreariness, and, as Hamilton paints it, "a great and terrible wilderness, where no soft features mitigated the unbroken horror, but dark and brown ridges, red peaks like pyramids of fire; no rounded hillocks or soft mountain curves, but monstrous and misshapen cliffs, rising tier above tier, and serrated for miles into rugged grandeur, and grooved by the winter torrents cutting into the veins of the fiery rock: a land dreary and desolate, yet sublime in its boldness and ruggedness, — a labyrinth of wild and blasted mountains, a terrific and howling desolation."

It is here that Moses seeks safety, and finds it in the home of a priest, where his affections may be cultivated, and where he may indulge in lofty speculations and commune with the Elohim whom he adores; isolated yet social, active in body but more active in mind, still fresh in all the learning of the schools of Egypt, and wise in all the experiences of forty years. And the result of his studies and inspirations was, it is supposed, the book of Genesis, in which he narrates more important events, and reveals more lofty truths than all the historians of Greece unfolded in their collective volumes, — a marvel of historic art, a model of composition, an immortal work of genius, the oldest and the greatest written history of which we have record.

And surely what poetry, pathos, and eloquence,

what simplicity and beauty, what rich and varied lessons of human experience, what treasures of moral wisdom, are revealed in that little book! How sublimely the poet-prophet narrates the misery of the Fall, and the promised glories of the Restoration! How concisely the historian compresses the incidents of patriarchal life, the rise of empires, the fall of cities, the certitudes of faith, of friendship, and of love! All that is vital in the history of thousands of years is condensed into a few chapters, — not dry and barren annals, but descriptions of character, and the unfolding of emotions and sensibilities, and insight into those principles of moral government which indicate a superintending Power, creating faith in a world of sin, and consolation amid the wreck of matter.

Thus when forty more years are passed in study, in literary composition, in religious meditation, and active duties, in sight of grand and barren mountains, amid affections and simplicities, — years which must have familiarized him with every road and cattle-drive and sheep-track, every hill and peak, every wady and watercourse, every timber-belt and oasis in the Sinaitic wilderness, through which his providentially trained military instincts were to safely conduct a vast multitude, — Moses, still strong and laborious, is fitted for his exalted mission as a deliverer. And now he is directly called by the voice of God himself, amid the wonders of the burning bush, — Him whom, thus far, he had, like Abraham, adored as the Elohim, the God Almighty, but whom henceforth he recognizes as Jehovah (Jahveh) in His special relations to the Jewish nation, rather than as the general Deity who unites the attributes ascribed to Him as the ruler of the universe. Moses quakes before that awful voice out of the midst of the bush, which commissions him to deliver his brethren. He is no longer bold, impetuous, impatient, but timid and modest. Long study and retirement from the busy haunts of men have made him self-distrustful. He replies to the great *I Am,* "Who am I, that *I* should bring forth the Children of Israel out of Egypt? Behold, I am not eloquent; they will not believe me, nor hearken to my voice." In spite of the miracle of the rod, Moses obeys reluctantly, and Aaron, his elder brother, is appointed as his spokesman.

Armed with the mysterious wonder-working rod, at length Moses and Aaron, as representatives of the Jewish people, appear in the presence of Pharaoh, and in the name of Jehovah request permission for Israel to go and hold a feast in the wilderness. They do not demand emancipation or emigration, which would of course be denied. I cannot dwell on the haughty scepticism and obdurate hardness of the King, — "Who is Jehovah, that I should obey *his* voice?" — the renewed persecution of the Hebrews, the successive plagues and calamities sent upon Egypt, which the magicians could not explain, and the final extorted and unwilling consent of Pharaoh to permit Israel to worship the God of Moses in the wilderness, lest greater evils should befall him than the destruction of the first-born throughout the land.

The deliverance of a nation of slaves is at last, it would seem, miraculously effected; and then begins the third period of the life of Moses, as the leader and governor of these superstitious, sensual, idolatrous, degraded slaves. Then begin the real labors and trials of Moses; for the people murmur, and are consumed with fears as soon as they have crossed the sea, and find themselves in the wilderness. And their unbelief and impatience are scarcely lessened by the tremendous miracle of the submersion of the pursuing host, and all successive miracles, — the mysterious manna, the pillar of cloud and of fire, the smitten rock at Horeb, and the still more impressive and awful wonders of Sinai.

The guidance of the Israelites during these forty years in the wilderness is marked by transcendent ability on the part of Moses, and by the most disgraceful conduct on the part of the Israelites. They are forgetful of mercies, ungrateful, rebellious, childish in their hankerings for a country where they had been more oppressed than Spartan Helots, idolatrous, and superstitious. They murmur for flesh to eat; they make golden calves to worship; they seek a new leader when Moses is longer on the Mount than they expect. When any new danger threatens they lay the blame on Moses; they even foolishly regret that they had not died in Egypt.

Obviously such a people were not fit for freedom, or even for the conquest of the promised land. They were as timid and cowardly as they were rebellious. Even the picked men sent out to explore Canaan, with the exception of Caleb and Joshua, reported nations of giants impossible to subdue. A new generation must arise, disciplined by forty years' experience, made hardy and strong by exposure and suffering. Yet what nation, in the world's history, ever improved so much in forty years? What ruler ever did so much for a people in a single reign? This abject race of slaves in forty years was transformed into a nation of valiant warriors, made subject to law and familiar with the fundamental principles of civilization. What a marvellous change, effected by the genius and wisdom of one man, in communion with Almighty power!

But the distinguishing labor of Moses during these forty years, by which he linked his name with all subsequent ages, and became the greatest benefactor of mind the world has seen until Christ, was his system of Jurisprudence. It is this which especially demands our notice, and hence will form the main subject of this lecture.

In reviewing the Mosaic legislation, we notice both those ordinances which are based on immutable truth for the rule of all nations to the end of time, and those prescribed for the peculiar situation and exigencies of the Jews as a theocratic state, isolated from other nations.

The moral code of Moses, by far the most important and universally accepted, rests on the fundamental principles of theology and morality. How lofty, how impressive, how solemn this code! How it appeals at once to the consciousness of all minds in every age and nation, producing convictions that no sophistry can weaken, binding the conscience with irresistible and terrific bonds, — those immortal Ten Commandments, engraven on the two tables of stone, and preserved in the holy and innermost sanctuary of the Jews, yet reappearing in all their literature, accepted and reaffirmed by Christ, entering into the religious system of every nation that has received them, and forming the cardinal principles of all theological belief! Yet it was by Moses that these Commandments came. He is the first, the favored man, commissioned by God to declare to the world, clearly and authoritatively, His supreme power and majesty, whom alone all nations and tribes and people are to worship to remotest generations. In it he fearfully exposes the sin of idolatry, to which all nations are prone, — the one sin which the Almighty visits with such dreadful penalties, since this involves, and implies logically, rebellion against Him, the supreme ruler of the universe, and disloyalty to Him as a personal sovereign, in whatever form this idolatry may appear, whether in graven images of tutelary deities, or in the worship of Nature (ever blind and indefinite), or in the exaltation of self, in the varied search for pleasure, ambition, or wealth, to which the debased soul bows down with grovelling instincts, and in the pursuit of which the soul forgets its higher destiny and its paramount obligations. Moses is the first to expose with terrific force and solemn earnestness this universal tendency to the oblivion of the One God amid the temptations, the pleasures, and the glories of the world, and the certain displeasure of the universal sovereign which must follow, as seen in the fall of empires and the misery of individuals from his time to ours, the uniform doom of people and nations, whatever the special form of idolatry, whenever it reaches a peculiar fulness and development, — the ultimate law of all decline and ruin, from which there is no escape, "for the Lord God is a jealous God, visiting the iniquities of the fathers upon the children unto the third and fourth

HEBREW JURISPRUDENCE.

generation." So sacred and awful is this controlling Deity, that it is made a cardinal sin even to utter His name in vain, in levity or blasphemy. In order also to keep Him before the minds of men, a day is especially appointed — one in seven — which it is the bounden duty as well as privilege of all generations to keep with peculiar sanctity, — a day of rest from labor as well as of adoration; an entirely new institution, which no Pagan nation, and no other ancient nation, ever recognized. After thus laying solemn injunctions upon all men to render supreme allegiance to this personal God, — for we can find no better word, although Matthew Arnold calls it "the Power which maketh for righteousness," — Moses presents the duties of men to each other, chiefly those which pertain to the abstaining from injuries they are most tempted to commit, extending to the innermost feelings of the heart, for "thou shalt not covet anything which is thy neighbor's;" thus covering, in a few sentences, the primal obligations of mankind to God and to society, afterward expanded by a greater teacher into the more comprehensive law of Love, which is to bind together mortals on earth, as it binds together immortals in heaven.

All Christian nations have accepted these Ten Commandments, even Mohammedan nations, as appealing to the universal conscience, — not a mere Jewish code, but a primary law, susceptible of boundless obligation, never to be abrogated; a direct injunction of the Almighty to the end of time.

The Ten Commandments seem to be the foundation of the subsequent and more minute code which Moses gave to the Jews; and it is interesting to see how its great principles have entered, more or less, into the laws of Christian nations from the decline of the Roman Empire, into the Theodosian code, the laws of Charlemagne, of Ina, of Alfred, and especially into the institutions of the Puritans, and of all other sects and parties wherever the Bible is studied and revered. They seem to be designed not merely for Jews, but for Gentiles also, since there is no escape from their obligation. They may seem severe in some of their applications, but never unjust; and as long as the world endures, the relations between man and man are to be settled on lofty moral grounds. An elevated morality is the professed aim of all enlightened lawgivers; and the prosperity of nations is built upon it, for it is righteousness which exalteth them. Culture is desirable; but the welfare of nations is based on morals rather than on æsthetics. On this point Moses, or even Epictetus, is a greater authority than Goethe. All the ordinances of Moses tend to this end. They are the publication of natural religion, — that God is a rewarder of virtuous actions, and punishes wicked deeds. Moses, from first to last,

HEBREW JURISPRUDENCE.

insists imperatively on the doctrine of personal responsibility to God, which doctrine is the logical sequence of belief in Him as the moral governor of the world. And in enforcing this cardinal truth he is dogmatic and dictatorial, as a prophet and ambassador of the Most High should be.

It is a waste of time to use arguments in the teaching of the primal principles which appeal to consciousness; and I am not certain but that elaborate and metaphysical reasoning on the nature and attributes of God weakens rather than strengthens the belief in Him, since He is a power made known by revelation, and received and accepted by the soul at once, if received at all. Among the earliest noticeable corruptions of the Church was the introduction of Greek philosophy to harmonize and reconcile with it the truths of the gospel, which to a certain class ever have been, and ever will be, foolishness. The speculations and metaphysics of theologians, I verily believe, have done more harm than good, — from Athanasius to Jonathan Edwards, — whenever they have brought the aid of finite reason to support the ultimate truths declared by an infinite and almighty mind. Moses does not reason, nor speculate, nor refine; he affirms, and appeals to the law written on the heart, — to the consciousness of mankind. What he declares to be duties are not even to be discussed. They are to be obeyed with unhesitating obedience, since no discussion or argument can make them clearer or more imperative. The obligation to obey them is seen and felt at once, as soon as they are declared. What he says in regard to the relations of master and servant; to injuries inflicted on the body; to the respect due to parents; to the protection of the widow, the fatherless, and the unfortunate; to delicacy in the treatment of women; to unjust judgments; to bribery and corruption; to revenge, hatred, and covetousness; to falsehood and tale-bearing; to unchastity, theft, murder, and adultery, — can never be gainsaid, and would have been accepted by Roman jurists as readily as by modern legislators; yea, they would not be disputed by savages, if they acknowledged a God at all. The elevated morality of the ethical code of Moses is its most striking feature, since it appeals to the universal heart. and does not conflict with some of the ethical teachings of those great lights of the Pagan world to whose consciousness God has been revealed. Moses differs from them only in the completion and scope and elevation of his system, and in its freedom from the puerilities and superstitions which they blended with their truths, and from which he was emancipated by inspiration. Brahma and Confucius and Socrates taught some great truths which Moses would accept, but they taught errors likewise. He taught no errors, though he permitted some sins which in the beginning did not exist, — such, for instance, as polygamy. Christ came not to destroy his law, but to fulfil it and complete it. In two things especially, how emphatic his teaching and how permanent his influence! — in respect to the observance of the Sabbath and the relations of the sexes. To him, more than to any man in the world's history, do we owe the elevation of woman, and the sanctity and blessing of a day of rest. In the awful sacredness of the person, and in the regular resort to the sanctuary of God, we see his immortal authority and his permanent influence.

The other laws which Moses promulgated are more special and minute, and seem to be intended to preserve the Jews from idolatry, the peculiar sin of the surrounding nations; and also, more directly, to keep alive the recognition of a theocratic government.

Thus the ceremonial or ritualistic law — an important part of the Mosaic Code — constantly points to Jehovah as the King of the Jews, as well as their Supreme Deity, for whose worship the rites and ceremonies are devised with great minuteness, to keep His *personality* constantly before their minds. Moreover, all their rites and ceremonies were typical and emblematical of the promised Saviour who was to arise; in a more emphatic sense their King, and not merely their own Messiah, but the Redeemer of the whole race, who should reign finally as King of kings and Lord of lords. And hence these rites and sacrifices, typical of Him who should offer Himself as a sacrifice for the sins of the world, are not supposed to be binding on other nations after the great sacrifice has been made, and the law of Moses has been fulfilled by Jesus and the new dispensation has been established. We see a complicated and imposing service, with psalms and hymns, and beautiful robes, and smoking altars, — all that could inspire awe and reverence. We behold a blazing tabernacle of gold and silver and precious woods and gorgeous tapestries, with inner and secret recesses to contain the ark and the tables of stone, the mysterious rod, the urn of manna, the book of the covenant, the golden throne over-canopied by cherubs with outstretched wings, and the mercy-seat for the Shekinah who sat between the cherubim. The sacred and costly vessels, the candlesticks of pure and beaten gold, the lamps, the brazen sea, the embroidered vestments of the priests, the breastplate of precious stones, the golden chains, the emblematic rings, the ephods and mitres and girdles, the various altars for sacrifice, the burnt-offerings, peace-offerings, meat-offerings, and sin-offerings, the consecrated cakes and animals for sacrifice, the rites for cleansing leprosy and all uncleanliness, the grand atonements and solemn fasts and festivals, — all were calculated to make a strong

HEBREW JURISPRUDENCE.

impression on a superstitious people. The rites and ceremonies of the Jews were so attractive that they made up for all other amusements and spectacles; they answered the purpose of the Gothic churches and cathedrals of Europe in the Middle Ages, when these were the chief attractions of the period. There is nothing absurd in ritualism among ignorant and superstitious people, who are ever most easily impressed through their senses and imagination. It was the wisdom of the Middle Ages, — the device of popes and bishops and abbots to attract and influence the people. But ritualism — useful in certain ages and circumstances, certainly in its most imposing forms, if I may say it — does not seem to be one of the peculiarities of enlightened ages; even the ritualism of the wilderness lost much of its hold upon the Jews themselves after their captivity, and still more when Greek and Roman civilization had penetrated to Jerusalem. The people who listened to Peter and Paul could no longer be moved by imposing rites, even as the European nations — under the preaching of Luther, Knox, and Latimer — lost all relish for the ceremonies of the Middle Ages. What, then, are we to think of the revival of observances which lost their force three hundred years ago, unless connected with artistic music? It is music which vitalizes ritualistic worship in our times, as it did in the times of David and Solomon. The vitality of the Jewish ritual, when the nation had emerged from barbarism, was in its connections with a magnificent psalmody. The Psalms of David appeal to the heart and not to the senses. The ritualism of the wilderness appealed to the senses and not to the heart; and this was necessary when the people had scarcely emerged from barbarism, even as it was deemed necessary amid the turbulence and ignorance of the tenth century.

In the ritualism which Moses established there was the absence of everything which would recall the superstitions and rites, or even the doctrines, of the Egyptians. In view of this, we account partially for the almost studied reticence in respect to a future state, upon which hinged many of the peculiarities of Egyptian worship. It would have been difficult for Moses to have recognized the future state, in the degrading ignorance and sensualism of the Jews, without associating with it the tutelary deities of the Egyptians and all the absurdities connected with the doctrine of metempsychosis, which consigned the victims of future punishment to enter the forms of disgusting and hideous animals, thereby blending with the sublime doctrine of a future state the most degrading superstitions. Bishop Warburton seizes on the silence of Moses respecting a future state to prove, by a learned yet sophistical argument, his divine legation, *because* he ignored what so essentially entered into the religion of Egypt. But whether Moses purposely ignored this great truth for fear it would be perverted, or because it was a part of the Egyptian economy which he wished his people to forget, still it is also possible that this doctrine of immortality was so deeply engraved on the minds of the people that there was no need to recognize it while giving a system of ritualistic observances. The comparative silence of the Old Testament concerning immortality is one of its most impressive mysteries. However dimly shadowed by Job and David and Isaiah, it seems to have been brought to light only by the gospel. There is more in the writings of Plato and Cicero about immortality than in the whole of the Old Testament. And this fact is so remarkable, that some trace to the sages of Greece and Egypt the doctrine itself, as ordinarily understood; that is, a *necessary* existence of the soul after death. And they fortify themselves with those declarations of the apostles which represent a happy immortality as the special gift of God, — not a necessary existence, but given only to those who obey his laws. If immortality be not a gift, but a necessary existence, as Socrates supposed, it seems strange that heathen philosophers should have speculated more profoundly than the patriarchs of the East on this mysterious subject. We cannot suppose that Plato was more profoundly instructed on such a subject than Abraham and Moses. It is to be noted, however, that God seems to have chosen different races for various missions in the education of his children. As Saint Paul puts it, "There are diversities of gifts, but the same Spirit, ... diversities of workings, but the same God who worketh in all." The Hebrew genius was that of discerning and declaring moral and spiritual truth; while that of the Greeks was essentially philosophic and speculative, searching into the reasons and causes of existing phenomena. And it is possible, after all, that the loftiest of the Greek philosophers derived their opinions from those who had been admitted to the secret schools of Egypt, where it is probable that the traditions of primitive ages were preserved, and only communicated to a chosen few; for the ancient schools were esoteric and not popular. The great masters of knowledge believed one thing and the people another. The popular religion was always held in contempt by the wise in all countries, although upheld by them in external rites and emblems and sacrifices, from patriotic purposes. The last act of Socrates was to sacrifice a cock to Esculapius, with a different meaning from that which was understood by the people.

The social and civil code of Moses seems to have had primary reference to the necessary isolation of the Jews, to keep them from the abominations of other nations, and especially idolatry, and even to make them repulsive and disagreeable to foreigners, in order to keep them a peculiar people. The Jew wore an uncouth dress. When he visited strangers he abstained from their customs, and even meats. When a stranger visited the Jew he was compelled to submit to Jewish restraints. So that the Jew ever seems uncourteous, narrow, obstinate, and grotesque: even as others appeared to him to be pagan and unclean. Moses lays down laws best calculated to keep the nation separated and esoteric; but there is marvellous wisdom in those which were directed to the development of national resources and general prosperity in an isolated state. The nation was made strong for defence, not for aggression. It must depend upon its militia, and not on horses and chariots, which are designed for distant expeditions, for the pomp of kings, for offensive war, and military aggrandizement. The legislation of Moses recognized the peaceful virtues rather than the warlike, — agricultural industry, the network of trades and professions, manufacturing skill, production, not waste and destruction. He discouraged commerce, not because it was in itself demoralizing, but because it brought the Jews too much in contact with corrupt nations. And he closely defined political power, and divided it among different magistrates, instituting a wise balance which would do credit to modern legislation. He gave dignity to the people by making them the ultimate source of authority, next to the authority of God. He instituted legislative assemblies to discuss peace and war, and elect the great officers of state. While he made the Church support the State, and the State the Church, yet he separated civil power from the religious, as Calvin did at Geneva. The functions of the priest and the functions of the magistrate were made forever distinct, — a radical change from the polity of Egypt, where kings were priests, and priests were civil rulers as well as a literary class; a predominating power to whom all vital interests were intrusted. The kingly power among the Jews was checked and hedged by other powers, so that an overgrown tyranny was difficult and unusual. But above all kingly and priestly power was the power of the Invisible King, to whom the judges and monarchs and supreme magistrates were responsible, as simply His delegates and vicegerents. Upon Him alone the Jews were to rely in all crises of danger; in Him alone was help. And it is remarkable that whenever Jewish rulers relied on chariots and horses and foreign allies, they were delivered into the hands of their enemies. It was only when they fell back upon the protecting arms of their Eternal Lord that they were rescued and saved. The mightiest monarch ruled only with delegated powers from Him; and it was the memorable loyalty of David to his King which kept him on the throne, as it was self-reliance — the exhibition of independent power — which caused the sceptre to depart from Saul.

I cannot dwell on the humanity and wisdom which marked the social economy of the Jews, as given by Moses, — in the treatment of slaves (emancipated every fifty years), in the sanctity of human life, in the liberation of debtors every seven years, in kindness to the poor (who were allowed to glean the fields), in the education of the people, in the division of inherited property, in the inalienation of paternal inheritances, in the discouragement of all luxury and extravagance, in those regulations which made disproportionate fortunes difficult, the vast accumulation of which was one of the main causes of the decline of the Roman Empire, and is now one of the most threatening evils of modern civilization. All the civil and social laws of the Jewish commonwealth tended to the elevation of woman and the cultivation of domestic life. What virtues were gradually developed among those sensual slaves whom Moses led through the desert! In what ancient nation were seen such respect to parents, such fidelity to husbands, such charming delights of home, such beautiful simplicities, such ardent loves, such glorious friendships, such regard to the happiness of others!

Such, in brief, was the great work which Moses performed, the marvellous legislation which he gave to the Israelites, involving principles accepted by the Christian world in every age of its history. Now, whence had this man this wisdom? Was it the result of his studies and reflections and experiences, or was it a wisdom supernaturally taught him by the Almighty? On the solution of this inquiry into the divine legation of Moses hang momentous issues. It is too grand and important an inquiry to be disregarded by any one who studies the writings of Moses; it is too suggestive a subject to be passed over even in a literary discourse, for this age is grappling with it in most earnest struggles. No matter whether or not Moses was gifted in a most extraordinary degree to write his code. Nobody doubts his transcendent genius; nobody doubts his wonderful preparation. If any uninspired man could have written it, doubtless it was he. It was the most learned and accomplished of the apostles who was selected to be the expounder of the gospel among the Gentiles; so it was the ablest man born among the Jews who was chosen to give them a national polity. Nor does it detract from his fame as a man of genius that he did not originate the most profound of his declarations. It was fame enough to be the oracle and prophet of Jehovah. I would not dishonor the source of all wisdom, even to magnify the abilities of a great man, fond as critics are of exalting the wisdom of Moses as a triumph of human genius. It is natural to worship strength, human or divine. We adore mind;

HEBREW JURISPRUDENCE. 123

we glorify oracles. But neither written history nor philosophy will support the work of Moses as a wonder of mere human intellect, without ignoring the declarations of Moses himself and the settled belief of all Christian ages.

It is not my object to make an argument in defence of the divine legation of Moses; nor is it my design to reply to the learned criticisms of those who doubt or deny his statements. I would not run a-tilt against modern science, which may hereafter explain and accept what it now rejects. Science — whether physical or metaphysical — has its great truths, and so has Revelation; the realm of each is distinct while yet their processes are incomplete: and it is the hope and firm belief of many God-fearing scientists that the patient, reverent searching of to-day into God's works, of matter and of mind, as it collects the myriad facts and classifies them into such orderly sequences as indicate the laws of their being, will confirm to men's reason their faith in the revealed Word. Certainly this is a consummation devoutly to be wished. I am not scientist enough to judge of its probability, but it is within my province to present a few deductions which can be fairly drawn from the denial of the inspiration of the Mosaic Code. I wish to show to what conclusions this denial logically leads.

We must remember that Moses himself most distinctly and most emphatically affirms his own divine legation; for is not almost every chapter prefaced with these remarkable words, "And the Lord spake unto Moses"? Jehovah himself, in some incomprehensible way, amid the lightnings and the wonders of the sacred Mount, communicated His wisdom. Now, if we disbelieve this direct and impressive affirmation made by Moses, — that Jehovah directed him what to say to the people he was called to govern, — why should we believe his other statements, which involve supernatural agency or influence pertaining to the early history of the race? Where, then, is his authority? What is it worth? He has indeed no authority at all, except so far as his statements harmonize with our own definite knowledge, and perhaps with scientific speculations. We then make our own reason and knowledge, not the declarations of Moses, the ultimate authority. As a divine oracle to us, his voice is silent; ay, his august voice is drowned by the discordant and contradictory opinions that are ever blended with the speculations of the schools. He tells us, in language of the most impressive simplicity and grandeur, that he *was* directly instructed and commissioned by Jehovah to communicate moral truths, — truths, we should remember, which no one before him is known to have uttered, and truths so important that the prosperity of nations is identified with them, and will be so identified as long as men shall speculate and dream. If we deny this testimony, then his narration of other facts, which we accept, is not to be fully credited; like other ancient histories, it may be and it may not be true, — but there is no certainty. However we may interpret his detailed narration of the genesis of our world and our race, — whether as chronicle or as symbolic poem, — its central theme and thought, the direct creative agency of Jehovah, which it was his privilege to announce, stands forth clear and unmistakable. Yet if we deny the supernaturalism of the code, we may also deny the supernaturalism of the creation, in so far as both rest on the authority of Moses.

And, further, if Moses was not inspired directly from God to write his code, then it follows that he — a man pre-eminent for wisdom, piety, and knowledge — was an impostor, or at least, like Mohammed and George Fox, a self-deceived and visionary man, since he himself affirms his divine legation, and traces to the direct agency of Jehovah not merely his code, but even the various deliverances of the Israelites. And not only was Moses mistaken, but the Jewish nation, and Christ and the apostles, and the greatest lights of the Church from Augustine to Bossuet.

Hence it follows necessarily that all the miracles by which the divine legation of Moses is supported and credited, have no firm foundation, and a belief in them is superstitious, — as indeed it is in all other miracles recorded in the Scriptures, since they rest on testimony no more firmly believed than that believed by Christ and the apostles respecting Moses. Sweep away his authority as an inspiration, and you undermine the whole authority of the Bible; you bring it down to the level of all other books; you make it valuable only as a thesaurus of interesting stories and impressive moral truths, which we accept as we do all other kinds of knowledge, leaving us free to reject what we cannot understand or appreciate, or even what we dislike.

Then what follows? Is it not the rejection of many of the most precious revelations of the Bible, to which we *wish* to cling, and without a belief in which there would be the old despair of Paganism, the dreary unsettlement of all religious opinions, even a disbelief in an intelligent First Cause of the universe, certainly of a personal God, — and thus a gradual drifting away to the dismal shores of that godless Epicureanism which Socrates derided, and Paul and Augustine combated? Do you ask for a confirmation of the truths thus deduced from the denial of the supernaturalism of the Mosaic Code? I ask you to look around. I call no names; I invoke no theological hatreds; I seek to inflame no prejudices. I appeal to facts as incontrovertible as the phenomena of the heavens. I stand on the platform of truth itself, which we all seek to know and are proud to confess. Look to the developments of modern thought, to some of the speculations of modern science, to the spirit which animates much of our popular literature, not in our country but in all countries, even in the schools of the prophets and among men who are "more advanced," as they think, in learning, and if you do not see a tendency to the revival of an attractive but exploded philosophy, — the philosophy of Democritus; the philosophy of Epicurus, — then I am in an error as to the signs of the times. But if I am correct in this position, — if scepticism, or rationalism, or pantheism, or even science, in the audacity of its denials, or all these combined, are in conflict with the supernaturalism which shines and glows in every book of the Bible, and are bringing back for our acceptance what our fathers scorned, — then we must be allowed to show the practical results, the results on life, which of necessity followed the triumph of the speculative opinions of the popular idols of the ancient world in the realm of thought. Oh, what a life was that! what a poor exchange for the certitudes of faith and the simplicities of patriarchal times! I do not know whether an Epicurean philosophy grows out of an Epicurean life, or the life from the philosophy; but both are indissolubly and logically connected. The triumph of one is the triumph of the other, and the triumph of both is equally pointed out in the writings of Paul as a degeneracy, a misfortune, — yea, a sin to be wiped out only by the destruction of nations, or some terrible and unexpected catastrophe, and the obscuration of all that is glorious and proud among the works of men.

I make these, as I conceive, necessary digressions, because a discourse on Moses would be pointless without them; at best only a survey of that marvellous and favored legislator from the standpoint of secular history. I would not pull him down from the lofty pedestal whence he has given laws to all successive generations; a man, indeed, but shrouded in those awful mysteries which the great soul of Michael Angelo loved to ponder, and which gave to his creations the power of supernal majesty.

Thus did Moses, instructed by God, — for this is the great fact revealed in his testimony, — lead the inconstant Israelites through a forty years' pilgrimage, securing their veneration to the last. Thus did he keep them from the idolatries for which they hankered, and preserved among them allegiance to an invisible King. Thus did he impress his own mind and character upon them, and shape their institutions with matchless wisdom. Thus did he give them a system of laws — moral, ceremonial, and civil — which kept them a powerful and peculiar people for more than a thousand years, and secured a prosperity which culminated in the glorious reigns of David and Solomon and a political power unsurpassed in Western Asia, to see which the Queen of Sheba came from the uttermost part of the earth, — nay, more, which first formulated for that little corner of the world principles and precepts concerning the relations of men to God and to one another which have been an inspiration to all mankind for thousands of years.

Thus did this good and great man fulfil his task and deliver his message, with no other drawbacks on his part than occasional bursts of anger at the unparalleled folly and wickedness of his people. What disinterestedness marks his whole career, from the time when he flies from Pharaoh to the appointment of his successor, relinquishing without regret the virtual government of Egypt, accepting cheerfully the austerities and privations of the land of Midian, never elevating his own family to power, never complaining in his herculean tasks! With what eloquence does he plead for his people when the anger of the Lord is kindled against them, ever regarding them as mere children who know no self-control! How patient he is in the performance of his duties, accepting counsel from Jethro and listening to the voice of Aaron! With what stern and awful majesty does he lay down the law! What inspiration gilds his features as he descends the

Mount with the Tables in his hands! How terrible he is amid the thunders and lightnings of Sinai, at the rock of Horeb, at the dances around the golden calf, at the rebellion of Korah and Dathan, at the waters of Meribah, at the burning of Nadab and Abihu! How efficient he is in the administration of justice, in the assemblies of the people, in the great councils of rulers and princes, and in all the crises of the State; and yet how gentle, forgiving, tender, and accessible! How sad he is when the people weary of manna and seek flesh to eat! How nobly does he plead with the king of Edom for a passage through his territories! How humbly does he call on God for help amid perplexing cares! Never was a man armed with such authority so patient and so self-distrustful. Never was so experienced and learned a man so little conscious of his greatness.

> "This was the truest warrior
>   That ever buckled sword;
> This the most gifted poet
>   That ever breathed a word:
> And never earth's philosopher
>   Traced with his golden pen,
> On the deathless page, truths half so sage,
>   As he wrote down for men."

At length — at one hundred and twenty years of age, with undimmed eye and unabated strength, after having done more for his nation and for posterity than any ruler or king in the world's history, and won a fame which shall last through all the generations of men, growing brighter and brighter as his vast labors and genius are appreciated — the time comes to lay down his burdens. So he assembles together the princes and elders of Israel, recapitulates his laws, enumerates the mercies of the God to whom he has ever been loyal, and gives his final instructions. He appoints Joshua as his successor, adds words of encouragement to the people, whom he so fervently loves, sings his final song, and ascends the mountain above the plains of Moab, from which he is permitted to see, but not to enter, the promised land; not pensive and sad like Godfrey, because he cannot enter Jerusalem, but full of joyous visions of the future glories of his nation, and breaking out in the language of exultation, "Who is like unto thee, O people saved by Jehovah, the shield of thy help and the sword of thy excellency!" So Moses, the like of whom no prophet has since arisen (except that later One whom he himself foretold), the greatest man in Jewish annals, passes away from mortal sight, and Jehovah buries him in a valley of the land of Moab, and no man knoweth his sepulchre until this day.

> "That was the grandest funeral
> That ever passed on earth;
> But no one heard the trampling,
> Or saw the train go forth, —

Perchance the bald old eagle
  On gray Bethpeor's height,
Out of his lonely eyrie
  Looked on the wondrous sight.
. . . .

"And had he not high honor —
  The hillside for a pall —
To lie in state, while angels wait
  With stars for tapers tall;
And the dark rock-pines, like tossing plumes,
  Over his bier to wave,
And God's own hand, in that lonely land,
  To lay him in the grave?
. . . .

"O lonely grave in Moab's land!
  O dark Bethpeor's hill!
Speak to these curious hearts of ours,
  And teach them to be still!
God hath his mysteries of grace,
  Ways that we cannot tell;
He hides them deep, like the hidden sleep
  Of him he loved so well."

SAMUEL.

1100 B.C.

THE HEBREW THEOCRACY UNDER JUDGES.

SAMUEL.

THE HEBREW THEOCRACY, UNDER JUDGES.

AFTER Moses, and until David arose, it would be difficult to select any man who rendered greater services to the Israelitish nation than Samuel. He does not stand out in history as a man of dazzling intellectual qualities; but during a long life he efficiently labored to give to the nation political unity and power, and to reclaim it from idolatries. He was both a political and moral reformer, — an organizer of new forces, a man of great executive ability, a judge and a prophet. He made no mistakes, and committed no crimes. In view of his wisdom and sanctity it is evident that he would have adorned the office of high-priest; but as he did not belong to the family of Aaron, this great dignity could not be conferred on him. His character was reproachless. He was, indeed, one of the best men that ever lived, universally revered while living, and equally mourned when he died. He ruled the nation in a great crisis, and his influence was irresistible, because favored alike by God and man.

Samuel lived in one of the most tumultuous and unsettled periods of Jewish history, when the nation was in a transition state from anarchy to law, from political slavery to national independence. When he appeared, there was no settled government; the surrounding nations were still unconquered, and had reduced the Israelites to humiliating dependence. Deliverers had arisen occasionally from the time of Joshua, — like Gideon, Jephthah, and Samson, — but their victories were not decisive or permanent. Midianites, Amorites, and Philistines successively oppressed Israel, from generation to generation; they even succeeded in taking away their weapons of war. Resistance to this tyranny was apparently hopeless, and the nation would have sunk into despair but for occasional providential aid. The sacred ark was for a time in the hands of enemies, and Shiloh, the religious capital, — abode of the tabernacle and the ark, — had been burned. Every smith's forge where a sword or a spear-head could be rudely made was shut up, and the people were forced to go to the forges of their oppressors to get even their ploughshares sharpened.

On the death of Joshua (about 1350 B. C.), who had succeeded Moses and led the Israelites into Canaan, " nearly the whole of the sea-coast, all the strongholds in the rich plain of Esdraelon, and, in the heart of the country, the invincible fortress of Jebus [later site of Jerusalem], were still in the hands of the unbelievers." The conquest therefore was yet imperfect, like that of the Christianized Saxons in the time of Alfred over the pagan Danes in England. The times were full of peril and fear. They developed the military energies of the Israelites, but bred license, robbery, and crime, — a wild spirit of personal independence unfavorable to law and order. In those days "every man did that which was right in his own eyes." It was a period of utter disorder, anarchy, and lawlessness, like the condition of Germany and Italy in the Middle Ages. The persons who bore rule permanently were the princes or heads of the several tribes, the judges, and the high-priest; and in that primitive state of society these dignitaries rode on asses, and lived in tents. The virtues of the people were rough, and their habits warlike. Their great men were fighters. Samson was a sort of Hercules, and Jephthah an Idomeneus, — a lawless freebooter. The house of Micah was like a feudal castle; the Benjamite war was like the strife of Highland clans. Jael was a Hebrew Boadicea; Gideon, at the head of his three hundred men, might have been a hero of mediæval romance.

The saddest thing among these social and political evils was a great decline of religious life. The priesthood was disgraced by the prevailing vices of the times. The Mosaic rites may have been technically observed, but the officiating priests were sensual and worldly, while gross darkness covered the land. The high-priests exercised but a feeble influence; and even Eli could not, or did not, restrain the glaring immoralities of his own sons. In those evil days there were no revelations from Jehovah, and there was no divine vision among the prophets. Never did a nation have greater need of a deliverer.

It was then that Samuel arose, and he first appears as a pious boy, consecrated to priestly duties by a remarkable mother. His childhood was passed in the sacred tent of Shiloh, as an attendant, or servant, of the aged high-priest, or what would be called by the Catholic Church an acolyte. He belonged to the great tribe of Ephraim, being the son of Elkanah, of whom nothing is worthy of notice except that he was a polygamist. His mother Hannah (or Anna), however, was a Hebrew Saint Theresa, almost a Nazarite in her asceticism and a prophetess in her gifts; her song of thanksgiving on the birth of Samuel, for a special answer to her prayer, is one of the most beautiful remains of Hebrew poetry. From his infancy Samuel was especially dedicated to the service of God. He was not a priest, since he did not belong to the priestly caste; but the Lord was with him, and raised

HEBREW THEOCRACY, UNDER JUDGES.

him up to be more than priest, — even a prophet and a judge. When a mere child, it was he who declared to Eli the ruin of his house, since he had not restrained the wickedness and cruelty of his sons. From that time the prophetic character of Samuel was established, and his influence constantly increased until he became the foremost man of his nation, second to no one in power and dignity since the time of Moses.

But there is not much recorded of him until twenty years after the death of Eli, who lived to be ninety. It was during this period that the Philistines had carried away the sacred ark from Shiloh, and had overrun the country and oppressed the Hebrews, who it seems had fallen into idolatry, worshipping Ashtaroth and other strange gods. It was Samuel, already recognized as a great prophet and judge, who aroused the nation from its idolatry and delivered it from the hand of the Philistines at Mizpeh, where a great battle was fought, so that these terrible foes were subdued, and came no more into the borders of Israel during the days of Samuel; and all the cities they had taken, from Ekron unto Gath, were restored. The subjection of the Philistines was followed by the undisputed rule of Samuel, under the name of Judge, during his life, even after the consecration of Saul.

The Israelitish Judge seems to have been a sort of dictator, called to power by the will of the people in times of great emergency and peril, as among the Romans. "The Theocracy," says Ewald, "by pronouncing any human ruler unnecessary as a permanent element of the State, lapsed into anarchy and weakness. When a nation is without a government strong enough to repress lawlessness within and to protect from foes without, the whole people very soon divides once more into the two ranks of master and servant. In Deborah's songs all Israel, so far as lay in her circle of vision, was divided into princes and people. Hence the nation consisted of innumerable self-constituted and self-sustained kingdoms, formed whenever some chieftain elevated himself whom individuals or the body of citizens in a town were willing to serve. Gaal, son of Zobah, entered Shechem with troops raised by himself, just like a condottiere in Italy in the Middle Ages. As it became evident that the nation could not permanently dispense with an earthly government, it was forced to rally round some powerful leader; and as the Theocracy was still acknowledged by the best of the nation, these leaders, who owed their power to circumstances, could not easily be transformed into regular kings, but to exceptional dictators the State offered no strong resistance."

And yet these rulers arose not solely by force of individual prowess, but were expressly raised up by God as deliverers of the nation in times of peculiar peril. And further, the spirit of Jehovah came upon them, as it did upon Deborah the prophetess, and as it did still more remarkably upon Moses himself.

The last and greatest of these extemporized leaders called Judges, was Samuel. In him the people learned to put their trust; and the national assembly which he summoned was completely guided by him. No one of the Judges, it would seem, had his seat of government in any central city, but where he happened to live. So the residence of Samuel was at his native town of Ramah, where he married. It would seem that he travelled from city to city to administer justice, like the judges of England on their circuits; but, unlike them, on his own supreme authority, — not with power delegated by a king, but acknowledging no superior except God himself, from whom he received his commission. We know not at what time and whom he married; but his two sons, who in his old age shared power with him, did not discharge their delegated functions more honorably than the sons of Eli, who had been a disgrace to their office, to their father, and to the nation. One of the greatest mysteries of human life is the seeming inability of pious fathers to check the vices of their children, who often go astray under an apparently irresistible impulse or innate depravity, in spite of parental precept and example, — thus seeming to show that neither virtue nor vice can be surely transmitted, and that every human being stands on his individual responsibility, with peculiar temptations to combat, and peculiar circumstances to influence him. The son of a saint becomes mysteriously a drunkard or a fraud, and the son of a sensualist becomes an ascetic. This does not uniformly occur: in fact, the sons of good men are more likely to be an honor to their families than the sons of the wicked; but why are exceptions so common as to be proverbial?

It was no light work which was imposed on the shoulders of Samuel, — to establish law and order among the demoralized tribes of the Jews, and to prepare them for political independence; and it was a still greater labor to effect a moral reformation and reintroduce the worship of Jehovah. Both of these objects he seems to have accomplished; and his success places him in the list of great reformers, like Mohammed and Luther, — but greater and better than either, since he did not attempt, like the former, to bring about a good end by bad means; nor was he stained by personal defects, like the latter. "It was his object to re-enkindle the national life of the nation, so as to combat successfully its enemies in the field, which could be attained by rousing a common religious feeling;" for he saw that there could be no true enthusiasm without a sense of dependence on the God of battles, and that heroism could be stimulated only by exalted sentiments, both of patriotism and religion.

But how was Samuel to rekindle a fervent religious life among the degenerate Israelites in such unsettled times? Only by rousing the people by his teachings and his eloquence. He was a preacher of righteousness, and in all probability went from city to city and village to village, — as Saint Bernard did when he preached a crusade against the infidels, as John the Baptist did when he preached repentance, as Whitefield did when he sought to kindle religious enthusiasm in England. So he set himself to educate his countrymen in the great truths which appealed to the inner life, — to the heart and conscience. This he did, first by rousing the slumbering spirits of the elders of tribes when they sought his counsel as a prophet, the like of whom had not appeared since Moses, so gifted and so earnest; and secondly, by founding a school for the education of young men who should go with his instructions wherever he chose to send them, like the early missionaries, to hamlets and villages which he was unable to visit in person. The first "school of the prophets" was a seminary of missionaries, animated by the spirit of a teacher whom they feared and admired as no prophet had been revered in the whole history of the nation since Moses.

Samuel communicated his own burning spirit wherever he went, and the burden of his eloquence was zeal and loyalty for Jehovah. Before his time the prophets had been known as seers; but Samuel superadded the duties of a religious teacher, — the spokesman of the Almighty. The number of his disciples, whom he doubtless commissioned as evangelists, must have been very large. They lived in communities and ate in common, like the primitive monks. They probably resembled the early Dominican and Franciscan friars of the Middle Ages, who were kindled to enthusiasm by such teachers as Thomas Aquinas and Bonaventura. Like them they were ascetics in their habits and dress, wearing sheepskins, and living on locusts and wild honey, — on the fruits which grew spontaneously in the rich valleys of their well-watered country. It did not require much learning to arouse the common people to new duties and a higher religious life. The Bible does not inform us as to the details by which Samuel made his influence felt, but there can be no doubt that by some means he kindled a religious life before unknown among his countrymen. He infused courage and hope into their despairing hearts, and laid the foundation of military enthusiasm by combining with it religious ardor; so that by the discipline of forty years, — the same period employed by Moses in transmuting a horde of slaves into a national host of warriors; a period long enough to drop out the corrupted elements and replace them with the better trained rising generation,— the nation was prepared for accomplishing the victories of Saul and David. But for Samuel no great captains would have arisen to lead the scattered and dispirited hosts of Israel against the Philistines and other enemies. He was thus a political leader as well as a religious teacher, combining the offices of judge and prophet. Everybody felt that he was directly commissioned by God, and his words had the force of inspiration. He reigned with as much power as a king over all the tribes, though clad in the garments of humility. Who in all Israel was greater than he, even after he had anointed Saul to the kingly office?

The great outward event in the life of Samuel was the transition of the Israelites from a theocratic to a monarchical government. It was a political revolution, and like all revolutions was fraught with both good and evil, yet seemingly demanded by the spirit of the times,— in one sense an advance in civilization, in another a retrogression in primeval virtues. It resulted in a great progress in material arts, culture, and power, but also in a decline in those simplicities that favor a religious life, on which the strength of man is apparently built,— that is, a state of society in which man in his ordinary life draws nearest to his Maker, to his kindred, and his home; to which luxury and demoralizing pleasures are unknown; a life free from temptations and intellectual snares, from political ambition and social unrest, from recognized injustice and stinging inequalities. The historian with his theory of development might call this revolution the change from national youth to manhood, the emerging from the dark ages of Hebrew history to a period of national aggrandizement and growth in civilization, — one of the necessary changes which must take place if a nation would become strong, powerful, and cultivated. To the eye of the contemplative, conservative, and God-fearing Samuel this change of government seemed full of perils and dangers, for which the nation was not fully prepared. He felt it to be a change which might wean the Israelites from their new sense of dependence on God, the only hope of nations, and which might favor another lapse to pagan idolatries and a decline in household virtues, such as had been illustrated in the life of Ruth and Boaz, — and hence might prove a mere exchange of that rugged life which elevates the soul, for those gilded glories which adorn and pamper the mortal body. He certainly foresaw and knew that the change in government would produce tyranny, oppression, and injustice, from which there could be no escape and for which there could be no redress, for he told the people in detail just what they should suffer at the hands of any king whom they might have; and these were in his eyes evils which nothing could compensate, — the loss of liberty, the extinction of personal independence, and a probable rebellion against the Supreme Jehovah in the degrading worship of the gods of idolatrous nations.

When the people, therefore, under the guidance of so-called "progressive leaders," hankered for a government which would make them like other nations, and demanded a king, the prophet was greatly moved and sore displeased; and this displeasure was heightened by a bitter humiliation when the elders reproached him because of the misgovernment of his own sons. He could not at first say a word, in view of a demand apparently justified by the conduct of the existing rulers. There was a just cause of complaint. If his own sons would take bribes in rendering judgment, who could be trusted? Civilization would say that there was needed a stronger arm to punish crime and enforce the laws.

So Samuel, perplexed and disheartened, fearing that the political changes would be evil rather than good, and yet feeling unable to combat the popular voice, sought wisdom in prayer. "And the Lord said, hearken unto the voice of the people in all that they say unto thee, for they have not rejected thee, but they have rejected me, that I should reign over them. Now therefore hearken unto their voice; howbeit yet protest solemnly unto them, and show them the manner of the king that shall reign over them." The Almighty would not take away the free-will of the people; but Samuel is required to show them the perversity of their will, and that if they should choose evil the consequences would be on their heads and the heads of their children, from generation to generation.

Samuel therefore spake unto the people, — probably the elders and leading men, for the aristocratic element of society prevailed, as in the Middle Ages of feudal Europe, when even royal power was merely nominal, and barons and bishops ruled, — and said : " This will be the manner of the king that shall reign over you: He shall take your sons and appoint them for himself for his chariots, and to be his horsemen; and some shall run before his chariots; and he shall appoint captains over thousands and captains over fifties, and will set them to ear [plough] his ground and reap his harvest, and to make his instruments of war, and the instruments of his chariots. And he will take your daughters to be confectioners [or perfumers] and cooks and bakers. And he will take your fields and your vineyards and your olive-yards, even the best of them, and give them to his servants; and he will take the tenth of your seed and of your vineyards, and give to his officers and to his servants. And he will take your men-servants and your maid-servants, and your goodliest young men, and your asses, and put them to his work. And he will take the tenth of your sheep; and ye shall be his servants. And ye will cry out in that day because of your king which ye have chosen you, and the Lord will not hear you in that day."

Nevertheless the people refused to obey the voice of Samuel; and they said, "Nay, but we will have a king over us, that we also may be like all the nations; and that our king may judge us, and go out before us, and fight our battles." It would thus appear that the monarchy which the people sought would necessarily become nearly absolute, limited only by the will of God as interpreted by priests and prophets,— for the theocracy was not to be destroyed, but still maintained as even superior to the royal authority. The future king was to be supreme in affairs of state, in the direction of armies, in the appointment of captains and commanders, in the general superintendence of the realm in worldly matters; but he could not go contrary to the divine commands as they would be revealed to him, without incurring a fearful penalty. He could not interfere with the functions of the priesthood under any pretence whatever; and further, he was required to rule on principles of equity and immutable justice. He could not repel the divine voice, whether it spake to his consciousness or was revealed to him by divinely commissioned prophets, without the certainty of divine chastisement. Thus was his power limited, even by invisible forces superior to his own; for Jehovah had not withdrawn his special jurisdiction over the chosen people for whom he was preparing a splendid destiny, — that is, through them, the redemption of the world.

Whether the people of Israel did not believe the predictions of the prophet, or wished to have a kingly government in spite of its evils, in order to become more powerful as a nation, we do not know. All that we know is that they persisted in their demand, and that God granted their request. With all the memories and traditions of their slavery in the land of Egypt, and the grinding despotism incident to an absolute monarchy of which their ancestors bore witness, they preferred despotism with its evils to the independence they had enjoyed under the Judges; for nationality, to which the Jewish people were casting longing eyes, demands law and order as the first condition of society. In obedience to this same principle the grinding monarchy of Louis XIV. seemed preferable to the turbulence and anarchy of the Middle Ages, since unarmed and obscure citizens felt safe in their humble avocations. In like manner, after the license of the French Revolution the people said, "Give us a king once more!" and seated Napoleon on the throne of the Bourbons, — a ruler who took one man out of every five adults to recruit his armies and consolidate his power, which he called the glory of France. Thus kings have reigned by the will of the people, — or, as they call it, by the grace of God, — from Saul and David to our own times, except in those few countries where liberty is preferred to material power and military laurels.

The peculiar situation of the Israelites in a narrow strip of territory which was the highway between Syria and Egypt, likely to be overrun by Aramæans, Assyrians, Babylonians, and Egyptians, to say nothing of the hostile nations which surrounded them, such as Moabites and Philistines, necessarily made them a warlike people (like the inhabitants of the Swiss Cantons five or six hundred years ago), and they were hence led to put a high estimate on military qualities, especially on the general who led them to battle. They accordingly desired a greater centralized power than the Judges wielded, which could be exercised only by a king, intrenched in a strong capital. Their desire for a king was natural, and almost excusable if they were willing to pay the inevitable price. They simply wished to surrender liberty for protection and political safety. They did not repudiate the fundamental doctrine of their religion; they simply wanted a change of government, — a more efficient administration.

The selection of a king did not rest with the people.

however, but with the great prophet who had ruled them with so much wisdom and ability, and who was regarded as the interpreter of the will of God.

Samuel, by the direction of God, did not go into the powerful tribe of Ephraim, which possessed one half of the Israelitish territory, to select a sovereign, but to the smallest of the tribes, that of Benjamin, — the most warlike, however, — and to one of the least of the families of that tribe, dwelling in very humble life. Kish, the Benjamite, had sent out his son Saul in quest of three asses which had strayed away from the farm, — a man so poor that he had no money to give to the seer who should direct his search, as was customary, and was obliged to borrow a quarter of a shekel from his servant when they went together to seek the counsel of Samuel. But this obscure youth was "a choice young man, and a goodly." He had a commanding presence, was very beautiful, and was head and shoulders taller than any other man of his tribe, — a man every way likely to succeed in war. Samuel no sooner saw the commanding figure and intelligent countenance of Saul than he was assured that this was the man whom the Lord had chosen to be the future captain and champion of Israel. He at once treated him with distinguished honor, and made him sit at his own table, much to the amazement of the thirty nobles who also were bidden to a banquet. The prophet took the young man aside, conducted him to the top of his house, anointed him with the sacred oil, kissed him (a form of allegiance), and communicated to him the will of God. But Saul was only privately consecrated, and with rare discretion told no man of his good fortune, — for he had not yet distinguished himself in any way, and would have been laughed to scorn by his relatives, as Joseph was by his brothers, had he revealed his destiny.

Nor did Samuel dare to tell the people of the man whom the Lord had chosen to rule over them, but assembled all the tribes, that the choice might be publicly indicated. Probably to their astonishment the little tribe of Benjamin was "taken," — that is pointed out, presumably by lot, as was their custom when appealing for divine direction; and out of the tribe of Benjamin the family of Matri was chosen, and Saul the son of Kish was selected. But Saul could not be found. With rare modesty and humility he had hidden himself. When at length they brought him from his hiding-place Samuel said unto the people, "See ye him whom the Lord hath chosen, that there is none like him among all the people!" And such was the authority of Samuel that the people shouted, saying, "God save the king!" — a circumstance interesting as being the first recorded utterance of a cry that has been echoed the world over by many a loyal people.

Not yet, however, was Saul clothed with full power as a king. Samuel still remained the acknowledged ruler until Saul should distinguish himself in battle. This soon took place. With heroic valor he delivered Jabesh-Gilead from the hosts of the Ammonites when that city was about to fall into their hands, and silenced the envy of his enemies. In a burst of popular enthusiasm Samuel collected the people in Gilgal, and there formally installed Saul as King of Israel.

Samuel was now an old man, and was glad to lay down his heavy burden and put it on the shoulders of Saul. Yet he did not retire from the active government without making a memorable speech to the assembled nation, in which with transcendent dignity he appealed to the people in attestation of his incorruptible integrity as a judge and ruler. "Behold, here I am! Witness against me before the Lord, and before his anointed. Whose ox have I taken, or whose ass have I taken, or whom have I defrauded? Or of whose hand have I received any bribe to blind my eyes therewith? And they said, Thou hast not defrauded us, nor oppressed us; neither hast thou taken aught of any man's hand." Then Samuel closed his address with an injunction to both king and people to obey the commandments of God, and denouncing the penalty of disobedience: "Only fear the Lord, and serve Him in truth and with all your heart, for consider what great things He hath done for you; but if ye shall do wickedly, ye shall be consumed,— both ye and your king."

Saul for a time gave no offence worthy of rebuke, but was a valiant captain, smiting the Philistines, who were the most powerful enemies that the Israelites had yet encountered. But in an evil day he forgot his true vocation, and took upon himself the function of a priest by offering burnt sacrifices, which was not lawful but for the priest alone. For this he was rebuked by Samuel. "Thou hast done foolishly," he said to the King; "for which thy kingdom shall not continue. The Lord hath sought him a man after his own heart, and the Lord hath commanded him to be captain over his people, because thou hast not kept that which the Lord commanded thee." We here see the blending of the theocratic with the kingly rule.

Nevertheless Saul was prospered in his wars. He fought successfully the Moabites, the Ammonites, the Edomites, the Amalekites, and the Philistines, aided by his cousin Abner, whom he made captain of his host. He did much to establish the kingdom; but he was rather a great captain than a great man. He did not fully perceive his mission, which was to fight, but meddled with affairs which belonged to the priests. Nor was he always true to his mission as a warrior. He weakly spared Agag, King of the Amalekites, which again called forth the displeasure and denunciation of Samuel, who regarded the conduct of the King as direct rebellion against God, since he was commanded to spare none of that people, they having shown an uncompromising hostility to the Israelites in their days of weakness, when first entering Canaan. This, and similar commands laid upon the Israelites at various times, to "utterly destroy" certain tribes or individuals and all of their possessions, have been justified on the ground of the bestial grossness and corruption of those pagan idolaters and the vileness of their religious rites and social customs, which unfortunately always found a temptable side on the part of the Israelites, and repeatedly brought to nought the efforts of Jehovah's prophets to bring up their people in the fear of the Lord, to recognize Him, only, as God. It was not easy for that sensual race to stand on the height of Moses, and "endure as seeing him who is invisible." They too easily fell into idolatry; hence the necessity of the extermination of some of the nests of iniquity in Canaan.

Whether Saul spared Agag because of his personal beauty, to grace his royal triumph, or whatever the motive, it was a direct disobedience; and when the king attempted to exculpate himself, inasmuch as he had made a sacrifice of the spoil to the Lord, Samuel replied: "Hath the Lord as great delight in burnt-offerings and sacrifices as in obeying his voice? . . . Behold, to obey is better than sacrifice, and to hearken than the fat of rams,— for rebellion is as the sin of witchcraft, and stubbornness as an iniquity and idolatry." The prophet here sets forth, as did Isaiah in later times, the great principles of moral obligation as paramount over all ceremonial observances. He strikes a blow at all pharisaism and all self-righteousness, and inculcates obedience to direct commands as the highest duty of man.

Saul, perceiving that he had sinned, confessed his transgression, but palliated it by saying that he feared the people. But this policy of expediency had no weight with the prophet, although Saul repented and sought pardon. Samuel continued his stern rebuke, and uttered his fearful message, saying, "Jehovah hath rent the kingdom of Israel from thee this day, and hath given it to a neighbor of thine that is better than thou." Furthermore Samuel demanded that Agag, whom Saul had spared, should be brought before him; and he took upon himself with his aged hand the work of executioner, and hewed the king of the Amalekites in pieces in Gilgal. He then finally departed from Saul, and mournfully went to his own house in Ramah, and Saul saw him no more. As the king was the "Lord's anointed," Samuel could not openly rebel against kingly authority, but he would henceforth have nothing to do with the headstrong ruler. He withdrew from him all spiritual guidance, and left him to his follies and madness; for the inextinguishable jealousy of Saul, that now began to appear, was a species of insanity, which poisoned his whole subsequent life. The people continued loyal to a king whom God had selected, but Samuel "came no more to see Saul until the day of his death." To be deserted by such a counsellor as Samuel, was no small calamity.

Meanwhile, in obedience to instructions from God, Samuel proceeded to Bethlehem, to the humble abode of Jesse, of the tribe of Judah, one of whose sons he was required to anoint as the future king of Israel. He naturally was about to select the largest and finest looking of the seven sons; but God looketh on the heart rather than the outward appearance, and David, a mere youth, and the youngest of the family, was the one indicated by Jehovah, and was privately anointed by the prophet.

Saul, of course, did not know on whom the choice had fallen as his successor, but from that day on which he was warned of the penalty of his disobedience divine favor departed from him, and he became jealous, fitful, and cruel. He presented a striking contrast to the character he had shown in his early days, — being no longer modest and humble, but proud and tyrannical. Prosperity and power had turned his head, and developed all that was evil in him. Nero was not more unreasonable and bloodthirsty than was Saul in his latter days. Prosperity developed in Solomon a love of magnificence, in Nebuchadnezzar a towering vanity, but in Saul a malignant envy of all extraordinary merit, and a sullen determination to destroy the persons it adorned. The last person in his kingdom of whom apparently he had reason to be jealous, was the ruddy and beardless youth whom he had sent for to drive away his melancholy by his songs and music. Nor was it until David killed Goliath that Saul became jealous; before this he had no cause of envy, for kings do not envy musicians, but reward them. David's reward was as extravagant as that which Russian emperors shower upon singers and dancers: he was made armor-bearer to the King, — an office bestowed only upon favorites and those who were implicitly trusted and beloved. Little did the moody and jealous King imagine that the youth whom he had brought from obscurity to amuse his melancholy hours by his music, and probably his wit and humor, would so soon, by his own sanction, become the champion of Israel, and ultimately his successor on the throne.

In the latter part of the reign of Saul the enemies with whom he had to contend were the various Canaanitish nations that had remained unconquered during the hard struggle of four hundred years after the Hebrews had been led by Joshua to the promised land. The most powerful of these nations were the Philistines. "Strong in their military organization, fierce in their warlike spirit, and rich by their position and commercial instincts, they even threatened the ancient supremacy of the Phœnicians of the north. Their cities were the restless centres of every form of activity. Ashdod and Gaza, as the keys of Egypt, commanded the carrying trade to and from the Nile, and formed the great depots for its imports and exports. All the cities, moreover, traded in slaves with Edom and southern Arabia, and their commerce in other directions flourished so greatly as to gain for the people at large the name of Canaanites, — which was synonymous with 'merchant.' Even the word 'Palestine' is derived from the Philistines. Their skill as smiths and armorers was noted; the strength of their cities attest their strength as builders, and their idols and golden mice and emerods show their respect for the arts of peace." It is supposed that they had settled in Canaan about the time of Abraham, and were originally a pastoral people in the neighborhood of Gesar, or emigrants from Crete. When the Israelites under Joshua arrived, they were in full possession of the southern part of Palestine, and had formed a confederacy of five powerful cities,— Gaza, Ashdod, Askelon, Gath, and Ekron. In the time of the Judges they had become so prosperous and powerful that they held the Israelites in partial subjection, broken at intervals by heroes like Shamgar and Samson. Under Eli there was an organized but unsuccessful resistance to these prosperous and warlike heathen. Under Samuel the tide of success was turned in Israel's favor at the battle of Mizpeh, when the Israelites erected their pillar at Ebenezer as a token of victory. The battle of Michmash, gained by Saul and Jonathan after an immense slaughter of their foes, was so decisive that for twenty-five years the Israelites were unmolested. In the latter part of the reign of Saul the Philistines attempted to regain their ascendency, but on the death of Goliath at the hand of David they were driven to their own territories. The battle of Gilboa, where Saul and Jonathan were slain, again turned the scale in favor of the Philistines. Under David the Israelites resumed the aggressive, took Gath, and completely broke forever the ascendency of their powerful foes. Under Solomon it would appear that the whole of Philistia was incorporated with the Hebrew monarchy, and remained so until the calamities of the Jews gave Philistia to the Assyrian conquerors of Jerusalem, and finally it fell into the hands of the Romans. The Philistines were zealous idolaters, and in times of great religious apostasy they succeeded in introducing the worship of their gods among the Israelites, especially that of Baal and Ashtaroth.

Samuel did not live to see the complete humiliation of his nation which succeeded the bloody battle when Saul was slain; but he lived to a good old age, and never lost his influence over the Israelites, whom he had rescued from idolatry and to whom he had given political unity. Although Saul was king, we are told that Samuel judged Israel all the days of his life. He died universally lamented. There is no record in the Scriptures of a death attended with such profound and general mourning. All Israel mourned for him. They mourned because he was a good man, unstained by crime or folly; they mourned because their judge and oracle and friend had passed away; they mourned because he had been their intercessor with God himself, and the interpreter of the divine will. His like would never appear again in Israel. "He represents the independence of the moral law, as distinct from regal and sacerdotal enactments. If a Levite, he was not a priest. He was a prophet, the first in the regular succession of prophets. He was also the founder of the first regular institutions of religious instruction, and communities for the purposes of education. From these institutions were developed the universities of Christendom."

In a spiritual and religious sense the prophet takes the highest rank in the kingdom of God on earth. Among the Hebrews he was the interpreter of the divine will; he predicted future events. He was a preacher of righteousness; he was the counsellor of kings and princes; he was a sage and oracle among the people. He was a reformer, teaching the highest truths and restoring the worship of God when nations were sunk in idolatry; he was the mouthpiece of the Eternal, for warning, for rebuke, for encouragement, for chastisement. He was divinely inspired, armed with supernatural powers, — a man whom the people feared and obeyed, sometimes honored, sometimes stoned; one who bore heavy responsibilities, and of whom were demanded disagreeable duties. We associate with the idea of a prophet both wisdom and virtue, great gifts and great personal piety. We think of him as a man who lived a secluded life of meditation and prayer, in constant communion with God and removed from all worldly rewards, — a man indifferent to ordinary pleasures, to outward pomp and show, free from personal vanity, lofty in his bearing, independent in his mode of life, spiritual in his aims, fervent and earnest in his exhortations, living above the world in the higher regions of faith and love, disdaining praises and honors, soft raiment and luxurious food, and maintaining a proud equality with the greatest personages; a man not to be bought, and not to be deterred from his purpose by threatenings or intimidation or flatteries, commanding reverence, and exalted as a favorite of heaven. It was not necessary that the prophet should be a priest or even a Levite. He was greater than any impersonation of sacerdotalism, sacred in his person and awful in his utterances, unassisted by ritualistic forms, declaring truths which appealed to consciousness, — a kind of spiritual dictator who inspired awe and reverence.

In one sense or another most of the august characters of the Old Testament were prophets, — Abraham, Moses, Joseph, David, Elijah, Daniel, Isaiah, Jeremiah, Ezekiel. They either foretold the future, or rebuked kings as messengers of omnipotence, or taught the people great truths, or uttered inspired melodies, or interpreted dreams, or in some way revealed the ways and will of God. Among them were patriarchs, kings, and priests, and sages uninvested with official functions. Some lived in cities and others in villages, and others again in the wilderness and desert places; some reigned in the palaces of pride, and others in the huts of poverty, — yet all alike exercised a tremendous moral power. They were the national poets and historians of Judæa, preachers of patriotism as well as of religion and morals, exercising political as well as spiritual power. Those who stand out pre-eminently in the sacred writings were gifted with the power of revealing the future destinies of nations, and above all other things the peculiarities of the Messianic reign.

Samuel was not called to declare those profound truths which relate to the appearance and reign of Christ as the Saviour of mankind, nor the fate of idolatrous nations, nor even the future vicissitudes connected with the Hebrew nation, but to found a school of religious teachers, to revive the worship of Jehovah, guide the conduct of princes, and direct the general affairs of the nation as commanded by God. He was the first and most favored of the great prophets, and exercised an influence as a prophet never equalled by any who succeeded him. He was a great prophet, since for forty years he ruled Israel by direct divine illumination, — a holy man who communed with God, great in speech and great in action. He did not rise to the lofty eloquence of Isaiah, nor foresee the fate of nations like Daniel and Ezekiel; but he was consulted and obeyed as a man who knew the divine will, gifted beyond any other man of his age in spiritual insight, and trusted implicitly for his wisdom and sanctity. These were the excellences which made him one of the most extraordinary men in Jewish history, rendering services to his nation which cannot easily be exaggerated.

in the sacred writings were gifted with the power of revealing the future destinies of nations, and above all other things the peculiarities of the Messianic reign. Samuel was not called to declare those profound truths which relate to the appearance and reign of Christ as the Saviour of mankind, nor the fate of idolatrous nations, nor even the future vicissitudes connected with the Hebrew nation, but to found a school of religious teachers, to revive the worship of Jehovah, guide the conduct of princes, and direct the general affairs of the nation as commanded by God. He was the first and most favored of the great prophets, and exercised an influence as a prophet never equalled by any who succeeded him. He was a great prophet, since for forty years he ruled Israel by direct divine illumination. — a holy man who communed with God, great in speech and great in action. He did not rise to the lofty eloquence of Isaiah, nor foresee the fate of nations like Daniel and Ezekiel; but he was consulted and obeyed as a man who knew the divine will, gifted beyond any other man of his age in spiritual insight, and trusted implicitly for his wisdom and sanctity. These were the excellences which made him one of the most extraordinary men in Jewish history, rendering services to his nation which cannot easily be exaggerated.

DAVID.

1055–1015 B. C.

ISRAELITISH CONQUESTS.

DAVID.

ISRAELITISH CONQUESTS.

CONSIDERING how much has been written about David in all the nations of Christendom, and how familiar Christian people are with his life and writings, it would seem presumptuous to attempt a lecture on this remarkable man, especially since it is impossible to add anything essentially new to the subject. The utmost that I can do is to select, condense, and rearrange from the enormous quantity of matter which learned and eloquent writers have already furnished.

The warrior-king who conquered the enemies of Israel in a dark and desponding period; the sagacious statesman who gave unity to its various tribes, and formed them into a powerful monarchy; the matchless poet who bequeathed to all ages a lofty and beautiful psalmody; the saint, who with all his backslidings and inconsistencies was a man after God's own heart, — is well worthy of our study. David was the most illustrious of all the kings of whom the Jewish nation was proud, and was a striking type of a good man occasionally enslaved by sin, yet breaking its bonds and rising above subsequent temptations to a higher plane of goodness. A man so elevated, with almost every virtue which makes a man beloved, and yet with defects which will forever stain his memory, cannot easily be portrayed. What character in history presents such wide contradictions? What career was ever more varied? What recorded experiences are more interesting and instructive? — a life of heroism, of adventures, of triumphs, of humiliations, of outward and inward conflicts. Who ever loved and hated with more intensity than David? — tender yet fierce, brave yet weak, magnanimous yet unrelenting, exultant yet sad, committing crimes yet triumphantly rising after disgraceful falls by the force of a piety so ardent that even his backslidings now appear but as spots upon a sun. His varied experiences call out our sympathy and admiration more than the life of any secular hero whom poetry and history have immortalized. He was an Achilles and a Ulysses, a Marcus Aurelius and a Theodosius, an Alfred and a Saint Louis combined; equally great in war and in peace, in action and in meditation; creating an empire, yet transmitting to posterity a collection of poems identified forever with the spiritual life of individuals and nations. Interesting to us as are the events of David's memorable career, and the sentiments and sorrows which extort our sympathy, yet it is the relation of a sinful soul with its Maker, by which he infuses his inner life into all other souls, and furnishes materials of thought for all generations.

David was the youngest and seventh son of Jesse, a prominent man of the tribe of Judah, whose great-grandmother was Ruth, the interesting wife of Boaz the Jew. He was born in Bethlehem, near Jerusalem, — a town rendered afterward so illustrious as the birthplace of our Lord, who was himself of the house and lineage of David. He first appears in history at the sacrificial feast which his townspeople periodically held, presided over by his father, when the prophet Samuel unexpectedly appeared at the festival to select from the sons of Jesse a successor to Saul. He was not tall and commanding like the Benjamite hero, but was ruddy of countenance, with auburn hair, beautiful eyes, and graceful figure, equally remarkable for strength and agility. He had the charge of his father's sheep, — not the most honorable employment in the eyes of his brothers, who, according to Ewald, treated him with little consideration; but even as a shepherd boy he had already proved his strength and courage by an encounter with a bear and a lion.

Until David was thirty years of age his life was identified with the fading glories of the reign of Saul, who laid the foundation of the military power of his successors,—a man who lacked only the one quality imperative on the vicegerent of a supreme but invisible Power, that of unquestioning obedience to the divine directions as interpreted by the voice of prophets. Had Saul been loyal in his heart, as David was, to the God of Israel, the sceptre might not have departed from his house,—for he showed some of the highest qualities of a general and a ruler, until his jealousy was excited by the brilliant exploits of the son of Jesse. On these exploits and subsequent adventures, which invest David's early career with the fascinations of a knight of chivalry, I need not dwell. All are familiar with his encounter with Goliath, and with his slaughter of the Philistines after he had slain the giant, which called out the admiration of the haughty daughter of the king, the love of the heir-apparent to the throne, and the applause of the whole nation. I need not speak of his musical melodies, which drove the fatal demon of melancholy from the royal palace; of his jealous expulsion by the King, his hairbreadth escapes, his trials and difficulties as a wanderer and exile, as a fugitive retreating to solitudes and caves of the earth, parched with heat and thirst, exhausted with hunger and fatigue, surrounded with increasing dangers, — yet all the while forgiving and magnanimous, sparing the life of his deadly enemy, unstained by a single vice or weakness, and soothing his stricken soul with bursts of pious song unequalled for pathos and loftiness in the whole realm of lyric poetry. He is never so interesting as amid caverns and blasted desolations and serrated rocks and dried-up rivulets, when his life is in constant danger. But he knows that he is the anointed of the Lord, and has faith that in due time he will be called to the throne.

It was not until the bloody battle with the Philistines, which terminated the lives of both Saul and Jonathan, that David's reign began in about his thirtieth year,[1] — first at Hebron, where he reigned seven and one half years over his own tribe of Judah, — but not without the deepest lamentations for the disaster which had caused his own elevation. To the grief of David for the death of Saul and Jonathan we owe one of the finest odes in Hebrew poetry. At this crisis in national affairs, David had sought shelter with Achish, King of Gath, in whose territory he, with the famous band of six hundred warriors whom he had collected in his wanderings, dwelt in safety and peace. This apparent alliance with the deadly enemy of the Israelites had displeased the people. Notwithstanding

[1] Authorities differ as to the precise date of David's accession.

all his victories and exploits, his anointment at the hand of Samuel, his noble lyrics, his marriage with the daughter of Saul, and the death of both Saul and Jonathan, there had been at first no popular movement in David's behalf. The taking of decisive action, however, was one of his striking peculiarities from youth to old age, and he promptly decided, after consulting the Urim and Thummim, to go at once to Hebron, the ancient sacred city of the tribe of Judah, and there await the course of events. His faithful band of six hundred devoted men formed the nucleus of an army; and a reaction in his favor having set in, he was chosen king. But he was king only of the tribe to which he belonged. Northern and central Palestine were in the hands of the Philistines,— ten of the tribes still adhering to the house of Saul, under the leadership of Abner, the cousin of Saul, who proclaimed Ishbosheth king. This prince, the youngest of Saul's four sons, chose for his capital Mahanaim, on the east of the Jordan.

Ishbosheth was, however, a weak prince, and little more than a puppet in the hands of Abner, the most famous general of the day, who, organizing what forces remained after the fatal battle of Gilboa, was quite a match for David. For five years civil war raged between the rivals for the ascendency, but success gradually secured for David the promised throne of united Israel. Abner, seeing how hopeless was the contest, and wishing to prevent further slaughter, made overtures to David and the elders of Judah and Benjamin. The generous monarch received him graciously, and promised his friendship; but, out of jealousy, — or perhaps in revenge for the death of his brother Asahel, whom Abner had slain in battle, — Joab, the captain of the King's chosen band, treacherously murdered him. David's grief at the foul deed was profound and sincere, but he could not afford to punish the general on whom he chiefly relied. "Know ye," said David to his intimate friends, "that a great prince in Israel has fallen to-day; but I am too weak to avenge him, for I am not yet anointed king over the tribes." He secretly disliked Joab from this time, and waited for God himself to repay the evil-doer according to his wickedness. The fate of the unhappy and abandoned Ishbosheth could not now long be delayed. He also was murdered by two of his body-guard, who hoped to be rewarded by David for their treachery; but instead of gaining a reward, they were summarily ordered to execution. The sole surviving member of Saul's family was now Mephibosheth, the only son of Jonathan,— a boy of twelve, impotent, and lame. This prince, to the honor of David, was protected and kindly cared for. David's magnanimity appears in that he made special search, asking "Is there any that is left of the house of Saul, that I may show him the kindness of God for

Jonathan's sake?" The memory of the triumphant conqueror was still tender and loyal to the covenant of friendship he had made in youth, with the son of the man who for long years had pursued him with the hate of a lifetime.

David was at this time thirty-eight years of age, in the prime of his manhood, and his dearest wish was now accomplished; for on the burial of Ishbosheth "came all the tribes of Israel to David unto Hebron," formally reminded him of his early anointing to succeed Saul, and tendered their allegiance. He was solemnly consecrated king, more than eight thousand priests joining in the ceremony; and, thus far without a stain on his character, he began his reign over united Israel. The kingdom over which he was called to reign was the most powerful in Palestine. Assyria, Egypt, China, and India were already empires; but Greece was in its infancy, and Homer and Buddha were unborn.

The first great act of David after his second anointment was to transfer his capital from Hebron to Jerusalem, then a strong fortress in the hands of the Jebusites. It was nearer the centre of his new kingdom than Hebron, and yet still within the limits of the tribe of Judah. He took it by assault, in which Joab so greatly distinguished himself that he was made captain-general of the King's forces. From that time "David went on growing great, and the Lord God of Hosts was with him." After fortifying his strong position, he built a palace worthy of his capital, with the aid of Phœnician workmen whom Hiram, King of Tyre, wisely furnished him. The Philistines looked with jealousy on this impregnable stronghold, and declared war; but after two invasions they were so badly beaten that Gath, the old capital of Achish, passed into the hands of the King of Israel, and the power of these formidable enemies was broken forever.

The next important event in the reign of David was the transfer of the sacred ark from Kirjath-jearim, where it had remained from the time of Samuel, to Jerusalem. It was a proud day when the royal hero, enthroned in his new palace on that rocky summit from which he could survey both Judah and Samaria, received the symbol of divine holiness amid all the demonstrations which popular enthusiasm could express. "And as the long and imposing procession, headed by nobles, priests, and generals, passed through the gates of the city, with shouts of praise and songs and sacred dances and sacrificial rites and symbolic ceremonies and bands of exciting music, the exultant soul of David burst out in the most rapturous of his songs: 'Lift up your heads, O ye gates; and be ye lift up ye everlasting doors; and the King of Glory shall come in!'" — thus reiterating the fundamental

truth which Moses taught, that the King of Glory is
the Lord Jehovah, to be forever worshipped both as
a personal God and the real Captain of the hosts of
Israel.

"One heart alone," says Stanley, "amid the festivities which attended this joyful and magnificent occasion, seemed to be unmoved. Whether she failed to enter into its spirit, or was disgusted with the mystic dances in which her husband shared, the stately daughter of Saul assailed David on his return to his palace — not clad in his royal robes, but in the linen ephod of the priests — with these bitter and disdainful words: 'How glorious was the King of Israel to-day, as he uncovered himself in the eyes of his handmaidens!'— an insult which forever afterward rankled in his soul, and undermined his love." Thus was the most glorious day which David ever saw, clouded by a domestic quarrel; and the proud princess retired, until her death, to the neglected apartments of a dishonored home. How one word of bitter scorn or harsh reproach will sometimes sunder the closest ties between man and woman, and cause an alienation which never can be healed, and which may perchance end in a domestic ruin!

David had now passed from the obscurity of a chief of a wandering and exiled band of followers to the dignity of an Oriental monarch, and turned his attention to the organization of his kingdom and the development of its resources. His army was raised to two hundred and eighty thousand regular soldiers. His intimate friends and best-tried supporters were made generals, governors, and ministers. Joab was commander-in-chief; and Benaiah, son of the high-priest, was captain of his body-guard, — composed chiefly of foreigners, after the custom of princes in most ages. His most trusted counsellors were the prophets Gad and Nathan. Zadok and Abiathar were the high-priests, who also superintended the music, to which David gave special attention. Singing men and women celebrated his victories. The royal household was regulated by different grades of officers. But David departed from the stern simplicity of Saul, and surrounded himself with pomps and guards. None were admitted to his presence without announcement or without obeisance, while he himself was seated on a throne, with a golden sceptre in his hands and a jewelled crown upon his brow, clothed in robes of purple and gold. He made alliances with powerful chieftains and kings, and imitated their fashion of instituting a harem for his wives and concubines, — becoming in every sense an Oriental monarch, except that his power was limited by the constitution which had been given by Moses. He reigned, it would seem, in justice and equity, and in obedience to the commands of Jehovah, whose servant he felt himself to be. Nor did he violate any known laws of morality, unless it were the practice of polygamy, in accordance with the custom of all Eastern potentates, permitted to them if not to their ordinary subjects. We infer from all incidental notices of the habits of the Israelites at this period that they were a remarkably virtuous people, with primitive tastes and love of domestic life, among whom female chastity was esteemed the highest virtue; and it is a matter of surprise that the loose habits of the King in regard to women provoked so little comment among his subjects, and called out so few rebukes from his advisers.

But he did not surrender himself to the inglorious luxury in which Oriental monarchs lived. He retained his warlike habits, and in great national crises he headed his own troops in battle. It would seem that he was not much molested by external enemies for twenty years after making Jerusalem his capital, but reigned in peace, devoting himself to the welfare of his subjects, and collecting materials for the future building of the Temple, — its actual erection being denied to him as a man of blood. Everything favored the national prosperity of the Israelites. There was no great power in western Asia to prevent them founding a permanent monarchy; Assyria had been humbled; and Egypt, under the last kings of the twentieth dynasty, had lost its ancient prestige; the Philistines were driven to a narrow portion of their old dominion, and the king of Tyre sought friendly alliance with David.

In the course of time, however, war broke out with Moab, followed by other wars, which required all the resources of the Jewish kingdom, and taxed to the utmost the energies of its bravest generals. Moab, lying east of the Dead Sea, had at one time given refuge to David when pursued by Saul, and he was even allied by blood to some of its people, — being descended from Ruth, a Moabitish woman. The sacred writings shed but little light on this war, or on its causes; but it was carried on with unusual severity, only a third part of the people being spared alive, and they reduced to slavery. A more important contest took place with the kingdom of Ammon on the north, on the confines of Syria, caused by the insults heaped on the ambassadors of David, whom he sent on a friendly message to Hanun the King. The campaign was conducted by Joab, who gained brilliant victories, without however crushing the Ammonites, who again rallied with a vast array of mercenaries gathered in their support. David himself took the field with the whole force of his kingdom, and achieved a series of splendid successes by which he extended his empire to the Euphrates, including Damascus, besides securing invaluable spoils from the cities of Syria, — among them chariots and horses, for which Syria was celebrated. Among these spoils also were a thousand shields overlaid with gold, and great quantities of brass afterward used by Solomon in the construction of the Temple. Yet even these conquests, which now made David the most powerful monarch of western Asia, did not secure peace. The Edomites, south of the Dead Sea, alarmed in view of the increasing greatness of Israel, rose against David, but were routed by Abishai, who penetrated to Petra and became master of the country, the inhabitants of which were put to the sword with unrelenting vengeance. This war of the Edomites took place simultaneously with that of the Ammonites, who, deprived of their allies, retreated with desperation to their strong capital, — Rabbah Ammon, twenty-eight hundred feet above the sea, and twenty miles east of the Jordan, — where they made a memorable but unsuccessful resistance.

It was during the siege of this stronghold, which lasted a year, that David, no longer young, oppressed with cares, and unable personally to bear the fatigues of war, forgot his duties as a king and as a man. For fifty years he had borne an unsullied name; for more than thirty years he had been a model of reproachless chivalry. If polygamy and ferocity in war are not drawbacks to our admiration, certain it is that no recorded crime or folly that called out divine censure can be laid to his charge. But in an hour of temptation, or from strange infatuation, he added murder to adultery, — covering up a great crime by one of still greater enormity, evincing meanness and treachery as well as ungoverned passion, and creating a scandal which was considered disgraceful even in an Oriental palace. "We read," says South in one of his most brilliant paragraphs, "of nothing like adultery in a persecuted David in the wilderness, when he fled hither and thither like a chased doe upon the mountains; but when the delicacies of his palace softened and ungirt his spirit, then it was that this great hero fell by a glance, and buried his glories in nocturnal shame, giving to his name a lasting stain, and to his conscience a fearful wound." Nor did he come to himself until a child was born, and the prophet Nathan had ingeniously pointed out to him his flagrant sin. He manifested no wrath against his accuser, as some despots would have done but sank to the ground in the greatest anguish and grief.

Then it was that David's repentance was more marvellous than his transgression, offering the most memorable instance of contrition recorded in history, — surpassing in moral sublimity, a thousand times over, the grief of Theodosius under the rebuke of Ambrose, or the sorrow of the haughty Plantagenet for the murder of Becket. His repentance was so profound, so sincere, so remarkable, that it is embalmed forever in the heart of a sinful world. Its wondrous depth and intensity almost make us forget the crime itself, which nevertheless pursued him into the immensity of eternal night, and was visited upon the third and fourth generation in treason, rebellion, and wars. "Be sure your sin will find you out," is a natural law as well as a divine decree. It was not only because David added Bathsheba to the catalogue of his wives; it was not only because he coveted, like Ahab, that which was not his own, — but because he violated the most sacred of all laws, and treacherously stained his hands in the blood of an innocent, confiding, and loyal subject, that his soul was filled with shame and anguish. It was this blood-guiltiness which was the burden of his confession and his agonized grief, as an offence not merely against society and all moral laws, but also against his Maker, in whose pure eyes he had committed his crimes of lust, deceit, and murder. "Against Thee, Thee only, have I sinned, and have done this evil in Thy sight!" What a volume of theological truth blazes from this single expression, so difficult for reason to fathom, that it was against God that the royal penitent felt that he had sinned, even more than against Uriah himself, whose life and property, in a certain sense, belonged to an Oriental king.

"Nor do we charge ourselves," says Edward Irving,

"with the defence of those backslidings which David more keenly scrutinized and more bitterly lamented than any of his censors, because they were necessary in a measure, that he might be the full-orbed man to utter every form of spiritual feeling. And if the penitential psalms discover the deepest hell of agony, and if they bow the head which utters them, then let us keep those records of the psalmist's grief and despondency as the most precious of his utterances, and sure to be needed by every man who essayeth to lead a spiritual life; for it is not until a man, however pure, honest, and honorable he may have thought himself, and have been thought by others, discovereth himself to be utterly fallen, defiled, and sinful before God, — not until he can, for expression of utter worthlessness, seek those psalms in which David describes his self-abasement, that he will realize the first beginning of spiritual life in his own soul."

Should we seek for the cause of David's fall, for that easy descent in the path of rectitude, — may we not find it in that fatal custom of Eastern kings to have more wives than was divinely instituted in the Garden of Eden, — an indulgence which weakened the moral sense and unchained the passions? Polygamy, under any circumstances, is the folly and weakness of kings, as well as the misfortune and curse of nations. It divided and distracted the household of David, and gave rise to incessant intrigues and conspiracies in his palace, which embittered his latter days and even undermined his throne.

We read of no further backslidings which seemed to call forth the divine displeasure, unless it were the census, or numbering of the people, even against the expostulations of Joab. Why this census, in which we can see no harm, should have been followed by so dire a calamity as a pestilence in which seventy thousand persons perished in four days, we cannot see by the light of reason, unless it indicated the purpose of establishing an absolute monarchy for personal aggrandizement, or the extension of unnecessary conquests, and hence an infringement of the theocratic character of the Hebrew commonwealth. The conquests of David had thus far been so brilliant, and his kingdom was so prosperous, that had he been a pagan monarch he might have meditated the establishment of a military monarchy, or have laid the foundation of an empire, like Cyrus in after-times. From a less beginning than the Jewish commonwealth at the time of David, the Greeks and Romans advanced to sovereignty over both neighboring and distant States. The numbering of the Israelitish nation seemed to indicate a desire for extended empire against the plain indications of the divine will. But whatever was the nature of that sin, it seems to have been one of no ordinary magnitude; and in view of its consequences, David's heart was profoundly touched. "O God!" he cried, in a generous burst of penitence, "I have sinned. But these sheep, what have they done? Let thine hand be upon me, I pray thee, and upon my father's house!"

If David committed no more sins which we are forced to condemn, and which were not irreconcilable with his piety, he was subject to great trials and misfortunes. The wickedness of his children, especially of his eldest son Amnon, must have nearly broken his heart. Amnon's offence was not only a terrible scandal, but cost the life of the heir to the throne. It would be hard to conceive how David's latter days could have been more embittered than by the crime of his eldest son,—a crime he could neither pardon nor punish, and which disgraced his family in the eyes of the nation. As to Absalom, it must have been exceedingly painful and humiliating to the aged and pious king to be a witness of the pride, insolence, extravagance, and folly of his favorite son, who had nothing to commend him to the people but his good looks; and still harder to bear was his rebellion, and his reckless attempt to steal his father's sceptre. What a pathetic sight to see the old warrior driven from his capital, and forced to flee for his life beyond the Jordan! How humiliating to witness also the alienation of his subjects, and their willingness to accept a brainless youth as his successor, after all the glorious victories he had won, and the services he had rendered to the nation! David's history reveals the sorrows and burdens of all kings and rulers. Outward grandeur and power, after all, are a poor compensation for the incessant cares, vexations, and humiliations which even the most favored monarchs are compelled to accept, — troubles, disappointments, and burdens which oppress both soul and body, and induce fears, suspicions, jealousies, and animosities. Who would envy a Tiberius or a Louis XIV. if he were obliged to carry their load, knowing well what that burden was?

Then again the kingdom of David was afflicted with a grievous famine, which lasted three years, decimating the people, and giving a check to the national prosperity; and the Philistines, too, whom he thought he had finally subdued, renewed their ancient warfare. But these calamities were not all that the old king had to endure. A new rebellion more dangerous even than that of Absalom broke out under Sheba, a Benjamite, who sounded the trumpet of defiance from the mountains of Ephraim, and who rallied under his standard ten of the tribes. To Amasa, it seems, was intrusted the honor and the task of defending David and the tribe of Judah, to which he belonged, — the king being alienated from Joab for the slaying of Absalom, although it had ended that undutiful son's rebellion.

The bloodthirsty Joab, as implacable as Achilles, who had rendered such signal services to his sovereign, was consumed with jealousy at this new appointment, and going up to the new general-in-chief as if to salute him, treacherously stabbed him with his sword, — but continued, however, to support David. He succeeded in suppressing the rebellion by intrigue, and on the promise that the city should be spared, the head of the rebel was thrown over the wall of the fortress to which he had retired. Even this rebellion did not end the trials of David, since Adonijah, the heir presumptive after the death of Absalom, conspired to steal the royal sceptre, which David had sworn to Bathsheba he would bequeath to her son Solomon. Joab even favored the succession of Adonijah; but the astute monarch, amid the infirmities of age, still possessed a large measure of the intellect and decision of his heroic days, and secured, by a rapid movement, the transfer of his kingdom to Solomon, who was crowned in the lifetime of his father.

In all these foul treacheries and crimes within his own household may be seen the distinct fulfilment of the punishment foretold by Nathan the prophet, as prepared for David's own "great transgression." God's providence is unerring, and men indeed prepare for themselves the retribution which, in spite of sincere repentance, is the inevitable consequence of their own violations of law, — physical, moral, and spiritual. God gave David the new heart he longed for; but the evil seeds sown bore nevertheless evil fruit for him and his children.

Aside from these troubles, we know but little of the latter days of David. After the death of Absalom, it would seem that he reigned ten years, on the whole tranquilly, turning his attention to the development of the resources of his kingdom, and collecting treasure for the Temple, which he was not to build. He was able to set aside, as we read in the twenty-second chapter of the Chronicles, a hundred thousand talents of gold and a million talents of silver, — an almost incredible sum.

If a talent of silver is, as estimated, about £390, or $1950, it would seem that the silver accumulated by David would have amounted to nearly two billion dollars, and the gold to a like sum, — altogether four billions, which is plainly impossible. Probably there is a mistake in the figures. We read in the twenty-ninth chapter of Chronicles that David gave to Solomon, out of his own private property, three thousand talents of gold and seven thousand talents of silver, — together, nearly $74,000,000. His nobles added what would be equal to $120,000,000 in gold and silver alone, besides brass and iron, — altogether about $194,000,000, which is not incredible when we bear in

ISRAELITISH CONQUESTS.

mind that a single family in New York has accumulated a larger sum in two generations. But even this sum, — nearly two hundred million dollars, — would have more than built all the temples of Athens, or St. Peter's Church at Rome. Whether the author of the Chronicles has exaggerated the amount of the national contribution for the building of the Temple or not, we yet are impressed with the vast wealth which was accumulated in the lifetime of David; and hence we infer that the wealth of his kingdom was enormous. And it was perhaps the excessive taxation of the people to raise this money, outside of the spoils of successful wars, that alienated them in the latter days of David, and induced them to rally under the standards of usurpers. Certain it is that he became unpopular in the feebleness of old age, and was forced to abdicate his throne.

David's premature old age presented a sad contrast to the vigor of his early days. He was not a very old man when he died, — younger than many monarchs and statesmen who in our times have retained their vigor, their popularity, and their power. But the intense labors and sorrows of forty years may have proved too great a strain on his nervous energies, and made him as timid as he once was bold. The man who had slain Goliath ran away from Absalom. He was completely under the domination of an intriguing wife.

He showed a singular weakness in reference to the crimes of his favorite son, so as to merit the bitter reproaches of his captain-general. "Thou hast shamed this day," said Joab, "the faces of all thy servants; for I perceive had Absalom lived, and all of us had died this day, then it had pleased thee well." In David's case, his last days do not seem to have been his best days, although he retained his piety and had conquered all his enemies. His glorious sun set in clouds after a reign of thirty-three years over united Israel, and the nation hailed the accession of a boy whose character was undeveloped.

The final years of this great monarch present an impressive lesson of the vanity even of a successful life, whatever services a man may have rendered to his country and to civilization. Few kings have ever accomplished more than David; but his glory was succeeded, if not by shame, at least by clouds and darkness. And this eclipse is all the more mournful when we remember not only his services but his exalted virtues. He was the most successful and the most admired of all the monarchs who reigned at Jerusalem. He was one of the greatest and best men who ever lived in any nation or at any period. "When, before or since, has there lived an outlaw who did not despoil his country?" Where has there reigned a king whose head was less giddy on a throne, or who retained more humility in the midst of riches and glories, unless it were Marcus Aurelius or Alfred the Great? David had an inborn aptitude for government, and a power like Julius Cæsar of fascinating every one who came in contact with him. His self-denial and devotion to the interests of the nation were marvellous. We do not read that he took any time for pleasure or recreation; the heavy load of responsibility and care never for a moment was thrown from his shoulders. His penetration of character was so remarkable that all stood in fear of him; yet fear gave place to admiration. Never had a monarch more devoted servants and followers than David in his palmy days; he was the nation's idol and pride for thirty years. In every successive vicissitude he was great; and were it not for his cruelty in war and severity to his enemies, and his one great lapse into criminal self-indulgence, his reign would have been faultless. Contrast David with the other conquerors of the world; compare him with classical and mediæval heroes,— how far do they fall beneath him in deeds of magnanimity and self-sacrifice! What monarch has transmitted to posterity such inestimable treasures of thought and language?

It is consoling to feel that David, whether exultant in riches and honors, or bowed down to the earth with grief and wrath, both in the years of adversity and in his prosperous manhood, in strength and in weakness, with unfailing constancy and loyalty turned his thoughts to God as the source of all hope and consolation. "As the hart panteth after the water-brooks, so panteth my soul after Thee, O God!" He has no doubts, no scepticism, no forgetfulness. His piety has the seal of an all-pervading sense of the constant presence and aid of a personal God whom it is his supremest glory to acknowledge, — his staff, his rock, his fortress, his shield, his deliverer, his friend; the One with whom he sought to commune, both day and night, on the field of battle and in the guarded recesses of his palace. In the very depths of humiliation he never sinks into despair. His piety is both tender and exultant. In the ecstasy of his raptures he calls even upon inanimate nature to utter God's praises, — upon the sun and moon, the mountains and valleys, fire and hail, storms and winds, yea, upon the stars of night. "Bless ye the Lord, O my soul! for his mercy endureth forever." And this is why he was a man after God's own heart. Let cynics and critics, and unbelievers like Bayle, delight to pick flaws in David's life. Who denies his faults? He was loved because his soul was permeated with exalted loyalty, because he hungered and thirsted after righteousness, because he could not find words to express sufficiently his sense of sin and his longing for forgiveness, his consciousness of littleness and unworthiness when contrasted with the majesty of Jehovah. Let not our eyes be fixed upon his defects, but upon the general tenor of his life. It is true he is in war merciless and cruel; he hurls anathemas on his enemies. His wrath is as supernal as his love; he is inspired with the fiercest resentments; he exhibits the mighty anger of Homer's heroes; he never could forgive Joab for the slaughter of Abner and Absalom. But the abiding sentiments of his heart are gentleness and magnanimity. How affectionately his soul clung to Jonathan! What a power of self-denial, when he was faint and thirsty, in refusing the water which his brave companions brought him at the risk of their lives! How generously he spared the life of Saul! How patiently he bore the rebukes of Nathan! How nobly he treated the aged Barzillai! His impulses were all generous. He was affectionate to weakness. He had no egotistic ends. He forgot his own sorrows in the sufferings of his people. He had no pride in all the pomp of power, although he never forgot that he was the Lord's anointed.

When we pass from David's personal character to the services he rendered, how exalted his record! He laid the foundation of the prosperity of his nation. Where would have been the glories of Solomon but for the genius and deeds of David? But more than any material greatness are the imperishable lyrics he bequeathed to all ages and nations, in which are unfolded the varied experiences of a good man in his warfare with the world, the flesh, and the devil, — those priceless utterances which portray every passion that can move the human soul. He has left bare to the contemplation of all ages all that a lofty soul can suffer or enjoy, all that can be learned from folly and sin, all that can stimulate religious life, all that can console in sorrow and affliction. These experiences and aspirations he has embodied in lyric poetry, on the whole the most exquisite in the Hebrew language, creating a new world of religious thought and feeling, and furnishing the foundation for Christian psalmody, to be sung from age to age throughout the world. His kingdom passed away, but his Psalms remain, — a realm which no civilization can afford to lose. As Moses lives in his jurisprudence, Solomon in his proverbs, Isaiah in his prophecies, and Paul in his epistles, so David lives in those poems that are still the most expressive of all the forms in which the public worship of God is still continued. Such poetry could not have been written, had not the author experienced in his own life every variety of suffering and joy.

The literary excellence of the Psalms cannot be measured by the standard of Greek and Roman lyrics. It is not seen in any of our present forms of metrical composition. It is the mighty soaring of an exalted soul which makes the Psalms so dear to us, and not their artificial structure. They were made to reveal the ways of God to man and the life of the human soul, not to immortalize heroes or dignify a human love. We may not be able to appreciate in English form their original metrical skill; but it is impossible that a people so musical as the Hebrews were kindled into passionate admiration of them, had they not possessed great rhythmic beauty. We may not comprehend the force of the melodic forms, but we can appreciate the tenderness, the pathos, the sublimity, and the intensity of the sentiments expressed. "In pathetic dirges, in songs of jubilee, in outbursts of praise, in prophetic announcements, in the agonies of contrition, in bursts of adoration, in the beatitudes of holy bliss, in the enchanting calmness of Christian life," no one has ever surpassed David, so that he was called "the sweet singer of Israel." There is nothing pathetic in national difficulties, or endearing in family relations, or profound in inward experience, or triumphant over the fall of wickedness, or beatific in divine worship, which he does not intensify. He raises mortals to the skies, though he brings no angels down. Never does he introduce dogmas, yet his songs are permeated with fundamental truths, and are a perpetual rebuke to pharisaism, rationalism, epicureanism, and every form of infidel speculation that with "the fool hath said in his heart, There is no God." As the Psalter was held to be the most inspiring poetry in the palmy days of the Hebrew commonwealth, so it proved the most impressive part of the ritual of the mediæval Church, and is still the most valued of all the lyrics which Protestantism has appropriated in the worship of God. And how potent, how lasting, how valued is a good song! The psalmody of the Church will last longer than its sermons; and when a song stimulates the loftiest sentiments of which men are capable, how priceless it is, how permanently it is embalmed in the heart of the world! "Thus have his songs become the treasured property of mankind, resounding in the anthems of different creeds, and carrying into every land that same voice which on Mount Zion was raised in sorrowful longings or ecstatic praise."

What a mighty power the songs of the son of Jesse still wield over the affections of mankind! We lose sight at times of Moses, of Solomon, and of Isaiah; but we never lose sight of David.

> Such is the tribute which all nations bring,
> O warrior, prophet, bard, and sainted king,
> From distant ages to thy hallowed name,
> Transcending far all Greek and Roman fame?
> No pagan gods thy sacred songs invoke,
> No loves degrading do thy strains provoke.
> Thy soul to heaven in holy rapture mounts,
> And joys seraphic in its bliss recounts.

O thou sweet singer of a favored race,
What vast results to thy pure songs we trace!
How varied and how rich are all thy lays
On Nature's glories and Jehovah's ways!
In loftiest flight thy kindling soul surveys
The promised glories of the latter days,
When peace and love this fallen world shall bind,
And richest blessings all the race shall find.

O thou sweet singer of a favored race,
What vast results to thy pure songs we trace!
How varied and how rich are all thy lays
On Nature's glories and Jehovah's ways!
In loftiest flight thy kindling soul surveys
The promised glories of the latter days,
When peace and love this fallen world shall bind,
And richest blessings all the race shall find.

SOLOMON.

THE GLORY OF THE MONARCHY.

ABOUT 993–953 B.C.

SOLOMON.

THE GLORY OF THE MONARCHY.

WE associate with Solomon the culmination of the Jewish monarchy, and a reign of unexampled prosperity and glory. He not only surpassed all his predecessors and successors in those things which strike the imagination as brilliant and imposing, but he had such extraordinary intellectual gifts that he has passed into history as the wisest of ancient kings, and one of the most favored of mortals.

Amid the evils which saddened the latter days of his father David, this remarkable man grew up. His interests were protected by his mother Bathsheba, an intriguing, ambitious, and beautiful woman, and his education was directed by the prophet Nathan. He was ten years of age when his elder brother Absalom rebelled, and a youth of fifteen to twenty when he was placed upon the throne, during the lifetime of his father and with his sanction, aided by the cabals of his mother, the connivance of the high-priest Zadok, the spiritual authority of Nathan, and the political ascendency of Benaiah, the most valiant of the captains of Israel after Joab. He became king in a great national crisis, when unfilial rebellion had undermined the throne of David, and Adonijah, next in age to Absalom, had sought to steal the royal sceptre, supported by the veteran Joab and Abiathar, the elder high-priest.

Solomon's first acts as monarch were to remove the great enemies of his father and the various heads of faction, not sparing even Joab, the most successful general that ever brought lustre on the Jewish arms. With Abiathar, who died in exile, expired the last glory of the house of Eli; and with Shimei, who was slain with Adonijah, passed away the last representative of the royal family of Saul. Soon after Solomon repaired to the heights of Gibeon, six miles from Jerusalem, — a lofty eminence which overlooks Judæa, and where stood the Tabernacle of the Congregation, the original Tent of the Wanderings, in front of which was the brazen altar on which the young king, as a royal holocaust, offered the sacrifice of one thousand victims. It was on the night of that sacrificial offering that, in a dream, a divine voice offered to the youthful king whatsoever his heart should crave. He prayed for wisdom, which was granted, — the first evidence of which was his celebrated judgment between the two women who claimed the living child, which made a powerful impression on the whole nation, and doubtless strengthened his throne.

The kingdom which Solomon inherited was probably at that time the most powerful in western Asia, the fruit of the conquests of Saul and David, of Abner and Joab. It was bounded by Lebanon on the north, the Euphrates on the east, Egypt on the south, and the Mediterranean on the west. Its territorial extent was small compared with the Assyrian or Persian empire; but it had already defeated the surrounding nations,— the Philistines, the Edomites, the Syrians, and the Ammonites. It hemmed in Phœnicia on the sea-coast, and controlled the great trade-routes to the East, which made it politic for the King of Tyre to cultivate the friendship of both David and Solomon. If Palestine was small in extent, it was then exceedingly fertile, and sustained a large population. Its hills were crested with fortresses, and covered with cedars and oaks. The land was favorable to both tillage and pasture, abounding in grapes, figs, olives, dates, and every species of grain; the numerous springs and streams favored a perfect system of irrigation, so that the country presented a picture in striking contrast to its present blasted and dreary desolation. The nation was also enriched by commerce as well as by agriculture. Caravans brought from Eastern cities the most valuable of their manufactures. From Tarshish in Spain ships brought gold and silver; Egypt sent chariots and fine linen; Syria sold her purple cloths and robes of varied colors; Arabia furnished horses and costly trappings. All the luxuries and riches which Tyre had collected in her warehouses found their way to Jerusalem. Even silver was as plenty as the stones in the streets. Long voyages to the mouth of the Indus resulted in a vast accumulation of treasure, — gold, ivory, spices, gums, perfumes, and precious stones. The nations and tribes subject to Solomon from the river of Egypt to the Euphrates, and from Syria to the Red Sea, paid a fixed tribute, while their kings and princes sent rich presents, — vessels of gold and silver, costly arms and armor, rich garments and robes, horses and mules, perfumes and spices.

But the prosperity of the realm was not altogether inherited; it was firmly and prudently promoted by the young king. Solomon made alliances with Egypt and Syria, as well as with Phœnicia, and peace and plenty enriched all classes, so that every man sat under his own vine and fig-tree in perfect security. Never was such prosperity seen in Israel before or since. Strong fortresses were built on Lebanon to protect the caravans, and Tadmor in the wilderness to the east became a great centre of trade, and ultimately a splendid city under Zenobia. The royal stables contained forty thousand horses and fourteen hundred chariots. The royal palace glistened with plates of gold, and the parks and gardens were watered from immense reservoirs. "When the youthful monarch repaired to these gardens in his gorgeous chariot, he was attended," says Stanley, "by nobles whose robes of purple floated in the wind, and whose long black hair, powdered with gold dust, glistened in the sun, while he himself, clothed in white, blazing with jewels, scented with perfumes, wearing both crown and sceptre, presented a scene of gladness and glory. When he travelled, he was borne on a splendid litter of precious woods, inlaid with gold and hung with purple curtains, preceded by mounted guards, with princes for his companions, and women for his idolaters, so that all Israel rejoiced in him."

We infer that Solomon reigned for several years in justice and equity, without striking faults,— a wise and benevolent prince, who feared God and sought from him wisdom, which was bestowed in such a remarkable degree that princes came from remote countries to see him, including the famous Queen of Sheba, who was both dazzled and enchanted.

Yet while he was, on the whole, loyal to the God of his fathers, and was the pride and admiration of his subjects, especially for his wisdom and knowledge, Solomon was not exempted from grave mistakes. He was scarcely seated on his throne before he married an Egyptian princess, doubtless with the view of strengthening his political power. But while this splendid alliance brought wealth and influence, and secured chariots and horses, it violated one of the settled principles of the Jewish commonwealth, and prevented that isolation which was so necessary to keep uncorrupted the manners and habits of the people. The alliance doubtless favored commerce, and in one sense enlarged the minds of his subjects, removing from them many prejudices; but the nation was not intended by the divine founder to be politically or commercially great, but rather to preserve the worship of Jehovah. Moreover, the daughter of Pharaoh was an idolater, and her influence, so far as it went, tended to wean the king from his religious duties, — at least to make him tolerant of false gods.

The enlargement of the king's harem was another mistake, for although polygamy was not condemned, and was practised even by David, it made Solomon prominent among Eastern monarchs for an absurd ostentation, allied with enervating effeminacy, and thus gradually undermined the healthy tone of his character. It may have prepared the way for the apostasy of his later years, and certainly led to a great increase of the royal expenses. The support of seven hundred wives and three hundred concubines must have been a scandal and a burden for which the nation was not prepared. The pomp in which he lived presupposes a change in the government itself, even to an absolute monarchy and a grinding despotism, fatal to the liberties which the Israelites had enjoyed under Saul and David. The predictions and warnings of Samuel were realized for the first time in the reign of Solomon, so that wealth, prosperity, and luxury were but a poor exchange for that ancient religious ardor and intense patriotism which had led the Hebrew nation to victory over surrounding idolatrous nations. The heroic ages of Jewish history passed away when ships navigated by Phœnician sailors brought gold from Ophir and silver from Tarshish, and did not return until the Maccabees rallied the hunted and decimated tribes of Israel against the armies of the Syrian kings.

Solomon's peaceful and prosperous reign of forty years was, however, favorable to one grand enterprise which David had longed to accomplish, but to whom it was denied. This was the building of the Temple, for so long a time identified with the glory of Jerusalem, and common interest in which might have bound the twelve tribes together but for the excessive taxation which the extravagance and ostentation of the monarch had rendered necessary.

We can form but an inadequate idea of the magnificence of this Temple from its description in the sacred annals. An edifice which taxed the mighty resources of Solomon and consumed the spoils of forty years' successful warfare, must have been in that age without a parallel in splendor and beauty. If the figures are not exaggerated, it required the constant labors of ten thousand men in the mountains of Lebanon alone to cut down and hew the timber, and this for a period of eleven years. Of ordinary laborers there were seventy thousand; and of those who worked in the quarries and squared the stones there were eighty thousand more, besides overseers. It took three years to prepare the foundations. As Mount Moriah, on which the Temple was built, did not furnish level space enough, a wall of solid masonry was erected on the eastern and southern sides nearly three hundred feet in height, the stones of which, in some instances, were more than twenty feet long and six feet thick, so perfectly squared that no mortar was required. The buried foundations for the courts of the Temple and the vast treasure-houses still remain to attest the strength and solidity of the work, seemingly as indestructible as are the pyramids of Egypt, and only paralleled by the uncovered ruins of the palaces of the Cæsars on the Palatine Hill at Rome, which fill all travellers with astonishment. Vast cisterns also had to be hewn in the rocks to supply water for the sacrifices, capable of holding ten millions of gallons. The Temple proper was small compared with the Egyptian temples, or with mediæval cathedrals; but the courts which surrounded it were vast, enclosing a quadrangle larger than the area on which St Peter's Church at Rome is built. It was, however, the richness of the decorations and of the sacred vessels and the altars for sacrifice, which consumed immense quantities of gold, silver, and brass, that made the Temple especially remarkable. The treasures alone which David collected were so enormous that we think there must be errors in the calculation, — thirteen million pounds Troy of gold, and one hundred and twenty-seven million pounds of silver, — an amount not easy to estimate. But the plates of gold which overlaid the building, and the cherubim or symbolical winged figures, the precious woods, the rich hangings and curtains of crimson and purple, the brazen altars, the lamps, the sacred vessels of solid gold and silver, the elaborate carvings and castings, the rare gems, — these all together must have required a greater expenditure than is seen in the most famous temples of Greece or Asia Minor, whose value and beauty chiefly consisted in their exquisite proportions and their marble pillars and figures of men or animals. But no representation of man, no statue to the Deity, was seen in the Temple of Solomon;

no idol or sacred animal profaned it. There was no symbol to indicate even the presence of Jehovah, whose dwelling-place was in the heavens, and whom the heaven of heavens could not contain. There were rites and sacrifices, but these were offered to an unseen divinity, whose presence was everywhere, and who alone reigned as King of Kings and Lord of Lords, forever and forever. The Temple, however, with its courts and porticos, its vast foundations of stones squared in distant quarries, and the immense treasures everywhere displayed, impressed both the senses and the imagination of a people never distinguished for art or science. And not only so, but Fergusson says: "The whole Mohammedan world look to it as the foundation of all architectural knowledge, and the Jews still recall its glories, and sigh over their loss with a constant tenacity unmatched by that of any other people to any other building of the ancient world." Whether or not we are able to explain the architecture of the Temple, or are in error respecting its size, or the amount of gold and silver expended, or the number of men employed, we know that it was the pride and glory of that age, and was large enough, with its enclosures, to contain a representation of five millions of people, the heads of all the families and tribes of the nation, such as were collected together at its dedication.

As the great event of David's reign was the removal of the Ark to Jerusalem, so the culminating glory of Solomon was the dedication of the Temple he had built to the worship of Jehovah. The ceremony equalled in brilliancy the glories of a Roman triumph, and infinitely surpassed them in popular enthusiasm. The whole population of the kingdom, — some four or five millions, — or their picked representatives, came to Jerusalem to witness or to take part in it. "And as the long array of dignitaries, with thousands of musicians clothed in white, and the monarch himself arrayed in pontifical robes, and the royal household in embroidered mantles, and the guards with their golden shields, and the priests bearing the sacred but tattered tabernacle, with the ark and the cherubim, and the altar of sacrifice, and the golden candlesticks and table of shew bread, and the brazen serpent of the wilderness and the venerated tables of stone on which were engraved by the hand of God himself the ten commandments," — as this splendid procession swept along the road, strewed with flowers and fragrant with incense, how must the hearts of the people have been lifted up! Then the royal pontiff arose from the brazen scaffold on which he had seated himself, and amid clouds of incense and the smoke of burning sacrifice offered unto God the tribute of national praise, and implored His divine protection. And then, rising from his knees, with hands outstretched to heaven, he blessed the congregation, saying with a loud voice, "Let the Lord our God be with us as he was with our fathers, so that all the earth may know that Jehovah is God and that there is none else!"

Then followed the sacrifices for this grand occasion, — twenty thousand oxen and one hundred and twenty thousand sheep and goats were offered up on successive days. Only a portion of these animals was actually consumed on the altar by the officiating priests: the greater part furnished meat for the assembled multitude. The Festival of the Dedication lasted a week, and this was succeeded by the Feast of the Tabernacles; and from that time the Temple became the pride and glory of the nation. To see it periodically and worship in its courts became the intensest desire of every Hebrew. Three times a year some great festival was held, attended by a vast concourse of the people. The command was that every male Israelite should "appear before the Lord" and make his offering; but this of course had its necessary exceptions, as multitudes of women and children could not go, and had to be cared for at home. We cannot easily understand how on any other supposition they were all accommodated, spacious as were the various courts of the Temple; and we conclude that only a large representation of the tribes and families took place, for how could four or five millions of people assemble together at any festival?

Contemporaneous with the building of the Temple, or immediately after it was dedicated, were other gigantic works, including the royal palace, which it took thirteen years to complete, and upon which, as upon the Sacred House, Syrian artists and workmen were employed. The principal building was only one hundred and fifty feet long, seventy-five broad, and forty-five feet high, in three stories, with a grand porch supported on lofty pillars; but connected with the palace were other edifices to support the magnificence in which the king lived with his court and his harem. Around the tower of the House of David were hung the famous golden shields, one thousand in number, which had been made for the body-guard, with other glittering ornaments, which were likened by the poets to the neck of a bride decked with rays of golden coins. In the great Judgment Hall, built of cedar and squared stone, was the throne of the monarch, made of ivory, inlaid with gold. A special mansion was erected for Solomon's Egyptian queen, of squared stones twelve to fifteen feet in length. Connected with these various palaces were extensive gardens constructed at great expense, filled with all the triumphs of horticultural art, and watered by streams from vast reservoirs. In these the luxurious king and court could wander among beds of spices and flowers and fruits. But these did not content the royal family. A summer palace was erected on the heights of Mount Lebanon, having gardens filled with everything which could delight the eye or captivate the senses. Here, surrounded with learned men, women, and courtiers, with bands of music, costly litters, horses and chariots, and every luxury which unbounded means could command, the magnificent monarch beguiled his leisure hours, abandoned equally to pleasure and study, — for his inquiring mind sought to master all the knowledge that was known, especially in the realm of natural history, since "he was wiser than all men, and spake of trees, from the cedar-tree that is on Lebanon even unto the hyssop that springeth out of the wall." We can get some idea of the expenses of his household, in the fact that it daily consumed sixty measures of flour and meal and thirty oxen and one hundred sheep, besides venison, game, and fatted fowls. The king never appeared in public except with crown and sceptre, in royal robes redolent of the richest perfumes of India and Arabia, and sparkling with gold and gems. He lived in a constant blaze of splendor, whether travelling in his gorgeous litter, surrounded with his guards, or seated on his throne to dispense justice and equity, or feasting with his nobles to the sound of joyous music.

To keep up this regal splendor, to support seven hundred wives and three hundred concubines on the fattest of the land, and deck them all in robes of purple and gold; to build magnificent palaces, to dig canals, and construct gigantic reservoirs for parks and gardens; to maintain a large standing army in time of peace; to erect strong fortresses wherever caravans were in danger of pillage; to found cities in the wilderness; to level mountains and fill up valleys, — to accomplish all this even the resources of Solomon were insufficient. What were six hundred and sixty-six talents of gold, yearly received (thirty-five million dollars), besides the taxes on all merchants and travellers, and the vast gifts which flowed from kings and princes, when that constant drain on the royal treasury is considered! Even a Louis XIV. was impoverished by his court and palace building, though he controlled the fortunes of twenty-five millions of people. King Solomon, in all his glory, became embarrassed, and was obliged to make forced contributions, — to levy a heavy tribute on his own subjects from Dan to Beersheba, and make bondmen of all the people that were left of the Amorites, Hittites, Perizites, Hivites, and Jebusites. The people were virtually enslaved to aggrandize a single person. The burdens laid on all classes and the excessive taxation at last alienated the nation. "The division of the whole country into twelve revenue districts was a serious grievance,—especially as the high official over each could make large profits from the excess of contributions demanded." A poll-tax, from which the nation in the olden times was freed, was levied on Israelite and Canaanite alike. The virtual slave-labor by which the great public improvements were made, sapped the loyalty of the people and produced discontent. This forced labor was as fatal as war to the real property of the nation, for wealth is ever based on private industry, on farms and vineyards, rather than on the palaces of kings. Moreover, the friendly relations which Solomon established with the neighboring heathen nations disgusted the old religious leaders, while the tendency to Oriental luxury which outward prosperity favored alarmed the more thoughtful. It was not a pleasant sight for the princes of Israel to see the whole land overrun with Phœnicians, Arabs, Babylonians, Egyptians, caravan drivers, strangers and travellers, camels and dromedaries from Midian and Sheba, traders to the fairs, pedlers with their foreign cloths and trinkets, all spreading immorality and heresy, and filling the cities with strange customs and degrading dances.

Nor was there, in that absolute monarchy which Solomon centralized around his throne, any remedy for all this, save assassination or revolution. The king had become debauched and effeminate. The love of pomp and extravagance was followed by worldliness, luxury, and folly. From agricultural pursuits the people had passed to commercial; the Israelites had become merchants and traders, and the foul idolatries of Phœnicians and Syrians had overspread the land. The king having lost the respect and affection of the nation, the rebellion of Jeroboam was a logical sequence.

I have not read of any king who so belied the promises of his early days, and on whom prosperity produced so fatal an apostasy as Solomon. With all his wisdom and early piety, he became an egotist, a sensualist, and a tyrant. What vanity he displayed before the Queen of Sheba! What a slave he became to wicked women! How disgraceful was his toleration of the gods of Phœnicia and Egypt! How hard was the bondage to which he subjected his subjects! How different was his ordinary life from that of his illustrious father, with no repentance, no remorse, no self-abasement! He was a Nebuchadnezzar and a Sardanapalus combined, going from bad to worse. And he was not only a sensualist and a tyrant, an egotist, and to some extent an idolater, but he was a cynic, sceptical of all good, and of the very attainments which had made him famous. We read of no illustrious name whose glory passed through so dark an eclipse. The satiated, disenchanted, disappointed monarch, prematurely old, and worn out by self-indulgence, passed away without honor or regret, at the age of sixty, and was buried in the City of David; and Rehoboam, his son, reigned in his stead.

The Christian fathers and many subsequent theological writers have puzzled their brains with unsatisfactory speculations whether Solomon finally repented or not; but the Scriptures are silent on that point. We have no means of knowing at what period of his life his heart was weaned from the religion of David, or when he entered upon a life of pleasure. There are some passages in the Book of Ecclesiastes which lead us to suppose that before he died he came to himself, and was a preacher of righteousness. This is the more charitable and humane view to take; yet even so, his moral teachings and warnings are not imbued with the personal contrition that endeared David's soul to God; they are unimpassioned, cold-hearted, intellectual, impersonal. Moreover, it may be that even in the midst of his follies he retained the perception of moral distinctions. His will was probably enslaved, so that he had not the power to restrain his passions, and his head may have become giddy in his high elevation. How few men could have resisted such powerful temptations as assailed Solomon on every side! The heart of the Christian world cannot but feel that so gifted a man, endowed with every intellectual attraction, who reigned for a time with so much wisdom, who recognized Jehovah as the guide and Lord of Israel, as especially appears at the dedication of the Temple, and who wrote such profound lessons of moral wisdom, would not be suffered to descend to the grave without the divine forgiveness. All that we know is that he was wise, and favored beyond all precedent, but that he adopted the habits and fell in with the vices of Oriental kings, and lost the affections of his people. He was exalted to the highest pinnacle of glory; he descended to an abyss of shame, — a sad example of the infirmity of human nature which all ages will lament.

In one sense Solomon left nothing to his nation but monuments of despotic power, and trophies of a material civilization which implied the decay of primitive virtues. He did not perpetuate his greatness; he did not even enlarge the boundaries of his kingdom. Like Louis XIV. he simply squandered a great inheritance. He did not leave his kingdom morally so strong as it was under David; it was even dismembered under his legitimate successor. The grand Temple indeed remained the pride of every Jew, but David had bequeathed the treasures to build it. The national resources had been wasted in palaces and in court festivities; and although these had contributed to a material civilization, especially the sums expended on fortresses, aqueducts, reservoirs, and roads for the caravans, this civilization, so highly and justly prized in our age, may — under the peculiar circumstances of the Jews, and the end for which, by the Mosaic dispensation, they were intended to be kept isolated — have weakened those simpler habits and sentiments which favored the establishment of their religion. It must never be lost sight of that the isolation of the Hebrew race, unfavorable to such developments of civilization as commerce and the arts, was providentially designed (as is evidenced by the fact of accomplishment in spite of all obstacles) to keep alive the worship of Jehovah until the fulness of time should come, — until the Messiah should appear to establish a new dispensation. The glory and grandeur of Solomon did not contribute to this end, but on the other hand favored idolatrous rites and corrupting foreign customs; and this is proved by the rapid decline of the Jews in religious life, patriotic ardor, and primitive virtues under the succeeding kings, both of Judah and Israel, which led ultimately to their captivity. Politically, Solomon may have added to the temporary power of the nation, but spiritually, and so fundamentally, he caused an eclipse of glory. And this is why his kingdom departed from his house, and he left a sullied name.

Nevertheless, in many important respects Solomon rendered great services to humanity, which redeemed his memory from shame and made him a truly immortal man, and even a great benefactor. He left writings which are still among the most treasured inheritances of his nation and of mankind. It is recorded that he spoke three thousand proverbs, and his songs were a thousand and five. Only a small portion of these have descended to us in the sacred writings, but they doubtless entered into the literature of the Jews. Enough remains, whenever they were compiled and collected, to establish his fame as one of the wisest and most gifted of mortals. And these writings, whatever may have been his backslidings, are pervaded with moral wisdom. Whether written in youth or in old age, on the summit of human glory or in the depths of despair, they are generally accepted as among the most precious gems of the Old Testament. His profound experience, conveyed to us in proverbs and songs, remains as a guide in life through all generations. The dignity of intellect shines triumphantly through all the obscuration of virtues. Thus do poets live even when buried in ignominious graves; thus do philosophers instruct the world even though, like Seneca, and possibly Bacon, their lives present a sad contrast to their precepts. Great thoughts emancipate the soul, from age to age, while he who uttered them may have been enslaved by vices. Who knows what the private life of Shakspeare and Goethe may have been, but who would part with the writings they have left us? How soon the personal peculiarities of Coleridge and Carlyle will be forgotten, yet how permanent and healthy their utterances! It is truth, rather than man, that lives and conquers and triumphs. Man is nothing, except as the instrument of almighty power.

Of the writings ascribed to Solomon, there are three books, each of which corresponds to the different periods of his life, — to his pious youth, to his prosperous manhood, and to his later years of cynicism and despair. They all alike blaze with moral truth, and appeal to universal experience. They present different features of human life, at different periods, and suggest sentiments which most people have realized at some time or another. And if in some cases they are apparently contradictory, like the Proverbs and Ecclesiastes, they are equally striking and convincing, and are not more inconsistent than the man himself. Who does not change, and yet remain individually the same? Is there not a change between youth and old age? Do not most great men utter sentiments hard to be reconciled with one another, yet with equal sincerity? Webster enforces free-trade at one time and a high tariff at another, as light or circumstances change. Gladstone was in youth and middle age a pillar of the aristocracy; later he was the oracle of the masses, yet a lofty realism underlay all his utterances. The writings of

Solomon present life in different aspects, and yet they are alike true. They are not divine revelations, like the commandments given to Moses amid the lightnings of Sinai, or like the visions of the prophets respecting the future glories of the Church. They do not exalt the soul into inspiring ecstasies like the psalms of David, or kindle a holy awe like the lofty meditations of Job; but they are yet such impressive truths pertaining to human life that we invest them with more than human wisdom.

The Song of Songs, long ascribed to King Solomon, has been attended with some difficulty of explanation. It is a poem liable to be perverted by an unsanctified soul, since it is foreign to our modes of expression. For two hundred years it has been variously interpreted. It was the delight of Saint Bernard the ascetic, and a stumbling-block to Ewald the critic. To many German scholars, who have rendered great services by their learning and genius, it is only the expression of physical love, like the amatory songs of Greece. To others of more piety yet equal scholarship, like Origen, Grotius, and Bossuet, it is symbolic of the love which exists between Christ and the Church. It seems, at least, to be a contrast with the impure love of the heathen world. But whether it describes the ardent affection which Solomon bore to his young Egyptian bride; or the still more beautiful love of the innocent

Shulamite maiden for her betrothed shepherd feeding his flock among the lilies, unseduced by all the influences of the royal court, and triumphant over the seductions of rank and power; or whether it is the rapt soul of the believer bursting out in holy transports of joy, like a Saint Theresa in the anticipated union with her divine Spouse, — it is still a noble tribute to what is most enchanting of the great certitudes on earth or in heaven; and it is expressed in language of exquisite and incomparable elegance. "Arise, my fair one, and come away! for the winter is past and gone, and the flowers appear upon the earth, and the voice of the turtle is heard in the land. Make haste, my beloved! Be thou like a roe on the mountains of spices, for many waters cannot quench love, nor the floods drown it; yea, were a man to offer all that he hath for it, it would be utterly despised." How tender, how innocent, how fervent, how beautiful, is this description of a lofty love, at rest in its happiness, in the society of the charmer, exultant in the certainty of that glorious sentiment which nothing can corrupt and nothing can destroy!

If this unique and beautiful Song was the work of Solomon in his early days of innocence and piety, the book of Proverbs seems to be the result of his profound observations when he was still uncorrupted by prosperity, ruling his kingdom with sagacity and amazing the world with his wisdom. How many of those acute sayings were uttered by Solomon we know not, but probably most of them are his, collected, it is supposed, during the reign of Hezekiah. They are written on almost every subject pertaining to ethics, to nature, to science, and to society. Some are allusions to God, and others to the duties between man and man. Many are devoted to the duties of women, applicable to the sex in all times. They are not on a level of the Psalms in piety, nor of the Prophecies in grandeur, but they recognize the immutable principles of moral obligation. In some cases they seem to be worldly-wise, — such as we might suppose to fall from the mouth of Benjamin Franklin or Cobbett, — recognizing worldly prosperity as the greatest of blessings. Sometimes they are witty, again ironical, but always forcible. In some of them there is awful solemnity.

There are no more terrific warnings and exhortations in the sacred writings than are found in the Proverbs of Solomon. The sins of idleness, of anger, of covetousness, of gossip, of falsehood, of oppression, of injustice, of intemperance, of unchastity, are uniformly denounced as leading to destruction; while prudence, temperance, chastity, obedience to parents, and loyalty to truth are enjoined with the earnestness of a man who believes in personal accountability to God. The ethics of the Proverbs are based on everlasting righteousness, and are imbued with the spirit of divine philosophy; their great peculiarity is the constant exhortation to wisdom and knowledge, to which young men are especially exhorted. Like Socrates, Solomon never separates wisdom from virtue, but makes one the foundation of the other. He shows the connection between virtue and happiness, vice and misery. The Proverbs are inexhaustible in moral force, and have universal application. There is nothing cynical or gloomy in them. They form a fitting study for youth and old age, an incentive to virtue and a terror to evil-doers, a thesaurus of moral wisdom: they speak in every line a lofty and comprehensive intellect, acquainted with all the experiences of life. Such moral wisdom would be imperishable in any literature. Such utterances go far to redeem all personal defects; they show how unclouded is a mind trained in equity, even when the will is enslaved by iniquity. What is still more remarkable, the Proverbs never apologize for the force of temptation, and never blend error with truth; they uniformly exalt wisdom, and declare that the beginning of it is the fear of the Lord. There is not one of them which seeks to cover up vice with sophistical excuses; they show that the author or authors of them love moral beauty and truth, and exalt the same, — as many great men, with questionable morals, give their testimony to the truths of Christianity, and utterly abhor those who poison the soul by plausible sophistries, — as Lord Brougham detested Rousseau. The famous writings of our modern times which nearest approach the Proverbs in love of truth and moral wisdom are those of Bacon and Shakspeare.

In striking contrast with the praises of knowledge which permeate the Proverbs, is the book of Ecclesiastes, supposed to have been written in the decline of Solomon's life, when the pleasures of sin had saddened his soul, and filled his mind with cynicism. Unless the book of Ecclesiastes is to be interpreted as ironical, nothing can be more dreary than many of its declarations. It even seems to pour contempt on all knowledge and all enjoyments. "In much knowledge is much grief, and he that increaseth knowledge increaseth sorrow. . . . What profit hath a man of all his labor? . . . There is no remembrance of the wise more than of the fool. . . . There is nothing better for a man than that he should eat and drink. . . . A man hath no pre-eminence over a beast; all go to the same place. . . . What hath the wise man more than the fool? . . . There is a just man that perisheth in his righteousness, and there is a wicked man that prolongeth his life in wickedness. . . . One man among a thousand have I found, but a woman among all those have I not found. . . . The race is not to the swift, the battle to the strong; neither bread to the wise, nor riches to the man of understanding. . . . On all things is written vanity." Such are some of the dismal and cynical utterances of Solomon in his old age. The Ecclesiastes contrasted with the Proverbs is discouraging and sad, although there is great seriousness and even loftiness in many of its sayings. It seems to be the record of a disenchanted old man, to whom all things are a folly and vanity. There is a suppressed contempt expressed for what young men and the worldly regard as desirable, equalled only by a sort of proud disdain of success and fame. There is great bitterness in reference to women. Some of the sayings are as mournful jeremiads as any uttered by Carlyle, showing great scorn of what ninety-nine in one hundred are vain of, and pursue after, as all ending in vanity and vexation of spirit. We can understand how riches may prove a snare, how pleasure-seeking ends in disappointment, how the smiles of a deceitful woman may lead to the chamber of death, how little the treasures of wickedness profit, how sins will find out the transgressor, how the heart may be sad in the midst of laughter, how wine is a mocker, how ambition is Babel-building, how he who pursueth evil pursueth it to his death; we can understand how abundance will produce satiety, and satiety lead to disgust, — how disappointment attends our most cherished plans, and how all mortal pursuits fail to satisfy the cravings of an immortal soul. But why does the favored and princely Solomon, in sadness and bitterness, pronounce knowledge also to be a vanity like power and riches, especially when in his earlier writings he so highly commends it? Is it true that in much wisdom is much grief, and that the increase of knowledge is the increase of sorrow? Can it be that the book of Ecclesiastes is the mere record of the miserable experiences of an embittered and disappointed sensualist, or is it the profound and searching exposition of the vanities of this world as they appear to a lofty searcher after truth and God, measured by the realities of a future and endless life, which the soul emancipated from pollution pants and aspires after with all the intensity of a renovated nature? When I bear in mind the impressive lessons that are declared at the close of this remarkable book, the earnest exhortation to remember God before the dust shall return to the earth as it was, I cannot but feel that there are great moral truths underlying the sarcasm and irony in which the writer indulged. And these come with increased force from the mouth of a man who had tasted every mortal good, and found it all, when not properly used, a confirmation of the impossibility of earth to satisfy the soul of man. The writer calls himself "the preacher," and surely a great preacher he was, — not to a throng of "fashionable worshippers" or a crowd of listless pleasure-seekers, but to all ages and nations. And if he really was a living speaker to the young men who caught the inspiration of his voice, how terribly eloquent he must have been!

I fancy that I can see that unhappy old man, worn out, saddened, embittered, yet at last rising above the decrepitude of age and the infirmities which sin had hastened, and speaking in tones that could never be forgotten. "Behold, ye young men! I have tasted every enjoyment of this earth; I have indulged in every pleasure forbidden or permitted. I have explored the world of thought and the realm of nature. I have been favored beyond any mortal that ever lived; I have been flattered and honored beyond all precedent; I have consumed the treasures of kings and princes. I builded me houses, I planted me vineyards; I made me gardens and orchards, I made me pools of water; I got me servants and maidens. I gathered me also silver and gold; I got me men-singers and women-singers and musical instruments; whatsoever my eyes desired I kept not from them; I withheld not my heart from any joy,— and now, lo! I solemnly declare unto you, with my fading strength and my eyes suffused with tears and my knees trembling with weakness, and in view of that future and higher life which I neglected to seek amid the dazzling glories of my throne, and the bewilderment of fascinating joys, — I now most earnestly declare unto you that all these things which men seek and prize are a vanity, a delusion, and a snare; that there is no wisdom but in the fear of God."

So this saddest of books closes with lofty exhortations, and recognizes moral obligations which are in harmony with the great principle enforced in the Proverbs, — that there is no escape from the penalty of sin and folly; that whatsoever a man sows that shall he also reap. The last recorded words of the preacher are concerning the vanity of life, — that is, the hopeless failure of worldly pleasures and egotistical pursuits in themselves alone to secure happiness; the impossibility of lasting good disconnected with righteousness; the fact that even knowledge, the greatest possession and the highest joy which a man can have, does not satisfy the soul.

These final utterances of Solomon are not dogmas nor speculations, they are experiences, — the experiences of one of the most favored mortals who has lived upon our earth, and one of the wisest. If, measured by the eternal standards, his glory was less than that of the flower which withers in a day, what hope have ordinary men in the pursuit of pleasure, or gain, or honor? Utter vanity and vexation of spirit! Nothing brings a true reward but virtue, — unselfish labors for others, supreme loyalty to conscience, obedience to God. Hence, such profound experience so frankly published, such sad confessions uttered from the depths of the heart, and the summing up of the whole question of human life, enforced with the earnestness and eloquence of an old man soon to die, have peculiar force, and are among the greatest treasures of the Old Testament.

The fundamental truth to be deduced from the book of Ecclesiastes is that whatsoever is born of vanity must end in vanity. If vanity is the seed, so vanity is the fruit. It is, in fact, one of the most impressive of all the truths that appeal either to consciousness or experience. If a man builds a house from vanity, or makes a party from vanity, or gives a present from vanity, or writes a book from vanity, or seeks an office from vanity, — then, as certainly as the bite of an asp will poison the body, will the expected good be turned into a bitter disappointment. Self-love cannot be the basis of human action without alienation from God, without weariness, disgust, and ultimate sorrow. The soul can be fed only by divine certitudes; it can be enlarged only by walking according to the divine commandments.

Confucius, Socrates, Epictetus, and Marcus Aurelius declared the same truths, but not so impressively. Not for one's self, not for friends, not even for children alone must one live. There is a higher law still which speaks to the universal conscience, asking, What is your duty? With this is identified all that is precious in life, on earth or in heaven, for time and eternity. Anything in this world which is sought as a good, whose end is selfish, is an impressive failure; so that self-aggrandizement becomes as absurd and fatal as self-indulgence. One can no more escape from the operation of this law than he can take the wings of the morning and fly to the uttermost parts of the sea. The commonest experiences of every-day life confirm the wisdom which Solomon uttered out of his lonely and saddened soul. If ye will not hear him, be instructed by your own broken friendships, your own dispelled illusions, your own fallen idols; by the heartlessness which too often lurks in the smiles of beauty, by the poison concealed in polished flatteries, by the deceitfulness hidden beneath the warmest praises, by the demons of envy, jealousy, and pride which take from success itself its promised joys.

Who is happy with any amount of wealth? Who is free from corroding cares? Who can escape anxiety and fear? How hard to shake off the burdens which even a rich man is compelled to bear? There is a fly in every ointment, a skeleton in every closet, solitude in the midst of crowds, isolation in the joy of festivals. The wrecks of happiness are strewn in every path that the world has envied.

Read the lives of illustrious men; how melancholy often are the latter days of those who have climbed the highest! Cæsar is stabbed when he has conquered the world. Diocletian retires in disgust from the government of an empire. Godfrey languishes in grief when he has taken Jerusalem. Charles V. shuts himself up in a convent. Galileo, whose spirit has roamed the heavens, is a prisoner of the Inquisition. Napoleon masters a continent, and expires on a rock in the ocean. Mirabeau dies of despair when he has kindled the torch of revolution. The poetic soul of Burns passes away in poverty and moral eclipse. Madness overtakes the cool satirist Swift, and mental degeneracy is the final condition of the fertile-minded Scott. The high-souled Hamilton perishes in a petty quarrel, and curses overwhelm Webster in the halls of his early triumphs. What a confirmation of the experience of Solomon! "Vanity of vanities" write on all walls, in all the chambers of pleasure, in all the palaces of pride!

This is the burden of the preaching of Solomon; but it is also the lesson which is taught by all the records of the past, and all the experiences of mankind. Yet it is not sad when one considers the dignity of the soul and its immortal destinies. It is sad only when the disenchantment of illusions is not followed by that holy fear which is the beginning of wisdom, — that exalted realism which we believe at last sustained the soul of the Preacher as he was hastening to that country from whose bourn no traveller returns.

ELIJAH.

Ninth Century b. c.

DIVISION OF THE JEWISH KINGDOM.

ELIJAH.

ELIJAH.

THE DIVISION OF THE KINGDOM.

EVIL days fell upon the Israelites after the death of Solomon. In the first place their country was rent by political divisions, disorders, and civil wars. Ten of the tribes, or three quarters of the population, revolted from Rehoboam, Solomon's son and successor, and took for their king Jeroboam, — a valiant man, who had been living for several years at the court of Shishak, king of Egypt, exiled by Solomon for his too great ambition. Jeroboam had been an industrious, active-minded, strong-natured youth, whom Solomon had promoted and made much of. The prophet Ahijah had privately foretold to him that, on account of the idolatries tolerated by Solomon, ten of the tribes should be rent away from the royal house and given to him. The Lord promised him the kingdom of Israel, and (if he would be loyal to the faith) the establishment of a dynasty, — "a sure house." Jeroboam made choice of Shechem for his capital; and from political reasons, — for fear that the people should, according to their custom, go up to Jerusalem to worship at the great festivals of the nation, and perhaps return to their allegiance to the house of David, while perhaps also to compromise with their already corrupted and unspiritualized religious sense, — he made two golden calves and set them up for religious worship: one in Bethel, at the southern end of the kingdom; the other in Dan, at the far north.

It does not appear that the people of Israel as yet ignored Jehovah as God; but they worshipped him in the form of the same Egyptian symbol that Aaron had set up in the wilderness, — a grave offence, although not an utter apostasy. Moreover, this was the act of the king rather than of the priests or his own subjects.

Stanley makes a significant comment on this act of the new king, which the sacred narrative refers to as "the sin of Jeroboam, the son of Nebat, who made Israel to sin." He says: "The Golden Image was doubtless intended as a likeness of the One True God. But the mere fact of setting up such a likeness broke down the sacred awe which had hitherto marked the Divine Presence, and accustomed the minds of the Israelites to the very sin against which the new form was intended to be a safeguard. From worshipping God under a false and unauthorized form they gradually learned to worship other gods altogether. . . . 'The sin of Jeroboam, the son of Nebat,' is the sin again and again repeated in the policy — half-worldly, half-religious — which has prevailed through large tracts of ecclesiastical history. . . . For the sake of supporting the faith of the multitude, lest they should fall away to rival sects, . . . false arguments have been used in support of religious truths, false miracles promulgated or tolerated, false readings in the sacred text defended. And so the faith of mankind has been undermined by the very means intended to preserve it."

For priests, Jeroboam selected the lowest of the people, — whoever could be induced to offer idolatrous sacrifices in the high places, — since the old priests and Levites remained with the tribe of Judah at Jerusalem.

These abominations and political rivalries caused incessant war between the two kingdoms for several reigns. The northern kingdom, including the great tribe of Ephraim or Joseph, was the richest, most fertile, and most powerful; but the southern kingdom was the most strongly fortified. And yet even in the fifth year of the reign of Rehoboam, the king of Egypt, probably incited by Jeroboam, invaded Judah with an immense army, including sixty thousand cavalry and twelve hundred chariots, and invested Jerusalem. The city escaped capture only by submitting to the most humiliating conditions. The vast wealth which was stored in the Temple, — the famous gold shields which David had taken from the Syrians, and those also made by Solomon for his body-guard, together with the treasures of the royal palace, — became spoil for the Egyptians. This disaster happened when Solomon had been dead but five years. The solitary tribe left to his son, despoiled by Egypt and overrun by other enemies, became of but little account politically for several generations, although it still possessed the Temple and was proud of its traditions. After this great humiliation, the proud king of Judah, it seems, became a better man; and his descendants for a hundred years were, on the whole, worthy sovereigns, and did good in the sight of the Lord.

Political interest now centres in the larger kingdom, called Israel. Judah for a time passes out of sight, but is gradually enriched under the reigns of virtuous princes, who preserved the worship of the true God at Jerusalem. Nations, like individuals, seldom grow in real strength except in adversity. The prosperity of Solomon undermined his throne. The little kingdom of Judah lasted one hundred and fifty years after the ten tribes were carried into captivity.

Yet what remained of power and wealth among the Jews after the rebellion under Jeroboam, was to be found in the northern kingdom. It was still exceedingly fertile, and was well watered. It was "a land of brooks of water, of fountains, of barley and wheat, of vines and fig-trees, of olives and honey." It boasted of numerous fortified cities, and had a population as dense as that in Belgium at the present time. The nobles were powerful and warlike; while the army was well organized, and included chariots and horses. The monarchy was purely military, and was surrounded by powerful nations, whom it was necessary to conciliate. Among these were the Phœnicians on the west, and the Syrians on the north. From the first the army was the great power of the state, its chief being more powerful than Joab was in the undivided kingdom of David. He stood next after the king, and was the channel of royal favor.

The history of the northern kingdom which has come down to us is very meagre. From Jeroboam to Ahab — a period of sixty-six years — there were six kings, three of whom were assassinated. There was a succession of usurpers, who destroyed all the members of the preceding reigning family. They were all idolaters, violent and bloodthirsty men, whom the army had raised to the throne. No one of them was marked by signal ability, unless it were Omri, who built the city of Samaria on a high hill, and so strongly fortified it that it remained the capital until the fall of the kingdom. He also made a close alliance with

Tyre, the great centre of commerce in that age, and one of the wealthiest cities of antiquity. To cement this political alliance, Omri married his son Ahab — the heir-apparent to the throne — to a daughter of the Tyrian king, afterward so infamous as a religious fanatic and persecutor, under the name of Jezebel, — one of the worst women in history

On the accession of Ahab, nine hundred and nineteen years before Christ, the kingdom of Israel was rapidly tending to idolatry. Jeroboam had set up golden calves chiefly for a political end, but Ahab built a temple to Baal, the sun-god, the chief divinity of the Phœnicians, and erected an altar therein for pagan sacrifices, thus abjuring Jehovah as the Supreme and only God. The established religion was now idolatry in its worst form; it was simply the worship of the powers of Nature, under the auspices of a foreign woman stained with every vice, who controlled her husband. For Ahab himself was bad enough, but he was not the wickedest of the monarchs of Israel, nor was he insignificant as a man. It was his misfortune to be completely under the influence of his Phœnician bride, as many stronger men than he have been enslaved by women before and since his day. Ahab, bad as he was, was brave in battle, patriotic in his aims, and magnificent in his tastes. To please his wife he added to his royal residences a summer retreat called Jezreel, which was of great beauty, and contained within its grounds an ivory palace of great splendor. Amid its gardens and parks and all the luxuries then known, the youthful monarch with his queen and attendant nobles abandoned themselves to pleasure and folly, as Oriental monarchs are wont to do. It would seem that he was unusually licentious in his habits, since he left seventy children, — afterward to be massacred.

The ascendency of a wicked woman over this luxurious monarch has made her infamous. She was an incarnation of pride, sensuality, and cruelty; and with all her other vices she was a religious persecutor who has had no equal. We may perhaps give to her, as to many other tiger-like persecutors in the cause of what they call their "religion," the meagre credit of conscientious devotion in their cruelty; for she feasted at her own table at Jezreel four hundred priests of Baal, besides four hundred and fifty others at Samaria, while she erected two great sanctuaries for the Phœnician deities, at which the officiating priests were clad in splendid vestments. The few remaining prophets of Jehovah in the kingdom hid themselves in caves and deserts to escape the murderous fury of the idolatrous queen. We infer that she was distinguished for her beauty, and was bewitching in her manners like Catherine de' Medici, that Italian bigot whom her courtiers likened both to Aurora and Venus. Jezebel, like the Florentine princess, is an illustration of the wickedness which is so often concealed by enchanting smiles, especially when armed with power. The priests of Baal undoubtedly regarded their great protectress as one of the most fascinating women that ever adorned a royal palace, and in the blaze of her beauty and the magnificence of her bounty were blind to her innumerable sorceries and the wild license of her life.

The fearful apostasy of Israel, which had been increasing for sixty years under wicked kings, had now reached a point which called for special divine intervention. There were only seven thousand men in the whole kingdom who had not bowed the knee to Baal, and God sent a prophet, — a prophet such as had not appeared in Israel since Samuel; more august, more terrible even than he; indeed, the most unique and imposing character in Jewish history.

Almost nothing is known of the early history of Elijah. The Bible simply speaks of him as "the Tishbite," — one of the inhabitants of Gilead, at the east of the Jordan. He evidently was a man accustomed to a wild and solitary life. His stature was large, and his features were fierce and stern. His long hair flowed upon his brawny shoulders, and he was clothed with a mantle of sheepskin or hair-cloth, and carried in his hand a rugged staff. He was probably unlearned, being rude and rough in both manners and speech. His first appearance was marked and extraordinary. He suddenly and unannounced stood before Ahab; and abruptly delivered his awful message. He was an apparition calculated to strike with terror the boldest of kings in that superstitious age. He makes no set speech, he offers no apology, he disdains all forms and ceremonies; he does not even render the customary homage. He utters only a few words, preceded by an oath: "As Jehovah the God of Israel liveth, there shall not be dew nor rain these years but according to my word." What arrogance before a king! Elijah, an utterly unknown man, in a sheepskin mantle, apparently a peasant, dares to utter a curse on the land without even deigning to give a reason, although the conscience of Ahab must have told him that he could not with impunity introduce idolatry into Israel.

Elijah doubtless attacked the king in the presence of his wife and court. To the cynical and haughty queen, born in idolatry, he probably seemed a madman of the desert, — shaggy, unwashed, fierce, repulsive. To the Israelitish king, however, with better knowledge of the ways of God, the prophet appeared armed with supernal powers, whom he both feared and hated, and desired to put out of the way. But Elijah mysteriously disappears from the royal presence as suddenly as he had entered it, and no one knows whither he has fled. He cannot be found. The royal emissaries go into every land, but are utterly baffled in their search. The whole power of the realm was doubtless put forth to discover his retreat, and had he been found, no mercy would have been shown him; he would have been summarily executed, not only as a prophet of the detested religion, but as one who had insulted the royal station. He was forced to flee and hide after delivering his unwelcome message.

And whither did the prophet fly? He fled with the swiftness of a Bedouin, accustomed to traverse barren rocks and scorching sands, to a retired valley of one of the streams that emptied into the Jordan near Samaria. Amid the clefts of the rocks which marked the deep valley, did the man of God hide himself from his furious and numerous persecutors. He does not escape to his native deserts, where he would most probably have been hunted like a wild beast, but remains near the capital in which Ahab reigns, in a deeply secluded spot, where he quenches his thirst from the waters of the brook, and eats the food which the ravens deposit amid the steep cliffs he knows how to climb.

The bravest and most undaunted man in Israel, shielded and protected by God, was probably warned by the divine voice to make his escape, since his life was needful to the execution of Providential purposes. He was the only one of all the prophets of his day who dared to give utterance to his convictions. Some four or five hundred there were in the kingdom, all believers in Jehovah; but all sought to please the reigning power, or timidly concealed themselves They had been trained in the schools which Samuel had established, and were probably teachers of the people on theological subjects, and hence an antagonistic force to idolatrous kings. Their great defect in the time of Ahab was timidity. There was needed some one who under all circumstances would be undaunted, and would not hesitate to tell the truth even to the king and queen, however unpleasant it might be. So this rough, fierce unlettered man of few words was sent by God, armed with terrible powers.

It was now the rainy season, when rain was confidently expected by the people throughout Palestine. Yet strangely no rain fell, though sixty inches were the usual quantity in the course of the year. The streams from the mountains were dried up; the land, long parched by the summer sun, became like dust and ashes; the hills presented a blasted and dreary desolation; the very trees were withered and discolored. At last even the sheltered brook failed from which Elijah drank, and it became necessary for the man of God to seek another retreat. The Lord therefore sent him to the last place in which his enemies would naturally search for him, even to a city of Phœnicia, where the worship of Baal was the only religion of the land. As in his tattered and strange apparel he approached Sarepta, or Zarephath, a town between Tyre and Sidon, worn out with fatigue, parched with thirst, and overcome with hunger, — everything around him being depressed and forlorn, the rivers and brooks showing only beds of stone, the trees and grass withered, the sky lurid, and of unnatural brightness like that of brass, and the sun burning and scorching every remnant of vegetation, — he beheld a woman issuing from the town to gather sticks, in order to cook what she supposed would be her last meal. To this sad and discouraged woman, doubtless a worshipper of Baal, the prophet thus spoke: "Fetch me, I pray you, a little water in a vessel that I may drink;" and as she turned sympathetically to look upon him, he added, "Bring me, I pray thee, a morsel of bread in thine hand."

This was no small request to make of a woman who was herself on the borders of starvation, and of a pagan woman too. But there was a mysterious affinity between these two suffering souls. A common woman would not have appreciated the greatness of the beggar and vagrant before her. Only a discerning and sympathetic woman would have seen in the tones of his voice, and in his lofty bearing, despite all his rags and dirt, an unusual and marked character. She

THE DIVISION OF THE KINGDOM. 251

probably belonged to a respectable class, reduced to poverty by the famine, and her keen intelligence recognized at once in the hungry and needy stranger a superior person, — even as the humble friar of Palos saw in Columbus a nobleman by nature, when, wearied and disappointed, he sought food and shelter. She took the prophet by the hand, conducted him to her home, gave him the best chamber in her house, and in a strange devotion of generosity divided with him the last remnant of her meal and oil.

It is probable that a lasting friendship sprang up between the pagan woman and the solemn man of God, such as bound together the no less austere Jerome and his disciple Paula. For two or three years the prophet dwelt in peace and safety in the heathen town, protected by an admiring woman, — for his soul was great, if his body was emaciated and his dress repulsive. In return for her hospitality he miraculously caused her meal and oil to be daily renewed; and more than this, he restored her only son to life, when he had succumbed to a dangerous illness, — the first recorded instance of such a miracle.

The German critics would probably say that the boy was only seemingly dead, even as they would deny the miracle of the meal and oil. It is not my purpose to discuss this matter, but to narrate the recorded incidents that filled the soul of the woman of Sarepta with gratitude, with wonder, and with boundless devotion. "Verily, I say unto you," said a greater than Elijah, "whosoever shall give a cup of cold water in the name of a prophet, shall in no way lose his reward." Her reward was immeasurably greater than she had dared to hope. She received both spiritual and temporal blessings, and doubtless became a convert to the true faith. Tradition asserts that her boy, whom Elijah saved, — whether by natural or supernatural means, it is alike indifferent, — became in after years the prophet Jonah, who was sent to Nineveh. In all great friendships the favors are reciprocal. A noble-hearted woman was saved from starvation, and the life of a great man was preserved for future usefulness. Austerity and tenderness met together and became a cord of love; and when the land was perishing from famine, the favored members of a retired household were shielded from harm, and had all that was necessary for comfort.

Meanwhile the abnormal drought and consequent famine continued. The northern kingdom was reduced to despair. So dried up were the wells and exhausted the cisterns and reservoirs that even the king's household began to suffer, and it was feared that the horses of the royal stables would perish. In this dire extremity the king himself set forth from his palace to seek patches of vegetation and pools of water in the valleys, while his prime minister Obadiah — a secret worshipper of Jehovah — was sent in an opposite direction for a like purpose. On his way, in the almost hopeless search for grass and water, Obadiah met Elijah, who had been sent from his retreat once more to confront Ahab, and this time to promise rain. As the most diligent search had been made in every direction, but in vain, to find Elijah, with a view to his destruction as the man who "troubled Israel," Obadiah did not believe that the hunted prophet would voluntarily put himself again in the power of an angry and hostile tyrant. Yet the prime minister, having encountered the prophet, was desirous that he should keep his word to appear before the king, and promise to remove the calamity which even in a pagan land was felt to be a divine judgment. Elijah having reassured him of his sincerity, the minister informed his master that the man he sought to destroy was near at hand, and demanded an interview. The wrathful and puzzled king went out to meet the prophet, not to take vengeance, but to secure relief from a sore calamity, — for Ahab reasoned that if Elijah had power, as the messenger of Omnipotence, to send a drought, he also had the power to remove it. Moreover, had he not said that there should be neither rain nor dew but according to his word? So Ahab addressed the prophet as the author of national calamities, but without threats or insults. "Art thou he who troubleth Israel?" Elijah loftily, fearlessly, and reproachfully replied : "I have not troubled Israel, but thou and thy father's house, in that thou hast forsaken the commandments of Jehovah, and hast followed Baalim." He then assumes the haughty attitude of a messenger of divine omnipotence, and orders the king to assemble all his people, together with the eight hundred and fifty priests of Baal, at Mount Carmel, — a beautiful hill sixteen hundred feet high, near the Mediterranean, usually covered with oaks and flowering shrubs and fragrant herbs. He gives no reasons, — he sternly commands ; and the king obeys, being evidently awed by the imperious voice of the divine ambassador.

The representatives of the whole nation are now assembled at Mount Carmel, with their idolatrous priests. The prophet appears in their midst as a preacher armed with irresistible power. He addresses the people, who seemed to have no firm convictions, but were swayed to and fro by changing circumstances, being not yet hopelessly sunk into the idolatry of their rulers. "How long," cried the preacher, with a loud voice and fierce aspect, "halt ye between two opinions ? If Jehovah be God, *follow* him; but if Baal be God, then follow *him*." The undecided, crestfallen, intimidated people did not answer a word.

Then Elijah stoops to argument. He reminds the people, among whom probably were many influential men, that he stood alone in opposition to eight hundred and fifty idolatrous priests protected by the king and queen. He proposes to test their claims in comparison with his as ministers of the true God. This seems reasonable, and the king makes no objection. The test is to be supernatural, even to bring down fire from heaven to consume the sacrificial bullock on the altar. The priests of Baal select their bullock, cut it in pieces, put it on the wood, and invoke their supreme deity to send fire to consume the sacrifice. With all their arts and incantations and magical sorceries, the fire does not descend. They then perform their wild and fantastic dances, screaming aloud, from early morn to noon, "O Baal, hear us!" We do not read whether Ahab was present or not, but if he were he must have quaked with blended sentiments of curiosity and fear. His anxiety must have been terrible. Elijah alone is calm; but he is also stern. He mocks them with provoking irony, and ridicules their want of success. His grim sarcasms become more and more bitter. "Cry with a loud voice!" said he, "yea, louder and yet louder! for ye cry to a god; either he is talking, or he is hunting, or he is on a journey, or peradventure he sleepeth and must be awakened." And they cried aloud, and cut themselves, after their manner, with knives and spears, till the blood gushed out upon them.

Then Elijah, when midday was past, and the priests

continued to call unto their god until the time of the offering of the evening sacrifice, and there was neither voice nor answer, assembled the people around him, as he stood alone by the ruins of an ancient altar. With his own hands he gathered twelve stones, piled them together to represent the twelve tribes, cut a bullock in pieces, laid it on the wood, made a trench around the rude altar, which he filled with water from an adjacent well, and then offered up this prayer to the God of his fathers: "O Jehovah, God of Abraham, Isaac, and Jacob, hear me! and let all the people know that thou art the God of Israel, and that I am thy servant, and that I have done all these things at thy word. Hear me, Jehovah, hear me! that this people may know that thou, Jehovah, art God, and that thou hast turned their hearts back again." Then immediately the fire of Jehovah fell and consumed the bullock and the wood, even melted the very stones, and licked up the water in the trench. And when the people saw it, they fell on their faces, and cried aloud, "Jehovah, he is the God! Jehovah, he is the God!"

Elijah then commanded to take the prophets of Baal, all of them, so that not even one of them should escape. And they took them, by the direction of Elijah, down the mountain side to the brook Kishon, and slew them there. His triumph was complete. He had asserted the majesty and proved the power of Jehovah.

THE DIVISION OF THE KINGDOM.

The prophet then turned to the king, who seems to have been completely subjected by this tremendous proof of the prophetic authority, and said: "Get thee up, eat and drink, for there is the sound of abundance of rain." And Ahab ascended the hill, to eat and drink with his nobles at the sacrificial feast,— a venerable symbol by which, from the most primitive antiquity to our own day, by so universal an impulse that it would seem to be divinely imparted, every form of religion known to man has sought to typify the human desire to commune with Deity.

Elijah also went to the top of Carmel, not to the symbolic feast, but in spirit and in truth to commune with God, reverentially hiding his face between his knees. He felt the approach of the coming storm, even when the sky was clear, and not a cloud was to be seen over the blue waters of the Mediterranean. So he said to his servant: "Go up now, and look toward the sea." And the servant went to still higher ground and looked, and reported that nothing was to be seen. Six times the order was impatiently repeated and obeyed; but at the seventh time, the youthful servant — as some think, the very boy he had saved — reported a cloud in the distant horizon, no bigger seemingly than a man's hand. At once Elijah sent word to Ahab to prepare for the coming tempest; and both he and the king began to descend the hill, for the clouds rapidly gathered in the heavens, and that mighty wind arose which in Eastern countries precedes a furious storm. With incredible rapidity the tempest spread, and the king hastened for his life to his chariot at the foot of the hill, to cross the brook before it became a flood; and Elijah, remembering that he was king, ran before his chariot more rapidly than the Arab steeds. As the servant of Jehovah, he performs his mission with dignity and without fear; as a subject, he renders due respect to rank and power.

Ahab has now witnessed with his own eyes the impotency of the prophets of Baal, and the marvellous power of the messenger of Jehovah. The desire of the nation was to be gratified; the rains were falling, the cisterns and reservoirs were filling, and the fields once more would soon rejoice in their wonted beauty, and the famine would soon be at an end. In view of the great deliverance, and awe-stricken by the supernatural gifts of the prophet, one would suppose that the king would have taken Elijah to his confidence and loaded him with favors, and been guided by his counsels. But, no. He had been subjected to deep humiliation before his own people; his religion had been brought into contempt, and he was afraid of his cruel and inexorable wife, who had incited him to debasing idolatries. So he hastens to his palace in Jezreel and acquaints Jezebel of the wonderful things he had seen, and which he could not prevent. She was transported with fury and vengeance, and vowing a tremendous oath, she sent a messenger to the prophet with these terrible words: "As surely as thou art Elijah and I am Jezebel, so may God do to me and more also, if I make not thy life to-morrow, about this time, as the life of one of them." In her unbounded rage she forgot all policy, for she should have struck the blow without giving her enemy time to escape. It may also be noted that she is no atheist, but believes in God according to Phœnician notions. She reflects that eight hundred and fifty of Baal's prophets had been slain, and that the nation might return to their allegiance to the god of their fathers, who had wrought the greatest calamity her proud heart could endure. Unlike her husband, she knows no fear, and is as unscrupulous as she is fanatical. Elijah, she resolved, should surely die.

And how did the prophet receive her message? He had not feared to encounter Ahab and all the priests of Baal, yet he quailed before the wrath of this terrible woman, — this incarnate fiend, who cared neither for Jehovah nor his prophet. Even such a hero as Elijah felt that he must now flee for his life, and, attended only by his boy-servant, he did not halt until he had crossed the kingdom of Judah, and reached the utmost southern bounds of the Holy Land. At Beersheba he left his faithful attendant, and sought refuge in the desert,— the ancient wilderness of Sinai, with its rocky wastes. Under the shade of a solitary tree, exhausted and faint, he lay down to die. "It is enough, O Jehovah! now take away my life, for I am no better than my fathers." He had outstripped all pursuers, and was apparently safe, yet he wished to die. It was the reaction of a mighty excitement, the lassitude produced by a rapid and weary flight. He was physically exhausted, and with this exhaustion came despondency. He was a strong man unnerved, and his will succumbed to unspeakable weariness. He lay down and slept, and when he awoke he was fed and comforted by an angelic visitor, who commanded him to arise and penetrate still farther into the dreary wilderness. For forty days and nights he journeyed, until he reached the awful solitudes of Sinai and Horeb, and sought shelter in a cave. Enclosed between granite rocks, he entered upon a new crisis of his career.

It does not appear that the future destinies of Samaria and Jerusalem were revealed to Elijah, nor the fate of the surrounding nations, as seen by Isaiah, Jeremiah, and Daniel. He was not called to foretell the retribution which would surely be inflicted on degenerate and idolatrous nations, nor even to declare those impressive truths which should instruct all future generations. He therefore does not soar in his dreary solitude to those lofty regions of thought which marked the meditations of Moses. He is not a man of genius; he is no poet; he has no eloquence or learning; he commits no precious truths to writing for the instruction of distant generations. He is a man of intensely earnest convictions, gifted with extraordinary powers resulting from that peculiar combination of physical and spiritual qualities known as the prophetic temperament. The instruments of the Divine Will on earth are selected with unerring judgment. Elijah was sent by the Almighty to deliver special messages of reproof and correction to wicked rulers; he was a reformer. But his character was august, his person was weird and remarkable, his words were earnest and delivered with an indomitable courage, a terrific force. He was just the man to make a strong impression on a superstitious and weak king; but he had done more than that, — he had roused a whole nation from their foul debasement, and left them quaking in terror before their offended Deity.

But the phase of exaltation and potent energy had passed for the time, and we now see him faint and despondent, yet, with the sure instinct of mighty spiritual natures, seeking recuperation in solitary companionship with the all-present Spirit.

We do not know how long Elijah remained in his dismal cavern, — long enough, however, to recover his physical energies and his moral courage. As he wanders to and fro amid the hoary rocks and impenetrable solitudes of Horeb, he seeks to commune with God. He listens for some manifestation of the deity; he is ready to do His bidding. He hears the sound of a rushing hurricane; but God is not in the wind. The mountain then is shaken by a fearful earthquake; but Jehovah is not in the earthquake. Again the mountain seems to flash with fire; but the signs he seeks are not in the fire. At last, after the uproar of contending physical forces had died away, in the profound silence of the solitude he hears the whisper of a still small voice in gentle accents; and by this voice in the soul Jehovah speaks: "What doest thou here, Elijah?" Was this voice reproachful? Had the prophet been told to flee? Had he acted with the courage of a man sure of divine protection? Had he not been faint-hearted when he wished to die? How does he reply to the mysterious voice? He justifies himself. But strengthened, comforted, uplifted by the exaltation of the consciousness of God's presence, Elijah feels his resilient powers again upspringing. His courage returns; his perceptions grow sharp again; the inspiration of a new line of action opens up to him He hears the word of the Lord: "Go, return on thy way to the wilderness of Damascus; and when thou comest, anoint Hazael to be king over Syria, and Jehu the son of Nimshi to be king over Israel, and Elisha the son of Shaphat to be prophet in thy room. And it shall come to pass that him who escapeth the sword of Hazael shall Jehu destroy, and him that escapeth the sword of Jehu shall Elisha slay. Yet I have left me seven thousand in Israel, who have not bowed the knee unto Baal."

Elijah still knows that his life is in peril, but is ready, nevertheless, to obey his master's call. He is not designated as the power to effect the great revolution which should root out idolatry and destroy the house of Omri; but Jehu, an unscrupulous yet jealous warrior, was to found a new dynasty, and the king of Syria was to punish and afflict the ten tribes, and Elisha was to be the mouth-piece of the Almighty in the court of kings. It would appear that Elijah did not himself anoint either the general of Benhadad or of Ahab as future kings,—instruments of punishment on idolatrous Israel, — but on Elisha did his mantle fall.

Elisha was the son of a farmer, and, according to Ewald, when Elijah selected him for his companion and servant, had just been ploughing his twelve yoke of land (not of oxen), and was at work on the twelfth and last. Passing by the place, Elijah, without stopping, took off his shaggy mantle of skins, and cast it upon Elisha. The young man, who doubtless was familiar with the appearance of the great prophet, recognized and accepted this significant call, and without remonstrance, even as others in later days devoted themselves to a greater Prophet, "left all and followed" the one who had chosen him. He became Elijah's constant companion and pupil and ministrant, until the great man's departure. He belonged to "the sons of the prophets," among whom Elijah sojourned in his latter days, — a community of young men, for the most part poor, and compelled to combine manual labor with theological studies. Very few of these prophets seem to have been favored with especial gifts or messages from God, in the sense that Samuel and Elijah were. They were teachers and preachers rather than prophets, performing duties not dissimilar to those of Franciscan friars in the Middle Ages. They were ascetics like the monks, abstaining from wine and luxuries, as Samson and the Nazarites and Rechabites did. Religious asceticism goes back to a period that we cannot trace.

After Elijah had gone from the scenes of his earthly labors, Elisha became a man of the city, and had a house in Samaria. His dress was that of ordinary life, and he was bland in manners. His nature, unlike that of Elijah, was gentle and affectionate. He became a man of great influence, and was the friend of three kings. Jehoshaphat consulted him in war; Joram sought his advice, and Benhadad in sickness sent to him to be healed, for he exercised miraculous powers. He cured Naaman of leprosy and performed many wonderful deeds, chiefly beneficent in character.

Elisha took no part in the revolutions of the palace, but he anointed Jehu to be king over Israel, and predicted to Hazael his future elevation. His chief business was as president of a school of the prophets. His career as prophet lasted fifty-five years. He lived to a good old age, and when he died, was buried with great pomp as a man of rank, in favor with the court, for it was through him that Jehu subsequently reigned. During the life of Elijah, however, Elisha was his companion and coadjutor. More is said in Jewish history of Elisha than of Elijah, though the former was not so lofty and original a character as the latter. We are told that though Elisha inherited the mantle of his master, he received only two-thirds of his master's spirit. But he was regarded as a great prophet for over fifty years, even beyond the limits of Israel. Unlike Elijah, Elisha preferred the companionship of men rather than life in a desert. He fixed his residence in Samaria, and was highly honored and revered by all classes; he exercised a great influence on the king of Israel, and carried on the work which Elijah began. He was statesman as well as prophet, and the trusted adviser of the king; but his distinguished career did not begin till after Elijah had ascended to heaven.

After the consecration of Elisha there is nothing said about Elijah for some years, during which Ahab was involved in war with Benhadad, king of Damascus. After that unfortunate contest it would seem that Ahab had resigned himself to pleasure, and amused himself with his gardens at Jezreel. During this time Elijah had probably lived in retirement; but was again summoned to declare the judgment of God on Ahab for a most atrocious murder.

In his desire to improve his grounds Ahab cast his eyes on a fertile vineyard belonging to a distinguished and wealthy citizen named Naboth, which had been in the possession of his family even since the conquest. The king at first offered a large price for this vineyard, which he wished to convert into a garden of flowers, but Naboth refused to sell it for any price. "God forbid," said he, with religious scruples blended with the pride of ancestry, "that I should give to thee the inheritance of my fathers." Powerful and despotic as was the king, he knew he could not obtain this coveted vineyard except by gross injustice and an act of violence, which even he dared not commit. It would be an open violation of the Jewish Constitution. By

THE DIVISION OF THE KINGDOM.

the laws of Moses the lands of the Israelites, from the conquest, were inalienable. Even if they were sold for debt, after fifty years they would return to the family. The pride of ownership in real estate was one of the peculiarities of the Hebrews until after their final dispersion. After the fall of Jerusalem by Titus, personal property came to be more valued than real estate, and the Jews became the money lenders and the bankers of the world. They might be oppressed and robbed, but they could hide away their treasures. A scrap of paper, they soon discovered, was enough to transfer in safety the largest sums. A Jew had only to give a letter of credit on another Jewish house, and a king could find ready money, if he gave sufficient security, for any enterprise. Thus rare jewels pledged for gold accumulated among the Hebrew merchants at an early date.

Ahab, disappointed in not being able without a crime to get possession of Naboth's vineyard, abandoned himself to melancholy. In his deep chagrin he laid himself down on his bed, turned his face to the wall, and refused to eat. This seems strange to us, since he had more than enough, and there was no check on his ordinary pleasures. But covetous men never are satisfied. Ahab was miserable with all his possessions so long as Naboth was resolved to retain his paternal acres. It seems that it did not occur even to this unprincipled king that he could get possession of the coveted vineyard if he resorted to craft and violence.

But his clever and unscrupulous wife came to his assistance. In her active brain she devised the means of success. She saw only the end; she cared nothing for the means. It is probable, indeed, that Jezebel hankered even more than Ahab for a garden of flowers. Yet even she dared not openly seize the vineyard. Such an outrage might have caused a rebellion; it would, at least, have created a great scandal and injured her popularity, of which this artful woman was as tenacious as the Jew was of his property. Moreover, Naboth was a very influential and wealthy citizen, and had friends to support him. How could she remove the grievous eye-sore? She pondered and consulted the doctors of the law, as Henry VIII. made use of Cranmer when he wished to marry Anne Boleyn. They told her that if it could be proved that any one, however high his rank, had blasphemed God and the king, he could legally be executed, and that his property would revert to the Crown. So she suborned false witnesses, who swore at the trial of Naboth, already seized for high treason, that he had blasphemed God and the king. Sentence, according to law, was passed upon the innocent man, and according to law he was stoned to death, and the vineyard according to law became the property of the Crown. Jezebel, who had managed the whole affair, did not undertake the prosecution in her own name; as a woman, she had not the legal power. So she stole the king's ring, and sealed the indictment with the royal seal.

Thus by force and fraud under skilful technicalities, and by usurpation of the royal authority, the crime was consummated, and had the sanction of the law. Oh, what crimes have been perpetrated in every age and country under cover of the law! The Holy Inquisition was according to law; the early Christian persecutions were according to law; usurpers and murderers have reigned according to law; the Quakers were put in prison, and witches were burned according to law. Slavery was sustained by legal enactments; the rum shops are all under the protection of the law. There is scarcely a public scandal and wrong in any civilized country which the law does not somehow countenance or sustain. All public robbers appeal to legal technicalities. How could city officials steal princely revenues, how could lawyers collect exorbitant fees, if it were not for the law? Neither Ahab nor Jezebel would have ventured to seize Naboth's vineyard except under legal pretences; false witnesses swore to a lie, and the law condemned the accused. Ahab in this instance was not as bad as his wife. He may not even have known by what diabolical craft the vineyard became his.

But such crimes, striking at the root of justice, cry to heaven for vengeance. On Ahab as king rested the responsibility, and he as well as his more guilty partner was made to pay the penalty. God in his providence avenged the death of Naboth. The whole affair was widely known. As Naboth's reputed offence was unusual, and the gravest known to the Jewish laws, there was so great a sensation that a fast was proclaimed. The false trial and murderous execution were accomplished "before all the people." But this very ostentation of legal form made the outrage notorious. It reached the ears of Elijah. The prophet's keen sense of right detected such an outrageous combination of hypocrisy, covetousness, fraud, usurpation, cruelty, robbery, and murder, that he once more heard the Divine voice which summoned him from his retirement and sent him to the court with an awful message. Suddenly, unannounced and unexpected, the man of God appeared before the king in his newly acquired possession, surrounded by his gardeners and artificers, and accompanied by two of his officers, — Bidkar, and Jehu the son of Nimshi, — destined to be both instrument and witness of the retribution. With unwonted austerity, without preface or waste of words, Elijah broke forth: "Thus saith Jehovah!" — how the monarch must have quaked at this awful name: "In the place where dogs licked the blood of Naboth, shall dogs also lick thine, even thine." The conscience-stricken, affrighted monarch could only say, "Hast thou found me, oh mine enemy!" And terrible was the response: 'Yes, I have found thee! and because thou hast sold thyself to work evil in the sight of the Lord, behold, I will take away thy posterity, and will make thy house like the house of Jeroboam, who made Israel to sin. And as to thy wife also, saith Jehovah, the dogs shall eat Jezebel by the wall of Jezreel. Him that dieth of Ahab in the city shall the dogs eat, and him that dieth in the field shall the fowls of the air eat."

When and where, in the annals of the great, has such a dreadful imprecation been uttered? It was more awful than the doom pronounced on Belshazzar. The blood of Ahab and his wife was to be licked up by dogs, their dynasty to be overthrown, and their whole house destroyed. This dire punishment was inflicted probably not only on account of the crime pertaining to Naboth, but for a whole life devoted to idolatry. The sentence was not to be executed immediately, — possibly a time was given for repentance; but it would surely be inflicted at last. This Ahab knew better than any man in his kingdom. He was thrown into the depths of the most abject despair. He rent his clothes; he put ashes on his head and sackcloth on his flesh, and refused to eat or drink. He repented after the fashion of criminals, and humbled himself.

as Nebuchadnezzar did, before the Most High God. God in mercy delayed, but did not annul, the punishment. Ahab lived long enough to fight the king of Syria successfully, so that for three years there was peace in Israel. But Ramoth in Gilead, belonging to the northern kingdom, remained in the hands of the Syrians.

In the mean time Jehoshaphat, king of Judah, whose son Jehoram had married Athaliah, daughter of Ahab, and who was therefore in friendly social and political relations with Ahab, came to visit him. They naturally talked about the war, and lamented the fall of Ramoth-Gilead. Ahab proposed a united expedition to recover it, to which Jehoshaphat was consenting; but before embarking in an offensive war against a powerful state, the two monarchs consulted the prophets. It is not to be supposed that they were the priests of Baal, but ordinary prophets who wished to please. False prophets and false friends are very much alike,— they give advice according to the inclinations and wishes of those who consult them. They are afraid of incurring displeasure, knowing well that no one likes to have his plans opposed by candid advisers. Therefore they all gave their voices for war, foretelling a grand success. But one prophet, more honest and bold — perhaps more gifted — than the rest, Micaiah by name, took a different view of the matter. He was constrained to speak his honest convictions, and prophesied evil, and was thrown into prison for his honesty and boldness.

Nevertheless Ahab in his heart was afraid, and had sad forebodings. Knowing his peril, and alarmed at the words of a true prophet, he disguised himself for the battle; but a chance arrow, shot at a venture, penetrated through the joints of his armor, and he was mortally wounded. His blood ran from his wound into the chariot, and when the chariot was washed in the pool of Samaria, after Ahab had expired, the dogs licked up his blood, as Elijah had predicted.

The death of Ahab put an end to the fighting; nor was Jehoshaphat injured, although he wore his royal robes. The Syrian general had given orders to slay only the king of Israel. At one time, however, the king of Judah was in great peril, being mistaken for Ahab; but when his pursuers discovered their mistake, they turned from the pursuit.

It seems that Jezebel survived her husband fourteen years, and virtually ruled the kingdom, for she was a woman of ability. She exercised the same influence over her son Ahaziah that she had over her husband, so that the son like the father served Baal and made Israel to sin.

To this young king was Elijah also sent. Ahaziah had been seriously injured by an accidental fall from his upper chamber, through the lattice, to the court yard below. He sent to the priests of Baal, to inquire whether he should recover or not. But Elijah by command of God had intercepted the king's messengers, and suddenly appearing before them, as was his custom, confronted them with these words: "Is there no God in Israel, that ye go to inquire of Baalzebub, the God of Ekron? Now, therefore, say unto the king, Thou shalt not come down from the bed on which thou art gone up, but shalt surely die." On their return to Ahaziah, without delivering their message to the god of the Phœnicians or Philistines, the king said: "Why are ye now turned back?" They repeated the words of the strange man who had turned them back; and the king said: "What manner of man was he who came up to meet you?" They answered, "He was a hairy man, and girt with a girdle of leather around his loins." The king cried, "It is Elijah the Tishbite." Again his enemy had found him!

Whereupon Ahaziah sent a band of fifty chosen soldiers to arrest the prophet, who had retired to the top of a steep and rugged hill, probably Carmel. The captain of the troop approached, and commanded him in the name of the king to come down, addressing him as the man of God. "If I am a man of God," said Elijah, "let fire come down from heaven and consume thee and thy fifty." The fire came down and consumed them. Again the king sent another band of fifty with their captain, who met with the same fate. Again the king sent another band of fifty men, the captain of which came and fell on his knees before Elijah and besought him, saying, "O man of God! I pray thee let my life and the lives of these fifty thy servants be precious in thy sight." And the angel of the Lord said unto Elijah, "Go down with him; be not afraid of him." And he arose and went with the soldiers to the king, repeating to him the words he had sent before, that he should not recover, but should surely die.

So Ahaziah died, as Elijah prophesied, and Jehoram (or Joram) reigned in his stead, — a brother of the late king, who did not personally worship Baal, but who allowed the queen-mother to continue to protect idolatry. The war which had been begun by Ahab against the Syrians still continued, to recover Ramoth-Gilead, and the stronghold was finally taken by the united efforts of Judah and Israel; but Joram was wounded, and returned to Jezreel to be cured.

With the advent of Elijah a reaction against idolatry had set in. The people were awed by his terrible power, and also by the influence of Elisha, on whom his mantle fell. It does not appear that the people had utterly abandoned the religion of their fathers, for they had not hesitated to slay the eight hundred and fifty priests of Baal at the command of Elijah. The introduction of idolatry had been the work of princes, chiefly through the influence of Jezebel; and as the establishment of a false religion still continued to be the policy of the court, the prophets now favored the revolution which should overturn the house of Ahab, and exterminate it root and branch. The instrument of the Almighty who was selected for this work was Jehu, one of the prominent generals of the army; and his task was made comparatively easy from the popular disaffection. That a woman, a foreigner, a pagan, and a female demon should control the government during two reigns was intolerable. Only a spark was needed to kindle a general revolt, and restore the religion of Jehovah.

This was the appearance of a young prophet at Ramoth-Gilead, whom Elisha had sent with an important message. Forcing his way to the house where Jehu and his brother officers were sitting in council, he called Jehu apart, led him to an innermost chamber of the house, took out a small horn of sacred oil, and poured it on Jehu's head, telling him that God had anointed him king to cut off the whole house of Ahab, and destroy idolatry. On his return to the room where the generals were sitting, Jehu communicated to them the message he had received. As the discontent of the nation had spread to the army, it was regarded as a favorable time to revolt from Joram, who lay sick at Jezreel. The army, following the chief officers, at once hailed Jehu as king. It was supremely necessary that no time should be lost, and that the news of the rebellion should not reach the king until Jehu himself should appear with a portion of the army. Jehu was just the man for such an occasion, — rapid in his movements, unscrupulous, yet zealous to uphold the law of Moses. So mounting his chariot, and taking with him a detachment of his most reliable troops, he furiously drove toward Jezreel, turning everybody back on the road. It was a drive of about fifty miles. When within six miles of Jezreel the sentinels on the towers of the walls noticed an unusual cloud of dust, and a rider was at once despatched to know the meaning of the approach of chariots and horses. The rider, as he approached, was ordered to fall back in the rear of Jehu's force. Another rider was sent, with the same result. But Joram, discovering that the one who drove so rapidly must be his own impetuous captain of the host, and suspecting no treachery from him, ordered out his own chariot to meet Jehu, accompanied by his uncle Ahaziah, king of Judah. He expected stirring news from the army, and was eager to learn it. He supposed that Hazael, then king of Damascus, who had murdered Benhadad, had proposed peace. So as he approached Jehu — the frightful irony of fate halting him for the interview in the very vineyard of Naboth — he cried out, "Is it peace, Jehu?" "Peace!"

replied Jehu; "what peace can be made so long as Jezebel bears rule?" In an instant the king understood the ominous words of his general, turned back his chariot, and fled toward his palace, crying, "There is treachery, O Ahaziah!" An arrow from Jehu pierced the monarch in the back, and he sank dead in his chariot. Ahaziah also was mortally wounded by another arrow from Jehu, but he succeeded in reaching Megiddo, where he died. Jehu spoke to Bidkar, his captain, and recalling the dread prophecy of Elijah, commanded the body of Ahab's son to be cast out into the dearly-bought field of Naboth.

In the mean time, Jezebel from her palace window at Jezreel had seen the murder of her son. She was then sixty years of age. The first thing she did was to paint her eyelids, and put on her most attractive apparel, to appear as beautiful as possible, with the hope doubtless of attracting Jehu, — as Cleopatra, after the death of Antony, sought to win Augustus. Will a flattered woman, once beautiful, ever admit that her charms have passed away? But if the painted and bedizened queen anticipated her fate, she determined to die as she had lived, — without fear, imperious, and disdainful. So from her open window she tauntingly accosted Jehu as he approached: "What came of Zimri, who murdered his master as thou hast done?" "Are there any on my side?" was the only reply he deigned to make, as he looked up to a window of the palace, which was a part of the wall of the city. Two or three eunuchs, looking out from behind her, answered the summons, for the wicked and haughty queen had no real friends. "Throw her down!" ordered Jehu; and in a moment the blood from her mangled body splashed upon the walls and upon the horses. In another instant the wheels of the chariot passed over her lifeless remains. Jehu would have permitted a decent burial, "for," said he, "she is a king's daughter;" but before her mangled corpse could be collected, in the general confusion, the dogs of the city had devoured all that remained of her but the skull, the feet, and hands.

So perished the most infamous woman that ever wore a royal diadem, as had been predicted. With her also perished the seventy sons of Ahab, all indeed that survived of the royal house of Omri. And the work of destruction did not end until the courtiers of the late king and all connected with them, even the palace priests, were killed. Then followed the massacre of the other priests of Baal, the destruction of the idolatrous temples, and the restoration of the worship of Jehovah, not only at Samaria, but at Jerusalem, for the revolution extended far and wide on the death of Ahaziah as of Joram. Athaliah the daughter of Jezebel, who reigned over Judah, also perished in those revolutionary times.

It is not to be supposed that the relentless and savage Jehu was altogether moved by a zeal for Jehovah in these revolting slaughters. He was an ambitious and successful rebel; but like all notable forces, he may be regarded as an instrument of Providence, whose ways are "mysterious," because men are not large enough and wise enough to trace effects to their causes under His immutable laws. Jehu was a necessary consequence of Ahab and Jezebel. Jehovah, as the national deity of the Jews, was the natural and necessary rallying cry of the revolt against Phœnician idolatry and foulness. The missionary sermons of those crude days were preached with the sword and the strong arm. God's revelations of himself and his purposes to man have always been through men, and by His laws the medium always colors the light which it transmits. The splendor of the noonday sun cannot shine clearly through rough, imperfect glass; and so the conceptions of Deity and of the divine will, as delivered by the prophets, in every case show the nature of the man receiving and delivering the inspired message. And yet, through all the turmoil of those times, and the startling contrast between the conceptions presented by the "Jehovah" of Elijah and the "Father" of Jesus, the one grand central truth which the seed of Abraham were chosen to conserve stands out distinctly from first to last, — the unity and purity of God. However obscured by human passions and interests, that principle always retained a vital hold upon some — if only a "remnant" — of the Hebrew race.

The influence of Elijah, then, acting personally through him and his successor Elisha, had caused the extermination of the worship of Baal. But the golden calves still remained; and there was no improvement in the political affairs of the kingdom. It was steadily declining as a political power, whether on account of the degeneracy which succeeded prosperity, or the warlike enterprises of the empires and states which were hostile equally to Judah and Israel. Jehu was forced to pay tribute to Assyria to secure protection against Syria; and after his death Israel was reduced to the lowest depression by Hazael, and had not the power of Syria soon after been broken by Assyria, the northern kingdom would have been utterly destroyed.

It was not given to Elijah to foresee the future calamities of the Jews, or to declare them, as Isaiah and Jeremiah did. It was his mission, and also Elisha's, to destroy the worship of Baal and punish the apostate kings who had introduced it. He was the messenger and instrument of Jehovah to remove idolatry, not to predict the future destiny of his nation. He is to be viewed, like Elisha, as a reformer, as a man of action, armed with supernatural gifts to awe kings and influence the people, rather than as a seer or a poet, or even as a writer to instruct future generations. His mission seems to have ended shortly after he had thrown his mantle on a man more accomplished than himself in knowledge of the world. But his last days are associated with unspeakable grandeur as well as pathetic interest.

Elijah seems to have known that the day of his departure was at hand. So, departing from Gilgal in company with his beloved companion, he proceeded toward Bethel. As he approached the city he besought Elisha to leave him alone; but Elisha refused to part with the master whom he both loved and revered. Onward they proceeded from Bethel to Jericho, and from Jericho to the Jordan. It was a mournful journey to Elisha, for he knew as well as the sons of the prophets at Jericho that he and his master, and friend more than master, were to part for the last time on earth. The waters of the Jordan happened to be swollen, and the two prophets, and the fifty sons of the prophets — their pupils, who came to say farewell — could not pass over. But the sacred narrative tells us that Elijah, wrapping his mantle together like a staff, smote the waters, so that they were divided, and the two passed over to the eastern bank, in view of the disciples. In loving intercourse Elijah promises to give to his companion as token of his love whatever Elisha may

THE DIVISION OF THE KINGDOM.

choose. Elisha asks simply for a double portion of his master's spirit, which Elijah grants in case Elisha shall see him distinctly when taken away.

"And it came to pass, as they still went on and talked, that behold there appeared a chariot of fire and horses of fire, which parted them both asunder. And Elijah went up by a whirlwind into heaven. And Elisha saw it, and he cried 'My father, my father! the chariot of Israel, and the horsemen thereof!'" — Thou art the chariot of Israel; thou hast been its horsemen! And then there fell from Elijah, as he vanished from human sight, the mantle by which he had been so well known; and it became the sign of that fulness of divine favor which was given to his successor in his arduous labors to restore the worship of Jehovah, "and to prepare the way for Him in whom all prophecy is fulfilled."

ISAIAH.

PROPHESIED 740–701 B. C.

NATIONAL DEGENERACY.

ISAIAH.

ISAIAH.

NATIONAL DEGENERACY.

TO understand the mission of Isaiah, one should be familiar with the history of the kingdom of Judah from the time of Jeroboam, founder of the separate kingdom of Israel, to that of Uzziah, in whose reign Isaiah was born, 760 B. C.

Judah had doubtless degenerated in virtue and spiritual life, but this degeneracy was not so marked as that of the northern kingdom, — called Israel. Judah had been favored by a succession of kings, most of whom were able and good men. Out of nine kings, five of them "did right in the sight of the Lord;" and during the two hundred and sixteen years when these monarchs reigned, one hundred and eighty-seven were years when the worship of Jehovah was maintained by virtuous princes, all of whom were of the house of David. The reigns of those kings who did evil in the sight of the Lord were short.

During this period there were nineteen kings of Israel, most of whom did evil. They introduced idolatry; many of them were usurpers, and died violent deaths If the northern kingdom was larger and more fertile than the southern, it was more afflicted with disastrous wars and divine judgments for the sins into which it had fallen. It was to the wicked kings of Israel, throned in the Samarian Shechem, that Elijah and Elisha were sent; and the interest we feel in their reigns is chiefly directed to the acts and sayings of those two great prophets.

The kingdom of Judah, blessed on the whole with virtuous rulers, and comparatively free from idolatry, continually increased in wealth and political power. Rehoboam, the son of Solomon, after the rebellion of the ten tribes, seems to have changed somewhat his course of life, although the high places and graven images were not removed; but his grandson Asa destroyed the idols, and made fortunate alliances. Asa's son Jehoshaphat terminated the civil wars that had raged between Judah and Israel from the accession of Rehoboam, and almost rivalled Solomon in his outward prosperity. Jerusalem became the strongest fortress in western Asia; the Temple service was continued in its former splendor; all that was vital in the strength of nations pertained to the smaller kingdom. The dark spot in the history of Judah for nearly two hundred years was the ascendency gained by Athaliah, the daughter of Jezebel, over her husband Jehoram, who introduced the gods of Phœnicia. She seems to have exercised the same malign influence in Jerusalem that Jezebel did in Samaria, and was as unscrupulous as her pagan mother. She even succeeded in usurping the throne, and in destroying the whole race of David, with the exception of Joash, an infant, whom Jehoiada the high-priest contrived to hide until the unscrupulous Athaliah was slain, having reigned as queen six years,— the first instance in Jewish history of a female sovereign.

Both Judah and Israel in these years had the danger of a Syrian war constantly threatening them. Under Hazael, who reigned at Damascus, great conquests were made by the Syrians of Jewish territory, and the capture of Jerusalem was averted only by buying off the enemy, to whom were surrendered the gifts to the Temple accumulating since the days of Jehoshaphat. The whole land was overrun and pillaged. Nor were calamities confined to the miseries of war. A long drouth burned the fields; seed rotted under the clods; the cattle moaned in the barren and dried-up pastures; while locusts devoured what the drouth had spared. Says Stanley: "The purple vine, the green fig-tree, the gray olive, the scarlet pomegranate, the golden corn, the waving palm, the fragrant citron, vanished before them, and the trunks and branches were left bare and white by their devouring teeth," — a brilliant sentence, by the way, which Geikie quotes without acknowledgment, as well as many others, which lays him open to the charge of plagiarism. Both Stanley and Geikie, however, seem to be indebted to Ewald for all that is striking and original in their histories, — so true is Solomon's saying that there is nothing new under the sun. The rarest thing in literature is a truly original history.

In this mournful crisis the prophet Joel, who was a priest at Jerusalem, demanded a solemn fast, which the entire kingdom devoutly celebrated, the whole body of the priests crying aloud before the gates of the Temple, "Spare Thy people, O Lord! give not Thine heritage to reproach, lest the heathen make us a by-word, and ask, Where is now thy God?" But Joel, the oldest, and in many respects the most eloquent, Hebrew prophet whose utterances have come down to us, did not speak in vain, and a great religious revival followed, attended naturally by renewed prosperity, — for among the Jews a "revival of religion" meant a practical return from vice to virtue, personal holiness, and the just and wholesome requirements of their law; so that "under Amaziah, Uzziah, and Jotham, Judah rose once more to a pitch of honor and glory which almost recalled the golden age of David."

A greater power than that of Syria threatened the peace and welfare of the kingdom of Judah, as it also did that of Israel; and this was the empire of Assyria. During the reigns of David and Solomon this empire was passing through so many disasters that it was not regarded as dangerous, and both of the Jewish kingdoms were left free to avail themselves of every facility afforded for national development. Ewald notices emphatically this outward prosperity, which introduced luxury and pride throughout the kingdom. It was the golden age of merchants, usurers, and money-mongers. Then appeared that extraordinary greed for riches which never afterward left the nation, even in seasons of calamity, and which is the most striking peculiarity of the modern Hebrew. This was a period not only of prosperity and luxury, but of vanity and ostentation, especially among women. The insidious influences of wealth more than balanced the good effected by a long succession of virtuous and gifted princes. I read of no country that, on the whole, was ever favored by a more remarkable constellation of absolute kings than that of Judah. Most of them had long reigns, took prophets and wise men for their counsellors, developed the resources of their kingdoms, strengthened Jerusalem, avoided entangling wars, and enjoyed the love and veneration of the people. Most of them, unlike the kings of Israel, were true to their exalted mission, were loyal to Jehovah, and discouraged idolatry, if they did not root out the scandal by persecuting violence. Some of these kings were poets, and others were saints, like their great ancestor David; and yet, in spite of all their efforts, corruption and infidelity gained ground, and ultimately undermined the state and prepared the way for Babylonian conquests. Though Jerusalem survived the fall of Samaria for nearly five generations, divine judgment was delayed, but not withdrawn. The chastisement was sent at last at the hands of warriors whom no nation could successfully resist.

The old enemies who had in the early days overwhelmed the Hebrews with calamities under the Judges had been conquered by Saul and David, — the Moabites, the Edomites, the Hittites, the Jebusites, and the Philistines, — and they never afterward seriously menaced the kingdom, although there were occasional wars. But in the eighth century before Christ the Assyrian empire, whose capital was Nineveh, had become very formidable under warlike sovereigns, who aimed to extend their dominion to the Mediterranean and to Egypt. In the reign of Jehoash, the son of Athaliah, an Assyrian monarch had exacted tribute from Tyre and Sidon, and Syria was overrun. When Pul, or Tiglath-pileser, seized the throne of Nineveh, he pushed his conquests to the Caspian Sea on the north

NATIONAL DEGENERACY.

and the Indus on the east, to the frontier of Egypt and the deserts of Sinai on the west and south. In 739 B. C. he appeared in Syria to break up a confederation which Uzziah of Judah had formed to resist him, and succeeded in destroying the power of Syria, and carrying its people as captives to Assyria. Menahem, king of Samaria, submitted to the enormous tribute of one thousand talents of silver. In 733 B. C. this great conqueror again invaded Syria, beheaded Rezin its king, took Damascus, reduced five hundred and eighteen cities and towns to ashes, and carried back to Nineveh an immense spoil. In 728 B. C. Shalmanezer IV. appeared in Palestine, and invested Samaria. The city made an heroic defence; but after a siege of three years it yielded to Sargon, who carried away into captivity the ten tribes of Israel, from which they never returned.

Judah survived by reason of its greater military skill and its strong fortresses, with which Asa, Jehoshaphat, and Uzziah had fortified the country, especially Jerusalem. But the fate of western Asia was sealed when Rezin of Damascus, Menahem of Samaria, Hiram of Tyre, and the king of Hamath moodily consented to pay tribute to the king of Assyria; the downfall of the sturdy Judah was in preparation.

Greater evils than those of war threatened the stability of the state. In Judah as in Ephraim drunkenness was a national vice, and the nobles abandoned themselves to disgraceful debauchery. There was a general demoralization of the people more fearful in its consequences than even idolatry. Judah was no exception to the ordinary fate of nations; the everlasting sequence — pertaining to institutions as well as nations, to religious as well as merely political communities — was here seen, — " Inwardness, outwardness, worldliness, and rottenness."

It was in this state of political danger and a general decline in morals, with a tendency to idolatry, that Isaiah — preacher, statesman, historian, poet, and prophet — was born.

Less is said of the personal history of this great man than of Moses or David, of Daniel or Elisha, and it is only in his writings that we see the solemn grandeur of his character. We infer that he was allied with the royal family of David; he certainly held a high position in the courts of Jotham, Ahaz, and Hezekiah. He was a man of great dignity, experience, and wisdom, but ascetic in his habits and dress. Although he associated with the great in courts and palaces, a cell was his delight. He was a retiring, contemplative, rapt, austere man, severe on passing follies, and not sparing in his rebukes of sin in high places, — something like Savonarola at Florence, both as preacher and prophet, — and exercising a commanding influence on political affairs and on the people directly, especially during the reigns of Ahaz and Hezekiah. He denounced woes and calamities, yet escaped persecution from the grandeur of his character and the importance of his utterances. He was a favorite of King Hezekiah, and was contemporary with the prophets Hosea, Amos, and Jonah. He lived in Jerusalem, not far from the Temple, and had a wife and two sons. He wrote the life of Uzziah, and died at the age of eighty-four, in the reign of Manasseh. It is generally supposed that although Isaiah had lived in honor during the reigns of four kings, he suffered martyrdom at last. It is the fate of prophets to be stoned when they are in antagonism with men in power, or with popular sentiments. His prophetic ministry extended over a period of about fifty years, and he was continually consulted by the reigning monarchs.

The great outward events that took place during Isaiah's public career were the invasion of Judah by the combined forces of Israel and Syria in the reign of Ahaz, and the great Assyrian invasion in the reign of Hezekiah.

In regard to the first, it was disastrous to Judah. The weak king, the twelfth from David, was inclined to the idolatries of the surrounding nations, but was not signally bad like Ahab. Yet he was no match for Pekah, who reigned at Samaria, or for Rezin, who reigned at Damascus. Their combined armies slew in one day one hundred and twenty thousand of the subjects of Ahaz, and carried away into captivity two hundred thousand women and children, with immense spoil. The conqueror then advanced to the siege of Jerusalem. In his distress Ahaz invoked the aid of Pul, or Tiglath-pileser II., one of the most warlike of the Assyrian kings, whose kingdom stretched from the Armenian mountains on the north to Bagdad on the south, and from the Zagros chain on the east to the Euphrates on the west. Earnestly did the prophet-statesman expostulate with Ahaz, telling him that the king of Assyria would prove "a razor to shave but too clean his desolate land." The inspired advice was rejected; and the result of the alliance was that Judah, like Israel, fell to the rank of a subject nation, and became tributary to Assyria, and Ahaz, a mere vassal of Tiglath-pileser. The whole of Palestine became the border-land of the Assyrian empire, easy to be invaded and liable to be conquered.

The consequences which Isaiah feared, took place in the time of Hezekiah, in the actual invasion of Judah by the Assyrian hosts under Sennacherib. Not the splendid prosperity of Hezekiah, little short of that enjoyed by Solomon, — not his allegiance to Jehovah, nor his grand reforms and magnificent feasts averted the calamities which were the legitimate result of the blindness of his father Ahaz. Sennacherib, the most powerful of all the Assyrian kings, after suppressing a revolt in Babylon and conquering various Eastern states, turned his eyes and steps to Palestine, which had revolted. Hezekiah, in mortal fear, made humble submission, and consented to a tribute of three hundred talents of silver and thirty of gold, and the loss of two hundred thousand of his people as captives, and a cession of a part of his territory, — as great a calamity as France suffered in the war (1870–71) with Prussia. Considering the prosperity of the kingdom of Judah under Hezekiah, it is a difficult thing to be explained that the king could raise but three hundred talents of silver and thirty of gold, although David had contributed out of his private fortune, for the future erection of the Temple, three thousand talents of gold and seven thousand talents of silver, besides the one million talents of silver and one hundred thousand talents of gold which he collected as sovereign. It would seem probable that an error has crept into the estimates of the wealth of the kingdom under Solomon and under the subsequent kings; either that of Solomon is exaggerated, or that of Hezekiah is underrated.

Notwithstanding his former defeat and losses, Hezekiah again revolted, and again was Judah invaded by a still greater Assyrian force. The king of Judah in this emergency showed extraordinary energy, stopped the supply of water outside his capital, strengthened his defences, gathered together his fighting men, and encouraged them with the assurance that help would come from the Lord, in whom they trusted, and whom Sennacherib boastfully defied. For the ringing words of Isaiah roused and animated the hearts of both king and people to a noble courage, announcing the aid of Jehovah and the overthrow of the heathen invader. As we have seen, the men of Judah showed their faith in the divine help by preparing to help themselves. But from an unexpected quarter the asssistance came, as Isaiah had predicted. A pestilence destroyed in a single night one hundred and eighty-five thousand of the Assyrian warriors,— the most signal overthrow of the enemies of Israel since Pharaoh and his host were swallowed up by the waters of the Red Sea, and also the most signal deliverance which Jerusalem ever had. The calamity created such a fearful demoralization among the invaders that the over-confident Assyrian monarch retired to his capital with utter loss of prestige, and soon after was assassinated by his own sons. No Assyrian king after this invaded Judah, and Nineveh itself in a few years was conquered by Babylon.

The fall of Jerusalem at the hands of the Babylonians was delayed one hundred years. But such were the moral and social evils of the times succeeding the Ninevite invasion that Isaiah saw that retribution would come sooner or later, unless the nation repented and a radical reform should take place. He saw the people stricken with judicial blindness; so he clothed himself in sackcloth and cried aloud, with fervid eloquence, upon the people to repent. He is now the popular preacher, and his theme is repentance. In his earnest exhortations he foreshadows John the Baptist: "Unless ye repent, ye shall all likewise perish." It would seem that Savonarola makes him the model of his own eloquence. "Thy crimes, O Florence! thy crimes, O Rome! thy crimes, O Italy! are the causes of these chastisements. O Rome! thou shalt be put to the sword, since thou wilt not be converted! O harlot Church! I will stretch forth mine hand upon thee, saith the Lord." The burden of the soul of the Florentine monk is sin, especially sin in high places. He sees only degeneracy in life, and alarms the people by threats of divine vengeance. So Isaiah cries aloud upon the people to seek the Lord while he may be found. He does not invoke divine wrath, as David did upon his enemies; but he shows that this wrath will surely overtake the sinner. In no respect does he glory in this retribution: he is sad; he is oppressed; he is filled with grief, especially in view of the prevailing infatuation. "My people," said he, "do not consider." He denounces all classes alike, and spares not even women. In sarcastic language he rebukes their love of dress, their abandonment to vanities, their finery, their very gait and mincing attitude. Still more contemptuously does the preacher speak of the men, over whom the women rule and children oppress. He is severe on corrupt judges, on usurers; on all who are conceited in their own eyes; on those who are mighty to drink wine; on those who join house to house and field to field; on those whose glorious beauty is a fading flower; on those who call good evil and evil good, that put darkness for light, that take away the righteousness of the righteous from him. His terrible denunciation and enumeration of evil indicate a very lax morality in every quarter, added to hypocrisy and pharisaism. He shows what a poor thing is sacrifice unaccompanied with virtue. "To what purpose," said he, "is the multitude of sacrifices? Bring no more vain oblations. Incense is an abomination to me, saith the Lord. Therefore wash you, make you clean, put away the evil of your doings; cease to do evil, learn to do well; seek judgment, relieve the oppressed, judge the fatherless, plead for the widow." Isaiah does not preach dogmas, still less metaphysical distinctions; he preaches against sin and demands repentance, and predicts calamity.

There are two points in his preaching which stand

out with great vividness, — the certain judgments of God in view of sin, retribution on all offenders; and secondly, the mercy and forgiveness of God in case of repentance. Retribution, however, is not in Isaiah usually presented as the penalty of transgression according to natural law; not, as in the Proverbs, as the inevitable sequence of sin, — "Whatsoever ye sow, that shall ye also reap," — but as direct punishment from God. Jehovah's awful personality is everywhere recognized, — a being who rules the universe as "the living God," who loves and abhors, who punishes and rewards, who gives power to the faint, who judges among the nations, who takes away from Judah and Jerusalem the stay and the staff of bread and water. "To whom then will ye liken God? Have ye not known, have ye not heard, hath it not been told you from the beginning? It is He that sitteth upon the circle of the earth, and the inhabitants thereof are as grasshoppers; that stretcheth out the heavens as a curtain, that bringeth the princes to nothing. Hast thou not known, hast thou not heard, that the everlasting God, the Lord, the Creator of the ends of the earth, fainteth not, neither is weary? He giveth power to the faint and weary, so that they who wait upon Him shall renew their strength, mount up with wings as eagles, run and not be weary, walk and not faint." Can stronger or more comforting language be made use of to assert the personality and providence of God? And where in the whole circuit of Hebrew poetry is there more sublimity of language, greater eloquence, or more profound conviction of the evil and punishment of sin? Isaiah, the greatest of all the prophets in his spiritual discernment, in his profound insight of the future, is not behind the author of Job in majestic and sublime description.

Whatever may be the severity of language with which Isaiah denounces sin, and awful the judgments he pronounces in view of it, as coming directly from God, yet he seldom closes one of his dreadful sentences without holding out the hope of divine forgiveness in case of repentance, and the peace and comfort which will follow. In his view the mercy of the Lord is more impressive than his judgments. Isaiah is anything but a prophet of wrath; his soul overflows with tender sentiments and loving exhortation. "Ho, every one that thirsteth, come to the waters! Come ye, buy and eat! Yea, come, buy wine and milk without money and without price! . . . Let the wicked forsake his way, and the unrighteous man his thoughts, and let him return unto the Lord, and he will have mercy upon him, and to our God, for he will abundantly pardon. . . . Behold, the Lord's hand is not shortened that it cannot save; neither his ear heavy that it cannot hear. . . . Though your sins be as scarlet, they shall be white as snow; though they be red like crimson, they shall be as wool."

According to modern standards, we are struck with the absence of what we call art, in the writings of Isaiah. History, woes, promises, hopes, aspirations, and exultations are all mingled together in scarcely logical sequence. He exhorts, he threatens, he reproaches, he promises, often in the same chapter. The transition between preacher and prophet is very sudden. But it is as prophet that Isaiah is most frequently spoken of; and he is the prophet of hope and consolation, although he denounces woes upon the nations of the earth. In his prophetic office he predicts the future of all the people known to the Hebrews. He does not preach to *them:* they do not hear his voice; they do not know what tribulations shall be sent upon them. He commits his prophecies to writing for the benefit of future ages, in which he gives reasons for the judgments to be sent upon wicked nations, so that the great principles seen in the moral government of God may remain of perpetual significance. These principles centre around the great truth that national wickedness will certainly be followed by national calamities, which is also one of the most impressive truths that all history teaches; and so uniform is the operation of this great law that it is safe to make deductions from it for the guidance of statesmen and the teachings of moralists. National effeminacy which follows luxury, great injustices which cry to heaven for vengeance, and practical atheism and idolatry are certain to call forth divine judgments, — sometimes in the form of destructive wars, sometimes in pestilence and famine, and at other times in the gradual wasting away of national resources and political power. In conformity with this settled law in the moral government of God, we read the fate of Nineveh, of Babylon, of Tyre, of Jerusalem, of Carthage, of Antioch, of Corinth, of Athens, of Rome; and I would even add of Venice, of Turkey, of Spain. Nor is there anything which can save modern cities and countries, however magnificent their civilization, from a like visitation of Almighty power, if they continue in the iniquity which all the world perceives, and sometimes deplores. It must have seemed as absurd to the readers of Isaiah's predictions twenty-five hundred years ago that Babylon and Tyre should fall, as it would to the people of our day should one predict the future ruin of Paris or London or New York, if the vices which now flourish in these cities should reach an overwhelming preponderance, but which we hope may be wholly overcome by the influence of Christianity and the spirit and interference of God himself; for He governs the world by the same principles that He did two thousand years ago, — a fact which seldom is ignored by any profound and religious inquirer.

I have no faith in the permanence of any form of civilization, or of any government, where a certain depth of infamy and depravity is reached; because the impressive lesson of history is that righteousness exalteth a nation, and iniquity brings it low. Isaiah predicted woes which came to pass, since the cities and peoples against whom he denounced them remained obstinately perverse in their iniquity and atheism. Their doom was certain, without that repentance which would lead to a radical change of life and opinions. He held out no hope unless they turned to the Lord; nor did any of the prophets. Jeremiah was sad because he knew they would not repent, even as Christ himself wept over Jerusalem. No maledictions came from the pen or voice of Isaiah such as David breathed against his enemies, only the expression of the sad and solemn conviction that unless the people and the nation repented, they would all equally and surely perish, in accordance with the stern laws written on the two tables of Moses,—for "I, thy God, am a jealous God, visiting the iniquities of the fathers upon the children, even to the third and fourth generation;"—yea, written before Moses, and to be read unto this day in the very constitution of man, physical, mental, spiritual, and social.

The prophet first announces the calamities which both Judah and Ephraim — the southern and the northern kingdoms — shall suffer from Assyrian invasions. "The Lord shall shave Judah with a razor, not only the head, but the beard,"— thus declaring that the land would be not only depopulated, but become a desert, and that men should no longer live by agriculture, or by trade and commerce, but by grazing alone. "Woe to the crown of pride, to the drunkards of Ephraim, whose glorious beauty is a fading flower; it shall be trodden under foot." The sins of pride and drunkenness are especially enumerated as the cause of their chastisement. "Woe to Ariel [that is Jerusalem]! I will camp against thee round about, and lay siege against thee with a mount, and I will raise forts against thee, and thou shalt be brought down. . . . Forasmuch as this people draw near me with their mouth, and with lips do they honor me, but have removed their heart far from me," — hereby showing that hypocrisy at Jerusalem was as prevalent as drunkenness in Samaria, and as difficult to be removed.

Isaiah also reproves Judah for relying on the aid of Egypt in the threatened Assyrian invasion, instead of putting confidence in God, but declares that the evil day will be deferred in case that Judah repents; however, he holds out no hope that her people may escape the final captivity to Babylon. All that the prophet predicted in reference to the desolation of Palestine by Syrians, Assyrians, and Babylonians, as instruments of punishment, came to pass.

From the calamities which both Judah and Israel should suffer for their pride, hypocrisy, drunkenness, and idolatry, Isaiah turns to predict the fall of other nations. "Wherefore it shall come to pass that when the Lord hath performed his whole work upon Jerusalem, I will punish the fruit of the stout heart of the king of Assyria, and the glory of his high looks. . . . For he saith, By the strength of my hand I have done it, and by my wisdom; for I am prudent, and I have removed the bounds of the people, and have robbed their treasures, and put down the inhabitants like a valiant man: and as I have gathered all the earth, as one gathereth eggs, therefore shall the Lord of Hosts send among his fat ones leanness, and under his glory He shall kindle a burning like the burning of a fire." In the inscriptions which have recently been deciphered on the broken and decayed monuments of Nineveh nothing is more remarkable than the boastful spirit, pride, and arrogance of the Assyrian kings and conquerors.

The fall of still prouder Babylon is next predicted. "Since thou hast said in thine heart, I will ascend into heaven, I will exalt my throne above the stars of God, thou shalt be brought down to hell. . . . Babylon, the glory of kingdoms, the beauty of the Chaldean excellency, shall be as when God overthrew Sodom and Gomorrah. It shall never be inhabited, neither shall it be dwelt in from generation to generation; neither shall the Arabians pitch tent there, neither shall the shepherds make their fold there; but wild beasts of the deserts shall lie there, and the owls shall dwell there, and satyrs shall dance there." Both Nineveh and Babylon arose to glory and power by unscrupulous conquests, for their kings and people were military in their tastes and habits; and with dominion cruelly and wickedly obtained came arrogance and pride unbounded, and with these luxury and sensuality. The wickedest city of antiquity meets with the most terrible punishment that is recorded of any city in the world's history. Not only were pride and cruelty the peculiar vices of its kings and princes, but a gross and degrading idolatry, allied with all the vices that we call infamous, marked the inhabitants of the doomed capital; so that the Hebrew language was exhausted to find a word sufficiently expressive to mark its foul depravity, or sufficiently exultant to rejoice over its predicted fall. Most cities have recovered more or less from their calamities, — Jerusalem, Athens, Rome, — but Babylon was utterly destroyed, as by fire from heaven, and never has been rebuilt or again inhabited, except by wild beasts. Its very ruins, the remains of walls three hundred and fifty feet in height, and of hanging gardens, and of palaces a mile in circuit, and of majestic temples, are now with difficulty determined. Truly has that wicked city been swept with the besom of destruction, as Isaiah predicted.

The prophet then predicts the desolation of Moab on account of its pride, which seems to have been its peculiar offense. It is to be noted that the sin of pride has ever called forth a severe judgment. "It goeth before destruction." Pride was one of the peculiarities of both Nineveh and Babylon. But that which is exalted shall be brought low. A bitter humiliation, at least, has ever been visited upon those who have arrogated a lofty superiority. It presupposes an independence utterly inconsistent with the real condition of men in the eyes of the Omnipotent; in the eyes of men, even, it is offensive in the extreme, and ends in isolation. We can tolerate certain great defects and weaknesses, but no one ever got reconciled to pride. It led to the ruin of Napoleon, as well as of Cæsar; it creates innumerable enemies, even in the most retired village; it separates and alienates families; and when the punishment for it comes, everybody rejoices. People say contemptuously, "Is this the man that made the earth to tremble?" There is seldom pity for a fallen greatness that rejoiced in its strength, and despised the weakness of the unfortunate. If anything is foreign to the spirit of Christianity it is boastful pride, and yet it is one of those things which it is difficult for conscience to reach, as it is generally baptized with the name of self-respect.

The next woe which Isaiah denounced was on Egypt, which had played so great a part in the history of ancient nations. The judgments sent on this civilized country were severe, but were not so appalling as those to be visited upon Babylon. With Egypt was included Ethiopia. Civil war should desolate both nations, and it should rage so fiercely that "every one should fight against his brother, and every one against his neighbor, city against city, and kingdom against kingdom." Moreover, the famed wisdom of Egypt should fail; the people in their distress should seek to gain direction from wizards and charmers and soothsayers. It always was a country of magicians, from the time that Aaron's rod swallowed up the rods of those boastful enchanters who sought to repeat his miracles; it was a country of soothsayers and sorcerers when finally conquered by the Romans; it was the fruitful land of religious superstitions in every age. It was governed in the earliest times by pagan priests; the early kings were priests, — even Moses and Joseph were initiated into the occult arts of the priests. It was not wholly given to idolatry, since it is supposed that there was an esoteric wisdom among the higher priests which held to the One Supreme God and the immortality of the soul, as well as to future rewards and punishments. Nevertheless, the disgusting ceremonies connected with the worship of animals were far below the level of true religion, and the sorceries and magical incantations and superstitious rites which kept the people in ignorance, bondage, and degradation called loudly for rebuke. By reason of these things the nation was to be still farther subjected to the grinding rule of tyrants. It was a fertile and fruitful land, in which all the arts known to antiquity flourished; but the rains of Ethiopia were to be withheld, and such should be the unusual and abnormal drouth that the Nile should be dried up, and the reeds upon its banks should wither and decay. The river was stocked with fish, but the fishermen should cast their hooks and arrange their nets in vain. Even the workers in flax (one great source of Egyptian wealth and luxury) should be confounded. The princes were to become fools; there was to be general confusion, and no work was to be done in manufactures. Even Judah should become a terror to Egypt, and fear should overspread the land. To these calamities there was to be some palliation. Five cities should speak the language of Canaan, and swear by the Lord of Hosts; and an altar should be erected in the middle of the land which should be a witness unto the Lord of Hosts, to whom the people should cry amid their oppressions and miseries; and Jehovah should be known in Egypt. "He shall smite it, but he also shall heal it." And when we remember what a refuge the Jews found in Alexandria and other cities in the no very distant future, keeping alive there the worship of the true God, and what a hold Christianity itself took in the second and third centuries in that old country of priests and sorcerers, producing a Clement, a Cyprian, a Tertullian, an Athanasius, and an Augustine; yea, that when conquered by the Mohammedans, the worship of the one true God was everywhere maintained from that time to the present,— we feel that the mercy of God followed close upon his justice. Isaiah predicted even the divine blessing on the land, which it should share with Palestine: " Blessed be Egypt my people, and Israel mine inheritance."

It is not to be supposed that Tyre would escape from the calamities which were to be sent on the various heathen nations. Tyre was the great commercial centre of the world at that time, as Babylon was the centre of imperial power. Babylon ruled over the land, and Tyre over the sea; the one was the capital of a vast empire, the other was a maritime power, whose ships were to be seen in every part of the Mediterranean. Tyre, by its wealth and commerce, gained the supremacy in Phœnicia, although Sidon was an older city, five miles distant. But Tyre was defiled by the worship of Baal and Astarte; it was a city of exceeding dissoluteness. It was not only proud and luxurious, but abominably licentious; it was a city of harlots. And what was to be its fate? It was to be destroyed, and its merchandise was to be scattered. "Howl, ye ships of Tarshish! for your strength is laid waste, so that there is no house, no entering in. . . . The Lord of Hosts hath purposed it, to stain the pride of glory, and bring to contempt all the honorable of the earth." The inhabitants of the city who sought escape from death were compelled to take refuge in the colonies at Cyprus, Carthage, and Tartessus in Spain. The destruction of Tyre has been complete. There are no remains of its former grandeur; its palaces are indistinguishable ruins. Its traffic was transferred to Carthage. Yet how strong must have been a city which took Nebuchadnezzar thirteen years to subdue! It arose from its ashes, but was reduced again by Alexander.

Isaiah condenses his judgment in reference to the other wicked nations of his time in a few rapid, vigorous, and comprehensive clauses. "Behold, Jehovah emptieth the earth, and layeth it waste, and scattereth its inhabitants And it happeneth, as to the people, so to the priest; as to the servant, so to the master; as to the maid, so to her mistress; as to the buyer, so to the seller; as to the lender, so to the borrower; as to the creditor, so to the debtor. The earth has become wicked among its inhabitants, therefore hath the curse devoured the earth, and they who dwelt in it make expiation." We observe that these severe calamities are not uttered in wrath. They are not maledictions; they are simply divine revelations to the gifted prophet, or logical deductions which the inspired statesman declares from incontrovertible facts. In this latter sense, all profound observations on the tendency of passing events partake of the nature of prophecy. A sage is necessarily a prophet. Men even prophesy rain or heat or cold from natural phenomena, and their predictions often come to pass. Much more to be relied on is the prophetic wisdom which is seen among great thinkers and writers, like Burke, Webster, and Carlyle, since they rely on the operation of unchanging laws, both moral and physical. When a nation is wholly given over to lying and cheating in trade, or to hypocritical observances in religion, or to practical atheism, or to gross superstitions, or abominable dissoluteness in morals, or to the rule of feeble kings controlled by hypocritical priests and harlots, is it presumptuous to predict the consequences? Is it difficult to predict the ultimate effect on a nation of overwhelming standing armies eating up the resources of kings, or of the general prevalence of luxury, effeminacy, and vice?

Isaiah having declared the judgment of God on apostate, idolatrous, and wicked nations; having emphasized the great principle of retribution, even on nations that in his day were prosperous and powerful; having rebuked the sins of the people among whom he dwelt, and exposed hypocrisy and dead-letter piety, — lays down the fundamental law that chastisements are sent to lead men to repentance, and that where there is repentance there is forgiveness. Severe as are his denunciations of sin, and certain as is the punishment of it, yet his soul dwells on the mercy and love of God more than even on His justice. He never loses sight of reconciliation, although he holds out but little hope for people wedded to their idols. There is no hope for Babylon or Tyre; they are doomed. Nor is there much encouragement for Ephraim, which composed so large a part of the kingdom of Israel; its people were to be dispersed, to become captives, and never were to return to their native hills. But he holds out great hope for Judah. It will be conquered, and its people carried away in slavery to Babylon, — that is their chastisement for apostasy; but a remnant of them shall return. They had not utterly forgotten God, therefore a part of the nation shall be rescued from captivity. So full of hope is Isaiah that the nation shall not utterly be destroyed, that he names his son Shear-jashub, — "a remnant shall return." This is his watchword. Certain is it that the Lord will have mercy on Jacob whom he hath chosen; his promises will not fail. Judah shall be chastised; but a part of Judah shall return to Jerusalem, purified, wiser, and shall again in due time flourish as a nation.

Isaiah is the prophet of hope, of forgiveness, and of love. Not only on Judah shall a blessing be bestowed, but upon the whole world. Forgiveness is unbounded if there is repentance, no matter what the sin may be. He almost anticipates the message of Jesus by saying, "Though your sins be as scarlet, they shall be white as snow." God's mercy is past finding out. "Ho, every one that thirsteth, come ye to the waters!" So full is he of the boundless love of God, extended to all created things, that he calls on the hills and the mountains to rejoice. Here he soars beyond the Jew; he takes in the whole world in his rapturous expectation of deliverance. He comforts all good people under chastisement. He is as cheerful as Jeremiah is sad.

Having laid down the conditions of forgiveness, and expatiated on the divine benevolence, Isaiah now sings another song, and ascends to loftier heights. He is jubilant over the promised glories of God's people; he speaks of the redemption of both Jew and Gentile. His prophetic mission is now more distinctly unfolded. He blends the forgiveness of sins with the promised

Deliverer; he unfolds the advent of the Messiah. He even foretells in what form He shall come; he predicts the main facts of His personal history. Not only shall there " come forth a rod out of the stem of Jesse, and a branch out of its roots," but he shall be " a man despised and rejected, a man of sorrows and acquainted with grief; who shall be wounded for our transgressions and bruised for our iniquities, brought as a lamb to the slaughter, cut off from the living, making his grave with the wicked and with the rich in his death; yet bruised because it pleased the Lord, and because he made his soul an offering for sin, and made intercession with the transgressors." Who is this stricken, persecuted, martyred personage, bearing the iniquity of the race, and thus providing a way for future salvation? Isaiah, with transcendent majesty of style, clear and luminous as it is poetical, declares that this person who is still unborn, this light which shall appear in Galilee, is no less than he on whose shoulders shall be the government, " whose name shall be called Wonderful, Counsellor, the mighty God, the Everlasting Father, the Prince of Peace; of the increase of whose kingdom and peace there shall be no end, upon the throne of David and upon his kingdom, to order it, and to establish it with judgment and justice forever."

Only in some of the Messianic Psalms do we meet with kindred passages, indicating the reign of the Christ upon the earth, expressed with such emphatic clearness. How marvellous and wonderful this prophecy! Seven hundred years before its fulfilment, it is expressed with such minuteness, that, had the prophet lived in the Apostolic age, he could not have described the Messiah more accurately. The devout Jew, especially after the Captivity, believed in a future deliverer, who should arise from the seed of David, establish a great empire, and reign as a temporal monarch; but he had no lofty and spiritual views of this predicted reign. To Isaiah, more even than to Abraham or David or any other person in Jewish history, was it revealed that the reign of the Christ was to be spiritual; that he was not to be a temporal deliverer, but a Saviour redeeming mankind from the curse of sin. Hence Isaiah is quoted more than all the other prophets combined, especially by the writers of the New Testament.

Having announced this glorious prediction of the advent into our world of a divine Redeemer in the form of a man, by whose life and suffering and death the world should be saved, the prophet-poet breaks out in rhapsodies. He cannot contain his exultation. He loses sight of the judgments he had declared, in his unbounded rejoicings that there was to be a deliverance; that not only a remnant would return to Jerusalem and become a renewed power, but that the Messiah should ultimately reign over all the nations of the earth, should establish a reign of peace, so that warriors "should beat their swords into ploughshares, and their spears into pruning-hooks." Heretofore the history of kings had been a history of wars, — of oppression, of injustice, of cruelty. Miseries overspread the earth from this scourge more than from all other causes combined. The world was decimated by war, producing not only wholesale slaughter, but captivity and slavery, the utter extinction of nations. Isaiah had himself dwelt upon the woes to be visited on mankind by war more than any other prophet who had preceded him. All the leading nations and capitals were to be utterly destroyed or severely punished; calamity and misery should be nearly universal; only "a remnant should be saved." Now, however, he takes the most cheerful and joyous views. So marked is the contrast between the first and latter parts of the Book of Isaiah, that many great critics suppose that they were written by different persons and at different times. But whether there were two persons or one, the most comforting and cheering doctrines to be found in the Scriptures, before the Sermon on the Mount was preached, are declared by Isaiah. The breadth and catholicity of them are amazing from the pen of a Jew. The whole world was to share with him in the promises of a Saviour; the whole world was to be finally redeemed. As recipients of divine privileges there was to be no difference between Jew and Gentile. Paul himself shows no greater mental illumination. "The glory of the Lord shall be revealed, and all flesh shall see it."

In view of this glorious reign of peace and universal redemption, Isaiah calls upon the earth to be joyful and all the mountains to break forth in singing, and Zion to awake, and Jerusalem to put on her beautiful garments, and all waste places to break forth in joy; for the glory of the Lord is risen upon the City of David. How rapturously does the prophet, in the most glowing and lofty flights of poetry, dwell upon the time when the redeemed of the Lord shall return to Zion with songs and thanksgivings, no more to be called "forsaken," but a city to be renewed in beauties and glories, and in which kings shall be nursing fathers to its sons and daughters, and queens nursing mothers. These are the tidings which the prophet brings, and which the poet sings in matchless lyrics. To the Zion of the Holy One of Israel shall the Gentiles come with their precious offerings. "Violence shall no more be heard in thy land," saith the poet, "wasting nor destruction within thy borders; but thou shalt call thy walls Salvation and thy gates Praise. . . . Thy sun shall no more go down, neither shall thy moon withdraw itself, for the Lord shall be thine everlasting light, and the day of thy mourning shall be ended. . . . Thy people shall be all righteous; they shall inherit the land forever, the branch of my planting, the work of my hands, that I may be glorified. A little one shall become a thousand, and a small one a strong nation: I the Lord will hasten it in its time."

Salvation, peace, the glory of Zion! — these are the words which Isaiah reiterates. With these are identified the spiritual kingdom of Christ, which is to spread over the whole earth. The prophet does not specify when that time shall come, when peace shall be universal, and when all the people shall be righteous; that part of the prophecy remains unfulfilled, as well as the renewed glories of Jerusalem. Yet a thousand years with the Lord are as one day. No believing Christian doubts that it will be fulfilled, as certainly as that Babylon should be destroyed, or that a Messiah should appear among the Jews. The day of deliverance began to dawn when Christianity was proclaimed among the Gentiles. From that time a great progress has been seen among the nations. First, wars began to cease in the Roman world. They were renewed when the empire of the Cæsars fell, but their ferocity and cruelty diminished; conquered people were not carried away as slaves, nor were women and children put to death, except in extraordinary cases which called out universal grief, compassion, and indignation. With all the progress of truth and civilization, it is amazing that Christian nations should still be armed to the teeth, and that wars are still so frequent. We fear that they will not cease until those who govern shall be conscientious Christians. But that the time will come when rulers shall be righteous and nations learn war no more, is a truth which Christians everywhere accept. When, how,—by the gradual spread of knowledge, or by supernatural intervention,—who can tell? "Zion shall arise and shine. . . . The Gentiles shall come to its light, and kings to the brightness of its rising. . . Violence shall no more be heard in the land, nor wasting and destruction within its borders. . . . They shall not hurt or destroy in all my holy mountain, saith the Lord. . . . And it shall come to pass that from one new moon to another, and from one Sabbath to another, shall all flesh come to worship before me, saith the Lord."

This is the sublime faith of Christendom set forth by the most sublime of the prophets, from the most gifted and eloquent of the poets. On this faith rests the consolation of the righteous in view of the prevalence of iniquity. This prophecy is full of encouragement and joy amid afflictions and sorrows. It proclaims liberty to captives, and the opening of the prison to those that are bound; it preaches glad tidings to the meek, and binds up the broken-hearted; it gives beauty for ashes, the oil of joy for mourning, and the garment of praise for the spirit of heaviness. This prediction has inspired the religious poets of all nations; on this is based the beauty and glory of the lyrical stanzas we sing in our churches. The hymns and melodies of the Church, the most immortal of human writings, are inspired with this cheering anticipation. The psalmody of the Church is rapturous, like Isaiah, over the triumphant and peaceful reign of Christ, coming sooner perhaps than we dream when we see the triumphal career of wicked men. In the temporal fall of a monstrous despotism, in the decline of wicked cities and empires, in the light which is penetrating all lands, in the shaking of Mohammedan thrones, in the opening of the most distant East, in the arbitration of national difficulties, in the terrible inventions which make nations fear to go to war, in the wonderful network of philanthropic enterprises, in the renewed interest in sacred literature, in the recognition of law and order as the first condition of civilized society, in that general love of truth which science has stimulated and rarely mocked, and which casts its searching eye into all creeds and all hypocrisies and all false philosophy, — we share the exultant spirit of the prophet, and in the language of one of our great poets we repeat the promised joy : —

> " Rise, crowned with light, imperial Salem, rise!
> Exalt thy towering head and lift thine eyes!

See a long race thy spacious courts adorn,
See future sons and daughters yet unborn!
See barbarous nations at thy gates attend,
Walk in thy light, and in thy temple bend!
See thy bright altars thronged with prostrate kings,
And heaped with products of Sabæan springs!
No more the rising sun shall gild the morn,
Nor evening Cynthia fill her silver horn;
But lost, dissolved in thy superior rays,
One tide of glory, one unclouded blaze
O'erflow thy courts; the Light himself shall shine
Revealed, and God's eternal day be thine!
The seas shall waste, the skies to smoke decay,
Rocks fall to dust, and mountains melt away;
But fixed His word, His saving power remains:
Thy realm forever lasts; thy own Messiah reigns!"

JEREMIAH.

About 629–580 b. c.

THE FALL OF JERUSALEM.

JEREMIAH.

THE FALL OF JERUSALEM.

JEREMIAH is a study to those who would know the history of the latter days of the Jewish monarchy, before it finally succumbed to the Babylonian conqueror. He was a sad and isolated man, who uttered his prophetic warnings to a perverse and scornful generation; persecuted because he was truthful, yet not entirely neglected or disregarded, since he was consulted in great national dangers by the monarchs with whom he was contemporary. So important were his utterances, it is matter of great satisfaction that they were committed to writing, for the benefit of future generations, — not of Jews only, but of the Gentiles, — on account of the fundamental truths contained in them. Next to Isaiah, Jeremiah was the most prominent of the prophets who were commissioned to declare the will and judgments of Jehovah on a degenerate and backsliding people. He was a preacher of righteousness, as well as a prophet of impending woes. As a reformer he was unsuccessful, since the Hebrew nation was incorrigibly joined to its idols. His public career extended over a period of forty years. He was neither popular with the people, nor a favorite of kings and princes; the nation was against him and the times were against him. He exasperated alike the priests, the nobles, and the populace by his rebukes. As a prophet he had no honor in his native place. He uniformly opposed the current of popular prejudices, and denounced every form of selfishness and superstition; but all his protests and rebukes were in vain. There were very few to encourage him or comfort him. Like Noah, he was alone amidst universal derision and scorn, so that he was sad beyond measure, more filled with grief than with indignation.

Jeremiah was not bold and stern, like Elijah, but retiring, plaintive, mournful, tender. As he surveyed the downward descent of Judah, which nothing apparently could arrest, he exclaimed: "Oh that my head were waters, and mine eyes a fountain of tears, that I might weep day and night for the daughter of my people!" Is it possible for language to express a deeper despondency, or a more tender grief? Pathos and unselfishness are blended with his despair. It is not for himself that he is overwhelmed with gloom, but for the sins of the people. It is because the people would not hear, would not consider, and would persist in their folly and wickedness, that grief pierces his soul. He weeps for them, as Christ wept over Jerusalem. Yet at times he is stung into bitter imprecations, he becomes fierce and impatient; and then again he rises over the gloom which envelops him, in the conviction that there will be a new covenant between God and man, after the punishment for sin shall have been inflicted. But his prevailing feelings are grief and despair, since he has no hopes of national reform. So he predicts woes and calamities at no distant day, which are to be so overwhelming that his soul is crushed in the anticipation of them. He cannot laugh, he cannot rejoice, he cannot sing, he cannot eat and drink like other men. He seeks solitude; he longs for the desert; he abstains from marriage, he is ascetic in all his ways; he sits alone and keeps silence, and communes only with his God; and when forced into the streets and courts of the city, it is only with the faint hope that he may find an honest man. No persons command his respect save the Arabian Rechabites, who have the austere habits of the wilderness, like those of the early Syrian monks. Yet his gloom is different from theirs: they seek to avert divine wrath for their own sins; he sees this wrath about to descend for the sins of others, and overwhelm the whole nation in misery and shame.

Jeremiah was born in the little ecclesiastical town of Anathoth, about three miles from Jerusalem, and was the son of a priest. We do not know the exact year of his birth, but he was a very young man when he received his divine commission as a prophet, about six hundred and twenty-seven years before Christ. Josiah had then been on the throne of Judah twelve years. The kingdom was apparently prosperous, and was unmolested by external enemies. For seventy-five years Assyria had given but little trouble, and Egypt was occupied with the siege of Ashdod, which had been going on for twenty-nine years, so strong was that Philistine city. But in the absence of external dangers corruption, following wealth, was making fearful strides among the people, and impiety was nearly universal. Every one was bent on pleasure or gain, and prophet and priest were worldly and deceitful. From the time when Jeremiah was first called to the prophetic office until the fall of Jerusalem there was an unbroken series of national misfortunes, gradually darkening into utter ruin and exile. He may have shrunk from the perils and mortifications which attended him for forty years, as his nature was sensitive and tender; but during this long ministry he was incessant in his labors, lifting up his voice in the courts of the Temple, in the palace of the king, in prison, in private houses, in the country around

Jerusalem. The burden of his utterances was a denunciation of idolatry, and a lamentation over its consequences. "My people, saith Jehovah, have forsaken me, the fountain of living waters, and hewn out for themselves underground cisterns, full of rents, that can hold no water. . . . Behold, O Judah! thou shalt be brought to shame by thy new alliance with Egypt, as thou wast in the past by thy old alliance with Assyria."

In this denunciation by the prophet we see that he mingled in political affairs, and opposed the alliance which Judah made with Egypt, which ever proved a broken reed. Egypt was a vain support against the new power that was rising on the Euphrates, carrying all before it, even to the destruction of Nineveh, and was threatening Damascus and Tyre as well as Jerusalem. The power which Judah had now to fear was Babylon, not Assyria. If any alliance was to be formed, it was better to conciliate Babylon than Egypt.

Roused by the earnest eloquence of Jeremiah, and of those of the group of earnest followers of Jehovah who stood with him, — Huldah the prophetess, Shallum her husband, keeper of the royal wardrobe, Hilkiah the high-priest, and Shaphan the scribe, or secretary, — the youthful king Josiah, in the eighteenth year of his reign, when he was himself but twenty-six years old, set about reforms, which the nobles and priests bitterly opposed. Idolatry had been the fashionable religion for nearly seventy years, and the Law was nearly forgotten. The corruption of the priesthood and of the great body of the prophets kept pace with the degeneracy of the people. The Temple was dilapidated, and its gold and bronze decorations had been despoiled. The king undertook a thorough repair of the great Sanctuary, and during its progress a discovery was made by the high-priest Hilkiah of a copy of the Law, hidden amid the rubbish of one of the cells or chambers of the Temple. It is generally supposed to have been the Book of Deuteronomy. When it was lost, and how, it is not easy to ascertain, — probably during the reign of some one of the idolatrous kings. It seems to have been entirely forgotten, — a proof of the general apostasy of the nation. But the discovery of the book was hailed by Josiah as a very important event ; and its effect was to give a renewed impetus to his reforms, and a renewed study of patriarchal history. He forthwith assembled the leading men of the nation, — prophets, priests, Levites, nobles, and heads of tribes. He read to them the details of the ancient covenant, and solemnly declared his purpose to keep the commandments and statutes of Jehovah as laid down in the precious book. The assembled elders and priests gave their eager concurrence to the act of the king, and Judah once more, outwardly at least, became the people of God.

Nor can it be questioned that the renewed study of the Law, as brought about by Josiah, produced a great influence on the future of the Hebrew nation, especially in the renunciation of idolatry. Yet this reform, great as it was, did not prevent the fall of Jerusalem and the exile of the leading people among the Hebrews to the land of the Chaldeans, whence Abraham their great progenitor had emigrated.

Josiah, who was thoroughly aroused by "the words of the book," and its denunciations of the wrath of Jehovah upon the people if they should forsake his ways, in spite of the secret opposition of the nobles and priests, zealously pursued the work of reform. The "high places," on which were heathen altars, were levelled with the ground; the images of the gods were overthrown; the Temple was purified, and the abominations which had disgraced it were removed. His reforms extended even to the scattered population of Samaria whom the Assyrians had spared, and all the buildings connected with the worship of Baal and Astaroth at Bethel were destroyed. Their very stones were broken in pieces, under the eyes of Josiah himself. The skeletons of the pagan priests were dragged from their burial places and burned.

An elaborate celebration of the feast of the Passover followed soon after the discovery of the copy of the Law, whether confined to Deuteronomy or including other additional writings ascribed to Moses, we know not. This great Passover was the leading internal event of the reign of Josiah. Having "taken away all the abominations out of all the countries that belonged to the children of Israel," even as the earlier keepers of the Law cleansed their premises, especially of all remains of leaven, — the symbol of corruption, — the king commanded a celebration of the feast of deliverance. Priests and Levites were sent throughout the country to instruct the people in the preparations demanded for the Passover. The sacred ark, hidden during the reigns of Manasseh and Amon, was restored to its old place in the Temple, where it remained until the Temple was destroyed. On the approach of the festival, which was to be held with unusual solemnities, great multitudes from all parts of Palestine assembled at Jerusalem, and three thousand bullocks and thirty thousand lambs were provided by the king for the seven days' feast which followed the Passover. The princes also added eight hundred oxen and seven thousand six hundred small cattle as a gift to priests and people. After the priests in their white robes, with bare feet and uncovered heads, and the Levites at their side according to the king's commandment, had "killed the passover" and "sprinkled the blood from their hands," each Levite having first washed himself in the Temple laver, the part of the animal required for the burnt-offering was laid on the altar flames, and the remainder was cooked by the Levites for the people, either baked, roasted, or boiled. And this continued for seven days; during all the while the services of the Temple choir were conducted by the singers, chanting the psalms of David and of Asaph. Such a Passover had not been held since the days of Samuel. No king, not even David or Solomon, had celebrated the festival on so grand a scale. The minutest details of the requirements of the Law were attended to. The festival proclaimed the full restoration of the worship of Jehovah, and kindled enthusiasm for his service. So great was this event that Ezekiel dates the opening of his prophecies from it. "It seems probable that we have in the eighty-fifth psalm a relic of this great solemnity. . . . Its tone is sad amidst all the great public rejoicings; it bewails the stubborn ungodliness of the people as a whole."

After the great Passover, which took place in the year 622, when Josiah was twenty-six years of age, little is said of the pious king, who reigned twelve years after this memorable event. One of the best, though not one of the wisest, kings of Judah, he did his best to eradicate every trace of idolatry; but the hearts of the people responded faintly to his efforts. Reform was only outward and superficial, — an illustration of the inability even of an absolute monarch to remove evils to which the people cling in their hearts. To the eyes of Jeremiah, there was no hope while the hearts of the people were unchanged. "Can the Ethiopian change his skin, or the leopard his spots?" he mournfully exclaims. "Much less can those who are accustomed to do evil learn to do well." He had no illusions; he saw the true state of affairs, and was not misled by mere outward and enforced reforms, which partook of the nature of religious persecution, and irritated the people rather than led to a true religious life among them. There was nothing left to him but to declare woes and approaching calamities, to which the people were insensible. They mocked and reviled him. His lofty position secured him a hearing, but he preached to stones. The people believed nothing but lies; many were indifferent and some were secretly hostile, and he must have been pained and disappointed in view of the incompleteness of his work through the secret opposition of the popular leaders.

Josiah was the most virtuous monarch of Judah. It was a great public misfortune that his life was cut short prematurely at the age of thirty-eight, and in consequence of his own imprudence. He undertook to oppose the encroachments of Necho II., king of Egypt, an able, warlike, and enterprising monarch, distinguished for his naval expeditions, whose ships doubled the Cape of Good Hope, and returned to Egypt in safety, after a three years' voyage. Necho was not so successful in digging a canal across the Isthmus of Suez, in which enterprise one hundred and twenty thousand men perished from hunger, fatigue, and disease. But his great aim was to extend his empire to the limits reached by Rameses II., the Sesostris of the Greeks. The great Assyrian empire was then breaking up, and Nineveh was about to fall before the Babylonians; so he seized the opportunity to invade Syria, a province of the Assyrian empire He must of course pass through Palestine, the great highway between Egypt and the East. Josiah opposed his enterprise, fearing that if the Egyptian king conquered Syria, he himself would become the vassal of Egypt. Jeremiah earnestly endeavored to dissuade his sovereign from embarking in so doubtful a war; even Necho tried to convince him through his envoys that he made war on Nineveh, not on Jerusalem, invoking — as most intensely earnest men did in those days of tremendous impulse — the sacred name of Deity as his authentication. Said he: "What have I to do with thee, thou King of Judah? I come not against thee this day, but against the house wherewith

I have war; for God commanded me to make haste. Forbear thee from meddling with God, who is with me, that he destroy thee not." But nothing could induce Josiah to give up his warlike enterprise. He had the piety of Saint Louis, and also his patriotic and chivalric heroism. He marched his forces to the plain of Esdraelon, the great battle field where Rameses II. had triumphed over the Hittites centuries before. The battle was fought at Megiddo. Although Josiah took the precaution to disguise himself, he was mortally wounded by the Egyptian archers, and was driven back in his splendid chariot toward Jerusalem, which he did not live to reach.

The lamentations for this brave and pious monarch remind us of the universal grief of the Hebrew nation on the death of Samuel. He was buried in a tomb which he had prepared for himself, amid universal mourning. A funeral oration was composed by Jeremiah, or rather an elegy, afterward sung by the nation on the anniversary of the battle. Nor did the nation ever forget a king so virtuous in his life and so zealous for the Law. Long after the return from captivity the singers of Israel sang his praises, and popular veneration for him increased with the lapse of time; for in virtues and piety, and uninterrupted zeal for Jehovah, Josiah never had an equal among the kings of Judah.

The services of this good king were long remembered. To him may be traced the unyielding devotion of the Jews, after the Captivity, for the rites and forms and ceremonies which are found in the books of the Law. The legalisms of the Scribes may be traced to him. He reigned but twelve years after his great reformation, — not long enough to root out the heathenism which had prevailed unchecked for nearly seventy years. With him perished the hopes of the kingdom.

After his death the decline was rapid. A great reaction set in, and faction was accompanied with violence. The heathen party triumphed over the orthodox party. The passions which had been suppressed since the death of Manasseh burst out with all the frenzy and savage hatred which have ever marked the Jews in their religious contentions, and these were unrestrained by the four kings who succeeded Josiah. The people were devoured by religious animosities, and split up into hostile factions. Had the nation been united, it is possible that later it might have successfully resisted the armies of Nebuchadnezzar. Jeremiah gave vent to his despairing sentiments, and held out no hope. When Elijah had appealed to the people to choose between Jehovah and Baal, he was successful, because they were then undecided and wavering in their belief, and it required only an evidence of superior power to bring them back to their allegiance. But when Jeremiah appeared, idolatry was the popular religion. It had become so firmly established by a succession of wicked kings, added to the universal degeneracy, that even Josiah could work but a temporary reform.

Hence the voice of Jeremiah was drowned. Even the prophets of his day had become men of the world. They fawned on the rich and powerful whose favor they sought, and prophesied "smooth things" to them. They were the optimists of a decaying nation and a godless, pleasure-seeking generation. They were to Jerusalem what the Sophists were to Athens when Demosthenes thundered his disregarded warnings. There were, indeed, a few prophets left who labored for the truth; but their words fell on listless ears. Nor could the priests arrest the ruin, for they were as corrupt as the people. The most learned among them were zealous only for the letter of the law, and fostered among the people a hypocritical formalism. True religious life had departed: and the noble Jeremiah, the only great statesman as well as prophet who remained, saw his influence progressively declining, until at last he was utterly disregarded. Yet he maintained his dignity, and fearlessly declared his message

In the meantime the triumphant Necho, after the defeat and dispersion of Josiah's army, pursued his way toward Damascus, which he at once overpowered.

From thence he invaded Assyria, and stripped Nineveh of its most fertile provinces. The capital itself was besieged by Nabopolassar and Cyaxares the Mede, and Necho was left for a time in possession of his newly-acquired dominion.

Josiah was succeeded by his son Shallum, who assumed the crown under the name of Jehoaz, which event it seems gave umbrage to the king of Egypt. So he despatched an army to Jerusalem, which yielded at once, and King Jehoaz was sent as a captive to the banks of the Nile. His elder brother Eliakim was appointed king in his place, under the name of Jehoiakim, who thus became the vassal of Necho. He was a young man of twenty-five, self-indulgent, proud, despotic, and extravagant. There could be no more impressive comment on the infatuation and folly of the times than the embellishment of Jerusalem with palaces and public buildings, with the view to imitate the glory of Solomon. In everything the king differed from his father Josiah, especially in his treatment of Jeremiah, whom he would have killed. He headed the movement to restore paganism; altars were erected on every hill to heathen deities, so that there were more gods in Judah than there were towns. Even the sacred animals of Egypt were worshipped in the dark chambers beneath the Temple. In the most sacred places of the Temple itself idolatrous priests worshipped the rising sun, and the obscene rites of Phœnician idolatry were performed in private houses. The decline in morals kept pace with the decline of spiritual religion. There was no vice which was not rampant throughout the land, — adultery, oppression of foreigners, venality in judges, falsehood, dishonesty in trade, usury, cruelty to debtors, robbery and murder, the loosing of the ties of kindred, general suspicion of neighbors, — all the crimes enumerated by the Apostle Paul among the Romans. Judah in reality had become an idolatrous nation like Tyre and Syria and Egypt, with only here and there a witness to the truth, like Jeremiah, the prophetess Huldah, and Baruch the scribe.

This relapse into heathenism filled the soul of Jeremiah with grief and indignation, but gave to him a courage foreign to his timid and shrinking nature. In the presence of the king, the princes, and priests he was defiant, immovable, and fearless, uttering his solemn warnings from day to day with noble fidelity. All classes turned against him; the nobles were furious at his exposure of their license and robberies, the priests hated him for his denunciation of hypocrisy, and the people for his gloomy prophecies that the Temple should be destroyed, Jerusalem reduced to ashes, and they themselves led into captivity.

Not only were crime and idolatry rampant, but the

THE FALL OF JERUSALEM.

death of Josiah was followed by droughts and famine. In vain were the prayers of Jeremiah to avert calamity. Jehovah replied to him: "Pray not for this people! Though they fast, I will not hear their cry; though they offer sacrifice I have no pleasure in them, but will consume them by the sword, by famine, and pestilence." Jeremiah piteously gives way to despairing lamentations. "Hast thou, O Lord, utterly rejected Judah? Is thy soul tired of Zion? Why hast thou smitten us so that there is no healing for us?" Jehovah replies: "If Moses and Samuel stood pleading before me, my soul could not be toward this people. I appoint four destroyers, — the sword to slay, the dogs to tear and fight over the corpse, the birds of the air, and the beasts of the field; for who will have pity on thee, O Jerusalem? Thou hast rejected me. I am weary of relenting. I will scatter them as with a broad winnowing-shovel, as men scatter the chaff on the threshing-floor."

Such, amid general depravity and derision, were some of the utterances of the prophet, during the reign of Jehoiakim. Among other evils which he denounced was the neglect of the Sabbath, so faithfully observed in earlier and better times. At the gates of the city he cried aloud against the general profanation of the sacred day, which instead of being a day of rest was the busiest day of the week, when the city was like

a great fair and holiday. On this day the people of
the neighboring villages brought for sale their figs
and grapes and wine and vegetables ; on this day
the wine-presses were trodden in the country, and
the harvest was carried to the threshing-floors. The
preacher made himself especially odious for his rebuke for the violation of the Sabbath. "Come," said
his enemies to the crowd, "let us lay a plot against
him; let us smite him with the tongue by reporting his
words to the king, and bearing false witness against
him." On this renewed persecution the prophet does
not as usual give way to lamentation, but hurls his
maledictions. "O Jehovah ! give thou their sons to
hunger, deliver them to the sword ; let their wives be
made childless and widows ; let their strong men be
given over to death, and their young men be smitten
with the sword."

And to consummate, as it were, his threats of divine
punishment so soon to be visited on the degenerate
city, Jeremiah is directed to buy an earthenware bottle,
such as was used by the peasants to hold their drink-
ing-water, and to summon the elders and priests of
Jerusalem to the southwestern corner of the city, and
to throw before their feet the bottle and shiver it in
pieces, as a significant symbol of the approaching fall
of the city, to be destroyed as utterly as the shattered
jar. "And I will empty out in the dust, says Jehovah,

the counsels of Judah and Jerusalem, as this water is now poured from the bottle. And I will cause them to fall by the sword before their enemies and by the hands of those that seek their lives; and I will give their corpses for meat to the birds of heaven and the beasts of the earth; and I will make this city an astonishment and a scoffing. Every one that passes by it will be astonished and hiss at its misfortunes. Even so will I shatter this people and this city, as this bottle, which cannot be made whole again, has been shattered." Nor was Jeremiah contented to utter these fearful maledictions to the priests and elders; he made his way to the Temple, and taking his stand among the people, he reiterated, amid a storm of hisses, mockeries, and threats, what he had just declared to a smaller audience in reference to Jerusalem.

Such an appalling announcement of calamities, and in such strong and plain language, must have transported his hearers with fear or with wrath. He was either the ambassador of Heaven, before whose voice the people in the time of Elijah would have quaked with unutterable anguish, or a madman who was no longer to be endured. We have no record of any prophet or any preacher who ever used language so terrible or so daring. Even Luther never hurled such maledictions on the church which he called the " scarlet mother." Jeremiah uttered no vague generalities, but brought the matter home with awful directness. Among his auditors was Pashur, the chief governor of the Temple, and a priest by birth. He at once ordered the Temple police to seize the bold and outspoken prophet, who was forthwith punished for his plain speaking by the bastinado, and then hurried bleeding to the stocks, into which his head and feet and hands were rudely thrust, to spend the night amid the jeers of the crowd and the cold dews of the season. In the morning he was set free, his enemies thinking that he now would hold his tongue; but Jeremiah, so far from keeping silence, renewed his threats of divine vengeance. "For thus saith Jehovah, I will give all Judah into the hands of the king of Babylon, and he shall carry them captive to Babylon, and slay them with the sword." And then turning to Pashur, before the astonished attendants, he exclaimed: 'And thou, Pashur, and all that dwell in thy house, will be dragged off into captivity; and thou wilt come to Babylon, and thou wilt die and be buried there, — thou and all thy partisans to whom thou hast prophesied lies."

We observe in these angry words of Jeremiah great directness and great minuteness, so that his meaning could not be mistaken; also that the instrument of punishment on the degenerate and godless city was

THE FALL OF JERUSALEM.

to be the king of Babylon, a new power from whom Judah as yet had received no harm. The old enemies of the Hebrews were the Assyrians and Egyptians, not the Babylonians and Medes.

Whatever may have been the malignant animosity of Pashur, he was evidently afraid to molest the awful prophet and preacher any further, for Jeremiah was no insignificant person at Jerusalem. He was not only recognized as a prophet of Jehovah, but he had been the friend and counsellor of King Josiah, and was the leading statesman of the day in the ranks of the opposition. But distinguished as he was, his voice was disregarded, and he was probably looked upon as an old croaker, whose gloomy views had no reason to sustain them. Was not Jerusalem strong in her defences, and impregnable in the eyes of the people; and was she not regarded as under the special protection of the Deity? Suppose some austere priest — say such a man as the Abbé Lacordaire — had risen from the pulpit of Notre Dame or the Madeleine, a year before the battle of Sedan, and announced to the fashionable congregation assembled to hear his eloquence, and among them the ministers of Louis Napoleon, that in a short time Paris would be surrounded by conquering armies, and would endure all the horrors of a siege, and that the famine would be so great that the city would surrender and be at the entire mercy of the conquerors, — would he have been believed? Would not the people have regarded him as a madman, great as was his eloquence, or as the most gloomy of pessimists, for whom they would have felt contempt or bitter wrath? And had he added to his predictions of ruin, utterly inconceivable by the giddy, pleasure-seeking, atheistic people, the most scathing denunciations of the prevailing sins of that godless city, all the more powerful because they were true, addressed to all classes alike, positive, direct, bold, without favor and without fear, — would they not have been stirred to violence, and subjected him to any chastisement in their power? If Socrates, by provoking questions and fearless irony, drove the Athenians to such wrath that they took his life, even when everybody knew that he was the greatest and best man at Athens, how much more savage and malignant must have been the narrow-minded Jews when Jeremiah laid bare to them their sins and the impotency of their gods, and the certainty of retribution!

Yet vehement, or direct, or plain as were Jeremiah's denunciations to the idol-worshippers of Jerusalem in the seventh century before it was finally destroyed by Titus, he was no more severe than when Jesus denounced the hypocrisy of the Scribes and Pharisees, no more mournful than when he lamented over the approaching ruin of the Temple. Therefore they sought to kill him, as the princes and priests of Judah would have sacrificed the greatest prophet that had appeared since Elisha, the greatest statesman since Samuel, the greatest poet since David, if Isaiah alone be excepted. No wonder he was driven to a state of despondency and grief that reminds us of Job upon his ash-heap. "Cursed be the day," he exclaims, in his lonely chamber, "on which I was born! Cursed be the man who brought tidings to my father, saying, A man-child is born to thee, making him very glad! Why did I come forth from the womb that my days might be spent in shame?" A great and good man may be urged by the sense of duty to declare truths which he knows will lead to martyrdom; but no martyr was ever insensible to suffering or shame. All the glories of his future crown cannot sweeten the bitterness of the cup he is compelled to drain; even the greatest of martyrs prayed in his agony that the cup might pass from him. How could a man help being sad and even bitter, if ever so exalted in soul, when he saw that his warnings were utterly disregarded, and that no mortal influence or power could avert the doom he was compelled to pronounce as an ambassador of God? And when in addition to his grief as a patriot he was unjustly made to suffer reproach, scourgings, imprisonment, and probable death, how can we wonder that his patience was exhausted? He felt as if a burning fire consumed his very bones, and he could refrain no longer. He cried aloud in the intensity of his grief and pain, and Jehovah, in whom he trusted, appeared to him as a mighty champion and an everlasting support.

Jeremiah at this time, during the early years of the reign of Jehoiakim, the period of the most active part of his ministry, was about forty-five years of age. Great events were then taking place. Nineveh was besieged by one of its former generals, — Nabopolassar, now king of Babylon. The siege lasted two years, and the city fell in the year 606 B.C., when Jehoiakim had been about four years on the throne. The fall of this great capital enabled the son of the king of Babylonia, Nebuchadnezzar, to advance against Necho, the king of Egypt, who had taken Carchemish about three years before. Near that ancient capital of the Hittites, on the banks of the Euphrates, one of the most important battles of antiquity was fought, — and Necho, whose armies a few years before had so successfully invaded the Assyrian empire, was forced to retreat to Egypt. The battle of Carchemish put an end to Egyptian conquests in the East, and enabled the young sovereign of Babylonia to attain a power and elevation such as no Oriental monarch had ever before enjoyed. Babylon became the centre of a new empire, which embraced the countries that had bowed down to the Assyrian yoke. Nebuchadnezzar in the pride of victory now meditated the conquest of Egypt, and must needs pass through Palestine. But Jehoiakim was a vassal of Egypt, and had probably furnished troops for Necho at the fatal battle of Carchemish. Of course the Babylonian monarch would invade Judah on his way to Egypt, and punish its king, whom he could only look upon as an enemy.

It was then that Jeremiah, sad and desponding over the fate of Jerusalem, which he knew was doomed, committed his precious utterances to writing by the assistance of his friend and companion Baruch. He had lately been living in retirement, feeling that his message was delivered; possibly he feared that the king would put him to death as he had the prophet Urijah. But he wished to make one more attempt to call the people to repentance, as the only way to escape impending calamities; and he prevailed upon his secretary to read the scroll, containing all his verbal utterances, to the assembled people in the Temple, who, in view of their political dangers, were celebrating a solemn fast. The priests and people alike, clad in black hair-cloth mantles, with ashes on their heads, lay prostrate on the ground, and by numerous sacrifices hoped to propitiate the Deity. But not by sacrifices and fasts were they to be saved from Nebuchadnezzar's army, as Jeremiah had foretold years before. The recital by

Baruch of the calamities he had predicted made a profound impression on the crowd. A young man, awed by what he had heard, hastened to the hall in which the princes were assembled, and told them what had been read from the prophet's scroll. They in their turn were alarmed, and commanded Baruch to read the contents to them also. So intense was the excitement that the matter was laid before the king, who ordered the roll to be read to him: he would hear the words that Jeremiah had caused to be written down. But scarcely had the reading of the roll begun before he flew into a violent rage, and seizing the manuscript he cut it to pieces with the scribe's knife, and burned it upon a brazier of coals. Orders were instantly given to arrest both Jeremiah and Baruch; but they had been warned and fled, and the place of their concealment could not be found.

Jehoiakim thus rejected the last offer of mercy with scorn and anger, although many of his officers were filled with fear. His heart was hardened, like that of Pharaoh before Moses. Jeremiah having learned the fate of the roll, dictated its contents anew to his faithful secretary, and a second roll was preserved, not, however, without contriving to send to the king this awful message. "Thus saith Jehovah of thee Jehoiakim: He shall have no son to sit on the throne of David, and his dead body will be cast out to lie in the heat by day and the frost by night; and no one shall raise a lament for him when he dies. He shall be buried with the burial of an ass, drawn out of Jerusalem, and cast down from its gates."

No wonder that we lose sight of Jeremiah during the remainder of the reign of Jehoiakim; it was not safe for him to appear anywhere in public. For a time his voice was not heard; yet his predictions had such weight that the king dared not defy Nebuchadnezzar when he demanded the submission of Jerusalem. He was forced to become the vassal of the king of Babylonia, and furnish a contingent to his army. But this vassalage bore heavily on the arrogant soul of Jehoiakim, and he seized the first occasion to rebel, especially as Necho promised him protection. This rebellion was suicidal and fatal, since Babylon was the stronger power. Nebuchadnezzar, after the three years of forced submission, appeared before the gates of Jerusalem with an irresistible army. There was no resistance, as resistance was folly. Jehoiakim was put in chains, and avoided being carried captive to Babylon only by the most abject submission to the conqueror. All that was valuable in the Temple and the palaces was seized as spoil. Jerusalem was spared for a while; and in the mean time Jehoiakim died, and so intensely was he hated and despised that no dirge was sung over his remains, while his dishonored body was thrown outside the walls of his capital like that of a dead ass, as Jeremiah had foretold.

On his death, B. C. 598, after a reign of eight years, his son Jehoiachin, at the age of eighteen, ascended his nominal throne. He also, like his father, followed the lead of the heathen party. The bitterness of the Babylonian rule, united with the intrigues of Egypt, led to a fresh revolt, and Jerusalem was invested by a powerful Chaldean army.

Jeremiah now appears again upon the stage, but only to reaffirm the calamities which impended over his nation, — all of which he traced to the decay of religion and morality. The mission and the work of the Jews were to keep alive the worship of the One God amid universal idolatry. Outside of this, they were nothing as a nation. They numbered only four or five millions of people, and lived in a country not much larger than one of the northern counties of England and smaller than the state of New Hampshire or Vermont; they gave no impulse to art or science. Yet as the guardians of the central theme of the only true religion and of the sacred literature of the Bible, their history is an important link in the world's history. Take away the only thing which made them an object of divine favor, and they were of no more account than Hittites, or Moabites, or Philistines. The chosen people had become idolatrous like the surrounding nations, hopelessly degenerate and wicked, and they were to receive a dreadful chastisement as the only way by which they would return to the One God, and thus act their appointed part in the great drama of humanity. Jeremiah predicted this chastisement. The chosen people were to suffer a seventy years' captivity, and then city and Temple were to be destroyed. But Jeremiah, sad as he was over the fate of his nation, and terribly severe as he was in his denunciations of the national sins, knew that his people would repent by the river of Babylon, and be finally restored to their old inheritance. Yet nothing could avert their punishment.

In less than three months after Jehoiachin became king of Judah, its capital was unconditionally surrendered to the Chaldean hosts, since resistance was vain. No pity was shown to the rebels, though the king and nobles had appeared before Nebuchadnezzar with every mark and emblem of humiliation and submission. The king and his court and his wives, and all the principal people of the nation, were sent to Babylon as captives and slaves. The prompt capitulation saved the city for a time from complete destruction; but its glory was turned to shame and grief. All that was of any value in the Temple and city was carried to the banks of the Euphrates, nearly one hundred and fifty years after Samaria had fallen from a protracted siege, and its inhabitants finally dispersed among the nations that were subject to Nineveh.

One would suppose that after so great a calamity the few remaining people in Jerusalem and in the desolate villages of Judah would have given no further molestation to their powerful and triumphant enemies. The land was exhausted; the towns were stripped of their fighting population, and only the shadow of a kingdom remained. Instead of appointing a governor from his own court over the conquered province, Nebuchadnezzar gave the government into the hands of Mattaniah, the third son of Josiah, a youth of twenty, changing his name to Zedekiah. He was for a time faithful to his allegiance, and took much pains to quiet the mind of the powerful sovereign who ruled the Eastern world, and even made a journey to Babylon to pay his homage. He was a weak prince, however, alternately swayed by the different parties, — those that counselled resistance to Babylon, and those, like Jeremiah, that advised submission. This long-headed statesman saw clearly that rebellion against Nebuchadnezzar, flushed with victory, and with the whole Eastern world at his feet, was absurd; but that the time would come when Babylon in turn should be humbled, and then the captive Hebrews would probably return to their own land, made wiser by their captivity of seventy years. The other party, leagued with Moabites, Tyrians, Egyptians, and other nations, thought themselves strong enough to break their allegiance to Nebuchadnezzar; and bitter were the contentions of these parties. Jeremiah had great influence with the king, who was weak rather than wicked, and had his counsels been consistently followed, Jerusalem would probably have been spared, and the Temple would have remained. He preferred vassalage to utter ruin. With Babylon pressing on one side and Egypt on the other, — both great monarchies, — vassalage to one or the other of these powers was inevitable. Indeed, vassalage had been the unhappy condition of Judah since the death of Josiah. Of the two powers Jeremiah preferred the Chaldean rule, and persistently advised submission to it, as the only way to save Jerusalem from utter destruction.

Unfortunately Zedekiah temporized; he courted all parties in turn, and listened to the schemes of rebellion, — for all the nations of Palestine were either conquered or invaded by the Chaldeans, and wished to shake off the yoke. Nebuchadnezzar lost faith in Zedekiah; and being irritated by his intrigues, he resolved to attack Jerusalem while he was conducting the siege of Tyre and fighting with Egypt, a rival power. Jerusalem was in his way. It was a small city, but it gave him annoyance, and he resolved to crush it. It was to him what Tyre became to Alex-

ander in his conquests. It lay between him and
Egypt, and might be dangerous by its alliances. It
was a strong citadel which he had unwisely spared,
but determined to spare no longer.

The suspicions of the king of Babylonia were probably increased by the disaffection of the Jewish exiles themselves, who believed in the overthrow of Nebuchadnezzar and their own speedy return to their native hills. A joint embassy was sent from Edom, from Moab, the Ammonites, and the kings of Tyre and Sidon, to Jerusalem, with the hope that Zedekiah would unite with them in shaking off the Babylonian yoke; and these intrigues were encouraged by Egypt. Jeremiah, who foresaw the consequences of all this, earnestly protested. And to make his protest more forcible, he procured a number of common ox-yokes, and having put one on his own neck while the embassy was in the city, he sent one to each of the envoys, with the following message to their masters: "Thus saith Jehovah, the God of Israel. I have made the earth and man and the beasts on the face of the earth by my great power, and I give it to whom I see fit. And now I have given all these lands into the hands of Nebuchadnezzar, king of Babylon, to serve him. And all nations shall serve him, till the time of his own land comes; and then many nations and great kings shall make him their servant. And

THE FALL OF JERUSALEM.

the nation and people that will not serve him, and that does not give its own neck to the yoke, that nation I will punish with sword, famine, and pestilence, till I have consumed them by his hand." A similar message he sent to Zedekiah and the princes who seemed to have influenced him. "Bring your necks under the yoke of the king of Babylon, and serve him, and ye shall live. Do not listen to the words of the prophets who say to you, Ye shall not serve the king of Babylon. They prophesy a lie to you." The same message in substance he sent to the priests and people, urging them not to listen to the voice of the false prophets, who based their opinions on the anticipated interference of God to save Jerusalem from destruction; for that destruction would surely come if its people did not serve the king of Babylonia until the appointed time should come, when Babylon itself should fall into the hands of enemies more powerful than itself, even the Medes and Persians.

Jeremiah, thus brought into direct opposition to the false prophets, was exposed to their bitterest wrath. But he was undaunted, although alone, and thus boldly addressed Hananiah, one of their leaders and himself a priest: "Hear the words that I speak in your ears. Not I alone, but all the prophets who have been before me, have prophesied long ago war, captivity, and pestilence, while you prophesy peace."

On this, Hananiah snatched the ox-yoke from the neck of Jeremiah, and broke it, saying, "Thus saith Jehovah, Even so will I break the yoke of Nebuchadnezzar from the neck of all nations within two years." Jeremiah in reply said to this false prophet that he had broken a wooden yoke only to prepare an iron one for the people; for thus saith Jehovah: "I have put a yoke of iron on the neck of all these nations, that they shall serve the king of Babylon. . . . And further, hear this, O Hananiah! Jehovah has not sent thee, but thou makest this people trust in a lie; therefore thou shalt die this very year, because thou hast spoken rebellion against Jehovah." In two months the lying prophet was dead.

Zedekiah, now awe-struck by the death of his counsellor, made up his mind to resist the Egyptian party and remain true to Nebuchadnezzar, and resolved to send an embassy to Babylon to vindicate himself from any suspicion of disloyalty; and further, he sought to win the favor of Jeremiah by a special gift to the Temple of a set of silver vessels to replace the golden ones that had been carried to Babylon. Jeremiah entered into his views, and sent with the embassy a letter to the exiles to warn them of the hopelessness of their cause. It was not well received, and created great excitement and indignation, since it seemed to exhort them to settle down contentedly in their slavery. The words of Jeremiah were, however, indorsed by the prophet Ezekiel, and he addressed the exiles from the place where he lived in Chaldæa, confirming the destruction which Jeremiah prophesied to unwilling ears. "Behold the day! See, it comes! The fierceness of Chaldæa has shot up into a rod to punish the wickedness of the people of Judah. Nothing shall remain of them. The time is come! Forge the chains to lead off the people captive. Destruction comes; calamity will follow calamity!"

Meanwhile, in spite of all these warnings from both Jeremiah and Ezekiel, things were passing at Jerusalem from bad to worse, until Nebuchadnezzar resolved on taking final vengeance on a rebellious city and people that refused to look on things as they were. Never was there a more infatuated people. One would suppose that a city already decimated, and its principal people already in bondage in Babylon, would not dare to resist the mightiest monarch who ever reigned in the East before the time of Cyrus. But "whom the gods wish to destroy they first make mad." Every preparation was made to defend the city. The general of Nebuchadnezzar with a great force surrounded it, and erected towers against the walls. But so strong were the fortifications that the inhabitants were able to stand a siege of eighteen months. At the end of this time they were driven to desperation, and fought with the energy of despair. They could resist battering rams, but they could not resist famine and pestilence. After dreadful sufferings, the besieged found the soldiers of Chaldæa within their Temple, a breach in the walls having been made, and the stubborn city was taken by assault. The few who were spared were carried away captive to Babylon with what spoil could be found, and the Temple and the walls were levelled to the ground. The predictions of the prophets were fulfilled, — the holy city was a heap of desolation. Zedekiah, with his wives and children, had escaped through a passage made in the wall, at a corner of the city which the Chaldeans had not been able to invest, and made his way toward Jericho, but was overtaken and carried in chains to Riblah, where Nebuchadnezzar was encamped. As he had broken a solemn oath to remain faithful, a severe judgment was pronounced upon him. His courtiers and his sons were executed in his sight, his own eyes were put out, and then he was taken to Babylon, where he was made to work like a slave in a mill. Thus ended the dynasty of David, in the year 588 B. C., about the time that Draco gave laws to Athens, and Tarquinius Priscus was king of Rome.

As for Jeremiah, during the siege of the city he fell into the power of the nobles, who beat him and imprisoned him in a dungeon. The king was not able to

THE FALL OF JERUSALEM. 363

release him, so low had the royal power sunk in that disastrous age; but he secretly befriended him, and asked his counsel. The princes insisted on his removal to a place where no succor could reach him, and he was cast into a deep well from which the water was dried up, having at the bottom only slime and mud. From this pit of misery he was rescued by one of the royal guards, and once again he had a secret interview with Zedekiah, and remained secluded in the palace until the city fell. He was spared by the conqueror in view of his fidelity and his earnest efforts to prevent the rebellion, and perhaps also for his lofty character, the last of the great statesmen of Judah and the most distinguished man of the city. Nebuchadnezzar gave him the choice, to accompany him to Babylon with the promise of high favor at his court, or remain at home among the few that were not deemed of sufficient importance to carry away. Jeremiah preferred to remain amid the ruins of his country; for although Jerusalem was destroyed, the mountains and valleys remained, and the humble classes — the peasants — were left to cultivate the neglected vineyards and cornfields.

From Mizpeh, the city which he had selected as his last resting-place, Jeremiah was carried into Egypt, and his subsequent history is unknown. According to tradition he was stoned to death by his fellow-exiles in Egypt. He died as he had lived, a martyr for the truth, but left behind a great name and fame. None of the prophets was more venerated in after ages. And no one more than he resembled, in his sufferings and life, that greater Prophet and Sage who was led as a lamb to the slaughter, that the world through him might be saved.

JUDAS MACCABÆUS.

Died, 160 b. c.

RESTORATION OF THE JEWISH COMMONWEALTH.

JUDAS MACCABÆUS.

RESTORATION OF THE JEWISH COMMONWEALTH.

AFTER the heroic ages of Joshua, Gideon, and David, no warriors appeared in Jewish history equal to Judas Maccabæus and his brothers in bravery, in patriotism, and in noble deeds. They delivered the Hebrew nation when it had sunk to abject submission under the kings of Syria, and when its glory and strength alike had departed. The conquests of Judas especially were marvellous, considering the weakness of the Jewish nation and the strength of its enemies. No hero that chivalry has produced surpassed him in courage and ability; his exploits would be fabulous and incredible if not so well attested. He is not a familiar character, since the Apocrypha, from which our chief knowledge of his deeds is derived, is now rarely read. Jewish history resembles that of Europe in the Middle Ages in the sentiments which are born of danger, oppression, and trial. As a point of mere historical interest, the dark ages that preceded the coming of the Messiah furnish reproachless models of chivalry, courage, and magnanimity, and also the foundation of many of those institutions that cannot be traced to the laws of Moses.

But before I present the wonderful career of Judas Maccabæus, we must look to the circumstances which made that career remarkable and eventful.

On the return of the Jews from the Babylonian captivity there was among them only the nucleus of a nation: more remained in Persia and Assyria than returned to Judæa. We see an infant colony rather than a developed State; it was so feeble as scarcely to attract the notice of the surrounding monarchies. In all probability the population of Judæa did not number a quarter as many as those whom Moses led out of Egypt; it did not furnish a tenth part as many fighting men as were enrolled in the armies of Saul; it existed only under the protection afforded by the Persian monarchs. The Temple as rebuilt by Nehemiah bore but a feeble resemblance to that which Nebuchadnezzar destroyed; it had neither costly vessels nor golden ornaments nor precious woods to remind the scattered and impoverished people of the glory of Solomon. Although the walls of Jerusalem were partially restored, its streets were filled with the débris and ruins of ancient palaces. The city was indeed fortified, but the strong walls and lofty towers which made it almost impregnable were not again restored as in the times of the old monarchy. It took no great force to capture the city and demolish the fortifications. The vast and unnumbered treasures which David, Solomon, and Hezekiah had accumulated in the Temple and the palaces formed no inconsiderable part of the gold and silver that finally enriched Babylonian and Persian kings. The wealth of one of the richest countries of antiquity had been dispersed and re-collected at Babylon, Susa, Ecbatana, and other cities, to be again seized by Alexander in his conquest of the East, then again to be hoarded or spent by the Syrian and Egyptian kings who descended from Alexander's generals, and finally to be deposited in the treasuries of the Romans and the Byzantine Greeks. Whatever ruin warriors may make, whatever temples and palaces they may destroy, they always spare and seize the precious metals, and keep them until they spend them, or are robbed of them in their turn.

Not only was the Holy City a desolation on the return of the Jews, but the rich vineyards and olive-grounds and wheat-fields had run to waste, and there were but few to till and improve them. The few who returned felt their helpless condition, and were quiet and peaceable. Moreover, they had learned during their seventy years' exile to have an intense hatred of everything like idolatry, — a hatred amounting to fanatical fierceness, such as the Puritan Colonists of New England had toward Catholicism. In their dreary and humiliating captivity they at length perceived that idolatry was the great cause of all their calamities; that no national prosperity was possible for them, as the chosen people, except by sincere allegiance to Jehovah. At no period of their history were they more truly religious and loyal to their invisible King than for two hundred years after their return to the land of their ancestors. The terrible lesson of exile and sorrow was not lost on them. It is true that they were only a "remnant" of the nation, as Isaiah had predicted, but they believed that they were selected and saved for a great end. This end they seemed to appreciate now more than ever, and the idea that a great Deliverer was to arise among them, whose reign was to be permanent and glorious, was henceforth devoutly cherished.

A severe morality was practised among these returned exiles, as marked as their faith in God. They were especially tenacious of the laws and ceremonies that Moses had commanded. They kept the Sabbath with a strictness unknown to their ancestors. They preserved the traditions of their fathers, and conformed to them with scrupulous exactness; they even went beyond the requirements of Moses in outward ceremonials. Thus there gradually arose among them a sect ultimately known as the Pharisees, whose leading peculiarity was a slavish and fanatical observance of all the technicalities of the law, both Mosaic and traditional; a sect exceedingly narrow, but popular and powerful. They multiplied fasts and ritualistic observances as the superstitious monks of the Middle Ages did after them; they extended the payment of tithes (tenths) to the most minute and unimportant things, like the herbs which grew in their gardens; they began the Sabbath on Friday evening, and kept it so rigorously that no one was permitted to walk beyond one thousand steps from his own door.

A natural reaction to this severity in keeping minute ordinances, alike narrow, fanatical, and unreasonable, produced another sect called the Sadducees, — a revolutionary party with a more progressive spirit, which embraced the more cultivated and liberal part of the nation; a minority indeed, — a small party as far as numbers went, — but influential from the men of wealth, talent, and learning that belonged to it, containing as it did the nobility and gentry. The members of this party refused to acknowledge any Oral Law transmitted from Moses, and held themselves bound only by the Written Law; they were indifferent to dogmas that had not reason or Scriptures to support them. The writings of Moses have scarcely any recognition of a future life, and hence the Sadducees disbelieved in the resurrection of the dead, — for which reason the Pharisees accused them of looseness in religious opinions. They were more courteous and interesting than the great body of the people who favored the Pharisees, but were more luxurious in their habits of life. They had more social but less religious pride than their rivals, among whom pride took the form of a gloomy austerity and a self-satisfied righteousness.

Another thing pertaining to divine worship which marked the Jews on their return from captivity was the establishment of synagogues, in which the law was expounded by the Scribes, whose business it was to study tradition, as embodied in the Talmud. The Pharisees were the great patrons and teachers of these meetings, which became exceedingly numerous, especially in the cities. There were at one time four hundred synagogues in Jerusalem alone. To these the great body of the people resorted on the Sabbath, rather than to the Temple. The synagogue, popular, convenient, and social, almost supplanted the Temple, except on grand occasions and festivals. The Temple was for great ceremonies and celebrations, like a mediæval cathedral, — an object of pride and awe, adorned and glorious; the synagogue was a sort of church, humble and modest, for the use of the people in ordinary worship, — a place of religious instruction, where decent strangers were allowed to address the meetings, and where social congratulations and inquiries were exchanged. Hence, the synagogue represented the democratic element in Judaism, while it did not ignore the Temple.

Nearly contemporaneous with the synagogue was the Sanhedrim, or Grand Council, composed of seventy-one members, made up of elders, scribes, and priests,—men learned in the law, both Pharisees and Sadducees. It was the business of this aristocratic court to settle disputed texts of Scripture; also questions relating to marriage, inheritance, and contracts. It met in one of the buildings connected with the Temple. It was presided over by the high-priest, and was a dignified and powerful body, its decisions being binding on the Jews outside Palestine. It was not unlike a great council in the early Christian Church for the settlement of theological questions, except that it was not temporary but permanent; and it was more ecclesiastical than civil. Jesus was summoned before it for assuming to be the Messiah; Peter and John, for teaching false doctrine; and Paul, for transgressing the rules of the Temple.

Thus in one hundred and fifty or two hundred years after the Jews returned to their own country, we see the rise of institutions adapted to their circumstances as a religious people, small in numbers, poor but free, — for they were protected by the Persian monarchs against their powerful neighbors. The largest part of the nation was still scattered in every city of the world, especially at Alexandria, where there was a very large Jewish colony, plying their various occupations unmolested by the civil power. In this period Ewald thinks there was a great stride made in sacred literature, especially in recasting ancient books that we accept as canonical. Some of the most beautiful of the Psalms were supposed to have been written at this time; also Apocalypses, books of combined history and revelatory prophecy, — like Daniel, and simple histories like Esther, — written by gifted, lofty, and spiritual men whose names have perished, embodying vivid conceptions of the agency of Jehovah in the affairs of men, so popular, so interesting, and so religious that they soon took their place among the canonical books.

The most noted point in the history of the Jews in the dark ages of their history, for two hundred years after their return from Babylon and Persia, was the external peace and tranquillity of the country, favorable to a quiet and uneventful growth, like that of Puritan New England for one hundred and fifty years after the settlement at Plymouth, — making no history outside of their own peaceful and prosperous life. They had no intercourse with surrounding nations, but were contented to resettle ancient villages, and devote themselves to agricultural pursuits. They were thus trained by labor and poverty — possibly by dangers — to manly energies and heroic courage. They formed a material from which armies could be extemporized on any sudden emergencies. There was no standing army as in the times of David and Solomon, but the whole people were trained to the use of military weapons. Thus the hardy and pious agriculturists of Palestine grew imperceptibly in numbers and wealth, so as to become once more a nation. In all probability this unhistorical period, of which we know almost nothing, was the most fruitful period in Jewish history for the development of great virtues. If they had no heathen literature, they could still discuss theological dogmas; if they had no amusements, they could meet together in their synagogues; if they had no king, they accepted the government of the high-priest; if they had no powerful nobles, they had the aristocratic Sanhedrim, which represented their leading men; if they were disposed to contention, as so many persons are, they could dispute about the unimportant shibboleths which their religious parties set up as matters of difference, — and the more minute, technical, and insoluble these questions were, the fiercer probably grew their contests.

Such was the Hebrew commonwealth in the dark ages of its history, under the protection of the Persian kings. It formed a part of the province of Syria, but the internal government was administered by the high-priests. After the return from exile Joshua, Joachim, and Eliashib successively filled the pontifical office. The government thus was not unlike that of the popes, abating their claims to universal spiritual dominion, although the office of high-priest was hereditary. Jehoiada, son of Eliashib, reigned from 413 to 373, and he was succeeded by his son Johanan, under whose administration important changes took place during the reign of Artaxerxes III., called Ochus, the last but two of the Persian monarchs before the conquest of Persia by Alexander.

The Persians had in the mean time greatly degenerated in their religious faith and observances. Magian rites became mingled with the purer religion of Zoroaster, and even the worship of Venus was not uncommon. Under Cyrus and Darius there was nothing peculiarly offensive to the Jews in the theism of Ormuzd, which was the old religion of the Persians; but when images of ancient divinities were set up by royal authority in Persepolis, Susa, Babylon, and Damascus, the allegiance of the Jews was weakened, and repugnance took the place of sympathy. Moreover, a creature of Artaxerxes III., by the name of Bagoses, became Satrap of Syria, and presumed to appoint as the high-priest at Jerusalem Joshua, another son of Jehoiada, and severely taxed the Jews, and even forced his way into the Holy of Holies, the innermost sanctuary of the Temple, — a sacrilege hard to be endured. This Bagoses poisoned his master, and in the year 338 B. C. elevated to the throne of Persia his son Arses, who had a brief reign, being dethroned and murdered by his father. In 336 Darius III. became king, under whom the Persian monarchy collapsed before the victories of Alexander.

Judæa now came under the dominion of this great conqueror, who favored the Jews, and on his death, 323 B. C., it fell to the possession of Laomedon, one of his generals; while Egypt was assigned to Ptolemy Soter, son of Lagus. Between these princes a war soon broke out, and Laomedon was defeated by Nicanor, one of Ptolemy's generals; and Palestine refusing to submit to the king of Egypt, Ptolemy invaded Judæa, besieged Jerusalem, and took it by assault on the Sabbath, when the Jews refused to fight. A large number of Jews were sent to Alexandria, and the Jewish colony ultimately formed no small part of the population of the new capital. Some eighty thousand Jews, it is said, were settled in Alexandria when Palestine was governed by Greek generals and princes. But Judæa was wrested from Ptolemy Lagus by Antigonus, and again recovered by Ptolemy after the battle of Ipsus, in 301 B. C. Under Ptolemy Egypt became a powerful kingdom, and still more so under his son Philadelphus, who made Alexandria the second capital of the world, — commercially, indeed, the first. It became also a great intellectual centre, and its famous library was the largest ever collected in classical antiquity. This city was the home of scholars and philosophers from all parts of the world. Under the auspices of an enlightened monarch, the Hebrew Scriptures were translated into Greek, the version being called the Septuagint, — an immense service to sacred literature. The Jews enjoyed great prosperity under this Grecian prince, and Palestine was at peace with powerful neighbors, protected by the great king who favored the Jews as the Persian monarchs had done. Under his successor, Ptolemy Euergetes, a still more powerful king, the empire reached its culminating glory, and was extended as far as Antioch and Babylon. Under the next Ptolemy, — Philopater, — degeneracy set in; but the empire was not diminished, and the Syrian monarch Antiochus III., called the Great, was defeated at the battle of Raphia, 217. Under the successor of the enervated Egyptian king, Ptolemy V., a child five years old, Antiochus the Great retrieved the disaster at Raphia, and in 199 won a victory over Scopas the Egyptian general, in consequence of which Judæa, with Phœnicia and Coele-Syria, passed from the Ptolemies to the Seleucidæ.

Judæa now became the battle-ground for the con-

JEWISH COMMONWEALTH RESTORED. 379

tending Syrian and Egyptian armies, and after two hundred years of peace and prosperity her calamities began afresh. She was cruelly deceived and oppressed by the Syrian kings and their generals, for the "kings of the North" were more hostile to the Jews than the "kings of the South." In consequence of the incessant wars between Syria and Egypt, many Jews emigrated, and became merchants, bankers, and artisans in all the great cities of the world, especially in Syria, Asia Minor, Greece, Italy, and Egypt, where all departments of industry were freely opened to them. In the time of Philo there were more than a million of Jews in these various countries; but they remained Jews, and tenaciously kept the laws and traditions of their nation. In every large city were Jewish synagogues.

It was under the reign of Antiochus IV., called Epiphanes, when Judæa was tributary to Syria, that those calamities and miseries befell the Jews which rendered it necessary for a deliverer to arise. Though enlightened and a lover of art, this monarch was one of the most cruel, rapacious, and tyrannical princes that have achieved an infamous immortality. He began his reign with usurpation and treachery. Being unsuccessful in his Egyptian campaigns, he vented his wrath upon the Jews, as if he were mad. Onias III. was the high-priest at the time. Antiochus dispossessed him of his great office and gave it to his brother Jason, a Hellenized Jew, who erected in Jerusalem a gymnasium after the Greek style. But the king, a zealot in paganism, bitterly and scornfully detested the Jewish religion, and resolved to root it out. His general, Apollonius, had orders to massacre the people in the observance of their rites, to abolish the Temple service and the Sabbath, to destroy the sacred books, and introduce idol worship. The altar on Mount Moriah was especially desecrated, and afterward dedicated to Jupiter. A herd of swine were driven into the Temple, and there sacrificed. This outrage was to the Jews "the abomination of desolation," which could never be forgotten or forgiven. The nation rallied and defied the power of a king who could thus wantonly trample on what was most sacred and venerable.

Two hundred years earlier, resistance would have been hopeless; but in the mean time the population had quietly increased, and in the practice of those virtues and labors which agricultural life called out, the people had been strengthened and prepared to rally and defend their lives and liberties. They were still unwarlike, without organization or military habits; but they were brave, hardy, and patriotic. Compared, however, with the forces which could be arrayed against them by the Syrian monarch, who was supreme in western Asia, they were numerically insignificant; and they were also despised and undervalued. They seemed to be as sheep among wolves,— easy to be intimidated and even exterminated.

The outrage in the Temple was the consummation of a series of humiliations and crimes; for in addition to the desecration of the Jewish religion, Antiochus had taken Jerusalem with a great army, had entered into the Temple, where the national treasures were deposited (for it was the custom even among Greeks and Romans to deposit the public money in the temples), and had taken away to his capital the golden candlesticks, the altar of incense, the table of shew bread, and the various vessels and censers and crowns which were used in the service of God,— treasures that amounted to one thousand eight hundred talents, spared by Alexander. So that there came great mourning upon Israel throughout the land, both for the desecration of sacred places, the plunder of the Temple, and the massacre of the people. Jerusalem was sacked and burned, women and children were carried away as captives, and a great fortress was erected on an eminence that overlooked the Temple and city, in which was placed a strong garrison. The plundered inhabitants fled from Jerusalem, which became the habitation of strangers, with all its glory gone. "Her sanctuary was laid waste, her feasts were turned into mourning, her Sabbath into a reproach, and her honor into contempt." Many even of the Jews became apostate, profaned the Sabbath, and sacrificed to idols, rather than lose their lives; for the persecution was the most unrelenting in the annals of martyrdom, even to the destruction of women and children.

The insulted and decimated Jews now rallied under Mattathias, the founder of the Asmonean dynasty.

The immediate occasion of the Jewish uprising, which was ultimately to end in national independence and in the rule of a line of native princes, was as unpremeditated as the throwing out of the window at the council chamber at Prague those deputies who supported the Emperor of Germany in his persecution of the Protestants, which led to the Thirty Years' War and the establishment of religious liberty in Germany. At this crisis among the Jews, a hero arose in their midst as marvellous as Gustavus Adolphus.

In Modin, or Modein, a town near the sea, but the site of which is now unknown, there lived an old man of a priestly family named Asmon, who was rich and influential. His name was Mattathias, and he had five grown-up sons, each distinguished for bravery, piety, and patriotism. He was so prominent in his little city for fidelity to the faith of his fathers, as well as for social position, that when an officer of Antiochus came to Modin to enforce the decrees of his royal master, he made splendid offers to Mattathias to induce him to favor the crusade against his countrymen. Mattathias not only contemptuously rejected these overtures, but he openly proclaimed his resolution to adhere to his religion, — a man who could not be bribed, and who could not be intimidated. "Be it far from us," he said, "to forsake law and ordinances. We will not hearken to the king's words, to turn aside to the right hand or to the left."

When he had thus given noble attestation of his resolution to adhere to the faith of his fathers, there came forward an apostate Jew to sacrifice on the heathen altar, which it seems was erected by royal command in all the cities and towns of Judæa. This so inflamed the indignation of the brave old man that he ran and slew the Jew upon the altar, together with the king's commissioner, and pulled down the altar.

For this, Mattathias was obliged to flee, and he escaped to the mountains, taking with him his five sons and all who would join his standard of revolt, crying with a loud voice, "Let every one zealous for the Law follow me!" A considerable multitude fled with him to the wilderness of Judæa, on the west of the Dead Sea, taking with them their wives and children and cattle. But this flight from persecution speedily became known to the troops that were quartered on Mount Zion, a strong fortress which controlled the Temple and city, and a detachment was sent in pursuit. The fugitives, zealous for the Law, refused to defend themselves on the Sabbath day, and the result was that they all perished, with their wives and children. Their fate made such a powerful impression on Mattathias, that it was resolved henceforth to fight on the Sabbath day, if attacked. The patriots had to choose between two alternatives, — to be utterly rooted out, or to defend themselves on the Sabbath, and thus violate the letter of the Law. Mattathias was sufficiently enlightened to perceive that fighting on the Sabbath, if attacked, was a supreme necessity, remembering doubtless that Moses recognized the right of necessary work even on the sacred day of rest. The law of self-defence is an ultimate one, and appeals to the consciousness of universal humanity. Strange as it may seem, the Sabbath has ever been a favorite day with generals to fight grand battles in every Christian country.

Mattathias, although a very old man, now put forth superhuman energies, raised an army, drove the persecuting soldiers out of the country, pulled down the heathen altars, and restored the Law; and when the time came for him to die, at the age of one hundred and forty-five years, — if we may credit the history, for Josephus and the Apocrypha are here our chief authorities, — he collected around him his five sons. all wise and valiant men, and enjoined them to be united among themselves, and to be faithful to the Law,—calling to their minds the noted examples from the Hebrew Scriptures, Abraham, Joseph, Joshua, David, Elijah, who were obedient to the commandments of God. He did not speak of patriotism, although an intense lover of his country. He exhorted his sons to be simply obedient to the Law,—not, probably, in the restricted and literal sense of the word, but in the idea of being faithful to God, even as Abraham was obedient before the Law was given. The glory which he assured them they would thus win was not the *éclat* of victory, or even of national deliverance, but the imperishable renown which comes from righteousness. He promised a glorious immortality to those who fell in battle in defence of the truth and of their liberties, reminding us of the promises which Mohammed made to his followers. But the great incentive to bravery which he urged was the ultimate reward of virtue, which runs through the Scriptures, even the favor of God. The heroes of chivalry fought for the favor of ladies, the praises of knights, and the friendship of princes; the reward of modern generals is exaltation in popular estimation, the increase of political power, the accumulation of wealth, and sometimes the consciousness of rendering important services to their country,— an exalted patriotism, such as marked Washington and Cromwell. But the reward which the Jewish hero promised was loftier, — even that of the divine favor.

The aged Mattathias, having thus given his last counsels to his sons, recommended the second one, Simon, or Simeon, as the future head of the family, to whose wisdom the other brothers were to defer, — a man whose counsel would be invaluable. The third brother, Judas, a mighty warrior from his youth, was appointed as the leader of the forces to fight the battles of the people, — the peculiar vocations of Saul and of David, for which they were selected to be kings.

On the death of Mattathias, mourned by all Israel as Samuel was mourned, at the age of one hundred and forty-five, and buried in the sepulchre of his fathers at Modin, Judas, called "The Maccabæus" ("The Hammer," as some suppose), rose up in his stead; and all his brothers helped him, and all his father's friends, and he fought with cheerfulness the battles of Israel. He put on armor as a hero, and was like a lion in his acts, and like a lion's whelp roaring for prey. He pursued and punished the Jewish transgressors of the Law, so that they lost courage, and all the workers of inquity were thrown into disorder, and the work of deliverance prospered in his hands. Like Josiah he went through the cities of Judah, destroying the heathen and the ungodly. The fame of his exploits rapidly spread through the land, and Apollonius, military governor of Samaria, collected an army and marched against a man who with his small forces set at defiance the sovereignty of a mighty monarchy. Judas attacked Apollonius, slew him, and dispersed his army. Ever afterward he was girded with the sword of the Syrian, — a weapon probably adorned with jewels, and tempered like the famous Damascus blades.

Seron, a general of higher rank, the commander-in-chief of the Syrian forces in Palestine, irritated at the defeat and death of Apollonius, the following year marched with a still larger army against Judas. The latter had with him only a small company, who were despondent in view of the great array of their heathen enemies, and moreover faint from having not eaten anything that day. But the heroic leader encouraged his men, and, undaunted in the midst of overwhelming danger, resolved to fight, trusting for aid from the God of battles; for "victory," said he, "is not through the multitude of an army, but from heaven cometh the strength." This resolution to fight against overwhelming odds would be audacity in modern warfare, which is perfected machinery, making one man with reliable weapons as good as another, and success to be chiefly determined by numbers skilfully posted and manœuvred according to strategic science; but in ancient times personal bravery, directed by military genius and aided by fortunate circumstances, frequently prevailed over the force of multitudes, especially if the latter were undisciplined or intimidated by superstitious omens, — as evinced by Alexander's victories, and those of Charles Martel and the Black Prince in the Middle Ages. The desperate valor of Judas and his small band was crowned with complete success. Seron was defeated with great loss, his army fled, and the fame of Judas spread far and wide. His name became a terror to the nations.

King Antiochus now saw that the subjection of this valiant Jew was no easy matter; and filled with wrath and vengeance he gathered together all the forces of his kingdom, opened his treasury, paid his soldiers a year in advance, and resolved to root out the rebellious nation by a war of extermination. Crippled, however, in resources, and in great need of money, he concluded to go in person to Persia and collect tribute from the various provinces, and seize the treasures which were supposed to be deposited in royal cities beyond the Euphrates. He left behind, as regent or lieutenant, Lysias, a man of royal descent, with orders to prosecute the war against the Jews with the utmost severity, while with half his forces he proceeded in person to Persia. Lysias chose Ptolemy, Nicanor, and Gorgias, experienced generals, to conduct the war, with forty thousand foot and seven thousand horsemen, besides

JEWISH COMMONWEALTH RESTORED. 389

elephants, with orders to exterminate the rebels, take possession of their lands, and settle heathen aliens in their place. So confident were these generals of success that merchants accompanied the army with gold and silver to purchase the Jews from the conquerors, and fetters in which to make them slaves. A large force from the land of the Philistines also joined the attacking army.

Jerusalem at this time was a forsaken city, uninhabited, like a wilderness; the Sanctuary was trodden down, and heathen foreigners occupied the citadel on Mount Zion. It was a time of general mourning and desolation, and the sound of the harp and the pipe ceased throughout the land. But Judas was not discouraged; and the warriors with him were bent upon redeeming the land from desolation. They however put on sackcloth, and prayed to the God of their fathers, and made every effort to rally their forces, feeling that it was better to die in battle than see the pollution of the Sanctuary and the evils which overspread the land. Judas succeeded in collecting altogether three thousand men, who however were poorly armed, and intrenched himself among the mountains, about twenty miles from Jerusalem. Learning this, Gorgias took five thousand men, one thousand horsemen, under guides from the castle on Mount Zion, and departed from his camp at Emmaus by night, with a view of surprising and capturing the Jewish force. But Judas was on the alert, and obtained information of the intended attack. So he broke up his own camp, and resolved to attack the main force of the enemy, weakened by the absence of Gorgias and his chosen band. After reminding his soldiers of God's mercies in times of old, he ordered the trumpets to sound, and unexpectedly rushed upon the unsuspecting and unprepared Syrians, totally routed them, pursued them as far as to the plains of Idumæa, killed about three thousand men, took immense spoil, — gold and silver, purple garments and military weapons, — and returned in triumph to the forsaken camp, singing songs and blessing Heaven for the great victory.

Many of the Syrians that escaped came and told Lysias all that had happened, and he on hearing it was confounded and discouraged. But in the year following he collected an army of sixty thousand chosen footmen and five thousand horsemen to renew the attack, and marched to the Idumæan border. Here Judas met him at Bethsura, near to Jerusalem, with ten thousand men, now inspirited by victory, and again defeated the Syrian forces, with a loss to the enemy of five thousand men. Lysias, who commanded this army in person, returned to Antioch and made preparations to raise a still greater force, while the victorious Jews took possession of the capital.

Judas had now leisure to cleanse the Sanctuary and dedicate it. When his army saw the desolation of their holy city, — trees growing in the very courts of the Temple as in a forest, the altars profaned, the gates burned, — they were filled with grief, and rent their garments and cried aloud to Heaven. But Judas proceeded with his sacred work, pulled down the defiled altar of burnt sacrifice and rebuilt it, cleansed the Sanctuary, hallowed the desecrated courts, made new holy vessels, decked the front of the Temple with crowns and shields of gold, and restored the gates and chambers. Judas also fortified the Temple with high walls and towers, and placed in it a strong garrison, for the Syrians still held possession of the Tower, — a strong fortress near the mount of the Temple.

When all was cleansed and renewed, a solemn service of reconsecration was celebrated; the sacred fire was kindled afresh on the altar, thousands of lamps were lighted, the sacrifices were offered, the people thronged the courts of Jehovah, and with psalms of praise, festive dances, harps, lutes, and cymbals made a joyful noise unto the Lord. This triumphant restoration was celebrated three years, to the very day, from the day of desecration; it was forever after — as long as the Temple stood — held a sacred yearly festival, and called the Feast of the Dedication, or sometimes, from its peculiar ceremonies, the Feast of Lights.

The successes of Judas and the restoration of the Temple worship inflamed with renewed anger the heathen population of the countries in the near vicinity of Judæa; and there seems to have been a general confederacy of Idumæans, — descendants of Esau, — with sundry of the Bedouin tribes, and of the heathen settled east of the Jordan in the land of Gilead, and of Phœnicians and heathen strangers in Galilee, to recover what the Syrians had lost, and to restore idol worship. Judas had now an army of eleven thousand men, which he divided between himself and his brother Simon, and they marched in different directions to the attack of their numerous enemies. They were both eminently successful, gaining bloody battles, capturing cities and fortresses, taking immense spoils, mingling the sound of trumpets with prayers to Almighty God, — heroes as religious as they were brave, an unexampled band of warriors, rivalling Joshua, Saul, and David in the brilliancy of their victories. All the Jews who remained true to their faith in the districts which he overran and desolated, Judas brought back with him to Jerusalem for greater safety.

Only one misfortune sullied the glory of these exploits. Judas had left behind him at Jerusalem, when he and Simon went forth to fight the idolaters, a garrison of two thousand men under the command of Joseph and Azarias, leaders of the people, with the strict command to remain in the city until he should return. But these popular leaders, dazzled by the victories of Judas and Simon, and wishing to earn a fame like theirs, issued from their stronghold with two thousand men to attack Jamnia, and were met by Gorgias the Syrian general and completely annihilated, — a just punishment for military disobedience. The loss of two thousand men was a calamity, but Judas pursued his victories, finally turning against the Philistines, who at this point disappear from sacred history.

In the meantime King Antiochus, who, as already stated, had gone on a plundering expedition to Persia, was defeated in the attempt, and returned in great grief and disappointment to Ecbatana. Here he heard that his armies under Lysias had been disgracefully beaten, and that Judæa was in a fair way to achieve its independence under the heroic Judas; and, worse still, that all the pagan temples and altars which he had set up in Jerusalem were removed and destroyed. This especially filled him with rage, for he was a fanatic in his religion, and utterly detested the monotheism of the Jews. So oppressed with grief was this heathen persecutor that he took to his bed; and in addition to his humiliation he was afflicted with a loathsome disease, called elephantiasis, so that he was avoided and neglected by his own servants. He now saw that he must die, and calling for his friend Philip, made him regent of his kingdom during the minority of his son, whom he had left at Antioch.

The Jews were thus delivered from the worst enemy that had afflicted them since the Babylonian captivity. Neither Assyrians nor Egyptians nor Persians had so ruthlessly swept away religious institutions. Those conquerors were contented with conquest and its political results, — namely, the enslavement and spoliation of the people; they did not pollute the sacred places like the Syrian persecutor. By the rivers of Babylon the Jews had sat down and wept when they remembered Zion, but their sad wailing was over the fact that they were captives in a strange land. Ground down to the dust by Antiochus, however, they bewailed not only their external misfortunes, but far more bitterly the desecration of their Sanctuary and the attempt to root out their religion, which was their life.

The death of Antiochus Epiphanes was therefore a great relief and rejoicing to the struggling Jews. He left as heir to his throne a boy nine years of age; but though he had made his friend Philip guardian of his son and regent of his kingdom, his lieutenant at Antioch, Lysias, also claimed the guardianship and the regency. These rival claims of course led to civil wars between Lysias and Philip, in consequence of which the Jews were comparatively unmolested, and had leisure to organize their forces, fortify their strongholds, and prepare for complete independence. Among other things, Judas Maccabæus attacked the citadel or tower on Mount Zion, overlooking the Temple, in which a large garrison of the enemy had long been stationed, and which was a perpetual menace. The attack or siege of this strong fortress alarmed the heathen, who made complaint to the young king, called Eupator, or more probably to the regent Lysias, who sent an overwhelming army into Judæa, consisting of one hundred thousand foot, twenty thousand horse, and thirty-two elephants. But Judas did not hesitate to give battle to this great force, and again gained a victory. It was won, however, at the expense of his brother Eleazer. Seeing one of the elephants armed with royal armor, he supposed that it carried the king himself; and heroically forcing his way through the ranks of the enemy, he slipped under the elephant, and gave the beast a mortal wound, so that it fell to the ground, crushing to death the courageous Maccabæus, — for the brothers of Judas, worthy compatriots and fellow-soldiers with him, were also called by his special name; and although the family name was Asmon, they are famous as "the Maccabees."

This battle however was not decisive. Lysias advanced to Jerusalem and laid siege to it. But hearing that Philip had succeeded in gaining authority at Antioch, he made peace with Judas, and hastily returned to his capital, where he found Philip master of the city. Although he recovered his capital, it was only for a short time, since Demetrius, son of Seleucus, who had been sojourning at Rome, returned to the palace of his ancestors, and slaying both Lysias and the young king, reigned in their stead.

With this king the Jews were soon involved in war. Evil-minded men, hostile to Judas (for in such unsettled times treachery was everywhere), went to Antioch with their complaints, headed by Alcimus, who wished to be high-priest, and inflamed the anger of King Demetrius. The new monarch sent one of his ablest generals, called Bacchides, with an army to chastise the Jews and reinstate Alcimus, who had been ejected from his high office. This wicked high-priest overran the country with the forces of Bacchides, who had returned to Antioch, but did not prevail; so the king sent Nicanor, already experienced in this Jewish war, with a still larger army against Judas. The gallant Maccabæus, however, gained a great victory, and slew Nicanor himself. This battle gave another rest for a time to the afflicted land of Judah.

Meanwhile Judas, fearing that the Syrian forces would ultimately overpower him, sent an embassy to Rome to invoke protection. It was a long journey in those times. A century and a half later it took

Saint Paul six months to make it. The conquests of the Romans were known throughout the East, and better known than the policy they pursued of devouring the countries that sought their protection when it suited their convenience. At this time, 162 B. C., Italy was subdued, Spain had been added to the empire, Macedonia was conquered, Syria was threatened, and Carthage was soon to fall. The Senate was then the ruling power at Rome, and was in the height of its dignity, not controlled by either generals or demagogues. The Senate received with favor the Jewish ambassadors, and promised their protection. Had Judas known what that protection meant, he would have been the last man to seek it.

Nor did the treaty of alliance with Rome save Judæa from the continued hostilities of Syria. Demetrius sent Bacchides with another army, which encamped against Jerusalem, where **Judas** had only eight hundred men to resist an **army of twenty** thousand foot and two thousand horse. We infer that his forces had dwindled away by perpetual contests. His heart of hope was now well-nigh broken, but his lion courage remained. Against the solicitation of his companions in war he resolved to fight; gallantly and stubbornly contested the field from morning to night, and at last, hemmed in between two wings of the Syrian foe, fell in the battle.

The heroic career of Judas Maccabæus was ended. He had done marvellous things. He had for six years resisted and often defeated overwhelming forces; he had fought more battles than David; he had kept the enemy at bay while his prostrate country arose from the dust; he had put to flight and slain tens of thousands of the heathen; he had recovered and fortified Jerusalem, and restored the Temple worship; he had trained his people to be warlike and heroic. At last he was slain only when his followers were scattered by successive calamities. He bore the brunt of six years' successful war against the most powerful monarchy in Asia, bent on the extermination of his countrymen. And amid all his labors he had kept the Law, being revered for his virtues as much as for his heroism. Not a single crime sullied his glorious name. And when he fell at last, exhausted, the nation lamented him as David mourned for Jonathan, saying, "How is the valiant fallen!" A greater hero than he never adorned an age of heroism. Judas was not only a mighty captain, but a wise statesman, — so revered, that, according to Josephus, in his closing years he was made high-priest also, thus uniting in his person both spiritual and temporal authority. It was a very small country that he ruled, but it is in small countries that genius is often most fully developed, either for war or for peace. We know but little of his private life. He had no time for what the world calls pleasures; his life was rough, full of dangers and embarrassments. His only aim seems to have been to shake off the Syrian yoke that oppressed his native land, to redeem the holy places of the nation from the pollutions of the obscene rites of heathenism, and to restore the worship of Jehovah according to the consecrated ritual established in the Mosaic Law.

The death of Judas was of course followed by great disorders and universal despondency. His mantle fell on his brother Jonathan, who became the leader of the scattered forces of the Jews. He also prevailed over Bacchides in several engagements, so that the Syrian leader returned to Antioch, and the Jews had rest for two years. Jonathan was now clothed with honor and dignity, wore a purple garment and other emblems of high rank, and was almost an acknowledged sovereign. He improved his opportunities and fortified Jerusalem. But his prosperous career was cut short by treachery. He was enticed by the Syrian general, even when he had an army of forty thousand men, — so largely had the forces of Judæa increased, — into Ptolemais with a few followers, under blandishing promises, and slain.

Simon was now the only remaining son of Mattathias; and on him devolved the high-priesthood, as well as the executive duties of supreme ruler. He wisely devoted himself to the internal affairs of the State which he ruled. He fortified Joppa, the only port of Judæa, reduced hostile cities, and made himself master of the famous fortress of Mount Zion, so long held in threatening vicinity by the Syrians, which he not only levelled with the ground, but also razed the summit of the hill on which it stood, so that it should no longer overlook the Temple area. The Temple became not only the Sanctuary, but also one of the strongest fortresses in the world. At a later period it held out for some time against the army of Titus, even after Jerusalem itself had fallen.

Simon executed the laws with rigorous impartiality repaired the Temple, restored the sacred vessels, and secured general peace, order, and security. Even the lands desolated by the wasting wars with several successive Syrian monarchs again rejoiced in fertility. Every man sat under his own vine and fig-tree in safety. The friendly alliance with Rome was renewed by a present to that greedy republic of a golden shield, weighing one thousand pounds, and worth fifty talents, thus showing how much wealth had increased under Judas and his brothers. Even the ambassadors of the Syrian monarch were astonished at the splendor of Simon's palace, and at the riches of the Temple, again restored, not in the glory of Solomon, but in a magnificence of which few temples could boast, —

the pride once more of the now prosperous Jews, who had by their persistent bravery earned their independence. In the year 143 B. C., the Jews began a new epoch in their history, after twenty-three years of almost incessant warfare.

Yet Simon was destined, like his brothers, to end his days by violence. He also, together with two of his sons, was treacherously murdered by his son-in-law Ptolemy, who aspired to the exalted office of high-priest, leaving his son John Hyrcanus to reign in his stead, in the year 136 B. C. The rule of the Maccabees, — the five sons of Mattathias, — lasted thirty years. They were the founders of the Asmonean princes, who ruled both as kings and high-priests.

With the death of Simon, the last remaining son of Mattathias, this lecture properly should end; yet a rapid glance at the Jewish nation, under the rule of the Asmonean princes and the Idumæan Herod, may not be uninteresting.

John Hyrcanus, the first of the Asmonean kings, was an able sovereign, and reigned twenty-nine years. He threw off the Syrian yoke, and the Jewish kingdom maintained its independence until it fell under the Roman sway. His most memorable feat was the destruction of the Samaritan Temple on Mount Gerizim, which had been an eye-sore to the people of

Jerusalem for two hundred years. He then subdued Idumæa, and compelled the people of that country to adopt the Jewish religion. He maintained a strict alliance with the Romans, and became master of Samaria and of Galilee, which were incorporated with his kingdom, so that the ancient limits of the kingdom of David were nearly restored. He built the castle of Baris on a rock within the fortifications that surrounded the hill of the Temple, which afterward was known as the tower of Antonia.

On his death, 105 B. C., Hyrcanus was succeeded by his son Aristobulus,—a weak and wicked prince, who assassinated his brother, and starved to death his mother in a dungeon. The next king of the Asmonean line, Alexander Jannæus, was brave, but unsuccessful, and died after an unquiet and turbulent reign of twenty-seven years, 77 B. C. His widow, Alexandra, ruled as regent with great tact and energy for nine years, and was succeeded by her son Hyrcanus II. This feeble and unfortunate prince had to contend with the intrigues and violence of his more able but unscrupulous brother, Aristobulus, who sought to steal his sceptre, and who at one time even drove him from his kingdom. Hyrcanus put himself under the protection of the Romans. They came as arbiters; they remained as masters. It was when Judæa was under the nominal rule of Hyrcanus II., driven hither and thither by his enemies, and when his capital was in their hands, that Pompey, triumphant over the armies of the East, took Jerusalem after a desperate resistance, entered the Temple, and even penetrated to the Holy of Holies. To his credit he left untouched the treasures accumulated in the Temple, but he demolished the walls of the city and imposed a tribute. Judæa was now virtually under the dominion of the Romans, although the sovereignty of Hyrcanus was not completely taken away. On the fall of Pompey, Crassus the triumvir plundered the Temple of ten thousand talents, as was estimated, and the fate of Judæa, during the memorable civil war of which Cæsar was the hero and victor, hung in trembling suspense. I will not enumerate the contentions, the deeds of violence, the acts of treachery, and the strife of rival parties which marked the tumultuous period in Judæa while Cæsar and Pompey were contending for the sovereignty of the world. These came to an end at last by the dethronement of the last of the Asmonean princes, and the accession of the Idumæan Herod by the aid of Antony (40 B. C.).

Herod, called the Great, was the last independent sovereign of Palestine. He was the son of Antipater, a noble Idumæan, who had ingratiated himself in the favor of Hyrcanus II., high-priest and sovereign, and who ruled as the prime minister of this feeble and incapable prince. By rendering some service to Cæsar, Antipater was made procurator of Judæa, and appointed his son Herod to the government of Galilee, where he developed remarkable administrative talents. Soon after, he was raised by Sextus Cæsar to the military command of Cœle-Syria. After the battle of Philippi, Herod secured the favor of Antony by an enormous bribe, as he had that of Cassius on the death of Cæsar, and was made one of the tetrarchs of the province. In the mean time his father, Alexander, was poisoned at Jerusalem, and Antigonus, son of Aristobulus, who had gained ascendency, cut off the ears of Hyrcanus, and not only deprived him of the office of high-priest, but usurped his authority. Herod himself proceeded to Rome, and was successful in his intrigues, being by the favor of Antony made king of Judæa. But a severe contest was before him, since Antigonus was resolved to defend his crown. With the aid of the Romans, Herod, after a war of three years, subdued his rival and put him to death, together with every member of the Sanhedrim but two. His power was cemented by his marriage with Mariamne, the beautiful sister of Aristobulus, whom he made high-priest.

The Asmonean princes were now, by the death of Antigonus, reduced to Aristobulus and the aged Hyrcanus, both of whom were murdered by the suspicious tyrant who had triumphed over so many enemies. In a fit of jealousy Herod even caused the execution of his beautiful wife, whom he passionately loved, as he had already destroyed her grandfather, father, brother, and uncle. Supported by Augustus, whom he had managed to conciliate after the death of Antony, Herod reigned with undisputed authority over even an increase of territory. He doubtless reigned with great ability, tyrant and murderer as he was, and detested by the Jews as an Idumæan. He reigned in a state of magnificence unknown to the Asmonean princes. He built a new and magnificent palace on the hill of Zion, and rebuilt the fortress of Baris, which he called Antonia in honor of his friend and patron, Antony. He also erected strong citadels in different cities of his kingdom, and rebuilt Samaria; he founded Cæsarea and colonized it with Greeks, so that it became a great maritime city, rivalling Tyre in magnificence and strength. But Herod's greatest work, by which he hoped to ingratiate himself in the favor of the Jews, was the rebuilding of the Temple on a scale of unexampled magnificence. He was also very liberal in the distribution of corn during a severe famine. He was in such high favor with Augustus by his presents and his devotion to the imperial interests, that, next to Agrippa, he was the emperor's greatest favorite. His two sons by Mariamne were educated at Rome with great care, and were lodged in the palace of the Emperor.

Herod's latter days however were clouded by the intrigues of his court, by treason and conspiracies, in consequence of which his sons, favorites with the people on account of their accomplishments and their Asmonean blood, were executed by the suspicious and savage despot. Antipater, another son, by his first wife, whom he had chosen as his successor, conspired against his life, and the proof of his guilt was so clear that he also was summarily executed. In addition to these troubles Herod was tormented by remorse for the execution of the murdered Mariamne. He was the victim of jealousy, suspicion, and wrath. One of his last acts was the order to destroy the infants in the vicinity of Jerusalem in the vain hope of destroying the predicted Messiah, — him who should be "born king of the Jews." He died of a loathsome and excruciating disease, in his seventieth year, having reigned nearly forty years. His kingdom, by his will, was divided between the children of his later wife, a Samaritan woman, — the eldest of whom, Archelaus, became monarch of Judæa; and the second, Antipas, became tetrarch of Galilee. The former married the widow of his half-brother Alexander, who was executed; and the latter married Herodias, wife of Philip, also his half-brother.

Archelaus ruled Judæa with such injustice and cruelty, that, after nine years, he was summoned to Rome and exiled to Vienne in Gaul, and Judæa became a Roman province under the prefecture of Syria. The supreme judicial authority was exercised by the Jewish Sanhedrim, the great ecclesiastical and civil council, composed of seventy-one persons presided over by the high-priest. The Sanhedrim, under the name of chief priests, scribes, and elders of the people, now took the lead in all public transactions pertaining to the internal administration of the province, being inferior only to the tribunal of the governor, who resided in Cæsarea.

Meanwhile the long expectation of the Jews, especially during the reign of Herod, of a promised Deliverer, was fulfilled, and one claiming to be the Messiah appeared, — not a temporal prince and mighty hero of war, a greater Judas Maccabæus, as the Jews had supposed, but a helpless infant, born in a manger, and brought up as a peasant-carpenter. Yet he it was who should found a spiritual kingdom never to be destroyed, going on from conquering to conquer, until the whole world shall be subdued. With the advent of Jesus of Nazareth, in which we see the fulfilment of all the promises made to the chosen people from Abraham to Isaiah, Jewish history loses its chief interest. The mission of the Hebrew nation seems to stand accomplished; the conception of one, holy, spiritual God was kept alive in the world until, in "the fulness of time," the mighty Romans subdued and united all lands under one rule, drawing them nearer together by great highroads ; the flexible Greek language gave all peoples a common tongue, in which already the Hebrew Scriptures had been familiarized among scholars; the life and teachings of Jesus entered with vital power into the heart and brain of those devoted followers who recognized him as the Christ, — the revelator of the universal fatherhood of the One true God; and thenceforward Christianity becomes the great spiritual power of the world.

SAINT PAUL.

Died, about 67 a.d.

THE SPREAD OF CHRISTIANITY.

SAINT PAUL.

THE SPREAD OF CHRISTIANITY.

THE Scriptures say but little of the life of Saul from the time he was a student, at the age of fifteen, at the feet of Gamaliel, one of the most learned rabbis of the Jewish Sanhedrim at Jerusalem, until he appeared at the martyrdom of Stephen, when about thirty years of age.

Saul, as he was originally named, was born at Tarsus, a city of Cilicia, about the fourth year of our era. His father was a Jew, a pharisee, and a man of respectable social position. In some way not explained, he was able to transmit to his son the rights of Roman citizenship, — a valuable inheritance, as it proved. He took great pains in the education of his gifted son, who early gave promise of great talents and attainments in rabbinical lore, and who gained also some knowledge, although probably not a very deep one, of the Greek language and literature. Saul's great peculiarity as a young man was his extreme pharisaism, — devotion to the Jewish Law in all its minuteness of ceremonial rites. We gather from his own confessions that at that period, when he was engrossed in the study of the Jewish scriptures and religious institutions, he was narrow and intolerant, and zealous almost to fanaticism to perpetuate ritualistic conventionalities and the exclusiveness of his sect. He was austere and conscientious, but his conscience was unenlightened. He exhibited nothing of that large-hearted charity and breadth of mind for which he was afterward distinguished; he was in fact a bitter persecutor of those who professed the religion of Jesus, which he detested as an innovation. His morality being always irreproachable, and his character and zeal giving him great influence, he was sent to Damascus, with authority to bring to Jerusalem for trial or punishment those who had embraced the new faith. He is supposed to have been absent from Jerusalem during the ministry of our Lord, and probably never saw him who was despised and rejected of men. We are told that Saul, in the virulence of his persecuting spirit, consented to the death of Stephen, who was no ignorant Galilean, but a learned Hellenist; nor is there evidence that the bitter and relentless young pharisee was touched either by the eloquence or blameless life or terrible sufferings of the distinguished martyr.

The next memorable event in the life of Saul — at

that time probably a member of the Jewish Sanhedrim — was his conversion to Christianity, as sudden and unexpected as it was profound and lasting, while on his way to Damascus on the errand already mentioned. The sudden light from heaven which exceeded in brilliancy the torrid midday sun, the voice of Jesus which came to the trembling persecutor as he lay prostrate on the ground, the blindness which came upon him, — all point to the supernatural; for he was no inquirer after truth like Luther and Augustine, but bent on a persistent course of cruel persecution. At once he is a changed man in his spirit, in his aims, in his entire attitude toward the followers of the Nazarene. The proud man becomes as docile and humble as a child; the intolerant zealot for the Law becomes broad and charitable; and only one purpose animates his whole subsequent life, — which is to spend his strength, amid perils and difficult labors, in defence of the doctrines he had spurned. His leading idea now is to preach salvation, not by pharisaical works by which no man can be justified, but by faith in the crucified one who was sent into the world to save it by new teachings and by his death upon the cross. He will go anywhere in his sublime enthusiasm, among Jews or among Gentiles, to plant the precious seeds of the new faith in every pagan city which he can reach.

It is thought by Conybeare and Howson, Farrar and others that the new convert spent three years in retirement in Arabia, in profound meditation and communion with God, before the serious labors of his life began as a preacher and missionary. After his conversion it would seem that Saul preached the divinity of Christ with so much zeal that the Jews in Damascus were filled with wrath, and sought to take his life, and even guarded the gates of the city for fear that he might escape. The conspiracy being detected, the friends of Saul put him into a basket made of ropes, and let him down from a window in a house built upon the city wall, so that he escaped, and thereupon proceeded to Jerusalem to be indorsed as a Christian brother. He was especially desirous to see Peter, as the foremost man among the Christians, though James had greater dignity. Peter received him kindly, though not enthusiastically, for the remembrance of his relentless persecutions was still fresh in the minds of the Christians. It was impossible, however, that two such warmhearted, honest, and enthusiastic men should not love each other, when the common leading principle of their lives was mutually understood.

Among the disciples, however, it was only Peter who took Saul cordially by the hand. The other leaders held aloof; not one so much as spoke to him. He was regarded with general mistrust; even James, the

Lord's brother, the first bishop of Jerusalem, would hold no communion with him. At length Joseph, a Levite of Cyprus, afterward called Barnabas, — a man of large heart, who sold his possessions to give to the poor, — recognizing Saul's sincerity and superior talents, extended to him the right hand of fellowship, and later became his companion in the missionary journeys which he undertook. He used his great influence in removing the prejudices of the brethren, and Saul henceforth was admitted to their friendship and confidence.

Saul at first did not venture to preach in Hebrew synagogues, but sought the synagogue of the Hellenists, in which the voice of Stephen had first been heard. But his preaching was again cut short by a conspiracy to murder him, so fierce was the animosity which his conversion had created among the Jews, and he was compelled to flee. The brethren conducted him to the little coast village of Cæsarea, whence he sailed for his native city Tarsus, in Cilicia.

How long Saul remained in Tarsus, and what he did there, we do not know. Not long, probably, for he was sought out by Barnabas as his associate for missionary work in Antioch. It would seem that on the persecution which succeeded Stephen's death, many of the disciples fled to various cities; and among others, to that great capital of the East, — the third city of the Roman Empire.

Thither Barnabas had gone as their spiritual guide; but he soon found out that among the Greeks of that luxurious and elegant city there were demanded greater learning, wisdom, and culture than he himself possessed. He turned his eyes upon Saul, then living quietly at Tarsus, whose superior tact and trained skill in disputation, large and liberal mind, and indefatigable zeal marked him out as the fittest man he could find as a coadjutor in his laborious work. Thus Saul came to Antioch to assist Barnabas.

No city could have been chosen more suitable for the peculiar talents of Saul than this great Eastern emporium, containing a population of five hundred thousand. I need not speak of its works of art, — its palaces, its baths, its aqueducts, its bridges, its basilicas, its theatres, which called out even the admiration of the citizens of the imperial capital. These were nothing to Saul, who thought only of the souls he could convert to the religion of Jesus; but they indicate the importance and wealth of the population. In this pagan city were half a million people steeped in all the vices of the Oriental world, — a great influx of heterogeneous races, mostly debased by various superstitions and degrading habits, whose religion, so far as they had any, was a crude form of Nature-worship. And yet among them were wits, philosophers, rhetoricians, poets, and satirists, as was to be expected in a city where Greek was the prevailing language. But these were not the people who listened to Saul and Barnabas. The apostles found hearers chiefly among the poor and despised, — artisans, servants, soldiers, sailors, — although occasionally persons of moderate independence became converts, especially women of the middle ranks. Poor as they were, the Christians at Antioch found means to send a large contribution in money to their brethren at Jerusalem, who were suffering from a grievous famine.

A year was spent by Barnabas and Saul at Antioch in founding a Christian community, or congregation, or "church," as it was called. And it was in this city that the new followers of Christ were first called "Christians," mostly made up as they were of Gentiles. The missionaries had not much success with the Jews, although it was their custom first to preach in the Jewish synagogues on the Sabbath. It was only the common people of Antioch who heard the word gladly, for it was to them tidings of joy, which raised them above their degradation and misery.

With the contributions which the Christians of Antioch, and probably of other cities, made to their poorer and afflicted brethren, Barnabas and Saul set out for Jerusalem, soon returning however to Antioch, not to resume their labors, but to make preparations for an extended missionary tour. Saul was then thirty-seven years of age, and had been a Christian seven years.

In spite of many disadvantages, such as ill-health, a mean personal appearance, and a nervous temperament, without a ready utterance, Saul had a tolerable mastery of Greek, familiarity with the habits of different classes, and a profound knowledge of human nature. As a widower and childless, he was unincumbered by domestic ties and duties; and although physically weak, he had great endurance and patience. He was courteous in his address, liberal in his views, charitable to faults, abounding in love, adapting himself to people's weaknesses and prejudices, — a man of infinite tact, the loftiest, most courageous, most magnanimous of missionaries, setting an example to the Xaviers and Judsons of modern times. He doubtless felt that to preach the gospel to the heathen was his peculiar mission; so that his duty coincided with his inclination, for he seems to have been very fond of travelling. He made his journeys on foot, accompanied by a congenial companion, when he could not go by water, which was attended with less discomfort, and was freer from perils and dangers than a land journey.

The first missionary journey of Barnabas and Saul, accompanied by Mark, was to the isle of Cyprus. They embarked at Seleucia, the port of Antioch, and landed at Salamis, where they remained awhile, preaching in the Jewish synagogue, and then traversed the whole island, which is about one hundred miles in length. Whenever they made a lengthened stay, Saul worked at his trade as a sail and tent maker, so as not to be burdensome to any one. His life was very simple and inexpensive, thus enabling him to maintain that independence so essential to self-respect.

No notable incident occurred to the three missionaries until they reached the town of Nea-Paphos, celebrated for the worship of Venus, the residence of the Roman pro-consul, Sergius Paulus, — a man of illustrious birth, who amused himself with the popular superstitions of the country. He sought, probably from curiosity, to hear Barnabas and Saul preach; but the missionaries were bitterly opposed by a Jewish sorcerer called Elymas, who was stricken with blindness by Saul, the miracle producing such an effect on the governor that he became a convert to the new faith. There is no evidence that he was baptized, but he was respected and beloved as a good man. From that time the apostle assumed the name of Paul; and he also assumed the control of the mission, Barnabas gracefully yielding the first rank, which till then he had himself enjoyed. He had been the patron of Saul, but now became his subordinate; for genius ever will work its way to ascendency. Then are no outward advantages which can long compete with intellectual supremacy.

From Cyprus the missionaries went to Perga, in Pamphylia, one of the provinces of Asia Minor. In this city, famed for the worship of Diana, their stay was short. Here Mark separated from his companions and returned to Jerusalem, much to the mortification of his cousin Barnabas and the grief of Paul, since we have a right to infer that this brilliant young man was appalled by the dangers of the journey, or had more sympathy with his brethren at Jerusalem than with the liberal yet overbearing spirit of Paul.

From Perga the two travellers proceeded to Antioch in Pisidia, in the heart of the high table-lands of the Peninsula, and, according to their custom, went on Saturday to the Jewish synagogue. Paul, invited to address the meeting, set forth the mystery of Jesus, his death, his resurrection, and the salvation which he promised to believers. But the address raised a storm, and Paul retired from the synagogue to preach to the Gentile population, many of whom were favorably disposed, and became converted. The same thing subsequently took place at Philippi, at Alexandria, at Troas, and in general throughout the Roman colonies. But the influence of the Jews was sufficient to secure the expulsion of Paul and Barnabas from the city; and they departed, shaking off the dust from their feet, and turning their steps to Iconium, a city of Lycaonia, where a church was organized. Here the apostles tarried some time, until forced to leave by the orthodox Jews, who stirred up the heathen population against them. The little city of Lystra was the scene of their next labors, and as there were but few Jews there the missionaries not only had rest, but were very successful.

The sojourn at Lystra was marked by the miraculous cure of a cripple, which so impressed the people that they took the missionaries for divinities, calling Barnabas Jupiter, and Paul Mercury; and a priest of the city absolutely would have offered up sacrifices to the supposed deities, had he not been severely rebuked by Paul for his superstition.

At Lystra a great addition was made to the Christian ranks by the conversion of Timothy, a youth of fifteen, and of his excellent mother Eunice; but the report of these conversions reached Iconium and Antioch of Pisidia, which so enraged the Jews of these cities that they sent emissaries to Lystra, zealous fanatics, who made such a disturbance that Paul was stoned, and left for dead. His wounds, however, were not so serious as were supposed, and the next day he departed with Barnabas for Derbe, where he made a long stay. The two churches of Lystra and Derbe were composed almost wholly of heathen.

From Derbe the apostles retraced their steps, A. D. 46, to Antioch, by the way they had come, — a journey of one hundred and twenty miles, and full of perils, — instead of crossing Mount Taurus through the famous pass of the Cilician Gates, and then through Tarsus to Antioch, an easier journey.

One of the noticeable things which marked this first missionary journey of Paul, was the opposition of the Jews wherever he went. He was forced to turn to the Gentiles, and it was among them that converts were chiefly made. It is true that his custom was first to address the Jewish synagogues on Saturday, but the Jews opposed and hated and persecuted him the moment he announced the grand principle which animated his life, — salvation through Jesus Christ, instead of through obedience to the venerated Law of Moses.

On his return to Antioch with his beloved companion, Paul continued for a time in the peaceful ministration of apostolic duties, until it became necessary for him to go to Jerusalem to consult with the other apostles in reference to a controversy which began seriously to threaten the welfare of their common cause. This controversy was in reference to the rite of circumcision, — a rite ever held in supreme importance by the Jews. The Jewish converts to Christianity had all been previously circumcised according to the Mosaic Law, and they insisted on the circumcision of the Gentile converts also, as a mark of Christian fraternity. Paul, emancipated from Jewish prejudices and customs, regarded this rite as unessential; he believed that it was abrogated by Christ, with other technical observances of the Law, and that it was not consistent with the liberty of the Gospel to impose rites exclusively Jewish on the Pagan converts. The elders at Jerusalem, good men as they were, did not take this view; they could not bear to receive into complete Christian fellowship men who offended their prejudices in regard to matters which they regarded as sacred and obligatory as baptism itself. They would measure Christianity by their traditions; and the smaller the point of difference seemed to the enlightened Paul, the bitterer were the contests,—even as many of the schisms which subsequently divided the Church originated in questions that appear to us to be absolutely frivolous. The question very early arose, whether Christianity should be a formal and ritualistic religion,— a religion of ablutions and purifications, of distinctions between ceremonially pure and impure things, — or, rather, a religion of the spirit; whether it should be a sect or a universal religion. Paul took the latter view; declared circumcision to be useless, and freely admitted heathen converts into the Church without it, in opposition to those who virtually insisted on a Gentile becoming a Jew before he could become a Christian.

So, to settle this miserable dispute, Paul went to Jerusalem, taking with him Barnabas and Titus, who had never been circumcised, — eighteen years after the death of Jesus, when the apostles were old men, and when Peter, James, and John, having remained at Jerusalem, were the real leaders of the Jewish Church. James in particular, called the Just, was a strenuous observer of the law of circumcision, — a severe and ascetic man, and very narrow in his prejudices, but held in great veneration for his piety. Before the question was brought up in a general assembly of the brethren for discussion, Paul separately visited Peter, James, and John, and argued with them in his broad and catholic spirit, and won them over to his cause; so that through their influence it was decided that it was not essential for a Gentile to be circumcised on admission to the Church, only that he must abstain from meats offered to idols, and from eating the meat of any animal containing the blood (forbidden by Moses), — a sort of compromise, a measure by which most quarrels are finally settled; and the title of Paul as "Apostle to the Gentiles" was officially confirmed.

The controversy being settled amicably by the leaders of the infant Church, Paul and Barnabas returned to Antioch, and for a while longer continued their labors there, as the most important centre of missionary operations. But the ardent soul of Paul could not bear repose. He set about forming new plans; and the result was his second and more important missionary tour.

The relations between Paul and Barnabas had been thus far of the most intimate and affectionate kind. But now the two apostles disagreed, — Barnabas wishing to associate with them his cousin Mark, and Paul determining that the young man, however estimable, should not accompany them, because he had turned back on the former journey. It must be confessed that Paul was not very amiable and conciliatory in this matter; but his nature was earnest and stern, and he was resolved not to have a companion under his trying circumstances who had once put his hand to the plough and looked back. Neither apostle would yield, and they were obliged to separate, — reluctantly, doubtless, — Paul choosing Silas as his future companion, while Barnabas took Mark. Both were probably in the right, and both in the wrong; for the best of men have faults, and the strongest characters the most. Perhaps Paul thought that as he was now recognized as the leading apostle to the Gentiles, Barnabas should yield to him; and perhaps Barnabas felt aggrieved at the haughty dictation of one who was once his inferior in standing.

The choice of Paul, however, was admirable. Silas was a broad and liberal man, who had great influence at Jerusalem, and was entirely devoted to his superior.

"The first object of Paul was to confirm the churches he had already founded; and accordingly he began his mission by visiting the churches of Syria and Cilicia," crossing the Taurus range by the famous Cilician Gates, — one of the most frightful mountain passes in the world, — penetrating thus into Lycaonia, and reaching Derbe, Lystra, and Iconium. At Lystra he found Timothy, whom he greatly loved, modest and timid, and made him his deacon and secretary, although he had never been circumcised. To prevent giving offence to Jewish Christians, Paul himself circumcised Timothy, in accordance with his custom of yielding to prejudices when no vital principles were involved, — which concession laid him open to the charge of inconsistency on the part of his enemies. Expediency was not disdained by Paul when the means were unobjectionable, but he did not use bad means to accomplish good ends. He always had tenderness and charity for the weaknesses of his brethren, especially intellectual weakness. What would have been intolerable to some was patiently submitted to by him, if by any means he could win even the feeble; so that he seemed to be all things to all men. No one ever exceeded him in tact.

After Paul had finished his visit to the principal cities of Galatia, he resolved to explore new lands. We next find him, after a long journey through Mysia of three hundred miles, travelling to the south of Mount Olympus, at Troas, near the ancient city of Troy. Here he fell in with Luke, a physician, who had received a careful Hellenic and Jewish education Like Timothy, the future historian of the Acts of the Apostles was admirably fitted to be the companion of Paul. He was gentle, sympathetic, submissive, and devoted to his superior. Through Luke's suggestion, Renan thinks, Paul determined to go to Macedonia.

So, without making a long stay at Troas, the four missionaries — Paul, Silas, Luke, and Timothy — took ship and landed at Neapolis, the seaport of Philippi on the borders of Thrace at the extreme northern shores of the Ægean Sea. They were now on European ground, — the most healthy region of the ancient world, where the people, largely of Celtic origin, were honest, earnest, and primitive in their habits. The travellers proceeded at once to Philippi, a city more Latin than Grecian, and began their work; making converts, chiefly women, among whom Lydia was the most distinguished, a wealthy woman who traded in purple. She and her whole household were baptized, and it was from her that Paul consented against his custom to accept pecuniary aid.

While the work of conversion was going on favorably, an incident occurred which hastened the departure of the missionaries. Paul exorcised a poor female slave, who brought, by her divinations and ventriloquism, great gain to her masters; and because of this destruction of the source of their income they brought suit against Paul and Silas before the magistrates, who condemned them to be beaten in the presence of the superstitious people, and then sent them to prison and put their feet fast in the stocks. The jailer and the duumvirs, however, ascertaining that the prisoners were Roman citizens and hence exempt from corporal punishment, released them, and hurried them out of the city.

Leaving Timothy and Luke at Philippi, Paul and Silas proceeded to Thessalonica, the largest and most important city of Macedonia, where there was a Jewish synagogue in which Paul preached for three consecutive Sabbaths. A few Jews were converted, but the converts were chiefly Greeks, of whom the larger part were women belonging to the best society of the city. By these converts the apostles were treated with extraordinary deference and devotion, and the church of Thessalonica soon rivalled that of Philippi in the piety and unity of its converts, becoming a model Christian church. As usual, however, the Jews stirred up animosities, and Paul and Silas were obliged to leave, spending several days at Berea and preaching successfully among the Greeks. These conquests were the most brilliant that Paul had yet made, — not among enervated Asiatics, but bright, elegant, and intelligent Europeans, where women were less degraded than in the Orient.

Leaving Timothy and Silas behind him, Paul, accompanied by some faithful Bereans, embarked for Athens, — the centre of philosophy and art, whose wonderful prestige had induced its Roman conquerors to preserve its ancient glories. But in the first century Athens was neither the fascinating capital of the time of Cicero, nor of the age of Chrysostom. Its temples and statues remained intact, but its schools could not then boast of a single man of genius. There remained only dilettante philosophers, rhetoricians, grammarians, pedagogues, and pedants, puffed up with conceit and arrogance, with very few real inquirers after truth, such as marked the times of Socrates and Plato. Paul, like Luther, cared nothing for art; and the thousands of statues which ornamented every part of the city seemed to him to be nothing but idols. Still, he was not mistaken in the intense paganism of the city, the absence of all earnestness of character and true religious life. He was disappointed, as afterward Augustine was when he went to Rome. He expected to find intellectual life at least, but the pretenders to superior knowledge in that degenerate university town merely traded on the achievements of their ancestors, repeating with dead lips the echo of the old philosophies. They were marked only by levity, mockery, sneers, and contemptuous arrogance; idlers were they, in quest of some new amusement.

The utter absence of sympathy among all classes given over to frivolities made Paul exceedingly lonely in Athens, and he wrote to Timothy and Silas to join him with all haste. He wandered about the streets distressed and miserable. There was no field for his labors. Who would listen to him? What ear could he reach? He was as forlorn and unheeded as a temperance lecturer would be on the boulevards of Paris. His work among the Jews was next to nothing, for where trade did not flourish there were but few Jews. Still, amid all this discouragement, it would seem that Paul attracted sufficient notice, from his conversation with the idlers and chatterers of the Agora, to be invited to address the Athenians at the Areopagus. They listened with courtesy so long as they thought he was praising their religious habits, or was making a philosophical argument against the doctrines of rival sects; but when he began to tell them of that Cross which was to them foolishness, and of that Resurrection from the dead which was alien to all their various beliefs, they were filled with scorn or relapsed into indifference. Paul's masterly discourse on Mars Hill was an obvious failure, so far as any immediate impression was concerned. The Pagans did not persecute him,— they let him alone; they killed him with indifference. He could stand opposition, but to be laughed at as a fanatic and neglected by bright and intellectual people was more than even Paul could stand. He left Athens a lonely man, without founding a church. It was the last city in the world to receive his doctrines,— that city of grammarians, of pedants, of gymnasts, of fencing masters, of play-goers, and babblers about words. "As well might a humanitarian socialist declaim against English prejudices to the proud and exclusive fellows of Oxford and Cambridge."

Paul, disappointed and disgusted, without waiting for Timothy, then set out for Corinth,— a much wickeder and more luxurious city than Athens, but not puffed up with intellectual pride. Here there were sailors and artisans, and slaves bearing heavy burdens, who would gladly hear the tidings of a salvation preached to the poor and miserable. Not yet was the alliance to be formed between Philosophy and Christianity. Not to the intellect was the apostolic appeal to be made, but to the conscience and the heart of those who knew and owned that they were sinners in need of forgiveness.

Paul instinctively perceived that Corinth, with its

gross and shameless immoralities, was the place for him to work in. He therefore decided on a long stay, and went to live with Aquila and Priscilla, converted Jews, who followed the same trade as himself, that of tent and sail making, — a very humble calling, but one which was well patronized in that busy mart of commerce. Timothy soon joined him, with Silas. As usual, Paul preached to the Jews until they repulsed him with insults and blasphemy, when he turned to the heathen, among whom he had great success, converting the common people, including some whose names have been preserved, — Titus, Justius, Crispus, Chloe, and Phœbe. He remained in Corinth eighteen months, not without difficulties and impediments. The Jews, unable to vent their wrath upon him as fully as they wished in a city under the Roman government, appealed to the governor of the province of which Corinth was the capital. This governor is best known to us as Gallio, — a man of fine intellect, and a friend of scholars.

When Sosthenes, chief of the synagogue, led Paul before Gallio's tribunal, accusing him of preaching a religion against the law, the proconsul interrupted him with this admirable reply: "If it were a matter of wrong, or moral outrage, it would be reasonable in me to hear you; but if it be a question of words and names and of your Law, look ye to it, for I will be no judge of such matters." He thus summarily and contemptuously dismissed the complaint, without however taking any notice of Paul. The mistake of Gallio was that he did not comprehend that Christianity was a subject infinitely greater than a mere Jewish sect, with which, in common with educated Romans, he confounded it. In his indifference however he was not unlike other Roman governors, of whom he was one of the justest and most enlightened. In reference to the whole scene, Canon Farrar forcibly remarks that this distinguished and cultivated Gallio "flung away the greatest opportunity of his life, when he closed the lips of the haggard Jewish prisoner whom his decision had rescued from the clutches of his countrymen;" for Paul was prepared with a speech which would have been more valued, and would have been more memorable, than all the acts of Gallio's whole government.

While Paul was pursuing his humble labors with the poor converts of Corinth, about the year 53 A. D., a memorable event took place in his career, which has had an immeasurable influence on the Christian world. Being unable personally to visit, as he desired, the churches he had founded, Paul began to write to them letters to instruct and confirm them in the faith.

The apostle's first epistle was to his beloved brethren in Thessalonica, — the first of that remarkable series of theological essays which in all subsequent ages have held their position as fundamentally important in the establishment of Christian doctrine. They are luminous, profound, original, remarkable alike for vigor of style and depth of spiritual significance. They are not moral essays like those of Confucius, nor mystic and obscure speculations like those of Buddha, but grand treatises on revealed truth, written, as it were, with his heart's blood, and vivid as fire in a dark night. In these epistles we see also Paul's intense personality, his frank egotism, his devotion to his work, his sincerity and earnestness, his affectionate nature, his tolerant and catholic spirit, and also his power of sarcasm, his warm passions, and his unbending will. He enjoins the necessity of faith, which is a gift, with the practice of virtues that appeal to consciousness and emanate from love and purity of heart. These letters are exhortations to a lofty life and childlike acceptance of revealed truths. The apostle warns his little flock against the evils that surrounded them, and which so easily beset them, — especially unchastity and drunkenness, and strifes, bickerings, slanders, and retaliations. He exhorts them to unceasing prayer, the feeling of constant dependence, and hence the supreme need of divine grace to keep them from falling, and to enable them to grow in spiritual strength. He promises as the fruit of spiritual victories immeasurable joys, not only amid present evils, but in the glorious future when the mortal shall put on immortality. Especially and repeatedly does he urge them to "have also that mind which was in Christ Jesus," showing itself in humility, willingness to serve others, unselfish consideration of others, even the preference of others' interests before their own, — a combination of the homely practical with the divinely ideal, such as the world had never learned from any earlier philosophy of life.

Paul at last felt that he must revisit the earlier churches, especially those of Syria. It was three years since he had left Antioch. But more than all, he wished to consult with his brethren in Jerusalem, and to be present at the feast of the Passover. Bidding an affectionate adieu to his Christian friends, he set out for the little seaport of Cenchrea, accompanied by Aquila and his wife Priscilla, and then set sail for Ephesus, on his way to Jerusalem. In his haste to reach the end of his journey he did not tarry at Ephesus, but took another vessel, and arrived at Cæsarea without any recorded accident. Nor did he make a long visit at Jerusalem, probably to avoid a rupture with James, the head of the church in that city, whose views about Jewish ceremonials, as already noted, differed from his.

Paul returned again to Ephesus, where he made a sojourn of three years, following his trade for a living, while he founded a church in that city of necromancers, sorcerers, magicians, courtesans, mimics, flute-players,

— a city abandoned to Asiatic sensualities and superstitious rites; an exceedingly wicked and luxurious city, yet famous for arts, especially for the grandest temple ever erected by the Greeks, one of the seven wonders of the world. It was in the most abandoned capitals, with mixed populations, that the greatest triumphs of Christianity were achieved. Antioch, Corinth, and Ephesus were more favorable to the establishment of Christian churches than Jerusalem and Athens.

But the trials of Paul in Ephesus, the capital of Asia Minor, the most celebrated of all the Ionian cities, — "more Hellenic than Antioch, more Oriental than Corinth, more wealthy than Thessalonica, more populous than Athens," — were incessant and discouraging, since it was the headquarters of pagan superstitions, and of all forms of magical imposture. As usual, he was reviled and slandered by the Jews; but he was also at this time an object of intense hatred to the priests and image-makers of the Temple of Diana, troubled in mind by evil reports concerning the converts he had made in other cities, physically weak and depressed by repeated attacks of sickness, oppressed by cares and labors, exposed to constant dangers, his life an incessant mortification and suffering, "killed all the day long," carrying about him wherever he went "the deadness of the crucified Christ."

Paul's labors in Ephesus were nevertheless successful. He made many converts and exercised an extraordinary influence, — among other things causing magicians voluntarily to burn their own costly books, as Savonarola afterward made a bonfire of vanities at Florence. His sojourn was cut short at length by the riot which was made by the various persons who were directly or indirectly supported by the revenues of the Temple, — a mongrel mob, brought to terms by the tact of the town clerk, who reminded the howling dervishes and angry silversmiths of the punishment which might be inflicted on them by the Roman proconsul for raising a disturbance and breaking the law.

Yet Paul with difficulty escaped from Ephesus and departed again for Greece, not however until he had written his extraordinary Epistles to the Corinthians, who had sadly departed from his teachings both in morals and doctrine, either through ignorance, or in consequence of the depravity which they had but imperfectly conquered. The infant churches were deplorably split into factions, "the result of the visits from various teachers who succeeded Paul, and who built on his foundations very dubious materials by way of superstructure," — even Apollos himself, an Alexandrian Jew baptized by the Apostle John, the most eloquent and attractive preacher of the day, who turned everybody's head. In the churches women rose to give their opinions without being veiled, as if they were Greek courtesans; the Agapæ, or love-feasts, had degenerated into luxurious banquets; and unchastity, the peculiar vice of the Corinthians, went unrebuked. These evils Paul rebukes, and lays down rules for the faithful in reference to marriage, to the position of women, to the observance of the Lord's Supper, and sundry other things, enjoining forbearance and love. His chapter in reference to charity is justly regarded by all writers and commentators as the nearest approach in Christian literature to the Sermon on the Mount. Scarcely less remarkable is the chapter on death and the resurrection, shedding more light on that great subject than all other writers combined in heathen and Christian annals, — one of the profoundest treatises ever written by mortal man, and which can be explained only as the result of a supernatural revelation.

Paul's second sojourn in Macedonia lasted only six months; this time he spent in going from city to city confirming the infant churches, remaining longest in Thessalonica and Philippi, where his most faithful converts were found. Here Titus joined him, bringing good news from Corinth. Still, there were dissensions and evils in that troublesome church which called for a second letter. In this letter he sets forth, not in the spirit of egotism, the various sufferings and perils he

had endured, few of which are alluded to by Luke:
"Of the Jews five times received I forty stripes save
one; thrice was I beaten with rods; once was I stoned;
thrice I suffered shipwreck; a night and a day have I
spent in the deep; in journeyings often; in perils of
rivers, in perils of robbers, in perils from my own race,
in perils from the Gentiles, in perils in the city, in
perils in the wilderness, in perils in the sea, in perils
among false brethren; in toil and weariness, in sleep-
lessness often, in hunger and thirst, in fastings often;
besides anxiety for all the churches."

It was probably at the close of the year 57 A. D.
that Paul set out for Corinth, with Titus, Timothy,
Sosthenes, and other companions. During the three
months he remained in that city he probably wrote his
Epistle to the Galatians and his Epistle to the Romans,
— the latter the most profound of all his writings, setting forth the sum and substance of his theology, in
which the great doctrine of justification by faith is
severely elaborated. The whole epistle is a war on
pagan philosophy, the insufficiency of good works without faith, — the lever by which in later times Wyclif,
Huss, Luther, Calvin, Knox, and Saint Cyran overthrew
a pharisaic system of outward righteousness. In the
Epistle to the Galatians Paul speaks with unusual boldness and earnestness, severely rebuking them for their
departure from the truth, and reiterating with dog-

matic ardor the inutility of circumcision as of the Law abrogated by Christ, with whom, in the liberty which he proclaimed, there is neither Jew nor Greek, neither bond nor free, neither male nor female, but all are one in Him. And Paul reminds them, — a bitter pill to the Jews, — that this is taught in the promise made to Abraham four hundred and fifty years before the Law was declared by Moses, by which promise all races and tribes and people are to be blessed to remotest generations. This epistle not only breathes the largest Christian liberty, — the equality of all men before God, — but it asserts, as in the Epistle to the Romans, with terrible distinctness, that salvation is by faith in Christ and not by deeds of the Law, which is only a schoolmaster to prepare the way for the ascendency of Jesus.

I need not dwell on these two great epistles, which embody the substance of the Pauline theology received by the Church for eighteen hundred years, and which can never be abrogated so long as Paul is regarded as an authority in Christian doctrine.

I return to a brief notice of Paul's last visit to Jerusalem, which was made against the expostulations of his friends and disciples in Ephesus, who gathered around him weeping, knowing well that they never would see his face again. But he was inflexible in his resolution, declaring that he had no fear of chains, and was ready to die at Jerusalem for the name of Jesus. Why he should have persisted in his resolution, so full of danger; why he should again have thrown himself into the hands of his bitterest enemies, thirsty for his blood, — we do not know, for he had no new truth to declare. But the brethren were forced to yield to his strong will, and all they could do was to provide him with a sufficient escort to shield him from ordinary dangers on the way.

The long voyage from Ephesus was prosperous but tedious, and on the last day before the Pentecostal feast, in May, in the year 58 A. D., Paul for the fifth time entered Jerusalem. His meeting with the elders, under the presidency of James, — "the stern, white-robed, ascetic, mysterious prophet," — was cold. His personal friends in Jerusalem were few, and his enemies were numerous, powerful, and bitter; for he had not only emancipated himself from the Jewish Law, with all its rites and ceremonies, but had made it of no account in all the churches he had founded. What had he naturally to expect from the zealots for that Law but a renewed persecution? Even the Jewish Christians gave no thanks for the splendid contribution which Paul had gathered in Asia for the relief of their poor. Nor was there any exultation among them when Paul narrated his successful labors among the Gentiles. They pretended to rejoice, but added, "You observe, brother, how many myriads of the Jews there are that have embraced the faith, and they are all zealots for the Law. And we are informed that thou teachest all the Jews that are among the Gentiles to forsake Moses." There was no cordiality among the Jewish elders of the Christian community, and deadly hostility among the unconverted Jews, for they had doubtless heard of Paul's marvellous career.

Jerusalem was then full of strangers, and the Jews of Asia recognizing Paul in the Temple, raised a disturbance, pretending that he was a profaner of the sacred edifice. The crowd of fanatics seized him, dragged him out of the Temple, and set about to kill him. But the Roman authorities interfered, and rescuing him from the hands of the infuriated mob, bore him to the castle, the tower of Antonia. When they arrived at the stairs of the tower, Paul begged the tribune to be allowed to speak to the angry and demented crowd. The request was granted, and he made a speech in Hebrew, narrating his early history and conversion; but when he came to his mission to the Gentiles, the uproar was renewed, the people shouting, "Away with such a fellow from the earth, for it is not fit that he should live!" And Paul would have been bound and scourged, had he not proclaimed that he was a Roman citizen.

On the next day the Roman magistrate summoned

the chief priests and the Sanhedrim, to give Paul an opportunity to make his defence in the matter of which he was accused. Ananias the high-priest presided, and the Roman tribune was present at the proceedings, which were tumultuous and angry. Paul seeing that the assembly was made up of Pharisees, Sadducees, and hostile parties, made no elaborate defence, and the tribune dissolved the assembly; but forty of the most hostile and fanatical formed a conspiracy, and took a solemn oath not to eat or drink until they had assassinated him. The plot reached the ears of a nephew of Paul, who revealed it to the tribune. The officer listened attentively to all the details, and at once took his resolution to send Paul to Cæsarea, both to get him out of the hands of the Jews, and to have him judged by the procurator Felix. Accordingly, accompanied by an escort of two hundred soldiers, seventy horsemen, and two hundred spearmen of the guard, Paul was sent by night, secretly, to the Roman capital of the Province. He entered the city in the course of the next day, and was at once led to the presence of the governor.

Felix, as procurator, ruled over Judæa with the power of a king. He had been a freedman of the Emperor Claudius, and was allied by marriage to Claudius himself, — an ambitious, extortionate, and infamous governor. Felix was obliged to give Paul a fair trial, and after five days the indomitable missionary was confronted with accusers, among whom appeared the high-priest Ananias. They associated with them a lawyer called Tertullus, of oratorical gifts, who conducted the case. The principal charges made against Paul were that he was a public pest and leader of seditions; that he was a ringleader of the Nazarenes (the contemptuous name which the Jews gave to the Christians); and that he had attempted to profane the Temple, which was a capital offence according to the Jewish law. Paul easily refuted these charges, and had Felix been an upright judge he would have dismissed the case; but supposing the apostle to be rich because of the handsome contributions he had brought from Asia Minor for the poor converts at Jerusalem, Felix retained Paul in the hope of a bribe. A few days after, Drusilla, a young woman of great beauty and accomplishments, who had eloped from her husband to be married to Felix, was desirous to hear so famous a man as Paul explain his faith; and Felix, to gratify her curiosity, summoned his distinguished prisoner to discourse before them. Paul eagerly embraced the opportunity; but instead of explaining the Christian mysteries, he reasoned about righteousness, self-control, and retribution, — moral truths which even intelligent heathen accepted, and as to which the consciences of both his hearers must have tingled; indeed, he discoursed with such matchless boldness and power that Felix trembled with fear as he remembered the arts by which he had risen from the condition of a slave, and the extortions and cruelties by which he had become enriched, to say nothing of the lusts and abominations which had disgraced his career. However, he did not set Paul free, but kept him a prisoner for two years, in order to gain favor with the Jews, or to receive a bribe.

Porcius Festus, the successor of Felix, was a just and inflexible man, who arrived at Cæsarea in the year 60 A.D., when Paul was fifty-eight years of age. Immediately the enemies of Paul, especially the Sadducees, renewed their demands to have him again tried; and Festus, wishing to be just, ordered the second trial. Again Paul defended himself with masterly ability, proving that he had done nothing against the Jewish law or Temple, or against the Roman Emperor. Festus, probably not seeing the aim of the conspirators, was disposed to send Paul back to Jerusalem to be tried by a Jewish court. To prevent this, as at Jerusalem condemnation and death would be certain, Paul, remembering that he was a Roman citizen, fell back on his privilege, and at once appealed to Cæsar himself. The governor, at first surprised by such an unexpected demand, consulted with his assistants for a moment, and then replied: "Thou hast appealed unto Cæsar, and unto Cæsar shalt thou go." Thus ended the trial of Paul; and thus providentially was the way open to him, without expense to himself, to go to Rome, which of all cities he wished to visit, and where he hoped to continue, even under bonds and restrictions, his missionary labors.

In the meantime, before a ship could be got in readiness to transport him and other prisoners to Rome, Herod Agrippa II., with his sister Bernice, came to Cæsarea to pay a visit to the new governor. Conversation naturally turned upon the late extraordinary trial, and Agrippa expressed a desire to hear the prisoner speak, for he had heard much about him. Festus willingly acceded to this wish, and the next day Paul was again summoned before the king and the procurator. Agrippa and Bernice appeared in great pomp with their attendants; all the officers of the army and the principal men of the city were also present. It was the most splendid audience that Paul had ever addressed. He was equal to the occasion, and delivered a discourse on his familiar topics, — his own miraculous conversion and his mission to the Gentiles to preach the crucified and risen Christ, — things new to Festus, who thought that Paul was visionary, and had lost his balance from excess of learning. Agrippa, however, familiar with Jewish law and the prophecies concerning the Messiah, was much impressed with Paul's eloquence, and exclaimed: "Almost thou persuadest me to be a Christian!" When the assembly broke up, Agrippa said, "This man might have been set at liberty, if he had not appealed unto Cæsar." Paul, however, did not wish to be set at liberty among bitter and howling enemies; he preferred to go to Rome, and would not withdraw his appeal. So in due time he embarked for Italy under the charge of a centurion, accompanied with other prisoners and his friends Timothy, Luke, and Aristarchus of Thessalonica.

The voyage from Cæsarea to Italy was a long one, and in the autumn was a dangerous one, as in Paul's case it unfortunately proved.

The following spring, however, after shipwreck and divers perils and manifold fatigues, Paul arrived at Rome, in the year 61 A. D., in the seventh year of the Emperor Nero. Here the centurion handed Paul over to the prefect of the prætorian guards, by whom he was subjected to a merely nominal custody, although, according to Roman custom, he was chained to a soldier. But he was treated with great lenity, was allowed to have lodgings, to receive his friends freely, and to hold Christian meetings in his own house; and no one molested him. For two years Paul remained at Rome, a fettered prisoner it is true, but cheered by friendly visits, and attended by Luke, his "beloved physician" and biographer, by Timothy and other devoted disciples. During this second imprisonment Paul could see very little outside the prætorian barracks, but his friends brought him the news, and he had ample time to write letters. He had no intercourse with gifted and fortunate Romans; his acquaintance was probably confined to the prætorian soldiers, and some of the humbler classes who sought Christian instruction. But from this period we date many of his epistles, on which his fame and influence largely rest as a theologian and man of genius. Among those which he wrote from Rome were the Epistles to the Colossians, the Ephesians, and many pastoral letters like those written to Philemon, Titus, and Timothy.

We know but little of the life of Paul after his arrival at Rome, for at this point Saint Luke closes his narrative, and all after this is conjecture and tradition.[1]

---

[1] There has been much doubt as to whether Paul was martyred during the three years of this imprisonment, or whether he was acquitted, left Rome, visited his beloved churches in Macedonia and Asia Minor, went to preach the gospel in Spain, and was again arrested, taken to Rome, and there beheaded. The earliest authorities seem to have been agreed upon the second hypothesis; and this is based chiefly upon a statement made by Paul's disciple Clement to the effect that the apostle had preached in "the extremity of the West" (an expression of Roman writers to denote Spain), and also on the impossibility of placing certain facts mentioned in the second letter to Timothy and the one to Titus in the period of the first imprisonment. He was certainly tried, defended himself, and he may have been at first acquitted.

But the main part of Paul's work was accomplished when he was first sent to Rome as a prisoner to be tried in the imperial courts; and there is but little doubt that he finally met the death he so heroically contemplated, at the hands of the monster Nero, who martyred such a vast multitude of Paul's fellow-Christians.

At Jerusalem and at Antioch he had vindicated the freedom of the Gentile from the yoke of the Levitical Law; in his letters to the Romans and Galatians he had proclaimed both to Jew and Gentile that they were not under the law, but under grace. During the space of twenty years Paul had preached the gospel of Jesus as the Christ in the chief cities of the world, and had formulated the truths of Christianity. What marvellous labors! But it does not appear that this apostle's extraordinary work was fully appreciated in his day, certainly not by the Jewish Christians at Jerusalem; nor does it appear even that his pre-eminence among the apostles was conceded until the third and fourth centuries. He himself was often sad and discouraged in not seeing a larger success, yet recognized himself as a layer of foundations. Like our modern missionaries, Paul simply sowed the seed; the fruit was not to be gathered in until centuries after his death. Before he died, as is seen in his second letter to Timothy, many of his friends and disciples deserted him, and he was left almost alone. He had to defend himself single-handed against the capricious tyrant who ruled the world, and who wished to cast on the Christians the stain of his greatest crime, the conflagration of his capital. As we have said, all details pertaining to the life of Paul after his arrival at Rome are simply conjectural, and although interesting, they cannot give us the satisfaction of certainty.

But in closing, after enumerating the labors and writings of this great apostle, it is not inopportune to say a few words about his remarkable character, although I have now and again alluded to his personal traits in the course of this narrative.

Paul is the most prominent figure of all the great men who have adorned, or advanced the interest of, the Christian Church. Great pulpit orators, renowned theologians, profound philosophers, immortal poets, successful reformers, and enlightened monarchs have never disputed his intellectual ascendency; to all alike he has been a model and a marvel. The grand old missionary stands out in history as a matchless example of Christian living, a sure guide in Christian doctrine. No more favored mortal is ever likely to appear; he is the counterpart of Moses as a divine teacher to all generations. The popes may exalt Saint Peter as the founder of their spiritual empire, but when their empire as an institution shall crumble away, as all institutions must which are not founded on the "Rock" which it was the mission of apostles to proclaim, Paul will stand out the most illustrious of all Christian teachers.

As a man Paul had his faults, but his virtues were transcendent; and these virtues he himself traced to divine grace, enabling him to conquer his infirmities and prejudices, and to perform astonishing labors, and to endure no less marvellous sufferings. His humanity was never lost in his discouraging warfare; he sympathized with human sorrows and afflictions; he was tolerant, after his conversion, of human infirmities, while enjoining a severe morality. He was a man of native genius, with profound insight into spiritual truth. Trained in philosophy and disputation, his gentleness and tact in dealing with those who opposed him are a lesson to all controversialists. His voluntary sufferings have endeared him to the heart of the world, since they were consecrated to the welfare of the world he sought to enlighten. As an encouragement to others, he enumerates the calamities which happened to him from his zeal to serve mankind, but he never complains of them or regards them as a mystery, or as anything but the natural result of unappreciated devotion. He was more cheerful than Confucius, who felt that his life had been a failure; more serene than Plato when surrounded by admiring followers. He regarded every Christian man as a brother and a friend. He associated freely with women, without even calling out a sneer or a reproach. He taught principles of self-control rather than rules of specific asceticism, and hence recommended wine to Timothy and encouraged friendship between men and women, when intemperance and unchastity were the scandal and disgrace of the age; although so far as himself was concerned, he would not eat meat, if thereby he should give offence to the weakest of his weak-minded brethren. He enjoined filial piety, obedience to rulers, and kindness to servants as among the highest duties of life. He was frugal, but independent and hospitable; he had but few wants, and submitted patiently to every inconvenience. He was the impersonation of gentleness, sympathy, and love, although a man of iron will and indomitable resolution. He claimed nothing but the right to speak his honest opinions, and the privilege to be judged according to the laws. He magnified his office, but only the more easily to win men to his noble cause. To this great cause he was devoted heart and soul, without ever losing courage, or turning back for a moment in despondency or fear. He was as courageous as he was faithful; as indifferent to reproach as he was eager for friendship. As a martyr he was peerless, since his life was a protracted martyrdom. He was a hero, always gallantly fighting for the truth whatever may have been the array and howling of his foes; and when wounded and battered by his enemies he returned to the fight for his principles with all the earnestness, but without the wrath, of a knight of chivalry. He never indulged in angry recriminations or used unseemly epithets, but was unsparing in his denunciation of sin, — as seen in his memorable description of the vices of the Romans. Self-sacrifice was the law of his life. His faith was unshaken in every crisis and in every danger. It was this which especially fitted him, as well as his ceaseless energies and superb intellect, to be a leader of mankind. To Paul, and to Paul more than to any other apostle, was given the exalted privilege of being the recognized interpreter of Christian doctrine for both philosophers and the people, for all coming ages; and at the close of his career, worn out with labor and suffering, yet conscious of the services which he had rendered and of the victories he had won, and possibly in view of approaching martyrdom, he was enabled triumphantly to say: "I have fought a good fight; I have finished my course; I have kept the faith. Henceforth there is laid up for me a crown of righteousness, which the Lord, the righteous judge, shall give me at that day."